KINGS OF MERCIA ACADEMY

BOOKS 1-4

✥

SOFIA DANIEL

Copyright © 2019 by Sofia Daniel.

All rights reserved. This book or any portion thereof may not be reproduced or used in any manner whatsoever without the express written permission of the publisher except for the use of brief quotations in a book review.

www.SofiaDaniel.com

OUTCAST

KINGS OF MERCIA ACADEMY BOOK 1

CHAPTER 1

Banished. That's what I was. Mom's new husband had banished me all the way to England. The worst part? She hadn't done a thing to stop him.

I sat back in the limousine's plush, leather seat, staring out at miles and miles of rolling green countryside. When Rudolph had proposed that I go to school in England, I'd immediately pictured London. But we'd left Heathrow airport three hours ago and I still couldn't find any signs of Mercia Academy.

I pulled at the starchy, burgundy blazer and sighed. Things could have been worse. At least I spoke the language.

Marissa, the personal assistant of my new stepfather's personal assistant, flipped through the academy brochure. "Remember, Rudolph said you have to complete a semester here to intern at any of the media companies of your choice within the Trommel Group. If you can complete the full two years, he'll pay for college." She beamed, revealing whitened teeth. "You won't even need to apply for a scholarship."

"Sure." I'd only known Marissa for the duration of our journey from Manhattan, so I couldn't share my true feelings with her.

The limo slowed through the narrow road of a village consisting of stone buildings and thatched roofs. All the stores stood along one stretch of road, with workers making morning preparations. My gaze caught an old woman placing a stacked plate of cupcakes in a window display. This had to be one of the Great British teashops Marissa had raved about on the journey.

"Oh," Marissa pressed her face against the window. "How quaint!"

"If this is the shopping district, what will the school be like?" I muttered.

She didn't reply, and I pressed the heel of my hand into my belly, which now ached with dread. It had been a mistake to tell Rudolph I wanted to be a journalist. The old man had taken advantage of my ambition and made me an offer so generous, it was impossible to refuse. I'd left my friends in New York for the opportunity of a millennium, but I'd never guessed the school would be so remote. Rudolph had probably had me sent away so Mom could focus all her attention on him. With thousands of miles of distance between us and a five-hour time difference, she'd likely forget about me… again.

"Emilia?" asked Marissa.

I pulled my gaze away from a butcher clad in a straw hat and a white shirt and tie under his blue-striped apron. "Yes?"

"You understand why you're being sent here and not to one of the prep schools back home?" She placed a hand on my knee.

"Not really." I couldn't help staring at her long, red nails.

"Mr. Trommel thinks the only way you'll get the mental toughness for a career in journalism is with a trial of fire."

My mind blanked. Where were they taking me? Fight Club School? "Trial of…"

Marissa gave me one of those slow blinks, as if she was trying to remember a rehearsed speech. One of her false eyelashes had come loose at the corner of her eyes. "Rudolph says if you can survive a British boarding school, you can survive anything."

Folding my arms across my chest, I asked, "Is this where he studied?"

She rubbed at her eye. "Of course not. Rudolph went to a run-down public school in Poughkeepsie, where he gained a sports scholarship to Harvard..."

I tuned her out and stared through the window. The Trommel history must be something all employees learned by rote. I'd read it on the company website, heard it from the man himself, and sat through it at his best man's speech two days ago at the wedding. Rudolph's trial of fire was B.S. He just wanted me out of the way because he needed Mom all to himself.

This backwater was so different from Park Prep, pangs of homesickness for Manhattan struck at my heart already. My best friend and former roommate, Noelle, would probably be sleeping now, so I couldn't even have someone to help me commiserate.

The limo turned left out of the village and into a two-lane road bordered by green wilderness. On the left, a black-and-white sheepdog ran around its flock, guiding them toward an open gate further into the field. I sat back into the leather seats and took in the sights. I could admit that Mercia county was a place of outstanding natural beauty. Nothing like noisy, built-up Manhattan, with its few pockets of peace, like Central Park. Mercia seemed the kind of place where people strolled around, doffing their caps at each other and saying 'good day, sir' in posh accents. It offered politeness and boredom, not trials of fire.

About ten minutes later, the road formed a boulevard of tall, leafy trees that stood like sentinels holding up their swords and forming an arch. Their branches stretched across the road, providing a canopy of dappled light. Up ahead loomed a stone archway emblazoned with a coat of arms and the words, MERCIA

ACADEMY. The opening was so grand it had a windowed room attached to each side and a wall that stretched for an eternity.

Through the arch were fields bisected by even more stretches of road, but no signs of a school. I ran damp palms down my pleated, gray skirt. "How big is Mercia Academy?"

Marissa flipped the brochure. "According to this, the entire site is seventeen-hundred acres. Twice the size of Central Park and bigger than Sherwood Forest!"

Dense forest bordered the fields, reminding me of a Robin Hood movie that had been fun to watch, but I'd never imagined living in a place like this. The thought of shivering in a drafty old castle with windowless rooms made my throat go dry. Would we need thick cloaks to stay warm? Candles to light our way? Chamberpots? I was going to miss the modern amenities of Park Prep.

I swallowed hard. "How old is this place?"

"Ummm…." Marissa furrowed her brow. "There were so many dates in its history, it's difficult to tell. I remember something in the fifteen-hundreds."

"That figures." I clutched my belly to hold in the riot of butterflies trying to escape.

Wasn't there an academy in London? One close to the subway and busses and other escape routes? We passed through the gates, and gravel rumbled under the limo's wheels, making the lining of my belly rumble like the thunderclaps in old horror movies. This was a trap. I pulled out my smartphone and checked its signal. One bar. I'd bet a fine old English institution like Mercia Academy didn't have cable or WiFi. I'd be isolated, which was exactly Rudolph's plan.

After a few minutes, Marissa gasped. "Oh… This is just like Downton Abbey!"

Ahead stood a three-story, stone-fronted building whose huge windows reflected the sunlight, making it all the more majestic. At each corner was a six-story tower, and at the roof a glass dome that was probably an atrium. My breath caught. This was nothing like I'd feared.

The limo stopped outside the building's mahogany double doors, and the driver stepped out and opened the limo's back door. "Mercia Academy," he said in the kind of smooth accent I'd only heard from TV butlers. "I will await your return outside, Miss Marissa."

Marissa stretched out her hand, indicating for him to help her step out. Clearly, the personal assistant of a personal assistant didn't get to ride in vehicles like this, and she wanted to milk the Cinderella experience. She placed her fingertips on the driver's palm, pointed the toe of her red stiletto and stepped out. I didn't blame her for acting like she'd won a fancy vacation to England. If I were returning to New York in a few days, I'd be delighted with the experience, too.

I stepped out and walked up the stone stairs and through ten-foot-tall double doors into a vast hallway that smelled of furniture polish. Kids of different ages, ranging from little eleven-year olds to those around seventeen, like me, rushed out of classrooms, each wearing burgundy blazers with the school crest, gray slacks for the boys and pleated skirts for the girls.

"Good morning?" Marissa waved her hand, jangling two rows of over-crowded charm bracelets. "Excuse me!"

None of the kids took any notice. Instead, they disappeared through doors, down hallways, and into stairwells. It was like a colony of oversized, burgundy ants. What was the rush?

"Excuse me!" Marissa strode toward a wide part of the hallway, where two corridors intersected. "Which way to the headmaster's office?"

A squat boy with pale, red hair bumped her to one side with his shoulder. "Bloody Yank. Too fucking loud."

My insides ached with dread. Is that what people would call me? Some of the kids gave Marissa filthy looks and eyed me up and down with curled lips, as though I was guilty of being a loud Yank by association. Which I was. Dread wrapped itself around my chest and squeezed like a vice. Was this the kind of treatment in store for me?

The last of the students disappeared into the classrooms, leaving the hallway a deserted oasis of marble and gilded, centuries-old portraits on white walls. I caught up with Marissa and placed an arm on her shoulder. "Let's walk around a little. I'm sure there'll be signs to the headmaster's office."

"I can't believe the rudeness of that kid!" Her voice echoed in the hallway along with the click-clack of her heels.

"Yeah," I whispered, hoping she would take the hint and also lower her voice. "I wasn't expecting that."

"I thought British people were polite!"

A door opened, and an old man with the kind of black, academic robes people wore during graduation, or at Hogwarts, stuck out his head and scowled. "Will you keep the noise down? Some of us are trying to teach."

Marissa's nostrils flared. "If someone would tell me where to find the headmaster, maybe I wouldn't need to talk so loud!"

"First floor." His head disappeared back into the room, and he shut the door with a click.

She shook her head. "What a snob!"

Wrapping my arms around my middle, I let out a shuddering breath. The people did have a point about her volume, but they didn't have to be so mean and condescending about it. I nodded at a stairwell and whispered, "Let's try over here."

Marissa stomped up the stone stairs, ranting about how the English were just rude, condescending snobs, and nothing like the genteel folk on TV. With each screeching word, her voice echoed in the stairwell. I trailed behind her and cringed. All the people in the classrooms could probably hear her, too.

"Marissa," I whispered.

She was too lost in her tirade to hear my whisper. I followed her onto the landing, where the staircase twisted forty-five degrees. At the top stood three of the most handsome boys I'd ever seen, making my heart splutter.

Each stood over six-feet tall with athletic builds and wore their school uniforms like tuxedos. I had to blink in case it was a hallucination. The trio had the grace and elegance of young kings.

When I opened my eyes, they were still there, still real, still handsome. My heart stopped, and my jaw unhinged.

The boy on the left bored into me with mischievous, chocolate-brown eyes that turned my insides to jelly. Glossy black hair curled around his ears. He looked like someone who'd stepped off a runway with his high cheekbones, strong jaw, and broad shoulders that tapered into a narrow waist and lean, muscular thighs. My gaze locked onto his full, kissable lips. I licked my own, imagining their touch against my skin.

He glanced at Marissa then gave me a sympathetic half-smile, which made my insides relax. Boys this good-looking were usually arrogant, but this one seemed a little friendly.

The second guy was a few inches taller, with a broad, football player's body I wanted to scale like King Kong on the Empire State building. His biceps and prominent pectoral muscles bulged tantalizingly under his uniform. He kept his blond, wavy hair slicked back off a face that could have been chiseled by a master sculptor. His cool, green eyes roved up and down my body as though assessing whether I was worth his time. My breath hitched, but the lack of reaction on his stony face told me I probably wasn't.

Ignoring my sinking heart, I turned my gaze to the third, a brunet built like he ran track and field. He didn't have the bulk of the blond or the willowy grace of the black-haired boy, but the way his blazer hung and curved and hugged his body promised lean, hard muscles that would melt a girl's panties. My gaze flickered to his face. He might have been the most handsome of the trio, with his startling sapphire eyes, straight nose, and strong jawline, if it wasn't for the scowl distorting his features.

Hatred burned in his eyes, and his lips curled into a snarl. It was enough to make my stomach twist into knots, and I glanced away, unable to withstand the weight of his stare.

"I must have a word with the headmaster about security," he said. They're letting in any old obnoxious tourist."

"Tourist?" Marissa screeched. She straightened herself to her full height of five feet five inches. "I'm the PA of Rudolph Trommel."

He stared down his nose at her and drawled, "Then I pity the man for not getting more decorous help."

"Wha—"

I rushed forward, stumbled over my feet, and grabbed the banister for balance. "Could you give us directions to the headmaster's office, please?"

"Mr. Chaloner can be found at the end of the first-floor hallway." He fixed me with a withering look. "And do keep your maid under control. This is an institution for education, not a baseball match."

The trio descended the stairs, and I pulled Marissa to one side. As they passed, I inhaled their mingled scents of sandalwood, citrus, and cedar, which filled me with a giddiness so heady, I had to brace myself against the wall of the stairwell. The black-haired one gave me a smile and a wink that promised a later, more intimate encounter.

I drew in a sharp breath through my nostrils, and the pulse between my legs pounded its approval. How could a tiny gesture like that have such a profound effect? I'd only just met these guys, and their intoxicating presence had mesmerized me into not getting offended that one of them had implied Marissa was my servant.

Marissa fumed in silence all the way to the headmaster's office. Guilt twanged at my heartstrings for not defending her. It wasn't like me to be so distracted by a guy's good looks, but there had been three of them, and my good sense had turned to mush.

The headmaster was a man in his early forties with pinched features topped by hair that had started to thin. Instead of black, academic robes, he wore a pinstriped suit and a dotted red tie—the kind of attire more suited to Wall Street.

"Welcome to Mercia Academy, Miss Hobson." Mr. Chaloner raised his bent arm to glance at his chunky gold watch, which also revealed matching, diamond-encrusted cufflinks. "Consider yourself fortunate to have been awarded a place at such short notice, as we're oversubscribed."

Marissa folded her arms across her chest. "Mr. Trommel made a sizable donation to the school for Emilia to jump the waiting list."

My brows drew together. The more they revealed, the more I thought my time here wasn't a last-minute decision. Rudolph had probably arranged my place here the moment Mom had accepted his proposal of marriage. He must have been desperate to get rid of me if he paid the school a bribe.

The headmaster's smiling facade dropped. "As a charitable institution that accepts donations, Mercia Academy is grateful to its many patrons and benefactors around the world." He turned to me. "Regardless of the generosity of your stepfather, Miss Hobson, while at Mercia, you will be subject to the same disciplinary procedures as all the other students."

My eyes bulged. How much exactly did Rudolph pay to keep me at the other side of the world? "Yes, sir."

He nodded. "In case you're thinking of using it to leverage preferential treatment, the donation is non-refundable even if you're expelled or decide to resign your place. Is that understood?"

"Y-yes, sir."

Mr. Chaloner curled his lip. "And I expect you to conduct yourself with the decorum befitting a student of a prestigious and ancient British institution steeped in tradition and history."

My teeth clenched. What kind of behavior did he expect from me?

"Is. That. Understood?" he asked.

A lead weight of dread pulled down my spirits. With warnings like that, what the hell could I expect from Mercia Academy? "Yes, sir."

CHAPTER 2

The headmaster explained that I would be rooming in Elder House, one of the two buildings dedicated to sixth-form students studying to take their Advanced Level exams. I nodded. He added that I would be in the lower-sixth, which was the equivalent of a high school senior in the States.

Without even making a phone call, he informed me that our housemaster, the man who would be in charge of my educational progress and welfare, was busy. I bristled as he escorted us out of the door and handed us over to his secretary. It was as if Marissa calling him out on acting like I was lucky to have been accepted had crushed his fragile ego.

Normally, I would have stewed at the affront, but I couldn't help thinking about the trio we'd met at the stairs. They had to be sixteen. Or seventeen, like me, which would make them sixth-formers. But would they be in Elder House, too? The black-haired runway-type looked friendly, but I wasn't sure about the blond. Jocks like him usually had girls scrambling after them and could sit back and take their pick.

I shook my head. Why was I even thinking about them? All three of them probably had every girl in Mercia Academy desperate to get into their pants. The last boy with the brown hair and sharp, blue eyes seemed to hate me already. If the contempt he displayed to Marissa was an indication of how he would treat me, I would stay away and keep a low profile.

The headmaster's secretary tapped my name into her computer and printed out the longest schedule I'd ever seen. Six days of classes, and 'prep' in the evenings before and after dinner. When did they expect a person to relax?

She returned to her computer. "Elder House… Elder. There's a prefect at the end of the hallway. Her name's Charlotte Underwood. Stay here, and I'll bring her over."

Marissa muttered, "At least someone has manners around here!"

I gave her a pat on the shoulder and what I hoped was a sympathetic smile. This was supposed to be such a classy institution, but so far, most people we had met had made an effort to make Marissa seem like she was disturbing their peace. All she'd wanted were directions.

She turned to me, brows furrowed. Somewhere between here and the limo, she'd lost her false eyelash. "I have to go now, but if you have any problems with these people, you call me. Alright? I'll be in London for the week and just a phone call away."

"Sure." My smile tightened. How could the assistant of an assistant help me if she was in another country in an even further away timezone? "I appreciate it."

Marissa walked down the hallway making as much noise as she could with her heels. I clasped my hands behind my back and turned to a portrait of a man dressed in armor, head bowed and holding a sword between his stretched hands. Hopefully, nobody would think the noise had come from my school loafers.

The secretary returned with a mousy-haired girl about my age whose Hooters girl curves strained through her blazer. Without meaning to, my gaze flickered down to my own B cups. Girls like her made me feel like a stalk of corn. Tall and thin with golden hair. At about five-feet-six, she stood four inches shorter than me, and yet somehow managed to look down her upturned nose at me as if I were a turd stuck to her Manolos. Her hazel eyes flickered up and down my body, then her thin lips tightened with disdain.

A rush of irritation scattered across my skin. Who did this girl think she was? The Queen of Mercia, probably.

"Emilia Hobson," said the secretary. "May I introduce you to Charlotte Underwood. Charlotte is a prefect at Elder House and will give you a tour of the grounds and show you to your room." The secretary scurried to her seat and picked up the phone. Probably to act as though she wasn't listening to whatever Charlotte would say.

I held out my hand. "Pleased to meet you."

The corners of her mouth twitched with disgust. "I have no doubt of that."

My hackles rose. "What does that mean?"

"Don't you observe social niceties in America, Hobson?" She tossed her head, nearly whacking me across the eyes with her ponytail, and strode down the hallway.

"Usually, we say that we're pleased to meet someone," I replied through clenched teeth.

Her head tilted to one side, lips stretched in a tight, condescending smile. "Here, we say, 'how do you do?'"

My brows furrowed. "How do you do what?"

She rolled her eyes. "Clearly, I'll have to sign you up for etiquette lessons. Where did you go to school?"

"New York." I was beginning to miss Park Prep already, where the mean girls threw insults, not patronizing puzzles.

She paused abruptly by a gold-framed portrait of a man in a long, white wig who seemed to look down at us with stern disapproval. "I mean *where* did you go to school? Charterhouse, Rugby, Shrewsbury?"

I'd be damned if I would admit to not knowing any of those places. "You wouldn't have heard of it. It's a small, *exclusive* prep school in Manhattan."

Charlotte sniffed. "I've heard the island is a rat-infested dump."

"Funny," I said. "Someone said the same about this place, but it's lovely. I guess only the gullible repeat unfounded rumors."

Charlotte gave me one of those tight smiles that said, *touché, bitch... stand by while I upgrade my shade-throwing game.* As we descended the stairs, she launched into an explanation that this was the main building, where all the classical lessons were taught, such as Latin, Classical Greek, Mathematics, Philosophy, and Literature.

We left through the back doors and walked along a pathway lined with magnolia trees, whose leaves had turned amber in the fall. The sun shone through their canopy, making the leaves glimmer like gold. On our left lay a square of lawn the size of ten football fields bordered by a number of old buildings that could have each been grand mansions.

She pointed out the art block, the drama block, the gymnasium, and the science block, explaining that wealthy alumni and other donors had funded the expansion of the school over the centuries. I clamped my lips together to hold back gasps at the historical sights. Even the newest of the buildings were older than anything found at home.

"Where did you say your family was from?" she asked, "New England?"

I tried not to gape at a building whose pillars reminded me of the New York Public Library. "Manhattan."

She wrinkled her nose. "I heard the—"

"Underwood," said a cultured voice from behind. It was as smooth as dark coffee, and gave me a jolt.

I turned around to find the trio of handsomeness walking a mere twenty feet behind us. My heart flip-flopped, and I took deep breaths to cool down the excited flush shooting up to my cheeks.

Charlotte smirked. "These three are also in Elder House."

"For our sins." The black-haired boy flashed a grin of gleaming, white teeth, making me catch my breath. He looked even more handsome in the sun with his tanned skin, thick eyebrows, and dimpled chin. If this was a production of Cinderella, he'd be Prince Charming. Tall, dark, and horny. "I'm Blake. Blake Simpson-West."

"How do you do?" My words came out a little stilted.

His face broke out into a wolfish smile, as though I'd said something stupid. I glanced at Charlotte, whose smirk of triumph made me want to slap myself upside the head. Who the hell asked people 'how do you do'? What did that even mean?

Blake gestured at the taller blond, who gazed down at me with expressionless eyes so green, they made the lawn look dull. "This handsome brute is Henry Bourneville of the Bournevilles."

My mind went blank. Was that supposed to mean something? I scrambled for an intelligible response, but all I could think of was Tess of the d'Urbervilles. I clamped my lips together to keep myself from blurting out something stupid.

His brows rose as though surprised I'd never heard of the name. With an amused quirk of his lips, he said, "How d'you do?"

My intestines formed several tight knots. Was he making fun of me or was there a specific reply to that nonsensical phrase? I kind of wished I'd sat through the Disney version of Alice in Wonderland or had at least skimmed through the book. It was the sort of thing the madcap characters would say to each other. "Ummm... I'm fine, thanks."

The last guy, the one with the mahogany hair whose ends shone like burnished copper and with eyes as blue and fathomless as the ocean, scowled, making the blood drain from my face. My stomach knots formed a noose I could use to hang myself. Maybe I'd used the wrong reply. Breached some kind of unbreachable British etiquette. Charlotte's huffed laugh was just background noise compared to the contempt screaming on his face.

"You're an American," he said in clipped tones. "Much like the woman who accompanied you into the main teaching block."

"Yes," I whispered, voice cracking.

"I haven't finished the introductions!" Blake's smooth voice sliced through the tension, making the knots in my stomach untighten. "This unfriendly bastard is Edward Mercia, heir to the Duchy of Mercia."

"And the de-facto owner of Mercia Academy," added Charlotte.

All the moisture evaporated from my mouth, leaving a tongue as stiff and as dry as pumice. Duchy meant duke, didn't it? What on earth did a person do when they met minor royalty? Bow, curtsey, or act like they were a regular person? My mind jumped back to what Blake had said. If Edward was the heir, that meant he wasn't yet the duke.

I cleared my throat. "I'm… pleased to meet you."

The smile he gave me was as cold as a snowdrift. "The pleasure is all yours, of that I am assured."

Charlotte stepped forward. "This is Emilia… Emilia…" She tapped her bottom lip. "Did you even have a last name?"

My hackles rose. The secretary had told her my full name, and she'd used it at least once. Through clenched teeth, I said, "Hobson."

"Emilia Hobson comes to us from an *exclusive* prep school in Manhattan which she refuses to name."

"Park Preparatory," I snarled. "And you didn't ask."

She waved away my correction like it was an annoying gnat. "Never heard of it."

Edward turned his cold gaze back to me. Even from the distance of six feet away, the glare lanced me through the gut like an icicle. "Emilia… whatever your name is." His voice was deep and smooth and resonant. The type that could slip through a girl's defenses and command her to do whatever he wanted. "We don't like Americans here at Mercia Academy."

My brows drew together. "Why not?"

"For reasons too numerous and too complex for a vacuous tart like you to understand. Save yourself a term of torment and turn away. We've never had an American last a term. Leave now, and you'll at least preserve your sanity."

I placed my hands on my hips. "And I suppose you're talking as the so-called owner of the academy?"

"I'm giving you a final warning." Edward stepped forward, close enough for his sandalwood and cypress scent to fill my nostrils. "Call back your Cadillac or whatever jalopy dragged you to our fine establishment and get out. If I have to tell you again, you won't like my methods."

Fury pumped hot blood into my veins, heating my skin. How dare this conceited asshole talk to me like he already owned the academy and decided who could stay and who could leave? If this was any indication of the kind of shit-talk I'd have to endure, I would turn around and go home. Why would I subject myself to such hateful, judgmental, and bigoted people?

I was about to tell him to pull the branch out of his ass when Marissa's words returned to the forefront of my mind. Rudolph had challenged me to endure two years of a British boarding school to develop the mental toughness I needed for a career in journalism. If I was going to let an arrogant asshole run me out of the academy after a day, then I didn't deserve the internship or the funding he would give me for an Ivy League college education.

Forcing my lips into a sweet smile, I tilted my head to the side. "Sorry, I forgot your name already, but thanks for the warning. I'll take it with a grain of salt."

Even with his face flushed and nostrils flared, Edward was breathtakingly handsome. "Don't say I didn't warn you."

I gave the school crest on his blazer a contemptuous pat and continued down the path, saying over my shoulder, "I take back what I said. There was no pleasure in meeting you at all."

Moments later, Charlotte caught up. "Ooooh! The boys are going to put you in your place, and I can't wait to watch."

"Really?" How else was I supposed to respond to a comment like that? Turn around, grab her shoulders and beg her to tell me what the boys had planned? It was probably nothing, given the grueling schedule of classes and sparse free periods.

Charlotte tired of gaping at my face for a reaction and continued her tour, explaining that Elder House was the original seat of the Duke of Mercia, who used his home to train elite soldiers for the hundred years war for King Henry V. I cast my mind back to history lessons. That would have been in the fifteenth century.

"The academy is now the training ground for the ruling classes of Great Britain," she said. "My family has attended for centuries. Father's the Secretary of State for the Supreme Court. He practically runs the country and makes all the most important decisions."

My brows rose. We'd also studied a bit of British politics at Park Prep. "Really, what do the Prime Minister and the rest of the cabinet do, while your father's the de-facto King of England?"

Blake, the runway model lookalike, snickered from behind. "Underwood's father is an administrator who barely serves on the cabinet."

My head jerked back. He was following us?

Charlotte's face turned purple with rage.

I smiled, imagining Noelle standing beside me. "We had insecure girls at Park Prep who tried to make themselves more important, too. I guess England isn't much different from the States."

She clenched her teeth. "Get out, you low-born Yank. You don't belong here."

I smoothed down the lapels of my blazer. "Mercia Academy can't be that exclusive if they let a lowly Yank jump the waiting list, can it?"

Charlotte paused beside a bench with a gold plaque etched with the name of the person who had donated it to the school. I don't know whether my timing was off, or if she'd deliberately paused at the bench with the name of an Underwood ancestor, or if her family had donated all the benches, but I would have colored myself impressed if I hadn't just been threatened and insulted.

She tossed her hair. "Hobson probably used her feminine wiles on the headmaster."

Blake grinned. "I'd let her in for a chance of those wiles."

I rolled my eyes and let out a weary sigh. "Can you stop the puerile speculations and just show me to my room, please?"

Charlotte turned on her heel. "Find it yourself. And enjoy a life of torment and solitude with rancid-Rita!"

I shook my head, watching her storm off down the path and back toward the main teaching block like an offended cat. She'd been so desperate to demonstrate her superiority, she'd exaggerated her father's importance in British politics. I might have kept quiet and not called her out if she hadn't been so disparaging.

"Emilia," murmured Blake in that smooth, smoky voice. "I'll escort you to Elder House and help you get comfortable."

I glanced around for someone—anyone not associated with either Charlotte and that hostile Edward Mercia, but nobody else was roaming the pathway. Twenty feet behind us, Edward and Henry stood shoulder-to-shoulder, probably planning their next bout of insults and glaring. I was left with Blake, the only friendly face, even if he did agree that I'd slept my way into the academy.

He placed a hand on the small of my back and leaned forward, his face so close to mine, the warmth of his skin and his intoxicating scent engulfed my senses. His gaze moved from my eyes to my mouth, and I felt myself staring at his sensual lips. A lash of hot desire whipped through my core as I imagined what they might taste like, and my body swayed towards him as if drawn by an invisible force.

"Come on, I won't bite..." he murmured. "Unless that's your kink."

I exhaled a shuddering breath and ignored my arousal. "Thank you. I'd appreciate it."

Edward crossed the distance and curled his lip. "Blake, if you return covered in fleas, I'll throw you into the lake."

"Fleas?" For reasons I couldn't even fathom, Edward's words hit like a slap. I jerked back from Blake, heart pounding with an odd mix of confusion and desire. "H-how old are you, five?"

Blake huffed out a laugh and looked at me as though I were a sugar-coated pretzel..

"When one lies down with a dog, the inevitable result is fleas." Edward's tight, wintry smile and frigid stare said it all. I was stupid for not understanding he'd indirectly called me a bitch. "Enjoy your next few hours of peace, Miss Hobson. Life at Mercia Academy is about to become unbearable."

CHAPTER 3

After casting that asshole, Edward, one last glare, I let Blake guide me down the magnolia tree path. He returned his hand to the small of my back and gave me an apologetic smile. Even through the thick, woolen blazer, the heat radiating from his fingertips penetrated my flesh. It spread around my back and down my belly, where it swirled around my core, making it pulse in time with the pounding of my heart. His spicy, sandalwood scent filled my nostrils and heightened my alertness.

I studied his features from the corner of my eye. The way those beautiful lips curved into an amused smile told me all I needed to know about Blake Simpson-West. This was a guy who knew the effect he had on women and enjoyed using it to get whatever he desired.

My breaths became shallow, and I bit down hard on my bottom lip from reacting to his touch. I willed myself to step away, to show him he wasn't as irresistible as he probably thought, but my traitorous body wouldn't move.

"Are you alright?" Blake asked with a chuckle. "You seem a little flushed."

"I'm fine." The words came out a little more clipped than I intended.

Blake's eyes bored into the side of my face as he ran his hand up and down my back, making my skin tingle. "I seem to have a peculiar effect on you. Why is that?"

The arrogance in his words snapped the sense back into my limbs, and I stepped away, face as hot and probably as red as coals. I was right. This was the playboy of the group. The guy who knew his way around a girl's mind and body to lure her to a humiliating downfall. I'd read about this type in hundreds of books. Women found him an irresistible challenge and fooled themselves into thinking they could tame his womanizing ways because their libidos took over.

Well, this was no fairytale, and I was no princess. As much as I wanted to snap out something to wipe that cocky grin off his handsome face and to stop those chocolate-brown eyes from twinkling with triumph, I still needed Blake to show me to my room.

"You're not affecting me." I straightened my blazer. "I'm just ticklish. I could have had that reaction with anyone."

His brows rose in the kind of incredulous expression people gave when humoring a bad liar. "Alright, then. I'll try not to tickle you while I escort you to your rooms."

"Rooms?" I pictured a suite with a living room, bedroom, bathroom, and kitchenette.

He waved a dismissive hand, wrapped it around my waist, and drew me close to his side. The one-two punch combination of a strong, muscled body and his incubus scent made my heart pound and my knees go weak.

"You seem a little unsteady on your feet, Emilia." His breath tickled my skin, and his low, smoky voice tickled me much lower down. "If there's anything you need. A helping hand, or some such, I'll be there. Ready and able to please."

A breath hissed through my teeth. I should push him away and tell him where to shove his offer. No one but a player ever came on that strong, but his touch, his words, even his hot breath made me feel alive in a way I'd never experienced. Every nerve ending vibrated with life, responding to his silent siren song.

"S-some such?" I asked.

We stopped at the double doors of a house in a different architectural style to the main teaching block. This one was a lot older, with smaller and fewer windows. Blake opened the door and bowed with a flourish. "Welcome to Elder House, my lady. Your home and mine for the next two years."

The absence of his body next to mine was both a loss and a relief. I took a steadying breath, willing the pounding in my heart to calm, and hoped the reception hall and its large, roaring fire would replace his missing heat. I stepped into the warm stone room, and my gaze swung to the mantle, above which hung a painting of what looked like the same armored man as the one outside the headmaster's office. A number of mahogany cabinets stood around the walls, each about the size of a breadbox with letter-sized slots.

"Is this some kind of mail room?" I asked.

"Yes." His hand returned to the small of my back, and he ushered me through the reception hall and into a corridor. "Our common room is at the end of this hallway. It's where some of the sixth formers like to relax after prep and before lights out. We're a lot quieter than the other houses that accommodate younger students."

"Why's that?" I was sure someone had explained this, but I couldn't think of anything else but that hand on my back and what it could do to the rest of my body.

"Only sixth formers are allowed in Elder and Hawthorn houses," he replied. "If you see anyone under the age of sixteen, feel free to give them a boot in the backside."

Blake took me to a room on the left side of the hallway and introduced me to Mr. Jenkins, the housemaster, who explained he was the keeper of the keys and in charge of the general welfare, academic or otherwise, of the people in Elder house. Mr. Jenkins was a kindly man of about five-food-eight, who was delighted that I would be sharing with Rita Yelverton. He pressed a key into my hand and wished me the best of luck.

Next, Blake ushered me up a set of stone stairs whose walls radiated the cold. Goosebumps rose on my flesh. It was no wonder they'd put the fire on despite it being a mild September day. These old buildings had no insulation.

"Female dorms are on the first and second floors. Male at the top." He reached the first flight and held the door open to a darkened hallway of mahogany floors. A large window at the end provided the only illumination. "By the way, who was the atrocious woman with the nauseating accent?"

He was referring to Marissa, but I snapped, "Charlotte Underhill."

His face split into a grin. "My apologies for the offense," he said in a voice that indicated he didn't give a shit but wanted to move the conversation past his insult. He brushed a lock of auburn hair off my face and let his gaze linger down my body. "Was the older lady your mother or another relative? I see no family resemblance."

My mouth dried. Marissa was short, much like Charlotte, with the kind of curves that made men turn around to check out her ass. I was like Mom. Tall and willowy, all angles and no jiggle. At five ten, I didn't exactly tower over most guys, but it was hard not to feel gangly around a group of smaller girls with perfect little figures.

My tongue darted out to lick my lips. His eyes tracked the movement. "Marissa… She's one of my stepfather's personal assistants."

"And your stepfather is?" He let the question hang in the air. "I didn't quite catch the name."

"Rudolph Trommel."

He tilted his head to the side. "I can't say I've heard of him. What industry is he in?"

I shrugged. "He buys media companies, mostly."

"Business must be lucrative if he's sent you here." He stepped into the hallway, as though the subject had bored him already.

I blinked hard. Rudolph Trommel was one of the most well-known tycoons in America. When pictures of him and Mom had appeared in the society pages, people I'd never heard from in years got in contact, asking for introductions, as though being the daughter of his current paramour granted me access to the man. I'd barely met him. Barely seen Mom during their whirlwind romance, and would likely barely hear from her until the inevitable divorce. A breath of relief slipped through my lips. It was nice to be in a place where nobody had heard of Rudolph Trommel.

When I caught up, Blake rested his hand on my hip and guided me through the hallway as though he was escorting me home from a date and expected to be invited in for coffee. His reaction to Edward's comment about fleas no longer stung. It hadn't been personal, and he seemed the type who would laugh at anything.

"So," he said, all business-like. "This is one of the female hallways. They house two-person dorms for the lower-sixth years."

"Are you in the upper-sixth?"

He grinned. "Thank you for the compliment, but I only turned seventeen a few days ago. If you'd like to give me a belated birthday kiss, I'll accept it with humble thanks."

My hand shot up to my mouth to hide a giggle. Blake was charming and funny, along with ridiculously handsome. A girl could fall for a rogue like him and probably not even regret it when he moved onto the next conquest. There was only one way to deal with such a flirt, and that was to never give him what he wanted until he swore off other women and meant it.

A smile curved my lips. All my knowledge of men was theoretical. During the times between divorces, Mom and I could get really close, and she would dish out nuggets of advice that I never thought I'd need... until now.

"Right." Blake furrowed his brows. "You'll be rooming with Rita Yelverton."

"Why did you say her name like that?"

He blinked. "I don't follow."

"You said her name as though there was a nasty smell under your nose."

"She's a scholarship student." He raised a shoulder. "Music and academics."

"What's wrong with that?"

"Nothing at all," he said too quickly to be true.

I narrowed my eyes. Either Rita was an innocent girl whose studious habits and scholarship offended him, or she was an unholy bitch who made Charlotte seem as cheerful and loving as Mary Poppins.

I placed my key in the lock and turned it, revealing a huge room, larger than my previous dorm in Park Prep. On the far left, four narrow windows streamed their light on two single beds arranged in a pair of alcoves. A fire burned in a stone fireplace, whose contents crackled and popped and spread dry warmth throughout the room. The side of the room farthest from the wall had posters of John Coltrane and Miles Davis, two of my favorite jazz musicians, and smaller pictures of Billie Holiday, Nina Simone, and Ella Fitzgerald.

I stepped into the room and exhaled a sigh of relief. No one who liked such great music could be a bad person. When Noelle got dumped, she and I had spent hours singing along with Billie Holiday's songs of heartache. A person who really understood those words couldn't ever inflict pain on others.

"There's something you're not telling me about my roommate." I turned and narrowed my eyes at Blake, who lounged against the doorjamb like he was a jazz singer. "What is it?"

He raised his palms. "There's nothing wrong with her. She's just… unpopular."

"Why?"

Blake stepped back into the hallway. "It's nothing I can place my finger on. Rita isn't just not very sociable."

I shrugged. "Antisocial I can deal with."

He clicked his heels in the parody of a devoted soldier and bowed with a flourish. "Then I will leave you to acquaint yourself with your new home."

Blake strode down the hallway, leaving me to study my side of the room. The white wall and white comforter on the wooden bed made for extremely dull accommodation. I'd have to buy a quilt or ask Mom to send something over from our storage unit.

With Rudolph's help, she had sold the Parkside apartment from the settlement she received from my previous stepfather, a man I'd barely met because I'd been sent away to school. Very few had bothered to ask why I didn't just walk the twenty minutes it would have taken each morning. But then I supposed a lot of us at Park Prep were in similar situations with parents too preoccupied or apathetic to care for their own kids.

My monogrammed, Louis Vuitton cases lay at the foot of the bed. They were Mom's way of apologizing for letting Rudolph send me halfway across the world. I shook my head. Did she think meaningless luggage could replace a mother?

I pulled out my smartphone and texted Mom, then Dad, then Noelle, to tell them I'd made it to my new school. Dad lived all the way in La Jolla, California, with his wife and young family, and couldn't afford to take care of a teen who would need college tuition and other equally as significant expenses.

After tying back my hair with one of the bands I kept around my wrist, I shut the door of my room and picked up the first case. I'd missed two weeks from the start of term. That was an eternity for someone who needed to take exams in a foreign country with foreign spelling and foreign study methods.

A knock sounded on the door, and the knob turned. Before I

could straighten, Charlotte stepped in with a pair of girls wearing headbands the same shade of burgundy as their blazers. Each stood with their chests thrust out, looking like they were in the middle of a boob-enhancement exercise. I imagined they were trying to appear as well-endowed as Charlotte, but they just looked pathetic. If I called them clones, it would suggest that Charlotte had a sense of style worth copying. The girls were more ghastly apparitions of Charlotte, or better still, doppelgängers.

"The British public school system is far more advanced than anything you've experienced," said Charlotte. "Go back to America."

I folded my arms across my chest. "I thought this was a private school."

Charlotte rolled her eyes, glanced back to her pair of doppelgängers for reassurance, before turning back to me. "In Great Britain, public schools are the most elite."

"Much like the British cabinet," I said with a smirk.

Charlotte turned to an unseen spot in the hallway. "Edward, tell the others what you found out."

Edward Mercia stepped into view. The window at the end of the hallway lit only one side of his face, casting the other side in mostly shadow. It brought out the prominence of his cheekbones, his strong jaw and the arch of his dark eyebrows. I drew in a sharp breath through my nostrils at the sight. As soon as he locked eyes with me, all that beauty morphed into a mask of hatred so fierce, it made my heart wrench.

He strolled forward, out of the spellbinding light. With both sides of his face fully lit, the effect was no less handsome. "Hobson's mother is a woman who slept with an ugly multi-millionaire to win her place here at the academy."

Charlotte's sycophants made loud gasps, acting as if they hadn't heard this information before and as if it was the most shocking revelation since Darth Vader revealed he was Luke's father.

My lips tightened. "She got married. It wasn't some kind of a tawdry transaction."

Edward held up his smartphone, showing a society picture of Mom looking stunning in a figure-hugging wedding gown standing outside on the steps of Rudolph's hotel. And there I was standing next to her in a mini-me bridesmaid's dress wearing the most obvious, pained smile.

His face twisted into a smirk. "Congratulations on the recent nuptials... *Trollop.*"

CHAPTER 4

I had to google the word trollop. It was a seventeenth century British word that meant I was a whore. The assholes here probably used obscure insults to make themselves feel sophisticated. It just made them look pathetic and pretentious.

The rest of the morning wasn't great. All of my classes were with Edward and his friends or with Charlotte and her doppelgängers. I didn't mind Blake so much. He was a harmless flirt only dangerous to anyone gullible enough to take his interest seriously. Despite the effect he had on my body, I wasn't deluded enough to believe someone who came on so strongly to a stranger would only have interest in one woman. So far, blond Henry was an enigma, observing me like being an American was a curious puzzle he needed to solve. As long as all he did was look, I would endure his stares.

My electives, the subjects I wanted to take for my Advanced Level exams, were English Literature, Creative Writing, Media Studies, and Spanish. Because the administration of Mercia Academy wanted to keep their students too busy to cause mischief, they'd added on Latin and Classical Greek, as though someone who had never studied ancient languages had a chance to catch up with those who had been taught it since they were eleven.

After English Lit, I followed the rest of the class back to Elder House, where lunch was served in an old-fashioned banqueting hall. Triple-height windows provided most of the illumination, and ten-foot-tall mahogany panels covered the walls. On the far left, a long table stood on a dais, and behind it hung the painting of the armored knight, flanked by a painting of the knights without his armor, and another of a king. Around the rest of the room stood smaller tables, seating four or six diners.

I blew out a breath of relief, glad that they weren't the long rows I'd seen in movies like Harry Potter.

Most of the tables were occupied, and people I approached whose tables had free seats glared at me until I went away. I found a scrawny boy with thick glasses and acne sitting at the back with a pile of newspapers next to his place setting.

"Excuse me," I said, "Is this seat taken?"

His gaze swept up and down my body, and with an accent so thick and posh, I could barely understand him, he said, "There are no seats in this dining room for yanks."

I folded my arms across my chest. Had Edward Mercia told him to say that, or was everyone in this room a raging xenophobe?

"You may sit with me if you like," drawled a bleached blonde wearing a velvet headband the same color as her blazer. She sat on her own at the next table down.

"Thanks." I offered her a smile and slid into the seat next to her.

"Wendy Radcliff." She stuck out her hand. "How d'you do?"

"Fine, I guess. How are you?"

"Curious." Her gray eyes gleamed. "News spread really fast about the newbie. I hear your mother married Rudolph Trommel."

People from nearby tables leaned across, listening out for tidbits of gossip. Bitterness coated my tongue. She'd only invited me to sit with her to gather information. I reached for the jug of water in the middle of the table and poured myself a glass. "That's true."

"What's he like, then?"

"Mom met him while I was in prep school. I barely got to see Rudolph before the wedding."

She nodded, as though not seeing one's parents and missing out on major life events was an average occurrence. It probably was with the boarding-school crowd. I nodded my thanks at a server who slipped a plate of grilled chicken and salad onto my setting. Wendy nibbled tiny morsels of shepherd's pie from her fork, which she explained was a dish of mashed potato atop minced lamb. "Mikkel Jensen is your biological father, isn't he?"

"How did you find that out?"

Wendy shrugged. "It was on the Mercia-Net."

"The what?"

"Our online bulletin board where we share all the latest news."

My pulse pounded in my ears, drowning out the sounds of forks and knives clinking on porcelain. "Who posted news about my dad?"

"Lots of people." She tapped her smartphone and scrolled down. "Take a look for yourself."

Several people, most names I didn't even recognize, had uploaded news reports about Mom. She was a popular model in the late nineties who left the profession when she married an up-and-coming Danish photographer and had me. They'd even posted a bunch of crap about Dad's drug problems, trips to rehab, and Mom finally leaving him when I was five. He was mostly clean now, with a small family, but people liked to focus on the negative.

I tore my gaze away. "Doesn't anyone have better things to do around here?"

Wendy mixed the shepherd's pie into mush and pointed the prongs of her messy fork in my face. "You're the biggest news we've had since the start of term."

"How nice for me," I muttered.

"Do tell." Her gray eyes darkened with malice. "Why would your mother marry a wrinkled, balding billionaire when she could have your handsome-beyond-belief father?"

I set down my silverware and rose out of my seat. "Apparently, you just looked at the pictures and came to your own conclusions."

Wendy stood and waved me away. "You might as well stay. I'm going to sit with friends."

She sashayed to the head table, where Edward, Blake, and Henry sat like they were a triumvirate of kings overseeing their court. Blake inclined his head, with an expression that said he acknowledged my interest in him, and if I was lucky, he'd grant me a night of satisfaction. I ground my teeth and scowled. To his right sat Charlotte, who smirked as though she was about to glean whatever I'd shared with Wendy. I forced my lips into a smirk. Too bad the creepy girl had been unsubtle with her line of questioning and didn't collect anything she hadn't already found on the Mercia-Net. From now on, I'd be careful answering any personal questions.

"Wait," I said.

Wendy turned around, gray eyes alight with excitement, and a smirk dancing on her lips. "Yes?"

"Where's Rita Yelverton?"

Her face split into the widest grin I'd seen outside of a crocodile. "She lacks the social graces to eat with the rest of the house. But I'm sure you'll find her scurrying about behind the skirting boards, looking for cheese."

I shook my head. From what I'd gleaned, Rita had been bullied and now stayed away from the rest of the school. The more these snobs dropped nasty hints about her, the more I liked the girl. She seemed to be the only decent person I'd be likely to meet in Elder House.

After lunch was compulsory Latin, taught by Mr. Frost, a red-haired man who didn't look much older than us. The lesson mostly centered on him focusing his attention on the triumvirate and ignoring the rest of the class, who worked from a textbook. At one stage, Edward whispered something to him that made the teacher's head snap up.

He fixed me with a leer, strode to the blackboard and wrote a three letter word in capitals. "Miss Hobson, conjugate the verb *sum*."

I raised a shoulder. There was a phrase we'd learned at Park Prep, *cogito ergo sum*, but I wouldn't admit that I knew it and give him any ammunition to use against me. It was clear that Edward had told him to catch me out. "We didn't study Latin in my old school, sir."

"All right." He rocked back on his heels, holding the ends of his academic robes, and smirked. "Try an easier verb: *amare*."

"The interesting thing about schools that don't teach Latin is that they don't. Teach. Latin," I said, channeling Noelle's Professor Snape impression.

Muffled laughter bubbled up from around the room.

His face turned red. "That's five demerits for rudeness!"

I raised a brow. It wasn't like they could cash in a demerit for a caning. He could give me a hundred, and I wouldn't care. I glared at Edward, who glared back, eyes blazing with animosity. Did he really think I was pathetic enough to catch the next plane crying because an ass-kissing teacher unfairly called me out in class? He'd have to try a lot harder to make me leave.

The next class was Spanish, where the only person I recognized was Henry, the blond who couldn't stop staring with those emerald-green eyes. A-level Spanish was more of a literature class than a language class, and the teacher discussed a book, *Maria*, by Jorge Isaac, in rapid Spanish. Although I struggled with his accent, it was harder to ignore the way Henry continued to gape at me, even when the teacher asked him a question. The way he smiled and didn't answer made me wonder if he was a dumb jock. He certainly had the physique of one.

I dipped my head, scribbled down notes, and focused on the lesson. Henry might well have the kind of body that made me wish I owned X-ray spectacles and had eight arms to roam over his expanse of taut muscles, but I wouldn't let him distract me from one of the few subjects I had a chance of passing.

After classes, a group of girls stepped into my path and asked if Mom had really screwed Rudolph Trommel to get me a place at Mercia Academy. I rolled my eyes and told them they were giving their educational institution too much credit. It was more likely someone would screw a multi-millionaire to be sent somewhere else. I stormed through the hallways, making snappy comebacks at whoever called me a trollop or suggested that Mom was a whore for achieving what all these bitchy types were probably sent here to do: marry up.

I reached Elder House, where the insults came thick and fast. By the time the twentieth person hissed the word trollop as I passed, my blood had reached boiling point, and I was ready to snap. I stormed through the first-floor hallway, heart pumping venom and mouth crammed with a barrage of insults I would spew at the next person who dared to call me a name.

I flung the door to my room open, startling a short girl with huge eyes such a deep brown, they appeared black. Her dark brown hair was tied back from her face and formed a luxurious braid that stretched down to her waist. She wore a headband the same shade of burgundy as her blazer, and held a plate of sandwiches covered in saran wrap.

"Who the fuck are you?" I snapped.

The girl shrank into the wall of jazz posters and clutched her plate to her chest. "R-Rita. Rita Yelverton."

All the anger drained out of me in a rush of guilt. "Oh, gosh. I'm sorry." Stepping forward, I held out my hand. "Emilia Hobson. Your new roommate."

Still pressed against the wall between her picture of Billie

Holiday and Nina Simone, she stared at my paltry peace offering and nodded. "P-pleased to meet you."

I stepped back. "You know, you're the only person who's said that to me."

Her arms dropped, and she held the plate at navel level with both hands. "W-what are they saying?"

"'How do you do' or something like that. I mean, how's a person supposed to respond to a question like that?"

Rita's full lips curved into a shy smile. She peered up from her lashes and said, "You're supposed to say, 'How do you do?' back."

My eyes bulged. "You're kidding me!"

She dipped her head into her shoulders. "No, really. That's the correct response."

"Then why did you say you were pleased to meet me?"

Rita raised a shoulder. "I'm not upper class. Not even lower middle. I wasn't brought up with people like that and only joined Mercia last year. It's a bit of a minefield here, but you get used to it eventually."

I chewed my lip. Eating sandwiches alone in a bedroom didn't strike me as someone getting used to life at Mercia Academy, but I held my tongue. After a day of mean girls, a triumvirate of excruciatingly handsome wanna-be kings, and the oddity of dozens of people with Downton Abbey accents calling me a trollop, I felt ground-down and ready to snap. I couldn't imagine surviving a year of this crap.

"Are you really going to eat that?" I gestured at a sandwich covered in saran wrap.

She frowned. "It's what I get every day."

"Come with me. We're going to the dining room and having a real dinner. Together."

"But no one ever allows me to sit with them."

I crooked my arm. "There was an empty table at lunchtime. We can sit there together like a pair of outcasts."

The hope that lit her eyes wrung my heart dry. "What if someone tells us to leave?"

"Then they'd have to carry us both out by our chairs because I'm not going anywhere."

A hush fell across the dining room as we entered. I couldn't tell whether it was for the trollop wanting a meal, for Rita's entrance, or because we'd formed an alliance. I was judging it was a combination of all three from the way everyone gaped. I straightened to my full five feet and ten inches and raised my chin, challenging anyone to tell me a Yank didn't deserve dinner. Nobody said a word as we walked through the dining room and sat at what I now deemed our table.

A server rushed over and took our order. The older woman beamed at Rita, seemingly delighted that she'd finally come to the dining room to eat. Blake, Edward, and Henry took their seats at the head table. I leaned over and asked in a low voice, "Why don't teachers sit up there?"

"We only have our housemaster, Mr. Jenkins. His wife's the matron of Elder House, and they prefer to eat together in private. All the other teachers eat in the staff dining room."

"That sucks," I muttered.

"It only works like that in the sixth form houses." She poured herself a glass of water then raised the jug in silent question. When I nodded, she poured me a glass, too. "I was in Sycamore last year, where the housemaster, his assistant, and the matron all dined with us." She dipped her head. "They made sure everyone was included."

"It's ike a civilized version of *Lord of the Flies* here. What gives those three the right to sit at the head table?"

The server placed two plates of salmon and steamed vegetables in front of us, while Rita whispered her answers. Edward was the only son of the Duke of Mercia, whose ancestor founded the academy. While the land and the ancient buildings belonged to the family, the academy was technically a charity funded by wealthy patrons, alumni, and parents. They lived off the academy's payments for the use of his land as well as other kickbacks related to ancient laws passed by long-dead kings.

I gaped. "That's why he's sitting on the head table like he owns the place?"

"He will one day."

I shook my head. No wonder he thought he had the right to dictate who got to stay at Mercia Academy and who got to leave. "What about Blake?"

Rita's eyes gleamed as she speared a new potato with her fork. "His mother is the second wife to the second in the line to the throne. I've heard him say that if his step-uncle dies, his stepfather will become the King of England."

I leaned forward. "Who, Prince—"

"Yes!" She popped the potato in her mouth.

"No!" My head reeled with the information. Why did people I'd only just met call me a trollop when Mom married rich, just like Blake's mother? I shook my head. "What about Henry?"

"His family owns the Bournville department store."

"Is that anything like Harrods?"

"Bigger. And the oldest department store in the world." Her voice dropped to a whisper. "His family also owns a quarter of the freeholds in central London."

My gaze flickered to the blond, who whispered something into Edward's ear. "He doesn't look super-rich."

"He's the only one of the three who doesn't flash his money about. They say he likes to be modest."

"How do you know all this?"

She gave me a rueful smile. "It's amazing what you can overhear in the back of the class when you're quiet."

I asked Rita about her life. She lived with her Mom in the English equivalent of the projects. Her dad was a Portuguese guitarist who died when she was five, and she was studying A Level

Music, History of Art, Music Technology, and Portuguese. When I asked her about how she liked Mercia Academy, she clammed up. I dropped the subject, deciding to wait until we knew each other better before asking again.

Rita accepted two servings of apple crumble, something that reminded me of peach cobbler but looked a lot more grainy. I stirred my bowl of custard, soaking in the history of this room. At some point, King Henry V would have sat here as the honored guest of the Duke of Mercia, and now, I got the chance to dine here. It was a pity so many of the people I'd met had been dicks.

Rita whimpered and shrank into herself. I turned to see what had made her so distressed. Blake, Edward, and Henry stepped down from their dais and strolled across the room, eyes fixed on our table. My heart accelerated, and all the moisture in my mouth vanished. I swallowed, willing myself to forget everything Rita had said about them. They were just people. Even if they were handsome, rich, and well-connected, I wouldn't act the fool and kiss their feet like Charlotte and her doppelgängers.

Edward took the lead. "You're keeping odd company, trollop."

"I enjoy hanging out with people who remember my name." I shook my head at his nerve. Did he expect me to beg for a set at his feet?

"Here." He threw a book in my dessert bowl, making custard splash on my blazer. "This should teach you how to address your betters."

Nervous chuckles came from other tables, along with hushed and scandalized whispers. I stared down at the mess, nostrils flaring, anger searing through my veins. That was the kind of prank people stopped doing at elementary school. I picked up the book by its clean corner and stood. Edward straightened, his cold, blue eyes challenging me to make my next move. Blake grinned, and Henry stared at me as though I was a fascinating new species he hadn't yet categorized.

I glanced at the cover. *"Debrett's Guide to Etiquette and Modern Manners?"*

Someone a few tables away choked with laughter, and one corner of Edward's mouth lifted into a smile. "Memorize it from cover to cover on the plane back to America."

I shoved the book, custard-first, into his chest. "It seems like you need its lessons more than me."

A hush fell across the dining room. Edward dropped the book onto the floor and glowered down at his smeared blazer. "Very well," he said, voice shaking with restrained anger. "I accept your declaration of war."

CHAPTER 5

That night, I couldn't help thinking about Edward and his dumb declaration. I lay in bed, eyes squeezed shut, haunted by those ocean-deep eyes looking through me and laying me bare. What did war mean, exactly? That they'd find a more hurtful thing to call me than trollop? Or would they post links to more trashy articles on the Mercia-Net?

I turned, pulling my comforter over my ears. I couldn't see them resorting to sticks and stones, but what could be so bad that they hadn't already said or dug up?

A sliver of moonlight flickered across my closed lids, and I snapped my eyes open and grabbed my smartphone. Four in the morning. Eleven at night in New York. Eight in the evening in California. Noelle had sent me a barrage of messages, demanding to know why I hadn't given her a minute-by-minute accounting of my first day of school. I sent her a quick reply, explaining that the schedule had been heavy and that most of the people I had met had been assholes.

Mom hadn't replied to my text, which was typical of her during the honeymoon phase of her marriages. Eventually, she would come back to earth and realize she had a daughter.

Dad had sent an email with pictures of his twins, Tamara and Tony. I tapped out a message, telling him the school grounds were unbelievably grand, and that I felt I was living in a fairytale. There was no need to specify that most of the original tales involved persecuted heroines. It would only worry him and set back his recovery.

When I eventually shut my eyes, the memory of Edward's glare still lingered. Except in my dream, he was declaring something else instead of war.

The bell broke me out of my sleep. I opened bleary eyes and shuddered at the erotic nightmare I'd had of Edward's eyes, Blake's roving hands, and Henry's body. What kind of sicko dreamed of the boys who were trying to make her life hell?

Rita was already dressed with her satchel of books over her shoulder. "Have a good day." She twisted the doorknob and paused. "That's strange."

I sat up. "What?"

"It won't budge." She twisted again, making a little straining noise in the back of her throat.

"Let me try." I swung my legs off the bed and strode to the door. Rita stepped aside, and I tried the knob. "It's totally jammed."

"Right." She bowed her head. "The war."

I closed my eyes for a couple of seconds and opened them, incredulity making my brows crinkle. "A prank war. Can't they think of anything more mature?"

Rita walked to her desk drawer and pulled out her smartphone. "We'll have to call someone."

"Who?" I asked.

"Mr. Carbuncle, the caretaker." She placed the phone to her ear and tapped her foot. After several moments, she said, "It's gone to voicemail."

"Ugh." I called Marissa, who answered in two rings. After explaining the situation to her, she assured me she would continue ringing the headmaster's office until someone dealt with the problem. My shoulders dropped with relief. She'd still been outraged from the rude treatment she'd received from the headmaster and the students. I'd let her take out her anger on them.

Less than half an hour later, after I'd showered and dressed, the door opened without a knock. A gorilla-sized janitor with a thick mustache with dirty-blond hair that skimmed the collar of his blue overalls stepped into the room as though we were invisible, tracking in dust with his boots.

He held the lock in his giant paw and shook his head. "This door is centuries old. I'll have to take it off its hinges for fixing."

"What was wrong with it?" I asked.

His nailbrush mustache twitched. "One of you girls must have jammed the lock. That's two demerits each for damaging school property."

I glanced at Rita, who cringed. Apparently, even the janitors could dish out punishments. "I locked the door last night, and I didn't jam it."

"If it weren't you, who did?" he asked.

"Try Edward Mercia. Or Blake Simpson-West and Henry Bourneville. The three of them declared war on me at dinner."

The janitor snorted. "Why would Mr. Edward damage his own property?"

I pursed my lips. Mr. Edward. That was all I needed to know. He'd probably ordered the janitor to sabotage our lock.

Mr. Carbuncle ran his tongue along the bristly underside of his mustache. "If I can't fix the lock, the door will need replacing, and you'll be billed for the damage. Should I split the invoice fifty-fifty?"

Rita made a pained warble in the back of her throat.

I stepped forward. "No. It was me they declared war on, not her."

We walked to breakfast, leaving Mr. Carbuncle in our room,

who tinkered with the door. The dining room was deserted, likely because we'd missed first period having to wait around for the janitor to arrive. One of the servers placed a *full English* in front of me, consisting of sausages, pale soggy bacon, beans in a tomato sauce, fried eggs, and blood sausage. My eyes bulged at the sheer amount of food.

Rita clapped her hand over her mouth and giggled. "You don't have to eat it all."

"Not if I want to fall into a coma." The breakfast actually tasted great, and after eating my full, I glanced at my schedule. "I have second period free. How about you?"

"Mine's free, too," she replied. "Do you want to study together?"

"Actually, I was thinking we could take a break. What do people do for fun around here?"

"There's the common room."

"Are there games?"

Her brows drew together. "I've never been there."

With a smile, I pulled her out of her seat, and we headed out of the dining room toward the common room. It would be empty at this time of the morning, and after the day I'd had yesterday, a game of cards or chess would be a relaxing break. The common room turned out to be a wood-paneled space warmed by a roaring fire, narrow windows and a mix of black sofas embroidered with silk thread and matching armchairs arranged around low tables. I whistled. This was really nice.

A chessboard already lay at a table close to the window with a box of pieces at its side. Rita and I sat at opposite armchairs around the table, and I slid the lid off the box, revealing elegantly carved pieces that could have been a century old. "Do you know how to play?"

She grinned. "Of course."

"You seem very confident about your abilities." I set out the pieces on the board. "We'll see who emerges the victor."

"Yelverton," snapped a male voice.

I glanced up to find Edward striding toward us, flanked by Blake and Charlotte. His cold, blue eyes blazed, and memories of last night's dream rose to the surface, causing the pulse between my legs to pound. Hot humiliation rose to my cheeks, and I bit down hard on my bottom lip. This wasn't right. I should be disgusted by him, not excited. I couldn't let them see my reaction—any of it. I jerked my head away and stared into the chessboard, breathing hard to stave off a full-body flush.

"Y-yes?" Rita replied.

"How do you address the future Duke of Mercia?"

She cleared her throat. "Yes, sir?"

Shame morphed into anger, and my nostrils flared. Until he inherited his stupid title and actually made something of himself apart from a mindless bully, he didn't deserve anything except contempt.

"Give Simpson-West your satchel," he said in cool tones.

Without any hesitation, Rita reached down and picked her bag off the ground.

I clenched my teeth. "What are you—?"

"Nobody's talking to you, trollop." His eyes flashed, and he bared straight, white teeth.

"Apart from you," I snapped back. "By your own admission, you're a nobody."

Edward's lips tightened into a thin line. "You'd better watch yourself, Yank."

"Or what?" I asked. "You'll bore me to death with lame pranks and mindless threats?"

The scent of burned leather filled the air. Rita clapped her hands over her mouth and smothered a cry. Tears filled her eyes, threatening to spill down her cheeks. I whirled around. Blake stood at the fireplace, dangling her satchel over the flames and scorching the leather.

I rushed out of my seat, across the room, and snatched the satchel out of his grip. "What the hell do you think you're doing?"

"It's all a bit of harmless fun, Hobson." He waggled his brows. "You ought to try it. Might loosen you up."

"I'm game any time you want me to push you in the fire. Because the next time you damage either of our property, I'll damage you." With a toss of my hair, I headed back to our table and passed Charlotte as though she didn't exist.

Edward let out a weary sigh. "Must you be such a melodramatic trollop?"

"Must you be such an attention-seeking asshole?" I tried mimicking his bored, English accent, but I sounded more like the evil uncle from the Lion King.

His lip curled. "Don't test me."

I sat on the armchair. Rita squeaked something, but I was too busy trying not to notice Edward's deep, blue eyes. If life was fair, they would be red and slitted. "I thought you'd already declared wa—" wetness seeped through my skirt and down my legs.

I leaped out of my seat and turned around, trying to examine the back of my lower half. "What the fuck did you do?"

He tilted his head to the side and smirked. "Don't blame me. Blame Mother Nature."

Charlotte wrinkled her nose. "Don't you have sanitary products in America, trollop? I swear, even the most primitive of women have the sense to stuff rags down their knickers."

I pulled the back of my skirt round to my side and snarled at the patch of reddish-brown liquid. The bastards had made it look so realistic. At least with bright red coloring, I could make people believe I'd been pranked.

Blake stood by the fireplace, grinning with mirth. "Smile for the camera, dear. You're on the Mercia-Net!"

I snatched up my satchel and stormed out of the common room.

A crowd of people gathered in the hallway jeering, insulting and recording my humiliation.

"Bloody trollop," shouted one boy.

"Ha-ha! Good one, Reeves," yelled someone else. "The Yank is a bloody trollop."

I took the stairs two at a time with Rita at my heels, holding up her charred satchel to hide the shame those idiots had foisted on me. Whatever they'd poured onto the sofa still hadn't dried, making the backs of my legs sticky and wet. I'd have to shower it off, put on my spare skirt, and tell anyone who wanted to talk about what was posted on the Mercia-Net to fuck off.

When we reached our room, Mr. Carbuncle still knelt at the doorway, squinting at the lock and adjusting it with a thin screwdriver.

"Excuse me," I said.

He shifted a foot to the side, giving me just enough room to pass by his bulk. "I see you've soiled yourself. Another demerit."

I whirled around, fists clenched. "This is the work of your precious Mr. Edward and his friends."

"I doubt that Mr. Edward is capable of changing a woman's tide," he muttered.

A scream of frustration stuck in my throat, and I flung open my case and pulled out one of my spare school skirts. It had the same patch of blood at its back, as did my other skirt, my track pants, regulation leggings, and every other piece of uniform I might have been able to wear instead of my skirt. I closed my eyes. "The stupid, vindictive assholes!"

"Another demerit for swearing," mumbled Mr. Carbuncle.

Rita placed her charred bag on the floor and wrung her hands. "I tried to say something, but you sat down too quickly."

I blew out my frustration in a long breath. "You're not to blame for any of this, all right?"

She turned her gaze to the satchel, not making any eye contact.

"Why don't we wash your clothes in cold water? That always works for me."

The janitor muttered something unintelligible from his position on the floor. I blinked. Blake, Charlotte, and Edward would have carried out their act of sabotage while we were at breakfast. While Mr. Carbuncle had been fixing our door.

I whirled on the kneeling man. "Who came here while we were gone?"

"I don't know what you're talking about," he replied.

"All my school skirts and pants were fine last night and this morning when the door was locked. Someone came in while we were at breakfast and tampered with my clothes. Who did it?"

"I was here all morning and didn't see a thing," he said without looking up.

"You're aiding and abetting vandalism." I stuck my finger under his nose. "If you don't tell me who came in here, I'll report you."

He pulled himself to his feet, mustache quivering like it had a life on its own. "Ungrateful. This whole job took me hours I could have spent not fixing your mistakes. Here. The lock is fixed. Next time, don't mess around with them."

"Drop dead." I shook my head. If he didn't let someone in to pour dye on my clothes, then Mr. Edward paid him to perform this act of sabotage. "Just drop dead."

He huffed. "Two demerits, and I'll be happy to tell the headmaster of your conduct."

"If you ever get a hold of him."

The next class was English Literature, all the way across campus in the teaching block. I wrapped my blazer around my waist and set off. A thousand demerits were better than being accused of not changing my tampon. It was the kind of thing that stained a girl's reputation for years.

Our teacher, an elderly woman named Miss Okeley, who wore her hair in a messy bun, took one look at my blazer around my waist. "One demerit, Miss Hobson, for not being properly dressed."

Charlotte raised her hand. "Please, Miss Okeley, please don't punish Hobson for something that wasn't even her fault!"

The old woman adjusted her black, academic robes, thin lips twisted with disapproval. "There are no exceptions to the rules, Miss Underwood. All students must wear proper attire unless permitted otherwise."

Charlotte stood and clasped her hands to her ample chest. "You see, Miss, poor Hobson is suffering from extremely heavy periods because she had to endure rough sex for money. It completely ruptured her cervix."

I drew in a shocked breath through my teeth. Amused gasps filled the room, and Miss Okely clapped her hand over her mouth, eyes swimming with tears. My eyes narrowed. Where were Charlotte's demerits for saying such outrageous lies in the middle of English Lit? Where was her demerit for slander? Or her demerit for putting realistic fake blood on the back of my skirt?

Miss Oakley handed me a rolled up newspaper. "You'd better sit on this, Miss Hobson."

Snickers spread around the classroom, making my insides want to shrivel up and die.

"This is no laughing matter," said the old woman. She turned to me with a kindly smile. "Ten credits for bravery, Miss Hobson, and five to Miss Underwood for defending your friend."

I groaned. The old woman had lost her mind if she believed Charlotte's filthy lie.

Miss Oakley's light blue eyes twinkled. "You know, there was a film a few years ago, starring a young woman like you. What was it called?"

"*Pretty Woman*," said someone at the back of the class.

My shoulders stiffened. Was my teacher calling me a prostitute now?

"Oh... it was starring Richard Newman." Miss Oakley's face broke into a smile of worn, yellowing teeth. "That's it. *Pretty Lady*! Keep your chin up, dear. Regardless of your previous circumstances, Mercia Academy will give you a chance for a better life."

I sat on the newspaper, hatred simmering like banked coals in my belly, trying not to react to the howls of laughter filling the room. If my hands weren't already convulsing with rage, I would have given Charlotte the finger... straight in her eye. I stared ahead, focusing on my breaths and willing the rest of the day to fast forward so I could seek out a spare uniform. I'd well and truly received their declaration of war, and I was ready to fight back with every dirty trick in my arsenal.

CHAPTER 6

I couldn't get the stains out of my skirts and neither could the house matron. For the rest of the week, I had to wear my blazer around my waist and to endure idiots throwing tampons at me while the school outfitters made up some new skirts. Each morning at mid-break, I would rush to the mailboxes in the entrance hall to see if the new skirts and pants had arrived, and each morning, I would find some kind of sanitary product or a note telling me to go home… trollop.

It was clear that Edward, one of the others in the triumvirate, or Charlotte and her doppelgängers had sabotaged my order. How long did it take to make up a gray skirt? They should have had them in stock. Twice, I called to check, but the snooty woman on the phone said she couldn't rush the process. Whatever that meant.

On Tuesday morning, I stepped into the entrance hall to find Edward, Blake, Charlotte and the doppelgängers huddled together around a table close to the mailboxes. As soon as I heard the words *bloody yank* and *trollop*, my heart flip-flopped. My package had arrived, and they were doing something to my clothes.

I strode over, fists clenched. "What's going on?"

Edward was the first to turn. His gaze flickered up and down my body, lingering on my B-cup breasts for longer than needed, then he tightened his lips as though to say he found them lacking. My insides writhed with shame, and a prickly heat rose from my chest and up my neck. I sucked in a breath and clenched my teeth, not daring to let him see how badly he'd upset me.

"What do you want, you bloody trollop?" he asked.

I flinched. Hearing those words flung at me in that commanding voice stung. I tried not to let the hurt show on my face and walked around him, acting like he didn't exist. "Is that my package?"

"Not everything revolves around you, Trollop." Charlotte twisted her body, hiding something behind her back.

I rushed forward, but Blake snatched the package out of reach, making me clamber after him with a snarl. "Give that to me!"

"With pleasure, my dear." He stepped back, holding it above his head, face split into a mischievous grin, chocolate-brown eyes sparkling with challenge. It was the sort of look that said, 'if you want it, come and get it.' The sort of look that made my nipples tighten and made heat pool low in my belly. Who wouldn't want the full attention of Blake Simpson-West? Especially when the loose curls framed his brow so perfectly, and that fine, sculpted chest already heaved in anticipation for a close contact wrestling match?

Somewhere, through the rush of blood through my eardrums, I heard the beep of a camera phone. I stopped advancing on Blake and glared at the taller doppelgänger who stood twelve feet away, holding a smartphone at the ready for the oncoming spectacle. She wanted me to rush forward and try to snatch my property while the others laughed and hooted at the trollop manhandling their friend. Well, I wouldn't give them the satisfaction… or the footage.

I feinted toward the doppelgänger, dodged left, spun Charlotte around, and snatched the bottle of ink out of her hands. "Is this what you used to ruin my clothes?"

She stepped back, red blotches appearing on her cheeks. "What are you talking about?"

I untwisted the cap off the bottle and wielded it like a weapon. "Give me my package, or this ink gets on all of you!"

"What?" she screeched.

Edward's nostrils flared. "Give it to her."

I straightened. Why were they giving up so easily?

"But I was having so much fun." Blake lowered the package to chest level and strode to the table, his dark eyes fixed on mine, and a smirk dancing across his full lips.

I stepped back, not trusting any of them to make a last-minute lunge, snatch the open bottle of ink, and pour it over me and my new clothes. "Don't try anything stupid, or you'll get a face-full of ink."

"Message received and understood." He placed the package on the table and backed away, palms up, as though I was holding a grenade.

"Crazy bitch," muttered one of Charlotte's doppelgängers.

I twisted around, but the doppelgänger scuttled back toward the door like a coward. Curling my lip, I said, "Nice try, bitches. The next time you touch my stuff, you'll be blinking ink out of your eyes for a month."

The girls muttered some disparaging remarks about my sanity and backed out of the door. Each of them moved slowly, as though one out of place gesture would have me charging at them, ink flying. Even Blake kept his hands up. He may have smiled, but his eyes remained trained on the bottle of ink. Triumph filled my chest with warmth, and I raised my chin, watching them file out of the front doors and into the crisp, autumn day.

Edward was the last to leave. Unlike the others, he didn't back away but crossed the room with a regal dignity as though he knew I wouldn't dare act against him. The arrogant prick paused at the door, fixing me with such an intense look of hatred, it made my stomach twist.

He was probably halfway to becoming a psychopath because that was the kind of look people reserved for monsters like Hitler, not Americans they found annoying. "This isn't over, Trollop. I've planned an attack that will make you run screaming back to your whore mother. Leave now, and you'll avoid the pain and humiliation."

"What makes you think I don't have something planned for you?" I snapped.

He jutted out a chin that could have been chiseled out of alabaster. "You're in my territory. Nothing happens here without my knowing."

I curled my lip. "We'll see about that."

He gave me a tight-lipped, wintry smile. "I wouldn't be too sure about your survival if I were you."

A barrel of dread rumbled through my belly, but I kept my features even. Edward Mercia would never know how much those words had affected me. He had to be talking about social survival. Nobody would go so far as to threaten someone's life. I replaced the lid on the bottle of ink and slipped it into my satchel. "What does that mean?"

Instead of an answer, he raised a brow and walked out through the double doors, leaving me alone in the entrance hall with my thoughts and the crack and pop of the fireplace. Whatever he planned next was probably going to be spectacularly humiliating. I strode to the table and cradled the package of clothes in my arms. If I didn't strike soon with something devastating that showed them I wasn't someone to be messed with, these snobs wouldn't stop.

Over the next few mealtimes, I observed the triumvirate and the stable of bitches who orbited them. Henry, the blond, I learned was the captain of the house rugby team. He was the most aloof of the three and only spoke to girls if they spoke to him first. Whenever Charlotte tried to engage him in conversation, he'd give her one-word answers and turn back to whatever he was doing, even if it was staring into space. Eventually, she'd get frustrated enough with Henry's lack of responses, flirt with Blake and cast Henry furtive glances to see if he was looking. Edward seemed to find the whole dynamic tedious and would often roll his eyes when Charlotte tried and failed to use Blake as a means to make Henry jealous.

Two of Charlotte's doppelgängers, Alice and Patricia, spent their time vying for Edward's attention. He seemed to be dating them both and noticed the conflict it caused the two friends but didn't care. Blake didn't have any favorites and would flirt with every girl, especially Charlotte and Wendy, the girl who had pretended to befriend me on my first day.

One lunchtime, I'd just sent Mom another text, when I noticed Henry jerk his arm away from Charlotte's touch. I whispered to Rita, "Why doesn't Henry like girls? Is he gay?"

"I heard a few of the others talk about it," she whispered back. "Some say he's in love with Blake, and others say he's insecure about being the least handsome in the group."

I glanced at the head table and met his startling green eyes. He blinked with surprise, then his blank expression sharpened into one of interest. A jolt of excitement shot through my heart and traveled down to my core. Henry had the looks of the sexiest kind of football player. Tall, broad, and heavily muscled without being too bulky. While Blake and Edward might be facially outstanding, Henry was still more handsome than any other boy in the school.

"I don't think he's insecure about his looks," I muttered.

"Others say he's careful of gold diggers," Rita whispered. "He's the only son of the Bourneville family and stands to inherit the department stores and all their properties in London. That's why so many of the girls want to get close to him."

"What do you think about Bourneville?"

She glanced down at her plate of mushroom risotto. "They're all terrible people."

"That's for sure," I muttered.

Up at the head table, Blake whispered into Wendy's ear. She giggled and slipped her hand under the table. Blake stared right at me and raised his brows in challenge. It was the kind of look that said, 'Don't you wish that was your hand down there?' Heat rushed to my face and spread down my neck and into my chest. I should have pulled my gaze away, shouldn't have played his game, but the gravity in his eyes held me mesmerized. My nipples tightened, and I shuddered as the intense warmth traveled south. His lips tweaked into a smile, and I almost growled. Damn him!

I dipped my head and plunged the tines of my fork into my spaghetti carbonara. Why did I waste so much time analyzing the love lives of those jerks? I needed to pay them back for the bloody clothes, not obsess over them and their bitches.

"You're planning something, aren't you?" asked Rita.

"Why do you ask?" I replied.

"Trust me. Fighting back will only escalate the bullying. Ignore them, and they'll get bored eventually and leave you alone."

"But what's the alternative?" I stared into my friend's dark brown eyes. Getting to eat real food in the dining room had filled out the hollowness of her cheeks, and the absence of negative attention on her had eased her skittishness. She'd spent her time hiding from the world, trying not to be noticed, and submitting to the bullies, but that hadn't helped her to thrive at Mercia Academy. "I can't just allow them to walk all over me."

She sipped her water. "I know it's hard, but they'll get bored eventually and move onto someone else."

"Why should they bully people at all?" I glared at the head table.

Blake leaned across and said something to Edward, who turned to stare in our direction. Edward said something back, and Blake rose from his seat.

"Oh, no," Rita slid further down her chair. "He's coming over."

I sat up and clenched my fork as though it was my only means of protection. As Blake stepped down off the podium, a hush spread across the dining room, broken only by the activation of multiple camera apps. I clenched my jaw. Whatever he said or did, I couldn't react and give these people more crap to post on the Mercia-Net. Blake walked across the room like he was in a grand ball about to ask the girl in the enchanted dress to dance. One of his brows rose, and a crooked smile curved his lips. It was obviously something he'd practiced in front of the mirror.

My breaths became shallow, and I glanced down at his empty hands. He'd come unarmed, but a jug of water sat in the middle of my table, something he could upend over my head. And I hadn't finished my carbonara, which he could use as a weapon of humiliation.

Rita made a pained noise in her throat and curled her shoulders, trying to make herself look small. As much as I wanted to tell her to sit up and stop giving the bullies the reactions they craved, I couldn't. Doing so would only draw more attention to Rita and make her return to eating sandwiches in her room. Instead, I rolled my eyes and faked a yawn.

After what felt like an eternity, Blake reached our table, pulled out a chair, spun it around, and straddled it. He turned to my friend. "Hello, Rita," he said in that deep, smoky voice. "It's nice to see you dining with us."

She dipped her head and wrapped her arms around her chest.

"What do you want?" I snapped.

"I couldn't help but notice you looking at us. At me, in particular."

"Can't a girl admire the paintings on the wall without being accused of lechery?" I drawled.

Blake leaned close, filling my nostrils with the intoxicating scent of sandalwood. "If there is anything you need," he said in a low voice. "*Anything*, I'm at your service."

The rumble in his voice started a tremor between my legs, and I imagined what kind of services a guy like Blake might be able to provide. On my first day, he'd placed his hand on the small of my back and set my libido on fire, then when he'd pulled me into his side, I had become so giddy with desire I might have let him do anything to me in my room. I inhaled a deep breath and let it out in a long whoosh.

Blake's eyes flashed, and his gaze dropped to my lips. "Is there anything you want?"

"Yes," I said, my voice breathy.

He leaned close. "Tell me."

I squeezed my legs together, blanked my mind, and put on my best irritated voice. "How about you go back to your table and stop interrupting my meal? My pasta's getting cold, and there's apple pie for dessert. I'd like to finish up so I can do my prep."

He had the nerve to flinch at my words. I blinked hard at the reaction. Was he so insecure that a rejection could affect him so much? Or was the flinch a ploy to lull me into thinking he was vulnerable?

Charlotte sauntered over with her hands on her hips. "What are you doing with the trollop, Blake? Everyone knows she's a gold-digging whore."

Blake straightened. "Trying to ascertain why she keeps looking at us."

"Actually," I said in a voice loud enough to carry. "I was curious."

"About what?" Charlotte snapped.

I tilted my head. "Does Charlotte have bad breath? She keeps wrinkling her nose."

Her cheeks turned bright red, and she rushed to the next table and grabbed their water jug. Before she could twist around and enact her plan, I leaped out of my seat, snatched my water jug and flung its contents into her face. I miscalculated somewhat, and water splattered over the front of her shirt, revealing a thick, red bra that looked more like a harness.

Titillated laughter filled the room. I stood back and admired my work. It was good to see her humbled for once.

"You bitch!" she screeched.

I raised a shoulder. "Sorry, you looked like you needed cooling down."

Charlotte threw the water in my direction, but I jumped out of the way, letting it hit my pasta.

"Give up on your stupid campaign." I placed the jug back on the table. "You're an annoying little mouse who can't muster up the style or originality to become a mean girl."

"Y-you trollop!"

"Says the girl looking like a contestant for a wet T-shirt contest," I snapped. "Does the guild of hookers make red bras your size, or did you have to order it specially?"

The dining hall erupted into laughter, and the best part was that I knew multiple spectators had recorded Charlotte's humiliation and would upload it on the Mercia-Net.

CHAPTER 7

Rita was right. The bullies escalated. Two mornings later, I was washing my hair in the shower, when my scalp felt like it had been doused with acid. Corrosive liquid seeped down my temple and into the seams of my eyelids. I screamed, "Rita!"

There was no response. She was usually dressed and out of the door by first bell. I was on my own. A rush of icy panic shot through my veins, and I stuck my face under the spray of water. Before I could wash the liquid out of my eyes, the stream dribbled to a halt.

A gasping sob escaped my throat. I'd threatened to throw ink in their eyes, and now, they meant to blind me! I scrambled out of the bath and groped around for the sink with trembling hands, breathing hard to stay calm. Panicking would only make me lose my sight. When my fingers met porcelain, I turned on the taps, pooled the warm water into my cupped hands, and splashed it onto my eyes. My scalp burned, and foul liquid poured down my shoulders and chest and back, but I ignored it. I had to protect my eyes.

Moments later, the tap spluttered, and the water stopped. All the breath left my lungs in a scream. What did I do next? My wet hair slapped me across the cheek and burned my skin. I had to cover it up. I rushed blindly to the right side of the bathroom, where we hung towels on a heated rail, and wrapped the nearest one I could find around my hair. I used another towel to dab at the sensitive skin on my face, then I groped around for a robe and threw it on.

By the time I stepped out of the bathroom, my face had dried, but my vision blurred.

A male voice huffed out a laugh.

I groped around for a weapon, but my hands only skimmed an empty table. "Who is that?"

He laughed again.

"I-I'm calling the police," I said. "This is assault."

Footsteps trod across the wooden floor, then the door slammed shut. I screamed and rushed after him, but he turned the key in the lock. The bastard, whoever he was, had trapped me so the liquid could take effect and eventually burn out my eyes. They'd gone too far. They needed to die.

I banged on the door. "Someone, help me!"

Footsteps shuffled outside in the hallway, most likely the bullies standing around to gloat, but I had to keep calling for help, even if it meant giving them what they wanted. My eyes were too important.

I slammed my fist on the wood over and over again, screaming, crying, pleading for someone to open the door and help me.

"What's wrong?" shouted a male voice. It sounded like Blake, but I couldn't be sure.

"There's something in my eye. Open the door. I need to get to the infirmary."

He paused, presumably to laugh. "Have you tried washing it out?"

"They've turned off the water."

"There's plenty in the toilet bowl."

My nostrils flared. This was their plan all along. To make me so desperate for water, I'd plunge my hands into the toilet to wash my face. There was no point in continuing the conversation. They had trapped me, and I had only one option left if I wanted to save my sight.

Pipes coughed and spluttered, and a stream of water gushed out of the taps. Relief burst through me like a geyser, and I rushed back into the bathroom, stood at the sink, and gathered the precious liquid between my cupped hands. The soothing water washed the tampered shampoo off my face, making me cry out my relief. When my vision cleared, I climbed back into the shower. Cold water streamed out, making me gasp, but I turned around, tilted my head back and let it wash away the doctored shampoo.

Tears gathered in my eyes, providing them with much needed relief, and I let out gasping sobs. How could they go so far? I hadn't done anything that warranted such a violent retaliation. These people were truly sick! Rita's words returned to the forefront of my mind. She'd told me things would get worse, but I'd thought they'd focus on more humiliation, not maiming.

I stood under the stream of cold water until my teeth chattered, and I'd lost all the sensation in my fingers and toes. Whatever they'd put in my shampoo had gone, but my eyes felt like they'd been rubbed with steel wool. I shut off the water, climbed out of the shower, and reached for a towel. There were none on the rack, none on the door hook, and none on the floor. A whimper reverberated in my throat. Someone must have come in while I was showering and stolen all the towels.

A cold rage surged through my veins. I hated them. Hated them with a passion. These people were truly evil, and the worst part was that there was nobody to stop them. I wrapped my arms around my middle and shivered. What was I going to do now?

The door leading to the hallway clicked shut, and I rushed out of the bathroom. The edges around my vision blurred, but I could see that no-one was in the room, and they hadn't left a towel for me, either. There was only one thing I could do: pull the sheets off my bed and use them to dry myself off.

It took an hour for sensation to return to my fingers, and I dried my hair as best as I could, put on my regulation sweatshirt and track pants, then tried the door. It opened. The hallway was deserted. I'd already missed the first period, and I expected everyone was in class. I eased myself down the stairs, walked through the hallway, and knocked on the housemaster's door.

"Enter," said a deep voice.

I stepped inside. Mr. Jenkins sat behind his desk, looking through a pile of papers. His thick mane of silvery hair flopped over his face. When I cleared my throat, he glanced up and frowned. "What can I do for you, Miss...?"

"Hobson," I rasped out through a throat raw from screaming. Couldn't he even remember me from when Blake had introduced us on our first day?

"Ah. The American." There was no contempt in his voice, and he gestured at the chair in front of his desk. "Do take a seat." The older man leaned forward, waiting for me to talk.

I coughed. "Someone put something in my shampoo this morning and shut off the water in my room."

His brows drew together. "Are you sure? Students don't have access to the plumbing."

"That's what happened," I replied.

"Do you know who might have done this?"

"Edward Mercia, Blake Simpson-West, Charlotte Underwood, and their friends."

Mr. Jenkins slumped back into his seat. "If Mr. Mercia is involved, there isn't much I can do about it, I'm afraid."

"What?" The word was more gasp than speech. I widened my eyes, trying to get a better look at the housemaster's expression. From the sag of his posture, he seemed defeated. There was no amusement or defiance in his eyes, just the kind of apathy a person developed in the face of an overwhelming situation they couldn't control. "Mercia threatened my life yesterday. Now it looks like he'll stoop to any level to make me leave."

The housemaster glanced away. "I'm sorry, but his family practically owns the school."

"Mercia Academy is a charity."

"Which exists because of the benevolence of the Duke of Mercia's estate. Without it, where would we hold lessons?" He reached for a stack of papers and pretended to sort them. "You may speak with the headmaster, but he'll give you the same answer."

"So, Edward Mercia is free to do as he pleases?" I spat. "Even terrorize and maim?"

Mr. Jenkins dipped his head. "There is always one authority he can't easily influence."

My heart skipped a beat. "Who?"

"God."

Shooting out of my seat, I yelled, "So, I should pray for a thunderbolt to strike him dead?" Angry blotches appeared on the man's face, and he opened his mouth to utter a rebuke, but I cut him off and headed out of the door. "Thanks for the advice. I'll know not to come here the next time they try to kill me."

I slammed the door and stormed through the downstairs hallway. Mr. Jenkins was right about one thing. There was another authority that wouldn't be as ineffective as him: the police. I took the stairs two at a time, rushed down my hallway and opened the door. Someone had made the bed. When I stepped into the bathroom, all the towels were back on the rack. I threw open the shower curtain to find the tampered shampoo was replaced by an unfamiliar British brand.

All the determination drained out of me in a wave of helplessness that made my legs buckle. I sat on the edge of the bath and rested my hands in my head. The bastards had even stolen my evidence.

I stayed in the bathroom, numb, hoarse and impotent with rage for hours. How could I report something that didn't look like it had happened? My vision had cleared, and the redness in my eyes faded into an innocuous pink. Whatever they'd put in the shampoo hadn't actually been as harmful as I'd thought. If I retaliated by throwing hot soup into their faces, I'd be the one facing charges. I shook my head. Splashing people with water was acceptable but scalding them was taking things too far.

At lunchtime, Rita stepped into the room and pushed the bathroom door ajar. "Why weren't you in classes this—?" She clapped her hands over her mouth. "You've been crying. What's wrong?"

Everything spilled out in a rush of emotion. Rita sat next to me on the rim of the bathtub and wrapped her thin arms around my back, giving me a measure of comfort. She listened to everything without any reminder that she'd warned me about the bullies' viciousness.

It was the psychological aspect of the trick that had hurt most. Turning off the water to heighten my panic, then leaving me to pound at the door for their amusement, only to take away the towels when they finally granted me cold water. If they hadn't mistimed the return of the plumbing, they might have caught me washing my face in the toilet. I hadn't thought them capable of such cruelty.

She took my hand and guided me out of the bathroom and to the bed. "What are you going to do?"

"Huh?"

"Telling you to ignore them won't work. They've taken their prank too far. Will you call your parents?"

I sighed. What could Dad do for me all the way in California and with no money? Mom was too busy with her new role as the millionaire mogul's wife to even reply to my texts, and Rudolph viewed my time here as a baptism of fire. He already knew about the brutality of British boarding schools, so complaining to him would only prove I wasn't strong enough for an internship in one of his companies or worthy enough for him to pay for my ivy league college.

"Install cameras around the room," I said.

Rita drew back. "Won't that give them something to spy on?"

"Not if we turn the cameras off during prep and while we're changing. The footage goes to the cloud, so only I will be able to access it."

"Alright," said Rita. "Then what?"

"Then we wait for the next person to enter the room without permission."

Rita guided me to the infirmary, where a medic took a look at my eyes and said I'd irritated my cornea but they were otherwise fine. He gave me a mild bottle of drops that would soothe my eyes and stop them from hurting.

I earned a string of demerits for missing classes, but no footage of me scrambling about the room, blind, naked, and with a towel over my head surfaced on the Mercia-Net. The shampoo prank had been designed to punish, not to humiliate.

The trollop and yank barbs continued, as did other more colorful insults, based on articles posted to the Mercia-Net whenever Mom appeared in the society pages with Rudolph. The level of vitriol thrown at me made me think the girls were jealous they hadn't snagged a millionaire for themselves.

One evening the next week, I'd finished my prep early and went down to the common room to rest. The room was deserted, and I lay in the semi-darkness on one of the plush sofas. Footsteps shuffled inside, accompanied by whispered voices.

"What did Henry say about me?" asked Charlotte's whiny voice.

"Oh, the usual." Low tones curled around my senses and made my nerve endings tingle. This had to be Blake. "You're beautiful, and he's too intimidated to make conversation."

I scrambled under a coffee table, pulled out my smartphone, and recorded.

"How do I get Henry to warm to me?" she asked.

"Give him time," replied Blake. "The more I bring you up in conversation, the more curious he becomes. He asked me if you fancied anyone."

"Really?" her voice rose several octaves. "What did you say?"

"I hinted that you might like him."

I furrowed my brow. Blake playing matchmaker? He seemed the type to sleep with the girls himself, not pass them onto his friends. None of this made sense. Why would anyone want to help Charlotte snag Henry? The girl had no redeeming features unless being bitchy was a virtue.

"Then what did he say?" Her voice was breathy with excitement.

"He was delighted." Blake's voice lost its seductive quality and now sounded flat.

I lay on my belly and rested my weight on my elbows. They made an odd pair. Blake stood a few feet away from the door in a white shirt with its sleeves rolled up to his elbows and dark, skinny jeans that showed off his lean, muscular figure. The huge fireplace to their right provided enough illumination to showcase the perfect curve of his ass. Charlotte stood about a foot away, clad in a white crewneck shirt that clung to her every curve and accentuated her breasts. Her miniskirt revealed stocky thighs that tapered off into thin calves.

She pressed her hands on Blake's chest. "What else—"

He placed a finger over her lips. "Enough, Lottie. I'm helping you with your campaign to ensnare Henry. What will you do for me?"

Charlotte tilted her head up and grinned. "Let's go to your room."

"No." He trailed his finger down her bottom lip and onto her chin. "Here."

"Why?" she panted.

He pulled her hand to his crotch. "Because I love the danger."

"Lock the door, so no one sees us."

He chuckled, the sound rich and dark. "Be quick, or someone will."

Before I could decipher his last comment, Charlotte giggled and dropped down to her knees. Blake unbuckled his belt, unzipped his fly, and pulled himself out. I drew in a breath through my teeth and dropped the camera face-down on the rug.

Before I got another look, Charlotte lunged forward and slobbered over the organ like a heifer taking her first salt lick. She lapped and slurped and pumped its base with her fist, groaning like was the best thing she'd ever tasted.

Blake threw his head back and moaned, the vibration in his voice going straight between my legs. My heart pounded so hard, they could probably hear it from where they stood. He snapped his hips in a deep thrust that I thought would have Charlotte gagging, but she sped up her ministrations, taking him in like she'd had years of practice. I bit down hard on my lip to stifle my own moan. Blake was losing his composure, and so was I.

My breathing went ragged. I'd never seen someone giving a blowjob. Not in real life, and not with so much enthusiastic abandon. Charlotte's lips and tongue slavered over his thickness, and Blake cupped his hand around the back of her neck and sped up his thrusts. She clung to his hips, and with a harsh, guttural grunt that made my nipples tighten, he climaxed. Thick globs of fluid poured out of the corner of her mouth, and her throat flexed as though she was swallowing bucketfuls.

Blake withdrew, still hard and flushed. "I'd say that was a job well done."

"Aren't I always good?"

"I can honestly say that Lottie Underwood is the very best fellator in Elder House."

She drew back. "Only in Elder?"

The good-natured bickering continued while Blake tucked himself back into his pants. I tried slowing my breathing, but my heart still galloped like an out-of-control racehorse. They were conspiring against Henry. Using Blake's influence to manipulate a relationship with Charlotte. I shook my head. This was spectacular ammunition, and I couldn't wait to use it as leverage.

CHAPTER 8

When Charlotte and Blake finally left the common room, I turned off the camera and crawled out from under the coffee table on trembling limbs. Each movement of my legs sent pleasure rippling up and down my core. That had been the most erotic experience of my life. I'd dated a few guys and we'd kissed and groped each other over our clothes, but this was something else.

I sat on the floor, leaning my head against a sofa, and gasped out panting breaths. If that had been me kneeling in front of Blake, I would have locked the door and leaned him against the wall. Taken my time and savored the experience. Wrapped my lips around him and drawn out every lick, every caress, every slurp.

I threw back my head and groaned. Now, whenever I saw Blake, I'd remember his caught breath, his thrusting hips, his sexy moans. I was supposed to hate him and his gang of psychopaths who had tampered with my shampoo, made me believe I was going blind, and then hidden all the evidence. Now, I couldn't stop thinking about Blake in the throes of passion.

It took several moments to regain my composure, but eventually, I pulled myself to my feet and stepped out into the dim hallway. As I took my first steps toward the staircase, strong arms wrapped around my shoulders and waist.

My heart stopped for a beat, making me stiffen, then it exploded into action. I struggled within the man's grip, breathing in the heady scent of sandalwood... and something else.

Blake's deep voice murmured, "Did you like what you saw?"

"W-what are you talking about?"

He rubbed his erection against my ass. "I heard your camera." He nuzzled my neck, sending ripples of pleasure down my spine. "Saw you under that table."

"I wasn't—"

He bit down on my ear, making me cry out with desire. "Don't lie to me. You're going straight to your room, and you'll touch yourself, thinking about my cock."

I clenched my teeth. "It was disgusting."

He chuckled, low and deep. The rumble went straight to my aching core. "That's why you're so aroused." He pressed his hardness into me with a firm thrust. "You want me. I've known it from the moment we met."

"Y-you're deluded. I hate you."

"Then why aren't you struggling? Why aren't you screaming for help?" He let go and stepped back.

The loss of his warmth and intoxicating scent hurt, left me feeling doused with ice water, but I pressed my lips together and jerked my head to the side. One glance at that cocky smile, those decadent, dark eyes, and I'd be weak. I ached for him, but I had enough good sense to know that letting Blake seduce me would open up a realm of torment.

"See." He took a step toward me. "That expression there is suppressed disappointment."

I turned on my heels and headed back to the stairs. "I'm going.

He grabbed my arm. "Give me that recording."

"No."

In that low, smoky voice he said, "If it's masturbation material you want—"

"It's leverage." I snatched my arm away. He didn't need to know I had dropped the camera just before the blow job. "If you don't stop this campaign against me, I'll show this to Henry."

Blake shrugged. "He likes an enthusiastic round of fellatio, same as any other chap."

"But would he appreciate you colluding with a gold digger to ensnare him?" When Blake's face dropped, victory surged through my chest. "I thought not."

His lips thinned. "What do you want?"

"For you, Edward, Charlotte and the others to leave me alone. Stop posting on the Mercia-Net about my family, and stop encouraging others to call me names."

He inclined his head. "I'll do what I can."

For the next few days, the triumvirate only glared at me from a distance. Charlotte sneered, and her doppelgängers muttered the occasional, half-hearted insults, but no one approached me. It seemed that my threat had scared Blake into telling his friends to back off.

Even though I saved the footage to the cloud and to a few email accounts, I kept my phone with me everywhere. Slept with it tucked into my bed-sock, took it to the bathroom, and even showered with it at my side. They had access to my room, and I wouldn't be stupid enough to neglect such a vital piece of leverage.

Battery-operated, motion-detection cameras also arrived that I connected via the internet to a secure network which would push the footage into a cloud server. I set up the cameras to record while we were at classes, meals, and after light's out, in case the bullies stormed the room in the middle of the night. But so far, the only things that triggered the motion sensitivity were the entry and exit of the matron and her cleaners. It was as if they'd given up.

In English Literature, Miss Oakley handed out copies of Chaucer's *Canterbury Tales* and told us to pair up. I glanced at the empty seat between mine and the wall, dreading having to ask someone to be my partner. As people got up and walked around, forming pairs, I glanced out, looking for a not-so-hostile face, when a huge body blocked my view of the class.

"Budge up," said Henry.

My insides shriveled with trepidation, along with the moisture in my throat. This was the most he'd ever said to me. Ever. Henry always stared, but always remained silent. He'd never even called me a yank or a trollop or some other combination of insult. My breath stuck in my gullet. Blake must have told him about the recording and he wanted to threaten me into handing over my phone and password.

"Hey, budge up," he repeated.

Charlotte, who hovered at the desk in front, fixed me with her filthiest glower. "There's a free space here."

Henry dropped his satchel onto the desk next to mine, walked around my chair, and lowered himself into the empty seat.

"What are you doing?" I hissed.

He stared straight ahead. "Miss Oakley said to pair up, didn't she?"

"Yes, but why are you sitting next to me?"

He fixed me with a blank stare. "Plebs don't get to make choices."

I folded my arms across my chest. "I'm surprised you know the meaning of that word, considering that you and your friends act the textbook definition of plebeian."

The corner of his lips curled into a smile.

Anger flared across my chest. He probably saw me and my suffering at his friends' hands, as a huge joke. "Oh, I know your type," I spat out what I thought would be the most degrading insult. "You're one of those weirdos who like being verbally humiliated. Do you need me to get Miss Oakley's cane?"

Henry barked out a laugh.

Charlotte spun around in her seat. "See, Henry? I told you she was a whore. She just offered you BDSM!"

Henry dipped his head and opened his satchel, acting as though he hadn't heard her. I glanced up at Charlotte and raised my brows. Perhaps she should have been trading insults for Henry's attention instead of trading blowjobs for crumbs with Blake. I itched to say the words, but clamped my lips shut. Revealing the illicit activities of that night would break our truce, and they would do much worse than the shampoo prank.

Miss Oakley got us to read aloud the medieval English and to translate it line by line.

"Right," said Henry. "You do the first few pages, and I'll jot down the notes."

Giving him a look that I hoped would project my skepticism, I said, "Nice try. We're doing this together or not at all."

He ran his fingers through his hair. "Here I was thinking you were intelligent."

I smirked. "Intelligent enough to recognize a slacker."

"Very well," he said with a mock grumble. "What does the first line say?"

"You read it out. It wouldn't sound authentic with my accent."

He chuckled. "I suppose not. Here we go: *What that Aprille with his shoures soote, the droghte of Marche hath perced to the roote.*"

I flipped to the glossary and looked up the words I didn't understand. "Ummm... When April with its sweet showers has pierced the drought of March to the root."

Charlotte turned around. "Wrong, trollop! It's sweet-smelling showers."

"Ah..." I gave her a sage nod. "Something you're sorely lacking. Thanks for the insight."

Henry jerked forward and choked on a laugh. Charlotte's face fell, and I would have felt bad for her if she and her pals hadn't nearly blinded me days before.

Throughout the rest of the exercise, Charlotte turned around to stare at Henry and to glare at me, but I focused on the work and ignored her attempts at distraction. It was the best way to hurt the little gold digger.

The truce continued for several more days until Mr. Jenkins walked into the dining hall and stood at the side of the head table. "Good evening, ladies and gentlemen."

Everyone stopped talking. We hardly ever saw our housemaster these days. I suspected he was lying low with shame after the shampoo incident.

Mr. Jenkins cleared his throat. "As you are aware, it's half-term in a fortnight."

Excited chatter spread across the room, and I blinked. Did that mean we got a mid-term break in two weeks? I'd have to check my bank balance, but if I could get a cheap flight, I might be able to make it to La Jolla and back without too much jet lag.

"This half-term, we're hiking in the peak district!" said our housemaster.

Everyone broke out into raucous cheers. I glanced at Rita, who dipped her head. This couldn't be good news.

"All special equipment will be provided from school stores, but for those of you wanting to maximize the experience, I've left a list of items you might find useful." He walked to the other side of the dining hall and placed a stack of papers on the table by the door.

I turned to Rita. "Is this trip compulsory?"

"They'll close down the house for the week. The only way to get out of it is by breaking a bone."

I shuddered. "Have you hiked before?"

"There was hiking in last year's whale watching trip," she said in a low voice. "But those three tied me to a tree when it was time to leave."

"What happened?"

"Apart from the boat having to come back for me an hour later, nothing." Her gaze flickered to the head table. "No one does anything against them."

I turned to glare at the triumvirate, only to find Edward walking over with Charlotte on one side, and Patricia, the taller doppelgänger he was currently dating, on the other. I narrowed my eyes. What happened to the truce? They were supposed to leave me alone, but the determination blazing in Edward's eyes told me he was about to restart this campaign of bullying. My hand patted for my blazer pocket and felt the reassuring bulge of my smartphone.

A malicious grin spread across Edward's face, revealing straight, white teeth that looked like they'd sprout fangs if I so much as exposed my neck. He certainly had the cruel beauty of a vampire. "I expect you've been wondering about the current ceasefire."

"Not really." I affected a bored voice, but on the inside, my stomach twisted into knots. I still had the recording. Wasn't that the reason why they'd stopped the bullying?

"Blake suggested we let things cool off for a bit," said Charlotte. "Save our energy for the school trip."

Clenching my teeth, I flicked my gaze to the head table. Blake leaned back in his seat, arms folded, brows raised with challenge. The lying bastard hadn't told Charlotte about the recording. He'd just been stalling for time!

I had to do something. With a deep breath, I leaned forward and rested my hand on my chin. "I heard something really interesting about you, Lottie."

"Don't call me that," she snapped.

"The best fellator in Elder House." I smirked.

Charlotte's face paled.

Edward turned to her. "What's the trollop talking about?"

She rolled her eyes. "Herself, most likely. Whores are supposed to have fellatio skills."

He smirked. "We have something extra special planned for you. It will send you running for the hills. Make sure you hone those trollop skills. You'll need them."

I folded my arms across my chest. "Let me guess? I can avoid all of this torment by booking the next flight to the States."

"I don't care where you go, as long as you leave my academy." His voice was glacier-hard.

"That's not going to happen." It hurt to say the words. I wasn't particularly enjoying my time here at. Even though Park Prep, had its share of mean girls, they hurt egos, not eyes.

"Very well." Edward straightened. "Then you give us tacit permission to torment you as we please." He spun on his heel and strode back to the head table. With a fake giggle, Patricia, his doppelgänger of the day. scurried after him.

Charlotte stood over us, nostrils flaring. "What did you mean earlier?"

"Me?" I widened my eyes. "Didn't Blake tell you about the recording of you sucking him off like a pornstar?" I shook my head. "Someone so quick to call others trollops really should be careful what they put in their mouths. Especially when they're looking to marry rich."

She bared her teeth. "I don't believe a word of what you're saying, bitch."

"Oh!" I imitated her accent. "What did Henry say about me? Why am I only the best fellator in Elder House, shouldn't I be the best in the academy?"

Red bloomed across her cheeks. "You..." She was probably going to call me a trollop again but thought better of it. "What do you want?"

"Get Edward to call off the prank."

"How?"

"I don't know. Fellate him into submission. You're a natural at that."

She turned to glare at Rita. "Utter a word of this to anyone, and I'll slit your throat."

"Touch my friend and I'll slit yours," I hissed back. "Now, fuck off and get to work, fellator."

Charlotte sucked in a deep breath through her flared nostrils, curled her lip to utter some kind of insult, and then deflated. After shooting us a hateful stare, she spun around and stomped back to the head table.

Rita leaned into me. "Was all that true?"

"I have a recording of Charlotte colluding with Blake to make Henry fall in love with her."

"Really?"

"But Charlotte thinks I recorded what happened later… the blow job she gave him in payment!"

Rita bit down on her lip. "That's… Oh my!"

I grinned. "Now, they'll leave me alone."

"I hope so." Her brows drew together. "But they always seem to find a way to win."

Two days later after lunch, my phone beeped during Creative Writing. Mr. Weatherford, our teacher, stopped talking. "Did someone bring a mobile phone into my class?"

"No," everyone chorused.

"Whoever did it will have their handset confiscated for the rest of the term."

I slid my hand into my pocket and squeezed the 'off' button. Next time, I wouldn't forget to put it on silent. For the rest of the class, I couldn't focus. The matron and cleaners usually came into the room between breakfast and first break. Whoever was in my room had to be there for malicious intent. The class trudged on for an eternity, and I longed to leave and check my phone. Since the cameras were positioned everywhere in the room, we'd see where the interloper went, and what he or she damaged.

"Homework," said Mr. Weatherford. "For next week, I'd like

poems in the following structures: iambic pentameter, limerick, and haiku. Extra credit for those who pen their works using the same subjects and the same vocabulary."

I bolted out of the class and into the nearest girl's bathroom, powered up the phone, and watched the videos. Mr. Carbuncle stepped into the room and folded his arms across his chest while Charlotte searched through my desk, pulled back my sheets, and rifled through my closet and drawers. She left Rita's side of the room untouched and didn't enter the bathroom. She'd been looking for my phone.

I curled my lip and headed for the headmaster's office. This was the evidence I needed to bury her. And that creepy, bribe-taking janitor. There was no point in calling on our housemaster as the man had clearly given up.

At first, the headmaster's secretary suggested I speak to Mr. Jenkins, as the headmaster was in meetings all day and couldn't see students. When I told her I would take the matter up with Rudolph Trommel, the door opened, and the headmaster stepped out and ushered me into his office. As with the last time I saw him, he didn't wear academic robes and donned a tailored, charcoal-colored suit with a bright blue tie.

"Miss Hobson." He leaned the backs of his legs against his desk, face pinched with distaste. "What can I do for you?"

"Are students allowed to break into other students' bedrooms?"

He straightened. "Of course, not. Theft is a punishable offense and will be disciplined both by the school and the police."

I pulled out my phone, pressed the security camera icon, and showed him the footage. "Then why is Charlotte Underwood ransacking my room with the janitor's help?"

His lips thinned when I said the word 'janitor.' As if saying 'caretaker' would make the situation any less dire. Without looking at my screen, he walked around to his desk and sat. "Miss Hobson, phones should be left in your bedrooms during class hours."

I spluttered. Was that all he could say in the face of a bribed janitor and a pillaging student? "Well, it looks like I'll have to take this matter to the authorities."

He rose from his seat. "Are you threatening me?"

"No, sir."

He stretched out his hand. "Give me that phone."

I stepped back. "If you want to look at the videos, I'll email them."

The headmaster jerked his arm, and in a voice laden with menace, he said, "I won't ask you again."

I took a few steps back and slipped the phone into the inner pocket of my blazer. If he wanted it, he'd have to tackle me to the floor and get it himself. With his secretary outside and staff teaching in nearby rooms, I doubted he would risk a scandal if I screamed.

He remained behind his desk, face so red, the flush showed through his thinning hair. "Recording devices are prohibited and violate the privacy of the students. Give me that phone."

"People upload videos on the Mercia-Net all the time, and you do nothing." I folded my arms across my chest. "You only seem to want to intervene when students are committing crimes that will bring your academy into disrepute."

His lips flattened, nostrils flared, eyes narrowed with disgust. "Five demerits. Ten, if you don't leave immediately!"

CHAPTER 9

By the time I rushed back to my room, Charlotte had already gone, and she'd straightened up her mess. It would be a futile effort, but I knocked on Mr. Jenkins' door anyway and showed him the evidence of the ransacking, but he also asked me to hand over my phone. I left his office without comment. Not only was he powerless against Edward and his friends, he actively tried to protect them from the consequences of their actions.

I found Charlotte at dinner, sitting next to Blake with her back ramrod straight, as though she was directing a lesson on perfect posture. Blake also spotted me and grinned. It was the kind of smile that would make a girl's toes curl up to her ankles and her thighs squeeze together with need. The kind that would get her to agree on anything... even something dangerously stupid like public fellatio.

Heat rushed to my cheeks, and I pressed my lips together to hold back my reaction. It didn't work, so I gave myself a mental slap and focused on the image of Charlotte going through my things under the watchful eye of Mr. Carbuncle.

She raised her chin. "Do you have something for me, Trollop?"

I tapped my smartphone and played the recording. "What were you doing in my room, Underwood?"

The haughty expression melted into slack horror. Her thin lips parted, and her vacuous, hazel eyes darted from side to side, looking for someone, anyone to throw me an insult and shut down this distasteful subject.

"Charlotte Underwood sneaks into people's rooms." I held up my phone like a beacon. Even if people couldn't see the video, they would know it existed. "Here's the evidence!"

"Hobson," she hissed through her teeth.

People around us craned their necks to see the video. Those at nearby tables stood to get a better view, then reported back to their friends on other tables. Within moments, loud chatter filled the room.

"Look at her!" I shouted for the benefit of those who were pretending I didn't exist.

Charlotte shot out of her seat. "Enough!"

I lowered the camera and folded my arms across my chest. "There's more where that came from. You make a clumsy cat burglar, but what you lack in stealth, you make up for in enthusiasm."

"How dare you," Edward's cold, resonant voice rang through the room, causing it to go silent. He rose from his seat with the grace of a panther and glared at me with cold, blue eyes just as predatory. "How dare you come here and disturb our peace."

I squared my shoulders. "Don't change the subject with faux-outrage. You're quick to tell me that this is your school, yet when you see thievery and corruption, you have the nerve to ask me how *I* dare expose it? Does the Duchy of Mercia have any integrity or did that wither over the past few generations?"

"Get out."

"So that's how it is. Defend your friends and ignore the evidence of their dirt?" I stuffed my phone in my pocket. "Let me tell you something. If you don't stop this asinine victimization campaign, I'll collect every scrap of evidence I have and use it to bring you down."

His face turned bright red, and he upturned the head table, making its contents crash toward me. "Leave!"

I jumped out of the way, heart thundering. Even Charlotte clapped her hand over her mouth. I looked to my left and right and even at the faces of the other two members of the triumvirate, but no one showed an ounce of concern that he'd nearly thrown a table at me.

A small hand wrapped around my arm. It was Rita's. "Let's go."

Even though my insides trembled, even though my knees wanted to buckle, I pulled my shoulders back and walked around the tables and out of the dining room with as much dignity as I could muster. We walked through the hallways and up the stairs, our footsteps echoing in the ensuing silence. Then Rita opened up the room and sat me on my bed. My body was so numb, I could barely feel myself sink into the mattress.

"I'm sorry," she whispered, dark eyes shimmering with unshed tears.

"Why?"

She lowered herself onto the mattress next to me. "I should have warned you about the cameras. They hate being outmaneuvered. Now, I'm afraid they'll do something terrible."

I swallowed hard. There was no way I could follow Rita's advice to accept any kind of bullying to stop it from worsening. I'd never be able to live with myself. Never feel any self-respect or be able to look myself in the mirror. "Whatever they do will be recorded."

"Don't go on the school trip," she said.

"It's compulsory, remember?"

Rita grabbed my hand. "But can't you ask your parents to call you back to the States on a family emergency? You saw how angry Edward got when you challenged his integrity in front of the whole house. He won't take that lying down. The school trip will be the perfect opportunity to get rid of you."

I shook my head. "They're not murderers." Rita didn't answer for several moments, and a palpitation rocked my chest. Was she gathering up her courage to tell me about a student they'd made disappear? I squeezed her hand. "What is it?"

"It isn't anything they've done, but last year, Edward wanted me to leave so badly, he threatened to poison my food. He hates anyone who isn't like him."

"But that's just bluffing."

"The next day, someone he disliked suffered a bout of explosive diarrhea in class. The teacher had to call an ambulance. All throughout the chaos, he gave me a meaningful look that said I'd be next if I didn't leave."

"But you're still here."

She shrugged. "The schools where I live are terrible, and the bullying is just as bad. At least here, I'll get four good A levels and a place at Oxbridge."

I nodded. It made sense that she would keep a low profile for a few years in exchange for a better future, but what was my motivation? An internship with one of Rudolph's companies? His respect for having endured this shitty school and its shitty bullies? I shook my head. Any sane person would leave. Even if he said he would pay for my university education, I could get loans or a part-time job to fund myself.

A knock sounded on the door, and Rita stiffened.

"Who is it?" I asked.

"Henry Bourneville," said a haughty voice. "May I come in?"

I glanced at Rita, who raised a shoulder as though to say she didn't mind.

"Come in," I said.

He hovered at the doorway, his huge silhouette taking up most of the space. After a moment of hesitation, he stepped in and gazed at the bare walls on my side of the room. "Edward's behavior was deplorable earlier, and he wishes to extend an apology."

"Why didn't he come here himself?" I asked.

Henry raised his brows. "Would you have let him in?"

"No."

The corner of his lips curled. "I expect you would have sent him packing with an iron candlestick holder."

"If only I had such an instrument of murder."

He took another step inside, letting the door click behind him. "Those recordings can't leave the school. They'd damage our reputation, and nobody would want to send their children here."

"I showed them to the headmaster, our housemaster, and the so-called owner of the school. Everyone's first instinct was to admonish me for recording a crime."

He glanced away. I hoped he was thinking about all the recording devices in his family's department store to catch criminals. These snobs seemed to think the rules of normal society didn't apply to them. That people were wrong for defending their property or for resorting to desperate measures to stop attacks against their person. I imagined that Henry agreed with my methods, but he needed a way to ask me for the recordings without sounding like a hypocritical asshole.

Eventually, he turned back, fixing me with earnest green eyes that melted my heart. "What if we removed Charlotte's prefect privileges?"

"That's a start." I folded my arms across my chest. "What about the big plan you have to ambush me on the school trip?"

"We can cancel that in exchange for deleting the recordings."

I stood. "All right."

He inclined his head. "Will you give me the memory cards?"

"The camera deletes the footage as soon as it's downloaded on my smartphone." I stood next to him, opened the app, and selected the recordings for deletion. "There. Done."

A huge breath heaved out of his lungs. "Thank you, Hobson."

I glanced up into his eyes. "You called me Hobson."

He smiled. "That's your name, or have you already adopted the other one?"

"Hobson is fine."

He gave me a curt bow, stepped out of the room, and shut the door. Rita and I stared at each other for about a minute, then she wrapped her hand around my wrist and pulled me into the bathroom. She turned on all the taps and the shower. I leaned on the door, brows raised at her caution.

"They'll break their promise, now," she said in hushed tones.

"I backed up those videos onto a completely different server."

Her eyes flashed. "But they don't know that!"

"He'll report back that he saw me delete the videos of Charlotte and Mr. Carbuncle in my room, but they'll know I have one more."

She tilted her head to the side. "The one that doesn't contain the you-know-what?"

I shrugged. "That video's going to protect me. Charlotte and Blake think I have it."

Her brows twisted with doubt. "I hope you're right."

Her skepticism made me text Mom and ask her to buy me a ticket to New York for the mid-term break. When she didn't reply, I called Marissa in New York, who said she would have to speak to her boss, who was on vacation. If I'd had enough money on my cards, I would have bought my own ticket, but I'd used several months' allowances to buy the security cameras.

Although the triumvirate and their hangers-on ignored me the next morning, with each passing day, Rita's warnings rattled in my skull. Edward and his group didn't like to be outmaneuvered, and with the cameras in my room and the recording, I'd done just that. Mom continued to ignore my texts, even when I told her it was an emergency. She'd never, ever been this negligent with any of her previous husbands. The last person I wanted to tell about my dire situation was Dad. If I triggered another relapse, I'd never forgive myself.

～

The school trip started with the ringing of a handbell early in the morning. After dressing, Rita and I sat in the front of a coach with Mr. and Mrs. Jenkins, Miss Oakley from English Lit, and our sycophantic Latin instructor, Mr. Frost. I slept through most of the journey, and just after midday, we arrived on the roadside at the middle of a landscape of breathtaking hills and valleys.

We all piled out of the coaches into the cold, windy afternoon and met our instructor, a burly army type called Bingham, and his six young assistants who seemed to know Mr. Frost. He told us we would hike up a hill, set up our tents, then have a barbecue dinner, followed by hot chocolate and a motivational movie. I shared a glance with Rita. We hadn't had our lunch yet. How long would this hike last?

While one of the assistants drove the teachers up the hill in a four by four, the rest of us shouldered on our backpacks and trudged behind the instructors. The wind blew droplets of rain onto our faces, and I kept my head down and gritted my teeth.

Blake hiked at my side, not even remotely out of breath. "Enjoying the view?"

Keeping my gaze away from the top of the interminable hill, I muttered, "Not really."

"You know," he murmured in a low voice, "I was looking forward to getting to know you on this trip."

I gulped and stared at him from the corner of my eye. The bastard looked good even in waterproof gear, but I was still smarting from his lack of reaction when Edward upturned the table at my feet. "How?"

"Well," he said in a tone both wheedling and seductive. "All those long walks, caves, and secret peaks. A couple could get lost for a very long time."

"Like in the Blue Lagoon?" It was an old movie where a boy and girl got marooned on a deserted island, grew up, fell in love and had a baby.

"The what?"

I turned my head away, and in my most dismissive tone, said, "Never mind."

Blake jogged up the hill and caught up with his friends, giving me the peace to walk up with Rita. She told me that she'd befriended an upper sixth year from the other house whose brother had gained a music scholarship for Oxford. I smiled, enjoying her company. It was rare for her to talk about herself.

After a brief lunch of store-bought sandwiches and bottled water, we set off again for the longest part of the hike. By the time we reached the campsite, the sun had dipped below the horizon and the scent of barbecued burgers lingered in the breeze. Bingham, our instructor, pointed out the kitchen, the toilet blocks, and the women's and men's shower blocks. Then he gestured at a huge space by a grove of oak trees and told us to set up our tents.

Rita and I managed to set up our groundsheet. We struggled so much with the tent, I became overheated and had to take off my waterproof jacket. Eventually, Blake took pity on us and set up our tent. I kept my eyes on each step on the printed-out instructions, making sure he didn't make a half-hearted attempt that would blow out in the wind. He didn't.

After hammering the last peg, he stepped back and grinned. "What do you think?"

"It looks great." I smiled, ignoring the twinges of guilt in my gut from having ignored him on the climb up. "Thanks."

"You know…" He sidled up to me. "Edward and Henry are sharing, and I'm all alone. You can have first dibs on warming me up tonight."

"Thanks," I said, voice flat and robotic. The long trek up the hill had sapped my energy, and I couldn't even get mildly excited about his indecent proposal. "I'll consider your tempting offer."

His grin widened, and he walked toward the barbecue. "Sleep with me tonight. You might not regret it."

I shook my head. The last place I wanted to end up was Blake's tent. The guy might be hot, but I couldn't trust him not to double-cross me in the middle of the night and let his friends do something nefarious to my sleeping body. Rita and I walked over to the barbecue and ate our burgers at one of the tables and chairs set up around the outdoor kitchen. A few feet away, Charlotte made a fool of herself flirting with an increasingly irritated Henry. The poor, deluded girl was so blinded by desperation, she couldn't pick up on even the most obvious of cues.

After dinner, all traces of sunlight had disappeared, leaving about six stone fire pits around the dining area for illumination. A cool breeze blew through the campsite, and Rita huddled close for warmth. Bingham and the instructors handed out steaming mugs of cocoa that tasted like melted chocolate with a dash of liqueur. Everyone, including Rita and me, hummed with appreciation at the rich, sweet beverages. Bingham set up a projector and a huge, outdoor screen, then announced the subject of the motivational movie. Himself.

I leaned into Rita. "This guy's got an ego the size of the Peak District."

She dipped her head and giggled into her cocoa.

His assistants walked around with huge, insulated carafes of cocoa, refilling our mugs. I sniffed at mine. "This tastes stronger than the previous version."

"They might be getting us drunk enough to endure his film," she whispered.

Since everyone was drinking the same thing, I took a few sips, enjoying its creamy, chocolatey goodness. The shot of alcohol gave it a kick that stopped the drink from becoming cloying.

A younger version of Bingham, clad in cut-off cargo pants, walked onto the screen, making everyone cheer. I couldn't hear whatever he talked about because of the hooting at his hairy shins and eighties-style haircut. Maybe it was the influence of the spiked cocoa, but I also giggled into my mug.

Then the video stopped, and a close up of Charlotte fellating Blake filled the screen. My stomach dropped, along with the contents of my mug. How many times had she done this with Blake, and why had she let him record it?

The hooting stopped, replaced by shocked silence. Everyone, including Rita and me, fixed our gazes on the mesmerizing sight of Charlotte's enthusiastic work on Blake's member. I shook my head. Who could have broadcasted this?

"You fucking bitch!" Charlotte sprinted out of the darkness and threw the contents of her mug in my face.

Hot cocoa scalded my skin, causing me to catch my breath in a loud gasp. Some of it seeped into my eyes, making me rear back and fall off my camp chair.

Before I could tell her the video wasn't my doing, a heavy boot landed in my diaphragm, causing the muscles around my ribs to spasm. All the air escaped my lungs in a rush, and when I inhaled, it got stuck at the bottom of my windpipe. My lungs wheezed out even more air, leaving me struggling. She kicked me again, this time, her boot landing in my gut. I cried out and curled into a ball.

"How dare you!" she booted me in the side of the stomach.

Her first strike had been so devastating, I couldn't even roll away or muster up the lung capacity to tell her it wasn't me. Before she could do any more damage, someone dragged her off.

Rita pulled me to my feet. "Are you alright?"

I doubled over, gasping for air with rapidly cooling chocolate dripping from my face. Before I could answer, Mrs. Jenkins, the house matron, whisked me to the bathroom block, muttering about the folly of broadcasting a young lady's indiscretion. She washed the chocolate off my face, made me take several sips of water, and walked me to my tent, telling me to go to bed and wait to until the morning for my punishment.

Trembling so hard I could barely function, I climbed into the sleeping bag, boots on, and lay on my side still reeling from the shock of having my phone stolen and from Charlotte's brutal attack. My head spun. My mind went around in circles. Who could possibly have done this? The only people I was certain could be innocent were Rita, because she wouldn't do such a terrible thing, and Charlotte, due to her fury at the video. Whoever it was had stolen my phone to make it look like I was the culprit because it was no longer in my pocket. Thoughts and suspicions swirled within my brain until exhaustion and alcohol dragged me into slumber.

∼

I awoke to the sun shining through my eyelids and the sound and feel of hot breaths in my ear. When I opened my eyes, I was no longer in my tent, and a sheep was chewing at my hair. I raised my hands to shove the beast away, but they were duct taped at the elbows and wrists.

CHAPTER 10

I shrieked and yanked my head away, but the sheep kept my hair in its teeth and jerked toward me. My heart pounded to the beat of a war drum. What had they done? Covered me in sheep pellets? Another sheep, this one with long, floppy ears, nibbled at my feet. I shoved the animal away, making it bolt. The one at my hair bleated and continued chewing. Its hot breath heated the side of my face, filling my nostrils with the musky scent of grass and lanolin.

"Get the fuck off me, now!" I screamed the last word.

Sheep-face finally got the message and walked away, releasing wet, grassy strands of hair to slap into my face. I growled. The bastards who had brought me out here had woven clumps of grass into my hair along with something earthy, hoping I'd be eaten alive by a sheep.

Worst of all, they'd bound my wrists, thighs, and ankles with duct tape before zipping me into this insulated prison. I jerked my hands up through the tiny opening at the neck and chewed at the duct tape at my wrists. It was the type fortified with tiny strings of plastic, so it couldn't be easily ripped. I shot a glare at the wall of hedgerows at my back. Edward, Blake, Charlotte and her doppelgängers were probably crying with laughter, filming my ultimate humiliation.

Sweat poured down my brow, mingling with dew, sheep saliva, and goodness-knows what else. The wind blew across the meadow, chilling my damp skin until I shuddered with the cold. Up ahead, a quintet of sheep stood in a clump, watching my struggles with eyes that shone with intelligence.

I shook my head. Now wasn't the time for my mind to reimagine a dire situation supernatural. I had to get out of here before the triumvirate brought the sheepdog or some other kind of horror.

By the time I'd chewed through enough of the duct tape to break free, my jaw ached and felt ready to drop off its hinges. I had to admire Charlotte for her oral endurance. Mine was sorely lacking. I unzipped myself, jerked free of the tape around my elbows, and peeled off the layers securing my legs. My only saving grace was the shock of last night's attack forcing me to sleep fully clothed, otherwise, they'd be filming me in my pajamas.

As soon as I got free, I jumped to my feet and ignored the ache in my shoulders and hamstrings from the struggle. A fallen branch lay on the side. Small enough for me to lift and large enough to wield like a club and break some heads. They had promised. Promised a ceasefire in exchange for the deleted videos, and broken their agreement on the first night of the camp.

"Assholes!" I picked up the branch and dragged it along the meadow, looking for an opening in the hedgerow.

There were none.

Nobody laughed, nobody moved, and nobody called me trollop. They'd somehow removed me from my tent, transported me here and left me all alone with the sheep.

My shoulders drooped, and all the anger spilled out of my chest, replaced by the cold realization that they hadn't cared if I'd been attacked by a wild animal or taken by a lunatic.

They'd left me out here bound and vulnerable and alone.

I closed my eyes and let out a shuddering breath. Rita had warned me, but I'd thought she had exaggerated by hinting that they could be capable of murder. She'd been right. They really didn't care about anyone but themselves. The branch slipped from my fingers. I trudged back to the sleeping bag and picked it up. Grass-covered hills surrounded me on three sides, with the hedgerow at my back, giving me three choices of direction to travel. From the position of the sun, it was probably about nine, but none of that mattered since I was completely and utterly lost.

Dark streaks in the grass lay several feet ahead that looked like tire tracks, and I followed the trail they'd left. Maybe they would lead me to a road or a house, where I could make a call and get someone to collect me.

I reached the bottom of the hill, and after about an hour of aimless wandering, a tall, thin man who looked more scarecrow than farmer stepped out from behind a hedgerow. His beady eyes widened at the sight of me, and his cracked lips spread into a grin of crooked, yellowed teeth. "Are you lost, love?"

"Yes." I glanced down the windy road. "I'm looking for a campsite."

He rubbed the back of his neck. "Which one?"

"I'm with an outward bound company run by a man called Bingham. Is there any way of telling which one he booked?"

His lips turned down. "Can't say there is."

"Do you have a phone I can borrow?" I asked.

"Can't say I have, but you can warm up in my shed if you like." He thrust out his hips and jangled something in his pocket. "I've got whiskey."

My jaw tightened. No phone, no car, but a supply of whiskey for two? No thanks. "Can't say I have the time."

I walked down the dirt road at double speed, ready to club scarecrow man in the face with my fist if he snuck up from behind.

By the time I mustered the courage to turn around, he'd disappeared back into the hedgerows. I continued down the narrow road until it opened up into a slightly larger road, bordered by hedges on both sides and with space for two directions of traffic. I walked until my stomach growled, my feet throbbed, and my chest ached.

Tears rolled down my cheeks. How could they do this? Who would dump a person where they couldn't even flag down a vehicle for help? I had no idea where they'd left me, or the location of the campsite. I could be halfway to Scotland or Wales by now, and nobody would find me.

Midday came and went, and I was still trudging through this maze of back roads. But as the sun hung halfway from its zenith, a white police car rolled past. I let go of the sleeping bag and broke into a run.

It took moments to reach the road, and I stood in the middle of it, waving my arms and screaming like a lunatic. The police car's brake lights went on, then it reversed and stopped a few feet away. I stumbled to the passenger side and crouched down.

The policeman frowned at my face, let me into his car, and asked me what had happened. The dam I had over my emotions broke, and the entire story came out in a rush, starting from getting blamed for the recording of Charlotte, waking up in a field with my hair munched on by sheep, to finding an occupied road after hours of trudging through hedges. He reached for his radio, and the mechanical voice told him the location of my campsite.

"How do I report a crime?" I asked.

"You should be more worried about the young lady making a complaint about you," he replied.

"What?"

"It's illegal to record people without their consent. Depending on your age, she might be able to press charges against you."

My stomach plummeted. I'd just confessed to committing a

crime to a police officer. "Even though she was part of the group that left me out here?"

"Can you identify any of the people behind the prank?"

I clenched my jaw. Leaving someone tied, bound, and at the mercy of fate should be classified as assault at the very least. "No. I was asleep when it happened."

He raised a shoulder. "There you go. Unless she's willing to own up, there's little you can do."

I stopped talking after that. It seemed that the justice system was stacked against victims of bullying and favored those who pushed the boundaries of morality and decency to dressed up their acts as jokes. I stared out of the window at the green wilderness. Someone with a car must have helped them. There was no way even Henry could carry a person this far.

About an hour later, the policeman dropped me off at the campsite. Miss Oakley sat alone on a camp chair with two phones on her lap. The old woman raised her head and stood, letting them both fall to the ground. The policeman explained where he had found me and went back into his car without asking for a witness statement or even the names of the suspects.

Miss Oakley tilted her head to the side. "I'm afraid it's natural for people to become hostile to your sort."

My mouth fell open, but no words came out. What the hell did that mean?

She patted me on the back. "Not to worry. Get yourself cleaned up, and I'll make you a cup of tea."

My nostrils flared. "Tea? Don't you want to know who did this to me?"

She pursed her lips. "The sooner you clean it off, the sooner you'll forget about it!"

I shook my head and walked to our tent. When a sane teacher arrived, I would tell them what had happened. Miss Oakley had clearly lost her last marble. I unzipped the opening of our tent to find the entire left side empty. They'd taken all my stuff, too. Typical.

Nothing of Rita's would fit me, so I walked to the shower block and stared at the mirror. The words, WHORE, TROLLOP, and YANK were scrawled on my face with permanent blue marker. My shoulders drooped with defeat. Now I understood why Miss Oakley had taken my complaint lightly. She'd thought I'd left because of the writing on my face. The bastards had taken my things and made it look like I'd run away. No wonder she had been unimpressed.

I rubbed at the insults with my fingers but couldn't even get the ink to fade. Instead, I combed through my hair, dislodging grass, twigs, and the occasional sheep pellet. Did Rudolph know how bad these boarding schools could get? I doubted he would let me suffer this much torment if it meant risking my life.

Miss Oakley entered with a steaming cup of tea, a towel, and some shower gel. "I found you some spares, but we'll have to invoice your parents for the supplies you left behind on your travels."

"T-thanks." My voice cracked. By now, I'd learned to pick my battles and wouldn't dispute the invoice. At least I could have a shower.

After undressing, I stepped into the only working cubicle and let the warm water wash away my aches, sweat, and all the other things I'd accumulated in the past twelve hours. Dipping my head, I let out a long breath and stared at the water swirling at my feet.

It was red.

A sob escaped my throat. The bastards had put red dye into the shower head, and I'd been too incautious to let the water run beforehand. I'd already cried myself dry on the long walk through the countryside, and only an empty well of despair filled my chest. Their cruelty was relentless, and it wouldn't stop until I'd left Mercia Academy. Forget Rudolph, forget the internship, his college money, and the promised job in journalism. I was going home, but not before I'd avenged myself with something vindictive.

I shut off the water and dried my artificially reddened skin, praying that they hadn't stolen my clothes while I'd showered. They hadn't. After dressing, and after choking down a shitty meal of tomato soup and miniature frankfurters, one of the instructors started up a barbecue, and the rest of the house returned through the woods, hooting at me as if my red skin and hair was the funniest thing they'd ever seen.

My hands tightened into fists. Right now, I wished I was Carrie, so I could drop some trees on their heads.

Blake broke through the crowd of idiots, his handsome face split into the biggest, shit-eating grin. "What happened to you?"

The mirth in his eyes made me want to spit. How could I have ever found him attractive? Right now, I wanted to slam my metal bowl into his face and enjoy seeing him grin through broken teeth and a bent nose.

Edward appeared at his side. "This won't end until you leave Mercia Academy. If you think last night was bad, things are about to get worse."

Behind them, Henry looked to the side, not able to meet my eyes. He'd been the one to negotiate the truce, but I'd been stupid enough to believe he was representing Edward. Who knew? He might have made up the apology and gone over to my room to say anything he needed to get those photos deleted.

The triumvirate strolled away to cheers and whistles, leaving me sitting alone like a discarded rag doll that had been washed in the hot cycle with a red sock. Every ounce of fight had left my body, and I was ready to give up. I looked around for my only friend, but she wasn't standing among the crowd. Maybe they'd done something to her, too.

Mr. Jenkins pulled up a chair.

"Miss Hobson, may I ask why you saw fit to leave us last night?"

When I explained what had happened, he shook his head, sighed, and patted me on the wrist.

"Sir?" I asked.

"Perhaps you should leave." He leaned forward and furrowed his brows. "The staff can't protect you, and the level of attacks against your person are escalating to unreasonable proportions. Think about your future. The last time, you came to me with eyes as red as tomatoes, and today, you were left to the elements."

My mouth dropped open. What kind of teacherly advice was this?

Mr. Jenkins shook his head. "I fear you may not be able to endure whatever they do next."

A boulder of dread made my entire body slump. Mr. Jenkins might have been an ineffective housemaster, but he had a point. Edward had promised to make things worse.

He raised his head. "Ah, there she is."

Rita trudged out from behind the trees, her entire front covered in mud. Someone had obviously pushed her into a puddle. A lump formed in my throat. I'd been so concerned about myself and hadn't even raised the alarm about my friend. Mrs. Jenkins rushed over, handed her a steaming mug, and guided her to the washroom. It was as if they knew their jobs were to clean up the triumvirate's messes with cups of tea and gentle words.

"Will you excuse me?" Mr. Jenkins rose and trailed after his wife.

I clenched the arms of my chair and glowered across the campsite at the students crowding around the barbecue. Something had to be done about Charlotte and the triumvirate. They couldn't be allowed to continue tormenting people. Before I left Mercia Academy, I would show them the pain of being vilified for no reason except that someone found their existence offensive.

Henry broke away from the crowd and strolled through the trees in the exact direction Rita had emerged. I shot out of my seat and followed after him, ready to demand answers. After passing through a small grove of oaks, I entered a clearing covered in leaf litter and acorns. Henry disappeared behind a clump of hazel and I quickened my pace, hoping to catch him with this pants down so he would be easier to intimidate.

When I rounded the coppice, it was to find two men in black had grabbed Henry's arms and were marching him away.

I raised my arm and called out. "Hey—"

Something hard cracked against the back of my head, and everything went black.

CHAPTER 11

My entire skull throbbed so hard, the vibrations traveled down my brainstem. Forcing myself out of unconsciousness was like swimming through jello wearing lead boots. A boulder of grogginess and pain kept forcing me back down. I don't know how long it continued, this cycle of struggling to wake then passing out again, or why, but every so often, I felt the surface beneath me rumble, as though I'd been laid out on a conveyor belt.

When I finally fought my way to the waking world and opened my eyes, Henry's were glaring back at me from a distance of about a foot. I drew back, wrists duct taped together, and kicked out with bound legs. We were in some kind of confined space. The trunk of a large vehicle with the smallest of light bulbs providing scant illumination.

"What are you doing?" he hissed.

A wave of fatigue wrapped around my mind, slowing it to halt. "Trying to… get free."

"You've gotten yourself kidnapped. Why?"

"What?" I blinked.

"Why did you have to follow me?" I'd never heard him speak so harshly.

"Kidnapped? What do you mean?" The words came out slow as molasses. My heavy eyelids pulled themselves shut, and I breathed hard to gather my strength. Being hit in the back of the head was brutal. This was probably a concussion.

If Henry explained what he meant, I didn't hear it. Another bout of head throbbing took over and dragged me back to sleep.

"Hobson," Henry hissed.

"Huh?" I yawned.

"Are you awake?"

"No."

I don't know how long this cycle of waking and immediately falling to sleep continued, but at some time, realization hit like a branch to the back of the head. Someone had abducted Henry, and because I'd witnessed it, they had taken me along. My heart jolted into action, pumping blood to my trembling limbs. The vehicle no longer rumbled beneath us. It was the smooth kind of vibration from driving along a trafficless road, like the freeway. The kidnappers were probably moving us to another location far out of reach of local search parties. Sweat broke out across my skin, and my breaths became shallow. Nobody would ever find us!

My eyes snapped open. "B-Bourneville?"

Henry sniffed. The dim light in the trunk darkened his blond hair and created harsh shadows across his face. "Now you're awake. What the hell did you think you were doing last night, Hobson? You could have gotten yourself killed!"

A rush of anger pushed my fear aside, flexing the muscles in my jaw and neck. I would never have ended up into this shitty predicament if he hadn't negotiated a fake ceasefire. I jerked in my bonds, and bumped my ass on the wall of the trunk. "That's rich, coming from the man who left me duct taped in a sleeping bag to be eaten alive by sheep!"

"I had nothing to do with that," he hissed.

"You could have stopped them, but you did nothing!" I hissed back.

Henry didn't reply because it was true. Even though he hardly participated in the bullying, he was always there with the others, observing me as though everything I'd suffered was some big TV social experiment. Not laughing along with his friends didn't make him innocent. At any time, he could have expressed his disapproval but he was probably too concerned with fitting into the triumvirate or didn't care enough to speak up. Either way, he was guilty by association.

He cleared his throat. "That prank would—"

"You call leaving someone to the elements a prank?" I shook my bound fists into his face. "Some pervert cornered me in a hedgerow and wanted to take me back to his shed for whiskey!"

He flinched. What did he think was going to happen to a young woman on her own? "I'm… are you alright?"

"No thanks to you! And now I'm kidnapped with a head that won't stop throbbing."

"Perhaps you shouldn't have broadcasted Underhill's—"

"That wasn't me." I thrashed about and accidentally kicked him in the shins.

"Shhh! It's best that they think you're unconscious, or they'll drug you again."

All the blood and anger drained from my face, leaving me with a mouth and throat as dry as sand. "D-drug?"

"Just after they taped you up, one of them injected you with something. They said it was to keep you calm for the journey."

I swallowed hard and stared at the dark walls of the trunk. No wonder it had taken so long to awaken. I'd thought it was a combination of pain and the mother of all concussions, but drugs? I shuddered. What if it was heroin or some other kind of addictive substance? What if they gave me an overdose?

Twisting around in the darkened space, I rasped, "W-we have to get out of here."

"This boot is secure. I tried kicking it open earlier. It wouldn't budge, and the kidnappers stopped at the roadside and said they'd kill you if I tried again."

A bone-deep shudder rocked my entire body. Drugs, murder, and a large getaway vehicle? These kidnappers were the real deal. "T-they did?"

He gave me a grim nod. "So, I'd keep quiet and cooperate, in case they work out you're more trouble than you're worth as a hostage."

"Is that what they want?" I asked. "Ransom?"

"Most likely. I can't see them abducting me and taking me this far for my body."

My gaze swept down his muscled chest. I couldn't see much of it in the dark, but if I was the kidnapping type and wanted to keep someone chained to a hideout for a little guilty pleasure, it would probably be a guy with a physique like Henry's. I pushed away the stray thought. Obviously, the drugs they'd injected into me were trying to derail my plans of escape.

The only way I could survive this ordeal was to become a hostage in my own right, not the hostage's whipping girl. "Did you tell them I was Rudolph Trommel's stepdaughter?"

"I kept quiet about that," he replied.

"Why?" It was a struggle to keep the screech out of my voice.

"If Trommel valued you enough as a daughter, you'd be in an American school, close to your family. Obviously, he shipped you to England because he didn't want you getting in the way of his beautiful, new wife."

His words hit harder than Charlotte's boot to the stomach, and I flinched. That was exactly why Rudolph sent me here. He'd just added the crap about studying overseas being character-building so he could impress Mom. Had Henry gleaned all this from his careful observations, or did the whole school know I'd been thrown away like trash? My throat thickened, and a tingling heat crept up my cheeks, settled around my eyes, and made them well with tears. Even if we'd been abducted by violent, drug-wielding kidnappers, I wouldn't let him see me cry. I rolled onto my other side and blinked the tears away.

"Hobson?"

I closed my eyes. As far as I was concerned, his trunk-time entertainment was over.

"Hobson."

I ignored his nudge.

"Hobson?"

It was insane. Here I was, duct taped for the second time in twenty-four hours, still suffering from being injected with a mystery drug, but it felt good to be the one doing the snubbing for once. The more Henry called out, the more I ignored him. He and the triumvirate were used to being the center of Mercia Academy. Let him see what it felt like to be the one clamoring for attention. I'd bet he didn't feel quite so kingly now. Eventually, whatever drugs still remained in my system kicked in again, and I fell back to sleep.

The next time I woke, a large someone was carrying me over his shoulder. I cracked my eyes open. It was sunrise, but the streetlights still shone. We seemed to be in a residential area of terraced houses fronted by ridiculously tiny front gardens with brick walls. This wasn't Mercia village. The distant traffic sounds and the lack of fresh air made me think we were in a large city.

Between parked cars, I caught glimpses of pot-holes in the road, indicating that this was a run-down part of town. Then we passed a street sign that said MULBERRY TERRACE. Whoever was carrying me stopped at a house with lots of broken furniture and black, plastic bags piled into its front garden. My nose twitched at the stench of trash.

The door opened, wafting out the warm, sickly-sweet smell of marijuana. The chatter of young people filled the air along with the strains of Bob Marley playing on a smartphone. My abductor's heavy tread made every floorboard creak underfoot. I counted three flights of what felt like woodworm-infested stairs.

"Caz!" shouted a slurred voice.

"Chat later," one of the kidnappers snapped.

"Oi, Stokes?" the voice said. "What are you two doing?"

I bit down hard on my lip and memorized those names. From the party atmosphere and lack of DJ, this place appeared to be some sort of commune for hippy criminals. At the end of the third floor hallway, someone up ahead opened a creaking door, and we entered a musty room filled with broken furniture. The man whose shoulder I'd been lounging on placed me onto a bed topped with a bare, urine-scented mattress.

"Keep her quiet, or we'll do it for you," said a rough voice.

I drew in a sharp breath through my teeth. More drugs?

"Don't worry about Hobson," Henry replied, resignation in his voice. "She's stronger than she looks."

When the door clicked shut and a key turned in the lock, Henry rushed to my side.

"Hobson? Are you alright?"

I tried to sit up, but the pain swirling inside my skull shoved me back down. "Headache." I squeezed my eyes shut, reciting a list of everything I'd seen: large city, pot-holes, Mulberry Terrace, broken furniture in the front garden, a three-story house occupied by hippies, the scent of marijuana, woodworm, Caz and Stokes. "But I'm fine."

Henry lowered himself onto the mattress, making its springs groan. "Hopefully, they'll let us out once the ransom is paid." He glanced around the room. "Although I think the squalor may kill us first."

CHAPTER 12

I must have fallen asleep again because the next thing I knew, I was propped up on the mattress with my back against the wall while someone took photos of me with a flash camera. My entire skull felt like it was made of iron, and each flare of the camera flash sent searing pain through its contents. They must have injected me again while I'd dozed off.

Cold despair filled my heart, seeped out into my chest and settled in my stomach, adding to its thickening dread. If the kidnappers kept me drugged like this, I'd probably be an addict by the time they'd convinced Rudolph to pay my ransom. Then I'd have to drop out of school and go to rehab, then spend the rest of my life relapsing like Dad. Then Mom would abandon me, and I'd end up a burden to Dad's new family, and he'd probably also start taking drugs again. Tears stung the back of my eyes. Why had I chased after Henry last night? It wasn't like the liar would have been willing to straighten things out.

The grimy photo shoot came to an end, and I cracked my eyes open. A pale blonde woman in her mid-thirties leaned against the far wall holding an SLR camera with a large flash. Thick, unkempt dreadlocks framed her scrawny face, and dark circles ringed her eyes. She wore a black sweater over a miniskirt that did nothing to flatter her thin, blotchy legs.

The photographer showed the screen of her digital camera to a clean-shaven man in his early twenties wearing a beanie. Thin wisps of fluff covered his jawline, and I re-evaluated his age. He was probably just a couple of years older than me. The pair discussed the images in hushed voices, working out which ones to send with their demand for ransom.

I closed my eyes again, not wanting them to know I'd seen their faces.

There was no sign of Henry in the room. Perhaps they'd taken him somewhere to make a ransom video.

Eventually, they shuffled out into the hallway. When the door clicked shut, and the key turned in the lock, I snapped my eyes open and surveyed my surroundings. Broken furniture lined the wall, piled to the ceiling in front of the windows. They were boarded up, but chinks of sunlight shone through a gap in the wood. At the side of the bed stood an oak chair, where they'd left two bottles of water and a pack of paracetamol. I ignored the tablets and checked the seal on the bottle. It was still intact, so I cracked it open and took several gulps of warm liquid.

Moments later, the door was unlocked, and Henry stumbled through. Behind him stood a pair of men in balaclavas. I drew my knees to my chest and breathed hard. It had been a good call to pretend I'd been asleep for the photo shoot. These kidnappers might not have let me out of their house alive otherwise.

The smallest of the balaclava men pointed at me. "Stay quiet, and no one gets hurt."

I nodded and gulped.

"How much do you think Trommel will pay for you? Five million? Ten?"

Warm water regurgitated to the back of my throat, making me cough. "What?"

The short kidnapper stepped forward and pointed his finger under my nose. "You're his stepdaughter, aren't you?"

I glanced at Henry, whose face stiffened. Had he been telling the kidnappers about me?

"Well?" snapped the short kidnapper.

"I am, but they only got married less than two months ago. We barely know each other."

"Right," he said in a tone that implied he was making recalculations. "Well, if he decides not to cough up, we'll send him body parts."

The dread lining my stomach formed a spike of fear. "They won't allow human flesh through the mail!"

He tossed his head and stepped out of the room with his companions, leaving me gasping at their brutal stupidity. It was going to get me killed, maimed, and addicted to whatever had been in that syringe.

As soon as the key turned in the lock, I whirled on Henry. "Why did you overestimate my worth like that? Now they'll be disappointed with anything they get!"

Henry stepped back, palms raised. "I said nothing of the sort."

"Then what were you doing out of the room with them?"

"Bathroom break." He picked up the paracetamol and water, then sat on the oak chair, which strained under his weight. "Look, there's no point in blaming me for anything that's happened. I didn't ask you to trail after me and get caught in the kidnapping. If we're going to survive, we'll have to work together, alright?"

I pressed my lips tight and huffed out a frustrated breath. Henry was right. Yesterday, he was my worst enemy, but today he was the only ally I had in a den of kidnappers. "Did they take your photo, too?"

"Yes. And I expect the school will raise the alarm when Edward tells them I didn't go to bed last night. There'll be search parties and everything."

"Of course." A bitter taste formed in the back of my throat as I remembered waking up being eaten alive by a sheep and then discovered the triumvirate and their sycophants had left me to my fate in the middle of nowhere. I rested my chin on my knees and wrapped my arms tight around my legs. "No one will raise the alarm for me. They thought I'd run away last night."

"Really?" Amusement laced his voice. "How did you find your way back?"

Hearing the mirth in his voice was like a fist to the heart. Anything could have happened to me out there. I jerked my head away. "If you're going to laugh, I'll stop talking."

Henry lowered himself onto the mattress, his weight making me topple to the side toward him. One of my hands stretched down for balance and sank into its filthy surface. Ugh. I'd eat left-handed for the entirety of my stay… if they ever fed us.

"Hobson, look at me." He paused, not speaking until I raised my head and glared at him from the corner of my eye. Even after a night in the trunk of a vehicle and with his blond hair tousled over his face, he still looked like Michelangelo's David come to life. "What happened at the academy is in the past. The situation we're in is far worse. Can you focus on the kidnapping and work with me?"

My eyes shuttered closed, and I gave my head a little shake. Not in response to his question, but at my single-minded fixation on the bullying. "Sorry."

"That's quite alright. Do you have any clues you can share with the police?"

I repeated a version of the mantra I'd memorized from being carried from the trunk, through the house, and into the room, adding that I'd seen the face of the photographer and the man in the beanie hat.

Henry nodded. "That will be helpful. What about—?"

The key turned in the lock, and a female kidnapper in a white balaclava walked in, holding a plate of sandwiches. From the bulk around her head, I would guess this was the photographer trying to hide her dreadlocks.

"Food." She placed the plate on the oak chair, reached into her pocket, and dropped two Snickers bars on top. Then she headed for the hallway.

I glanced at Henry, silently urging him to spring forward, commando-style, snap her neck, and make a break for the exit, but he was too busy eyeing the sandwiches to read my eye signal.

"Which do you want?" he asked, "Cheese, ham, or egg?"

I took in the chipped plate. "Neither."

The female kidnapper paused at the door. "Don't even think of going on hunger strike."

"How do I know you didn't grind pills into the butter or something?" I asked.

She rolled her eyes. "Fine. Someone will make a trip to Marks and Sparks, but it might take a few hours. That all right for you, Princess?"

"No sandwiches," I said. "Just potato chips and packaged food."

She walked out of the room and locked the door, muttering something about the bourgeoisie. I clamped my lips shut. If she'd seen some of the apartments Mom and I shared in the early days, she wouldn't compare me to the likes of Henry, who had grown up stinking rich.

I turned to bourgeoisie boy, who was already halfway through the second round of sandwiches. "What are you doing?"

"I'm hungry." He threw a Snickers bar onto my lap.

I picked it up and held it to the light, examining its wrapper for puncture marks, breaks in its seams or any other signs of tampering.

Henry snatched it out of my hands, pulled it open and gave it back. "Eat something and keep up your strength. If they want to drug you, they'd hold you down or do it while you're sleeping."

After sniffing for chemical scents, I bit into the chocolate and rolled it on my tongue, checking for unusual flavors. Yesterday, I'd been too busy freaking out about having been left in the middle of a field to think about how I'd slept through the duct taping, but now, I had a few ideas. "Did you drug my cocoa?"

"Hobson," he snapped.

Right. Forget about the past and focus on the current situation. "Why are you so calm? Have you been kidnapped before?"

"Twice." He pulled open his Snickers bar and took a huge bite. "The first I barely remember because I was five, but the second happened just before my first day at Mercia."

"You were eleven?"

He paused and gave me a strange look. "Ten. My birthday's on the first of September."

"What happened?"

"Cars ambushed the limo on a country road, and they snatched me." He shrugged. "It was in all the papers."

I chewed the chocolate and swallowed. "I didn't keep abreast on the international news circuit at that age, so sorry I missed it."

His face split into a crooked grin and his eyes flashed to mine with a mixture of mirth and desire. "You're actually quite amusing."

"Thanks." I tried to ignore the sleeping butterflies that stirred in my stomach, picked out a peanut and held it to the light. "I always wanted to be the side entertainment during a kidnapping."

Henry chuckled, drawing my gaze to his smiling face. He finished his Snickers bar in two more bites and shrugged off his waterproof jacket. Then he unzipped his thermal jacket and pulled off his sweater. The fabric rode up, revealing a stomach that could have been carved out of marble. His abs rippled with his movements, a contour of peaks and valleys I longed to explore with my fingertips and tongue.

All the moisture in my throat rushed south and gathered between my legs. What caught my attention most was the golden treasure trail that led down into the waistband of his cargo pants. When the fabric rode up to the bottom of his pectoral muscles, a little gasp escaped my throat. "What… What are you doing?"

"It's hot." He pulled down his long-sleeved T-shirt, abruptly ending the show. "You'll get dehydrated if you keep on all that outdoor gear. Take something off."

Heat rushed to my cheeks as I imagined his bare skin pressed against my own, and I clutched the Snickers bar to my chest. "I'll keep on what I have, thanks."

He rolled his eyes. "Suit yourself." Then his gaze landed on my chocolate. "Are you going to eat that?"

"Yes!" I took a larger than average bite of the Snickers and chewed hard.

Henry laughed and lowered himself back onto the mattress. The see-saw effect of his weight had me rolling onto his side and inhaling his comforting citrus and mint scent. "Oh, Hobson," he said with a chuckle. "If I had to be kidnapped, I could think of no more an amusing companion than you."

I longed to snap at him and demand to know if that was why he'd stood back and watched me get bullied and tormented, but he'd remind me to focus on the present. Instead, I asked, "What do you mean?"

"You're stubborn. The average person would have left the school with all that pressure. I know Yelverton stayed out of financial desperation. Someone living in her kind of squalor can't afford to leave when things get tough, but you could have gone anywhere with the Trommel fortune. Why?"

"You've answered your own question." I shifted to the other side of the mattress.

"What are you talking about?"

"Trommel fortune. There's no Hobson fortune. My father's a

fashion photographer with a young family. He can't afford boarding schools."

"Is that why your mother left? She was a model, wasn't she?"

I bit down hard on my Snickers bar. Of course, someone like him would see all women as shameless gold diggers who walked out on perfectly good men for those with more money.

Mom left when Dad's recreational drug habit turned into a dangerous addiction that drained their savings, dried up his work, and brought unsavory characters to our home. Even though it would leave her destitute and penniless, she took herself and five-year-old me out of the dangerous situation. She had stayed with friends, rented shitty apartments, and tried to get work, but I'd been a millstone around her neck. Mom had never explained any of this to me, but our fortunes only changed when she remarried, but that guy eventually left her for someone younger and without a surly kid.

Henry glanced down at me. "It was a simple question, Hobson. Your mother married an extremely wealthy man."

"And yours didn't?"

After a pause, he inclined his head. "Touché."

Maybe it was the chocolate, or the remnants of whatever the kidnappers' drugged me with, but my eyes became heavy, and a yawn ripped from my lips. I blinked several times to try and stay awake, but I felt myself falling fast. I turned to Henry. "Let's talk about sleeping arrangements."

His eyes narrowed. "Don't even suggest I take the floor or that rickety chair."

"I wasn't going to," I snapped. My mind scrambled for ideas because that's exactly what I'd thought of proposing.

His gaze lingered on the queen-sized mattress. "Good, because if you're not amenable to either of those options for yourself, we'll share the bed."

"Fine." I eyed the bitten part of the Snickers bar. Did they usually look this messy? "But we're sleeping top to tail and back to back with no wandering past the halfway dividing line."

"Don't flatter yourself," he drawled. "I wouldn't dream of pouncing on you in the middle of the night. I intend to be the perfect gentleman."

A flush bloomed down my entire front, and I jerked my head away and folded my arms across my chest. The image of a shirtless Henry and his treasure trail pouncing on me in the middle of the night brought a wave of heat crashing between my thighs. I squeezed my legs together and harrumphed. My mind was taking me to strange and dark places, and it was all because of the concussion and the kidnappers' drugs.

CHAPTER 13

I wasn't sure how much time had passed, but when I awoke, sunlight still shone through the gaps of the boards covering the window. Henry's booted feet lay two inches away from my face, and I shoved away his ankles, making him snort in his sleep. I propped myself on my elbows, letting my gaze linger on the fabric pulled taut against his muscular ass. A tiny growl of appreciation rumbled in my throat. At least he'd kept his promise and mostly remained on his side of the bed.

Later, one of the kidnappers let me out into the darkened hallway for a bathroom break, telling me to go to the door at the end. On my left was the handrail, which led to the top of the stairs. I made a mad dash for freedom, but two balaclava-clad men standing halfway up the stairs blocked my path and shoved me back up to the third-floor landing. Even though they mocked my pitiful attempt, I held my head high and strode to my destination. At least I'd tried.

The bathroom was a tiny, avocado-colored room with a threadbare, burgundy brocade carpet that hid the rotten floorboards. I tried not to look into the toilet bowl as I squatted over it to relieve myself, but I couldn't help glimpsing decades of built-up grime around the walls. Dust covered the bathroom mirror, which I wiped off with the sleeve of my waterproof jacket.

A cerise-pink, straggly-haired mess stared back at me, looking like something out of a Stephen King novel. The blue insults TROLLOP, WHORE, and YANK still stood out like words on a whiteboard. I sighed and turned on the rusty taps with my fingertips. Brown water spluttered out.

I shook my head and left the water running until it turned yellow. I muttered, "What else should I have expected from this dump?"

Someone banged on the door. "Hurry up. This isn't America's Top Model!"

"Clearly." I glowered at the filthy water swirling around a plughole clogged with limestone.

Eventually, the water turned a less poisonous shade, and I stuck my fingers under it and tried rubbing the crap off my face. The color, along with the epithets, remained fast.

This routine continued into the next day. Our captors had been kind enough to supply us with a bar of soap, a tube of toothpaste, and a washcloth, making getting clean in cold water a little more pleasant, even if it did mean brushing my teeth with my index finger.

Henry and I maintained a truce of sorts. We'd lie side by side on the bed, and the heat of his body caused my own to rise. He had revealed that most of the pranks had been instigated by Edward and Charlotte, with Patricia and Blake providing assistance. Whenever I'd ask why he did nothing to stop them, he'd draw away, clam up or change the subject.

About a week into our captivity, it was Henry's turn to bathe, and he'd been gone for nearly three hours. The photographer was late arriving with breakfast, and my heart flipped summersaults. I paced the room and clutched my stomach to still the nausea churning inside.

Something had happened. Perhaps his parents had paid the ransom, and the kidnappers had let him go. My mind whirled. Had he escaped and left me behind? Or… or his parents refused to pay, and our captors had decided to kill us.

My breaths became shallow. Anything could have happened. I knocked on the door for attention. "Hey!"

Nobody came.

I banged on the door with both fists, pounding to match the rhythm of my heart. "Somebody, help!"

Still, nobody came. Not even to tell me to shut the fuck up.

My eyes shuttered closed, and I rested my head on the wooden door, thumping my fist against it until my arm ached. Palpitations reverberated through my chest and my head swam. Something terrible had happened to Henry, and when they had discarded his body, they would come after me.

Even though I resented him for standing by the bullies, I couldn't survive captivity without his company. When my knees buckled, I staggered back to the mattress and lowered my spinning head between my knees. I gulped as much air as I could fit in my lungs and gave myself a mental slap. Panicking wouldn't help me ensure this torment. I had to stay calm. Had to survive so I could escape and tell the police everything I knew about the kidnappers.

"City, pot-holes, Mulberry Terrace, broken furniture in the front garden, a three-story house, hippies, the marijuana, Caz and Stokes, blonde dreadlocked photographer, man in the beanie hat." I rocked back and forth and recited the mantra over and over, whispering it until the words formed a groove in my memory. I knew all their voices. Knew their body shapes. I'd be able to pick each of the kidnapping bastards out in an identity parade… As long as I remained calm.

Another spasm of fear rattled my bones. Where was Henry? What had they done with him? I pushed away the questions and repeated the mantra. I had to stay focused. I had to survive. I don't know how long they kept me alone in that room and without food or water, but panic subsided into exhausted despair. My vision blurred, and my mantra became a blur of jumbled sound. Numbness overtook my senses, and my eyes dropped shut. I dozed, dreaming of myself running from room to room in an abandoned house, looking for Henry.

After what felt like a day, the lock turned.

My heart jolted back to life. I sprang off the mattress and rushed to the door.

Henry stepped through, looking dazed and drawn. My heart burst with a warm mix of joy and relief, which flowed into my chest, thickened my throat, and brought happy tears to my eyes.

The whites of his eyes were bloodshot, as though they had kept him awake all night. He ran a hand over his face and groaned. I wrapped my arms around his huge frame. Marijuana masked most of his comforting scent, but I didn't care. He'd returned mostly unhurt.

"You're alive!" The last word came out as a sob.

Henry drew back and placed his large hands on my shoulders. A puzzled frown wrinkled his brow, but his eyes shone with warmth. "You were worried?"

I swallowed back the lump in my throat. "I-I thought they'd killed you. What happened?"

He let out a long, weary breath and guided me back to the mattress. The weight of his body created that effect where I fell onto his side, but instead of scrambling away as usual, I savored the closeness.

He wrapped his arm around my shoulder, bringing me even closer. My sinuses had long become accustomed to the stench of must and mold and marijuana, but what was left of Henry's mint and citrus scent filled my heart. He was here. This was real.

"They were asking about the department store," he said.

"Why?"

"Apparently, they're planning on robbing it while everyone's distracted by the kidnapping. They showed me plans of every floor, footage they'd taken with their phones, and even diagrams. Then they asked question after question about its security."

"Oh no." I shuddered. "What did you say?"

"What I'd been trained to do in a situation like this: I revealed everything."

Resting my head on his chest, I wrapped my arms around his middle and listened to his slow heartbeat. "I don't get it."

"Our security consultant told us that some of the questions are rigged to see whether you're telling the truth. If they catch you in a lie, they'll extract the next answers with violence. He showed us some examples of famous kidnappings, and what could go wrong."

"Like Stockholm syndrome?"

"Yes." He drew back and brushed a strand of hair off my face and stared at me with bloodshot, green eyes. Tears gathered in mine at the thought of something terrible happening to Henry. "You've been crying."

My bottom lip trembled. "I didn't know if you were alive or dead."

A smattering of golden stubble covered his chin, giving him the kind of rugged look that made the butterflies in my stomach flutter. The corner of his full lips lifted, and my heart melted into goo.

"I thought you hated me," he murmured, his gaze never leaving my own.

"It's the other way around." I slid my arm across his broad back. "You and your friends hate me because I'm American."

He shook his head. "Edward is the only one who might take issue with your nationality."

"Might?"

"He mostly wanted to humble you."

I shook my head. Did Rudolph think I'd have a difficult time at a British boarding school because the students would think I was an arrogant American? They certainly hadn't used that word to describe Marissa on our first day. I'd demonstrated that I wasn't loud or brash. What had there been to dislike?

"And the girls?" I asked.

"You're a threat. We've all known each other since we were eleven." He paused, seeming to work out how to phrase what he was going to say next. "It's taken years to settle into our roles, and Charlotte's popularity took an upturn when she developed those breasts."

"Really?" I rolled my eyes at their shallowness.

"We'd had newbies before, but none of them made an impact. But then you waltz in…." His eyes roamed the length of my body, and he licked his lips. "Looking like a model and putting every sixth former to shame. The girls had to keep you from breaking up the relationships they'd worked so hard to build."

"Model?' I spluttered, but warmth flooded my cheeks and the look in Henry's eyes woke the butterflies in my stomach again. "That's my Mom, not me."

He leaned his face closer. "Genetics."

I drew back, unable to believe his words and the way his saying them made me feel. "What does that even mean? Half the girls in my prep school look better than me. I don't even wear makeup!"

"Imagine what would happen if you actually made an effort to flirt. Charlotte and her friends wanted to keep you off-kilter because they couldn't compete. You could have any man in Elder House. Even those like Edward, who considered you a threat."

My lips trembled. There were lots of pretty girls at Mercia Academy. Charlotte wasn't even the best looking. Nothing Henry said made sense. "What about you?"

"I don't find you threatening in the least." He cupped my cheek and lifted my chin. Our eyes locked again, and for a heartbeat, time stood still. Nothing mattered except Henry and the intensity of his gaze… until he lowered his lips onto mine.

The kiss was soft at first, a slight caress of lips. Tentative, as though Henry was asking permission with his mouth instead of with words. His warm, familiar mint and citrus scent engulfed my senses, and I tilted my head back, parted my lips, silently telling him I wanted more. We'd become so close in the past few days, locked together in the room with only ourselves for company. He was different from his friends, kinder, more humble, relatable, and I could trust him. I needed this kiss. I needed Henry.

With a hum of approval, he threaded his fingers through my hair and ran his tongue along the seam of my lips, making me gasp. All thoughts of the triumvirate, the kidnapping, and even the squalor of the room melted away, and it was just me and Henry and my desperate desire for him to deepen our connection. His tongue caressed mine, the pleasurable sensations sending tingles to my pulsing core. I pressed my thighs together and writhed.

Henry lowered me onto the mattress, resting my head on one of the bundles of jackets we used as pillows. The weight of his body on mine and the arms around my back acted as the blanket of safety and warmth I craved. I ran my fingers over the corded muscles of his neck and arched onto his chest. Somehow, he'd positioned his legs between mine, and now his thick erection ground at my core, sparking bursts of pleasure with each movement. I threw my head back and gasped, then Henry buried his head into my neck, nipping, licking, and sucking at my flesh.

Panting and moaning, I writhed against his hardness, losing myself in a frenzy of pleasure. I dug my fingers into the muscles of his rippling shoulders and shuddered. If he continued like this, I would climax.

"Hobson," he whispered, voice breathy. "Have you ever?"

The words catapulted me to reality. I curled back into the mattress and examined his flushed features. I dismissed the way his wavy hair curled around his face, framing it like a work of art, and stared into the blown pupils of his verdant, green eyes. If he wanted to ask if I was a virgin, he could spell out the question with words.

With as much deliberation as I could muster, I asked, "Have I ever what?"

He nuzzled my cheek, leaving a trail of kisses and a tingling sensation in his wake. "Have you ever had sex?"

I slapped him hard on the chest. Things were going too far, too fast. 'If you believe I'll have my first time with no protection and on a filthy mattress with my worst enemy, you can think again." I tried to push him off, but he was too heavy. "Get off me."

Henry drew back, cheeks adorably flushed. "I'm not your worst enemy. That's Charlotte Underwood."

I sat up and glared into my lap. How the hell did I go from resenting Henry for doing nothing while his friends bullied me, to rutting against his erection like it was the last dick on earth? This kidnapping had turned my judgment upside-down. A week ago, or however many days they'd kept us here, I would never have even considered flirting with Henry, let alone kissing him.

"Hobson," he said, still out of breath.

"What?"

"Did I do something wrong?"

"I don't know," I snapped, fixing my gaze on his heaving chest. "Did you?"

"I don't follow."

I turned to him, heart thrumming, stomach tightening with anticipation. "If we get out of here, and Edward decides to pull another of his stunts, what would you do?"

He paused and drew his brows together. "I'd ask him to stop."

"Why?"

"I didn't know you before." He placed a hand on my shoulder and massaged a path of relaxation up my neck. "It's hard to explain the friends you make at schools like Mercia. We live with each other most of the year, eat, study, and play together. The relationships can run deeper than family. Your friends are the ones who see you through your hardest times, not the housemaster or your parents."

I tilted my neck to the side, giving him better access. "Go on."

"When you came, you were a stranger. Beautiful and fascinating, yes, but not someone I'd want to jeopardize a friendship I'd built for over half a decade."

I shrugged him off. "It's all right. I understand."

"Once Edward gets to know you, he'll back off."

"And the girls?"

"They want to marry rich. Most of them are that way inclined."

"I'm not, and neither is Rita."

He smiled and reached for my other shoulder. "I know that, now." His fingers made quick work of my tense muscles. "You have a well of inner strength I've never seen in another person, and it's more intoxicating than your beauty."

Henry lowered his lips onto mine, and I let my eyes flutter shut.

The key turned in the lock, and the door cracked open. "Good news, Bourneville. Your father paid the ransom. It's time to go."

CHAPTER 14

All the blood drained from my face into my spasming heart. I drew in a sharp breath, only for it to catch at the top of my lungs. They'd said Henry could go, not me. What happened to my ransom? Were the photos enough to convince Rudolph that I'd been captured? I clutched my hands to my chest. Or maybe he didn't care.

Henry wrapped his arm around my shoulder. "I'm not leaving without Hobson."

The taller of the kidnappers stepped into the room. "Don't be stupid. We've got the money. Now, we're holding our end of the bargain." He hooked his thumb over his shoulder. "Out."

"No," Henry snapped.

My breaths became shallow, my shoulders rose around my ears, and my elbows tucked into my sides. They wanted to keep me here on my own, where I would go insane from being cooped up without Henry's company. If Rudolph didn't pay whatever they'd asked, the kidnappers might take out their frustrations on my body and send the photographic evidence to his office.

The larger kidnapper wrapped a hand around Henry's wrist and yanked him to his feet. Although there wasn't much of a height difference between the two men, Henry's frame was broader and more athletic. He swung his fist into the other man's jaw, making his head rock back.

With a pained roar, the man shouted, "Loki!"

I stiffened. They'd just given up something else to add to my collection of facts.

As Loki rushed inside to help his friend, I looked around for a suitable weapon. Tables, empty wardrobes, drawers and other massive furniture littered the edges of the room, but nothing I could wield like a club. Not even a bottle of water.

I picked up the rickety chair and held it over my head. "Get out!"

"Easy." Loki raised his palms as though I was holding something more dangerous than a chair that looked about to fall apart. He pulled his friend toward the door and backed away. "No one's getting hurt, alright?"

"I won't leave until you free Hobson," said Henry.

The first kidnapper rubbed his balaclava-covered jaw. "Is that what you want me to tell your father?"

"Yes." Henry lifted his chin. "Either we both leave together, or we both stay."

A relieved breath shuddered out of my body, and I lowered the chair to the ground. Henry could have walked out of that door and left me to my fate, just as his friends had done the night before the kidnapping. Not only had he remained, but he'd arranged things for his father to pay my ransom, too. My heart made a happy thrum in my chest, and I reached down his arm for his hand. The touch of our fingers sent a jolt of pleasure into my heart, and I stared up into his determined expression.

"Fine." The kidnapper backed toward the door. "We'll call Mr. Bourneville, explain the situation, and arrange another ransom drop. If he gets pissed off and calls the police, and if any of my gang is arrested, you and the girl die."

Henry pulled back his shoulders. "It's a risk I'm willing to take for Hobson's freedom."

The kidnapper shrugged. "It's your fucking funeral."

"Wait." I stepped forward. "What's happening with Rudolph Trommel?"

"He's negotiating." The kidnapper stepped into the hallway. "It's taking longer because we have to go through a PA, who passes messages onto another PA, who speaks to him and vice-versa."

The words hit me like a wrecking ball, and I doubled over, holding my hands on my thighs to stay upright.

"How could he?" I gasped out. He wasn't my father. Wasn't my anything, but I thought his affection for Mom would have made him want to at least negotiate directly with the kidnappers. My heart twisted into knots, sending an ache straight to my gut.

Mom.

If she'd acted like I wasn't an imposition to be sent away to school, and if she'd insisted on keeping me close, Rudolph would never have had me sent so far away. If Mom acted like I was precious to her, he would never have relegated my abduction and ransom to an assistant of an assistant. "How much are you asking for?"

He rubbed his chin. "It started off as quarter of a mil. Not as much as with Bourneville here, but he's a natural-born son, the heir, and worth more."

I nodded. "What is it now?"

Even in the hallway and with a balaclava over his features, I could see his face twisting into a pained grimace. "He's negotiated us down to fifty thousand."

I reared back. Humiliation rippled through my insides, making them shrivel to dust. The engagement ring he bought Mom was reported to be worth ten times that much. "What will you do if he doesn't pay?"

"No need to answer that," said Henry. "If my father doesn't agree to pay that amount, tell them it can come out of my inheritance."

"We'll be back soon with news." The kidnapper shut the door and turned the key.

Henry gathered me into a warm embrace of strong arms and his comforting, minty scent. I leaned against his shoulder, relishing the safety he provided, and breathed hard. Henry had done more for me than Rudolph had in the entire time he'd been dating and married to Mom, and Henry had been my former enemy, not even my stepfather. This time, when the tears gathered in my eyes, I let them flow.

"Shhh," said Henry. "Rudolph Trommel is a hard man. Anyone who has read his history can gather that he's a bastard. His decisions are no reflection on you."

My throat spasmed. "But he's supposed to love my mom. This kidnapping isn't something he can hide, and it will come out eventually that he didn't deem me worth the price of one of his designer watches."

Henry drew back and swiped a tear from my cheek. "I'm sure he's keeping this information from her. No mother in the world would prolong a kidnapping to quibble over money."

"Huh," I said.

"What was that?"

"She didn't object when Rudolph decided to send me to England. What if she's not objecting to these lengthy negotiations?"

He cupped my face with both hands, tilting my head up, so we locked gazes. "You don't know that, Hobson. Being cooped here in this room is making you fear the worst. Hopelessness is part of being held hostage. I'm sure your mother is either completely ignorant of what's happened, or on a plane to England to pay your ransom personally."

The naive optimism of his words made me smile. If I ever got my smartphone back and searched the news, I'd find no pictures of

Mom rushing through the arrivals gate at Heathrow airport. She'd be in the society magazines, at some function or a party in the states, wearing a gown worth twice my ransom and acting like her only daughter wasn't being held by kidnappers.

"Hey." Henry lowered me to the bed and settled us onto the mattress, so my entire left side rested against his body. His chest rumbled as he spoke. "You're not the only one without a perfect family, and that doesn't make you less loved."

"But your father paid your ransom."

He snorted. "That man is more interested in making his mark on the family legacy than in spending time with his son. The only reason he's paid my ransom is that he needs someone to manage the businesses after he's gone."

I closed my eyes and smiled. Henry was right. Everyone's lives were a little blighted by family woes. Mom would probably never side with Rudolph when it came to a situation of life or death. Rudolph had likely withheld the information and was just being his usual, hard-nosed self.

Henry told me about the family situations of his other classmates. Edward's mother died a few months after he joined Mercia Academy, and his father was suffering from an early type of dementia and failing fast. Blake's father was a violent alcoholic who resented his mother's relationship with the prince. When they divorced, she married said prince, and his father died in a drink-driving accident that was covered up by the palace. Now, his mother was having an affair with someone else, and the prince was too smitten to divorce her.

I sighed. "Why do people with such unhappy backgrounds inflict pain on others?"

"I had a theory about that," he rumbled. "When one is too busy enjoying the suffering of others, one has no time to wallow in one's own misfortune."

I drew back and glared into his solemn, green eyes. "Is that why you do nothing? For the distraction?"

"Of course not."

He continued telling me about Charlotte. Her brother had also gone to Mercia Academy, and had emerged as a gambling addict who frequently got himself into trouble with casinos. Their father frittered away the family fortune to bail out his son, but nothing could get him to stop the gambling. Charlotte was both worried and resentful about her brother, but hid it by telling everyone he worked for the Saudi royal family. By the end of the conversation, I had learned more about the triumvirate than I'd had the weeks I'd attended the academy.

"You see." He wiped away my last tear. "You're not alone. We might seem like a happy, close-knit group, but it's a facade that hides a myriad of hurts."

"Thanks." I gave him a peck on the lips. "For fighting to stay with me. And for making me feel less awful."

That evening, I moved my makeshift pillows to his end of the bed, so we slept spooning each other. Henry's hand rested on my belly, rubbing it in gentle circles. It was the balm I needed to soothe the hurt of the day's disappointment and heartbreak. I let my eyes flutter closed and focused on the sensations of his large, warm palm and thick fingertips.

No one had ever caressed me to sleep like this. I'd been kissed before and petted, but this mattress and our conversations were the closest I'd ever been with another person except Noelle.

"You're so much different from how I expected," he murmured.

"Hmm?"

"Softer. Sweeter." A finger slipped under the hem of my top and skimmed the bare skin above the waistband of my cargo pants.

I smiled. "Really?"

"Really." The pads of his fingers made a soft, slow trail up to my bellybutton and rubbed gentle circles that made me squirm with delight. "I imagined someone as stunning as you would be arrogant and aloof, but you weren't." His warm breath on the back of my neck quickened, and he pushed his clothed erection into the backs of my thighs.

Arousal surged through my core, and I squeezed my legs together. He was only touching my belly and I could barely keep myself contained.

"You're so beautiful." He shifted on the bed, positioning his covered erection between the cleft of my clothed buttocks.

My right thigh slid over my left. Tiny pulses of my core muscles moved in time with the slow, steady movements of his hand on my belly. His hips moved in gentle circles, each stroke of his erection against my buttocks a form of sweet torture. If we were anywhere else, I would turn around, pull off his shirt and run my hands over those hard, thick muscles. But we were in this squalid room, where balaclava-clad kidnappers could walk in at any time.

"God, I want you so much," he murmured.

I bit down hard on my bottom lip to stop myself from reciprocating. That interrupted kiss had left me aching for more than his touch. Telling him I felt the same would only escalate something I couldn't bring myself to do until after we'd returned to the academy. After he'd proven that things wouldn't switch back to his siding with the bullies.

I gasped out. "Don't—"

"I heard you the first time. Not here. But you didn't say I couldn't touch." His other hand snaked under my arm, along my collarbones, and cupped my shoulder. "See? I'm being the resolute gentleman."

I huffed out a laugh. His hands might be staying within the realms of decency, but his hips weren't. And neither was that thick erection. Grinding back with my own hips, I let out a happy sigh. I had no complaints.

"Hobson," he gasped out.

"We should be on a first name basis by now, don't you think, Henry?" I said.

"Emilia…" he kissed my earlobe. "I like the sound of my name on your lips."

The heat pooling between my legs turned into an urgent ache, which wouldn't be relieved from squeezing my thighs together. I unbuttoned my cargo pants, slipped my hand into my panties and circled my nub. Pleasure streaked through my core, making me bite down hard on my bottom lip to stifle a moan.

"Let me do that for you," said Henry, his voice strained. His hand slipped into my panties and slid over mine. The weight of his fingers added pressure to my strokes, and I cried out. Henry's breath quickened. His hips jerked against mine. "Please."

"Alright." I pulled my hand back, letting his finger slide over my sensitive bundle of nerves. "But don't venture any further than this."

"Yes," he whispered.

Henry stroked and rubbed, making me buck against his fingers. At that moment, I could have stayed in that room with him forever, making each oncoming day an exploration of our minds and bodies. I'd opened myself to him, and he hadn't mocked or judged. He had accepted me, just as I had accepted him. His fingers never strayed from my clit, even though my body yearned for more.

He continued those clever caresses, grinding out his own pleasure against my ass until my world splintered into a million pieces and remade itself into one where things might actually work between Henry and me. I threw back my head and gasped out my orgasm in several shuddering breaths. Henry trembled through his climax, holding me so tight, we were nearly one.

As I panted through the aftershocks, sleepy and content and heart full to bursting, I wondered how much closer we would become in the morning.

CHAPTER 15

The next time I awoke, the sun shone through my eyelids. I cracked them open to find myself lying on a bench on a country road with my head in Henry's lap. When I lifted my head, it throbbed so hard, I had to slump back down.

Henry ran his fingers through my hair and murmured, "Welcome back."

"What happened? Did they drug me again?"

"They must have done it while we were sleeping. I woke up sitting next to you and rearranged us to make you more comfortable." A long, relieved breath heaved out from his lips. "I can't believe we survived that. And that you're safe. When they wanted to keep you with them…"

I glanced up into his pained face. The morning sun shone through his blond curls, making them glimmer like spun gold. Even the stubble on his cheeks shone like a smattering of gold dust. The muscles around his eyes tightened and I nearly choked at the sight of them so close and in the light. They weren't the color of emeralds but far richer. Bursts of blues and yellows and greens mingled from the pupils, where the colors coalesced around the edges into the deepest shade of peridot. Thick, golden lashes framed the entire effect, reminding me of the gilded portraits around the academy.

I could have lost myself forever in those orbs had the wind not blown a strand of auburn hair into my face. I squeezed my eyes shut and exhaled. Whatever was in that drug was exaggerating my perceptions. "Do you have a migraine, too?" I pulled myself up, this time, keeping my head down. "Because my head feels like it's been struck with a hammer."

"No, but I'm twice your size," he said. "I probably metabolized the drugs while I slept."

"Right." I stood and swayed on my feet. Transparent stars swam before my eyes, and I blinked several times to clear my vision. "Let's call the police."

Henry placed both hands on my shoulders and held me steady. "Don't. They warned me that they have an inside man at Mercia Academy. If we tell anyone anything about what we saw, they'll kill us."

"Who's going to pick us up if we don't call the police?"

He gave me a crooked smile. "Don't you know where we are?"

I glanced around at a field full of sheep. The land was flat and the air less crisp, so we couldn't be back in the Peak District. "Where?"

"Outside Mercia village. We can call the academy and ask for a car. There's a phone box at the end of the road. Let me carry you the distance."

I refused, of course. No matter how close I'd become to Henry during our captivity, things would change when we returned to Mercia Academy, and now was the time for a bit of distance to cushion the impact of his return to the triumvirate. He had said things wouldn't change, but he'd also expressed the importance of his friendships and the deep connection he had formed with Edward and Blake over the years. No matter how earnest he appeared, I wouldn't hold onto any foolish hope.

We spent the next half hour walking down a country road, through foot-deep piles of fallen leaves and under a canopy of skeletal branches with amber-colored leaves. When we spotted the red phone box at the corner of the village, we picked up our pace.

"Can we call collect?" I asked.

"No need." He jingled the change in his pocket. "I have enough for a quick phone call and a pot of tea for two at the village bakery."

I jogged to keep up with his long, fast strides. "I'll take that over another lukewarm bottle of plasticky water."

Of all the people Henry could have called for help, he chose our housemaster, the ineffective Mr. Jenkins, explaining that the headmaster was always too busy with outside matters to bother with a case of missing students.

While we waited, Henry placed both hands on my waist. "When we return, I'll acknowledge you as my friend."

A thin coating of ice formed on my heart. I hadn't given it much thought, but I'd hoped we'd be more than just friends after last night. I forced my lips into a smile. "Thanks. I appreciate that."

"And the others won't give you any trouble." He wrinkled his nose. "Although I can't make any promises about Charlotte."

"I can deal with her," I muttered.

About five minutes later, a four-by-four arrived with Mr. Carbuncle at the wheel. Even the sight of his shifty, mustached face couldn't dampen my relief. He rolled down the window on the passenger side and said, "You're back, then?"

Henry opened the back door, ushered me inside, sat next to me and laced his fingers through mine. I swept my gaze from our intertwined hands, up his arms, and to his face.

An earnestness shone in his green eyes that made my stomach quiver. "Thank you for making pleasant what could have been harrowing. I'm not sure if I would have survived it without you."

The ice around my heart melted, and warmth filled my chest. I'd been silly to have gotten upset at his declaration of friendship. We'd only been together for a few days, and I couldn't expect a proclamation of love. The village of thatched roofs and stone-brick buildings rushed past the corner of my eye, followed by huge fields bordered by trees whose leaves had yellowed or fallen off. Instead of looking at the autumn scenery, I kept my gaze fixed on Henry's as if searching into his soul. When my eyes traveled down to his lips, he leaned across the seat and gave me a chaste kiss.

"No canoodling at the back," snapped Mr. Carbuncle.

We both ignored him and shared a few more kisses.

Instead of dropping us at the double doors of the main building, the janitor drove past it and down a side road that looped around the vast estate. Butterflies stirred in my stomach. The morning we left the academy seemed an eternity ago. Henry squeezed my hand as though assuring me that things would be different.

Mr. Jenkins stood outside the doors to Elder House, hands clasped, rocking back and forth on the balls of his feet. As soon as the car stopped, he rushed down the steps. "Mr. Bourneville, Miss Hobson! Are you alright? Do you need medical attention? An associate of your parents informed us of your situation, but we've kept it quiet, as requested."

Edward and Blake emerged from the wooden doors and strode down the stairs like a pair of princes. Edward glanced from Henry to me, staring with an intensity I couldn't decipher. Whatever was on his mind, it wasn't the usual hatred.

Blake broke formation and grinned, wrapping his arms around Henry. "Welcome back, Henry." Then he broke away and gave me the longest, bone-crushing hug. "I couldn't stop thinking about you, Emilia. Are you hurt? Is there anything you need?"

He drew back, encasing the sides of my face in a lover's caress, chocolate brown eyes radiating genuine concern. All my words evaporated into thin air, leaving me slack-jawed. Blake had always been flirtatious, but that had been his womanizing. Other than a few half-hearted attempts to sleep with me, he had participated in most of the bullying. My gaze flickered to Henry, who nodded and gave me an encouraging smile.

I licked my dry lips. "I'm... fine. Thank you."

He closed his eyes, exhaled a relieved breath, and pressed a kiss on my forehead. I turned to Henry again, who shrugged. Did the triumvirate have a form of mental communication I knew nothing about, or was something else going on?

Edward's brows drew together in a pained expression, and his posture straightened in an English way I'd only seen in period TV dramas. Slightly regimented, polite, yet dashing. He cleared his throat. "Miss Hobson, I apologize unreservedly for the way I've conducted myself since you joined Mercia Academy. You were right. It was unbecoming of the Duchy of Mercia, unbecoming of the school, and unbecoming of me. From this moment onward, I swear you'll meet a different Edward Mercia."

My heels ground into the gravel path, and I had to blink a dozen times to let his words sink in. Edward... apologizing? I wanted to ask why now, but it was probably guilt at having gone too far with their bullying. I would have asked Rita, but I doubted that any occasion would have arisen for them to make such assurances to her.

"Thank you." I held out my hand to shake on his promise. "I accept your apology."

Edward wrapped his fingers around mine, sending a jolt of sensation into my heart. Instead of shaking my hand, he brought my knuckles to his lips for the lightest of pecks. The sensation quickened, and I sucked in a sharp breath through my nostrils. Whether the gallant kiss had excited me, or the fact that a future British duke had done it, or because it had been Edward, I didn't know, but I hoped that wouldn't be the last time he would kiss me.

Henry placed his large hand on the small of my back and guided me up the stairs, through the doors, and through the hallways and stairs, just as Blake had on my first day. Back then, I hadn't known what to expect from Mercia Academy. A little snobbery and a few barbed comments, perhaps, but none of the shockingly vicious attacks I'd suffered.

The footsteps of five men echoed through the hallways as Henry, Edward, Blake, Mr. Jenkins, and even Mr. Carbuncle, walked me to my room.

The janitor handed me my key and stepped back. "Here we are, Miss Hobson. It's all there like you left it."

I turned around and gave them what I hoped would be a bracing smile. "I'm fine, everyone. Just longing for a hot shower."

Mr. Jenkins beamed, while the other four had the decency to glance away. The adrenaline that had kept me going throughout the kidnapping had crashed, leaving my body and my spirits too heavy to even comment on the incident with the tampered shampoo.

"Thank you." I unlocked the door, stepped into the room, and rested my back against the closed door. A rush of mingled emotions swirled and expanded within my chest, threatening to spill out into tears. Relief at leaving that squalid room, sadness that Mom hadn't been here to welcome me, and confusion about the triumvirate.

I ran a hand down the side of my face and blew out a breath. The most optimistic part of me, the one that believed in Henry, thought he would take weeks to change his friends' opinions about me. Blake's reaction hadn't been completely out of character. He was never unpleasant if I encountered him alone. But Edward had shown me nothing but threats and hostility from the day we met. How could I believe he could change just because I got kidnapped?

I tore off my clothes, put on a robe, turned on the shower, and waited. Waited for the blue dye, for the water to turn cold, or for it to stop altogether, but it streamed down, hot and plentiful. My hair was a greasy mess from not having washed it for so long, and my skin a cesspool of sebum from a daily diet of Snickers bars and potato chips.

I stood underneath the hot spray, gasping with relief at the feel of clean, clear water. After testing my shower gel and shampoo for signs of tampering, I scrubbed myself raw. Washed myself of the grime, the mustiness, the squalor, and the fear of that awful place. There were only two things I held onto: the memories of my intimacy with Henry, and the list of items I'd been memorizing for days.

"City." I dug my nails into my scalp. "Pot-holes, Mulberry Terrace, broken furniture in the front garden, three-story house, hippies, marijuana, Caz and Stokes, blonde dreadlocked photographer, man in the beanie hat, Loki."

I repeated the words over and over until the steam and hot water made me so dizzy, I staggered out and scribbled the list out, along with everything else I could remember of my kidnapping.

The door burst open, and Rita ran inside. "Emilia!"

I shot to my feet. "Rita?"

She barreled into me, tiny body knocking me off my feet and onto my bed. "You've been gone for nine days. Everyone was talking about it, but the teachers were saying nothing." She drew back, dark eyes wild. "I thought—"

Her face crumpled and she burst into racking sobs.

"What's wrong?" I placed a hand on her trembling shoulder.

She shook her head and kept it bowed.

"Rita?" I pulled her next to me on the bed, wincing at the feel of her sharp bones. In the past week, she seemed to have lost all the weight she'd gained.

"I thought they'd kill you," she rasped.

I stayed silent and waited for her to continue. Maybe this was the time she would confide in me about the extent of the bullying she'd suffered last year.

She wiped her eyes with the back of her hand. "That morning, when you'd gone missing for the whole day, I'd thought they'd left you somewhere like the edge of a cliff, or in the middle of the motorway, where you'd be sure to have an accident and break your neck. But when you didn't turn up after following Bourneville into the forest, I thought he'd finished the job."

I gasped. "Rita!"

"I'm not the only one who came to that conclusion. A few of the other scholarship students approached me with their suspicions, too. They thought you were dead, and he'd flown to a country without an extradition treaty with the UK."

I shook my head. Normally, I would have smiled, but she'd seen more of the triumvirate and experienced more of their cruelty. "Don't mention this to anyone, but Bourneville was kidnapped, and they took me because I'd seen them and tried to raise the alarm."

Her eyes widened. "Is that where you've been?"

I nodded. "They kept us in a room together. We've…" A warm glow formed behind my ribs, and I couldn't help the tiny smile that curved my lips. "We've become friends, and Mercia and Simpson-West apologized. Things might be different from now on."

Rita drew back and pressed her lips together. Although she didn't speak, she might have scrawled the skepticism all over her face with blue marker pen.

CHAPTER 16

Despite Rita's belief that I'd been killed, she had asked Mr. Jenkins to collect notes and homework from all the classes I'd missed. Seeing it all piled up on the side of my desk made me realize how much work a student at Mercia Academy got done. Previously, I'd thrown myself into my studies as a distraction from the taunts and bullying. Now, with Henry on my side and the other members of the triumvirate remorseful, I hoped my fortunes would change for the better.

I didn't leave the room for the rest of the day. Couldn't face all the noise, the stares, and the demands to know where I'd been. Mrs. Jenkins, the matron, had been kind enough to bring food to my room, but I mostly crashed on the bed and slept off the remnants of the kidnappers' drugs.

The next morning, Rita didn't bolt toward the door before the bell. She waited around to escort me to the dining room. Perhaps she knew the day after such a major event like returning from a suspicious absence was the worst. I gave her a smile of gratitude, and we walked down the hallway to breakfast.

A hush spread across the dining room, and the students stopped eating to gape. For a second, I froze, meeting the ocean of expectant faces, but Rita nudged me toward our usual table.

"Miss Hobson," said an authoritative voice.

I glanced around to find Edward standing behind the head table. The stained glass windows cast him in slight silhouette, highlighting the breadth of his shoulders and the reddish highlights in his mahogany hair. The effect made him look so majestic my breath caught. His eyes, which were usually as cold and fathomless as the ocean, shone with warmth. On either side of him sat Blake and Henry, each of them giving me the kind of affectionate smiles I'd only imagined in my most fevered fantasies of acceptance. Charlotte, who sat next to Blake, leaned forward, eyes alight with anticipation.

A flock of butterflies took off in my stomach, and I had to force my arms to remain by my side so they wouldn't clutch the queasiness they'd left in the pit of my belly. Edward might have apologized in private yesterday, but he'd had a full day to change his mind and resume his war. I was still a Yank, and if Henry had spoken about what I'd allowed him to do on our last night, even more of a trollop.

A tight band of apprehension wrapped around my chest. I sucked in a breath, trying to keep the shake out of my voice. "Yes?"

"I'd like to invite you to breakfast with us at the head table." His gaze fell on Rita. "You and Miss Yelverton."

Rita squeaked and shook her head. I was about to muster up a polite refusal, when Charlotte drawled, "Really, Edward? There's only so much whorishness one can take before the first bell."

The warmth in Edward's eyes disappeared, and he turned to Charlotte, lips flattened in an angry line. In clipped tones, he said, "Yet here you are, sitting among us."

A bolt of triumph shot through my heart and exploded into fireworks of joy. Gasps, a few nervous chuckles, and exclamations of shock filled the room. Rita scuttled to our usual table, leaving me standing alone in the sea of spectators. Anticipation thrummed in my chest. This was a deciding moment. If I publicly refused his offer of friendship, Edward might restart the war.

I glanced at Rita, who shrugged. Her way of saying it was up to me. Last night, I'd half convinced her that things were different between Henry and me.

Henry smiled and gave his head a little, beckoning flick. All the tension around my chest unwound itself, and I smiled back. Whatever the triumvirate had planned for me, it wouldn't culminate in public humiliation… today.

In my clearest voice, I pulled back my shoulders and said, "Thank you, Mercia. I think I will take up your invitation."

Edward lowered himself into his seat, and I walked around to take the empty seat next to Henry. The peck on the cheek he gave me made my insides fizzle with joy, and elicited a round of even louder gasps from the onlookers.

"We missed you at lunch and dinner yesterday," Henry murmured. "I thought you might be hungry, so I sent Matron up with food. How are you feeling?"

I drew back and stared into those warm, green eyes, my heart filling with joy. "That was you?"

The corner of his lip quirked. "I thought you might want a change from your usual fare of Snickers and ready salted crisps."

Heat rushed to my cheeks. "Thank you."

"And you look particularly radiant this morning."

"Thank the wonders of a clean bed and a warm shower."

He poured me a glass of orange juice from a crystal jug. "Those were also two things I missed the most, but I'd swap them any time for another chance to sleep by your side."

The memories of his hand on my stomach and his fingers pleasuring me to distraction returned, making my nipples tighten and heat to surge between my legs. I dipped my head and squeezed my thighs together, murmuring, "Your company was the only upside to being in that room."

"Only my company?" he said in a low voice that was both seductive and teasing.

I picked up my glass and gulped down a mouthful of juice. "There were other benefits."

One of the servers brought my usual cooked breakfast but served on a plate of fine china instead of the porcelain. It was then that my gaze caught the extra knives, forks, and spoons at my place setting. My brows rose. The head table was more than an elevated platform, it was an exercise in fine dining.

I cut a piece of grilled tomato and hummed at the explosion of flavor. After a week of eating junk, real food was a welcome sight. Even the pale bacon and blood sausage were appealing.

Charlotte whined from Blake's end of the table, "What happened between them? Why did they go away for so long? Nobody's saying anything!"

I glanced up at Henry. "You didn't tell her?"

His lips tightened. "The fewer people who know, the better. Even in a closed-off environment like Mercia Academy, news can leak to the press and give people ideas."

"I told Rita," I whispered.

"We thought you might," he replied. "Yelverton knows to keep her mouth shut."

I lowered my knife and fork and glared at the side of his handsome face. Without the stubble, he looked less the rugged football player and more the dashing prince. "Is that a threat?"

Henry stopped eating to meet my gaze. "It's an observation. Unlike some of the girls around here, Yelverton isn't a gossip, and I expect that neither are you."

I let out a breath and returned to my breakfast. Perhaps the boys had been serious about changing, after all.

"Well?" snapped Charlotte. "Did they disappear to the same place?"

Her two doppelgängers at the end of the table murmured their agreement. Patricia said in a loud voice, "The trollop probably got recalled to her brothel for retraining."

The pair shared congratulatory giggles. From the way they acted, it was as though they'd never been able to produce an insult that hadn't already been uttered by someone with more wit.

Edward stood, shoulders tense and raised a few inches higher than usual. "Alice, Patricia, please find alternative seating arrangements. You are no longer welcome at my table."

I held my breath and froze. Those were the two girls he'd been dating. What was he saying? Patricia leaned forward and tried to catch Edward's eye. From the way she swung her neck from side to side, snake-charmer style, it looked like Edward stared through them. If she hadn't been involved in some of the pranks perpetrated against me, I might have felt sorry for the girl. Right now, I could only think thoughts of vindication.

"What?" said Charlotte. "You can't just banish them after everything they've done for you."

"You are free to leave with them," he said through clenched teeth.

Charlotte turned to Blake, who stared ahead. In a small voice, she said, "But I've sat at your table since third year. How could you eject my friends and me for insulting a low-life trollop?"

"And now, you've outstayed your welcome," Edward said, nostrils flaring. "Leave, Miss Underwood, or I will have you removed."

Charlotte was the first to stand. She tossed her ponytail, stuck her nose in the air and announced, "There's a foul stench in the air, and it's made me lose my appetite. Come on, girls."

Patricia and Alice stood, amidst a smattering of applause. I gaped at the looks of glee on the other students' faces. It looked like the girls weren't as popular as they'd thought. They sashayed, single file, to the dining room doors and walked out into the hallway. I hid my expression with my crystal glass of orange juice. This was a fitting end to Charlotte's reign as the Queen of Mercia Academy.

I turned to look for Rita at our usual table. She wasn't there but three tables across with a trio of students I'd never seen before. A black-haired girl with her hair tied back into a high ponytail, and two unremarkable-looking boys. My brows furrowed.

"Worrying about Yelverton?" asked Henry.

"Who are those people?"

"Other scholarship students."

"Oh." She had mentioned spending time with the other scholarship students while I'd been away. I straightened in my seat and smiled at her. Even if it had been to speculate on my grizzly fate, I was glad she'd connected with them.

Classes were a blur of trying to keep up with the lessons I'd missed. Fewer people in the hallways called me Trollop. I supposed the other houses hadn't yet gotten the message about my ceasefire with the triumvirate. It would probably not last. Good things never did. But I would savor the peace I got from not having to constantly be on alert for insults and pranks.

Later that day, Charlotte caught up with me on one of the tree-lined pathways as I walked back to Elder House. She grabbed my wrist. "What did you do, Trollop?"

I snatched my arm away, resisting the urge to shove her to the ground. "Watch it! I still owe you for throwing hot chocolate in my face and for kicking me in the stomach."

She bared her teeth and hissed, "What do you expect for showing off that video, whore?"

A snort caught in the back of my throat. "Says the girl caught on camera sword swallowing! Look, I didn't even record your blowjob. Maybe you've done it so many times, there's dozens of videos of you in circulation."

"I doubt that," she snapped.

I raised a shoulder. "All I ever wanted was a ceasefire. Why on earth would I have jeopardized that for a stupid prank?"

Charlotte pursed her lips, eyes burning with hatred. I shifted my weight onto my other hip and folded my arms. She could resent me all she wanted for encroaching on her imagined claim on the triumvirate, but I expect she couldn't deny the truth in my words. It wasn't me who broke the agreement.

Her lip curled. "If you're lying, I'll—"

"What? Have me wake up in the middle of a pond? Put arsenic in my tea? Someone who hates you just as much as you hate me shot and broadcasted that video to the entire house. Look elsewhere. I'm not your enemy."

"Then why did you take my place at the head table?" she screeched.

"If someone offers an olive branch, I'll take it. You're the ones who couldn't stop making uncouth comments."

Blake strolled up to us, looking the resolute playboy with the burgundy blazer skimming his lean physique. He placed his hands in his pockets and took his time in reaching where we stood. Tendrils of messy black hair framed his tanned features, and he flashed us a panty-melting grin.

"Problems, ladies?" he asked.

Charlotte whirled on him. "I can't believe you're being civil to her after what she did."

"Oh." His brows rose. "Care to elaborate?"

"That video," she hissed.

"The one I told Bingham's assistants to play on the projector?" Blake asked.

I clapped my hand over my mouth. Blake must have stolen my phone while helping us put up our tent. I had wondered why he was being so attentive, but after that tiring trek up the hills, and our multiple failed attempts at deciphering the instruction, I finally gave in and let Blake help us. I had been too busy scrutinizing him for signs of sabotaging our tent to notice him take my phone out of my waterproof jacket.

Charlotte staggered back, eyes bulging. "What?" Her bottom lip trembled. "Why?"

His grin widened. "I wanted to see the fallout. Wanted to show the world your prowess. Wanted to brighten up the evening. Take your pick."

I held out my hand. "Thanks for framing me. I found the fallout invigorating. Now, if you've quite finished with my phone, I'll take it back."

He reached into his inside pocket and pulled out my smartphone. "I didn't try to guess your passcode, I swear."

"Right." I didn't believe that for a minute. I turned to Charlotte, whose hazel eyes glistened with tears. Any pity I might have had for her public humiliation and subsequent betrayal spilled away with the hot chocolate she had thrown in my face. "You see? There's your pornographer. Now you know I didn't make or broadcast that video."

"No, but you claimed to have shot it," she spat.

My lips tightened. Wasn't she going to say anything to the guy who humiliated her in public? Apparently not. Another example of how the privileged got away with their crap.

I stepped back. "I'll leave the pair of you to work out your differences. If I were you, Underwood, I wouldn't call people trollop or whore when you're the one acting the part."

The look of hatred she shot me said that Edward might have announced a ceasefire, but she was determined to bury me six feet in the ground.

CHAPTER 17

For the rest of the week, I sat with the triumvirate at each mealtime, occasionally persuading Rita to take up their invitation. At those times, she remained quiet but answered their polite questions. When she didn't sit with us, she ate with the other scholarship students. Henry continued to kiss me on the cheek each time we met, then Blake started to greet me with a peck. It was bizarre. Not Blake's kiss. He was a natural flirt, and I expected no less from him, but the warmth I received, even from Edward, made me think they might be setting me up for a giant fall.

The boys sat with me in each class I shared with them, causing Charlotte and her doppelgängers to make disparaging remarks. On Friday morning, I sat between Edward and Henry at breakfast when Mr. Carbuncle brought Edward's mail to the head table.

I stared down at the letters arranged neatly on a silver plate. One of them was even secured with a golden, wax seal. "Why can't you go to the mailboxes yourself?"

"Edward's correspondence goes to the new house," said Henry.

"What's that?" I asked.

"You're aware that Elder House was the original duke's residence?" asked Edward.

I glanced at the painting of the first Duke of Mercia dining with King Henry V. "Yes, I heard about that."

"Over the centuries, the family has built additional residences on the grounds. Largely to keep out of the way of the expanding school. The new one is our fifth."

"What happens to the others?" I asked.

"They're turned into school accommodation." Edward broke open the seal of the fanciest looking letter, read its contents and turned to me, his blue eyes sparkling with excitement. "The Royal Academy is holding a charity ball on Christmas Eve. Will you be in the country or back in America?"

My brows drew together. I still hadn't heard from Mom, even after I'd texted her to find out if she'd known about the kidnapping. If she couldn't bother herself to find out if I was unhurt by the ordeal, she probably wouldn't send me money for a flight back to New York. Even then, I would have stayed home, but she'd sold that apartment to move in with Rudolph. The thought of her not caring about my whereabouts made my heart sink and my shoulders droop.

I stared at my roasted tomatoes and sighed. "I planned on staying here for the vacation."

"Accompany us," he said.

My head snapped up. "To the ball?"

"It will be fun," said Henry.

Blake leaned across the table. "Think about it… One of you and three of us. You'll have a full dance card."

I turned to Henry. "Isn't that a bit awkward? I can't go as all of your dates."

He grinned. "You'd be doing us all a favor. Taking a lady to a ball is hard work."

Blake wiped his hand over his brow in a theatric gesture. "The kissing of hands, the fetching of drinks, and all that dancing when you just want to stand in the corner and smoke a cigar."

"Not to mention the demands for promenades," said Henry.

I glanced from Blake, to Edward, to Henry. Although they all smiled, they each appeared serious about them all taking me as their date. "I don't have anything to wear."

Blake spluttered. "Look to your right, woman. You're sitting next to a man who can get you any gown you desire."

My heart flipped like a crepe, and I bit down on my bottom lip. Was this an impromptu re-enactment of Cinderella or Pretty Woman? I shook my head. "I don't dance."

Edward placed a hand on my wrist. The touch of his fingers on my skin sent a ripple of shock up my arm and into my heart, which made an extra-hard reverberation. In a low voice, he said, "We'd be delighted to help you practice the waltz. I, personally, would be honored if you accepted our invitation."

I glanced at Henry. Of all the members of the triumvirate, he was the one I knew best. The soft smile curving his lips said it all. A fun night out was the boys' way of showing me they were sorry. He'd promised to stop the bullying, and I believed him.

"Alright," I murmured. "I accept."

∽

After breakfast on Sunday, the triumvirate escorted me to a limousine that sped us out of Mercia county and to the center of London. Blake mixed us bucks fizz, a cocktail of orange juice and champagne for the journey, while Edward and Henry explained what typically happened during these Royal Academy charity balls. I gulped down my cocktail and listened to their explanations. There were so many rules, and for the first time, I wished I'd kept Edward's hurled copy of *The Debrett's Guide to Etiquette and Modern Manners*.

Bourneville's department store was located in the heart of

London on one of the roads leading from Piccadilly Circus. It was an imposing, palatial-looking building made of stone and arranged over five stories. Tall, symmetrical windows, each with multiple panels adorned the lower floors, while the ground floor boasted the kind of fashion displays found in major department stores worldwide. Its grand entrance consisted of Roman-style, stone pillars, sentineled by guards in old fashioned, blue livery.

My heart thrummed in my chest. One day, all this would belong to Henry, the boy who had become a close friend. I tried not to gasp, tried not to appear awed by the sheer size and grandeur of the department store, but it was a near impossible feat.

The limo driver opened the door, and Henry helped me out. "You're going to look beautiful in a ballgown."

I stared down at my leather jacket, tank top, and skinny jeans and gulped. Why hadn't they warned me to dress for the occasion?

The men at the door instantly recognized Henry and swept into low bows as they opened the door. Tingles of excitement ran up and down my spine, and I ignored the tiny voice screaming in the back of my head. Cinderella had a fairy godmother. Pretty woman had a rich benefactor. And today, it looked like I had three. But when I stepped in and my lungs filled with the subtle scents of mingled perfumes, and I took the splendor of the marble-floors, unbelievably huge, crystal chandeliers, and assistants selling all manner of luxury goods, even the voice in the back of my head turned mute.

"Shopping can be a tiring event," Edward drawled. "Shall we have lunch first?"

Henry led us through the store to a door where a pair of security guards stood. With their tailored suits, bullet-proof vests, and earpieces, they looked more like bodyguards. They probably carried at least two firearms. The kidnappers had held Henry for an entire day, demanding sensitive security information about the store. Had he been able to warn his parents in time? We hadn't spoken in depth about the ordeal, as Henry wanted to forget about it and move on.

The guards opened the door, which led to a carved, mahogany staircase, lit by a hexagonal skylight. Antique crystal adorned the walls between portraits of men who bore a resemblance to Henry. He explained that this part of the store led to private dining rooms and apartments used by the family whenever they returned to London.

After dining on coq au vin served with burgundy wine at an intimate dining room, we returned to the public area of the department store. Every major designer had a concession at Bournveilles: Chanel, Gucci, Yves St. Laurent, Prada... I stopped noticing after Dior because my head spun at all the choices.

Edward stepped back and swept his gaze up and down my body, making me flush. "What do you think, Blake? Is Hobson a Chanel girl?"

"Givenchy. She has that Audrey Hepburn chic."

I drew my elbows into my body and dipped my head. "Hardly."

Henry placed a hand on the small of my back, and I couldn't help thinking about our last night in that room, when he'd caressed my belly and... I gulped, bringing my attention back to the boys and back to the department store. He asked, "Is there a designer you particularly like, Emilia?"

I closed my eyes and pictured Mom's wedding dress. "Tom Ford."

Henry's lips spread into a grin of dimples, white teeth, and sparkling green eyes. "Tom Ford, it is, then."

The man at the Tom Ford concession store showed me his selection of ballgowns. None of them looked right. I'd always pictured myself with an asymmetrical neckline, like Mom on her wedding day to Dad. It was before her career had taken off, and neither of them had much money. She'd designed the dress with a student of fashion, basing it on Roman togas. I pulled out my smartphone, showed him the picture of Mom, and asked if he had anything with this silhouette.

He disappeared into the storeroom and brought back a dress from a previous season. It wouldn't be a perfect fit, but he took me into a mirrored fitting room the size of my dorm and pinned the dress in place. I clapped my hand to my mouth and gasped at the way he'd made the fabric skim my figure. This was exactly what I wanted.

When I stepped out, dressed in my skinny jeans, the boys' faces fell. Henry stepped forward, brows drawn. "Didn't you find anything you liked?"

Happiness bubbled up to my chest. "I did."

"Where is it?" He glanced around, looking for the assistant. "We wanted to see you in the gown."

"They're making alterations. You'll have to see the final version on the night of the ball."

Blake shook his head and smiled. "Always keeping us on our toes."

I smirked. "Don't I ever?"

After Henry paid the cashier with his ebony store card, we returned to the limousine. One side of it had been decked out with ice, slices of lemon, and condiments like an oyster bar, and a magnum of champagne in a special, ice-filed compartment. Blake leaned over, dark eyes smoldering. "You know why oysters are considered an aphrodisiac?"

"I'm sure you're going to tell me."

"It's the amino acids," he said in a smoky drawl. "They increase the production of sex hormones and stimulate sexual desire. But I like to think it's the slippery, sensual, slide of the oyster going down."

My gaze automatically the length of his body, but I forced it back to his eyes in case it reignited the arousal from the night I'd hidden under the coffee table.

Edward chuckled. "Stop teasing the girl and drink your champagne."

"It's no tease." He placed his glass to his lips. "If you're ever curious about how I can last all night on oysters, you only have to ask."

Henry's green eyes danced with excitement. "He's not joking about his staying power."

I sipped my champagne, inhaling the alcohol-scented bubbles popping at the surface. "How would you know?"

The corner of his mouth curved. "Let's put it this way. Best friends share everything."

Blake raised a brow. "Everything."

"Everything?" I glanced at Edward.

"They're exaggerating. I wouldn't share my last Rolo with anyone, but if there was something..." His gaze lingered on the neckline of my tank top, skimmed down my breasts, thighs, and then made a slow journey back to my eyes. "Or someone, we all adored, we wouldn't squabble over it. We would be gentlemen and share."

Blake rolled his eyes. "When he says 'it,' he means 'her.'"

"You." Henry pointed his flute at me.

My throat dried, and I gulped a mouthful of champagne. They had already gotten me to agree to be their shared date for the charity Christmas ball. My mind refused to believe they were suggesting anything else.

Blake leaned forward, chin raised, eyes glimmering with challenge. "I'd like to know your thoughts."

Was I imagining things, or was the triumvirate making me an indecent proposal?

CHAPTER 18

My gaze swept from Henry, who leaned forward, green eyes expectant, to Blake, who gave me a saucy wink, to Edward, who furrowed his brow. My throat flexed in time with my tightening stomach. This had to be a trick. Boys this handsome collected girls. They didn't vie for the attention of anyone, let alone a girl they'd called a trollop for weeks. The moment I asked if they were suggesting I date all three of them, they would chuckle and make a disparaging remark about my sexual appetite. Then Henry would tell them I was a virgin, and they'd all laugh.

After an awkward silence, Edward placed his glass of champagne in a special holder. "Perhaps a change in subject would be appropriate."

Blake lowered his glass. "But—"

"Tell me, Henry, what will you wear to the charity ball?"

Henry mentioned his green cummerbund and matching bowtie, and Blake laughed, saying that was what he wore to the last ball. The tightening of my stomach eased, but I couldn't help thinking about what I'd heard. They might have shared objects, but I'd seen no evidence of them sharing girls. Henry hadn't shown any interest in anyone until we had been forced together in a room for nine days. As far as I knew, Charlotte's relationship with Edward had been platonic. I glanced at Blake, who shucked an oyster like a pro. I didn't know how to describe the arrangement he'd had with Charlotte.

At the other end of the limo, Edward stretched out his long, muscled legs and took a slow sip of his champagne. Although he faced front, the blue of his eyes fixed on me. I probably stared back at him like a rabbit caught in the gaze of a wolf, but I had to work out what they'd proposed. If anything, Alice and Patricia shared Edward, so why would he want to share me with his friends?

I gave myself a mental shake. They had probably been talking about the dance.

The conversation continued as normal, with the boys wanting a hint at what I would wear to the ball and which accessories I would need. I kept tight-lipped but dropped useless hints that made them laugh. Blake showed me how to prepare and eat oysters, but he held off all that sexy talk the entire journey.

When we reached Mercia Academy, the limo sped past Elder House and through a small wood, to a mansion built in the same flat-fronted, symmetrical style as the main teaching block. It was significantly smaller, with four stories instead of five, but with tall, sash windows instead of four towers.

"Welcome to my home," said Edward.

With a gasp, I blurted, "Who lives here?"

For a second, his face fell, taking on the expression of an abandoned, little boy. "The butler, I suppose."

My stomach clenched. Henry had told me Edward's mother had died in his first year of the academy. I wanted to ask about the current Duke of Mercia, but I remembered that Henry mentioned the man's declining mental health. Blake grabbed my hand and pulled me out of the limo.

"Emilia," he said with a forced laugh. "You have to see Edward's gramophone. It's the most ridiculous thing!"

"What's a gramophone?"

Henry stepped out of the limo and placed an arm around my waist. "A record player of sorts."

Blake also looped his arm around my back. "Let's not waste time." He ushered me up the steps that lead to a paneled, wooden door with iron knockers taking the shape of an eagle. "Onwards and upwards!"

I glanced over my shoulder. The door to the limo lay open, but Edward still sat inside. I turned to Henry. "Did I say something wrong?"

"Don't ask about his family," said Blake in smooth tones. "It's a sore subject and not one we care to talk about."

I wouldn't push. I'd been on the receiving end of intrusive questions about my own family, and I didn't want to be that type of person who couldn't take a hint. We stepped through the doors and into a marble reception hall, much like the one in the main teaching block. Perhaps the buildings had been designed by the same architect.

An elderly butler stepped out from a wooden door beyond the reception hall. "Mr. Henry, Mr. Blake, how wonderful it is to see you."

"This is Emilia," said Blake. "Our new friend."

The butler's brows rose, and he inclined his head. "I'm delighted to make your acquaintance, Miss Emilia. How are you finding life at a British boarding school? A little different to what you're used to in America, I presume?"

"I..." Realization hit me like a slap in the face. Edward had spoken to his butler about me. I forced a smile. "It's great here. I love the architecture."

He nodded, made a comment about the buildings around the campus, and led us up a set of grand, marble stairs to Edward's suite on the first floor. The room was over six times the size of the dorm I shared with Rita with floor-to-ceiling windows giving a view of the mansion's manicured gardens. At one end of the room stood a four-poster bed, and in the other stood a roll-top bathtub with claw feet. Silk brocade sofas occupied the middle, where two magnums of champagne sat in buckets crammed with ice.

The butler bowed. "Mr. Edward will join you soon."

Blake rushed to the most bizarre-looking, wooden record player with a brass horn attached that curved and tapered into a needle. Beneath the gramophone was a cabinet of records. He pulled one out, settled it onto the turntable, turned a hand-crank, and placed the needle on the record. The strains of violins filled the room, making me giggle. The machine had to be over a hundred years old. Why wasn't it in a museum?

He strode toward me and bowed with a flourish. "Care to waltz, my lady?"

I giggled and glanced away. "This is silly."

Blake took my hand and swept me into a waltz. I'd taken dance lessons and had waltzed at Mom's weddings and other social events, but dancing didn't come naturally to me and I didn't particularly enjoy it. I counted out the steps in my head and followed the music and Blake's lead, remembering my dance instructor's barked-out demands to correct my posture.

Blake hummed. "Not bad for someone who claims to have never danced before."

"I said, I didn't dance. There's a huge difference."

He frowned. "You'll have to do something about your shoulders. They're practically bunched up around your ears." Before I could respond, he glanced over my shoulder. "Henry, stand behind Emilia and keep her in position."

Henry snarled. "You're the one who can lead and follow, remember?"

Blake let go of my hand and waist and stood at my back. He

slipped off my leather jacket and threw it on the sofa. Then with strong, deft hands, he massaged my shoulders. "Is that better?"

I closed my eyes, focusing on the sensations sparking from his fingertips. They penetrated my muscles, making them relax back down to a restful posture. A sigh slipped from my lips. "You're good with your hands."

"Better than me?" Henry took my hand and wrapped his arm around my waist in the closed position.

"I didn't say that."

We continued the waltz, with Blake mirroring my steps at my back and adjusting my posture.

When the music stopped, Blake leaned close and murmured, "Very good." His lips grazed my neck, eliciting a full body shudder.

Henry lifted my chin and brought his lips down onto mine in a dizzying kiss. Desire and relief flooded my body. I had wondered if our intimacy would continue. His kisses on the cheek had been nice, but nothing of the passion we'd shared on our last night. Henry's lips slid over mine, and the arm around my waist pressed me into his hard body. I slid my hand down from his shoulder over his huge biceps and round to his strong back and rested it just above the taut ass I'd ogled more than once while he'd curled up on that mattress. This was the first time we had kissed since the kidnapping —really kissed—and the slide of his lips against mine was as potent as any drug.

The butterflies in my stomach took flight, exploding like fireworks at the sheer excitement of being with him again. When he had told me we were friends, I hadn't expected much, but this was beyond any hope I dared to have harbored.

Henry's tongue swept across the seam of my mouth, demanding entrance. With a moan, I let him in. His tongue made the most delicious caresses, each one sending licks of pleasure between my legs and making me whimper. He pressed us so close, the thudding of his heart synchronized with mine.

"Henry." My tone was breathy, desperate. It was impossible to word my request. I wanted more. Needed it. But the words, *whore* and *trollop* echoed in my skull. If this was a trick, a test of my virtue, I would fail.

Blake stood so close to me his body heat warmed my back. Then butterfly kisses landed on my neck. Soft at first. The barest whisper of smoke on the breeze. I arched into the touch, and the kisses became more insistent. Hot. Open-mouthed. Another set of arms wrapped around me from behind, engulfing me in the intoxicating scent of cedar and spice.

"I've wanted you for an eternity, Emilia." Blake ran a hand down my side, skimming a path of fire along my breasts, waist, and settling on my hip. "You're the most exciting thing to have happened to this academy since we joined."

Henry broke away from the kiss, his pupils blown. I thought he would tell his friend to back off, but instead, he murmured, "Blake's turn."

I turned my head, and Blake's lips descended on mine. Unlike Henry's kiss, his started playfully. He caught my bottom lip between his teeth and pulled.

"Stop toying with her," said Henry.

"As you wish." Blake's arms wrapped around my middle, and he brought me into his body.

His full lips brushed mine in another tease that left me wanting more. With a moan, I parted my lips in a silent command for him to deepen the kiss. Blake's tongue flicked out to meet mine in short licks, each one making my core pulse with need. He was a tease, who acted like he enjoyed chasing girls, but this kiss told me everything I needed to know about this flirtation: he wanted the girls to crave him. My tongue darted out to meet his, in a series of mirroring licks, until he tired of the game and took control of the kiss.

Henry ran his tongue along the other side of my neck, making my core clench. I lowered my hand and squeezed his ass, the way I had wanted to do while he slept. Henry's large, warm hands roved my clothed body, stopping at my breasts, which he cupped and squeezed and caressed. Each touch brought me to a desire so dizzying, I could barely stay upright.

When Blake finally broke away, my gaze landed on Edward, who sat on the sofa, legs spread. He pressed the heel of his hand on his erection, and the movement sent a shudder down my spine.

"The three of us have wanted you since the day you joined the academy," murmured Blake.

"Oh," I gasped out. I'd gotten the hint by now. They really had made me an indecent proposal in the back of the limo.

"Can you handle us?" asked Henry.

I blinked hard. All my awareness had traveled down to my core, which ached for one of them—all of them to pleasure me until I splintered. But that was the champagne. It had gone to my head and made me giddy. I staggered back into Henry's arms.

"Emilia?"

"I'm..."

Edward got out of his seat and strolled across the room. "Back off, you two." He took my hand and wrapped an arm around my waist. "Sorry for the others' heavy-handedness. It wasn't our intention to get you inebriated and then overwhelm you."

"It's..." I swallowed. Words were becoming more and more difficult.

Edward walked me out of the room with a chaste arm at my back to keep me steady. Henry and Blake stood at the door, their eyes ablaze. Blake blew me a kiss, and Henry gave me a crooked smile. I suppose my wanton performance when the music had stopped gave them the answer to their question. I could handle them, but possibly not the alcohol at the same time.

Outside, the crisp air filled my lungs, cooled my overheated skin, and brought me to my senses.

Edward lifted my chin, meeting my eyes with an assessing gaze. "I couldn't let things go any further with you in that condition."

"T-thanks," I murmured. His rescue was appreciated but unnecessary. Every kiss, every touch, every caress of the two men's hands had set me aflame. I still wanted more, but a little voice in my head reminded me that this was the triumvirate. It would be foolish of me to give in to my desires when they might backfire.

Edward opened the door of the limousine, ushered me in, and climbed in after me.

"What about Blake and Henry?" My words came out slurred.

His lips formed a tiny smile. "They can entertain themselves."

The limousine sped us back to Elder House, and Edward walked me through the building. A few stragglers milled around the hallways, gaping at the sight of us together. At my door, he took my hand and pressed his lips onto my knuckles.

"Please take your time and consider our proposal." His smooth delivery made me wonder if he was talking about something other than sharing me with his two best friends. "Henry and Blake can be particularly persuasive. Try not to let them rush you into a decision."

He straightened, turned, and strolled down the hallway, leaving me both confused and aroused.

I cleared my throat. "Mercia?"

He turned. "Call me Edward."

"I don't understand. Why me?"

Edward's gaze lingered on my lips. "You know the three of us have been friends since we were eleven?"

"Yes."

"This is something we've wanted to do since we were thirteen and fourteen, but until you arrived, we'd never agreed on a fourth."

My breath caught. "Are you—?"

"That's a subject best left to the privacy of my home, don't you think?" He inclined his head. "Good night, Miss Hobson."

"Emilia."

A smile broke out across his face that made my heart melt. I'd seen him laugh, smirk, and even bare his teeth, but never anything so radiant. In a low, silky voice that made my toes curl, he said, "Good night, Emilia."

The next few weeks were a blur of classes, prep, and sexual frustration. I ate with the triumvirate each mealtime, sat with them in classes, but received nothing from them except the chastest of kisses on the knuckles or cheek. Even dance practices were proper and respectable, held in the school ballroom with Rita and three other scholarship students as chaperones.

Most nights, I went to bed, thinking about that champagne-fueled Sunday evening, where we'd nearly lost control. Memories of the boys' hands over my body, their erections grinding into my ass, and their lips on mine haunted my fantasies and morphed into dreams of the boys pleasuring me on Edward's velvet sofa.

They were either waiting for me to approach them or biding their time until the Christmas ball.

One morning after breakfast, we stood in the reception hall checking our mailboxes, when Henry dropped his satchel with a thud. He stared at a piece of paper which hung loosely from his fingers.

"What's wrong?" I tilted my head to read its contents.

Someone had printed out a photo of him shirtless and tied up. Beneath the picture was a scrawled note demanding twenty-five thousand pounds in cash to be deposited in the nearest phone box… or else.

My heart shuddered to a stop, and I gasped out, "The kidnappers."

A muscle in his jaw flexed, and his hand closed around the paper.

"Yes," he said, his voice tight. "It looks like they've already spent the ransom money."

"What are you going to do?"

He shrugged. "Track down Father for money, I suppose. And stay within the academy grounds."

I clenched my teeth. If he gave in to their threats, they would never leave him alone. The words I had etched into my brain tumbled to the forefront of my mind. It was time to call the police and tell them what had happened.

At first break, I rushed back from the main teaching block to Elder house and bumped into Blake in the reception hall. He grabbed onto my arms. "Emilia, are you alright? You look troubled."

I glanced over his shoulder. A group of students were approaching through the hallway. "Can we talk somewhere else?"

"Of course." He swung his arm out toward the open door.

I stepped out of Elder House, and Blake gestured to the right. "There's a quiet spot between here and the tuck shop."

"Right." I glanced in the direction of a one story building at the end of a long pathway that edged the lawn. A few buildings stood to the right of the path, but they weren't crowded with students. "Thanks."

Blake and I walked in silence, our feet crunching on the gravel. I folded my arms over my chest, holding down the anticipation thrumming in my heart. Maybe Blake would have a better idea of how to deal with the kidnappers. He had links to royalty, and had probably been briefed on what to do if under threat.

When we reached a building similar to Elder House, he stopped and gestured at a wooden bench opposite. "What's on your mind?"

"It's Henry." I lowered myself onto the seat and stared into my lap. "The kidnappers sent him a letter. They want twenty-five thousand pounds or they'll take him away again."

"I see…"

My head snapped up, and I stared into Blake's unconcerned, chocolate-brown eyes. "They have an inside man at the academy."

He nodded.

"Well?"

"It's a rather tricky subject." He tilted his head to the side. "Did they say anything else?"

My head jerked back and I blinked hard. "Isn't that enough?"

"You're right." He gave me a side-long look. "Maybe the four of us need to spend a little more time hidden away. Edward has a cozy, little study—"

"I have to call the police."

Blake winced. "I'm sure that will enrage the kidnappers."

I shot to my feet and paced up to the empty building. "They need to be behind bars where they can't hurt anyone else!"

"Come back." He patted the seat. "Emilia, you're over reacting."

"They're desperate and dangerous. I can't just do nothing while they're out there, circling the academy."

"You're underestimating Henry. He's the captain of the rugby team and tougher than any boy in our year. If a pair of kidnappers come close, he'd fight them off and raise the alarm." Blake grinned. "There's no need to call the police. Henry can take care of himself."

A frustrated breath pushed its way out of my nostrils. How could Blake be so stupidly optimistic? Henry had been all of those things during the school trip, and the kidnappers had managed to abduct him then. Now that these people had a sure way to extort money, they probably wouldn't leave Henry alone until they had accidentally overdosed him with those drugs.

Blake stood, placed his hands on my shoulders, and gazed in the direction of the main teaching block. "I'm glad you're calmer. It's time for class."

"I'm going back to Elder House."

"See you later." He gave me an absent smile and strolled away.

I stared at his retreating back. Even though Blake had said I shouldn't call the police, the reasons he gave me indicated that I should. Henry was in danger, and I wouldn't let him spend another day in captivity with those hippie assholes. I pulled out my smartphone and googled the number of the local police.

The sooner they arrested the kidnappers, the sooner Henry would be able to get on with his life and forget that the ordeal had ever happened.

CHAPTER 19

*E*arly on the Monday morning after I had called the police, Mr. Carbuncle knocked on my door, saying the headmaster wanted to see me urgently. I dressed as quickly as I could, threw on a coat, and hurried across the frost-covered campus with the janitor at my heels. My pulse pounded in my ears, drowning out the sounds of frozen twigs breaking underfoot. Had Mom and Rudolph finally arrived in England to complain about the school's negligence? The headmaster hadn't even visited Elder House to ask if Henry and I had recovered from our ordeal. I expected Mom would be livid when she heard about this.

We rushed into the main teaching block, up the stairs, and down the hallway. Mr. Chaloner's door was ajar, so I knocked and stepped inside. Instead of Mom and Rudolph, two men I'd never seen before sat in the seats opposite the desk, leaving me nowhere to sit. They didn't seem the academic types, so I focused my attention on the headmaster.

Mr. Chaloner stood. "Thank you for coming so quickly, Miss Hobson. May I introduce you to Chief Inspector Faust and Sergeant Sullivan, both Mercia Academy alumni."

Neither of the men stood, but the older one, who wore a black undertaker's suit that contrasted with his startling white hair and pencil mustache, gave me a nod of acknowledgment.

I sucked in a sharp breath. "Is this about the kidnapping? Did you catch the culprits?"

The headmaster crossed the room and pulled up a stool. "Do take a seat, Miss Hobson."

"Thanks," I kept my voice flat. I still hadn't forgiven him for trying to confiscate my phone.

When I settled onto the stool, Chief Inspector Faust spoke. "Let me get straight to the point, Miss Hobson. We used the information you gave us to track down the people you said abducted you and Mr. Bourneville."

I bristled at the tone of his voice. It implied that he doubted we'd been kidnapped at all. "Did you arrest them? I told you they'd threatened Henry and will strike again if he doesn't give in to their demands."

"We found a house full of squatters who confirm that you and Mr. Bourneville stayed with them, but as guests." He remained silent and folded his arms across his chest.

I stared into his gray eyes, wondering what he wanted me to say. That the kidnappers were liars? Anyone with an ounce of sense would know that criminals would say anything to get out of trouble. The silence continued like one of those whistling kettles where the pressure built and built until the sound became deafening. My heart thrummed with a painful mix of anticipation and dread, pulling every nerve in my body taut.

My head pounded in memory of what I had suffered at those people's hands. "What did they say happened, then? Why would any sane person leave a school trip to stay in that filthy, attic room?"

"They claim that you arranged to abduct Henry Bourneville in revenge for an altercation you had during a camping trip."

I shook my head. "They're lying. I've never argued with Henry, and even if I did, I wouldn't retaliate with a kidnapping."

Inspector Faust pursed his lips. "That might be the case, but the five-hundred thousand pounds they helped you to extort from Mr. Bourneville the elder gives you a strong motivation for arranging your classmate's abduction."

My breath caught. "But I didn't—"

"We found nearly ten thousand pounds in cash at the squat," said the sergeant, a red-haired man with thick brows that matched his trimmed beard. "What did you do with the rest?"

"Me?" I gasped out. "How could I arrange something as complicated as a kidnapping when I haven't spent more than half a day away from the academy since I came to England?"

"You tell me," he replied.

I spluttered. "I didn't do it. I didn't even know we'd be going to the Peak District until Mr. Jenkins announced the trip!"

Sergeant Sullivan folded his arms across his chest. "Why would the kidnappers identify you as their accomplice?"

"Revenge," I said.

His brow rose. "I beg your pardon?"

"They were pissed because they tried to get a ransom out of my stepfather, but he kept negotiating them down."

The look the inspector gave me was part boredom and part disgust. "All the evidence is stacked against you. The staff we interviewed told us of a campaign of bullying and harassment conducted against you by Mr. Bourneville and his friends. Your motivation for his abduction is financial gain and revenge."

I turned to the headmaster, hoping he would step in and tell these bungling policemen they were being ridiculous, but the man stood in the corner of the room, folding his arms as though this was no problem of his. My jaws gnashed together. The bastard had washed his hands of me, and I was on my own.

"Why would I report my so-called accomplices and incriminate myself?" I asked.

"They told me there was a dispute about money," replied Inspector Faust. "When they demanded a larger share for the efforts they had made, you threatened to have them arrested. It looks like you carried out that threat."

"No." I shot to my feet, letting the stool clatter on the floor. My heart pounded against my ribcage urging me to say something to convince them of my innocence. "Ask Henry what happened. He'll tell you I didn't do it."

Chief Inspector Faust also stood. "We spoke to Mr. Bourneville on Friday."

"What did he say?" My voice shook.

The sergeant flipped his notebook open. "He was shocked at the suggestion that you were involved but had to admit that the evidence against you is overwhelming."

All the blood drained from my face, and my heartbeat slowed to a dull, heavy thud. I'd seen him yesterday, the day before, and the day before that, but he'd never mentioned anything about being interviewed by the police. Had they told him to keep quiet while they finished their investigation? How could Henry have believed the kidnappers over me?

My insides trembled, and nausea crawled up the back of my throat. "Does he believe I was behind the kidnapping?"

"Let's continue this conversation after the arrest," said the inspector.

"Right," replied the sergeant.

The edges of my vision blurred, and the walls spun like I was stuck in the middle of a merry-go-round. Pressing my clammy palms to my temples, I squeezed my eyes shut to stop myself from falling. This couldn't be happening. I had contacted the police to protect Henry from the kidnappers' demands, not to have suspicion fall on me. I needed a lawyer. Mom. Anyone who could talk sense into these cops and explain that I could never have orchestrated the abduction of a classmate.

The headmaster stepped out of his corner, and relief washed over my fevered body. He was going to remind them I was underage, and to take the matter up with Mom.

He straightened the jacket of his pinstriped suit and said, "The academy can't afford a scandal. Miss Hobson only enrolled a little over two months ago." A nervous laugh warbled in his throat. "She isn't really one of us, and her indiscretions shouldn't tarnish the academy."

After the shock of all the other revelations, I wasn't surprised the headmaster wanted to throw me under the bus to save his school's precious reputation.

"What do you suggest, Headmaster?" Chief Inspector Faust scraped his chair back as though readying himself to pounce on me.

"Let me expel her before releasing her into your custody." He drummed his fingers on a cabinet by the wall.

"But I'm innocent," I gasped out.

The officers didn't even spare me a glance. Inspector Faust rubbed his chin as though considering the request. "How soon can you get her parents to come down and accompany her to the station?"

My knees knocked together, threatening to give way and have me crashing onto the silk rug. I rested my palms on the headmaster's desk, lowered my head, and breathed hard. The whoosh of blood rushing through my eardrums and the pulse reverberating in my skull muffled out their conversation. I could make out the headmaster explaining that my parents were in the USA, and the police refusing to take me without a guardian and demanding the identity of my housemaster. The conversation went back and forth until the headmaster agreed to keep me in a solitary room until Mom or Rudolph could come and get me.

Both officers left, and Mr. Carbuncle came in. After a short exchange with the headmaster, the janitor marched me out of the main teaching block. The journey across the lawn and under the skeletal trees felt like walking on cotton wool, I was that numb. This had to be a nightmare because there was no way anyone would believe me over a bunch of kidnapping hippies. As we passed through the wooden doors of Elder House, a little voice in the back of my head told me to go to the dining room and confront Henry. But I couldn't face him if he thought I'd arranged the kidnapping.

Mr. Carbuncle guided me down a staircase that lead to the basement and through a humid hallway. The matron and her staff bustled from room to room, oblivious of my predicament. I wanted to cry out. Ask for help, but I couldn't break through my wall of numb shock.

"I knew you were trouble the minute I laid eyes on you." The janitor stared into my face, his expression expectant.

I stared through him. If he wanted a bribe, he was out of luck.

He unhooked his giant ring of keys, fumbled about with its contents, and unlocked a door at the end of the hallway that consisted of a narrow cot. "In you go." He gave me a gentle shove on the back. "This is where you'll stay until your mum and stepdad come for you."

As soon as I stepped through the threshold, the door slammed shut, and the key turned in the lock.

My heart ached. It overflowed with bitter grief that filled my chest, caught in my throat, and spilled from my eyes in a torrent of tears. I was confined. Again. And this time, Henry wasn't there to keep me sane. He was upstairs, sitting at the head table, hating me for orchestrating his kidnapping. Charlotte was probably holding his hand, explaining that a trollop like me would take any desperate measures to access the Bourneville fortune and its heir.

I walked across the creaking floorboards, lowered myself onto the cot, and slumped. The mattress springs squeaked under my weight. What would Edward think? That I was a calculating whore who had worked out a way to infiltrate the triumvirate? And Blake? I couldn't even imagine his reaction to my impending arrest. I doubled over, resting my knees on the bed, pressed the heels of my hands into my temples, and dug my nails into my scalp.

Mom would disassociate herself from me if she hadn't done so already. Once they could arrest me, it would be all over the news that the daughter of Veronica Hobson had kidnapped a British aristocrat. Rudolph might divorce her for the scandal, and she'd have to find a new husband. I blew out a breath. Somehow, I needed to fix things.

In the bare, white room, each interval between the bells felt like days. I almost missed the musty attic room with its piles of broken furniture and curtain-like cobwebs. At least I hadn't been alone there. A few minutes into second break, the key turned in the lock. I leaped off the bed and rushed to the door.

Henry stepped in, flanked by Edward and Blake, each wearing stony expressions.

A sob formed in my throat, and I rushed to Henry and grabbed his biceps. "You've got to believe me, I didn't even know the kidnappers, let alone arrange for them to abduct you!"

He peeled my hands off his arms and held me at arm's length. "I told you not to call the police."

Tears welled in my eyes. "But they were threatening to take you again. I couldn't let that happen!"

He glanced at Edward, who shook his head. "She doesn't get it."

"Get what?" I asked.

Blake wrapped a hand around my arm, guided me across the room, and pulled me down to sit. Then he stepped back and said, "You meddled, and now you're paying the price."

"But I was trying to help." My voice broke.

Edward leaned against the wall. "We had it under control. The kidnappers were never a threat."

"How could you know that? You never even met them." I turned to Henry. "They were threatening to take you again!"

Henry sighed. "They were just trying their luck with empty threats."

I shook my head. Why did they seem so resigned? And why did they care more about my calling the police than my involvement in the kidnapping? Blake stood over me, brows raised with the kind of anticipation of a middle school teacher watching a slow kid struggling with a math problem. Edward pursed his lips, disapproval etched over his face, and Henry stared at a point on the floorboards next to my left foot. There was a piece of the puzzle that hadn't yet fallen in place, and none of them would tell me what I'd done wrong.

"I shouldn't have called the police." My voice was dull.

"Correct," said Edward.

"The kidnappers weren't as big a threat as I'd thought." I was just summarizing what the boys had told me. My mind was so thick with fog, I couldn't put together any conclusions. "Why?"

"That's a rather leading question, don't you think?" drawled Blake.

I glanced up at Henry. He was the least cruel of the group. The one I knew the most, but he wouldn't look into my eyes. I dropped my gaze to my knees. What was I missing? Just before the abduction, they'd been at their cruelest and had left me duct taped in a sleeping bag out where anything might have happened to me. But when I returned, Edward and Blake were immediately apologetic. I'd thought they had felt bad about their actions, and how they'd driven me to chase after Henry the day he'd been kidnapped.

My throat convulsed. What if there was a more nefarious motive?

An idea dropped into my head, making it snap up. "The school trip… T-that campsite… How did the kidnappers know where to find you?"

Blake grinned. "I think she's finally getting it."

"Oh, do be quiet," snapped Edward.

"You knew them, didn't you?" I glared at Henry, who still wouldn't look at me. My glare turned to Edward. "He arranged it himself. That's why the kidnappers drugged me and not him."

Edward stared back, blue eyes wintry. "You only have yourself to blame for your predicament."

My heart beat the tune of a war drum, and my hands balled into fists. I stood from the cot, ready to swing. "When you failed to kill me with sheep, you arranged for those hippies to abduct me!"

Edward rolled his eyes. "Don't be so melodramatic. Not everything we did revolved around you."

"Then why did you do it?" I spat.

"We needed the money," Henry finally said. "You weren't supposed to be there, but the chaps panicked and took you along with me before you could raise the alarm."

My arms drooped to the side. "What would you need that much money for?"

"That's none of your business," said Edward.

The sight of them made me sick, and I closed my eyes. Everything had been a lie, and they'd probably meant to frame me for the kidnapping all along.

The bell signifying the end of second break rang, and the boys filed out of my little prison without a backward glance. Mr. Carbuncle stepped into the doorway, keys in hand.

"Did you hear that?" I asked. "They arranged Henry's kidnapping. I'm innocent."

The huge man rolled his eyes and placed the key in the lock. "I don't get paid to eavesdrop, girl."

CHAPTER 20

I didn't see the boys again after that initial visit, but for the next few days, I stared at the white walls, going over every interaction I'd had with the triumvirate. All that bullshit about wanting a relationship with me had had a sole purpose: to keep me quiet when I eventually discovered they had scammed Henry's parents. They had even devised a contingency plan with the kidnappers in case I ever went to the police. For an extra share of the ransom, the kidnappers would say I had been working with them, keeping Henry and the rest of the triumvirate out of trouble.

I lay back on the cot, letting my arm trail off its edge to the floor. What an idiot I had been. What an arrogant fool. I had thought I was different. Special, somehow. That beneath their hatred and resentment for me was the suppressed desire for a relationship.

I snorted a bitter laugh. "Yeah, right."

Maybe Rita's strategy to keep to the shadows was the only way to survive Mercia Academy. She was the best of us all. Always cautious, always vigilant, always fearful of the wickedness that hid behind the triumvirate's handsome facades.

Each day blurred into the other with only the briefest interaction with the matron, who delivered plastic bottles of Evian and cheese sandwiches wrapped in paper, the upper-crust equivalent of bread and water rations, I supposed. After five days of captivity, I stopped counting and gave into despair.

Noelle and I had lost contact, but she was in no position to help. Mom had probably found a way to disassociate herself from me, Rudolph Trommel didn't care, and Dad was probably scrounging together the money for a plane ticket to England... if he hadn't already relapsed with the shock of discovering his daughter was a kidnapper.

I pushed the morbid image out of my head and fumbled under the bed for my water bottle. What were the triumvirate doing? Toasting themselves at their triumph over the trollop?

Of all the stunts they had pulled, this one had to be the cruelest because they had made me ache for them. The worst bit about it was that a part of me still did.

"Fool." I pushed myself up onto the bed, bent my knees to my chest and hugged my shins. "Fool." My rocking back and forth made the bedsprings creak. "I'm the biggest, fucking fool."

The key turned in the lock, and I sprang to my feet. Mrs. Jenkins usually knocked before entering. This had to be someone else.

Mr. Carbuncle filled the doorway, his lips twisted into a smirk. "Climbing the walls, then?"

"That's Spiderman."

He wrinkled his nose, spreading the bristles of his broom handle mustache. "Headmaster wants to see you."

"Right." I smoothed down my shirt. It was rumpled from near-constant wear.

"Now, unless you want to stay in there for another seven days."

"Seven—" I stopped myself from giving him a reaction. Mr. Carbuncle was the symbol of my oppression. He'd worked behind the scenes on at least three of the so-called pranks. The man was probably observing me so he could describe my every weakness to the triumvirate.

I kept my head up as I walked through the humid, basement hallway, past the cleaning and kitchen staff too busy with their duties to cast me a glance. Behind me, Mr. Carbuncle's keys jangled with every step. It was like the ringing of the bell to my walk of shame.

He ushered me up the stairs, and when I reached the ground floor, my heart stopped. Students stood in rows on both sides of the hallway, forming an obscene gauntlet of burgundy blazers.

"They all left the dining room to see you off," murmured Mr. Carbuncle into my ear. "Isn't that nice?"

I would have asked him why he was being such a sadistic dick, but I wouldn't give him the satisfaction of knowing his actions had gotten to me. At the end of the hallway, the double doors stood open, revealing a bright December morning. Cameraphones pinged into action, and a third of the goons turned their raised screens in my direction. I'd bet Rudolph's fortune that the videos of my leaving would grace the Mercia-Net before the hour was out.

I squared my shoulders. Whatever they said or did, I would not react. I'd die before I give them the satisfaction of a scene.

"Go on, then." Mr. Carbuncle prodded the small of my back with his this finger.

Disgust rippled through my spine, but I suppressed the reaction. The first step toward the gauntlet was agony. The second was excruciating. As I neared them, the students stepped away from the walls, narrowing my path.

"Trollop," hissed a voice.

"Whore," whispered another.

The chant spread, a cacophony of filthy slurs, all undeserved. A well of despair emptied into my gut, filling my innards with its foul contents. If I hadn't cared for Henry and tried to protect him, none of this would have happened. If I hadn't accepted Edward's invitation to sit at the head table, none of this would have happened. If I hadn't succumbed to Blake's seductive ways and let him demonstrate how good it could be with more than one boy, none of this would have happened.

Mr. Carbuncle gave me a harder poke in the back. "Hurry up, girl."

I clenched my teeth. One day, I'd make sure he felt the same misery as he'd arranged for me.

I swallowed hard and stepped through the crowd. The burgundy-clad vultures pounced. Some shoving, some punching me in the back, some pulling my hair. I clenched my teeth and grimaced through the pain, breathing hard to quieten the whimpers in my throat.

"Whore!"

"Slut!"

"Yank!"

"Trollop!"

"Gold digger!"

I kept my head down and continued on through the interminable crowd of bullies. Many of them didn't even belong to Elder House. Whoever had arranged this with Carbuncle, Edward perhaps, had wanted to send me off with maximum pain and humiliation.

A hand went up my skirt, and I jerked away, suppressing a scream. The crowd closed in, blocking my way, and I had to push through the attacks, the insults, the hatred. A little voice in the back of my mind noted that no one had called me a kidnapper, extortioner, fraudster or any combination of words related to the crime I'd supposedly have committed. Someone kicked at my ankle, and I stumbled forward. The crowd parted, leaving me to land hard on my hands and knees.

Hooting laughter filled my ears, as did comments that I was in the right position for whoring. My throat thickened. My heart rate tripled. And the well of despair rose to my throat, forcing out a sob.

The confusion of taunts and blows and groping hands drowned out the sound.

Mr. Carbuncle blew a whistle. "Everybody, stand back!"

The jeers and insults subsided, and the crowd parted, presumably to reform the gauntlet. I no longer cared. I'd reached the halfway point down the hallway, and anything, even the custody of Chief Inspector Faust and his sergeant, would be better than these upper-class savages.

"Get up," the janitor hissed.

My arms trembled, barely able to hold my weight.

He wrapped a strong arm around my bicep and yanked me to my feet. "Move!"

I stumbled to keep up with his fast strides through the hallway. Only one side of the gauntlet attacked. The other probably didn't want to incite Mr. Carbuncle's wrath by getting too close. I looked around for signs of Henry, Blake, and Edward, but they weren't in the crowd. The bastards probably couldn't show their faces after what they'd done.

Once we'd passed the double doors of Elder house, Charlotte stepped into my path, flanked by Wendy, Alice, Patricia, and a wannabe doppelgänger whose name I'd never learned. Her hazel eyes gleamed with a mix of curiosity and triumph. "I don't know what you did to our boys, but they don't even want to hear your name in their presence."

I shook my head. Even if I told her, she'd find a way to twist things around to her advantage.

"Don't you have any witty replies, Trollop?" she asked.

I stared straight ahead, heart beating in sync with the throbbing of my aches and bruises. Charlotte wasn't worth my time. She was just a stupid bitch gloating that she'd protected her territory. One day, she would discover that the triumvirate weren't worth the effort. I hoped it would be soon.

Mr. Carbuncle hurried me along the path of magnolia trees

stripped of their leaves and beautiful flowers. I couldn't help feeling an affinity with the branches. The gauntlet had laid me bare and stripped me of my dignity. Over something they didn't even know had taken place.

"How did you like the little send-off I organized?" asked Charlotte from behind.

I stopped and glanced over my shoulder. "You?"

"Come on!" Mr. Carbuncle dragged me through the back doors of the main teaching block.

I kicked myself for giving Charlotte a reaction.

∼

I'd expected Chief Inspector Faust and his sergeant in the headmaster's office, but Rudolph sat in the seat opposite Mr. Chaloner, clad in a similar suit. Perhaps they used the same designer.

The headmaster stood, but Rudolph remained seated with his arms folded over his chest.

"Where's Mom?" I asked.

"She couldn't face her daughter, the kidnapper," Rudolph said without looking at me.

"Where's Marissa, then?"

He turned livid, steel-gray eyes on me, anger etching his usually expressionless face. "Do you know what I had to do to clear up your little scandal?"

I parted my lips to tell him the truth, but he continued his rant.

"I repaid the Bournevilles the million pounds you extorted from them, and donated another fifty thousand to the school to erase your records. Even that Chief Inspector wanted a donation to his pet charity!"

My jaw dropped, but no words came out. I turned and stared at the headmaster, who narrowed his eyes, daring me to tell Rudolph he'd been the one who wanted to avoid the scandal and that Rudolph had paid for nothing.

Rudolph stood. "I'm taking you somewhere you will never tarnish our names!"

"W-where?" I pictured an institution deep in Siberia.

"Military school." He stood, walked out of the room and down the hallway, not even bothering to check that I was following him.

I hurried after him. "Rudolph… wait."

Ignoring my entreaties to stop and listen, Rudolph continued down the marble staircase, through the hallway, and out of the double doors.

Rita stood at the bottom of the stairs, her dark eyes large and solemn. "What happened to you? They packed all your things and wouldn't say where you'd gone."

I shook my head and wrapped my arms around her. "The less you know, the better."

She stepped back. "Have you been expelled?"

"More like wiped out of the academy's existence."

"Sorry." Rita left the rest unsaid. She'd tried to warn me. Several times, but I'd been too stubborn and too confident in my mental strength to listen. It had never occurred to me that the triumvirate would stoop so low.

"Thanks for being there for me," I said through the lump in my throat.

She pressed her lips together and nodded. "I'll never forget you."

We embraced once more, and I stepped out into the wintry day. Out on the courtyard, between the front door and the limo, Henry, Blake, and Edward stood in a form of one-sided gauntlet.

A fist clenched my heart so hard, tears welled in my eyes. I had no words for them. Anything I said would be taken as some kind of triumph over the Yank they never wanted in their precious academy. I held my head high and walked toward Rudolph's car, keeping my gaze fixed on the driver standing by the passenger seat.

"Emilia," said Henry.

My step faltered, but I refused to look at him.

"You shouldn't have called the police."

"There's a lot of things I regret," I breathed hard to keep the tremble out of my voice. "But considering you unworthy swine as anything but unlovable bastards was my biggest mistake."

Edward stepped forward. "You brought this onto yourself. We were serious about you being our fourth."

I shook my head and walked past. "Go to hell and take your pathetic friends with you."

The driver opened the door. I stepped in and took the seat opposite Rudolph who was on the phone, yelling at an employee who had failed to account for all the debts of a newspaper he'd just bought. Apparently, he was stuck with a staff of a hundred and would have to lay off half to make the venture break even.

The limo pulled out of the driveway, and I turned to stare at the triumvirate one last time. They stood in the same formation I'd originally met them on the top of the stairs. Blake on the left, Henry in the middle, and Edward at the end. If I had known then that they would give me half a term of hell, followed by half a term of companionship only to frame me for their own crimes, I would have left with Marissa and never turned back. If only there was a way to stick a proverbial knife in their guts, I would do it in a heartbeat.

Rudolph hung up, muttering about worthless investments, when an idea dropped into my head.

"Rudolph?"

"What?"

"Is the paper British?"

"Why?"

"I know of a few scandals that might be of interest to the British public." I paused, gathering the courage to continue. "One of them involves you."

He narrowed his eyes. "If it's about my stepdaughter who's going to military school, I already know it."

Greenery whizzed by the limo windows, but I focused on my new stepfather, counting off the scandals on my fingertips. "The Bourneville ransom was five-hundred thousand, but they tricked you into paying double."

His face drained of color. "What?"

"And Mr. Chaloner had expelled me a week ago and was desperate to avoid a scandal. He just fleeced you of fifty thousand pounds because he could." Rudolph's nostrils flared, and a shot of triumph heated my belly. He could have avoided every unnecessary payment by treating me like a person and not an object that needed to be discarded. "And I know the secrets of some of the most influential families in England, including the royals."

Rudolph leaned forward and listened to everything I had learned from Henry about our classmates. The royal scandal, the corrupt government minister, and the declining duke. With each revelation, his eyes took on a calculating gleam. His new paper would be profitable within weeks with my stories.

We were on the freeway before I'd finished, and Rudolph asked, "Do you have proof?"

"I can get it, but you'll have to send me back to Mercia Academy."

He gave me a sharp nod. "I'll put you in touch with the Saturday Correspondent's editor. You'd better come up with the goods, or I'll send you to military school."

"You'd better publish all the scandals I'll send you. Some of them will have the power to ruin lives."

Rudolph threw his head back and laughed. I smoothed out my features to hide my contempt for the man who had given me this shitty trial by fire. One day, he would get his, but for now, I was coming after the triumvirate and everyone who supported their reign of terror.

"Henry Bourneville... Edward Mercia... Blake Simpson-West... Charlotte Underhill," I muttered under my breath. "I'll ruin you, and this time, I'll show no mercy."

END OF BOOK ONE
READ BOOK TWO

REVENGE

KINGS OF MERCIA ACADEMY BOOK 2

CHAPTER 1

It was strange. Here I was, sitting in the open plan office of the Saturday Correspondent, working the exact job I'd been desperate to do, yet all I could think about was Mercia Academy. A group of young secretaries stood by the windows, laughing at some joke, and my insides cringed. I dipped my head, breathing hard to remind myself that people at the Correspondent didn't scheme against colleagues.

If I wasn't so antsy, I might have enjoyed the atmosphere. My desk was sandwiched between two enthusiastic, young journalists who were always willing to share war stories about working for a newspaper. Opposite was a gossip columnist who told the most scandalous stories, and on the other side was a girl five years older, who had graduated with a degree in journalism.

A red-haired intern wearing tinsel around her neck brought back coffees from her Starbucks run and placed a latte on my desk. I handed her my cash and checked the messages on my smartphone. Rudolph hadn't called or texted or emailed in two weeks to update me on his negotiations for my re-entry into the academy. I was beginning to think he'd forgotten about me.

On the far left, Jackie's door opened. She was our Editor-In-Chief. The older woman's bleached blonde hair flopped over her face as she peered out into the open-plan office. "Emilia? A word."

I pulled myself out of my seat, nearly knocking down an over-decorated Christmas tree. After steadying it on its stand, I circled the nest of desks and walked to the editor's office. Jackie was a petite woman with a heavily lined face who dressed in skinny jeans and tank tops.

It was hard to tell her age, as she smoked cigarillos that rasped her voice and puckered her lips. Since she'd taken me in as an intern, I'd stuck by her side, attending interviews, press conferences, and meetings. It had been a crash course in journalism.

She perched herself on the edge of her desk, palms spread on its surface. "What do you know about classical music?"

"Not much… Why?"

"Sergei Bachmann, the son of the late Vasily Bachmann, is making his debut in London. I want you to learn everything you can about his father's death and uncover why Sergei was unknown in the music circuit until now."

I nodded, my gaze traveling down to her desk. It landed on two tickets to the Royal Academy Charity Ball. The one Edward had invited me to attend as the triumvirate's date. A lump formed in my throat, and my shoulders drooped. The day I'd agreed to date all three of them marked the start of my downfall. If I had refused, the boys might have backed off. Instead, they tangled me further into their web, and my feelings for Henry now extended to Edward and Blake.

A sigh slid from my lips. How I yearned to rip their guts out and make them feel the gut-wrenching agony of such a horrific betrayal.

"Emilia?"

My gaze snapped up to Jackie. "Sorry… Yes… I'll read up on Bachmann."

The corner of her lips quirked into a smile. "What's wrong? Enthusiasm for journalism waning?"

"No." I shook my head, my gaze falling back onto the tickets. "But Rudolph said he'd have news by now, and—"

She held up a hand. "We're getting you back into Mercia Academy." She nodded to the desk outside the door, where a strawberry-blond haired man cross-referenced data from two screens. "Charlie is linking all the students you named to aristocratic families, government departments, and big business. "It's just going to take a little more time."

I dipped my head. "Right."

"Hey," she said.

My head snapped up.

"Enjoy your time here, because when you return to Mercia, it will be a hard slog."

"I don't know what you mean."

"Rudolph's making us do things differently around here." She pushed herself off the desk and strode across the room, bringing with her the scent of stale tobacco. "You'll have to record friends and classmates and send the files back to us, so we can put together stories based on insider information. Are you alright with that?"

I straightened. The triumvirate had framed me for kidnapping, and I thirsted for revenge. "That's fine with me."

"These methods aren't above board or even legal." She placed her hands on her hips. "Are you sure?"

My jaws clenched. Was she asking if I was having second thoughts? I gave her a sharp nod. "If that's what I have to do to take these guys down, I'll do it."

Jackie made a rasping chuckle and gave me a pat on the arm. "Good! In the meantime, you can learn the ropes of the profession. It's not all about undercover work."

I pulled my gaze away from the tickets. Even if I wanted to confront the boys about framing me for kidnapping Henry, it would mean standing outside the Royal Academy building in the freezing cold, waiting for them to arrive. And it probably might jeopardize our plan for me to get the dirt on their families to publish in the Saturday Correspondent.

Giving Jackie what I hoped was an enthusiastic smile, I chirped, "I'll get right on researching Bachmann!"

∽

Another week passed with still no word from Rudolph. I slouched at my desk, swirling the remnants of my hot chocolate and pushed away the memory of Mr. Carbuncle manhandling me through the crowd of angry sixth-formers. My arm throbbed in remembrance. The terrible janitor had acted as though he blamed me that the ambush *he'd* set up with Charlotte had turned violent and bloodthirsty.

I shook away those thoughts. Rudolph couldn't have forgotten about me. He had been just as eager to bring down the Bourneville family, who had lied about the ransom amount and asked for double to drop the criminal charges against me. He also wanted to hurt the headmaster of Mercia Academy for demanding an unnecessary donation to expunge my school records. I stared into my notepad, barely seeing the shorthand symbols. Jackie was right. I had to be patient.

One morning, I was putting the finishing touches to a piece on elitism within British public schools, when my cellphone rang. My heart thrummed with excitement as I scrambled to click the answer button. It was from an Unknown Caller, but that could mean anything. Even Rudolph from one of his many offices around the world or one of his many assistants.

"H-hello?"

"Hi, this is Frank from the Tom Ford concession at Bourneville's.

We've completed the adjustments to your gown, and it's ready to be picked up."

My heart flip-flopped. Regardless of what had happened, I still wanted that gown. "I-I'll come at lunchtime."

Bourneville's department store wasn't quite so magical when approached from Piccadilly Circus tube and with the cold wind mingling with exhaust fumes from double-decker buses, but its beautiful, stone Georgian exterior reminded me of Mercia Academy so much, my heart ached. Those weeks before everything had gone wrong had been a whirl of dancing lessons and of basking in the affection of the three most handsome and witty boys in the academy.

I closed my eyes, letting the cacophony of traffic fill my ears. But it did nothing to distract me from the painful truth. The triumvirate's affection and attention had been an illusion created to distract me from discovering the truth. I forced the memories out of my head and stepped through a set of automatic doors.

Ignoring the fragrant aromas from the perfume and makeup counters, I made my way toward the escalator. As soon as the device pulled me up to the first floor, I scanned the walls at the far distance, passing over security guards to catch a glimpse of Henry. My heart sank, as did my self-respect. Had I always been this pathetic?

The man who had originally fitted me into the dress wasn't at the Tom Ford concession, but the young woman advised me to try on the gown to see if it needed any last minute adjustments. I refused and took the dress away. It wasn't like I would ever use it. This wasn't Cinderella, and Jackie was no fairy godmother. She was more likely to take her husband to the charity ball than some intern who had been foisted on her by the tycoon who had bought her newspaper.

When I returned to her office, she had already started her interview with Sergei Bachmann, a young man who couldn't be more than nineteen. He sat on her leather sofa with his back ramrod straight, and his arms folded across his chest.

Sergei had the look of someone who would be distinctive when they were older: long black hair, strong eyebrows, and a patrician nose. Combined with high cheekbones and startling, aquamarine eyes, the effect was rather striking. Leaning against the wall was a handsome blond man who looked like a bodyguard.

"Sergei, may I introduce you to Emilia Hobson, our intern." There was an edge to Jackie's voice that said she was only tolerating my lateness because of my connection to Rudolph.

Shame crawled through my gut. My eagerness to grasp anything related to the triumvirate was now affecting my internship. What had made me think I could travel from Fleet Street to Piccadilly Circus and grab a sandwich in less than an hour? I held out my hand. "I'm pleased to meet you."

Sergei stood and brought my knuckles to his lips. "*Enchanté, Mademoiselle.*"

"Oh," I said. "I thought you were Russian."

He flicked his black hair off his face. "I spent most of my years at the *Institut de la Musique* in Paris. A fine school, but we did not have girls as charming as you."

I shot Jackie a nervous glance, but she gave me one of those subtle nods that told me to flirt back.

Batting my lashes, I twirled a strand of my light, auburn hair. "I heard you were playing at the Royal Academy charity ball in a few days, Mr. Bachmann."

"Call me Sergei." His lips quirked into a smile.

"I'd love to see you perform." My voice rose a few octaves.

His beautiful blue eyes twinkled, reminding me somewhat of Edward's. "Then you must come as my guest."

Butterflies took flight in my stomach. If I arrived at the ball on the arm of an up-and-coming musician, the triumvirate would have to notice me. I had expected one of them, maybe Blake or Henry, to call, but the three maintained a wall of silence that implied they had discarded me like used chewing gum.

A gust of triumph inflated my chest. Soon, the triumvirate would know I hadn't been packed of to the States like. My face broke into a smile. "Thank you, Sergei, I'd be delighted."

CHAPTER 2

*T*he next few days whizzed by, each evening spent trying on the Tom Ford gown in my hotel room and experimenting with different hairstyles and accessories. The silk ivory garment hugged my b-cup breasts, cradled my waist, and skimmed the swell of my hips, ending in a dramatic fall of bias-cut fabric to my ankles. I swept my light hair into a chignon, exposing my neck and teardrop gold earrings. The only other piece of jewelry in my ensemble was a matching, gold bracelet.

"Stunning, not desperate," I repeated a mantra I'd recited most nights. "Elegant and aloof."

I may have looked like a debutante, but I felt like an impostor. Jackie told me to gather whatever I could about Sergei, and I agreed but refused her offer of a recording device on the grounds that it would spoil the line of my dress.

On the evening of the ball, Sergei picked me up from the foyer of my hotel, a marble-floored space lit by dozens of chandeliers. The man looked devastatingly handsome in a tuxedo and one of those black capes lined in red silk worn by suave fiends like Dracula. His glossy, black hair hung over his shoulders, making me wonder what Edward would look like if he didn't keep his own short.

Sergei's gaze swept up and down my gown, settling on my shoes. I'd bought them two days before and had wiped out my bank account. "Emilia," he said in an accent that was a mix of French and Russian. "You look enchanting."

Pride made my chest swell. If I could impress a Paris-educated classical musician, I could probably impress the triumvirate. "Thanks. So do you."

He held out his arm, and we strolled out of the marble reception room, into the crisp, London evening, and to his limousine. I settled into the plush, leather seat, and he joined me opposite. Then the blond bodyguard from the interview stepped inside, sat to my right, and gave me a nod of greeting.

The limo pulled out from the curb and drove through central London. I'd seen it all before in the daytime, but after dark, the city looked magical lit up with Christmas lights fashioned in a multitude of festive shapes. I glanced at Sergei, wondering why someone as sophisticated as him had asked me out.

"How long have you been working with the newspaper?" he asked.

"A few weeks." I straightened in my seat. "It's sort of a holiday internship. I'm supposed to be going back to school in January."

His dark brows rose. "You study here in London?"

"No." I swallowed hard. "My academy is a boarding school in Mercia county."

The blond bodyguard twisted in his seat. "You have a boyfriend in this school?"

An iron fist of betrayal clutched at my heart and twisted. How did I answer a question like that? I'd had three, but they all turned out to be bastards, and now I can't stop thinking about them. Sorry, Mr. Bodyguard, but I'm dating your client under false pretenses.

Sergei patted my left hand. "Andreo is too curious. I can tell someone broke your heart. You don't have to talk about it if it still hurts."

I dipped my head. "Thanks."

Minutes later, the limo joined a line of similar vehicles outside the Royal Academy, an imposing building built like an opera house with a vaulted ceiling for acoustics. Dozens of paparazzi stood outside, snapping pictures of the guests. An empty pit opened up in my stomach, filled by the flutter of a flock of butterflies. I held my hand over my heart and gulped in lungfuls of air. How did Mom cope with being a society wife, going to function after function and finding her pictures plastered all over the news and the internet?

"My commission doesn't start until eleven." Sergei glanced at the time on his phone. "That gives us plenty of time to have fun at the ball."

I smiled and nodded, but my stomach churned as our limo rolled to the red carpet. Sergei stepped out first, then took my hand and helped me out of the vehicle.

Cameras flashed. I blinked into the blinding light. Photographers closed in on us like a gauntlet, and my chest tightened. The feel of hot, angry bodies pressing in on me, raining blows on my arms, my head, my back, returned as though I was still on the ground floor of Elder House.

"It's not real," I whispered under my breath with a fixed smile I hoped wouldn't look too strained. "It's only photos."

We walked arm in arm toward the building with Andreo and five other men in suits close behind.

I glanced at them over my shoulder and stiffened. "What's going on?"

"They're bodyguards," murmured Sergei. "My father made a lot of enemies before he died."

Oddly, the thought of these enemies didn't frighten me as much as the notion of photographers piling on top of me and crushing the air out of my lungs. The investigative journalist part of me itched to ask more questions, but I tamped down my curiosity. I hadn't heard from Mom since leaving New York, and the loss of contact was an ache that wouldn't go away. I couldn't imagine what it would be like to have a parent die, and I wouldn't probe.

I gave Sergei what I hoped was a sympathetic smile, and we followed the red carpet through a grand hallway that boasted pictures of musicians from all eras. Sergei pointed out a photo of a severe-looking man with strong, angular features, cast mostly in shadow. It was his father, Vasily Bachmann. I glanced at Sergei's softer features. Whoever his father had married, she must have been beautiful.

The Royal Academy ballroom had the feel of a cathedral. Tall pillars on the edges of the dance floor stretched up into arches that supported a vaulted ceiling three stories high. Behind them stretched dining tables and chairs, already occupied by those not dancing. Arched windows ran along the highest levels of the ceiling, which would have brought in a spectacular amount of light during the day. At the far end of the room stood a raised stage for the orchestra with a grand piano.

At the sight of the elegant couples swirling around the dance floor, my stomach flip-flopped. They were all dancing the Viennese waltz, a fast version of the dance where the female partner leaned backward and spun in circles around the dance floor. My dance instructor at Park Prep had said I didn't have the aptitude for this type of movement and had advised me to feign tiredness to avoid humiliating myself at a ball.

Sergei squeezed my hand. "I never asked...Do you waltz?"

I gave him an embarrassed smile. "Not the Viennese."

He patted me on the hand. "This piece is nearly finished. If the next one is to your liking, maybe we can dance."

I was about to ask how he knew the end of the song, then I stopped myself. Someone who went to a fancy music academy in Paris would have picked up the knowledge of more than a few pieces. As the music stopped, and people offered their applause, I spotted a figure who towered above most of the dancers. Blond, broad-shouldered, and breathtakingly stunning in a black tuxedo and a forest green cummerbund with a matching bowtie, he could only be one person: Henry.

The bastard looked even more handsome than I had remembered. His football player's body filled the outfit, which had clearly been tailored to give him long, sleek lines instead of bulk. Blond waves surrounded his face like gilded frames, setting off chiseled features and those verdant, green eyes.

My heart halted to a stop, and my gaze traveled down to the girl on his arm. It was Charlotte, wearing a silver, lace bodice that accentuated her voluptuous breasts. She'd darkened her long hair, letting it flow over her shoulders and down her back in loose curls. Henry escorted Charlotte off the dance floor, the pair of them chatting like old friends. As they'd known each other since they were eleven, they probably were.

The crowds covered my view, but between the throng, I caught sight of Edward walking off the dance floor with the doppelgänger, Patricia, on his arm, and Blake with Wendy, the girl who had pretended to be friendly with me on my first day.

Nausea with a side-order of jealousy crawled up my throat. A little part of me had taken what Edward had said to heart. That they had been serious about a relationship with me and I had spoiled everything by calling the police. But that tiny flame of hope was now doused by the evidence standing before me. The boys had moved on and had only cared about covering up the fake kidnapping.

"Emilia, are you well?" asked Sergei, his thick brows drawn together.

"Sure." I gave him my brightest smile.

The orchestra started up another piece. One I recognized from dancing lessons with the triumvirate.

"Ready for a slow waltz?" he asked.

I placed my hand in his and let him sweep me onto the dance floor. The strains of the orchestra filled the room, but my heart felt empty. Somewhere in the back of my mind, I had pictured the three boys attending the ball alone. My step faltered, and I muttered an apology, focusing on Sergei's lead, his aquamarine eyes, and his adoring smile.

"You seem distracted," he said. "What is wrong?"

"Are you sure you want to hear? It's a very long story."

"This is a very long piece."

As we danced, the sorry tale spilled from my lips, and Sergei listened with avid attention. It took about five waltzes for the story to finish, and by the time the last piece ended, he wrapped his arms around me and pressed a lingering kiss on my forehead. Whether it was out of genuine affection or out of pity, I couldn't be sure, but I relished in the comfort. Nobody but Rita had cared how much I'd suffered at the hands of the triumvirate and their cronies, and it felt good to have spoken about the ordeal with someone outside the academy.

We drank a few cocktails and glasses of champagne, danced a little more, then Sergei led me to the edge of the stage and kissed my hand. "It's time for my performance."

"Are you nervous?" I glanced around at the sea of expectant faces gathered on the dance floor to watch the London debut of the son of the recently deceased composer.

He grinned. "Every performance is nerve-wracking, but I will focus on those I love."

I offered him a smile and wished him an enjoyable performance. Andreo and the other bodyguards stood by my side. Some fixing their gazes on the stage, and others looking out for potential threats.

Sergei played one of his father's last compositions, a piano concerto that stirred my blood. It was a fast, angry piece that reminded me of all the injustices I'd endured at the hands of those snobs, and everything I planned to do to the triumvirate when I returned to Mercia Academy. By the time I finished with Henry, Blake, and Edward, the trio's lives would be in tatters, and they would wish they had never bullied anyone.

How many lives had they ruined with their pranks and taunts, and their incitement of others to victimize innocents? Too many, and soon, they would pay.

As Sergei transitioned to the second movement, a hand wrapped around my bicep. I glared at its owner.

Edward's wintry, blue eyes met mine. His mahogany hair was slicked off his face, accentuating the twist of his handsome features into a scowl. His tuxedo was a dark, gunmetal blue with black, silk lapels and a matching waistcoat. "What are you doing here with that Russian?"

"What business is it of yours?" I hissed. "As far as I know, you don't own the Royal Academy."

Behind him, Henry and Blake pushed through the crowd to make their presence known. For once, Blake didn't wear his usual mocking or knowing smirk. His brown eyes hardened into obsidian, and his full lips formed a thin, angry line. I clenched my teeth. Why the hell was he angry? As far as he knew, I was moving on with someone else. The boy wore a burgundy, one-button tuxedo that emphasized his broad shoulders and narrow waist and set off his beautiful, tan skin.

How I wanted to slam my fist in Blake's face for not properly warning me never to call the police. And for the glee he had expressed when I had been locked in that basement, lonely, miserable, and confused. He had delighted in my shock and anguish when I had guessed that they, and not the stoners, had framed me for the kidnapping.

Edward's nostrils flared, and his hand tightened around my bicep. "Come with us."

"What for?" I snapped. We had a plan. I was supposed to return to Mercia Academy, befriend the boys, and ruin them from the inside. But at the sight of their entitled faces and their awful dates, bitter resentment crawled up the back of my throat and coated my tongue. "Haven't you hurt me enough?"

Andreo turned toward me, eyes hard. "Is this man bothering you, Emilia?"

"Yes," I hissed. "Him and his two friends."

Andreo turned to the five men and gave them a sharp nod. A bald-headed brute about six-and-a-half-feet tall surged forward and wrapped his meaty fist around Edward's wrist. Edward released his grip from around my bicep, and I rubbed it for emphasis. Another equally as large man walked around and grabbed Blake by the back of the neck. His dark eyes widened, but he said nothing. Then two men each grabbed Henry around the arms.

"What are you doing?" hissed Edward. "Call off your thugs."

"They will not trouble you again," said Andreo.

Sergei's bodyguards escorted the triumvirate through the crowds and out of the ballroom. I would have rushed out to watch the spectacle, but I was sure the paparazzi would capture everything I needed to see. Warm triumph made my heart swell, and I turned back to the stage to listen to the rest of the second movement. I hoped the bodyguards hurt the triumvirate as much as they'd hurt me.

CHAPTER 3

After Sergei had finished his piece, we stayed for more dancing and to meet people in the classical music circuit. I fixed a smile on my face but couldn't enjoy the rest of the ball. The hostility in Edward's eyes confirmed everything I needed to know about the boys' intentions. It had all been a pretense, and my presence at the Royal Academy ball had been a blight on their evening. They had probably wanted to take me aside to threaten me not to reveal their criminal secret.

We stepped into the limo, and I checked my smartphone, expecting a barrage of angry texts and voicemails, but not one of them had gotten in contact. Not even a message from Charlotte and the doppelgängers to demand to know what I had done to their dates. It was as if they didn't deem me worthy enough for their attention.

The next morning, I arrived at the newspaper office to find Jackie rushing at me, brandishing a newspaper. My picture was plastered all over the society pages. I smiled and wondered if Mom had seen the picture.

"Come on, dish." Jackie dragged me straight into her office. "What did you find out about Sergei? I want all the gossip."

I gave her the blandest facts about his time at the Institut, which made her eyes glaze.

She huffed. "Will you be going out again?"

I shrugged. That incident with the triumvirate had been a disaster. I doubted whether a man like Sergei Bachmann would want to associate himself with a girl who had needed her own set of bodyguards.

To my surprise, he invited me to another evening function the next day and the day after that. Since I'd already studied everything I could about our biggest targets: the Duke of Mercia, the Bournevilles, and the former Mrs. Simpson-West, I accepted his invitations and entered London's society circuit. I found it glamorous at first, but the conversations and the people we met were superficial and dull. I totally understood why Sergei went out on the circuit. He was trying to drum up publicity and additional commissions, but it was hard to believe that Mom had swapped a family for such an empty life.

One morning, Jackie called me into her office. A tall man in a sweatshirt and jeans perched on her desk while she sat behind it on her ergonomic chair.

She leaned forward and steepled her fingers. "You need to put cameras in the school. Tom will show you what to do."

My stomach dropped, and I clapped my hand over my chest. "W-wait. They're letting me back in?"

"Rudolph is furious." Jackie rolled her eyes. "Your headmaster demanded a five-figure sum for your return."

I bit my lip. Mercia Academy had extorted so much from my stepfather. He would be determined more than ever to ruin them all.

Tom stood and opened his large palm, revealing small, white cubes. "These are wireless cameras that will record continuously and send footage to our servers. Since you've already supplied us with the passwords for the academy's internet service, they're all ready to go."

Jackie let out a hacking cough. "I want a few in strategic places like the common room, headmaster's office, the boys' bedrooms, and the home occupied by the Duke of Mercia."

Blood drained from my face and into my churning stomach. I'd agreed to do a little spying and reporting back of what I'd seen, but I'd imagined recording everything on my smartphone, just like I had done with Charlotte's scheme to ensnare Henry.

I stepped back toward the door. "How am I going to get into places like that without being detected?"

"Find a way," said Jackie, her voice sharp. "The headmaster has finally named a figure to take you back, and Rudolph is negotiating him down. He'll be livid if you back out now."

I eyed the small cameras in the man's hands. "I'm not backing..." My throat flexed. Rudolph had already threatened me with military school if I failed to follow through with the plan, and nightmares of being imprisoned in bare, filthy rooms made me cry out for vengeance in the middle of the night. "It might take some time."

She folded her arms across her chest. "Rudolph says he'll return you to New York and pay for a school and an Ivy League university of your choosing if you succeed. How's that for an incentive?"

"R-really?" My eyes bulged. "I'll find a way!"

Knowing that I'd soon return to Mercia made every society function more exciting. My pictures were probably all over the Mercia-Net, just as Mom's had been whenever she appeared in the papers. I'd make my smile extra bright and gaze adoringly into Sergei's eyes, acting the devoted girlfriend. He'd probably be happy to play along for the publicity.

Once the Saturday Correspondent published my name, all the

other papers followed suit. It was no longer 'Sergei Bachmann and companion' on the captions. One magazine even dug out some old photos of me at Mom's weddings and analyzed my fashions.

Dad sent me emails asking about Sergei, but I told him we were just friends. He insisted that a man didn't keep dating a pretty girl because he wanted to be her pal. I stared at Dad's message on my smartphone. I liked Sergei, but hadn't gotten over the triumvirate. Was I leading him on?

One evening, Sergei and I were riding in the limo with Andreo, his blond bodyguard. They were having a hushed conversation in rapid French. Every so often, Andreo would glance at me, giving the impression that I was the topic of their conversation.

I leaned forward, throat drying. "What's going on?"

"I apologize for fooling you," said Sergei.

My stomach dropped, and my gaze zoomed onto the passenger seat door. Was he not Sergei Bachmann? He certainly played like the son of a famous composer. After my experience with the triumvirate, I was ready to believe the worst.

The limo sped through London, but the second it stopped at the lights, I could jump out and run for safety. "What do you mean?"

"I cannot offer you anything but friendship." He nodded toward the bodyguard. "Andreo is my lover, but we cannot be open about our relationship. In Russia, that would mean the end of my career."

The muscles around my stomach relaxed. Maybe he'd seen something in my eyes, a lack of interest, preoccupation, or sadness that had prompted him to ask me out. "You want a beard?"

His brows drew together, and an incredulous smile curled his lips. "Beard?"

I sat back and explained that the term referred to a woman who agreed to date a gay man so he would appear straight to the rest of the world. They both chuckled and said that was exactly what they were looking for.

Sergei gave me a broad smile. "Emilia Hobson, will you consent to be my beard?"

I raised a shoulder. "As long as you don't expect me to be faithful."

∼

Rudolph finally paid Mr. Chaloner's demand, and I returned to Mercia Academy, armed with mini cameras I'd stuffed into the bottom of a pack of night-time sanitary pads in case someone entered my room and checked my things. The headmaster didn't even deem me worthy of a meeting. I expect he might have been sheepish at having accepted three sets of bribes: one to place me at the top of the waitlist, another to delete my records after he'd already expelled me, and the last to take me back.

Rudolph authorized the paper to pay for a limo to take me to the school in style. I directed the driver through the campus, around the imposing main building with frost covering its four towers, atrium, and huge windows. So much had changed since I had left. Even the magnolia trees that had formed the walkway through to the back of the campus had lost their leaves and now jutted out like naked umbrella spokes.

The limo pulled me into Elder House around first break, and I stepped through the mahogany doors into the warm reception hall, breathing in the warm and familiar scent of wood smoke. Although the crack and pop and sizzle of the fire felt welcoming, a tight band of panic wound around my ribcage. The last time I'd been here, Mr. Carbuncle had dragged me by the arm through a crowd of baying students. It had been harrowing and humiliating, and every part of my body had been hurt from their attacks.

Closing my eyes, I forced deep breaths in and out of my lungs, just as I had learned from a YouTube video on post-traumatic stress disorder. Things would be different, now. I would damage the triumvirate's reputations with such precision, they would have no time for their vicious plots.

"Emilia?" asked a small voice. I turned around. Rita hovered at the doorway, wringing her hands. Her shoulders curled into her petite frame, and her long braid hung down to her waist, making her appear even smaller.

A little of the tightness unwound itself to allow for a nervous chuckle. "I'm back."

"Why?" Her eyes widened to emphasize her question. "They haven't stopped talking about you since you left. Pictures of you are all over the society pages. Underwood and her group are hopping mad."

"Things will be different, now," I said. "You'll see."

She shook her head. "I would leave this place in the blink of an eye if it wasn't my best chance of a future. But you have a choice to go somewhere else."

My stomach twisted. All those fantasies of finding scandalous stories to humiliate the boys evaporated, leaving behind memories of struggling through my bedroom, naked with my eyes burning from something they'd put in my shampoo. The next time they pulled that prank, would they shove me out into the hallway to parade myself in front of the masses and their cameras? I pushed away that thought. This time, I wouldn't antagonize the triumvirate, and I still held their secret. Things had to go differently.

I forced a smile. "I'll be fine."

She glanced over her shoulder. "I heard about what happened to you when you left." Her voice lowered to a whisper. "If you're here for revenge, you should turn back. Nothing good ever came from defying those three."

The bell went, and Rita dashed to her mailbox, picked up a letter, and scurried back to classes. I went to Mr. Jenkins' office to pick up my keys. The man lowered his neck into his hunched shoulders and hid behind one of the many stacks of papers on his desk. He'd probably heard all about the violent send-off courtesy of the inhabitants of Elder House and their guests and couldn't look me in the face. After I picked up the keys, I returned to my room, lowered myself onto the bed, and sighed. In less than two hours, it would be time for me to make my grand entrance.

I stood in the bathroom mirror, checking my appearance. My pale auburn hair waved around my face, and the brown liner I'd placed on my lash line to frame my eyes was still intact. I reached into the inside pocket of my blazer, pulled out a red lipliner and placed it straight back. The objective of my look was desirable, not desperate. Instead, I applied a layer of rosebud liner on my lip line. I could have placed it outside like Charlotte did to make her thin lips look fuller, but anyone with a sharp pair of eyes would be able to see the fakery. I couldn't give the girls any ammunition against me.

The burner phone in my inside pocket vibrated. It was a text from Jackie, asking if I was in place. I texted back to say I would soon meet my classmates at lunch. Her next text was a demand for a story, and I slipped the phone back into my blazer. It had taken them weeks to get me back into the academy. Surely, she didn't want immediate results?

The lunch bell rang. I stayed in my room, calculating the amount of time it would take for a person to pack their things, walk across the campus, and settle into the dining room. After brushing down my uniform to remove any traces of lint and checking my teeth for signs of breakfast, I left the room and took the long walk down the stairs, across the hallway, and to the dining room.

My feet froze at the doorway. I had forgotten the majestic, triple-height windows, the mahogany-paneled walls, and the paintings of the king and the armored knight. Blake, Edward, and Henry sat in their usual seats at the head table like kings. Wendy and Patricia sat at Blake's end and Charlotte perched on the right next to Henry. A breath caught in my throat, combining shock and awe and outrage.

My stomach hardened. I could do this. Face the people who had treated me like the kind of disgrace to be tarred and feathered. I stepped inside, keeping my chin high.

A hush fell across the dining room, and every face turned to me. Apart from the faces I wanted. Edward glanced up from his meal to see what had caused everyone to fall silent. Our eyes locked for a millisecond, then he continued eating, not showing an ounce of anger or curiosity.

My throat dried. I could only describe his expression as indifference.

Henry stared straight through me as though he'd found the coat of arms over the door more fascinating than the girl he'd spent nine days in a dingy room. Part of me wanted to storm over and demand to know what he'd done with the five-hundred thousand dollars he'd scammed out of his parents, but I held back. If the boys had framed me for calling the police with a description of the kidnappers, what would they do if I announced their secret in front of the entire dining room? The memory of Edward upturning the table made me wince.

Not even Blake spared me a glance. He was pretending to be fascinated by Wendy's knuckles and placed kisses on each of them, making her giggle.

My shoulders drooped, and I trudged to my usual table. Rita wasn't there. Had she returned to eating sandwiches in her room? I hoped she'd deepened her friendship with the other scholarship students. The sweet girl deserved a break.

"Hobson?" said a voice. "Come and sit with us."

Alice, one of Charlotte's doppelgängers, sat with the scrawny boy with the thick glasses who had rejected me on my first day. With another sweep of the surrounding tables to check for signs of Rita, I crossed the room, hoping this wasn't a trick. A few people turned back to their meals, but most tracked my movement across the dining room. Nobody hissed insults as I passed, and I wondered if that was related to all the sightings of me on Sergei's arm at various functions.

"It's good to see you looking so well." Alice's face split into a wide smile. "Won't you join Duncan and me?"

I raised my brows at the bespectacled boy, hoping he would remember how he had refused to let me sit with him, claiming that there were no seats for Yanks. He cast a nervous glance at the head table, then nodded and stared into his bowl of tomato soup.

"Thanks," I replied. "Did I miss anything while I was gone?"

Alice glared at the head table. "When you left, the boys invited us back to their table, and after dinner, Edward asked me back to his room. I gave him an ultimatum. Patricia or me." Her gaze dropped down to the bread on her side-plate. "He chose Patricia."

I sat. "That might not necessarily be a bad thing."

Duncan's head snapped up, making his thick glasses bounce on the bridge of his nose. "That's what I keep telling her," he said in an accent so thick and posh, I had to strain to listen. "Those toss-pots aren't worth the effort."

I gave him a hard look. "Yet you told me Yanks weren't welcome at your table."

"That was before I knew what you were like. You're not nearly as bad as everyone said."

"Thanks," I muttered.

Alice nodded. "I was with Edward on and off for two years before he discarded me. All because I couldn't share him any longer with my best friend."

The server took my order and returned shortly after with a plate of asparagus and grilled trout. I glanced at Alice, whose features looked different. She wore her hair on her face instead of the usual ponytail, and her shoulders were no longer pushed back to emulate Charlotte's ample chest. Maybe she did have a grudge against the triumvirate and the doppelgängers. It was hard to tell.

"Have you seen Bourneville?" asked Duncan. "I used to think he was a decent sort, but now he's flashing his cash like a used car salesman. Underwood is milking him for what he's worth."

I swallowed hard. Now that Henry had nearly half a million pounds of spending money, he could afford to date a gold digger like Charlotte.

Alice leaned forward and fluttered her eyelashes. "I've read every society column about you. What's Sergei Bachmann like? Does he have any single musician friends?"

My lips curled into a smile. Alice really was outcast, and she'd only invited me to use as a stepping stone to a more glamorous life. She had been part of the group who had organized that terrible gauntlet, and the least I could do was use her to exact my revenge.

"He does, but none are as handsome as Sergei," I replied. "Sergei been invited to play at a singles party next month. I'll see if he can wrangle you an invitation."

Her eyes lit up. "If you can invite a few others, you'll be even more popular than Charlotte."

CHAPTER 4

Classes continued as usual, except that the triumvirate sat with each other or with Charlotte and the doppelgängers, and I sat alone, just as I had before the kidnapping. I'd thought that Blake, the usually flirtatious member of the trio, would break ranks and approach me, but even he acted as though I didn't exist. Occasionally in the hallway, someone from one of the lower years would mutter a half-hearted 'trollop' as I passed, but the new version of myself followed after them to demand they repeat their insult and to explain what I'd done to warrant it. Their pasty faces would turn pink, they would stammer, and they would scurry out of sight like cowards.

Despite Rita's entreaties to keep a low profile, I continued my regime of hair and subtle makeup and walked around the campus with my head high and my posture straight. Increasing amounts of students would greet me in the hallways, which was a welcome start. Alice explained that being in the British society pages made me an international celebrity rather than a common Yank, whatever that meant.

One Friday in English Lit, I felt the burn of someone's stare on the side of my face. Without making it too obvious, I turned my head a fraction and found Henry looking at me. Perhaps he was the weakest link. We had become close during our supposed captivity with the stoners. Maybe he felt bad about framing me for his own crime.

Miss Oakley told us to get into pairs, and Henry twisted in his seat, head turned to me. I held my breath, waiting for him to call out my name.

Someone knocked on the door, and a fifth-year prefect who wore her hair in a long braid like Rita's stepped inside. "Emilia Hobson has a visitor at reception."

My eyes widened. "Who?"

"It's something about a press conference." She swept her braid over her shoulder and left.

Whispers sussurated through the room like a sudden wind. I swallowed. Was this something Jackie had set up without telling me? I'd been back at the academy for a week and still hadn't produced anything she could use in her paper.

Miss Oakley clasped her hands to her chest. "You'd better go, Miss Hobson. It could be your handsome prince."

Suppressing the urge to roll my eyes, I stuffed my books into my satchel. Ever since Charlotte had implied I was some kind of slut for pay, the old woman slipped references to Cinderella and Pretty Woman into our every conversation. The annoying part was that she wasn't malicious, just a little addled.

I followed the prefect out of the room, down the hallway and into the reception area. It was empty. "Where's this press conference?"

"He said he'd be waiting for you outside."

"He?"

"Foreign fellow." The prefect headed back into her classroom.

I stepped through the double doors of the main teaching block, squinting against the cold rush of wind and expecting to see

Rudolph's limo, but it was Sergei, sitting in a red sports car. A bolt of excitement shot through my heart, and I rushed down the stone stairs to the passenger side. "What are you doing here?"

He grinned. "Jackie said you were lonely in school, so I thought I would come and see you and create a little publicity for myself."

"Where are Andreo and the others?" I glanced down the empty, forest-lined driveway.

"Not far behind." He leaned across the passenger seat and opened the door.

When I scooted inside and got myself settled into the warm, leather seat, Sergei held out a box and flipped open its lid. "Do not be excited. It's just a simulant."

I gaped at a solitaire encased in burgundy velvet. "Should I put it on?"

"There are people watching." He jerked his head toward the entrance of the academy, where a few stray students stood outside the doors. "It will give them something to report back to their friends." He pulled the ring out of its casing, slipped it on my finger and pressed his lips to my knuckles.

I smirked and fastened my seatbelt. Someone had likely recorded that for the Mercia-Net.

With a roar of the engine that made the onlookers jump, Sergei sped down the driveway and through the gates, where he slowed to take in the expanse of frost-covered fields. He tutted. "Why would a girl like you go to school so far from London? Do you ever feel trapped?"

"My stepfather sent me here." I swept my fingertips over the leather armrest and glanced through the tinted window at a herd of sheep huddled together against the cold. "He just wanted me out of the way to get all my mom's attention."

"A possessive man."

"Yeah. Controlling, too."

Sergei slowed to a stop outside the village tea shop, which was already swarming with paparazzi. "Whatever happened with those boys from your school?"

"They're ignoring me." I unbuckled my seatbelt.

"They are playing games." He stepped out of the car, walked around its hood, and helped me out.

A gust of cold wind hit me in the face, and a riot of camera flashes filled my ears, their flares of light making me blink. No matter how much I thought I'd gotten used to the paparazzi, their presence en masse was always disconcerting.

I turned to Sergei in an attempt to save my vision. "Did anything happen recently? You don't usually get so many following you around."

"The inquest into my Father's death was published today." He laced his fingers through mine and guided me across the road. "It concluded that he was poisoned."

My stomach dropped. "I'm so sorry. You must be devastated."

He shook his head and opened the door to the tea shop. "Father was more like a teacher than a parent." The scent of freshly baked cakes engulfed us, and we stepped inside, where four of his bodyguards sat at tables with empty cups. Behind us, a car door opened, and Andreo stepped in behind us, looking bored.

"Sergei!" shouted a reporter. "What do you think of today's inquest?"

He raised a hand. "I refuse to answer questions on that subject."

"Sergei!" shouted a reporter. "What brings you to Mercia county?"

He gestured at me. "Emilia returned to school, and I wanted to see her."

All the female reporters cooed at that comment, and I forced a wide smile for the camera. A disgruntled old lady brought a pot of tea and two cups the bodyguards must have ordered, and I sent her an apologetic smile. Although the reporters had also ordered tea, they were still disturbing the peace of her establishment.

"Emilia," shouted a reporter I recognized from the Saturday Correspondent. "Is that an engagement ring?"

Panic burst through my chest, and my mouth dried. Whatever I said next could either help or hinder my mission. I turned to Sergei. "You tell them."

He gave the reporters an enigmatic smile. "We are not ready to make any official announcements."

The reporters continued their barrage of questions, while Sergei poured us each a cup of tea. He redirected the conversation to his plans to conquer the classical music circuit in Europe and made a few diplomatic comments about other classical pianists.

Throughout the conversation, Mr. Carbuncle pushed his way through the crowd and walked up to the counter. The old woman gave him a box, presumably containing cake, but the janitor leaned on the counter, listening to the rest of the press conference, his oversized mustache twitching with disapproval. Disgust rippled through my belly at the sight of the man, but I forced a smile so wide, my cheeks ached.

∽

The next morning at breakfast, I walked to the table I shared with Alice and Duncan. Rita had awoken early to spend time with the upper-sixth year boy from Hawthorne House who she'd befriended the previous term. I was pleased for her, and suspected she kept her distance to avoid being caught up in the shit storm I would create when I finally enacted my revenge.

As soon as I sat, one of the girls jogged over with their smartphone open to a digital copy of the Saturday Correspondent. "Hobson, it's saying here that you're engaged to Sergei Bachmann. Is that true?"

"What?" I pulled out my own smartphone. "Let me see."

The reporter I'd met the day before had written a piece saying we were engaged but being tight-lipped about making an announcement. She had even managed to take a picture of the ring on my finger.

Alice gasped and grabbed my wrist. "How many carats is that?"

I slipped my hand under the table. "I didn't ask."

While I ate my cooked breakfast, people from other tables passed by to gape at the ring. Anxiety surged through my belly. If anyone knew about jewelry, they might work out the diamond was a fake.

"We're playing Hawthorn House today at rugby," said Alice. "Everyone's going to give their support. Want to come with us?"

"Umm..." I stared down at my plate. The last thing I wanted to see was Henry running about a field half-dressed. But with everyone out of the house, it would be a perfect opportunity to plant some cameras. I'd placed a few in the common room after lights-out, but Jackie had complained that they hadn't been positioned well enough to get any decent footage. I glanced up at Alice's face. "Actually, I need to stay behind to catch up on my prep."

After Saturday classes, I headed for the common room. The triumvirate preferred to hold court at the leather sofas closest to the fire. I lifted the camera I'd placed next to the clock on the mantle and glanced around for a better vantage point. If I could screw the device to the wall and tilt it downward, I'd get an amazing view of whoever sat on the sofa. I glanced at the sash window on the right. Any of the sills might work if nobody tried to open it.

The door clicked open, and Blake sauntered in with his hands in his pockets, looking like he was strolling into a yacht. His black hair hung about his temples, making his chocolate brown eyes stand out. He wore a shirt closely fitted to show off the contours of his chest, unbuttoned to the sternum to offer tantalizing glimpses of tanned skin. My heart stopped, and I stuffed the camera in the pocket of my denim jacket.

"You're not fooling anyone." He sauntered over with a lazy half smile.

I sucked in a breath through tightening lungs and backed away. Jackie's idea for me to install the cameras had been a horrible idea. Students hardly got the opportunity to tamper with walls unmolested, as there was always someone hanging about and asking awkward questions.

I headed through a row of sofas toward the door on the far side of the common room. "I don't know what you're talking about."

Blake caught up in a few long strides. "You're not over us. I can tell by the way you stare."

Relief lightened the tight hand of panic around my lungs. He hadn't noticed the cameras, after all. I exhaled a long breath before the offense in his words reached me with a hard slap. I stopped walking and turned around. "What the hell are you talking about?"

He advanced on me, arrogant smirk in full force. It was the kind of lazy, confident smile a guy made when he already knew a girl was hot for him, and he was just waiting to hear her say the words. "You want a relationship with the three of us, but you don't know how to get on your hands and knees to grovel."

"Are you smoking crack, or do you usually hallucinate that people are looking at you? I shoved the door open and rushed through the hallway.

Blake overtook me and stood on the first steps of the staircase, blocking my way. "Why did you return if it wasn't to rekindle our old flame?"

I made a one-hundred-and-eighty-degree turn and stormed through the reception hallway, out of the double doors and into the cold morning. Blake followed after me, keeping up with my fast strides. I shot him a filthy glare. "If you must know, my stepfather gave me the choice of Mercia or military school. But now you're making me think I made the wrong decision."

The wind blew over the lawn that stretched between Elder

House and the other buildings, and I sucked in a deep breath of bracing air. Although I was glad that Blake hadn't caught me with the camera, a pit of hatred opened up in my belly. He had only made the insulting overtures because he'd heard about the report of my supposed engagement. Now, he and the triumvirate would do anything to sabotage my fake progress with Sergei.

"I think you're lying," said Blake.

At the far left of the campus stood the academy tuck shop, a cafe that served hot and cold snacks. Wrapping my arms around my middle to protect from the cold, I headed left.

Blake kept up with my steps, staring into my face as though he had a right to question me about my relationship choices. "It's true, isn't it?"

I kept my eyes on the small building at the end of the gravel walkway. "Believe what you want, but I'm not here for you. Things are going well with Sergei, and I'm happy."

He stopped. "Are you?"

"Am I what?" I glared at him over my shoulder.

"Happy."

I rolled my eyes and continued walking. Predictably, he followed after me. A glow of triumph warmed my insides. Whoever had the idea to publish details of a fake engagement was a genius. The triumvirate were so malevolent, they were moving in to sabotage my happiness by sending Blake over to make a flirty overture.

"That evening in the new house, when it was you and Henry and me," Blake's voice became low and seductive. "Don't tell me you didn't enjoy it, because you did. It was the hottest night of your life, and you know it."

"I drank too much champagne that day," I inspected my nails. "It's all one blur, now."

"Liar. I'll bet you think about it all the time." His smoky voice curled around my eardrums, making my spine tingle. "I imagine you relive that experience every time you touch yourself. I know that's my go-to fantasy."

"You're disgusting," I spat.

"But you like it." Blake stepped in front of me, blocking my path. "I don't care if Sergei Bachmann has the fingers of a pianist. He has only two hands, and we have six. Do you know what else you can get from three men?"

"Two extra people to betray you when you try to help." I shoved him aside and continued toward the tuck shop.

A group of passing third-year girls giggled and scurried away. I stared after them, envying their simple lives.

Blake raised his palms. "That business had nothing to do with me."

"Are you throwing Henry under the bus, now?" I picked up my pace, feet stamping on the gravel.

"Throwing?" He shook his head and continued after me. "Why take second best when you can have us?"

I flared my nostrils and twisted my features to look hurt and offended. It wasn't a stretch, because they really had hurt me. The triumvirate had only cared about themselves and had used me as their sacrificial lamb. If it wasn't for my revenge plan, I would never have returned.

"What the fuck do you want?" I asked.

"We'll take you back into the fold."

I stopped, eyes wide. "What?"

Blake was no longer smirking. "But you'll have to break things off with the pianist."

Loud techno music boomed out of a building on our right. While it was of a similar architectural style of Elder House, wet laundry and plastic bags containing groceries hung out of the windows. It was as if this particular house didn't have a master or anyone tasked to keep the students under control. "What is this place?"

"International House."

"Are they celebrating something?" I eyed a scruffy young man who stared out of a ground floor window. He was probably a janitor.

Blake stuffed his hands into his jeans pockets and shrugged. "It's been like this ever since they occupied the building."

"I didn't notice them last term."

"That's because they only joined the academy in January."

My brows furrowed. Why would bullies target people doing their best to fit in, like Rita and me, and not rise up against those who turned the campus into an eyesore? If I had hung wet laundry out of the window, a mob would bay for my blood, but these students showed no respect for their building.

"Who are they?" I asked.

"That's a question best left unanswered." Blake turned around and strolled back toward Elder house.

I bit down on the inside of my cheek. This was certainly a subject I would raise with Jackie. If Rudolph was looking for an angle to avenge himself on the headmaster, there might be something in International House that could bring down the school.

CHAPTER 5

I sat in the tuck shop, nursing a cup of coffee. Blake's offer left me with a mix of conflicting feelings. The triumph of finally getting their attention was overshadowed by disgust. He'd only approached me after learning that Sergei had proposed. The usual anger that stuck in my craw whenever I thought of the triumvirate rose, and I tried to push it down when the server gave me a funny look for scowling into my teacup. I focused instead on making my plan come together.

To break the triumvirate, I needed to do it from the inside. But the invitation left a taste in my mouth more bitter than the coffee. I added a spoon of sugar to my drink and took another sip.

A couple of third years entered the shop, and the boy asked the girl what he could get her to drink. From the blush that rose on both their cheeks and her nervous answer, I guessed they were on a first date. Despite the fact the two had probably called me trollop at some time, I hoped things would work out okay for them. They certainly seemed happy with each other as they sat at a table towards the back of the room. But looks could be deceiving.

The triumvirate were a trojan horse, dressed up in ribbons and pretty promises but inside was a trio of boys who would stick the knife through my back. Again. They sought to take away what they thought was a promising relationship and leave me distraught, just as I had been last term.

∼

The next day, I took a stroll through the campus and headed toward International House. On the flowerbeds outside the building grew a clump of snowdrops through the frost, and I pulled out my cameraphone to take a picture.

"Look who it is," said a nasal voice. "The trollop."

I glared up. Edward and Patricia stood over me. My face twisted into a mask of annoyance. "What do you want?"

"To welcome you back to Mercia Academy, of course." Patricia wrapped both arms around Edward's bicep. "We should arrange a welcoming party. It's only fair, after all the effort we went to send her off."

My throat thickened, and I met Edward's wintry blue eyes. He stared down his perfect, straight nose at me, lips thinned into a grim line. Mahogany hair hung loose around his face, softening his stern features. Wasn't framing me for the kidnapping enough for him? All this time, I'd thought Charlotte had arranged the gauntlet with Mr. Carbuncle.

Edward's brows lowered into a scowl. "That was not my doing."

"No, but you didn't object," Patricia murmured.

He pulled his arm out of her grasp and stepped away. "Nobody could have guessed you would take your spite so far."

I straightened and placed the smartphone back in my pocket. Facing Edward like this was bad enough, but hearing this poor excuse for a doppelgänger brag about humiliating me was more than I could stand. "Excuse me, while I get some fresh air."

Patricia spluttered. "We're outside, you trollop. Are you trying to say I stink? Because there's only one person around here who—"

"You're tiresome," Edward snapped.

She reared back. "What?"

I continued toward International House, leaving them to argue amongst themselves. If Edward wanted to approach me, he could do so without a bitchy sycophant hanging off his arm like an overgrown leech. My feet skidded over the frost, so I slowed my steps, making sure to study the building that had fallen to disrepute. The strains of a cheesy techno tune drowned out Patricia's screechy voice, but it was clear from the pitch that she was unhappy about whatever he'd said to her.

"Emilia!" said Edward from several feet away.

I stopped and gazed into a window, where a group of smoking students sat in a room, watching television. "What?"

"I wanted to apologize for Patricia," he said.

"For what she said to me, the little send-off she organized last term, or her entire existence?"

His sapphire blue eyes twinkled, and his full lips quirked into a smile. "All of it, really."

"I find that hard to believe, since she's your girlfriend."

"Was." He shook his head. "It was never serious between us. She was just…"

"Convenient?" I placed my hands on my hips.

He turned his head. "I wouldn't put it quite so callously." After a moment's pause, he said, "Have you made your decision yet about what Blake proposed?"

"The answer is no." I headed back toward Elder House, stomping so hard, the ice crushed beneath my loafers. "I'm happy with Sergei. A musician who earns money from playing the piano isn't likely to frame me for his crimes."

Edward walked at my side with a silence that stretched so long, it made my stomach writhe with nerves. Tiny shards of ice blew in the wind, freezing the top layer of my skin. If I agreed to go back to them so quickly, they would be suspicious. I had to put up some resistance for them to overcome, so it would feel like they had the upper hand.

"Are you sure about this fellow?" he said at last. "What do you really know about him?"

"He's talented, handsome, and has a good heart. That's more than I can say about some of the men around here." I dodged a falling cigarette butt thrown by someone out of an open window.

Edward acted as though I hadn't replied. "I'm concerned you're jumping into a relationship before you're ready."

"Really," I drawled. "You said the same thing last term, and look where that got me."

I could have sworn he snorted a laugh, but the sound was over so quickly, I missed it. Not that it mattered. Edward and Blake were both full of shit and just wanted to break up my fake relationship, toy with me for a few weeks, before getting me expelled again and thrown out in disgrace.

At last, we reached Elder House, and I climbed the stone steps leading to its double doors. As soon as I stepped into the reception hall, the warm scent of burning pine engulfed my senses, making me inhale the sweet air. I turned to Edward. "Thanks for the unsolicited escort. While I enjoy a good stalking as much as the next girl, I can handle the rest of the journey from here."

"Actually, I have something to show you." He swept his arm toward the common room at the end of the corridor. "It's this way."

My heart pounded hard against my ribcage. Had he found the cameras I'd hidden in my bag of sanitary pads? A shuddering breath escaped my lungs. Blake hadn't mentioned catching me with recording devices, but he wasn't the type to broadcast his schemes. My gaze darted to the staircase, but running away would only postpone the problem. I followed him down the hallway and swallowed hard. But instead of going straight on when we passed Mr. Jenkins' office, he turned right and opened a door.

"What's this?"

The door led to a study with burgundy, Chesterfield sofas and a huge, mahogany desk topped with leather. Logs burned and crackled in the fireplace, filling the room with heat. Blake and Henry strode toward us from different sides of the room, each wearing lightweight shirts, open at the neck. My throat dried. Was this an ambush?

Edward placed his hand on the small of my back and guided me through the threshold of the study, letting the door click shut behind him.

I scowled. "What are you doing?"

Henry strode toward me and placed both hands on my shoulders. "I'm sorry for what happened last term. You were only trying to help."

"I told you to tell her everything." Blake said without inflection. Perhaps this was the expression he used when rehearsing a line.

"We've fought about this countless times," added Edward with an exaggerated frown. "Let's focus on making up with Emilia."

I bit down hard on the inside of my cheek. This sounded so scripted. They probably had a game plan for building up my trust and then shattering my spirits with a betrayal even greater than the one they had dished out in the previous term.

"We shouldn't keep arguing," Henry said to Edward. He turned to me, green eyes shining with earnestness. "Nothing has been right between the three of us since the headmaster locked you up."

"Right..." I would have laughed at his pathetic attempt to blame someone else for his actions if this new attempt to double-cross me again wasn't so transparent.

Blake stepped forward, his gaze lingering on my breasts. "Is there anything we can say... Anything we can do to convince you we're sorry?"

"Anything." Edward stepped closer, meeting my eyes.

Henry advanced on me, his gaze locked on my lips. "Anything."

The atmosphere in the room took on a charge that made the fine hairs on the back of my neck stand on edge and made the pulse between my legs twitch. I knew an indecent proposal when I heard one, and the triumvirate seemed willing to perform any act to prove their sincerity.

Squeezing together my trembling legs, I pointed at the Persian rug. "The three of you can go down on your knees."

When Edward turned away and walked to the window, I asked, "What are you doing?"

"Securing a level of privacy." He flashed me a smile over his shoulder. "If you want us to grovel, we will. But first, I'll shut the curtains."

Henry got down on his knees in front of me, and Blake knelt beside him. The pair stared up at me with wide-eyed, furrowed brows, and pleading expressions designed to melt a girl's heart. Blake shuffled forward, making me back into an armchair. "Would you like to sit and make yourself comfortable?"

I lowered myself into the leather seat and pointed out my loafer. "Kiss my feet."

Blake grinned and cradled my right ankle in his hands. The movement sent a jolt of pleasure up my leg. He slipped off my loafer and stared down at my stockinged foot. "How can I carry out my penance when you're all covered up?"

A tingle meandered up my spine. "Y-you don't have to."

"I insist," he said, voice husky.

Henry took my other leg, slipped off my shoe, placed my foot on his thigh, and swiped both hands from my toes to my ankles. His strong fingers caressed my flesh, making my insides squirm pleasantly, and memories of the night he had massaged my belly resurfaced. "You're stiff," he murmured. "Allow us to ease your tension."

I bit down hard on my lip and groaned. This is the point where I should tell them to go to hell and stop trying to take control, but this was how I would get them to trust me so I could learn enough of their secrets to bury them. I had to make it seem like they were manipulating me. Sensations rippled up my legs from their touches, and I clenched my core muscles and huffed out a breath.

The triumvirate had worked out a weakness I didn't even know I had. Having them both at my feet, both attentive and ready to give me pleasure made the pulse between my legs pound with need.

"Will you let me take off those tights?" asked Blake.

"Oh!" I panted. This wasn't fair. With a few deft movements, they'd broken through my defenses. The worst part was that they were doing exactly what I'd asked. I lifted my hips off the leather armchair and eased my thick tights down to the tops my thighs.

Blake chuckled, the sound low and deep. "Now, may we atone?"

Henry grinned. "Let us."

When I gave them the tiniest of nods, each took their time in pulling down my tights. Henry caressed each inch of flesh he exposed, while Blake kissed it. Edward pulled the last set of curtains closed, plunging the room into semi-darkness. Any inhibitions I had evaporated, and my muscles turned to mush.

While Henry worshipped my left foot with his fingers and thumbs, Blake kissed and nibbled and licked a path from my toes, past my ankle, and up my calves.

Pleasure trickled up my thighs and gathered between my legs, making me bite down on my lip to suppress a groan. This wasn't the reunion I'd expected, but I couldn't complain.

With strong, firm fingers, Edward kneaded the stiff knots out of my shoulders, making my head loll to one side. I closed my eyes, marveling at the attention of the three males. Henry's mouth engulfed my toes, and the low, ecstatic groans he made as he sucked them caused the muscles of my core to ripple. Blake wedged my leg open and lapped at a sensitive spot in the corner of my knee. His heavy breathing, in synch with my own panting breaths, broadcasted his arousal.

"See how good it can be with three men?" Edward murmured into my ear. He sucked my lobe between his lips, making me gasp. I didn't even know my ears could be that sensitive. "We can take your body places you never thought possible."

Blake's kisses traveled up my thighs, each promising the most intense pleasure if I parted my legs wide enough to let him reach the top. I squeezed my legs together, trapping his head. I might be enjoying myself, but I wouldn't lose control… yet.

"Let me in." Blake's voice was muffled.

Edward's hands slipped over the fabric covering my breasts, and he circled my nipples with the tips of his fingers. Little lightning bolts of pleasure sparked and added to the sensations building in my aching core.

"Relax, Emilia," he said in that low, commanding voice. "Let us give you what you need."

Henry drew back, releasing my toe from his mouth with a pop, then ran his tongue along the arch of my foot, setting every nerve ending alight.

"Oh!" My back arched, and my legs splayed out. That had been… intense.

Blake's head reached the juncture of my thighs, and he mouthed at my panties.

A breath caught in the back of my throat. "W-what are you doing?"

His low chuckle reverberated against my flesh. "Do I need to spell it out?"

My tongue darted out to wet my bottom lip.

He hooked his hand under both thighs and spread them further apart. "Permission to remove these pesky knickers."

"N-no." I regretted the words the moment I said them.

"Then you won't object to me pulling them to one side," he said, voice smug.

I bucked my hips in reply.

Blake mouthed at the fabric, applying the smallest amount of pressure against my throbbing nub. A frustrated groan resounded in the back of my throat, making him chuckle. "Impatient? I like that in a woman."

"Get on with it, or we'll swap places," snapped Henry.

Blake pulled my panties to the side, and a gust of air hit my wet folds. "Oh fuck," he moaned. "She's just as beautiful on the inside as she is on the outside."

A laugh huffed out from my throat. "Th-that phrase refers to personality."

"Not the way I use it." He moved in with a slow, sensual slide of his tongue that traveled up from my core to my throbbing bundle of nerves.

I cried out and shuddered under his ministrations. Blake showed no mercy and continued those wonderful, dizzying licks. Heat and moisture gathered in my core, which ached and twitched and throbbed. I'd never had sex before, but I had used toys, and right now, I needed to be filled.

Edward placed a fingertip on my lips and with his other hand, gave my nipple an admonishing squeeze. "We're next door to the common room. If you scream the house down, you'll have everyone at our door."

With a whimper, I nodded.

Henry rubbed a finger along my wet folds. I bucked my hips as he skimmed my core, and he slid it inside. Sparks of pleasure pulsed out from where his digit pushed and stretched my inner muscles. Then he slipped in another finger, and my mouth opened in a silent scream.

Blake quickened his licks into rapid flicks that made my eyes roll to the back of my head. What the hell were these three doing to me?

At that moment, with Henry pumping his fingers in and out of me, Edward tweaking and teasing my nipples to the point of distraction, and Blake torturing me with that clever tongue, I couldn't think about my plans, couldn't think of resentment or revenge. The triumvirate had me writhing like a trollop, suspended in pleasure on the leather armchair.

Ecstasy built and built until I thought my insides would implode. My mind blanked, and I became a sensitive ball of need, shaking, gasping and keening at their command. Blake continued the relentless lapping, making the muscles of my core clamp around Henry's finger in anticipation of an explosive climax.

Then he stopped.

My eyes flew open and I stared down at his smirking face, eyes wide with disbelief. "What?"

"Will you come back to us?" Blake's breath puffed against my quivering flesh.

I clenched my teeth. "Why?"

"What?" asked Henry.

"Why do you want me back?" I pressed my lips together and let out a shaky breath.

"We told you in the back of the limo that time we took you shopping." Henry slid another thick finger inside me, making my eyes roll to the back of my head. "We all want you equally, and we're going to share."

Edward sucked on the side of my neck. His fingers circled my nipples over my shirt. "It's just as I explained as you left the academy. We were serious about you becoming our fourth," he whispered. "Say yes, and they'll let you come."

I scrunched every muscle in my face and shook my head. They wouldn't get me so easily. Why had they framed someone they wanted so much? I was about to speak, but Henry scissored his thick fingers, making me clutch the leather of the Chesterfield.

Blake blew on my wet folds, and I gasped. Sweat beaded at my brow, and my breath came in panting, shuddering breaths. This was more than I could bear. No one had ever teased me so mercilessly. Blake held me at that knife-edge of pleasure and frustration with the gentlest of caresses, giving me the barest amount of sensation to stoke the flames of my desire but not enough to give me that sweet relief.

Sweat poured down my brow, and I squeezed around Henry's thick fingers and bucked my hips, trying to create some friction.

Henry placed a heavy hand on my pelvis, pinning me in place. "No cheating. Either Blake finishes you, or you continue to whimper."

"Well?" Edward pinched a nipple, and pulses of electricity shot down to my core. "Will you come back to us?"

"N-n-not until I find out why—"

Blake drew back, and I cried out with frustration.

"It's a simple decision," he said from between my legs. "Say yes. Say you forgive us, and come back."

I clamped down hard on Henry's fingers. If they were withholding my orgasm, I would do it on my own.

"She's trying to cheat again," said Henry. "I'd better slide my fingers out."

"N-no!" I couldn't stand more loss of contact. "I-I forgive you."

"That's all we wanted to hear," murmured Edward.

Blake repositioned himself between my legs and lapped at my sensitive nub with extra vigor. Henry pumped his fingers in and out of my aching core. Edward slipped his fingers under my sweater, into my bra and toyed with my nipples. I lay back on that armchair, eyes closed, submitting to the sensations. This time, when the pressure reached a feverish pitch, they continued pleasuring me until I splintered.

Just before I could cry out, Edward clamped his lips on mine and swallowed my scream. He explored my mouth with deep strokes, while I bucked and shuddered on the leather armchair. When my spasms ebbed to gentle ripples and my breathing calmed, he drew back.

"You're back in the fold," said Edward. "Any regrets?"

I shook my head.

Blake nipped at my inner thigh. "If there's anything you need. A friendly word. A hug. A pleasuring by the fireplace. We're here."

My throat went dry, and I stared down at Blake and Henry's crotches. Each man sported a huge erection. I swallowed hard. It was one thing to sit like a queen while the three of them pleasured me, but nothing had changed between us. I hadn't forgotten their betrayal, and I still resented them for trying to get between me and Sergei with their dirty tricks.

"W-what do you want from me?" I asked.

Edward squeezed my shoulder. "We'll take care of ourselves," he murmured. "Don't worry about us."

Henry helped me to my feet and held me steady while I slipped on my loafers. "Will you be alright going up the stairs?"

"Y-yes." I stuffed my tights in my pocket and backed toward the door. "Good night."

I hurried out of the room, down the hallway and up the stairs. That had been unbelievable. Now that they thought they'd persuaded me back into their inner circle, I needed to form a plan. The first of the triumvirate I wanted to destroy was Henry, but to do that, I needed to rid myself of the biggest obstacle: Charlotte.

CHAPTER 6

On Monday morning, I sat at the head table between Blake and Edward. Even though Henry's fingers had taken me to ecstasy and back, I still couldn't act like things were perfect between us. To make my deception real, I had to appear to hold on to a little resentment. Only a liar would forgive being abducted for nine days, framed for kidnapping, and the subsequent seven days I'd spent in the basement. As I was buttering my toast, Charlotte stepped into the dining room. She locked gazing with me and turned around, taking Patricia with her.

I narrowed my eyes. Someone as desperate as Charlotte would probably scheme something to match that ghastly goodbye gauntlet to get me out of the way. I had to strike before she could, and to do that, I would need more information on her.

Rita walked into the dining room, took one look at me, and jerked her head away. The tightening of her lips said it all. I was playing with gunpowder and the fall-out would be explosive. I lowered my gaze to my plate of scrambled eggs and smoked salmon and tried not to think about her warning. Even if I wanted to walk away, Rudolph still held the threat of military school over my head, and Jackie had sent a text, asking when I would be able to install all the cameras.

"Problems with Yelverton?" asked Edward.

"We're fine," I replied. "She didn't know we were all friends again."

He stared after her, lips pressed together. Rita settled herself at a table full of the scholarship students who had approached her last term with their theories that I'd been murdered by Henry. I was glad she was able to connect with them, but the hard look in Edward's eyes lined my stomach with dread. Was he so desperate to screw up people's lives that he was looking to rekindle a fresh round of bullying?

"If you act against her, we're finished."

"Of course," he said a little too smoothly. "Although it seems that you might be drifting apart."

"What do you expect her to do?" I picked up a slice of toast from the silver rack. "Sit around waiting for me to spare her a crumb of time between my three boyfriends?"

"I like the sound of that," murmured Blake. "Maybe you can see us tonight and finish what you started last night?"

I patted him on the knee. "Tempting... If only I hadn't missed so much prep and classwork from getting expelled."

Henry made a choking sound and turned his head away. I clamped my lips together to stop them from curling with disdain. He wasn't fooling anyone with that fake display of guilt.

Blake took a large bite of his toast and continued wolfing it down until he muttered something about going to classes early. Then he left. I narrowed my eyes at Edward, who was still staring at the table of scholarship students. What the hell was he planning? He might be thinking of cornering Rita to ask about my motives. But she had told me not to tell her my plans, and I had respected her request and kept our conversations away from the triumvirate.

My first class of the day was Creative Writing. Alice lowered herself into the seat next to mine and hissed, "What do you think you're doing with that wanker?"

"Edward?" I asked.

"Yes. And the other two. They're trouble."

I shrugged. "You saw what happened to me last term when I left. Befriending them is the only way I can survive here."

Alice had the decency to glance away. "T-that wasn't me." She swallowed. "I mean... I knew they would form lines and watch you leave, but I didn't think things would go out of control."

A furnace of resentment burned in my stomach, and I had to reach down and pull my satchel on the table to give myself time to smooth out my expression. Breathing hard to stop my hands from shaking, I asked, "What did you expect from the other students?"

Her tongue darted out to lick her lips. "Like I said, I didn't organize it. That was Charlotte. She's still paying off her debts to Carbuncle for all the work he did behind the scenes."

I was about to ask what she meant when Mr. Weatherford strolled into the room and told everyone to turn to a page in our textbooks and dissect a poem. I tried to focus on my work, but my thoughts kept rocking back to Charlotte. I owed that bitch for the gauntlet. Mr. Carbuncle, too. My hands balled into fists. If there was a way I could prove he was taking cash from students, I would expose him first.

Alice was the key to getting to Charlotte, and I had to be careful not to scare her away. I turned to her and whispered, "Sergei's playing in a concert hall in Sussex. He sent me two tickets. Do you want to come with me?"

Her eyes gleamed. "When?"

"This coming Sunday," I replied.

"I'd love to!"

"Great." I made a mental note to contact Jackie and ask her to authorize the purchase of alcohol. Alice was Charlotte's former friend and could tell me a lot about her father, the current Secretary of State for the Supreme Court.

～

At the end of the week, Jackie sent a limo to pick us up and take us to Sergei's concert. Alice drank copious glasses of champagne and was already tipsy by the time we reached the small, Victorian concert hall. I bought us some drinks and snacks for the show.

Sergei walked onto the stage to a round of applause, dressed in the most elegant tuxedo with a white waistcoat and a white bowtie.

Alice leaned into my side and whispered, "He's so dashing."

I smiled and leaned back in my seat. If only she knew the truth. "Thank you."

She took several sips of champagne before refilling her glass from the bottle I'd left in the ice bucket by our feet.

Sergei played one of his father's concertos, a tumultuous piece that roused my blood. I closed my eyes and surrendered myself to the emotional intensity of his playing. It was as though he was translating my thirst for revenge into music.

During the interval, Alice's eyes drooped, and she let out a pained sigh. "The girls all gather in my room in the evenings, talking loudly about how you've taken away their boys."

"Who do you room with?"

"Wendy. She wasn't even serious with any of them, but she goes along with Charlotte and Patricia just to see me cringe. It's like they don't care that they pushed me out of their group when I gave Edward that ultimatum."

While she poured herself another glass of champagne, I turned on the voice recorder app on my smartphone. "Why do they want Edward and Henry so much?"

Alice raised her brows. "You've seen them, haven't you? They're the hottest guys in the school, and that's counting the upper-sixth years."

"There must be something else," I said. "Charlotte's really into Henry."

She swirled her glass, and I topped it up with champagne. After taking a few delicate sips, she said. "She's after the Bourneville fortune."

"Why's that?"

"Her family is spiraling into debt. Peter—that's Charlotte's older brother—he has a gambling problem, and Mr. Underwood keeps bailing him out. Charlotte's livid about it because she doesn't even know if her father can afford to pay next year's fees." Alice shook her head.

Sergei walked back on the stage to tremendous applause, and I shut off the voice recorder. Alice's story was consistent with what Rita had told me the previous term, but I needed a few more bits of information: the name of the casinos Peter owed, and any hints of illegal behavior on the part of Charlotte's father.

At the end of the concert, we went backstage, and I introduced Sergei to a drunken, star-struck Alice. We took a few publicity photos, then Alice and I headed back to the car.

As she stepped through the doors and out into the cold evening, I pulled my phone out of my coat pocket and turned on the recording app. "It's a bit unfair that these casinos let Charlotte's brother gamble, even though they know he's an addict."

She sipped a can of diet coke. "They've completely ruined the family."

I made a show of pursing my lips. "I'd like to avoid those casinos. Can you remember which ones he visited?"

As the limo pulled out from the front of the concert hall, Alice rattled off a list of names and then added that Mr. Underwood's secretary had resigned due to spending more time negotiating with them than doing government work, leaving Charlotte's father scrambling for a new assistant.

I leaned back into the leather seat and smiled. This had been a very productive evening. The car sped along a seafront road lit by iron street lamps connected by long strings of bright lights that reflected on the surface of the sea. A drunken flush on Alice's face stood out in the reflection of the artificial illumination.

"Hey, if Charlotte's family is in such financial trouble, how can she afford to pay Mr. Carbuncle?"

Alice clapped her hands over her mouth and giggled. "He doesn't take money from girls."

"What does he want from them?" I cracked an eye open as if the answer wasn't obvious.

"He loves going down on them."

I twisted in my seat and gaped at Alice, who gave me a knowing smirk. "With that big, bristly mustache? No!"

"Don't knock it until you've tried it."

My eyes bulged. "You did?"

"Just once. It was after the girls gave me the cold shoulder."

"What did you want?"

She shrugged. "Company, I suppose."

I sucked in a breath. "You need to report him for taking advantage of school girls."

Alice's face hardened, and she reached into the open drinks cabinet for a miniature bottle of vodka and poured its contents into her coke. "He never goes further than fingers and oral, and he doesn't approach us. We approach him."

I clenched my teeth. Even if the girls did instigate these encounters, Mr. Carbuncle was the adult and should have turned them away. "How long has he been offering this… service?"

Alice shrugged. "I'm not sure. All the girls know about him. It's an open secret." She grabbed my arm. "You look angry. Don't get him into trouble. He's a decent sort."

I made a long, theatrical sigh. Alice was still useful for gathering information. There was no point in antagonizing her by letting her know I wanted her precious Mr. Carbuncle fired.

No, I wouldn't report Mr. Carbuncle yet. He had access to all the buildings in the academy and would be well-positioned to put up the cameras with the right motivation. I'd ask Jackie to use the knowledge of his extra-curricular activities to blackmail him into putting up those cameras. Alice's recording and the video of him letting Charlotte into my room would be enough evidence to convince him to work for the paper.

"Wasn't it an ordeal?" I made my voice as perky as I could. "That mustache has to be scratchy."

Alice's eyes sparkled. "Charlotte doesn't think so, and neither do some of the others."

"But it looks like a broom!"

Alice recited a list of girls who had offered themselves to Mr. Carbuncle. A few had just done it for the experience and others had requested favors, such as access to someone else's room. Each name and funny anecdote Alice told me became a nail in the janitor's coffin. He would be a useful person to blame in case anyone suspected me of spying or of passing information onto the Correspondent. Not only would he install those cameras, but I would ask Jackie to transfer small payments to his bank account and send thank you letters every time she published an article related to the academy... Just in case I needed someone to frame if everything went wrong.

I sat back and listened to Alice ramble about the janitor's sexual escapades with a whole host of girls. This was perfect. Not only had I found someone to complete the task of putting up the cameras, but I'd also found a fall guy who deserved to be framed.

Alice fell asleep in the back of the car, and I emailed the recordings to Jackie on my burner phone with my request. She replied immediately, congratulating me on a brilliant idea and saying she'd get someone down to visit Mr. Carbuncle in Mercia county as soon as possible.

When the car pulled into the driveway outside Elder House, I shook Alice awake.

Her eyes fluttered open. "Thanks for a fun evening."

I smiled down at her. "Glad you had a great time. We should do it again."

She opened the door and staggered out of the car. I let out a long, satisfied yawn. That had been a very satisfying evening. I followed her up the stairs and into the building. The reception hall was dark, only lit by the roaring and crackling fire. I stood in front of the mesmerizing sight when a hand grabbed my wrist.

"When will you let Bachmann know?" said Henry.

I pulled out of his grip and folded my arms across my chest. "Have you been waiting here all night for me, just to ask about Sergei?"

He loomed over me, his green eyes unusually stormy. The light of the fire made the ends of his hair glow like sunshine. "You said—"

"You can't expect me to throw away a good man for a foot massage with a happy ending," I hissed.

His face fell. "What about our agreement?"

"I said, I'd consider forgiving you." I prodded Henry in his hard pectoral muscle. "It's going to take a very long time to trust you after what you did."

He bowed his head. "If my father ever discovered I'd swindled the family out of a ransom, I'd be disinherited."

I growled with frustration. Why hadn't I turned on the recorder? That could have been excellent blackmail material. The next time I would bring up the subject, it would be in front of cameras or at least my smartphone's recording app.

"I'm not ready to talk about that yet," I snapped. "Good night."

As I stalked across the reception hall, he murmured, "I regret what I did, now."

"Now?" I stopped by the doorway. "That implies you had no regrets at the time."

He jerked his head back to the fire. "You're twisting my words."

"I'm interpreting them. It's called comprehending English."

"Well, I wasn't thinking straight last term, but I'll make it up to you."

I folded my arms across my chest and glared at him over his shoulder. "I'll need more than just an apology."

His Adam's apple bobbed up and down. "I know."

CHAPTER 7

It was strange. Telling Henry that he'd have to earn my forgiveness had deepened the trust of the triumvirate. The week before, they'd held me at arm's length, but with the realization that it would take a little more time and bonding for me to fully accept them, they accepted me back into the fold and insisted that I sit with them in classes again.

I spent most of my free time catching up on the work I missed in the previous term and using that as an excuse to avoid studying in Edward's office with the others. Their idea of prep was a repeat of what had happened the week before. While it had been the most explosive experience of my life, I had to be careful not to let them distract me. Distraction had been a tactic they had used so I wouldn't work out who had really been behind Henry's supposed kidnapping.

On Monday night, Jackie sent me a text on the burner phone telling me that Mr. Carbuncle had agreed to put up the cameras in exchange for not reporting him to the police. I texted back to ask if whoever she had sent had coerced him to stop his sexual activities with the girls, but Jackie didn't reply. My chest tightened at the implication that they hadn't told him to stop. If I caught him with a girl in his office, I'd have to do something about it.

The following Saturday, just before breakfast, I sat on the edge of my bed and checked the Correspondent's home page and found an animated gif of a young man stumbling out of a casino with the headline: SHAME OF SUPREME COURT SECRETARY OF STATE. A breath whooshed out of my lungs, and I flopped down onto the corner of my bed. That was Charlotte's brother!

"Did you get bad news?" Rita stepped out of the bathroom with a towel over her hair.

"Look." I turned the smartphone around and showed her the screen.

Her eyes widened. "B-but I told you about that."

"Did you tell me which casinos he visited?" I asked.

"No, but—"

"Then don't worry. No one will track that information to you."

She pulled the towel off her head and let her long, dark hair tumble down past her shoulder. "Underwood is going to work out that the leak came from the school."

"Or her father's secretary," I said. "She'll never know you eavesdropped on her conversation."

"Actually, I overheard Patricia telling Alice." She patted her hair dry.

"See? You're off the hook. Don't worry about it."

Rita chewed her lip. "She'll lash out. Everyone thinks her brother is an advisor for the Saudi Royal family. When they discover she was lying, people will ostracize her."

I pushed myself off the bed and headed for the bathroom. "Let her see what it feels like for a change."

∼

Charlotte didn't turn up at breakfast that day, although Patricia and

Wendy sat together in silence, not answering questions from the rest of the house about their friend. Students crowded around Duncan's table, as he had subscriptions for nearly every British newspaper.

I turned to Edward. "What's going on over there?"

"A scandal surrounding Charlotte's brother," said Blake. "Well, it's more focused on their father and how he's selling off his assets to pay his son's gambling debts."

I feigned a gasp. "Is that true?"

He shrugged. "She was always tight-lipped with me about her family."

Edward huffed a laugh. "It's a pity she wasn't tight-lipped in other respects."

Henry snorted his juice, making his friends chortle. I placed my own glass over my lips to hide my disgust at their double standards. Especially Blake, who had recorded Charlotte giving him a blow job and then made it look like I'd been the one who had broadcasted it on the school trip. It had resulted in me waking up in the middle of nowhere, then confronting Henry and getting myself embroiled in a kidnapping plot and subsequent framing.

Charlotte didn't turn up for any of her meals on Saturday, and she was missing at breakfast on Sunday. I hoped she was dining on plastic-wrapped sandwiches, just as the bullies had forced Rita to do until I had found an unoccupied table.

Later, I told the boys I wanted to buy tampons from the school's tuck shop. It was the only way they would leave me alone to walk around the campus. Frost still covered the grounds, but the weather was mild compared to what it would be like in New York.

I strolled over the lawn, admiring the snowdrops and Christmas roses sprouting from the flowerbeds. Mercia Academy would have been a paradise if it hadn't been for Charlotte and the Triumvirate. Most students only bullied to win the favor of the school's kings.

When I dethroned them, maybe the scourge of cruelty and snobbery would vanish.

A loud blast of heavy metal caused me to turn to the direction of International House. A young woman stepped out through the double doors, dabbing a handkerchief to her face. She wore a hooded jacket, a woolen mini skirt, and ankle boots. My gaze swept up and down her long legs. Either they were bare, or she was the queen of selecting perfectly nude pantyhose.

"Are you alright?" I jogged up to her.

She turned to me with doleful eyes. In a thick, Eastern European accent, she asked, "Do you have international phone card?"

I shook my head. "Sorry, no. Try the tuck shop."

Her over-plucked brows creased together. "Tuck?"

"Umm… It's a store that sells snacks and other things. Are you a teacher?" I asked.

"No. I am student of GCSE."

I examined her features. With her heavy makeup, bouffant hair, and crow's feet, there was no way she was fifteen or sixteen, the typical ages of GCSE students. She was at least twenty-five. Although Mom had signed me up for the International Baccalaureate in Park Prep, I knew enough about the British educational system to assume that people her age could go to a less prestigious university as a mature student instead of spending two years getting their GCSEs and then another two just to get their A levels.

"I'm Emilia." I gave her my warmest smile.

"Nadia."

"I'm going to the tuck shop, now. Should we go together?"

Nadia smiled back, and we strolled across the campus to the small building that held both a cafe and a general store. The assistant found a stack of phone cards, and Nadia paid from a wad of cash she kept in an envelope in her purse. I swallowed. Who carried about that much money these days?

We strolled over the path leading back to our houses, our feet crunching gravel underfoot. A cold shock of wind blew through my thick tights, and I glanced at Nadia to see how she was faring with her bare legs. Her face didn't even change expression.

"Aren't you freezing?" I asked.

"England is not so cold compared to the Sakha Republic."

"Where's that?"

Her face fell. "The north-east of Russia."

"What's wrong?" I asked. "Are you homesick?"

Edward approached from the other side of the path, bundled up in a scarf and hat. Even though I couldn't see most of his expression, it was hard to miss his wintry glare. He caught up with us outside International House, where two sets of stereos competed for attention.

"Emilia." His gaze flickered up and down Nadia's form. "You're wanted back in Elder House."

Nadia dipped her head. "Thank you for helping. I feel better now."

I gave her a friendly smile. "You're welcome."

As soon as she was out of earshot, Edward whirled on me. "Don't mix with the students of International House."

Excitement jolted through my chest. If I acted clueless, he might reveal something I could give Jackie. "What's wrong with Nadia?"

His brows furrowed. "If that's your idea of a nice girl, I seriously doubt your judgment."

"Because she's from Russia?"

He reared back. "Of course not. I wouldn't be so prejudiced."

"How do you explain all those Yank taunts you made last year?"

Edward's expression froze. In his little bout of self-aggrandizement, he'd forgotten how everyone had used my nationality as a slur. A wave of genuine anger crashed through my veins as I remembered looking into the mirror and finding words scrawled on my face in blue permanent marker. Then the shower of red dye that had broken my spirit. Even if he hadn't meant to be xenophobic in his warning about International House, I still despised the way he had treated me the previous term.

"How can you say you're not prejudiced when you bullied Rita," I spat. "She isn't what you'd call an English rose."

"Because she was a scholarship student," he replied in a tone that implied it was reasonable to victimized someone for being awarded a place on merit.

My nostrils flared. Did he think I was some kind of idiot? "I've met the other scholarship students, and none of them mentioned being bullied. What made Rita a target when the others weren't?"

He jerked his head away. "You're coming to the wrong conclusions on purpose."

"Don't gaslight me." I tossed my head with as much indignation as I could muster. I'd meant what I had said about him singling Rita and me out for bullying. We were outsiders, and he was a bigot. "You dislike the students of International House because they're not British."

I stormed off back toward Elder House, hoping he would chase after me and explain the reasons for his warnings, but I didn't hold out hope. Edward had one of those patient, calculating personalities. I would have to work on him a little more before finding out why such strange people occupied International House.

~

Days later, Henry leaned into my side in English Lit. "I haven't seen you alone in ages."

I pursed my lips. Whose fault was that? After the kidnapping, I had wanted to continue things as we'd left off, but he had kept a distance romantically, waiting for the opportunity to present itself to share me with his friends. As much as I wanted to spit that, and a few other choice words, into his face, I shrugged. "I've been trying to get my grades up."

"Don't you have the rest of the afternoon free? There's a French restaurant in the village. We could go there for an early dinner. Or I could get a car to take us to London. Then you'd be able to do whatever you like."

My eyes narrowed. Was the London trip a ploy on the part of these manipulative fucks to break up my pretend relationship with Sergei? He'd probably want to take me somewhere prominent, so the paparazzi could take pictures of Sergei's supposed fiancé on the arm of the Bourneville heir.

I placed my hand on his. "The French restaurant sounds lovely."

Henry was about to say something when Miss Oakley gave him a demerit for talking in class. He clammed up and turned his attention to the old lady. I rested my chin on my hand and listened to the rest of the lecture. I couldn't wait to gather information on him to share with Jackie. Of all the triumvirate, he had hurt me the most.

∼

The car stopped on the same stretch of road as the phone box we'd used to call for help after our supposed kidnapping. A pang of sadness hit me as I spotted the red structure. At the time, I had been so relieved to have my freedom, but it also reminded me that the kidnappers had injected me with a drug. Several times.

"Here it is." Henry placed a hand on the small of my back and led me to a store with darkened windows. He opened the door, letting out a waft of garlic-and-rosemary-scented air, and we stepped inside. "You'll love this place."

I gazed around the restaurant, eyes wide. The exposed brick walls, wooden beams, and baskets hanging on the walls gave it a homey, rustic feel, and I couldn't wait to try out the food. "It's so beautiful. Why are we here alone? Blake and Edward would adore this place."

The side of his lips quirked into the kind of smile that used to make my heart melt. Now it made my heart twist with sadness. The triumvirate had probably practiced all their facial expressions on girls over the years. How else could they attract so many hangers-on even when they showed them little interest?

"Jean-Paul and Françoise have been surrogate parents for the three of us. This is the perfect place to start our reconciliation." He guided me to a table close to the kitchens. "Nothing can be right between us until I fix things."

An elderly couple rushed out and both wrapped their arms around Henry.

"Henri," cried the woman. "Je suis heureuse de te voir! Comment ça va?"

He gave them a crooked smile. "Bien, merci. Êtes-vous?"

I shuffled my feet as the conversation in French continued, until the old lady gave me the widest grin and asked, "Et ta nouvelle fille?"

Henry straightened. "Jean-Paul, Françoise, may I present Emilia Hobson."

The old lady stepped close and gave me two kisses on the cheek. As I drew back, she said in a French accent, "We embrace four times in Loire Atlantique."

"Oh." We exchanged two more kisses before she drew back, and her husband gave me four.

Afterward, the couple disappeared into a back room while we looked over the menu.

"What would you like to order?" Henry asked. "The taster menu is sublime."

I raised a shoulder. "Sounds good."

When Jean-Paul returned, Henry proceeded to order for me in fluent French. I propped my chin on the heel of my hand, wondering how many other languages he spoke apart from French and Spanish. Did he speak German as well? I tamped down the giddy feeling of awe rising from my chest. With enough money and enough time, a school could drum any subject in their students. What they couldn't teach them was basic decency.

We stayed in the company of Jean-Paul and Françoise for hours, drinking red wine and eating samples of whatever the old couple brought out from the kitchens. If I hadn't been with Henry, it would have been a wonderful date.

After Henry paid the check, we strolled around the village, enjoying the sight of the quaint, stone buildings and their thatched roofs. The sun had already set, and old-fashioned iron lamps cast the street in warm, orange light. We reached the corner by the red telephone box, and Henry grabbed my hand.

"I can't express how much I regret my actions of last term." His Adam's apple bobbed up and down as he swallowed. "And I can't tell you how lucky I am that you're back."

I let out a long, deep breath and stared at the bridge of his nose. If this was where I was supposed to forgive him and say flattering words about feeling lucky to have three of the most handsome boys in the school, I would stay silent.

"I'm so sorry, Emilia." He threaded his fingers through my hair and gave me a look of such hunger, it made my heart pound in anticipation of a kiss. "Believe me when I tell you, I'll do whatever it takes to earn your forgiveness."

"Why don't you start by explaining who decided to frame me?"

"Pardon?" His brows drew together.

"All three of you were remorseful about getting me into so much trouble. But I still don't completely understand why you would let me take the blame for something I didn't do."

He pressed his lips onto my forehead. "It was never meant to be like this."

My heart skipped several beats. Was he finally going to open up to me? "Go on…"

"If I had known how badly things would end for you, I would never have let you take the blame for their actions."

"The kidnappers?"

He placed his finger on my lips. "Let's not dwell on such unpleasantness. We're sorry, and I'm going to make things up to you. Surely that's all that matters?"

"But—"

He leaned down, pressing soft lips against mine, and engulfing me in his citrus and mint scent. His arms snaked around my back, cradling me to his chest and to the warmth of his large body. The kiss was chaste and undemanding, as if he wasn't sure of my reaction. I sighed into it and wrapped my arms around his neck. Regardless of what he had done, my body couldn't help relaxing in his presence.

"I've wanted to do this for weeks," he murmured against my mouth.

Threading my fingers through his silken hair, I brought his head down for another kiss and parted my lips. Henry's tongue slid against mine, tasting of vanilla and red wine. His hand rubbed circles on the small of my back, reminding me of the last night we had spent together on that mattress.

This was madness. Kissing the guy who had betrayed me so mercilessly. I broke away, breathing hard. Henry leaned forward, pressing kisses on my neck, each one setting my skin aflame.

"H-Henry." I gave him a gentle shove on the chest.

"Sorry." He ran a hand through his hair. "I got carried away. Shall we go back?"

I let out a long, shuddering breath. Hardening my heart against him would be near impossible.

CHAPTER 8

We had Latin the next day, and I pulled out my notebook and worked on my Creative Writing assignment. The class was so advanced, I had no hope of catching up. Blake sat next to me and kept brushing the back of his hand against the side of my arm. I dipped my head, trying to concentrate on my homework, but I couldn't help thinking about that amazing afternoon in Edward's study where they had pleasured me to distraction. He had been right. Six hands were better than two.

"Where were you at breakfast?" Blake leaned close and murmured into my ear, sending shivers down my spine. "I heard about your date with Henry."

From the seat in front, Henry turned around from where he sat next to Edward and smirked.

"Shhh." I placed a finger on my lips.

"He got a date with you. What about me?" He reached under the desk and squeezed my thigh.

I shot him a hard look. Sometimes, it was hard to tell if Blake was the best of the triumvirate or the worst. Whereas Edward and Henry had their motives, Blake did not. Edward was fiercely protective of who attended Mercia Academy, with the strange exception to the people of International House. Henry had wanted to extort money out of his parents for reasons I hadn't yet discovered.

Blake, on the other hand, had never seemed dislike me. Yet he had participated in all of the pranks and had framed me for broadcasting the blowjob video he'd shot of himself and Charlotte. He had conveniently edited out all the incriminating parts where he had promised Charlotte a chance with Henry… and the Bourneville fortune.

Blake turned back to his notebook. I picked up my fountain pen and wrote the first sentence of my Creative Writing assignment. Moments later, his fingertips slid down my inner thigh, sending tingles shooting straight to my core.

I clamped my legs together, trapped his hand, and hissed, "Stop that!"

"Well, it isn't fair," he whispered. "I've been good to you all this time, and I want a date."

My teeth clacked together. Blake could have saved me a world of hurt by giving me a stronger warning not to contact the police. I'd gone to him, worried out of my mind for Henry, and Blake had given me the most unconvincing of reasons why I shouldn't worry about the kidnappers returning to abduct his friend. I held back a growl. It was almost as if he had goaded me into calling the police.

"Emilia…" he whispered into my ear.

Irritation fizzled up my spine. Everything was a joke to Blake. And when he wasn't amused, he would set in motion a shit storm and laugh at everyone scrambling about. My eyes shuttered closed. How many times had Henry snapped at him to stop teasing me? And that time I was locked in the basement, who had delighted in my struggle to work out that I had been framed?

Blake.

Wrapping my hand around his wrist, I pulled it off my thigh. It was time for me to teach Blake a little lesson. "There's no need for a date," I whispered. "You're the easy one."

His gaze hardened. "What do you mean?"

"Hobson!" Mr. Frost threw a piece of chalk at the patch of wall beside my head. It bounced off the surface and smacked me on the temple. "No talking in class."

"It's fine," said Edward. "She's not bothering anyone."

Mr. Frost inclined his head and continued his lecture on a Roman orator called Cicero.

Blake continued trying to wheedle a date out of me, but I didn't reply and kept a closed-lipped smile. My insides warmed with a sick sense of glee. He was an attention whore, and he hated not getting any. I would draw out this teasing for as long as I could before giving in to his demands.

I turned to Mr. Frost. Apart from red hair that thinned at the temples, he appeared to be in his early to mid twenties. Surely, he was too old to be a sycophant? Perhaps he deferred to Edward because the triumvirate had blackmailed him into submission. Even people like our housemaster, Mr. Jenkins, seemed resigned about Edward's rule over the academy, but Mr. Frost was much like Carbuncle, who enjoyed being subservient to the boys.

I wrote down some notes for Creative Writing and peered at the way Mr. Frost singled Edward out for personal attention. At least Carbuncle got the benefit of bribes. Why did Mr. Frost kiss Edward's ass?

After classes, I went to my room to unpack my books. Rita sat at her study desk, working on a musical score. As soon as I stepped inside, her entire back stiffened, then she bowed her head.

I closed the door. "What's wrong?"

"It's nothing," she whispered.

My brows drew together. It had been ages since I'd seen her act so timid. Ever since she had connected with the other scholarship students, Rita had smiled more and now had a friend in another house. This kind of jittery behavior was odd for her. "Rita?"

She twisted in her seat, looking ready to bolt. "Yes?"

"Is someone bothering you again?" Ever since the report on her brother, Charlotte had kept a low profile. I couldn't see her bullying Rita when everyone still gossiped about the Underwood family finances.

"It's nothing." Rita picked up her satchel and placed the scores into its depths. Then she slung it over her shoulder. "Just a few words."

"Who?"

She stood and bowed her head. "If you confront him, it will only get worse."

I stepped in front of her, blocking her path. "It's Edward, isn't it? I caught him giving you a funny look last week and told him to back off."

"It's Simpson-West," she whispered.

"Blake?"

Rita shrugged. "It wasn't much. He cornered me in the hallway and told some younger boys I looked nearly fuckable."

I clenched my teeth. Everything was a game to Blake. I would bet Rudolph's entire net worth that Blake knew I would find out what he had said to Rita. Then I would confront him, and he would demand a date in exchange for leaving her alone. He'd do it in a flirty, smiley way, but that had been his game plan in humiliating Rita.

I placed both hands on her thin shoulders. "I won't confront him directly, but can you hang on for a few more days?"

Her dark eyes widened. "What are you going to do?" Then she squeezed them shut and gave her head a minute shake. "It's best if you don't tell me."

"Trust me. When I've finished with Blake, he won't be in the mood to approach you with harassing comments."

Rita pressed her lips together as though holding back an objection. She probably didn't want me to act against Blake, but what I would do next was for my benefit as much as hers. If Blake craved attention, he would get it, but it might not be of the positive kind.

I let go of Rita's shoulders. "What do you know about Mr. Frost?"

"Not much." She scurried toward the door. "He's an ex-student who came here on a scholarship and went on to study Linguistics at Christ's College."

"Cambridge?"

She nodded. "I'm meeting the other scholarship students for dinner. Will you join us tonight?"

My shoulders drooped. I'd already planned to contact Jackie at the Correspondent in the evening. If I spent too many mealtimes away from the triumvirate, they'd get suspicious. "Another time?"

Rita gave me a sad smile and shrugged.

∾

At dinner, I sat between Edward and Henry, much to Henry's delight. Blake cast me a hurt look. When I raised my brows in question, he glanced away. He was probably too proud to admit to his friends that I wasn't giving him enough attention. It would continue that way until I had exacted my revenge, and I knew exactly how I would do it: by appealing to his sense of pride. I tamped down the tentacles of guilt writhing within my belly. In his own way, Blake was just as dangerous as his friends. He just had the most frivolous of reasons.

As we finished our coffee and after-dinner mints, one of the rugby players approached the head table. He was as tall as Henry but had a broad, stocky figure instead of Henry's defined muscles. His nose was flattened by at least one break, and edges of his ears were puffy and misshapen.

"I say, Mercia." He spoke with the same thick, posh accent as Duncan, Alice's friend with the thick glasses. "What are we going to do about those louts at International House? They're making a mockery of the academy."

Edward waved his hand. "Shouldn't you concern yourself with your studies, Coates? I hear you're failing abysmally."

Coates' face twisted into a scowl, and he stalked off to sit with his friends.

"He's right, you know," murmured Henry. "International House is bringing down the campus."

"I'll speak to the headmaster," Edward replied in a distracted tone that implied he'd do nothing of the sort. He turned to me. "Would you care to join me after dinner?"

My stomach flip. Our last conversation about International House had ended with me accusing him of bigotry and storming away. Maybe Edward wanted a chance to explain himself. I gave him a broad grin. "That depends on if you plan on having me in your study again."

He smirked. "Only if you ask nicely."

"Let's go for a walk."

He inclined his head. "I'll bring the hot chocolate."

Blake leaned forward. "When do I get to see you on my own?"

"Soon enough." I stood from my seat and smiled. "I'm just getting my coat."

For the briefest of moments, confusion crossed Blake's features, but he masked the expression with a smile. "When we meet, I insist you wear only the boots, coat and a dab of perfume."

"Keep dreaming." I walked out of the dining room with dozens of eyes boring holes into my back. Right now, Blake was probably staring also after me, wondering why I was paying his friends more attention than him.

∼

Later, Edward met me at the foot of the stairs, wearing a green waxed jacket with a flat cap, looking every bit the English country gentleman. An insulated tartan bag was slung over his shoulder, which I assumed contained hot chocolate. I glanced around for signs of Blake and Henry, but they were probably in their room or in Edward's study. It didn't matter. I'd already dented Blake's ego and intended to push him up my priority list for what he had said to Rita.

I took Edward's arm, and we walked out of Elder House into the crisp evening. The sun had long set, and a thick layer of frost covered the entire campus, making it look magical, all lit up by old-fashioned lamps on iron posts. While we strolled, Edward told me the history of all the buildings, including International House, which had been built during the Regency period. His recounting of the history of the estate was so enthralling, I forgot to ask why he had dismissed Coates' complaint about the rowdy students.

We continued beyond the campus, where we stopped at a huge, timber vehicle shed by a road that stretched out into the distance. Inside were mainly farm vehicles, but Edward opened the passenger door to a jeep.

"Do you have your license?" I stepped into the four-by-four and settled into its worn, leather seat.

He smirked. "Not yet, but I've been driving since I was thirteen."

I spluttered. "Isn't that illegal?"

"Not on private property." He jumped into the driver's seat, turned the ignition, and the engine sprung to life with a roar.

I fastened on my seatbelt, and Edward drove me through the estate, his floodlights on at full capacity. Marissa had been right about it being larger than Central Park. In the dark, I made out stables, a vast amount of farmland, cattle, sheep, a huge fishing lake, and several patches of forest. Within all of this were a number of buildings, which included accommodation for some of the estate's employees.

He turned his head toward me. "Does it impress you that I'll own all of this one day?"

I tilted my head to the side. "The grounds are impressive, and I think whoever owns them will be lucky to have access to such a vast estate, but am I impressed that you'll inherit it? No."

"May I ask your reasons why?"

"When I was growing up, my mom taught me the value of hard work."

"She was a model, wasn't she?"

"That's one of the hardest jobs a person can get. Early starts, long, irregular hours, not to mention a strict diet to look right for the camera. She recommended I find a less grueling career where the salaries increased with age and experience, and not the other way around"

"I hadn't thought of it that way," he murmured. "But she did marry Rudolph Trommel."

"At a very high price," I replied, heart sinking at the thought of her forgetting me. "Trophy wives have to sacrifice a lot for their rich husbands. I lived at home until Mom remarried. After that, she sent me away to school, and I barely saw her." A lump formed in my throat, and I swallowed hard. "That's not going to be me."

"What do you want to do?" He turned the jeep off the road, and up a bumpy hill.

"Write," I said as the vehicle jerked me from side to side. I gripped both sides of my seat and tightened my stomach muscles. That much was true, but I'd be damned if I revealed to him my desire for a career in journalism. "I love Hemingway, Orwell, and Twain."

His lips quirked into a smile. "You'll become a novelist?"

"Why not?"

"It's an honorable profession." We hit a ditch, and Edward reversed a few feet then put his foot down on the accelerator, revving up the engine to a roar and powering through the dip in the terrain.

"How about you?" I asked. "Will the Duchy allow you to have a career?"

He grimaced. "The estate is vast and includes properties within the county. If I hired a management company to take care of all the assets, there'd be very little to reinvest."

"That sounds like hard work."

"It's why I'm taking Economics, Law, and Accounting. They're subjects that will prepare me for managing the estate"

I would have asked whether his father was helping, but Henry had mentioned that his mental health had taken a decline soon after the death of his mother. Who was running the estate now? Last term, after our shopping trip, I'd asked who lived in his house, then Edward wouldn't get out of the limo for ages.

The terrain flattened, and we soon joined a road that led to a dozen of the largest greenhouses I'd ever seen, alongside a field, and to the edge of a forest, where a man wearing a hardhat and protective clothing threw large pieces of wood into a huge, metal barrel.

When we got out of the jeep, the man doffed his cap. "Good evening, Mr. Edward!"

"Good evening, Shanks," he replied. "How are the twins?"

Rocking back on his heels, the man puffed out his chest. "Doing well, young sir. Please pass on our thanks to His Grace for the bonus. Two sets of everything ain't cheap!"

Edward chuckled. "I imagine it isn't."

Shanks bundled up the firewood and continued to another metal barrel further on along the edge of the forest.

I followed the man with my eyes. It was clear that he worked for the estate, as he had thanked Edward's father for the extra money. Was Edward managing the estate in his father's illness, or did the old butler do the work?

Edward pulled out a flask from his backpack. "Time for a spot of hot chocolate, I think."

"I hope it's not spiked."

His brows drew together. "That was a rather childish prank to play on everyone. Mrs. Jenkins had to put poor Miss Oakley to bed after she'd passed out having had one too many mugs."

My brows drew together. "That wasn't you?"

"Widespread chaos via intoxication is more Blake's style." Edward grinned. "One time, he put hair remover in Coates' sunblock, dissolving all his body hair. The poor chap had to shower in private for weeks until it grew back."

"Nice," I muttered. At least I knew the identity of one of the culprits behind the tampered shampoo.

He pulled out two insulated mugs and poured two mugs of the most delicious-smelling hot cocoa I'd ever tasted. Then we stood together, watching the wood burn in the barrel, which Edward explained was used to make charcoal. Later, we returned to the jeep, and Edward drove us back a different route with a road that avoided the steep part of the hill.

When we returned to Elder House, Edward walked me up to the first floor, took my hand, and pressed his lips to my knuckles. "Good night, Emilia."

I tilted my head to the side and smiled. "You're not going to invite me to your study?"

"You're worth the wait." He drew back, walked down the hallway, and disappeared down the stairs, leaving me bewildered.

I stepped into my room. The bathroom door was open, and Rita's bed was still made. She was probably in Hawthorn House with her upper-sixth year friend. I sat on the edge of my bed and put my head in my hands. What kind of game was Edward playing? When we were alone, he was the perfect gentleman, and he only participated a little when Henry and Blake got hot and heavy. Was he really trying to play things slow, or was he differentiating himself from the others by holding back?

Blinking out the confusion, I shook my head. He'd bullied me just as much as the others, and he'd been involved in framing me for the kidnapping. Nobody would be immune from my wrath, not even those who acted gallant.

CHAPTER 9

I had hoped to be able to send something useful to Jackie from yesterday's date with Edward, but unfortunately I hadn't discovered anything except his fascinating relationship with his employees. And the beautiful grounds. And a secret strength and kindness, hidden behind his hard exterior. As to whether I was glad I had found no dirt on him… I didn't want to examine that too closely. Jackie forwarded me scanned plans of Elder House and key areas of the academy with red dots to indicate the locations of the cameras they had forced Carbuncle to install.

Later that evening, I sat between Edward and Henry in the common room, where the triumvirate held court at the sofas closest to the fire. Charlotte, Patricia, and Wendy sauntered into the room, holding marshmallows and long, metal prongs. This was the first time she had shown her face since the Correspondent had published the article on her brother's gambling addiction.

They had also delved into the financial activities of her father. Over the years, he had placed several family properties for auction, selling them for less than their worth. With so many people fixated on money and status in Mercia Academy, and with her lie about her brother working for the Saudi Royal family exposed, I wasn't surprised Charlotte had gone into hiding.

Patricia was the first to speak. "We brought marshmallows." She fluttered her lashes at Edward. "I know they're your favorite."

He wrapped an arm around my shoulder. "Some things are better than junk food."

"None for me, thanks." Henry stretched out on his side of the sofa, taking up all the space.

Blake scooted toward Edward. "Sit with me, if you like."

I narrowed my eyes. This was clearly a ploy to make me jealous. It was time to act, and I had a great idea. Rita had once told me that Blake liked to boast about his connection to the British Royal family. If I could prompt him into repeating his little speech, Jackie would have a nice little story, and I'd have my revenge. I locked eyes with Patricia and slid my hand on Edward's muscular thigh. He kissed me on the cheek.

The other girl's bottom lip wobbled. "Do you know what I hate the most?"

"What's that?" asked Charlotte.

"Gold diggers who follow the examples of their trollop mothers."

Wendy shook her head. "How true."

"Wow," I said. "You should be kinder to yourself, Pat—" I tapped my bottom lip. "Sorry, I forgot your last name. What is it again?"

Patricia's nostrils flared, and she pulled back her shoulders and stuck out her chest. I rolled my eyes. No matter how much she adjusted her posture, she would never have half of Charlotte's assets. I was about to tell her as much, but she bared her teeth. "I was talking about you, whore."

Edward sighed. "Must you make a scene?"

"Glass houses and all that," added Henry.

I rubbed my temples. "Can you stop the name-calling? It's tiresome and hypocritical."

Charlotte reared back. "Who are you calling a hypocrite?"

"You, mostly." I stood and let my voice carry, so everyone behind us in the common room could hear. I didn't give a damn about these idiots, their marshmallows, or their petty jibes. My target here was Blake, and I needed to word things correctly to prompt him into giving his infamous boast. "Henry is the heir to the Bourneville fortune, and you've tried every trick at your disposal to get at him."

"That's not true," she spat.

"Even I've noticed it," drawled Henry.

Charlotte's face turned purple. "What about you?"

"I'm not the one chasing after riches. Not like your little friend whose name I can't remember."

"It's Patricia. Patricia Darnley."

"Thank you, *Darling*." The boys snickered at that. "You're so desperate for Edward and his Duchy of Mercia wealth, you're prepared to fight your best friend over him. What kind of girl does that?"

"A gold digger!" shouted someone from deep within the common room.

"Out of the mouth of babes." I sat and held my breath, hoping Blake would take the bait.

"And there's me, of course," Blake drawled. "If anything happens to the Prince of Wales, my stepfather will become the King of England and make me a prince."

"Not this again," Henry muttered under his breath.

A tingle of excitement ran through my insides. Blake had fallen into my trap. Now, all I needed to do was give him the gentlest of prompts. "What's that?"

Blake sat straighter in his seat, chocolate eyes shining. "It's obvious, really. Her Majesty doesn't have long for this world, and the next in line is always going overseas and sticking his neck out for all sorts of international causes. With the rise of terrorism, something might happen to him and voila!" He stood, stretching his arms wide. "My stepfather gets the throne, and I'll be Prince Blake."

"Sit down, you twat," said Henry. "It's just a title."

Edward chuckled, blue eyes dancing with amusement.

Blake shook his head. "My stepfather says it won't be. I'll join the civil list and get my own wing in one of the palaces. If I endure a few charity events each year, I'll be set. An entire life of luxury funded by the taxpayer."

I rubbed my chin. This was excellent. I had one more question that if answered right would get him into a world of trouble. "Your stepfather, the prince, told you this?"

"Of course." Blake rocked back on his heels. "He's seen the writing on the wall, and he's told me more than once that he'll become the King of England."

"That explains why the gold diggers want you." I turned to Wendy. "Have you been setting your heart on becoming a princess?"

She curled her lip. "Oh, fuck off, you pathetic whore."

Triumph flared through my insides. Blake had said enough to hang himself. I took note of the time on the mantle to tell Jackie where to find the clip and fluttered my eyelashes at Wendy. "Did I hit a nerve?"

Charlotte grabbed the bag of marshmallows and threw their contents at me before storming out of the room with her doppelgängers.

"If that's your way of having the last word, I'll debate with you any time!" Snickers filled the common room, and I picked off a marshmallow and stuck it in my mouth. "I should have asked her for a prong. These are much better toasted."

∽

Days later, I sat at the head table between Edward and Henry, staring at the next article of the Saturday Correspondent on Henry's smartphone. A photo of Blake sitting on the sofa in front of the fire, smoking a joint, featured prominently on the page. Charlotte's head was at his crotch, but her face was obscured. I bit down hard on the inside of my cheek to hide my reaction. Blake had to be in serious trouble.

The entire room was abuzz with excitement. Yet again a small crowd formed around a beaming Duncan's table, who shouted out the headline, "Simpson-West plots Prince of Wales' demise!"

The paper had printed a transcript of Blake's speech, along with a link online where anyone could listen and verify that he'd actually spoken about how he would benefit from the death of a senior royal. A fourth year visiting his older sister pulled out his phone and broadcasted the recording to the room.

Charlotte trotted in with her two remaining doppelgängers. I guessed with the attention now on Blake, she felt safe enough to show her face in the dining room.

I reached for a pot, poured myself a cup of tea, and shook my head. "Someone's embellished this. I don't remember Blake saying that much. How's he taking the news?"

"He's left to see his mother," replied Henry.

"Is she in the palace?"

"One of them," he replied.

"Who could have done this to him?" I asked.

"I have an idea," Edward's gaze fixed on Charlotte, who stared back.

My brows rose. I picked up the milk jug and added a splash into my tea. Charlotte hadn't even been holding a camera on that evening. But if this stunt earned her the animosity of the triumvirate, I would consider it a bonus.

"You could be right," said Henry. "This is revenge for the time Blake posted that blow job on the projector."

I winced at the remembered pain of Charlotte kicking me in the diaphragm. That had been almost as bad as the mugful of hot cocoa in the face. "What about the photo? She couldn't have taken that."

"If she set up her camera on the mantelpiece and waited for

Blake to come in, she would have recorded the entire event." One side of Henry's lips quirked into a smile. "He could never resist fellatio."

Edward snorted. "Good old Blake."

I raised the teacup to my lips and scowled. They needed to stop talking about Blake's blow job escapades.

By the next day, news spread to the Sunday papers, who reprinted the article with a cropped picture featuring just Blake and the joint, and on Monday morning, Buckingham Palace issued a statement that Blake had been under the influence of drugs when he had made those boasts, and that they had not come from his stepfather as Blake had claimed. The statement concluded that he would receive counseling for his addiction.

At lunchtime, someone posted a video clip on the Mercia-Net of Blake's stepfather, the prince, issuing a statement denying that he had discussed his brother's death as Blake had claimed. Blake's mother stood at his side, clad in vintage Chanel, exuding elegance and silent dignity. Her black hair was swept up in a chignon, highlighting similar, prominent cheekbones and eyes as dark as Blake's. I chewed on my bottom lip, hiding my amusement. When Blake returned to the academy, he would be a pariah and too occupied with his own social ostracism to bother harassing the likes of Rita.

"The comments Blake made were his and his alone?" Henry spat. "Lying bastard! Do you remember that Easter we all spent in Scotland?"

Edward sipped his orange juice. "It's etched in my mind. Didn't His Highness say it the day after he caught Mrs. Simpson-West with the chauffeur?"

I gasped. "What?"

Edward pursed his lips. "The prince was so desperate to keep Mrs. Simpson-West in line, he blurted out that promise in front of us all, hoping she'd stay."

I held my breath and stared into my plate of kippers. It was one thing to get Blake into trouble, but I didn't want the royal family to fall into complete disgrace.

Blake didn't turn up for school the next day. As I took a stroll through the grounds, I pulled out my phone and sent him another text asking how he was coping with the scandal. I held it in my hands for a few minutes, waiting for his reply, but none came.

I moved to search the internet to see if the papers had any update on the story and soon found a report of Blake being escorted by his mother into a rehab facility.

My throat dried, so I went to the tuck shop and ordered a service of orange juice before gulping it down in one. My fingers trembled as I held the glass. I hadn't expected things to go that far. A bit of public humiliation and a harsh reprimanding from his parents was all I'd wanted from Blake, and now he was in some sort of institution.

I shuddered at the thought of the doctors giving him methadone or some other drug he didn't need. Apart from that photo, I'd never even seen Blake take drugs, and the boys assured me he wasn't an addict.

After returning to my room, I locked myself in the bathroom to call Jackie. "Emilia!" she slurred, sounding like she'd had too much to drink. "Do you know how much money we made from syndicating that photo and article?" Before I could answer, she said, "Enough to keep us afloat for a very long time, even if the Press Standards Organization decides to fine us for posting a lewd picture!"

"About that," I asked. "Did you take it from the camera?"

"It was from the night you went out with Edward Mercia. Why didn't you probe him on the dodgy goings-on at International House? Nobody but him seems to know what's happening."

I rubbed the back of my neck. "I'm working on it."

"Good. Rudolph says you need to top this and produce something explosive."

My shoulders sagged. If the Correspondent made so much from Blake's scandal, why was I now under even more pressure? "If I can encourage people to post about International House on the Mercia-Net, that should give you enough to write up a few articles, right?"

"Only when we find out why there's suddenly a brand new house filled with people who don't belong in a high school."

I pursed my lips. With Edward being so cagey about the new students, I would need more than a bit of luck to crack that mystery.

～

The following Monday, Blake returned to the academy. He stepped through the dining room doors to a round of applause and cheers. His stony expression melted into a grin that froze halfway to his eyes. The members of the rugby team hoisted him on their shoulders and carried him to the head table, calling him a stud and a fucking legend. By the time they had bolstered his ego, his face brightened, and the smile turned genuine.

He stood on a chair at the head table, raising his arms and waiting for the wolf-whistles to subside. "Ladies and Gentlemen," he announced. "News of my addiction to alcohol and drugs has been greatly exaggerated for the protection of the realm."

"He took one for the country!" yelled a voice from the back of the dining room.

"Nice one!"

All my previous concerns for Blake evaporated into the ether, and my lips tightened. I had meant to give him a taste of what I had suffered, not turn him into a living legend. When the triumvirate had framed me, all I received was a week's imprisonment, cheese sandwiches, and a brutal, humiliating send-off by the same people who now saluted Blake for getting caught talking treason.

Henry shook his head. "They shouldn't encourage him."

Since that little stunt didn't work, I would have to try something else.

My gaze caught Alice's, who rolled her eyes. The last time we had gone out, I'd mentioned that Sergei would be playing at an exclusive singles' event in London. What if I got Jackie to arrange an apartment with cameras and enough drink to make everyone spill their secrets? That would keep Rudolph off my back until I found something worth publishing about International House.

CHAPTER 10

The excitement about Blake's return from an unnecessary trip to rehab died down by the next day, and his mood became somber. Perhaps getting the blame for something that wasn't really his fault had given him something to think about. Or his stepfather had admonished him for embarrassing the royal family. Whatever it was, he now turned pensive and would spend moments staring off into space.

I stopped shunning him and acted the supportive friend. Partially out of curiosity about his fate, but mostly to see if there was any information I could gather for my next attack.

English lit was the last class of the day. As everyone got up to leave, I turned to Blake. "Want to go for a walk?"

He gave me a sad smile. "A date?"

"If you like." I shrugged.

Blake nodded and placed his books in his satchel. I twisted around, reached into my pocket, and turned on the recording app on my burner phone. When we'd both finished packing, I looped my arm through his, and we walked out of the main teaching block and across the lawn to the music block.

Throughout our journey, younger students whispered and gaped. A few mentioned Blake's recent appearances in the papers and on the TV, but at a sharp look from him, they clammed up.

"How are you coping?" I asked.

Blake dipped his head. "The worst part about this mess is my stepfather. He's denying ever saying the Prince of Wales might die before ascending to the throne, but Edward and Henry heard him."

"Henry told me as much," I murmured.

"Now the palace has labeled me a drug addict to save face."

"Do they believe your side of the story?" I shooed away a little first year who jogged up with a scrap of paper for an autograph, dared to by his giggling friends.

"The aide I spoke to said it didn't matter who said what. I shouldn't have repeated it in public. He was livid that someone had placed a recording device in our common room and has written to the headmaster, demanding answers."

My heart thudded in my chest, and I let out a long breath. Even if someone swept the room for hidden devices, they couldn't be traced back to me. Not when they'd been set up by Mr. Carbuncle.

We rounded the building and walked into a courtyard with a circular lawn. Around it grew winter jasmine shrubs. A glossy evergreen plant laden with thick white flowers climbed over all the walls. It was the kind of garden that was pleasant in winter but would look spectacular in the summer.

I shook my head. "Everyone's got smartphones these days. Even Charlotte."

His handsome features twisted. "She did this."

My brows drew together. As much as I wanted Charlotte shunned, it couldn't be for something she hadn't done. "Are you sure? What would she have to gain?"

"You heard me admit to broadcasting her blow job video. This is her revenge."

"How did you even get hold of that recording?" I asked. "That evening, when I hid under the common room table, I dropped my phone the moment I realized what you two were doing."

He smirked. "You were probably too fixated on my cock to notice my other hand. It was holding the smartphone. Charlotte always closes her eyes when she sucks me off... Something to do with her gag reflex not working if she multitasks. She isn't exactly the brightest of girls."

My stomach dropped. The more I got to know of him, the more I wanted him ruined. "Why did you set things up to make it look like I'd broadcasted the video?"

He grimaced. "Sorry about that... Before I became friends with Edward and Henry, Charlotte made my life here miserable. Even though she's forgotten about it, I never have."

"That still doesn't explain why you framed me."

"I thought it would hurt her more if the video came from someone she saw as a threat."

I folded my arms across my chest. "You must have known she would go psycho."

"She has never attacked anyone in the six years I've known her." He placed a hand on my shoulder and turned on the pleading eyes. "I thought she would rush out of the campsite in tears."

My nostrils flared, but I held my tongue. We were even now. Sort of. Even if Elder House saw Blake as some kind of hero, the rest of the country thought he was a scheming braggart and a drug addict. That had to be worse than Charlotte's kick to my guts and a mug of hot cocoa in the face.

I took his hand and gave it a gentle squeeze. In my most soothing voice, I said, "Sorry that this happened. I know what it's like to be slandered, and it isn't pleasant."

He squeezed back, likely too upset to take the hint. "Thanks for sticking by me."

"Anytime." I pulled him into an alcove and cupped his cheeks with both hands. "Anytime the pressure of being the royal family's fall guy becomes too much, speak to me."

He wrapped his arms around my waist. "This is nice."

"Hmmm?" I smiled into his soft gaze.

"Talking to you like this. I've only ever felt close to Henry and Edward."

I ran my thumb over his high cheekbone. After seeing footage of his stunning mother, I could understand how he got those handsome looks. He stared down at me with hooded eyes the color of molten chocolate.

A spasm of desire rippled through my heart. Blake had one of those faces that could make a girl fall into a stupor of lust and fascination. It was no wonder Charlotte had forgotten their tumultuous past. Before I let him mesmerize me, I raised myself to my tiptoes and placed a chaste kiss on his forehead.

Blake sighed and pulled me into his body, engulfing me in his sandalwood and spice scent. To make my facade of offering comfort complete, I wrapped my arms around his neck.

The comfort of his larger frame and strong muscles was deceptive. Why hadn't he confided in me that the kidnappers weren't a danger because Henry had arranged the entire abduction? I might have raged at them for a few days, but would never have gone behind their backs and called the police. Blake must have known that his flippant answer to my worries would never have convinced me of Henry's safety.

"You feel so good," he murmured into my neck.

"This is perfect," I lied.

Even though Blake had hurt me tremendously, my chest twinged with guilt. I was the biggest hypocrite, standing there, giving him comfort over something I had set into motion, but I had to follow through on this plan. Not only did Rudolph expect it, but I had sworn to myself that I wouldn't rest until I'd completed my revenge against the triumvirate.

The following week, a courier brought a dozen red roses to the head table. A hush fell across the dining room, and I glanced at Blake, wondering if they had come from him. He shook his head. A bulky envelope accompanied the roses, and when I opened it, a dozen invitations spilled out. I smiled. Jackie had organized this and hired Sergei to play, making it look like he'd sent the invitations and roses.

> ST VALENTINE'S DAY MASSACRE BALL
> Penthouse Suite - Waterloo Towers
> Performance by Sergei Bachmann
> Admits _____ plus guest
> Dress code: fancy dress
> RSVP stvdaymass@gmail.com

Edward took an invitation. "Why's Bachmann sending you invitations to a ball? I thought you would have broken up with him by now."

"You're still wearing his engagement ring." Henry took an invitation and turned it around in his fingers.

"Let's have a look." Blake reached over and grabbed one. "Why's he inviting you to a Valentine's ball?"

"Will you three stop whining?" I snapped. "A single date isn't enough for any girl to throw away an engagement to a sexy, musical genius. I said I'd give you a chance, not my future."

Blake snorted into his tea. "I distinctly heard you cry out that you'd give us everything."

I narrowed my eyes. "Obviously, your ears were muffled by my thighs because I said nothing of the sort."

Henry snickered and bit down on his toast, while Edward smiled.

"A man knows these things from the cadence of a woman's cries." Blake placed down his cup and waggled his eyebrows.

"Right." I held out my hand. "I'll take those back, please."

Henry slipped the invitation he stole into the inside pocket of his blazer. "I'm holding onto this."

"Me, too," said Blake.

I turned to Edward. "We only need two invitations between the four of us."

"This one is for Paul." He tapped the invitation.

"Paul who?"

"Mr. Frost, the Latin master."

A breath caught in the back of my throat. This was too good to be true. A teacher getting drunk with students wasn't on the same magnitude as Mr. Carbuncle's activities with sixth form girls, but it would be satisfying to embarrass Mr. Frost for a change. I eyed Edward. Had he said that as a test? The natural reaction to a suggestion like that was resistance, so I folded my arms across my chest. "Why him?"

"He's the best source for anything," said Blake. "Always has been."

I smiled. "What kind of things?"

Henry batted my nose. "You'll find out."

I didn't push the issue. Jackie would place cameras all over the apartment and capture Mr. Frost supplying students with alcohol or worse. "As long as he has absinthe, I don't care."

Blake leaned forward. "The off-license in the village stocks absinthe, I can get—"

"No." I licked my lips. To get the boys to loosen up, I needed the most potent version in existence. "The bottles available in the stores is watered down crap. I want the real thing. See if he can get a high thujone brand."

Later that day, Alice and I sat together in Creative Writing, the only class I didn't share with any of the triumvirate.

She gave me a nudge on the arm. "Who bought you the roses?"

"Sergei." I pulled out an invitation to the Valentine's ball. "This is the singles' event I was telling you about."

"Is that for me?"

I fanned myself with the invitation. "On two conditions."

"What are they?" Her voice became breathy.

"One. Take a photo of it and place it on the Mercia-Net."

"Why?"

I smirked. "How mad would Charlotte and the others get to know you'd been invited and they hadn't?"

"Oh, great!" She rubbed her hands together. "What's the other condition?"

"Nothing glamorous," I replied. "Could you start a post on International House, asking people to comment with examples of the students flouting the rules? I tried to speak to the headmaster about all the noise, but he didn't believe me."

Her lips tightened. "If he ever left that office of his, he'd see the evidence with his own eyes. Some of those men look like gangsters. The first years are terrified!"

I shrugged. "He can see the photos and recordings on the Mercia-Net. If we overwhelm him with facts, he'll have to do something, right?"

Alice pulled the invitation out from my fingers. "Consider them done."

Later that night, I checked in with Jackie to let her know I'd received the invitations, and she told me the email address had already received thirty messages from people claiming to be my close friend who needed an invitation. Some of the names came from members of prominent families in the United Kingdom. Alice's posting of the invitation to the Mercia-Net had worked.

I ran my hands through my hair and stared into the bathroom mirror. This would be a massacre of epic proportions.

With only a few weeks to go before the Valentine's Day party, I focused on my schoolwork and on getting to know each member of the triumvirate as individuals. Blake continued to be miserable about falling into disfavor with the royal family, and no matter how much we talked about the unfairness of him taking the blame for something his stepfather had said, it didn't dawn on him that he and his friends had done far worse to me.

It hurt my heart to spend time with Henry. I'd become so close to him, yet what had brought us together hadn't even been real. Those nights I'd spent in that terrible room, eating awful food, and being frightened out of my mind had been a facade. No matter how much he said he needed to atone, I couldn't forgive him until we were even. The kidnapping had been bad. I might have been able to let that go, but I'd never respect myself if I didn't punish him for framing me for his own crime.

The only member of the triumvirate I could stand was Edward. Perhaps it was because he had mostly shown his true colors from the start. And because he appreciated more than the other two that it would take time for things to heal between us. Unlike Blake and Henry, he didn't push for intimacy, just understanding.

A number of sixth-formers in both Elder and Hawthorn house approached me for tickets. I had nine remaining from what the triumvirate stole, and I wanted to ensure that the most deserving got the chance to be caught on camera doing something scandalous. I made sure to give the tickets to those I recognized from the gauntlet. Those who had been the vilest and cruelest. Those who had the nerve to pretend friendship when they would easily tear me apart at the barest provocation.

One Saturday after classes, we sat in Edward's study, reading through the Correspondent. I lay on one of the Chesterfield sofas, resting my head on Henry's lap with my bare feet on Blake's. Edward sat behind his desk with his feet up, reading Hemingway's *For Whom the Bell Tolls*. Today's edition featured an exposé on Patricia's aunt, who worked in the Home Office, yet was having an affair with a man who had entered England illegally. The reporters had even tracked them down to a hotel she had paid for with her government credit card.

"I don't know where all this information is coming from?" asked Henry.

"Charlotte," replied Blake. "Patricia confides in no one else."

Edward leaned back on his desk chair and folded his copy of the paper. "What should we do about her?"

"We could have her head shaved." Blake ran his thumb along the sole of my foot, making me arch my back. "It was very popular in France after World War Two."

"You can't do that," I gasped out.

"Why not?" asked Henry. "She's done a damned sight worse to you."

I propped myself up on my elbows. "Firstly, you don't know who is sending information to the newspapers, and secondly, it's too extreme."

Blake stopped massaging my feet. "I spent an entire week in rehab. Do you know what they had me doing? Group discussions half the time and one-to-one counseling for the rest of my stay. It was hell."

I clenched my teeth. "Try spending a week in a basement room with only a sandwich and a bottle of Evian for company."

They all fell silent. It was becoming a pattern. Blake would complain about the injustice he'd suffered, and then I would remind them of what they had inflicted on me. Then awkwardness would ensue. It was as if there was another party involved who they didn't want to expose. My jaws clenched with determination. If I worked on them individually, one of them would let something slip.

My shoulders slumped back into the leather sofa. Part of me longed for the days after the kidnapping when we were becoming closer, when I was oblivious to the terrible scheme they had hatched. At times, I looked at the boys for signs of true repentance, but it seemed that Blake and Henry just wanted me to forget about what they had done, so we could all start having sex.

"When are you seeing Sergei Bachmann next?" Henry twirled a lock of my hair with his fingers.

"Do you want to come along?" I stared up into his green eyes.

"You've been spending most of your free time with us," said Blake. "He's unwanted baggage that needs ditching."

My lips quirked into a tiny smile. They were jealous. "I plan on cooling it off with him at the party."

Edward peered at me over the top of his novel. "On Valentine's day? That will be fun."

"We should go shopping for your costume," said Henry. "Something red for heartbreak would be apt."

Blake's hands wandered up my ankles and into my skinny jeans. I closed my eyes and sighed. Since that afternoon I'd told them to kiss my feet, I had been wearing jeans or pants whenever I visited Edward's study. Henry and Blake seemed to want to rush intimacy, whereas I couldn't afford to fall prey to my passion. Blake's thumb rubbed the swell of my ankle, making me groan and pull my feet off his lap.

"I've already hired a costume." A lazy grin crossed my face. Jackie had picked it out for me and said the boys would never be able to undo it in front of the cameras. No matter how much I begged.

CHAPTER 11

*V*alentine's day fell on a Saturday this year. I left for London immediately after morning classes and caught the train to meet Jackie and her crew at Waterloo Towers, a high-rise building overlooking the River Thames. As soon as I walked through the door of the apartment, Jackie rushed at me with a box, not giving me time to marvel at the huge, open-plan room or its period furniture. "Your costume."

I lifted the Marie Antoinette gown complete with a corset and pannier petticoat and bit my lip. "How do I put this on?"

"You can change in the bathroom." Jackie ushered me and her new intern toward another door. "Hurry, as we have a lot to do before the party starts."

"This way." The intern, a tall, black girl with chin-length braids, gave me an apologetic smile and opened the door, revealing a white, marble bathroom the size of the space I shared with Rita at the academy. "Tom needs to get away to double-check the sounds of all the cameras, but he wants to show you their locations before he leaves."

She helped me into the underthings first, then the dress, then fastened up the bodice and secured it with a few stitches. Jackie must have told her about the boys and their roving hands.

"One more thing!" she rushed out of the room and returned with another box, containing a white wig and a lace mask. "Jackie wants you to wear these."

Afterward, Tom walked me through the apartment, starting with the main room, which had a grand piano in the middle and could hold two-hundred guests. He pointed out the location of all the cameras there before showing me a passage away from the main room, where a bookshelf formed a hidden door into a boudoir with a four-poster bed.

Jackie leaned against a tall, wooden cabinet. "You must get that information about International House. Based on what people are posting on the Mercia-Net, some of the characters are unsavory and not suitable to be allowed anywhere near children."

"Has anything happened?" I sat on the bed.

"Just a few thugs violently objecting to having their photos taken. The third year girls report that one creepy bastard keeps trying to strike up conversations. They're traveling in packs, now."

An unpleasant shudder ran down my spine. "What are the parents saying?"

"It's hard to tell." She coughed into her hand. "Everyone's tiptoeing around the subject, including Edward Mercia."

I nodded. "Yes, I noticed that too, but he just tells me to keep my distance and clams up whenever I bring up International House."

She stepped away from the cabinet and opened the door, revealing a refrigerator filled with ice and champagne. "Get them in here and get them talking. Use the drinks to loosen their tongues. This room's quiet, and we've fitted recording devices in the balcony in case you need to get Edward alone."

I breathed out a long breath, eyes scanning the splendor of the room. "I'll do my best."

Jackie clamped a hand on my shoulder and stared up at me, eyes laden with menace. "This is the groundbreaking story we've been waiting for. There's more to International House than a few noisy louts. You must make Edward Mercia spill everything."

"Right." I gulped. She'd left unsaid the threat of Rudolph sending me to military school if I failed, but I was well aware of the consequences. Forcing a smile, I said, "Results or ruin."

Jackie's lined face split into a grin. "That's the spirit. We've set up half our journalists to act as servers, and we're expecting big things."

My throat went dry. This was a lot of responsibility. "What if nobody comes?"

"We distributed fifty tickets to people from your school and a little over sixty to people who claim to be alumni. Each is likely to bring one or more guests. There's also a few undercover agents we like to use for events like this. Focus on your boys, and we'll take care of the rest."

By the time the first few arrivals trickled in, the undercover reporters were already in place. Some were clad in black and white as servers, while the others wore fancy dress. Sergei arrived a couple of hours after the start with his full complement of bodyguards. When we hugged hello, I warned him to be careful with Andreo, because there were cameras everywhere. He kissed me on the cheek and thanked me for the heads up.

Sergei played popular tunes to get the party going. I stood by the piano, nursing a glass of tonic water that had been made to look like it contained gin. Strangely, for a bunch of people who wrangled their invitations by claiming to know me, very few approached to say hello.

Andreo stood by my side. "Sergei tells me you are hurting those boys who betrayed you. Are you tempted to forgive them?"

My lips quirked into a smile. "Sometimes I have a great evening with one of them, then he says something that reminds me he hasn't changed and would betray me in a heartbeat if it benefitted them."

"They seemed like conceited brats to me."

I giggled into my drink. Andreo had kicked them out of the Royal Academy charity ball and had probably heard an earful of haughty objections. The next time I looked up to survey the guests, I found the three of them on the other side of the room, holding champagne flutes and glaring in my direction. The arrogant fucks probably thought I was responsible for their evening's entertainment, even though they had invited themselves to the party.

Edward wore a blue frock coat with white breeches, looking like the beast after Belle had broken the curse, and Blake wore the dark tunic and skirt of a gladiator, which showed off his muscular thighs and arms. I couldn't work out whether Henry had come as a fireman or a stripper dressed as a fireman, as he didn't wear a shirt under his jacket, revealing prominent pecs and tight abs.

I raised my glass and gave them my widest smile. They mirrored the movement but kept their faces stony, probably in a bad mood because I was still with Sergei.

"How are you doing it?" asked Andreo. "Divide and conquer?"

I shot Sergei an adoring look. "Their friendships are too deep for a tactic like that. I'm getting to know them each and finding out what will hurt them most."

"Aim for the heart, not the wallet or the reputation. Betrayal from someone you care about hurts the most."

I gulped a mouthful of lemony tonic water and grimaced. It was as though Andreo could read my mind. Nothing had hurt me more than knowing they had kept me close to secure their secret, never confided the reason why I shouldn't call the police, and then betrayed me when I did. From what I could glean from our interactions, they still kept me close so I wouldn't blurt out the truth to Henry's parents, and because they were fascinated by the idea of a foursome.

So far, only Blake had suffered my wrath and he had emerged from it a little battered but unscathed. Jackie was right. To produce results, I would step up my game.

While I stood by the piano, playing the role of the devoted fiancée, the triumvirate held court on a gold-embroidered, antique sofa held up by ornate, clawed feet. People swarmed around them as though they were the hosts of the party. I glanced around the room for more familiar faces and found Mr. Frost, dressed like Charlie Chaplin, slipping a small envelope to a young man I didn't recognize. He wore an academy uniform a couple of sizes too small, and I guessed he was one of the alumni who had emailed for an invitation.

Sergei finished playing to loud applause, and another pianist took over. He wrapped both arms around me and murmured, "Since this place is unsafe for us to relax, I will go home."

"Alright." I gazed into his dark eyes. "I'll try to stop by and see you in London before I leave."

He drew back. "You are going back?"

"My stepfather promised to pay for a school of my choosing if I survived the winter term at Mercia Academy. I want to return to New York."

He grinned. "You are thriving!"

Sergei gave me another hug goodbye and left with Andreo and his bodyguards. Their absence as a buffer between myself and my task for the evening sent a ripple of anxiety through my gut. The time for pretending to be his adoring fiancée was over. It was time to get results.

A hand slipped around my waist, and Blake's sandalwood scent engulfed my senses. "Why did he leave?"

I stepped away. "Not here."

"Where?"

"Follow me." Without looking at him, I crossed the room, passing the army of fake waiters pressing glasses of champagne into the hands of increasingly drunk guests. Everybody in the room was a sixth former and above the drinking age for the United Kingdom. I had made sure not to hand out invitations to younger students, and Jackie had checked the background of each person who had requested an invitation online.

When I reached the bookshelf, Blake wrapped his arms around the waist of my bodice and murmured, "You look gorgeous tonight."

My laugh was low and throaty. "I could say the same for you."

"Why did Bachmann leave?" He peppered my neck with kisses.

A pleasant shudder ran down my spine. "I told you. We're cooling things off." I fumbled with the lever of the bookshelf's secret door. Now was the time for me to get the facts on International House. "Where are the others?"

"Right behind Blake," said Henry.

"What are you doing?" asked Edward from further down the hallway.

"One second…" I pulled up the lever, and the door clicked open. "Get inside."

Blake swept past me and turned in a slow circle. Edward joined straight after, and Henry wrapped his arms around my waist and walked me inside. He shut the door with a click and ran his hands up and down my corset.

"We've decided," Henry murmured into my ear. "Tonight's the night you lose your virginity."

I giggled. "Oh? Which one of you is planning to penetrate me first?"

"Blake," said Edward with a chuckle. "He's the smallest and can ease you in."

"Oh, fuck off," Blake snapped. "Edward's going in first. He's the one they call mushroom-man."

I would have doubled over with laughter if my corset wasn't holding me upright. With my wig and little mask, I could appear on camera, and no one would know my identity.

I turned to face Henry, who still had his arms wrapped around my waist. "How about you?"

"If you don't mind, I could go first and break you in nice and gently for Blake and Edward." He pressed his lips onto mine, tasting of mint and champagne.

I stepped away from his embrace. "How generous. But I'm not nearly drunk enough to lose my virginity to three men."

"We brought absinthe," said Blake. "One hundred milligrams of thujone. Guaranteed to melt your inhibitions along with your pesky hymen."

My eyes widened. Absinthe that strong wasn't even sold in the UK. This would be perfect for making them loosen up. "You remembered."

"Paul did." Edward pulled the small bottle of fluorescent liquid out of his jacket pocket.

I pointed at the wooden cabinet on the wall. "There's plenty of champagne in there."

"How did you manage to get a room like this?" asked Blake.

"The host gave it to Sergei," the lie slipped from my lips like butter. "But when I told him I wasn't ready to spend the night with him, he decided to leave."

Henry squeezed me tighter and pressed a kiss on my temple. "You made the right choice."

Blake opened the fridge, pulled out two bottles of champagne, and handed one to Edward. With the greatest of care and very little spillage, they popped the corks and drank straight from the bottle. While the triumvirate downed their champagne in long, deep drags, I took tiny sips to coat my lips, but nowhere near enough to even get tipsy.

After they'd nearly finished their bottles, Henry spun me around and kissed me on the lips. Before he could slip me his tongue, Blake twisted me toward him and gave me a drunken, sloppy kiss. I placed my hands on his chest to give him a shove, but Henry wrapped his arms around my waist and lifted me off my feet. "Come on, virgin. Let's deflower you."

I threw my head back and laughed. Maybe I'd wait a little before bringing up International House. "Don't I get a say in this matter?"

"Only on the position." Blake scrambled onto the mattress. "Bring her here."

I rolled my eyes and let Henry place me smack in the middle of the bed. Then he crawled over and fumbled at my waist. "How do I take it off?"

"Roll her onto her front," said Blake.

I raised a hand and slurred my voice. "Here's where I exercise my choice over positions. I want to lie on my back, propped up with pillows, while you two take turns kissing me until I beg for it."

Blake growled. "Begging sounds good."

Henry's lips descended onto mine in an impatient kiss of teeth and tongue that sent jolts of excitement down my body. Blake kissed a trail down my neck, along my collar bone and over the swell of my breasts. I squeezed my legs together and groaned. Even sloppily drunk, the boy knew what to do with his lips.

Henry's fingers circled my right breast, moving over bare skin and the part of my chest encased within the bodice. His tongue slid against mine in a series of caresses that made me arch my back and grab at his broad shoulders. I'd barely had anything to drink, but the pulse between my legs pounded in time with my heart, and slickness gathered in my panties.

If I didn't slow down, I might lose control and show them how to unfasten my gown. Then we'd all get too distracted to talk about International House, and I would fail my assignment. I pushed away considerations of Rudolph's retribution. Thoughts about him didn't belong in any kind of boudoir.

I broke away from henry's lips and gasped. "Thirsty."

Blake reached for the champagne, but I said, "Absinthe." I needed to get them so drunk, they couldn't function. Then they would spill their guts and tell me everything Jackie needed to know. Clicking my fingers, I said in my most commanding voice, "Bring it here."

Edward appeared from behind the curtain and produced the opened bottle. He gulped a mouthful and passed it to Blake, who took a swig and passed it to me.

I let the tiniest of splashes land between my lips, then I stuck out my tongue. "Bleurgh! It doesn't taste right."

Henry took a long sip, grimaced and handed it to me. "It's fine."

I passed it to Blake. "What do you think?"

He took another sip. "Aniseed and licorice. What were you expecting?"

"You try it," I said to Edward who perched on the edge of the bed by our feet.

He reached down, tasted it and shrugged. "Maybe champagne's more to your liking."

By the time the boys finished half the small bottle of absinthe and the two bottles of champagne, their eyes glazed, but Henry and Blake still pawed at my bodice and made noises about deflowering me. They took turns landing increasingly sloppy kisses on my lips, but I kept staring at Edward, who didn't move any closer to us on the mattress.

A frustrated breath huffed out of my nostrils. Why wasn't he loosening up? I shoved Blake out of the way and pushed myself up on my elbows. "Edward, are you alright?"

"Ignore him." Henry pulled me back down. "He's melancholy tonight."

Edward ran a hand through his hair. "Maybe I shouldn't have had so much to drink. Sometimes, I forget alcohol is a depressant."

The boys each nuzzled at my neck, and I pushed myself onto my knees and crawled at the foot of the bed where Edward sat.

"What about us?" Henry slurred.

"Kiss Blake for a minute." I pressed my chest against Edward's back and wrapped my arms around his shoulders. "I'm going to see if I can do something about his melancholy."

Edward tilted his head and smiled. "Sorry."

"What for?"

"You were probably looking forward to this party, and I'm too preoccupied."

Behind us, someone groaned. I glanced over my shoulder to find Henry lying on top of Blake and kissing the life out of him. I blinked at the sight, not quite believing they had taken my suggestion so seriously.

"Help me off the bed," I said. "This petticoat is awkward."

Blake held my waist with both hands, lifted me off the bed and set me on my feet. "Let's get some fresh air."

I glanced at the two drunken boys kissing on the bed. Henry's fireman jacket had slipped over his shoulders, revealing his broad, muscular back. The pulse between my legs reverberated, sending a shockwave of arousal through my core. Blake moaned and cupped Henry's muscular ass with both hands.

My tongue darted out to lick my lips. "Will they be alright?"

Edward wrapped an arm around my waist and guided me toward the balcony. On the way, he picked up another bottle of champagne. "Blake's an equal-opportunity slut, and Henry's always happy to go along for the ride. They'll be fine."

Blake's hand slipped under the waistband Henry's pants, further piquing my interest. Instead of staying to gape, I grabbed a blanket at the foot of the bed and followed Edward toward the balcony. If there was an opportunity to hear about International House, I had to take it. Jackie's words about the unsavory characters being in proximity to children were ominous. She and Rudolph wouldn't forgive me if I turned down the opportunity for a huge scoop to watch two gorgeous boys make out.

Besides, they were doing it in front of one of the cameras, the last place I wanted to get down and dirty.

CHAPTER 12

The crisp air gave me a shock as I stepped through the balcony doors, and the view of the river caused a breath to catch in the back of my throat. On one side of the Thames, the London Eye glowed cornflower blue. Opposite and a little downstream, stood Big Ben and the Houses of Parliament, illuminated with yellow light. Maybe the few scraps of alcohol I'd imbibed had gotten to my head, but the entire city looked magical.

Perhaps some of the magic might rub off on Edward, and he would give me the information I needed to satisfy Jackie's fascination with International House.

Edward uncorked the champagne bottle with a soft pop and threw the cork into the night.

"What's wrong?" I asked.

"I don't want to burden you with my problems." He leaned against the edge of the balcony and stared down at a spot on the tiled floor.

I stepped forward but kept a distance of about three feet so as not to crowd him. Trying to keep the eagerness out of my voice, I said, "Maybe there's something I can do to help."

"It's doubtful." He took several long drags of the sparkling beverage and handed me the bottle.

"Get it off your chest." I let a thimbleful bubble onto my tongue. "It's clearly bothering you."

The faint sound of a foghorn caught my attention, and I glanced down into the Thames. A cruise boat, lit up by hundreds of multi-colored lightbulbs, made its slow journey through the river. It was probably filled with party-goers.

After a moment, Edward sighed. "My father has a condition which is worsening, and we're having trouble with round-the-clock care."

I held my breath. Henry had mentioned the duke's decline while we were in that dingy room, but so much had happened since then, I wasn't sure if I correctly remembered the details. "Your butler?"

"Gregson is too old, and Father has young-onset dementia. He needs a carer young and strong enough to keep up with him."

"Oh." I tried to picture Dad in that situation, but the image was too painful. With his mother deceased, the pressure on Edward had to be tremendous. I took a swig of champagne and handed it back. "I'm so sorry."

"So am I." He backed away, leaned against one of the balcony rails and drank a few gulps. Compared to the others, he was relatively sober. I wondered if he'd drunk enough of that absinthe.

"Is he in an institution?"

Edward raised his head, giving me the strangest look as though I'd said something ridiculous. I went over what I had asked. Since Edward was sixteen or seventeen and in full-time education with only an elderly butler at home, it made sense that the Duke of Mercia might go to a facility that could give him the treatment he needed.

After several moments, he said, "We're taking care of him at home."

"You and Gregson?"

"And a male nurse Henry was kind enough to hire." He gulped down several mouthfuls.

I gasped, just as a cold breeze blew across the balcony, sending a chill running down my back. "Wait! That's what you did with the ransom money?"

Edward let out a long, weary sigh. "We're in a similar situation to the Underwoods. Father made some very poor business decisions before his diagnosis. The accountant is picking through the ledgers and trying to decipher what exactly Father has done, but it's taking time."

Without meaning to, my gaze flickered to the direction of the camera, and I pulled it back to my lap. All this time, I had thought the boys wanted a bit of spending money. But they had staged the kidnapping to help the ailing duke. My heart twisted, and a tight band of panic wrapped around my chest. If I had known... I squeezed my eyes shut. Things might have been different.

A little voice in the back of my head, the one that cried out for vengeance, whispered that it still didn't explain why they had framed me when I would have kept their secret. My chest loosened, and I exhaled a long breath.

"That's terrible." I wrapped the blanket over my shoulders. "Is there a business manager?"

"Just the full-time accountant, Gregson, and me. We'd love to bring in an expert on estate management, but Father's going to live a long life, and that ransom money might only stretch a decade."

My brows drew together. "Can the school help?"

Edward placed the bottle to his mouth, tilted his head back and drank an unholy amount of champagne. I jerked forward to grab the bottle, but by the time I reached him, he had already straightened and pulled it off his lips. He turned his gaze to the tiled floor. "If it was just the troubles of the estate, I wouldn't mind to much, but the headmaster is my biggest source of stress."

"Isn't he paying for the use of the land?"

"The academy treasurer takes care of that." Edward sighed. "Mr. Chaloner approached me with the proposal of an expensive international summer school that would take in quality students who wanted a British education."

My breathing quickened, and I tried not to turn around to check on the camera Tom had placed on the wall behind me. This was exactly what Jackie had wanted me to uncover. I dared not speak for fear of derailing his train of thought, but when he continued staring at the balcony floor, I said, "Is that how International House started?"

"The bastard brought his plans forward to January," he said between clenched teeth.

I gulped. "Is International House part of Mercia Academy?"

"It's affiliated with the Duchy of Mercia, not the academy. The headmaster capitalized on most people not knowing the difference." Bitterness laced his voice.

I slipped a hand over my mouth. This was fraud… Sort of. While the Duchy owned the estate, the academy was run by a charitable trust that paid the Duchy for the use of the land. The headmaster's international school was a completely different venture not associated with the academy but using the Mercia name to make the international students believe they'd get the same level of education as the British students.

"International House is bringing down the academy," said Edward. "None of the staff will teach there, the younger students are frightened out of their wits at some of the residents, and the headmaster has to bring in substandard personnel to attend to the students."

I shook my head. "I can't believe he would do that to the school. Who are these students, anyway?"

Edward placed the bottle on the tiled floor and stared down into the Thames. The party boat had disappeared into the distance, and a calmness settled over our stretch of the water. "He assured me they would be children of diplomats, politicians, and international executives who wanted the prestige of a British education, but having seen some of them, I'm not sure."

I thought about Nadia, who looked around twenty-five and carried large amounts of cash, and some of the shady characters whose pictures had been uploaded on the Mercia-Net. "Don't dignitaries educate their children at the right age? The people I've seen look like grown adults."

"Whoever they are, the headmaster is losing control of them."

"Can they be deported?" I took a few steps closer and placed a hand on Edward's back.

"He's arranged student visas. The Home Office can do nothing about them."

My heart ached for Edward. Mr. Chaloner had clearly taken advantage of the Duchy's financial situation and its need to pay the duke's medical expenses. The tight band of panic snaked its way back around my chest, and I wrapped my arms around Edward and forced breaths in and out of my lungs.

If I had known his situation was so dire, I wouldn't have brought him out to the balcony where everything would be recorded. Guilt scoured through my insides. I'd set things in motion that could have terrible repercussions against Edward and his father. But I couldn't stop now. Something strange was happening in International House, and the headmaster seemed to have unleashed some kind of dangerous machination.

Also, Rudolph had invested a hefty sum to get me back into Mercia Academy, and he also threatened me with military school if I failed to deliver. I blinked hard and blew out a shuddering breath. Maybe it was the alcohol in my system affecting my mood, but all I could feel now was an impending sense of doom.

"Maybe it's time to get some outside help," I murmured.

Edward drew back. "The headmaster is counting on everybody

keeping quiet about International House. Anything that tarnishes the school also damages the prospects of the students."

I leaned across the balcony and squeezed his hand. "And what about their safety? Some of them are only eleven years old. What if Mr. Chaloner decides to fill more empty buildings with even worse people?"

"That's what scares me the most." He gazed up into into the sky. A dark haze settled overhead, with heavy clouds obscuring the moon. Not a single star was visible, unlike at Mercia Academy, where on crisp nights, the entire heavens were laid bare. "I'm sorry for burdening you with my problems."

"That's what friends are for."

"Are we?" He turned, meeting my gaze with eyes so a blue so deep they appeared black in the dim light of the balcony.

"What?"

"Friends."

My mouth opened and closed, and the bones of my corset tightened around my torso. Why would he hand me information that could bury him and his precious academy if he didn't trust me? "I don't know what you mean."

"I've been so cruel to you." He let go of my hand and drew away to rest his back against the balcony's corner railing. "Without knowing anything about you except you were an American whom I found attractive, I made you the campaign of underserved name-calling, and when that didn't succeed, we resorted to cruel and dangerous pranks. How could you stand in front of me and offer me friendship? I wouldn't be quite so forgiving."

The truth in his words crushed my lungs and left me struggling for air. Everything he said was right, but my motives weren't quite so pure as forgiveness. I had wanted to infiltrate the group, find their weaknesses, and bury them in exchange for what they did to me. Now… I wasn't quite so sure.

Edward shook his head. "What we did to you afterward was

reprehensible. It would have been the breaking of a lesser person." The corners of his eyes creased with pain. "Emilia, I'm so sor—"

"Why did you do it?" I had to change the subject. Fast. If he gave me a heartfelt apology for the events surrounding the fake kidnapping, my heart would shatter with guilt. "Why bully anyone?"

He lowered his head into his hands and heaved out a long sigh. The tightness around my lungs loosened. If he was talking about himself, he wouldn't ask me awkward questions I couldn't answer. Finally, Edward said, "The academy is the only part of my life where I feel in control."

"But it's so regimented."

"Work-wise, yes…" He glanced through the doors of the balcony. Although the four-poster was visible through the glass, the curtains obscured our view of Henry and Blake. "But the academy is a predictable environment and one where I'm the king and even the most learned of teachers fear me. As the future duke, anything I say holds sway with the board."

"And the students?"

"They're like sheep, really. Deep down, they all fear becoming the target of scrutiny and disapproval. It's far easier for them to gain acceptance by aligning themselves with a more powerful influence than in being an individual."

I swallowed down the bitter taste in the back of my throat. "So, you bullied everyone who didn't fit in?"

"Only a few examples, like Rita Yelverton."

"Why?"

"The conventional thinking is that she's an affront to everything that makes us better than your average pleb. She's poor, from the wrong background and doesn't speak like us, yet she gained an academic scholarship." He shook his head. "Academic. Any more Yelvertons, and people will stop believing they are a privileged elite that deserves to one day rule Britain."

Disgust rippled through my belly, throwing off my previous

panic and guilt. I pursed my lips and hoped the camera was recording this terrible confession. "That's what you think?"

"Certainly not. If anyone can excel without a single advantage, they deserve all the success in the world."

"Really," I said, keeping my voice flat with disbelief.

He nodded. "Mercia Academy was established to teach poor boys to become elite soldiers for King Henry V. I still stand by those general principles. But you have to understand that not everyone agrees."

I lowered myself into one of the seats at the other end of the balcony and folded my arms across my chest. "Parents send their children to Mercia Academy because they can afford the fees and want a prestigious education."

"True."

"It's not because they're better than anyone else." My knee bounced up and down in time with the agitation pumping through my veins. "The headmaster doesn't mind accepting a huge donation in exchange for letting someone jump the wait list. Why does having money make someone better than anyone else?"

"It doesn't." He placed a foot on the concrete that held up the balcony's iron posts.

"Then why did you go after Rita?"

"I told you."

"No." I shot out of my seat, temper flaring with heat. "That's the reason you gave to justify your actions. You weren't protecting a fine institution. You bullied her because it was fun."

He raised his shoulders. "She was an easy target. I meant it when I said the academy was the only time I felt in control. Turning her from a proud, accomplished girl into a trembling wreck made me feel powerful."

"Like a king."

He gave me a soft nod. "Part of me wanted to see the same happen to you."

"It was all a game," I whispered, heart plummeting.

"Something about you was so compelling. Each day, I would wake up excited about the prospect of sparring with you. When you got yourself kidnapped, I realized that your fire was the only thing keeping me sane in a world where everything was falling apart."

My jaw fell slack. Any lingering feelings of guilt I had about exposing International House and getting Edward into trouble blew away in the wind. Was he saying I was no better than a favorite lab experiment?

He lifted his gaze from the river and studied my features. Maybe it was paranoia or a fear of getting caught, but a tiny voice in the back of my mind wondered if this was a test. If I dismissed his confession and acted like I understood, he would become suspicious. He might even work out that I had infiltrated the triumvirate to bring it down and had partially succeeded by exposing Blake.

My posture sagged. Second-guessing the boys was exhausting. As was all this scheming. I turned back to the chair. "You shouldn't hurt innocent people to make yourself feel better."

"I realize that now," he replied.

"What changed?"

"Being your friend gives me more happiness than being your enemy."

A lump formed in my throat. Edward was so broken. Who else but a tortured soul would ruin people's lives to feel in control? Or show kindness to others because it made him feel good, not because it was the right thing to do? I would break him further with my actions, and there was not a thing I could do to stop it. The wheels of my betrayal had already been set in motion.

"It's hard, sometimes." I forced my features into a rueful smile. "But I keep holding out that we'll return to how we were before I called the police."

"Why did you ruin things?" he stared straight into my eyes.

Inside, I bristled. If there had been something to ruin, they wouldn't have set me up for the kidnapping. I closed my eyes, sucked a deep breath through my nostrils and exhaled.

"I thought the abduction would take Henry." My throat thickened as memories resurfaced of fighting through fear and horror and grogginess of waking up in a trunk. How could Henry allow that to happen to me? "Those people drugged me at least twice. They were dangerous, or so I thought."

Edward was silent for several moments. What could you say to a person in a situation like this? Oh, sorry. Our minions injected goodness-knows-what into your system to hide the fact that they were working for us? Hope you're not too sore about the violation. It was all in a good cause. Ours.

If I was going to convince him, the most skeptical of the triumvirate, then I needed to humble myself and act like every other woman they had cast aside and allowed back into the fold. "If I had known they wouldn't really take Henry, I wouldn't have called the police. Maybe next time, confide in me?"

He gave me a half-smile. "I suppose we could have been more forthcoming."

The words were like a punch to the gut. He supposed? We had been in a relationship. Any more of these lame justifications, half-apologies and attempts to push the blame on me, and I might shove him off the balcony. "Blake and Henry have been quiet. Do you think they're sleeping?"

He stood and pulled me up with him. "Let's hope they haven't passed out in their own fluids."

I would have asked what he meant, but we stepped into the boudoir and found Blake's head at Henry's crotch. Henry threw his head back and groaned, while Blake pumped up and down on his friend's erection. Warmth trickled between my legs. I'd never seen two guys together and I wanted more.

"Are they..." I struggled for words. "Usually like this?"

Edward smiled. "Only when drunk and horny."

"Do you ever join them?"

"When we were much younger. These days, I prefer girls." His arm curled around my waist, then he drew me close and murmured into my ear, "One in particular."

Groans and moans and gasps filled the air, and wetness gathered between my folds. Edward's lips skimmed over the shell of my ear, his hot, rapid breath adding to my excitement. He also found the two on the bed hot.

"Does it excite you to see them together?" he asked.

"Yes," I whispered back.

He ran his hand down my back, over the fastenings of the corset. "We can join them. Neither would mind."

Desire pulsed through my core, filling me with an aching heat. Then I remembered the camera attached to the frame of the fourposter. "Another time."

"What's wrong?"

"After everything you've said, I need some space."

Edward wrapped both arms around my waist. "You can't just leave. We haven't finished talking."

"Actually... I'm done."

His arms dropped away. "I knew you'd overreact."

I whirled on him, anger blazing through the vessels under my skin. "What did you expect from me? A declaration of love?"

"Understanding."

"You ruined other peoples' lives because your own life outside the Academy was chaotic, and you wanted to feel in control by manipulating others. I get it."

"And?" His brows drew together.

"Now I need a little space to let everything sink in."

Henry let out a deep, shuddering moan that made my nipples tighten. If Edward hadn't left me in such a foul mood, I would have asked him to join the others, so I could watch. Instead, I headed for the door. "Give me time, alright?

Edward inclined his head. "As you wish."

I turned the handle, stepped out into the hallway and closed the door. As soon as it clicked shut, the music of the party returned, reminding me of the outside world. I doubled over and steadied myself with my hands on my knees. What had I done to Henry and Blake? With all the recent scandals surrounding Blake, Jackie was bound to put stills of him and Henry on the front page of the Correspondent.

My breath came in shallow pants, ribs straining against my tight bodice. I blinked hard, trying not to collapse from a lack of oxygen. There was no need to panic until I'd discussed the footage with Jackie. I might be able to convince her that outing two boys under the age of eighteen was a step too far and might expose them to homophobic attacks, but I doubted that such a concern would bother Rudolph.

CHAPTER 13

I spent the rest of Saturday night crashing in a suite Jackie and her team had rented to observe the party. On Sunday, I went to the Correspondent office, where the whole team sifted through the footage. Her interns had identified each guest by name, so that if they found anything interesting, they could look the person up and see whether they were worth exposing in the paper.

Jackie and I sat behind her desk, watching my conversation with Edward on the balcony. She shook her head. "I'm not surprised you want to destroy this boy. What a selfish prick."

"Is there enough on International House?" I asked.

"It's a start." Jackie let out a rasping cough. "We now know it's the headmaster's lucrative sideline, and from what Edward Mercia says, they seem to be splitting the proceeds. It's a pity you didn't think to ask the ratios—"

"But I didn't want to sound like a journalist." My shoulders drooped. The footage I had captured was pretty damning. I didn't know if it was enough to get the headmaster into trouble, but considering Edward had been tight-lipped about International

House until now, I thought Jackie would have been a little more impressed.

She nodded and stared back at the screen. "He would have clammed up, then. The way you handled things was great, but I need more to finish the story."

"What are you looking for?" I held my breath, wondering what she would demand next.

"Evidence. How much are these students paying? Who are they? Where is the money going?"

I shifted in my seat. "That's a lot."

"There's a file somewhere with all the evidence. I need it."

Turning my head, I closed my eyes and let out a long, frustrated huff. "I'm not a cat burglar."

"You'll find a way."

I tried to suggest Mr. Carbuncle, but Jackie said the man was becoming agitated with her reporter's demands to install more cameras. Any more pressure, and he might leave the school and disappear. She said she would reword Edward's speech about bullying, change a few details, embellish it with real events taken from the Mercia-Net and publish a piece as an interview with an anonymous public schoolboy.

Next, we turned to the footage of Henry and Blake. She grimaced and fast-forward through most of it, slowing down when Edward came into the picture to talk.

"Buckingham Palace has threatened to have us investigated if we publish anything about Blake Simpson-West. He's off-limits unless we want to get shut down."

Relief whooshed out of my lungs. "So, you won't use the footage?"

Jackie shook her head. "But you might be able to use it to force a confession out of Henry Bourneville and get him to clear your name."

I glanced away. A video like that might get either of them

attacked by a homophobe. I wanted to see them humiliated, not physically hurt. Besides, after agreeing to be Sergei's beard, it would be awfully hypocritical of me to threaten to expose Henry's gay sex video. "It's too low a blow."

Jackie pushed her bleached hair behind her ears and fixed me with a hard stare. "So is framing an innocent girl for a crime she didn't commit. Do you know what would have happened to you if Rudolph didn't pay the Bourneville family to drop the charges?"

"No," I replied in a small voice.

"An institution for young offenders, followed by prison, depending on the length of your sentence. Henry Bourneville would never have guessed that Rudolph would pay to make the problem disappear. That's what's so terrible about what they did. Your whole life would have been blighted by their lies." She took a long sip from her mug of black coffee. "It's still blighted. Except now, everyone in the know thinks your rich stepfather bailed you out."

A newfound anger simmered in my belly. I clenched my teeth and stood. She was right, and I was pulling my punches. "I'll find another way to get the truth out of him. Maybe a video confession. Do you think you'll be able to track down the kidnappers based on the information I sent you?"

"They already left the squat, but we have photos of the room. If Henry can supply one name, we might be able to put together a sensational piece."

"Try Bingham's Outward Bound. That's the name of the company who arranged the hiking and camping during our trip." An idea hit me on the side of my head, knocking me back onto my seat. "Mr. Bingham's assistants knew Mr. Frost!"

She blinked. "I don't follow."

My hands shook, and I blurted out everything on my mind. "Paul Frost. Our Latin master. Edward gave him an invitation to the party. He supplies things, like absinthe. He knew the assistants on our hiking trip, who drove the vehicles up the hill. What if Mr.

Frost was involved? The boys needed a car for the first prank and for the kidnapping. What if he introduced the boys to the assistants?"

"Slow down!" Jackie raised her hand. "What?"

After a few deep breaths, I explained that Mr. Frost was a former scholarship student who appeared to be on good terms with Edward, partially because he supplied them with illicit items like the strongest kinds of absinthe. He also knew the assistants on the school trip and might have arranged the kidnapping for the boys.

Jackie licked her lips. "Leave it with me. We'll check the footage and see what he did at the party. If he supplied anyone with anything stronger than alcohol, we'll approach him and offer him a deal like we did with Carbuncle."

I took the train back to Mercia Academy in a daze. What if the kidnappers had bungled the doses? What if Rudolph hadn't bailed me out? The train sped through swathes of green countryside, the chug of its wheels on the track fueling my paranoia.

My head flopped down to my chest. By working with a small newspaper that now had the attention of the national press, I had the potential to ruin lives. But if I backed out, it would be military school and Rudolph's wrath.

And the boys... My feelings for them were murky. I had felt something for Henry, and I thought it had been real, but I couldn't help associating him with the brunt of the betrayal. Underneath Edward's cold exterior was a warm, sensitive soul, but beneath that lay I worldview I failed to understand.

I brought my coffee cup to my lips and stared out of the window at the fields whizzing by. Blake was the warmest of the three by far, and the most fun. He was the instigator and the one who brought us all together. But I hadn't seen anything of his true personality. Someone who disliked Charlotte had to have at least one redeeming feature, right?

A sigh slid from my lips. Every so often, I'd get glimpses of how things used to be between us, and my heart would melt... then my blood would boil when I remembered it had been a facade.

I rested my head in my hands and took several deep, calming breaths. I was in over my head, and now it was time to swim.

～

Monday morning at breakfast was abuzz with tales from the party. I sat between Edward and Blake, stealing glances at Blake and not quite believing how hot he had been that night. His black hair hung loose over his face, as though he hadn't had time to style it this morning. It framed his dark eyes and high-cheekbones perfectly. The top button of his shirt hadn't been fastened, and the knot of his tie hung half an inch below his collar. For Mercia Academy, he looked seductively disheveled.

"I missed you yesterday," he murmured. "And at the party."

"The absinthe went to my head, and I sat on the balcony with Edward. Did you have a good time?"

"Wonderful," he purred.

I would have asked what he did when he had finished sucking off Henry, but I'd seen footage of the three of them leaving the room together and joining the rest of the party. Jackie would email or text if they did something other than hold court.

Coates, the rugby player who had complained about International House, sauntered up to the table. "Great party," he said to Henry. "Thanks for snagging me an invite."

Henry grinned. "Did you get lucky?"

"You wouldn't believe me if I told you." He strolled out of the dining room with his hands in his pockets and nodded to Charlotte as she swept in with her nose in the air.

"Hobson." She placed her hands on her waist and thrust out her right hip. Wendy and Patricia flanked her and struck a similar pose but with far less attitude.

I picked up a jug of orange juice, which made her flinch, then made a show of pouring it into my glass. When I finished, I took a long sip and glanced up. "Sorry, Underwood, did you say something?"

"Nice party. I'll have to tell your fiancé that you disappeared with three boys."

"Do you want his email address or will you post it on his Facebook page?"

The smug twist of her face melted into slack disappointment. "You're a bitch."

"And by your own admission, you're a gatecrasher, but you don't see me complaining."

Her mouth opened and closed like a washed up blobfish, and she glanced from Henry to Blake, as though they might say something in her defense. I raised my brows and gave her a little smirk. When nobody spoke, she stormed off toward a table at the other end of the dining hall. I made a mental note to ask Jackie if Charlotte had done anything interesting during the party.

A few sycophants approached the head table, thanking the triumvirate for a good time. I bit hard into my toast. Never mind that I'd gotten the invitations because my fake fiancé had been playing at the venue. This kind of behavior was typical of the people in Elder House, though, as these were the people who had relished humiliating me in that gauntlet. I looked forward to reading about them in the Saturday Correspondent.

∼

After classes, I walked along the path bordered by bare magnolia trees. The pale winter sun shone down from a cloudless sky, softening the frost underfoot. In the distance, I spotted Nadia, the girl from International House who had needed phone cards. Her shoulders were drooped, and her bouffant had disappeared, replaced by limp, black hair that hung over the sides of her face like drapes. Obviously, life at Mercia Academy, or whatever the headmaster had called his scam, wasn't working out for her.

"Nadia!" I stood on my tiptoes and waved.

She stopped and gave me a half-hearted wave back.

I jogged over the frosty ground, careful not to slip. When I reached her, I asked, "Do you like hot chocolate? I'm going to the tuck shop to get some."

"I need more international phone cards." She raised her shoulders around her ears and walked alongside me. A couple of men in thick, sheepskin jackets stood outside the double doors of International House, smoking roll-up cigarettes. From their thick, five o'clock shadows, they were university age or older, and certainly not teachers.

"Didn't the cards you bought last long enough?" I asked. Lame question, but it might prompt her into explaining why she appeared so homesick.

"I worry for my fiancé," she said in a small voice. "The police in my city hate him and say he sells drugs."

"Oh no!" I turned to her. "Why aren't you with him to help him fight them?"

Her face crumpled, and I gave her a pat on the shoulder, ignoring the guilt churning in my stomach. Nadia wanted to get her problems off her chest, and whatever she said, I wouldn't repeat the details to anyone. I just needed enough information to work out how the headmaster was marketing the school overseas. We stepped into the tuck shop, which was modeled like the village tea shop with its wooden tables and chairs. Then I told her to wait for me, and I ordered two cups of steaming, hot cocoa.

Nadia stared into her cup. "His family sent me here, so the police would not hurt me."

I placed the cup to my lips. It was more likely that her fiancé's family sent her to Mercia Academy for her to avoid being forced to give evidence. "How long will you be here?"

She squeezed her eyes shut. "One year."

I took a sip of the sweet, chocolatey drink. So much for the headmaster's agreement that International House would be a summer school. Nadia was a nice woman who had been caught up in a situation not of her own making. But some of the others who had been featured in the Mercia-Net were awful. She was too upset to continue a conversation, so we sat in silence, nursing our drinks until she decided to call her fiancé.

⁓

Just before bedtime, I walked down to Edward's study and knocked. He appeared at the door, looking drawn. "Emilia?"

"I have something to tell you. Are you alone?"

He stepped aside. "What is it?"

I walked inside and glanced at the crackling fireplace. Jackie told me that Mr. Carbuncle had set up a couple of cameras in Edward's study so she would see my attempts to cajole him into handing over evidence. I lowered myself into the sofa adjacent to that fateful armchair and patted the seat next to me.

When he sat, I twisted around and took his hands. "I spoke to someone in International House," I said with a quavering note of worry. His brows furrowed, and he parted his lips, presumably to admonish me, but I spoke over him. "She's not like the others, but her family sent her here so she wouldn't testify against a drugs charge."

"What?" he whispered, face paling.

"I-I think the students might be connected to organized crime. You've seen them and how they act on camera. They're not right."

His chest heaved up and down in a series of shallow breaths. Then he turned away, blinking rapidly. "I suspected something like that, but if I report the headmaster, the school's reputation will be in ruins."

"He told you they were the children of dignitaries," I said. "Can he show you checks written from legitimate sources like foreign governments?"

"The accountant gave me a file and told me to read through it, but I haven't yet dared."

I gasped. "Why not?"

He clenched the edge of his leather seat cushion and squeezed his eyes shut. "I was afraid of what I might find."

I rubbed my thumb over his hand, giving him what comfort I could offer. It was an awful situation, but I still had a mission. Jackie needed evidence that the money was streaming to the headmaster and that it came from disreputable sources. I needed that file, and I would say anything to convince Edward to hand it over.

"Do you remember that woman who brought me here?" I asked. "Marissa, with the loud voice?"

His brows drew together, but he nodded.

"She's an accounts clerk who did bank reconciliations for a year. Maybe she can help. She's working in Rudolph's London office right now and could use a freelance side-gig. And she's American, so wouldn't know who to contact if she found something strange."

He dipped his head. "I'll think about it."

A shock of excitement rocked my insides. If I kept the pressure on, he would give me that file before the end of the month.

CHAPTER 14

On Monday, an old man filled in for Mr. Frost in Latin classes, explaining that our teacher had a death in his immediate family and had returned home to make funeral arrangements. I couldn't focus on my Creative Writing assignment, as I itched to speak to Jackie and find out if she had caused Mr. Frost's disappearance. With Blake already somewhat disgraced, and plans for the exposure of International House and Edward's involvement in the scam underway, I focused on my next target: Henry.

He sat next to Edward at the desk in front of Blake and me and had taken off his blazer. The cotton of his white shirt clung to every muscle, which bunched and stretched as he moved. I closed my eyes and cast my mind back to the time we had spent together in that filthy room. Lying within his strong embrace had been so comforting. When his beautiful body had engulfed mine and those fingers had teased me until I had splintered beneath his touch, I'd felt so protected and whole and fulfilled, even though we were both in a desperate situation.

My fingers closed around my fountain pen, and my nostrils flared. It had all been a lie.

That lying Henry.

That lying, fucking, scheming, backstabbing Henry, who I would bury alive.

How great would it feel if I exposed his treachery to the world, had him cast out by his parents, ostracized by his peers, broken, crying and pleading for forgiveness. My breaths became shallow, and a tiny smile played on my lips. I'd lay him out on his back, tie him to that filthy mattress and take my pleasure from his defeated, quivering body.

"What are you thinking about?" Blake murmured into my ear. "You look positively turned on."

"Henry."

Henry turned around. "What?"

Blake leaned forward. "She's thinking about you, and her nipples are standing to attention."

Edward twisted in his seat, glanced down at my chest, smirked, and turned back to his work.

Henry rocked his chair back on two legs, leaning its backrest against my desk. "What do you have in mind?"

I leaned forward and whispered, "Nothing I can say in public."

"You there," snapped the substitute teacher. "No talking in class."

"Yes, sir!" Henry shifted his chair back onto four legs.

Ignoring Blake's attempts at dirty talk, I dipped my head and scribbled a few lines of verse on my Creative Writing notebook. I might hate Henry with the passion of a thousand suns, but there was no denying how hot he had looked at the party when shuddering and trembling under Blake's touch.

After class, Henry caged me against the wall with his arms, a shit-eating grin on his face. His blonde hair flopped down over his temples, making him look like the fun kind of guy who wouldn't frame a girl for kidnapping. "Want to get hot and bothered over me tonight?"

"I don't know…" I let my gaze flicker from his lips to the hard pecs that strained through the cotton of his white shirt. "What do you have in mind?"

Blake sidled up to us with a smirk. "Come to our room. We have four different types of booze."

"Next time," I said.

Blake's face fell, and he stuffed his hands in his pockets. "See you later, then."

Henry spared him the barest of glances before turning back to me. "We can go to Edward's—"

I dipped out of his arm cage and walked around him. A gaggle of fifth-year girls who had been watching the spectacle giggled. "I need time alone with you to talk."

His brows furrowed. "We can do that. Just tell me what you want."

"Let's walk to the village for some of Jean-Paul's liqueur coffee."

"Alright." His shoulders drooped. What had he been expecting? A night at a local bed and breakfast?

"See you later," I replied in my breeziest tone. Henry walked to his next lesson, while I stayed back to watch him retreat.

He turned around and gave me a half-smile, which I returned with a wide grin. Mom always said that the way to a man's heart was to let him talk about himself and later paraphrase what he had said to make him think there was a connection. I would replicate that closeness we had in that room, get him to open his heart, and then crush him like he crushed me.

∽

I wore a close-fitting cashmere sweater with a wool miniskirt and thick tights to our date, with Ugg boots to keep my feet warm during the walk. A long, hooded coat finished off the outfit, and I dabbed on a bit of gloss to attract his attention to my lips.

Rita glanced up from her music scores she had laid out on her desk. "You look nice. Are you going out with one of them?"

"Henry. What are you working on?"

"A composition. My friend, whose brother got into Oxford on a musical scholarship, said that playing something original had made the difference."

"Can I hear it?"

She glanced at the door. "Won't you be late?"

"Do I care?"

She placed her fingers over her lips and giggled. "I still can't believe you came back."

"Sometimes, neither can I."

"They don't like me playing instruments in the dorm, but this is what I have so far." She pulled out her smartphone and tapped a few buttons. A piano concerto rang out, reminding me of Sergei's music.

I lowered myself onto the bed, feeling queasy. Why hadn't I brought Rita down to London on any of the times I had met Sergei? She probably hadn't asked because her enforced humility wouldn't allow it, but I knew she was devoted to music, and I still hadn't offered. Rita's playing was like escaping into another world where people laughed and danced and didn't play games with others' lives. The piece ended abruptly, and my head snapped up.

"That's all I have for now." She gave me a tight smile.

"It's wonderful!" I went to my closet mirror and fastened my long, woolen coat. "Can I show it to Sergei?"

Her face paled. "I-it isn't ready!"

"Next time I see him, I'll tell him about my roommate, who's a genius on the piano."

Her face scrunched up, but the little smile she gave me belied her true level of confidence. Anyone who got into a place like Mercia Academy on both a musical and an academic scholarship had to know they were good. That was the whole point of Edward's bullying.

She threw her arms around me and whispered, "When you've finished your plan, don't wait around to watch the damage. Run."

I nodded. "What happened to me last term will never happen again."

Rita stepped back and blew out a long breath. "Have a… productive evening."

"I'll try!" I stepped out of the door to find the triumvirate outside in the hallway. Henry stood in the middle, wearing a peacoat, hat and scarf, while Blake stood to his right still in his school uniform. Edward stood on Henry's left, wearing a faint smile.

All the blood drained from my face. How long had they been standing outside, and what had they heard? Rita had whispered the most incriminating part of our conversation, but I was sure there was a part where I'd implied I didn't care if I'd kept Henry waiting.

Blake stepped forward and whistled. "What are you wearing under the coat?"

"Chanel Number Five."

His gaze flickered down my body. "Good choice."

"What are the three of you doing up here?" I asked. "Shouldn't you be working on your prep or something?"

Blake smirked. "After that little display in Latin class, we thought you might need a pair of chaperones."

"Why?" I placed my hands on my hips.

Blake stepped forward, hooked his arms through mine, and wrapped them around my waist. "A girl walking alone in the dark with that beast might find herself set upon in the bushes."

I glanced up at Henry, who shook his head and smiled. I returned his smile with a smirk. These guys were a lot of fun when they weren't stabbing a girl in the back. Placing my hand over Blake's heart, I said, "It's tempting, but I'll take my chances with beastie boy."

With a theatrical sigh, Blake stepped back and grinned at Edward. "It was worth a try, eh, Woodie?"

I clapped my hand over my mouth. "I've never heard you use that nickname."

"And you never will." Edward wrapped an arm around Blake's neck and marched him down the hallway. "Do pop in and say goodnight on your way back."

"Sure."

Henry crooked an arm and flashed me a grin. "Shall we?"

Ignoring my aching heart, I stepped forward and took his arm. We walked down the stairs, past a livid Charlotte and her two remaining doppelgängers, through the entrance hall with its crackling, pine-scented fire, and out into the cold evening.

The entire campus was blanketed in white from a sudden bout of snow. I inhaled a breath of cold air and blew it out through my mouth, creating a cloud of condensation.

"What made you choose a walk when we could have liqueur coffee at Edward's study?" asked Henry.

I glanced down at the layer of snow staining my boots. "There's something about the three of you together. You're all bad influences on each other. Ten minutes, and you'll have me losing control."

"Perhaps you're the bad influence on us," he replied.

We walked under the path of magnolia trees, and I gazed up into the darkening sky through their skeletal branches. "I wouldn't be too sure about that. You and Blake put on a really hot show at the party."

"You should have joined us," he said.

"I wouldn't have been able to get out of my dress after drinking all that champagne."

"Next time, then." He pressed a kiss on my temple.

"Did Edward join you after I left?"

"He mostly likes to watch."

"Do you and Blake..." I chewed my lips, struggling for the right words. "Do you do that often?"

"It's not something we'd do these days sober unless there's a girl involved."

My eyes widened. Edward had implied they got together often, but he hadn't specified whether alcohol had been involved. I glanced over my shoulder at Elder House, which stood in the distance with its windowsills covered in snow. "Who have you all been with?"

"Just you, unfortunately. As adventurous as the girls around here might act, they're strictly monogamous." He pulled me close. "It's just one of the reasons we're all so crazy about you."

I dipped my head. "Then it's a pity you framed me for your kidnapping."

"I can't tell you how sorry I am about that." Sincerity shone in his green eyes. "You got knocked out, and we didn't know what to do with you. If you woke and raised the alarm, the police would take an inventory of who wasn't at the campsite and catch up with us. We had to take you along, and the others decided to rig things so that you'd be blamed if you ever spoke to the police and got anyone caught. I went along with it because I didn't know you back on the trip."

"The others?" I rolled over what he had said in my mind. Whoever had driven him to the squat needed to return to the campsite before Henry and Edward raised the alarm. "Who else was involved?"

He pressed another kiss on my temple. "Let's not dwell on that."

"It's hard not to when I spent so many days locked up." I gazed into his glistening eyes, pressing my gloved palms on his chest. "Henry, I need to know."

He glanced away and sighed. "Can't you be satisfied with the way things are right now? Your stepfather got the charges dropped, you're back at the academy, and we're all getting along so well. Bringing up this subject only jeopardizes what we have together."

"I don't want to lose you again." The lie felt like sandpaper on my vocal cords. How dare he act like I was the one making things awkward? My name was tarnished, I still had flashbacks from being locked up and beaten, and the threat of military school still hung over my head. I blinked several times to fake the effect of holding back tears. "But can't you see why these things might be important to me? I need to clear my name."

He swiped his thumb over my cheekbone. "You have to let it go, Emilia."

If my fingers could shoot out icicles, I would have plunged one into his chest and told him to let go of that. Easing out a breath of frustration, I said, "But the police have my name on record—"

"Which will be expunged the moment you turn eighteen." He kissed the tip of my nose. "That's in less than a year, and this mess will be a distant memory."

With a deep sigh, I lied, "Maybe you're right."

He wrapped his arms around me and pecked me on the lips. "Things will be great between us four. You'll see."

I hugged back, inhaling his fresh, minty scent. I'd give him one more chance. One more chance to fix things and clear my name, or I would unleash a torrent of shit that would make the selfish prick wish he was back in that dingy room.

CHAPTER 15

We continued arm in arm past the porter's lodge, a single-story building that marked the start of the campus. The frost underfoot piled inches deep and crunched with each of our steps. A cool breeze meandered through the trees lining the road that led to the academy gates, bringing with it the scent of juniper.

I stole a glance at Henry, who gazed down at me with eyes that shone with so much warmth, my heart ached. Who was he, really? A calculating bastard subduing me with affection and sweet promises, or a naive fool who thought he could fix the situation he'd created, without owning up to his misdeeds?

I fastened the top button of my coat and stared straight ahead into the grove of oaks on our left. None of that mattered. Henry would either clear my name and prove his apologies were heartfelt, or I would sit back and watch him burn. He'd writhe on the ground, shirtless in that sexy fireman's costume, shuddering and twitching and moaning… just as he had when Blake had sucked him off on the four-poster bed.

Heat rippled down to my core, and I let out a soft moan. That night at the party, Henry had been magnificent. I had almost wanted to crawl on that bed and join Blake in making him come undone.

"Are you alright?" he placed his cool fingertips on my hot cheek.

My chest heaved, and I glanced around. The porter's lodge was a quarter of a mile away, with no one wandering around its grounds. I didn't feel like walking miles to the village for a cup of coffee, not when there was nothing left to discuss. "No... I'm far from it."

Henry's brows drew together, and he dipped his head to meet my gaze with concerned, green eyes. "Do you want to—"

"I want you against a tree. Now."

His brows rose. "You're serious."

"Right now."

It took a few moments for realization to sink in, but his lips curled into a grin, and he glanced over his shoulder into the grove, presumably looking for a tree large enough for me to ravish him. A thick oak stood behind him to his left, and he backed into it, breathing hard, staring down at me with eyes that danced with excitement.

I shoved him as hard as he could against the tree trunk. A pair of robins flew out from the branches above, and thick chunks of unmelted snow fell onto the six-inch pile at our feet. I unbuttoned his pea coat and yanked his scarf to the side.

Henry's breath hitched. "What are you—"

"Silence." I pulled down his neck and slammed my lips onto his.

Henry pressed back with equal fervor, his tongue darting out to part my lips. He tasted of mint and warmth and deceptive familiarity. A snarl reverberated in the back of my throat. The wretched boy was trying to take control. I pressed my hip into the juncture of his thighs, reveling in the hardening of his flesh.

"Emilia," he groaned.

"Shut up." I clamped my gloved hands on the side of his face, brought our lips together, and pressed him harder against the tree trunk.

Henry moaned low and deep, seeming to get the hint. I was in charge, today. I fisted his hair and held him in place while I delved my tongue into his mouth. For that moment, he was mine. Mine to kiss, mine to arouse, and mine to command.

Above us, the robins released a stream of high pitched tweets, presumably telling us to get out of their territory. Ignoring the noisy birds, I ravished his mouth with my tongue with long, languid strokes, enjoying the heave of his chest, tightness of his arms around my waist, and the strain of his erection against my belly. My core pulsed and throbbed in time with my pounding heart, and warm, wet, slickness gathered between my folds.

His hands skimmed the placket of my coat, fingers reaching for the top button.

"No!" I gave him a sharp slap on the wrist. Betrayers didn't get to call the shots.

"Emilia," he said in a gasp.

My hand skimmed down his hot, heaving body, and I reached between his legs and squeezed his balls, delighting in his pained moan rumbling against my chest. "Quiet." I palmed his thickening erection, which pulsed and twitched at my command. "You're my plaything, and you don't get to do anything until I give you an order."

"Y-yes."

"Yes, what?"

"Yes, Emilia."

Since I didn't have a leather bodice, let alone a horsewhip to beat him into submission, I accepted that answer and groped at his firm ass. He bucked into my hand, trying to increase the friction.

"Stop," I snapped.

He drew back, eyes wide, panting through slackened, reddened lips. "What's wrong?"

"I know what you're trying to do, and you don't get to climax before me."

"What do you want?"

I pointed at the ground. "Kneel."

His head jerked back. "You're joking. There's half a foot of snow down there."

"Really?" I raised my brow, giving him a moment to reconsider. When he didn't kneel on the ground I made a one-shouldered shrug. "We can go back to Edward's study, and I'll have Blake—"

Before I could finish that sentence, he fell onto his knees and unfastened the bottom few buttons of my coat.

"That's enough." I eased down my woolen tights and panties. The cold air hit my damp folds, making me shudder. Before I could freeze off my extremities, I grabbed Henry by the back of his blond head and shoved his face into my crotch.

He stilled for a second, as though not knowing how he'd gone from walking to the gates to kneeling on the ground with a face full of auburn pubes, but then he huffed out a laugh. At his first lick, the combination of the cold air and his hot tongue made me cry out and twist my fingers into his hair. He grunted and circled my clit with his flattened tongue, generating a current of sparks with each movement. I closed my eyes, loosened my grip on his hair, and relaxed into his hot caresses.

Henry groaned against me, sending pleasurable vibrations up my core. My muscles clenched and unclenched, remembering the feel of those thick fingers inside me. As much as I yearned to be filled, I wanted to prolong the pleasure and have him on his knees, worshipping my slit until I splintered.

"That's it," I said between gritted teeth. "Put that lying tongue to use."

Henry pulled back, letting in a gust of cold air. "What did you say?"

"Did I tell you to stop?" I shoved his head back into my crotch.

He lapped at my nub, flicking that deceiver's tongue over and over again with relentless endurance. Shockwaves of pleasure darted down my legs, making them tremble so much, I had to hold onto Henry's shoulders for balance. He must have taken that as a signal to increase his efforts because his licks turned into the most intense, open-mouthed kisses.

Whimpers filled my throat as his tongue had me shuddering and spasming. I dug my fingers into him as the pleasure wound and coiled around my core like a spring. My head fell to my chest, and I panted through parted lips, parsing the intensifying sensations. Sweat gathered in my brow, and warmth built up beneath my woolen clothes. A breeze would chill my skin, but then the heat from beneath my coat would warm it. I swallowed hard and moaned.

Henry's thumbs pressed into the flesh of my inner thighs, the movement opening me further into his caresses. The pleasure spiked, and something deep within me broke, releasing wave upon wave of the most intense climax of my life.

"Yes!" I cried out.

The noise made the robins up above take flight.

His mouth clamped around me as I came, and his tongue flattened out as though not wanting to miss a drop of my undoing.

I rested the back of my head against the tree trunk, boneless and spent. There was something to be said about making out with someone when you were too pissed at them to give a shit about their own pleasure or what they thought. It was liberating, and the orgasms were more intense.

Henry pulled up my hose and panties, then adjusted my skirt back over my hips. He tried to rise, but I pushed him down.

"What about me?" He stared up at me with plaintive eyes. "Aren't you going to—"

"I want to watch you."

"A-alright." Excitement made his voice hitch. "No girl has ever made me do this. But how are you going to see everything when it's so dark?"

I pulled out my smartphone, tapped the flashlight button, and pointed the beam at his crotch.

Henry fumbled over his fly, pulled himself, out and let his gaze flicker from my eyes to my lips. "Are you recording this?"

Ignoring my watering mouth, I said, "Do you want me to?"

He chuckled. "Not really."

"Then don't put ideas into my head." I gave myself a mental slap. How could I not have thought to record it?

It took Henry less than a dozen pumps to bring himself to a moaning climax. The wretched fool didn't give me any warning and shot his junk over my coat. I kicked him in the thigh, and he promised to buy me a new one. After he tucked himself back into his pants, fastened his coat, and retrieved his scarf from where I'd dropped it, he stood and wrapped his arms around me, laughing like a look. "Oh Emilia, you really are the most amusing girl."

Annoyance rippled through my relaxed state, and I rolled my eyes. He had said something similar when he had pretended to be abducted, and look where that amusement got me.

"We may as well return to Elder House." I broke out of his embrace and headed back toward the campus.

"Are you sure?" he asked. "What about the liqueur coffee?"

"You're such an attentive date." I gave him a tight smile and grabbed his hand. It was a pity he was so lax about other things, like a girl's need to clear her name.

As we walked back toward the porter's lodge, Henry gushed about the way I had taken charge, how hot it had made him, and how he wanted me to do it again but include Edward and Blake. I pictured the triumvirate hard and naked at my feet, and a laugh huffed out of my throat. I would hurl an etiquette book at Edward, pour red ink over Blake and restrain Henry's hands in duct tape, so he couldn't climax.

When we reached the steps of Elder House, Henry invited me to Edward's study for coffee. From the excited gleam in his eyes, I could tell he wanted a repeat performance. A petty retort formed on my tongue to tell him to wait until he'd turned eighteen, but I didn't want to bring up my grievances again without a plan. Instead, I refused and walked through the reception hall and up the stairs.

∼

The next morning at first break, I returned to Elder House to find Charlotte and Patricia squealing over a huge package.

I peered into my mailbox to see if Mom had sent me a postcard or some sort of sign that she remembered having a daughter. It was empty.

"I ought to thank you, Hobson," said a nasal voice from behind my back. When I didn't turn around to ask what for, Charlotte continued. "I met the most amazing man because of your party. He's older, handsome, rich, and smitten."

Patricia sniffed. "Much better than the immature louts we have here."

I turned. Charlotte pulled back her shoulders, making her boobs strain against the burgundy blazer, and Patricia mimicked the action, looking like a mime artist imitating a chicken. I suppressed a smirk, and said in my calmest voice, "That's great."

Charlotte's mouth slackened. "What did you say?"

"I'm happy for you." I walked past them, through the doorway, and toward the stairs. "Excuse me, while I get some textbooks."

As soon as I reached the first run of the stairs, Patricia said, "Bitch."

My feet ground to a halt, and I whirled around. Patricia's eyes widened, and she took a step back, hiding half her taller, thinner body behind Charlotte's. My skin prickled with irritation. I hadn't said or done anything to her, yet she felt the need to call me names within my earshot.

"What was that?" I asked in a calm voice.

Patricia's hand shot out to hide her mouth. "Nothing."

"You called me a bitch." I walked back into the reception hall. "Why?"

Patricia glanced at Charlotte for support, but her friend's gaze dropped to the package she cradled in her arms. A silence stretched out, broken only by the crack and sizzle of the fire. As if spurred on by an invisible bout of courage, Patricia flared her nostrils. "What do you want?"

"I haven't repaid you for last term's stunt, and if you dare call me names again, I'll give you a taste of what I suffered."

Her mouth puckered like she had eaten a lemon, but she remained silent, and Charlotte seemed too lost in her admiration of whatever was in the package to comment. I turned back to the stairs and took them two at a time. Jackie might be able to tell me the identity of her generous benefactor and give me an update on the situation with Mr. Frost.

After picking up my books and sending a message on my burner phone, I headed out of Elder House to toward the main teaching block. The clouds cleared, and pale sunlight thinned the frost on the lawn, allowing patches of green to shine through. Rock salt lined the pathway leading to the main teaching block, making me wonder why they hadn't used it weeks ago.

"Emilia!" shouted a voice from the direction of the tuck shop.

I turned to find Nadia standing a few feet away from the entrance to International House. My stomach flip-flopped. I hadn't seen her for a few days, and had worried she might have regretted confiding in me about her fiancé's drug charges. The bouffant had returned to her hair, which had to mean things were going better at home.

I jogged across the lawn and grinned. "How are you?"

"I need some help." She stuffed her hands into her pockets.

"What's wrong?"

"Will you come to my room? I can show you there."

A boulder of apprehension rolled through my belly, but I suppressed the reaction. Nadia was a nice woman, alone and needing a favor from a friend. Nothing bad could come of going with her. "Sure."

I followed Nadia into the building. As it was more modern than Elder House, its entrance hall was warmed by radiators instead of fireplaces. The marble-floored hallways reminded me of the main teaching block, as did the small atrium where two corridors bisected. Cigarette buts littered the ground, making me shudder. Did Edward know the international students were treating his family property with such disrespect?

Nadia's room was on the first floor. Unlike the space I shared with Rita in Elder House, Nadia's was a single-study room with modern furniture and a door leading to the bathroom. No pictures adorned the desk or walls, making me wonder if she'd had to leave the country in a hurry and hadn't been able to pack keepsakes.

"How can I help you?" I asked.

"I do not understand this." She walked to her desk, opened up a folder and showed me a photocopy of this year's GCSE exam paper, the tests used in schools all over Britain. It was stamped by the educational authority and marked highly confidential.

My breath caught in the back of my throat, and I stiffened, pulling back every reaction, so as not to alarm Nadia. Students weren't supposed to see this until they sat their exams.

"What don't you understand?" I asked.

"The teacher said I had to learn this for exams in June, but it is just questions."

"He didn't explain what they were for?"

Nadia shook her head. "He does not come in every day."

I rubbed my chin, trying not to salivate. "Let me take a photo of these, and I can look on the internet and give you a list of books that can give you the answers."

"You would do that?"

I nodded. "Would you like me to order them on the internet for you? I can have them delivered to International House."

Her cheeks turned pink. "Thank you, Emilia!"

I swallowed hard. If the Correspondent published evidence of the headmaster basing a curriculum on public exam papers, it would be damning. But if I could get Edward's file, and have Jackie link this scandal to prove that he was also accepting candidates linked to organized crime, I would bury the headmaster along with Edward.

CHAPTER 16

The following Saturday morning, I sat between Henry and Edward, my gaze glued to my smartphone. A detailed article in the Correspondent revealed how Charlotte's father had falsely claimed expenses to bolster his ministerial salary. Mr. Underwood had gotten the government to pay for a luxury apartment he rented through an agency, but a quick search through the land registry showed that Mr. Underwood already owned it outright.

He also listed Charlotte as his secretary, earning a salary of twelve-thousand pounds a year, even though Charlotte was in full-time education. At the bottom of the article were links to reports on Charlotte's brother, the gambling addict, including a gallery of photos depicting the young man living the high life at various London casinos.

Chatter filled the air, and a small crowd gathered around Duncan's table to read a paper copy of the article over his shoulder.

Alice rushed into the room, cheeks bright. "She's walking down the stairs!"

A hush fell over the entire dining room, and my heart thrummed a steady beat. How would these vultures treat one of their own whose family had been disgraced? Memories of that terrible gauntlet rolled to the front of my mind, of fists raining down on my cowed body and the weight of the crowd crushing me to the ground. A tight band formed around my chest and throat, making my breaths shallow. Sweat gathered on my brow, and I closed my eyes, trying to force air in and out of my lungs. It was just a memory. It couldn't hurt me now.

"Emilia." Edward placed his fingertips on my arm. "Are you alright?"

"Just a cramp… It's nothing." I placed my hand on my stomach and grimaced.

Charlotte stepped through the wooden doors, flanked by Wendy and Patricia. She wore an ivory v-neck sweater that accentuated her figure and a skirt too short for her muscular thighs. Her steps faltered, and her gaze darted around her new audience. She creased her brow. "What's wrong?"

Those who weren't filming Charlotte turned to the head table. Edward, whose skin had turned as pale as milk, pretended to be too engrossed in his smartphone to notice. He was probably thinking about the scandal on his own doorstep. Blake glanced away. Whether it was because he had also been the victim of the newspaper, or because of his strange relationship with Charlotte, I wasn't sure.

Henry stood. "The Saturday Correspondent is making some damning accusations against your father."

Her eyes bulged. "They're not true."

Duncan, the boy with the thick glasses, scurried over to her with his physical copy of the paper, opened at the center spread. I could only guess this was where the reporter had published copies of the expense claim alongside evidence from the Land Registry that Charlotte's father had been claiming rents for an apartment he already owned and rented out to someone else.

Charlotte's bottom lip trembled as her eyes scanned its contents. Then she shook her head. "No... That's libel."

"Which part?" drawled Duncan.

"All of it!" She shoved the paper away, making Duncan stagger back into the nearest table. "And I'm not receiving any kind of salary."

Duncan folded up his copy of the Correspondent. "I'm sure the press will demand answers from your father on Monday. If you're part of the scam, you might also face criminal charges."

"She lied about her brother being an advisor to the Saudi Royal family," said Alice from Duncan's table.

Charlotte's eyes bulged, and her chest heaved up and down as though she was trying not to faint. "T-they'll clear him. He's done nothing wrong!"

"Let's hope so," said Henry. "Every single politician caught fiddling expenses has been imprisoned for false accounting."

For a moment, she froze, her eyes glassy. I thought I would enjoy seeing her suffer, but a well of pity opened up in my heart. Maybe it related to my younger years, when Dad had relapsed and ended up in the papers. Back then, the mean girls at school had acted as though I'd been the one to have taken drugs.

It was hard to watch someone ostracized for something they didn't do. Even if it was Charlotte. That didn't mean I forgave her or wanted to rush to her defense. Instead, I observed her the way a scientist watched an experiment for a chemical reaction. All I needed was a clipboard.

Charlotte tossed her head. "Don't you people have better things to do than read such low-brow publications? Come, Wendy and Patricia, I've suddenly lost my appetite."

The other two girls snubbed her, walking to their usual table and leaving Charlotte standing by the doorway, opening and closing her mouth like a trout left out of water to flounder.

Most of the students turned back to their conversations and meals, as though the matter was resolved and now old news.

I glanced around the room, breathing hard, and holding my features steady to hide my reaction. Was that it? A few drawled words and a mild shunning? I hadn't expected them to make her do a walk of penance, but I thought she would get a taste of what it was like to be blamed for something she didn't do. Now that the attention had left her, Charlotte's posture sagged, and she walked out of the dining room.

I blew out a long sigh. It looked like Charlotte might come out of this scandal unscathed.

Blake tried to make conversation with Edward, who seemed preoccupied. I peered at him through the corner of my eye. Color hadn't yet returned to his face, and the hand that held his teacup trembled.

I was about to ask if anything was the matter, when Mr. Carbuncle walked into the dining room, holding a giant box. I sat up. All mail was delivered to the entrance hall with packages placed on the table. For him to make a huge show of the boxes, it had to be one of Charlotte's mysterious gifts.

"Package for Hobson," he announced in a loud clear voice.

The chatter and clink of silverware on plates halted, plunging the room once again into silence. My brows drew together. Jackie was the only person likely to send me packages, but she wouldn't be so indiscreet as to have something delivered to Elder House.

"Are you sure it's for me?" I asked.

"Unless there's another Emilia Hobson here in the house," he snapped.

"Carbuncle, you overstep your place!" Edward's words were sharp.

The janitor dipped his head. "Begging your pardon, Miss Hobson. Yes, I'm sure it's for you."

Henry snickered. "I know what it is. Take it to her room, so she can go through them in her own time."

Mr. Carbuncle inclined his head and walked out of the dining room with the package. A sea of cold faces turned to me, their eyes demanding an explanation. I bristled and held my orange juice to my lips. They hadn't been so hostile to Charlotte, whose father had been caught stealing from the government, yet they shot me accusing stares because the janitor brought a simple package to stir up shit?

I leaned into Henry. "What is it?"

His grin widened. "Coats."

A pulse shot through my core, and my cheeks warmed. I could still feel the press of his thumbs on my inner thighs, and that relentless tongue on my nub. That encounter behind the oak tree had been incredible. The only thing hotter would to make Henry do it again after he had cleared my name.

Blake leaned forward. "What's the story behind this package? Anything I need to know?"

"Probably not," I muttered.

Gawkers still stared, and I clenched my teeth, longing to yell at them all to get screwed.

"I'm sure we'll hear about it when we don't have so much of an audience." Edward set down his teacup. "What's everyone doing tonight?"

∽

Edward's mood remained low for the rest of the day, and he returned to his family home for the weekend, needing to be alone to sort out a few things. I cornered him in his study on Monday night after dinner and asked what was on his mind.

He sat on the end of the leather Chesterfield with his elbow on the armrest. The light of the fire flickered across the room, softening his features. At that moment, Edward seemed younger and more vulnerable. I sat next to him and laced my fingers through his. My heart ached for him, even though I was still bitter from Henry's refusal to discuss the fake kidnapping plot.

A brandy-scented sigh escaped his lips. "More complaints about International House keep popping up on the Mercia-Net. How soon before students start posting them to a public forum like Facebook?"

"Do you think they would?" I made a mental note to check online to see if Mercia Academy had a Facebook group or an unofficial students or alumni page.

"If nothing gets done about the international students, yes."

I gave his hand a gentle squeeze. "Whatever happens, I'll be at your side."

He drew back and rubbed at his brow. "You think the information will leak outside the school?"

"I'm just going by what you've said." Scooting closer to him, I rested my head on his shoulder. "But you can't deny that the situation is escalating to a point that's worrying."

His Adam's apple bobbed. "I don't want to end up like Mr. Underwood, the subject of an official inquiry."

I bit back a smile. A committee of auditors had convened over the weekend to investigate the accusations, and by Monday, Charlotte's Father had already been suspended pending the results of an inquiry. A video of the Prime Minister's statement to the press on the subject was circulated on the Mercia-Net. And the best part was that Charlotte had disappeared from the campus.

"What do you think I should do?" he asked.

A bolt of excitement struck my chest, and I tried to keep still. Now was the time to persuade him to hand over those files.

"Did you read through those papers the headmaster sent?" I asked.

"I started to, but I can't make sense out of them."

"Oh, no." I wrapped an arm around his middle and squeezed. As much as I wanted to remind him about Marissa's supposed services, I couldn't afford to arouse his suspicion with a lack of subtlety. "Mr. Chaloner must have presented the information in a way that couldn't be understood by a student."

With a long sigh, he wrapped an arm around my shoulder and pulled me closer into his body. "I'm beginning to think you're right."

My eyes fluttered closed. Edward didn't have Henry's size and bulk, but his athletic frame and dizzying cedar-wood and cypress scent made my hands twitch to explore him. He placed a kiss on my forehead and murmured something about appreciating my support.

Warmth spread across my insides. The complaints I had asked Alice to start up against the International House were now flooding the Mercia-Net, giving Jackie and her team ample material for a sensational article and putting a reasonable amount of pressure on Edward.

He didn't ask me for any other advice on that evening, but over the next few days, I sat by Edward's side whenever I could, offering my silent support and encouraging him to read through the papers again or to ask his butler to help.

As more video clips of the louts of International House reached the Mercia-Net, Edward withdrew more into himself and skipped meals on the pretext of studying. I wondered if this was how Rita had felt when she had stopped going to the dining room. Hopefully the turmoil he was suffering matched hers.

The next Saturday, the Correspondent printed the photos I had taken of Nadia's exam papers along with snippets from the Mercia-Net of students, recognizable in our school blazers, lounging in front of International House, drinking beer and cigarettes. It was accompanied by an article explaining that their entire GCSE curriculum was based on getting the students to learn the questions on the exam paper.

The article concluded that there was no evidence that domestic students had received such an example, but the reporter cited the school's stellar exam results and demanded an inquiry.

When I reached the dining room, students crowded around the head table, demanding answers. I walked around to my side of the table. Blake and Henry were seated on Edward's left and right, telling people to back off.

Edward sat on his seat with the air of a disdainful king looking down on his subjects. His facial expression and posture broadcasted his confidence, but the darkened circles under his eyes spoke of a boy who had spent many sleepless nights wrestling with the problem.

I straightened and sucked in a deep breath. It was time for me to put on the performance of a lifetime.

"What's wrong with you all?" I snapped.

The crowd's attention turned to me, and a boy at the back of the crowd sneered, "Stay out of this, Hobson."

"If you have questions about International House, take them up with the headmaster or the board of governors. Edward's an A-Level student whose family happens to own the estate. He doesn't owe any of you an explanation!"

"She's right," said Henry. "Take your complaints elsewhere."

Most of the people crowding the head table walked away. I glanced at Edward, whose shoulders relaxed. I supposed years of acting like he owned the academy instead of its grounds, had caused people to believe he had the power to do anything, including fixing the problem with International House. He had certainly used that illusion of power to incite the students to victimize others, and now it was backfiring on him.

On Monday, Edward wasn't at breakfast, but someone had placed a pile of clippings from prominent British newspapers at his place setting. Each had picked up the Correspondent's story and were demanding to know what had happened to Mercia Academy.

I leaned into Henry. "Where's Edward?"

"Gone to see the headmaster," he murmured. "Poor chap hasn't slept a wink since the story about International House broke out. Somehow, he thinks the blame will fall onto him."

"Why?"

"Who do you think authorized the use of that empty building during the duke's absence? It's all gone horribly wrong, and now the whole country knows."

I clapped a hand over my mouth and widened my eyes to appear shocked. With this kind of pressure on him to provide answers, Edward might get desperate enough to give me the file of transactions to pass onto Marissa. "Poor Edward."

Henry gave me a solemn nod. "The past few years have been so hard on him."

I buttered a slice of toast and hummed my agreement. Decent people under pressure didn't lash out at vulnerable students and recruit others make their lives hell. I didn't know how this problem would unfold over the next few days, but it was bringing me closer to my goal. Once I got the evidence that the headmaster had received payments from international crooks, Rudolph would pay for my flight home, and I'd be back in Park Prep.

At second break, I knocked on the door to Edward's study.

"Come in," said a weary voice.

I stepped inside. Edward slumped on his desk, mahogany hair mussed, blazer open with the top three buttons of his shirt undone. He would have looked hot if it hadn't been for the red rims of his eyes.

"I'm glad you're here." His voice was cracked. "Your stepfather's assistant. Can you vouch for her trustworthiness?"

My heart spasmed, making me suck in a breath between my teeth. I smoothed my features, trying to keep from appearing over-eager. "Yes. Marissa is just interested in getting extra work to pay a few expenses. If we tell her we're worried about Mr. Chaloner giving you a false accounting, she won't even know to call the press."

He leaned back in his leather desk chair, closed his eyes and flexed his jaw, as though chewing over the problem. "You're sure about Marissa?"

My insides trembled with anticipation. "Absolutely."

Edward opened a drawer from under his desk and pulled out a large, manilla file. "Tell her to treat these papers with the utmost confidentiality."

Triumph exploded in my chest like fireworks, but I bit down hard on the inside of my cheek to keep my expression grave. "I'll take it to London, right now."

He reached for his phone. "Let me order you a car."

My stomach dropped. The Correspondent building was on Fleet Street, which was famous for newspapers. Any driver of his would report back to Edward with my activities. "It'll be faster by train."

He sighed and slid his hand through his hair. "All right."

I walked around his desk and wrapped my arms around his shoulders. Even though Edward had been one of my biggest tormentors and he and his friends had ruined my future, I would miss them when I returned to New York. "It will work out for the best." I pressed a kiss on his temple. "I promise."

CHAPTER 17

Later that day, I sat in Jackie's office, watching her leaf through the papers. An accountant called Greg stood beside her chair, reading over her shoulder and shaking his head every so often. I hadn't dared to open the folder until I reached her in case I dropped something in my nervousness.

She whistled. "Mr. Chaloner is something else."

I leaned forward. "What did you find?"

Jackie smirked. "Receipts for cash payments of fifty thousand pounds per student."

"Per term," added Greg.

"Transfers from numbered accounts in Nevis, Panama, and the Cayman Islands to an account in Switzerland."

My brows drew together. "What does that mean?"

Jackie licked her lips. "Your friend and his headmaster have received significant payments from sources that do not wish to be named. And most of them in cash. This is money laundering, which is very serious."

"We'll have to hand these over to the National Crime Agency," said Greg.

"After I publish the story," snapped Jackie.

The older man gulped and turned his gaze to me. "How on earth did you manage to get the headmaster to hand you such incriminating evidence?"

I cringed. "It's a long story."

"We should be able to get this article syndicated to a number of other publications," said Jackie. "You've made us a lot of money with your investigations. If you want to skip uni, let me know. You'd excel in investigative journalism."

"Thanks. Will you tell Rudolph I'm holding up my end of the bargain?"

She grinned, revealing yellowing teeth. "He knows and he's very impressed with how your research has turned around our paper. I'll let him know about this particular piece of research. You've delivered over a dozen ground-breaking stories, and he told me he only expected four."

∽

Now that Jackie had everything she needed for an article to expose the scam behind International House and Edward's contribution towards it, I focused on my more pressing target: Henry. Asking him directly to clear my name hadn't worked, so I thought a grand gesture might prompt him into doing the right thing.

We all sat together in English Literature while Miss Oakley stood in the front of the class talking about the great novels in literature. One of her examples was *A Tale of Two Cities*.

The old woman's black academic robes trailed on the ground as she paced the room. "Which themes do you think makes a book stand the test of time?"

I raised my hand. This was a great opportunity to place an idea into Henry's head. "Sacrifice, Miss."

She smiled. "Explain, dear girl."

"*In A Tale of Two Cities*, Carton sacrificed his life so Lucie could be happy with Darnay. And in *Bleak House*, John Jarndyce gave up on pursuing Esther because she loved Mr. Woodcourt. People who love others are prepared to make sacrifices, even if things work out to their detriment."

She pressed her hand on her chest. "An astute observation, and probably the most romantic gesture one person can make for another."

Henry gave me a nudge. "You're quite the expert on love."

"I have three guys," I whispered. "It's bound to give me a few insights."

He grinned and squeezed my thigh.

After English Lit, Henry and I both had free periods, so we walked back to Elder House together and settled in the triumvirate's common room sofa. Flames crackled and popped within the roaring fireplace, providing much-needed warmth and a cozy atmosphere to hold our conversation.

I threaded my fingers through his and stared into his earnest, green eyes. "I've been thinking a lot about love recently."

Henry grinned. "Anyone in particular?"

Lowering my lashes into what I hoped was a vulnerable expression, I said, "I'm not sure I can commit to a man who would let me take the blame for something as serious as a kidnapping."

"It wasn't just me," he replied.

"I know, but it was you they supposedly abducted, and your parents who paid the ransom. If Blake or Edward went to the police telling them I was innocent, they would dismiss their claim." I squeezed his hand. "That's why I need your help."

His brows drew together. "But my parents…"

"If they could drop the charges for me at Rudolph's request, they would forgive their only son."

He jerked his head away, breaking eye contact. "You don't know what they're like... they're always threatening me with disinheritance if I don't do exactly what they say."

I pressed my lips together, holding back the rage and disgust simmering in my belly. What an entitled prick. Not only did he think it was alright to trick his parents out of five-hundred thousand pounds, but he didn't want to jeopardize his claim to the Bourneville fortune by telling the truth. Did the wretched boy have no ambition other than to inherit the fruits of someone else's labors? I closed my eyes and exhaled my frustration, hoping my feelings wouldn't show in my voice. "Would it be so bad to be like the rest of us?"

"I'll tell you what." He cupped my face in both hands. "Break off your engagement with Bachmann and show us your commitment, and I'll take care of everything."

"You'd tell your parents it wasn't me?"

He nodded.

"Thank you!" I threw my hands around his neck, knocking him onto his back. Perhaps he wasn't so bad after all. "I'll speak to him tonight and tell you about it tomorrow."

∼

The next day after lunch, I stood in Edward's study in front of the triumvirate, who sat on the leather Chesterfield sofa like a panel of sexy judges. Butterfly wings tickled the lining of my stomach, making me wrap my hands around my belly. The Persian rug lay between us, not quite a barrier, but a marker of our positions on two sides of an unspoken war. The clock struck a quarter to one, giving me fifteen minutes until the next bell, and me an excuse to escape... just in case.

"What do you have to say?" Edward asked from the middle seat with Blake at his left and Henry at his right. All three of their faces were grim, as though they had spoken about me earlier and were dreading the worst.

Twisting a cheap ring I'd bought online on my finger, I walked past the desk to the fireplace, glancing at the boys from beneath my lashes. Each of their gazes locked onto the ring, a symbol that I didn't fully trust them with my heart.

"I-I'm ready to commit." I pulled off the ring and threw it into the fireplace. "Sergei and I spoke last night. He's upset—"

Henry rushed out of his seat and wrapped me in a tight hug. "I've been waiting all term for you to say those words."

I hugged back. "Sorry that it took so long."

He let go of me, and Blake stepped forward. "This is wonderful news." He grabbed me by the arms and kissed me on both cheeks. "Thank you."

I turned to Edward, making sure to blink a few times and swallow. They needed to think I was holding back intense happiness at this new stage of my life.

He cupped my cheek and pressed a kiss close to my ear. "I had dreamed of this moment but never thought it would happen. Thank you, Emilia."

"I-I think this is the right decision."

"It is," murmured Henry. "You'll never regret becoming our lover."

I suppressed a scowl. It wasn't like I'd expected one of them to fall to their knees and propose in exchange for having discarded a fake fiancé, but being just a lover seemed an uneven exchange. Maybe in their tiny minds, they thought I was making the upgrade. Three dicks in exchange for one. A bargain, if that was all I wanted out of life.

As soon as Edward drew back, Henry threaded his fingers through my hair, cupping the back of my head in his large, warm hands. I met his green eyes and pushed aside my misgivings with a smile. He might be a lying asshole, but he was a great kisser, who never failed to give me thrills of anticipation. His other hand stroked my back, making me arch into his touch.

"Thank you." He leaned down and pressed his lips against mine, tasting of lemon and mint.

I let my eyes flutter closed and parted my lips. Kissing Henry was so familiar, so safe, so spine-tinglingly sensual. His tongue slid into my mouth, curling around mine in caresses that made my head spin. I wrapped my arms around his muscular back, digging my fingers into his flesh and bringing us so close together, I felt myself melting into his beautiful, hard body.

Henry's erection pressed into my belly, making a thrill shoot up my spine. I slipped my hand between our bodies and brushed my fingers against his hardness. He groaned and jerked, then Blake spun me around.

"I've been waiting for this for so long." Blake made a playful growl and started off the kiss with gentle pecks, each sparking sensations across my lips that mirrored in pleasant tingles between my legs.

When Blake kissed me like this, it was hard to remember why I'd ignored him so much, especially when his arms wrapped around my waist and shoulder blades in a tight clinch that told me I was his. He deepened the kiss with long, slow caresses of his tongue.

I matched him move for move, eliciting deep, heavy groans from him that made the muscles of my core clench. Blake's hand slid down to cup my ass, and his fingers skimmed the crack between my cheeks. I broke the kiss to let out a quivering breath. I had never known I could be so sensitive there.

Blake's kisses moved across my cheek, and he nibbled on my earlobe before kissing a hot trail down my neck. At the same time, Henry stood behind me, his large body providing a wall of comfort at my back. He held my hips in place and rubbed his erection against them.

"My turn to kiss Emilia." Edward stepped forward. His lips slid against mine with a maddening gentleness compared to Blake's wet, open-mouthed kisses against my neck, and the grind of Henry's hardness against my ass.

A whimper reverberated in the back of my throat. Kissing him was like a warm, unhurried caress that said we had plenty of time to get to know each other. I slid my hand around the back of his neck to bring us closer.

"Emilia," he said between panting breaths. "I've wanted you for so long, I'm not sure I'll be able to hold back."

"Then don't," I murmured, anticipation making my nipples tingle.

His tongue slid between my lips and explored of my mouth, deep and demanding and devouring. Both arms wrapped around my waist and brought our bodies close. At this stage, with Blake and Henry arousing me with their mouths and erections, it was hard to keep track of who was doing what. Heat and wetness gathered between my legs, soaking my panties, and I moaned, needing more.

My insides felt like molten fire. Hands—I don't know whose—unfastened the buttons of my blazer and slid the garment over my shoulders. Edward continued to kiss me with a hunger that belied his cool exterior. All that politeness and the gentlemanly distance disappeared, replaced with a searing passion that felt beyond physical attraction.

"Thank you," he said, voice breathy. "For being here when I needed you most."

Blake pressed his body against my side and continued running sensual kisses along the column of my neck. I moaned into his caresses, never wanting them to stop.

The bell rang, indicating the end of lunch. A tiny voice in the back of my head said it was time to stop, but their touches and kisses had brought me well beyond the point of caring about nefarious plans and escape routes.

It took every ounce of self-control for me to draw back. "W-we have classes."

"Ignore it." Edward's voice held the kind of command I yearned to follow.

"A-alright," I gasped out.

Someone's hand slid over my breast, rolling my nipples between his fingers. Another hand slid under my skirt and rubbed the throbbing spot between my legs. Shivers ran down my spine and into my core. It was nice, but I needed more. Groaning, I wriggled against Henry's erection, urging him to pull it out of his pants.

A strange ringtone filled the air. Edward drew back and cursed. "That's the headmaster. If he's contacting me during the day, something disastrous must have happened."

The words were like a bucket of cold water, and I blinked myself back into awareness. Even Blake and Henry stepped back to gape at their friend. I gulped. "Do you want me to come with you for support?"

Edward gave me a sad, half-smile. "As much as I would appreciate your company, the headmaster would not. He is less likely to speak if you are there."

Taking a deep breath, Edward straightened his tie and blazer. I ran my fingers over his hair, smoothing it to perfection.

He swallowed and headed for the door. "Thank you."

My heart thudded in my chest. The most damning article about International House hadn't yet been published. What could be so urgent that the headmaster was summoning Edward?

CHAPTER 18

The door clicked shut behind Edward, and I stared at its wood panels as though that would give me an insight into why the headmaster wanted to see him. It couldn't have been because of the exam paper article. Days had passed since then.

Henry developed me in a mint-scented hug. "You're worried."

I leaned into his chest and murmured, "I don't trust Mr. Chaloner."

He kissed me on the tip of my nose. "Neither do I, but Edward will be safe with him."

I stepped away and locked eyes with Blake, who gave me the strangest look, almost as though he had come to some sort of realization. It might have been because of my concern for Edward and my closeness with Henry. I certainly hadn't given him any cause to suspect me of setting him up to be exposed in the national press for repeating his stepfather's treasonous words. Pushing away those thoughts, I buttoned up my shirt and fastened my tie.

"Let's go to lessons," I said. "It wouldn't feel right to continue without Edward."

Blake's face fell for a second, but he hid the expression with a smile. "You're right."

Henry pressed a kiss into my temple. "And we have to hand in that Spanish assignment."

The three of us walked out of Edward's study at the same time Mr. Jenkins was stepping out of his office. His eyes widened at the sight of our kiss-reddened lips, and he dove back through the door and shut it behind him.

I narrowed my eyes and muttered, "Is this what he does at any sign of inappropriate behavior?"

"He's been like this ever since we got to Elder House," said Blake. "It works out to our benefit."

As I walked through the hallway, I swallowed hard and pushed away memories from the gauntlet. Mr. Jenkins must have heard the noise from his office. He and the matron might have been able to talk sense into the baying crowd or at least ordered those from outside the house to leave. Or he could have called campus security, but he did nothing.

Mr. Carbuncle sorted a stack of mail in the reception hall, which he had upended on the large table. The man looked more haggard than usual, his cheekbones prominent, eyes sunken, and mustache thicker. He gave the boys a polite nod and went on with his work.

Outside, bass music boomed from International House, and a cold wind swirled in from the direction of the woods, bringing with it the scent of pine and juniper. The fresh air from the overcast day cleared my head and returned echoes of three sets of lips and hands caressing me to distraction. I ran a hand through my hair and sucked in a deep breath. If Mr. Chaloner hadn't called Edward when he had, I might have ended up sleeping with at least one of the triumvirate.

Blake headed off to the music block on the far right of the campus, while Henry and I walked down the path of bare magnolia trees toward the main teaching block.

As the gravel crunched underfoot, Henry shook his head. "I can't believe you got rid of Bachmann."

I smiled. "Why not?"

"After everything we put you through last term."

"But you apologized, didn't you?"

"And I meant every word." He placed his hand on my shoulder and squeezed.

I turned my head up to meet his gaze and smiled. As long as the apology was backed up with the clearing of my name, I would accept it. "What will you say to your parents?"

"That we're friends, of course." He smiled back, eyes shining with affection. "Summer's a slow time of year, and they usually visit the stores in the Middle East. Henry, Blake, and I spend most of our time in one of the villas. We'd be delighted to have you join us."

My jaws tightened with irritation, and my hands twitched and curled into fists. I stopped by a bench labeled TOBIAS UNDER-WOOD and grabbed Henry by the wrist. He furrowed his brow and peered down at me as though I was acting strangely.

"We had an agreement," I said through clenched teeth. "I would break up with Sergei, and you would tell your parents the truth."

His frown melted into a blank look. "And I will."

"What will you say?"

"That you weren't behind the kidnapping, of course."

I dropped his wrist as though brainlessness was contagious and folded my arms across my chest. My pulse thrashed in my eardrums, drowning out the sounds of music playing from International House. Anyone could make assurances. Pretty words and earnest utterances in the heat of passion were worthless in the cold light of day. "How will you convince them?"

Henry leaned down to give me a peck on the lips, but I stepped out of range. He had the nerve to droop his shoulders as though he'd been rejected for no reason and stared at me, eyes pained.

"Once they get to know you, they'll understand you could never be capable of such a crime."

"No," I snapped.

"I don't follow."

I prodded him in the chest. "You have to tell them who did it."

He turned his gaze toward the plaque on the bench. "I couldn't."

"That's what we agreed."

His brows drew together. "You wanted me to tell them you weren't the kidnapper."

"Right," I said between clenched teeth. There was no point in continuing this line of conversation when he was deliberately acting obtuse. "We'll be late for Spanish."

He grabbed my bicep. "What's wrong?"

I tried jerking my arm free, but his grip was too firm. "Rudolph still thinks I arranged a kidnapping, and he still thinks I'm harboring half a million pounds. If I step out of line one more time, he'll send me to military school."

"But you're here." He cupped both cheeks with his warm hands. Hands that now felt stifling.

I shook my head. "Why would he pay for the university education of a person who extorted a fortune from your parents? I won't get into any colleges with no money, and my grades aren't high enough for a scholarship."

"Shhh." He pressed a kiss on my forehead and wrapped his arms around my shoulders. "You worry too much. By then, I'll come into my fortune and take care of you."

I stepped out of his grasp. "Then I really will become a trollop."

His face fell. "Emilia."

I stormed off down the magnolia path. He could easily have caught up with me, but he didn't. Maybe he was thinking about what I'd said, or maybe he just didn't care. What kind of idiot would take the rap for someone else's crimes on the promise that they'd be taken care of at some point in the distant future?

Henry didn't know I'd made a deal with Rudolph and be safely in New York before the end of term, but his attempt at fulfilling his end of the bargain was insulting. As I neared the wood doors of the main teaching block, I remembered the most important flaw in his pathetic promise of financial support. Henry was one of the youngest people in our year. His birthday was on September first, which meant by the time the funds were due for colleges, he would still be only seventeen.

The thought of enduring two hours of Spanish with Henry at my side made my stomach churn, so I walked alongside the main teaching block toward the library. It was as old as Elder House, with its stone front and small windows. Its interior consisted of a single floor with mezzanines that stretched up to a vaulted, stained glass ceiling. Students sat at four-person, mahogany desks, each fitted with brass table lamps to provide additional illumination.

A few heads turned as I passed. All the crap that had been posted about me on the Mercia-Net had meant that few students didn't know the American trollop. I spotted a set of wooden stairs that led to the first mezzanine and tiptoed up them, trying not to make the structure creak. The mezzanine was about eight feet wide with stained glass windows every few feet between bookcases. An ornate, iron rail ran down one side, making it feel like an upstairs landing.

Lowering myself into the leather window seat with a view of the lawn and the row of magnolia trees, I let out a deep sigh. Was it time to leave Mercia Academy? I could have pressed Jackie to fund my return plane ticket to New York, but I had wanted the satisfaction of Henry clearing my name by confessing his crime to his parents. I lowered my head into my hands and sighed.

Moments later, footsteps padded toward me, and a quiet voice said, "Emilia?"

I glanced up. Blake stared down at me, his face solemn. My brow creased. "I thought you had Music."

"Henry asked me to speak to you. Will you come outside with me?"

"What's the point?" I asked.

"You might learn something that explains his behavior."

"Alright. Let me put these books away, and I'll meet you outside."

He smiled and headed toward the iron stairs that led to the ground floor. As soon as he disappeared down the steps, I pulled out my burner phone and turned on the recording app. I doubted that Blake would tell me anything that could possibly explain why Henry would let his supposed lover take the blame for his crime, but he might reveal something of use to Jackie and the team.

Outside, Blake placed a hand on the small of my back, and we strolled to a garden behind the music block where white-flowered, evergreen shrubs grew next to lavender. While we walked around a meandering, gravel path, he repeated things I had already heard weeks ago from Edward. That Henry had faked his own kidnapping to pay for the Duke of Mercia's full-time care and that the Duchy's finances were in a terrible state because of decisions the duke had made before his diagnosis of dementia.

"Why didn't you tell me this last term?" I shook my head. "If I'd known the kidnappers were only asking Henry for a larger share of the ransom, I wouldn't have interfered."

"I didn't think you'd actually call the police," Blake replied.

I stopped. "Why wouldn't I when your reasons not to worry were so flippant? Telling me that Henry strong and can take care of himself after I'd seen the men overpower him was almost goading me to get help."

He rubbed the back of his neck and grimaced. "I should have taken you more seriously. I realize that, now."

I turned away, swallowing back the bitterness crawling up my gullet. One flippant comment from Blake had set off a disastrous chain of events that had turned me from a regular person to someone who snuck about, pretending to be friends with others while planning their downfall. If my schemes backfired on me before I left, I'd face something worse than Charlotte's gauntlet.

Blake stepped in front of me and tilted his head to the side. "Why do you spend time alone with Edward and Henry but not with me?"

Because being ignored and considered less important than his friends drove him mad. I wouldn't tell him that, of course. Instead, I said, "You're the one whose motives I understand the least."

"Me?"

"Did you ever dislike or mistrust me?"

He stepped back. "Of course not."

"Yet you joined in on all the pranks. Why?"

He parted his lips, but no words came out.

"You made Charlotte believe you were arranging a relationship with Henry. Then you got her to pay you in fellatio and set up a camera to record her."

A smile twitched across his handsome face. "But that's Charlotte. We have a history."

"And then you played the video on the projector in front of everyone. You even went so far as to steal my phone to make it look like the recording came from me." I curled my lip. "You'll do anything to be entertained, even if people get hurt."

He turned away. Probably because my words were true. Edward had said that night on the balcony that Blake loved to create chaos. I could see that now.

"I don't know what you want from me," he said in a small voice.

I would have told him I wanted him to be less two-faced, but I was the most duplicitous of all. "Why don't we stop dwelling on this? When Edward returns, we can all go back to his study and continue where we left off."

He grinned. "I wouldn't be averse to that, although I have a suggestion."

"What's that?"

"We return to the new house and use his four-poster."

I closed my eyes and hummed. The triumvirate, hot and naked and all over me might be an explosive experience to take away when I left. "I'll think about it."

～

Edward didn't return to classes for the rest of the afternoon, nor was he at dinner. But the next evening, he walked into the dining room looking drawn.

I placed my hand on top of his wrist. "What's happened?"

"Inspectors..." He gulped. "Both from the examination boards and the charity commission have invaded the school."

"What for?" asked Henry.

"They're trying to ascertain whether International House is part of the academy." His hands shook as he reached for the teapot.

"Let me do that." I picked up the pot and poured him a cup of tea, all the while breathing hard. "What's the headmaster doing?"

"Trying to clean up his mess." Edward gulped down the steaming, hot tea. "If they deem International House part of the academy, then the examination board will revoke the school's ability to administer and invigilate A-Levels and GCSE examinations."

My blood turned to ice. Without the ability to administer exams, everyone from Mercia Academy would have to make a pilgrimage to a local school to sit their A-Levels and GCSEs. That had to be disruptive, and might affect students' grades.

I'd thought a few people would be publicly shamed from the exposure, but the fifth and upper-sixth years who were due to take their exams in the summer would be at risk. This wouldn't affect Rita yet, as we were all in the lower-sixth, but she'd probably worry about her friend from Hawthorn House. My mouth went dry, and I gulped down a glass of orange juice.

"Can't the Board of Directors put them right?" asked Henry.

Edward gave his head a minute shake. "At the rate things are going, if there's one more scandal, people will start withdrawing their children from the academy."

I stared down at my plate and swallowed the guilt writhing up my gullet. Before the end of term, Jackie would publish a scandal that would make the others seem like the mildest of misdemeanors.

CHAPTER 19

With a weary sigh, Edward rose from his seat. His shoulders hung several inches lower than usual, and he seemed shorter with his slumped posture. "The matter was out of my hands. Excuse me while I catch up on my sleep."

My stomach churned with a mixture of confusion and guilt and worry. I had only meant to embarrass Edward. To repay the pain and humiliation of leaving Mercia Academy beaten, broken and in disgrace. But I'd gone too far. Set into motion a national scandal that would hurt more than just Edward. Now, every student at the academy might suffer, and Edward would blame himself.

"I'll come with you." The words tumbled out of my mouth before I could stop them. "No one should be alone at a time like this."

He gave me a half-smile. "I'd appreciate the company."

We walked side-by-side out of the dining room, through the hallway laden with the disapproving stares of alumni and Mercia ancestors hanging on the wall. We ascended the stairs in silence, the tread of wood under our footsteps creaking in time with the thud of my heart. If I had any sense, I would leave Mercia Academy now.

There was no more information left to gather. Jackie and the others could complete their exposés without my help.

If I was honest with myself, I'd become a little too attached to the boys. Even when they made me angry, I still needed their presence. They'd burrowed into my heart like a trio of persistent maggots and now wouldn't leave. A tiny part of me also wanted to help Edward weather the upcoming shit storm, but it was ridiculous, since I'd been its cause.

Edward's bedroom was much like the one I shared with Rita, except there was a wooden-framed double bed instead of a single. The fire in the grate had reduced itself to embers, and a chill hung in the air.

"I'd better stoke that before it burns out." I rushed to the wood bucket, adding kindling to the fire with trembling hands. A month ago, I might have delighted in his misery. Mere days ago, I had rejoiced in having that last piece of information to bury Edward and Mr. Chaloner, but now, all I could think about was Edward's pain. And it was all because of me. The kindling caught fire, and I added some more logs. Moments later, large flames curled around them, and I stood.

"Thank you." Edward wrapped his arms around me from behind, filling my senses with his camphor wood scent.

He felt warm and comforting and so right at my back that my eyes fluttered shut, and I exhaled a long, shuddering breath. "What for?"

"I'm not sure how I might have survived this without your presence." His breath puffed against my neck, sending pleasant tingles down my spine. "These past few years have been an ordeal, but things have gotten worse, recently. Without you, I might have fallen apart."

His words were a knife through the heart. If he knew I'd set up his troubles and had stuck around to see him suffer, he'd revert back into the Edward I had met at the start of last term. I turned around, rested my head on his shoulder, and hugged back. Edward rubbed circles between my shoulder blades, as though I was the one who needed soothing.

"Edward..." I drew back, mind going blank. It wasn't like I would tell him I was the cause of his troubles, but I didn't deserve such high praise.

His eyes were as blue as the ocean reflecting storm clouds. Indigo around the edges with starbursts of pale light. "You're the only girl in Elder House who hasn't wanted something from me apart from friendship."

The intensity of his stare weighed my stomach with guilt, and I lowered my lashes. Unlike the other girls, I hadn't been interested in becoming the Duchess of Mercia — because I'd wanted to bury Edward for what he had done to me and leave him in ruins. Now that I was on my way to getting what I wanted, victory over such a broken soul felt hollow. "Let's go to bed."

"I'll be a gentleman," he said.

I smoothed my hands down the front of his blazer and gave him a peck on the lips. "You always are."

Edward kissed back, a slow brush of his lips against mine. It was warm, soft, unhurried, as though he wanted to savor this moment. He held me by the waist, and I wrapped my arms around his neck, bringing us closer.

His hands slid to my front, skimming the opening of my blazer. "May I?"

"Only if you let me take off yours." I slipped his buttons through their holes, reveling in the slow reveal of Edward's body.

I slid my hands under the fabric of his blazer, brushing over the hot skin of his neck and eliciting a groan. Once I had eased it off his shoulders and let it fall to the rug, I worked on the buttons of his shirt, pressing my lips on each new glimpse of alabaster skin stretched over taut muscles.

"Emilia, I want to see you." With deft fingers and the lightest of touches, Edward unbuttoned my shirt.

I let my arms fall to the side and stared into his eyes. Heat blazed within their blue depths, and his fingers shook as he pushed my shirt and blazer off my shoulders, revealing my cream, silk bra. "You're even more beautiful than I imagined."

My lips quirked into a smile. "I could say the same for you."

He peppered kisses down my neck, each sending sparks of pleasure across my skin and between my legs. I reached for his belt buckle, and he grabbed both hands. "I said I'd be a gentleman, and part of that means not taking advantage of your aroused state."

"You're right." I wrapped my arms around him, holding us close. It was already hypocritical to take all this pleasure from him while he was so upset, considering who had caused of his troubles. "Let's go to bed."

Spooning with Edward was nothing like spooning with Henry. Edward held my hips still when I tried to grind against his erection, and he didn't let his hands wander as Henry might. If I was skeptical, I would suspect he was banking my desire, keeping me simmering until I exploded from pent-up need and pounced on him. This might have been how he'd strung Alice and Patricia along for months. But then again, I might have spent so long mistrusting Edward that I looked for nefarious reasons in his every small action.

Later, I turned around and stared into his face. In slumber, and without the cruel twist of his features, Edward's beauty melted my heart. The light streaming in through the windows caught his mahogany hair, turning its ends coppery. The strands fell onto his face, framing thick brows and lashes, a straight nose, high cheekbones, kiss-swollen lips, and an angular jaw.

I pressed a kiss on the tip of his nose. How would he cope when the Saturday Correspondent published the article on money laundering? Poor Edward had signed a contract giving the headmaster permission to convert a disused building into an international summer school, and now it would be the center of an even worse scandal that would lead to a police investigation.

After several minutes, Edward's breathing deepened, and I slipped out of the bed.

"You're leaving?" he slurred.

"Not if you want me to stay."

"Stay."

I slid back into the warm bed and nestled in his arms, hoping he would have the strength to deal with the calamity I had set into motion.

∽

On Friday after classes, an e-ticket for a flight from London to New York arrived in my inbox, accompanied by a message from Rudolph's PA that asked where I would like to study the following semester. I squealed and dropped my phone on the mattress.

Rita raised her head from the marked-up music scores on the table. "What's happened?"

"I finally have my ticket out of here."

Her eyes bulged. "How soon can you leave?"

"One sec." I glanced at the date on the ticket. "Monday afternoon."

"Have you checked with the you-know-what about what they'll publish over the weekend?"

My eyes shuttered closed. If it was the money laundering article, Edward would know I had leaked it to the press. It wouldn't take long for him to work out that all the other articles about the school had come from me. This time, there would be no gauntlet, only a howling mob. I pulled out my burner phone and sent a message to Jackie. She replied immediately with a message that she and Greg were still sifting through the papers I had given them, and she had another article planned for Saturday.

A huge sigh of relief slipped from my lips, and I gave Rita a grateful smile. "That article I was afraid of won't be published tomorrow."

She nodded and fixed me with serious, dark eyes. "It might be fun to see their reactions, but be safe and get out before the paper publishes anything that can be linked back to you."

Wrapping my hands over my middle to settle the regret roiling through my stomach, I gave her a sharp nod.

※

Rita shook me awake in early in the morning, just as the first traces of light peeked through the chink in the curtains. Instead of night clothes, she wore a denim jacket over her sweater, meaning she had spent the night with her friend in Hawthorn house.

I blinked to clear my vision. "What's wrong?"

"Sit up," she whispered. "They've just published the latest article."

All traces of sleepiness vanished. This had to be serious if she had woken me. Maybe Jackie had changed her mind and published details from Edward's folder. Maybe Rudolph had told her to expose me as a slut who had three boyfriends she couldn't even stand.

I pushed myself up and rested my back against the headboard. "W-what is it?"

She placed her smartphone on my lap.

BOURNEVILLE £1M KIDNAP SCAM

All the blood drained from my face. "Am I mentioned?"

"No, but it won't take a genius to work out the identity of the unnamed female student. They've outlined everything. Did you know Mr. Frost organized it all? This is a confession."

I scanned the article, throat drying with each revelation. Henry had arranged a way with Mr. Frost to access some of the Bourneville fortune before his majority of eighteen. Frost used his influence as a schoolteacher to persuade the housemaster of Elder House to arrange a school trip facilitated by a friend who ran an outward bound company. They planned to take Henry to a hideout and demand a ransom of five hundred thousand pounds in cash, but had to bring along a female student who had witnessed the kidnapping and had tried to raise the alarm.

The paper published the names and photographs of each person involved, including Henry, Mr. Frost, two of the assistants from the outward bound company, the dreadlocked photographer, and a handful of stoners from the squat.

"It said they subdued you with ketamine," whispered Rita. "Is that true?"

Nausea slithered up my throat at the thought of such a powerful drug. "I don't know what they injected into me."

The article continued, stating that Henry had used the bulk of the funds to pay for the ailing Duke of Mercia's medical expenses, but that the gang had colluded to place the blame on the unnamed female student, who spent a week incarcerated within the school and had been facing criminal charges. It damned Mr. and Mrs. Bourneville for extorting double the ransom money from the girl's stepfather to drop the charges.

At the bottom of the article was another piece: CRIMINAL LATIN MASTER, which described how an intelligent boy who had gained a scholarship to study at Mercia Academy and then at Cambridge University had turned into a criminal mastermind. As a student, Paul Frost had supplied alcohol and marijuana to younger children and then returned to use his influence as a teacher to sell to the students. All the paper's claims were either backed up with camera footage or messages posted on the Mercia-Net.

My vision blurred, and I ran my fingers through my hair. "They're going to kill me."

"Didn't you read the first paragraph?" asked Rita. "It was Mr. Frost who confessed everything."

"Why?"

"He says he wanted to set the record straight about the kidnapping being ordered by Henry and Edward. I'll bet he thought he would be next in line to get the blame."

Anger washed through my veins. Jackie had recordings of Henry admitting that he and other accomplices had organized the kidnapping. She had probably caught footage of Mr. Frost selling his wares at the Valentine's party and blackmailed him into making a confession. "I'll bet Mr. Frost told the others to pin the kidnapping on me if anything went wrong."

Rita shrugged. "Probably. I'm guessing he thought his plan was watertight."

I couldn't look at the article anymore. It was a relief for all the evidence to be out there to clear my name, but the boys had treated me as though I had been disposable. Tears clouded my vision. Would Rudolph show it to Mom? She still hadn't contacted me. I couldn't ask Dad to call her. Ever since I was old enough to use a smartphone, Dad would call and email me directly instead of going through her, so they had lost touch.

"You should go down to the dining hall and hold your head up high," said Rita. "This time when you leave, it will be with dignity, and they'll be the ones in disgrace."

I swung my legs out of bed. "There's no point in going back to sleep. I couldn't even if I'd wanted."

~

As though Jackie had negotiated it beforehand, the tabloids immediately picked up the kidnapping story on the same day. Some focused on the Bourneville department store, minimizing Mr. Frost's involvement to focus on their high prices, unfair employment practices, and their sale of real animal fur. The tabloids had even dredged up whatever negative press they could find about the

Bourneville family, portraying them all as crooks. Others brought up the International House story, implying that Mr. Frost might have sold exam papers to students.

At breakfast, Blake was the only person sitting at the head table, looking forlorn without his friends.

I slid in the seat next to him. "Where's Henry?"

"London. I'm not sure we'll see him for a few days. Mother kept me out of the academy for a week when the Correspondent wrote an article about me."

"Oh." I stared down at my tea. "Are the tabloids leaving you alone?"

"A couple of reporters are suggesting Mr. Frost got me addicted to drugs and that's why I started talking treason." He blew out a long breath. "They're desperate."

"But you're not even an addict."

"Everyone who matters knows that, but it's in the interest of national security that I make a slow recovery from addiction." He said the last few words as though imitating an older woman. Then he took a long drag from his orange juice and sighed. "Otherwise, people might believe my stepfather will be a more pliable king, and something really will happen to the Prince of Wales."

"This is just like how Henry's kidnapping was blamed on me," I said in a small voice.

"Well, that article has cleared your name." The tone of his voice indicated his annoyance that Henry was now implicated in his own kidnapping.

"Not yet." I picked up a slice of toast and put it on my plate. "The police might not want to re-examine the case and expunge my file."

Blake didn't answer. Most likely because he was too preoccupied with Henry's troubles to care about mine.

Mr. Jenkins jogged into the dining room. "Miss Hobson! Two police officers are with the headmaster. They wish to see you immediately."

Blake's face twisted into a harsh smile. "You must have a fairy godmother. What luck!"

I stood. If I'd been lucky, I would never have gotten sent to Mercia Academy in the first place.

We walked out of Elder House, passing a shame-faced Mr. Carbuncle in the reception hall. He had overheard the boys telling me that they had arranged the kidnapping, yet he had kept their secret. He was just as corrupt as the others. Worse, considering what he did with female students.

Mr. Jenkins wrung his hands the entire journey across the campus, the March winds blowing through his thinning hair. A nervous laugh warbled from his throat. "I should never have believed the lies. The article in the paper explained everything, and now, I owe you the deepest of apologies."

"You never once visited me in that cell." I stared down at the gravel path.

"Mrs. Jenkins updated me on your wellbeing."

There wasn't any point in arguing. The man had already proven himself unfit for housemaster duties. Chastising him wouldn't make the slightest bit of difference.

As we walked through the rest of the path, I pictured Chief Inspector Faust's miserable face, and how he and his sergeant would stumble over their apology before expunging my record. I would tell him I understood that policing in England wasn't as thorough in the States and to go reread the Agatha Christie novels he'd used to learn detective work.

As soon as I entered the headmaster's office, two uniformed police officers stood. Mr. Chaloner stepped out from behind his desk. Edward leaned against the wall, staring at me with cold eyes.

The headmaster's eyes burned with fury. "Here's our little leak. Officers, arrest her for the production and distribution of indecent images of children."

CHAPTER 20

My heart beat so hard, it made my chest vibrate. I locked eyes with Edward, who stared back through eyes as cold and piercing as a winter wind. What had happened since we had lain together? The article about Mr. Frost's involvement in Henry's kidnapping couldn't be pinned on me. My gaze moved to the two uniformed police officers who scrutinized me with dispassionate gazes. Every bit of moisture dried up in my mouth, and I took a step back and bumped into Mr. Jenkins, knocking him into the door.

The movement jolted me out of my shock, and I blurted, "What the hell are you talking about? I didn't leak anything!"

The headmaster's face turned red, and veins stood out on his temples like thunderbolts. "Someone from outside the academy has been accessing the Mercia-Net with your username and password."

I clutched at my chest, feigning surprise. "Who?"

"You tell me." He rounded the desk. "We traced the IP address to a Virtual Private Network. Whoever was using your login details made great efforts to hide their location."

"W-what?"

He leaned forward. "Did you know that anyone accessing from the Saturday Correspondent could be traced to their offices in Fleet Street?"

"But you said the hacker used a VPN," I replied, trying to keep the tremor out of my voice.

"That's why they had to use a VPN," snapped the headmaster.

I gulped. It hadn't occurred to me that they would be so thorough in their investigations as to check on who had accessed the Mercia-Net from outside the academy.

"Well, Miss Hobson?" Mr. Chaloner loomed over me.

Excuses whirred through my mind, but the only thing I could think of was the time I had visited the headmaster asking for help, only for him to try to confiscate my phone.

My tongue darted out to lick my lips. "People have been breaking in and out of my room all year." I cast a glance at the police officers. If they weren't corrupt, this information should be of interest to them. "Do you remember? I reported the first incident to you, and you said nothing. How do you know they didn't steal my login details from my room? It was printed out on a piece of paper I received with my schedule."

The policemen glanced at each other. I swallowed hard. Hopefully, they would focus on the real crime that took place—entering a person's room without permission—and forget about the trumped up, not-even-criminal charge of leaking information to the press. I turned pleading eyes to Edward, who glanced away.

"Who entered your room, Miss Hobson?" asked the older policeman.

"Charlotte Underwood."

The headmaster folded his arms across his chest. "I doubt that one of the largest victims of the mole would hand the Saturday Correspondent information to bury her own father."

His words hit like a punch to the gut. If I didn't think fast, I'd end up locked in that basement room until Rudolph could bother himself to collect me. Of course, Charlotte couldn't be the leak. Her name was the first that popped into my mind. Before I could think another excuse, words spewed out of my mouth. "There's someone who has access to every room in Mercia Academy. He's corrupt and accepts bribes. I wouldn't be surprised if the Correspondent employed him to leak information."

"Who?" asked the headmaster.

"Mr. Carbuncle."

Mr. Jenkins placed a hand on my shoulder. "Are you sure about this, Miss Hobson? You're making a very serious accusation."

Anger flared through my veins. This asshole stood in the back of the room saying nothing while the headmaster accused me of leaking information, but now, he came forward to protect Mr. Carbuncle? If I ever got the chance to expose him to the press, I would do it in the blink of an eye.

My lip curled, and I shot the thin man my most withering stare. "Have you forgotten the camera footage I showed you of Mr. Carbuncle letting a student into my room to search my things? If anyone's the leak, it would be him."

Mr. Jenkins flinched and shrank back toward the wall like a cornered rat.

Edward narrowed his eyes into the kind of expression that told me he wanted to see how far I would take this lie before he delivered a piece of information that would cut through my bullshit and prove my guilt. Of all the people in this room, he would know why I had felt the need to hurt others in my house. Until I'd returned to Mercia Academy, he had been the worst of the bullies. He'd even told me he couldn't believe I had been so forgiving. I looked him squarely in the eye. If he had something to say, he could speak up now.

"Why don't we ask Mr. Carbuncle if those accusations are true?" said Mr. Jenkins.

I whirled on him, clenching my fists. "Last term, when I was falsely imprisoned in a dank basement, you never once visited to ask if I'd really arranged Henry's kidnapping. Why are you suddenly Mr. Carbuncle's biggest defender?"

The housemaster dipped his head. "I have learned from my mistakes. He who does nothing is just as much a sinner as he who does evil."

If two policemen hadn't been in the room, I would have swung at the pious hypocrite.

"Where do we find this…" The first policeman glanced at his notebook. "Mr. Carbuncle?"

My lips curled into a snarl. That uniformed bastard had heard me say I was falsely imprisoned and didn't even follow up with questions. I held my tongue. Right now, I was under suspicion for something that could be traced to me if they found my burner phone. If I distracted the topic of conversation from Mr. Carbuncle, they might return to thinking I was the leak.

"Follow me." Mr. Jenkins led a procession of us out of his office, through the main teaching block and out of the double doors at the back.

We trampled after him through the dew-covered campus. The morning sun shone brighter than it had in months, melting the last vestiges of frost. A fresh breeze mingled with the faint scent of blossoms budding on the trees, but I couldn't enjoy the pleasant atmosphere. Not when my heart pounded like it was about to burst.

I trailed at the end with Edward by my side, stiff as a tin soldier. He stared straight ahead as though the sight of me turned his stomach. "No matter what you say," he whispered, "I know it was you."

I shook my head. Anything I uttered now would fall on deaf ears.

"This morning's article cleared your name," he whispered. "That's what you wanted all along, isn't it?"

I opened my mouth to protest, but then I clapped it shut. There was no way anyone could link the article about me when Mr. Frost had confessed his crimes to the Saturday Correspondent. Edward was probably throwing random accusations, hoping to catch me out. Hoping I would tear up and blurt out my reasons for leaking stories to the press. Giving him another little head shake, I kept my eyes on the headmaster's clenching and unclenching fists. The man looked ready to strangle someone with his bare hands. I had to watch out for his temper. After a week of examination board inspectors on his back, I would bet he was looking for someone to blame.

Mr. Chaloner led us around the back of Elder House, to a building that reminded me of the gatehouses at the entrance of Mercia Academy. "This is Mr. Carbuncle's lodge."

"Is he usually in around this time of the day?" asked the taller policeman.

"He can be a little difficult to track down." Mr. Jenkins made a nervous laugh in the back of his throat. "Mr. Carbuncle's activities are far and wide."

A DO NOT DISTURB sign hung on the door.

Mr. Jenkins rocked back and forth on his feet. "He's probably restoring an antique and needs a bit of peace and quiet."

"Or he needs privacy to send images to the newspapers," I spat. "Don't give him a chance to cover his tracks."

The taller policeman knocked once, making me roll my eyes at his politeness. Then he tried the handle, which didn't budge.

"Force the door open," the headmaster snarled.

The policemen shared a glance as though wondering if they had permission to damage academy property.

"I'll do it!" Mr. Chaloner reared back, raised his suited leg and drove his heel into the panel by the lock. The wood splintered, and the door swung inward.

Just as my mouth dropped open at the man's prowess, a female shriek filled the air.

"Blimey," shouted the policeman. "He's got a schoolgirl in here!"

"No," cried Mr. Carbuncle from within the lodge. "This isn't what it looks like!"

Everybody, including me, rushed into the hut. The janitor's dungarees hung at his hips, the fabric fisted around his groin. He held out his other hand as though trying to stop traffic. A pair of pink panties lay on the table and beneath it, a red-haired upper-sixth year girl scrambled to pull on her skirt.

I clapped my hand over my mouth. This was turning out even better than I had hoped.

"Never mind the girl," snarled the headmaster. "I want to know who leaked information to the Saturday Correspondent."

The janitor spluttered. "Not me!"

I glanced around the room and found a filing cabinet in the corner. One of the drawers was marked PERSONAL. In seconds, I flung it open and rifled through sections containing snacks and letters. There was even a space for used panties at the back.

"What are you doing?" Edward hissed from behind.

I glared over my shoulder. The sobbing girl pushed past the dumbstruck officers and rushed out of the lodge. I turned back to the filing cabinet rifling through its sections with trembling hands. If I didn't find something while everyone who mattered was distracted by Mr. Carbuncle's indiscretion, suspicion would fall back to me.

"You can't just search through a man's things," added Mr. Jenkins.

Anger seared through my veins, turning the edges of my vision black. I whirled on my housemaster, hands trembling with the need to punch him hard in the face. "You've just caught Carbuncle half-naked with a student, and you're worried about *his* privacy?"

I stepped away from the filing cabinet and advanced on the paling housemaster. Whether he was an idiot or completely corrupt, I no longer cared. If I could get him into trouble, I would.

"It looks like you already knew what he did," I spat. "Why are you trying to protect him? Did he give you access to vulnerable girls?"

Mr. Jenkins cheeks turned red. "He most certainly did not, and I would never condone such activities between staff and students."

"I've found something," said Edward from the filing cabinet.

"No," shouted Mr. Carbuncle. "That wasn't me!"

I folded my arms across my chest and stepped back. Edward pulled out a fistful of checks from the Saturday Correspondent.

"I didn't cash any of them!"

"Why did they send you money?" I kept the glee out of my voice. The more confused I acted, the more people would believe in my innocence.

Mr. Carbuncle's glistening mustache quivered, and tears gathered in his eyes. "I-I don't know."

I ignored the pang of guilt piercing through my insides, even though I was about to condemn an innocent man for an act I had committed. The janitor had brought me through the main hallway of Elder House, and had organized that gauntlet with Charlotte. He had also smirked when he discovered the boys had framed me for Henry's kidnapping. But the most heinous of all was his disgusting, abusive arrangement with schoolgirls. With a bit of luck, more of them would come forward and make sure he rotted in prison.

The policemen circled around him, but Mr. Carbuncle dodged. Apparently, all this sexual activity made a man quick on his feet. He feinted left. Right. Ducked. Wove, all the while keeping up a complicated sequence of footwork I had only seen on a boxer during a heavyweight championship fight. I curled my lip. They should be hitting a pervert like him with clubs, not floating like butterflies around him.

Mr. Carbuncle ducked low, darted out of the room, knocked the headmaster to the ground as he sprinted for freedom. The policemen gave chase, and I turned to Edward, who pulled out a few bank statements from the filing cabinet.

"What did you find?" The headmaster pulled himself up and stalked across the lodge, eyeing the panties the girl had left on the table.

"There's a transaction here from the Saturday Correspondent." Edward handed the headmaster the evidence.

Mr. Chaloner looked at the uncashed checks and scanned the bank statements, scowl deepening with each passing moment. I held my breath, hoping this would be enough to convince him of Mr. Carbuncle's guilt and my innocence.

Without a word or a backward glance, the headmaster walked out of the caretaker's lodge and toward the main teaching block.

Edward shook his head. "That proves Carbuncle was behind some of the leaks, but I'm still convinced you were the cause of at least one."

"I'm disappointed in you." I stepped out of the lodge and into the fresh spring morning, heart soaring with victory. "If you can believe I was the culprit after seeing so much overwhelming evidence that proves my innocence, then I guess what we had together meant nothing."

He wrapped an arm around my wrist. "If you don't come with me now, I'll call back the headmaster and give him an alternative and more convincing theory of who really orchestrated those leaks."

CHAPTER 21

My stomach dropped, and my mind filled with the memory of Edward's fury the day he had flipped the table in my direction. But even at his worst, he was still preferable to the headmaster, who seemed to be more than a simple academic and had a file of transactions linking him to organized crime. I swallowed hard. There was no choice but to let Edward lead me back to Elder House.

Thud. Thud. Thud. My heavy heartbeat reverberated through my bones, shaking them to the marrow. They filled the silence between us as we passed the small lawn between the caretaker's lodge and Elder House. Overhead, tight buds formed on the tips of branches, marking the beginning of spring. I chewed on the inside of my lip, hoping Edward was bluffing and trying to shake a confession out of me.

A cool wind meandered across the gardens, filling my senses with the scent of laundry and cooking. It reminded me of the days I had spent locked in the basement of Elder House and my heart filled with the remembered despair. I glared down at my loafers and mentally kicked myself for returning to the academy the day I had gone to London with Edward's files. If I hadn't been so determined to get Henry to confess, I might already be in New York by now.

We passed by the last few students making their way out of Elder House. None cast me a glance, and I let out a long breath. At least he hadn't organized some kind of ambush.

The warmth of the entrance hall made the skin of my cheeks tingle. Edward led me through the hallway into his study. The second the door clicked shut behind us, he grabbed me by the arms and pressed me against the wall.

I gasped out. "Edward!"

His eyes flashed. "What did you do with those files I gave you?"

"M-Marissa has them."

He pulled out his phone. "Call her."

"I don't have her UK num—"

"Call her!" he roared.

My heart jumped into my throat, and my body stiffened. "I can't."

"Because there is no Marissa." He stepped back, giving me space to breathe. "She probably returned to America the day after she brought you here, and you used her as a ruse to obtain those files."

I made a show of rubbing my arms. Anything to garner a bit of sympathy. "If I did, the Saturday Correspondent would have published something by now. Instead, the articles all focused on Mr. Frost's confession. You've already found your moles."

"No," he snapped. "Paul and Carbuncle would never betray me like that unless cornered."

"Neither would I!"

His eyes narrowed, and he advanced on me, seeming to grow several inches. "After everything we did to you, why did you come back?"

"Rudolph gave me a choice." I lowered my gaze. The scrutiny of his frigid glare caused my stomach to knot. "Either I return to

Mercia Academy or go to a military academy somewhere in the States. Mercia was the better of two bad choices."

"I don't believe you," he murmured.

My throat convulsed. So far, he hadn't mentioned this convincing theory about why I was the leak and not Mr. Frost of Mr. Carbuncle. He had probably been bluffing, so I would follow him here to be interrogated. Or, he had been referring to the files he had handed me to pass on to Marissa.

"Edward…" I placed my hand on his heart, which pounded hard against my palm. "I don't know what I can say to convince you. This is like last term all over again where I couldn't convince anyone I hadn't kidnapped Henry."

He cupped my cheek with his large. "Tell me, Emilia, will I find extracts of those files I gave you in next week's Saturday Correspondent?"

A flock of butterflies in my stomach writhed and flailed about in a dizzying combination of nerves and nausea. "I didn't give them to the paper."

"You wouldn't stoop so low as to toy with the heart of another."

"No." I shook my head for emphasis. I hadn't set out to break hearts. I just needed to get close enough to the boys to exact my revenge. They had proven last term that they hadn't care about me, so I hadn't considered their feelings… Until it was too late. Now that I had my plane ticket, I needed to leave.

He cupped my other cheek. "You're the first woman I've felt close to since…"

My pulse quickened at the confession. His mother had died years ago, leaving him to cope alone with a declining father. My heart ached for Edward. He had trusted me in the end.

I wrapped my arms around him and murmured, "I care too much for you." Right now, I was telling the truth. Over the past few weeks, I had come to understand Edward. What came next was also sincere. "I would never add to your problems."

Edward hugged back. "I'm sorry for doubting you."

I raised my head. "Just kiss me. Make me forget about this unpleasant morning."

He drew back, eyes shining with remorse, and pressed his lips against mine in the softest and most bitter-sweet of kisses. Over the past weeks, I'd connected with Edward more deeply than I had with any other boy. He had opened his heart to me, laid himself bare, and I had used it to manipulate evidence against him that could result in a sentence for money laundering.

I moved my lips against his, luxuriating in our connection. The layers of resentment I'd used to wrap my heart unwound, leaving one that ached with the need to confess. I'd seen the broken soul behind his cruel majesty, and it was beautiful. His kiss filled my empty, treacherous heart, making my head spin. I couldn't tell him the truth. I couldn't cause him further pain, and I couldn't subject myself to another gauntlet.

"I love you," he murmured into the kiss.

My heart stilled. "What?"

"I'm sorry for ever doubting you."

"I…"

He placed a finger on my lips. "You don't have to speak. Just let me make it up to you."

This time, when we kissed, he gave me no assurances that he would be a gentleman, and I didn't ask for any. It was hot. Demanding. Arms of steel held me in place, and his tongue devoured my mouth as if committing me to memory. I threw my head back and surrendered. This would be our last kiss, and I would treasure it for an eternity.

I had defeated him. Defeated the entire triumvirate and exposed their weaknesses to the country. No longer was I that betrayed and beaten girl who had to be dragged to the headmaster's office, humiliated and disheveled. I would leave Mercia Academy triumphant.

But first, I would leave Edward with something that proved the extent of my true affection.

"Sofa," I gasped out between kisses.

He lowered me onto the leather Chesterfield and sat at my side. I placed both hands on his shoulders and pushed him onto his back. Edward's brows quirked up. "Taking charge?"

"Taking what I need." I straddled his hips, smoothing my hands over the planes and contours of his clothed torso.

Edward growled and pulled me down toward him, resuming our kiss. With hands so eager that they shook, I slipped off his tie, unbuttoned his shirt, and marveled at the tight muscles of his chest and abs. His nipples were pale and pink and puckered. I pinched one between my thumb and forefinger. His eyes rolled back, and the erection beneath me twitched. Heat flooded my core, accompanied by an aching, throbbing wetness.

A smile danced over my lips. Edward was so pliant, so responsive. I leaned forward and flicked my tongue over a nipple, enjoying his bucking and hisses. Then I reached for his belt.

"Emilia." The words came out like a gasp, and his hand encircled my wrists. "Are you sure—"

"I've wanted you for ages. Let me do this."

Excitement flared in his blue eyes like lightning reflecting over an ocean. He released my wrists and placed his hands on my hips. "As you wish."

Keeping my gaze locked on his, I scooted down off his hips, unbuckled his belt, unzipped his slacks, and pulled down the waistband of his underpants. The tip of his penis popped out, making my mouth water. I wrapped my fingers around his shaft. The skin was as smooth as gossamer, but veins pulsed beneath the warm, thickening flesh. Edward hissed through his teeth.

Triumph flared across my chest at having made Edward Mercia hiss. I pumped up and down, watching his expression for more changes. Puffs of air escaped his lips, and tiny beads of sweat gathered on his hairline.

"Emilia," he rasped.

Before he could complete his sentence, I lowered my lips to his pink, bulbous tip and darted out my tongue to taste him.

With a low moan, Edward's hips arched off the sofa.

I held him down. "Stay still, or I'll stop."

"Y-yes."

I ran my tongue up his shaft, enjoying the way Edward shook and twitched at my command. This was the guy with the regal grace and the commanding voice, lying beneath me, shivering under my touch. Seeing him so undone sent tingles up and down my core. I sucked the entire head into my mouth and made him whimper.

My other hand wrapped around his base, and I pumped up and down while savoring his reddened flesh.

"E-Emilia," he gasped out. "I won't last much longer if you continue to do this."

"Do you have a condom?" I asked.

Heat flared in his eyes. "There're in the inside pocket of my blazer."

"Get it, then." I rose onto my knees

Edward twisted about and fumbled with the garments bunched up around his arms. I continued my long, languid licks up and down his shaft, occasionally curling my tongue around his tip to make him moan. After a few moments, he produced the foil wrapper, tore it open with his teeth and rolled it down his erection.

"This is your first time." Edward propped himself up on his elbows. "Let me go on top and take care of you."

"No." I climbed off him, toed off my loafers, and pulled down my tights and panties. "It has to be like this."

He fisted his erection around the base, holding it upright. I returned to the sofa and lowered myself onto him. My muscles stretched around his thickness but after they adjusted, a ripple of pleasure fluttered around his length. Maybe it was the thought of dominating Edward like this and having him at my mercy, but this position felt right.

I rubbed my fingertips over his nipples, making him throw his head back and bare his clenched teeth. My throat thickened, and I swallowed down my guilt. Poor Edward. In less than a week, he'd realized I'd fucked him more than one way.

With deliberate slowness, both for my comfort and for the satisfaction of seeing him squirm, I lowered myself down his shaft and rolled my hips. Edward stared back at me, eyes wide with disbelief. A tiny voice in the back of my head mused that he would make a similar face when he had discovered what I had done with those files, and I snatched my gaze away from his.

If I had a shred of decency left, I would stop and confess, but I rode him, gently at first, and when the pleasure built, and my body demanded more, I picked up my pace.

Edward panted, sweated, thrashed his head from side to side, but I rode up and down, reveling at his undoing. Then his hands gripped my hips, and he pistoned up into me, making me cry out. Dominating him was wonderful, but his participation doubled my pleasure.

"I-I'm not sure how long I can last," he said from between clenched teeth.

I gripped his shoulders and ground my hips. "Kiss me."

Edward rose, wrapped a hand around my neck and brought me down into the warmest kiss I'd ever received. The new angle rubbed against a spot that sent lightning bolts of pleasure rippling through my core. A high pitched noise escaped my lips, but Edward swallowed it in a kiss that turned my insides to mush and made my toes curl. He thrust over and over against that spot, and I rolled my hips, increasing the friction.

Ecstasy sparked and spread with each movement, and I cried out, "Edward!"

A haze of pleasure fogged his reply. He might have been telling me he was about to climax, but my world had condensed into Edward's gorgeous shaft and the pleasure pulsing and rippling out from my quivering core.

I ground harder, increasing that sensation until pressure built behind my clit. The climax surged out, bursting through my torso, into my limbs, setting each nerve ending aflame. When it reached my neck, I threw my head back and screamed.

Edward stiffened, and with a howl, he convulsed underneath my thighs and collapsed back onto the Chesterfield. I followed him seconds afterward, then we lay tangled, staring into each other's souls.

I nuzzled the side of his face. "When I first saw you on the staircase, I thought you had the potential to be the most beautiful man I'd ever seen."

"And now?"

"You're heart-stopping."

Edward grinned and rubbed the small of my back. "You say the most flattering things."

"It's true."

"Seeing you for the first time was like a blow to the chest," he murmured.

"Why?"

"Those huge, gray eyes were unlike any I'd seen before. So intense. So beautiful. I feared that you could see into my heart and wrench it out of my chest.

"Is that why you kept your distance?" I asked.

He closed his eyes and turned his head away for a fraction. "I'd hardly describe the campaign we launched against you as distance, but I appreciate your understanding." He paused. "Yes, bullying you was a way to keep you at a distance and save myself for when you inevitably left."

I ran my fingers down the side of his face. An assurance that I would never leave him stuck in the back of my throat. My new life awaited me in New York, and I wouldn't be able to stick around Mercia Academy when Edward worked out that I really had handed those papers to the Saturday Correspondent.

We lay on the sofa until our eyes closed, and we both fell asleep. By the time I awoke, the sun had already set. I disentangled myself from his limbs, sighing with the loss of contact. What a pity Edward had decided to bully me and recruit others to do the same. My first term at Mercia Academy could have been paradise with him and the boys, instead of being the seventh circle of hell.

I slipped on my skirt and loafers then crept out of the door, not once looking over my shoulder in case the sight of naked, sleeping Edward tempted me to stay.

The Uber drove through the campus and past the main teaching block, where the two different policemen bundled the handcuffed headmaster into the back of a car. Either Jackie had passed the files onto the National Crime Agency or the headmaster had done something to hurt Mr. Carbuncle. As far as I was concerned, both men had gotten what they deserved.

I stared out of the window at the darkening campus. It would be a pity I wouldn't get to see it in spring, but staying here would be dangerous when someone traced the leaks back to me.

The taxi dropped me at the train station, and I wheeled my case full of casual clothes onto the platform. I had completed my mission, earned a trip back to New York, a place at Park Preparatory or any similar American institution, and Rudolph's scholarship to an Ivy League college. And I had avenged myself on the biggest of the bullies. The articles on Charlotte's brother had led to an investigation into how her father had been selling off assets to bail out his gambling son. It had also led to an exposé of his expenses fiddling, which would land him in prison and humiliate Charlotte.

Blake had disgraced himself with his treasonous comments, and the article was recycled and reintroduced to the press anytime someone mentioned his stepfather the prince in the papers. The exam-paper scandal of International House had upset Edward greatly, and he was about to become embroiled in a money laundering scandal. And Henry's lies had been exposed to both the public and his parents. I doubt that they would ever trust him again.

So why wasn't I happy?

I would miss the triumvirate, the treacherous wretches. Miss their banter, their kisses, and their caresses. I would even miss their anguished faces every time something got leaked to the press or to the Mercia-Net.

After boarding the train to London, I settled into my seat, pulled out my smartphone, and scrolled over to the email containing my e-ticket to New York. With a bit of careful finger work, I copied and pasted the booking code into the airline's website. After pressing 'send,' I got the following error message.

Code Invalid.

I returned to the email and tried again.

Code Invalid.

I shook my head. That couldn't be right. I called Jackie's cell. She answered after one ring.

"Jackie? It's Emilia. I just tried to check into my flight for New York. It says the ticket's invalid. Could you buy me a flight and claim the cost back from Rudolph's office?"

She was silent for several moment. "Actually, Rudolph is in London."

Relief huffed out of my lungs. "He wants to see me before I go?"

"He came to oversee our expansion into a daily paper, and he wants you to continue supplying new material."

My heart froze, and my blood turned to ice. This wasn't our

arrangement. The moment the Correspondent published Edward's paperwork, he would know that the real leak wasn't Carbuncle, but me.

"B-but I can't go back," I rasped.

"Sorry. His new plans involve you back in Mercia Academy, gathering information. Come down later today and speak to him if you like." Jackie hung up.

My nostrils flared.

Rudolph had gone back on our agreement.

The wretched bastard had betrayed me.

And now, I would have to return to Mercia Academy and face all those I had betrayed.

END OF BOOK TWO
READ BOOK THREE

DEPOSED

KINGS OF MERCIA ACADEMY BOOK 3

CHAPTER 1

I clutched my smartphone with numb fingers, and stared at my invalid e-ticket to New York for so long, my vision blurred. The editor-in-chief of the Saturday Correspondent's words echoed in my head and drowned out the roar of blood rushing through my eardrums.

The train sped over the tracks, creating a blur of green outside its huge windows, and making the lining of my stomach rumble with dread. It had taken tears, lies, and a whole lot of feminine wiles for Edward to believe that I hadn't leaked the academy's secrets to the Saturday Correspondent. And now, after I'd fulfilled my end of the bargain and given his paper some scandalous scoops, Rudolph wanted me to return.

To the wrath of Edward.

To the triumvirate.

And to Mercia Academy.

My throat spasmed, and my mind ran through everything I'd suffered during my first term. The gauntlet pushed itself to the front of my mind, as did the punches and kicks and hair-pulling. I squeezed my eyes shut, feeling the sting of the tampered shampoo.

If I returned to Mercia Academy, things would be much worse. I might not even make it out alive. Anger surged through my veins, making my limbs shake. Rudolph couldn't do this to me. The information I had given the Correspondent had taken it from a loss-making operation to one that syndicated articles to much larger papers. Jackie had even told me they'd made enough to pay off their corporate debt. I had done enough, and he couldn't demand any more.

The train pulled into an artificially lit platform in London, Victoria station. A muffled announcement sounded on the loudspeaker, and all the passengers bustled out toward the exit. I stared after them, still rooted to my seat. I had two choices. One, to return to Mercia Academy face the consequences when the article based on the file I took from Edward came out on Saturday. Or two, to storm Jackie's meeting with Rudolph and demand that he fulfill his end of our bargain.

Rudolph owed me a ticket back home to Manhattan, a place at a school of my choosing, an ivy league education, and an internship. I'd given his paper the information they had needed to create scandalous articles. He wouldn't get away with treating me like shit.

People boarded the train, indicating that it would soon head back south. I pulled myself out of my seat, grabbed my case, and eased my way through the stream of new passengers and out onto the platform. It was time to go to Fleet Street and confront Rudolph.

I passed the ticket barrier and walked through the busy station, avoiding near collisions with people running for their trains. The cacophony of traffic coming in from outside combined with announcements over multiple loudspeakers filled my ears and made my head pound. My phone vibrated. I stopped walking and pulled my smartphone out of my pocket.

A message from Edward flashed on the screen. *Where are you?*

Guilt surged up my gullet. Mere hours ago, I'd left him naked and sleeping in his study without so much as a goodbye. I stuffed the phone back into my pocket. Stuffed the guilt back down into my gut, and headed for the taxi rank.

∽

Jackie usually ushered me into her room every time I visited the Saturday Correspondent. Today, she kept me waiting. I sat at the only free seat in the open-plan room, which was next to a bank of six desks set up with huge computer screens for interns to watch through the camera footage. Chocolate Easter egg wrapping littered the surfaces of their desks.

"Mr. Underwood's daughter's going to a local comprehensive school now," whispered an Indian girl with a long braid she coiled into a thick bun.

"Charlotte?" Her colleague, a plump blonde, raised her head and grinned. "Why?"

"Her dad's diverting all his funds to hiring a lawyer. He's convinced he'll go to jail for fiddling expenses." She took a sip from her coffee mug. "What are you looking at?"

"Edward Mercia."

My heart jumped into my throat, and I whirled around. Both interns fixed their gazes on the computer screens, and each wore headphones.

"Oh." The blonde leaned back to stare at the Indian girl's screen. "I saw him rush through the common room, looking agitated. What's got his knickers in a twist?"

"He's frantic about Emilia and has just told Blake Simpson-West that she's moved out of her room."

Regret spasmed through my insides. Keeping my head down, I twisted in my seat and turned my back on the interns in case they recognized me. I wasn't in any kind of mood to discuss what I'd done to Edward with wide-eyed, young journalists. They continued discussing his sorry state until the sounds of their excited voices made my insides shrivel.

My spying probably caused Edward and the triumvirate more distress and public humiliation than they had originally caused me.

I pulled my attention away from the interns and back to Jackie's door. What could be so important that she couldn't spare a few minutes to see me? It felt like I'd been sitting here for at least an hour. My gaze flickered to the window, where a trio of red, double-decker buses headed toward St. Paul's Cathedral. My smartphone buzzed again, and a pit of dread opened up in my stomach.

I pulled it out of my pocket and stared at the screen. It was Edward. Again. *What kind of person leaves a place so suddenly and without a goodbye? A guilty one. You were the leak. Your actions are the only confession I need.*

My lips tightened. It looked like he had barged his way through the room I shared with Rita and found that I had taken some of my things and gone.

"Mr. Trommel!" exclaimed a voice at the other end of the open-plan office.

My head snapped up. Rudolph strolled in, flanked by two female assistants. He wore a navy blue, pinstriped suit with a silver tie that matched his startling, gray eyes. As usual, his face was devoid of expression, jowls and excess skin hanging off his bones like used-up crepe paper.

My heart pounded to the beat of the fury thrumming in my veins. This was the man who had seen my disheveled state after that gauntlet and hadn't given a damn. Now he wanted to send me back into the den of bullies and bastards and bitches. My nostrils flared. If he thought he could make me return to Mercia Academy, he was as addled as he looked.

"Rudolph?" I said.

He stopped in his tracks and narrowed his eyes. "Why aren't you at school?"

The interns at the nearby bank of desks all stopped watching their videos to gape. It was hard to tell if they were looking at Rudolph or kicking themselves that they hadn't noticed me sitting so close.

I rose to my feet. "Term ends in a week, and I've finished my assignment. I was on my way to Heathrow Airport when the airline's online check-in no longer recognized my e-ticket for New York as valid."

"Because you're staying in England and giving me more material for the Correspondent." Without so much as a knock, Rudolph pushed open Jackie's door and stepped inside.

I scrambled after him and clenched my teeth. "Rudolph—"

"Wait for your editor-in-chief." He waved me away.

Jackie sat at her desk with a booted foot on its surface and her phone wedged between her ear and shoulder. "No…" she rasped at the person on the other line. "I don't care that you represent the Sunday Times and that you think my money laundering article should debut in your Educational Supplement."

The other person replied with something that made her smirk. She tucked a lock of bleached-blonde hair behind her other ear. "It's tempting, but how will you publish that article without mentioning all the other goings-on in International House? Your readers will want context."

Seconds later, she interjected with, "No, way. If you want those articles, you're paying for them separately."

Another pause. Another smirk. A wink at Rudolph, who steepled his fingers like Mr. Burns, rocked back on his heels and beamed. Disgust curdled in my stomach. Jackie wouldn't be able to demand money from the Sunday Times without my hard work. She knew it, and Rudolph knew it, too. That was why he had canceled my ticket to New York. He hadn't finished milking his stepdaughter, the cash cow.

"Alright." She coughed into her hand. "Take that number, double it, and I'll let you run it before the Correspondent."

The person at the other end of the phone must have said yes because Jackie's lips spread into a smile that exposed her tobacco-stained teeth.

Rudolph lowered himself onto one of the chairs in front of her desk and beamed, giving her a hand signal to carry on.

I took the seat next to him and leaned in to whisper. "Does Mom know you're using me as a spy?"

His jovial expression morphed, slow as a turtle emerging from its shell, into a grimace of irritation. "She also doesn't know how her daughter obtained this information." He shook his head. "And it would break her to think you'd seduced three boys to get it."

His words hit like a punch in the stomach. Mom had probably washed her hands of me by now. I'd sent her dozens of texts and emails and hadn't gotten any response. These days, the only time I saw her was when she appeared at various charity events in the society pages.

I shook off those thoughts. There were cameras in Edward's study and his room, and I'd been careful not to do anything within its line of sight. But nothing could be done about the sounds. Maybe the interns monitoring the footage worked things out and told Jackie, who told Rudolph.

I clenched my teeth. If this was his attempt at blackmailing me, it wouldn't work. I wasn't ashamed of anything I'd done with the boys... Apart from what Rudolph wanted me to do.

Jackie hung up. "We're going to focus on Chaloner's dirty dealings, and the Times will take the educational angle. It works out more lucrative that way."

"Excellent." Rudolph tapped his steepled fingers, giving Jackie a bizarre round of silent applause. "How will we follow up this great performance, ladies?"

"I'm not going back to Mercia Academy," I said.

Jackie leaned forward, resting her forearms on her desk. Her gaze flickered to Rudolph, who sat back in his seat and gave her a gentle nod. A frustrated breath huffed out of my nostrils. She'd kept me waiting because she didn't want to make an unreasonable demand without my wretched stepfather as backup.

"We need you on the inside for one more term," she said. "After what's coming, they'll be reconstructing their reputa—"

"No!" My hands curled into fists. I glowered at Rudolph, but he kept his gaze on Jackie, as though whatever I said next wouldn't matter. "I agreed to provide stories on Edward Mercia, Henry Bourneville, Blake Simpson-West, and Charlotte Underwood. That was the deal. I delivered on that and more, now it's time for you to uphold your end of the bargain."

Jackie slid back into her seat and shot Rudolph a pleading look.

The wretched old man puckered his lips. "Return to the academy, gather more information about those kids, and I won't tell your mother you're in a relationship with three boys."

"Tell her," I snapped.

He turned his sharp, silvery eyes on me and stared.

"She hasn't responded to any of my texts." I reached into my pocket and pulled out my smartphone. "Maybe she'll remember she has a daughter if she finds out I've turned to boys to fill the maternal gap."

His silent stare continued for so long, my stomach twisted. I pressed my lips together and held his gaze. A tactic like that probably intimidated a whole bunch of people in the business world, but so what? His disapproval was nothing compared to the crowd of violent assholes at Mercia Academy who would bay for my blood when they discovered what I'd done to their precious school.

Nobody in the room spoke. My heart pounded in synch with Jackie's drumming of the pads of her fingers on the wooden desk, and one of the personal assistants standing behind us shifted on her feet. The silence built and built like a pressure cooker about to explode. Rudolph showed no signs of wanting to speak to me, so I caved.

"Did you know Headmaster Chaloner cornered me this morning and nearly had me arrested by two police officers? Or that he's insane enough to kick a door off its hinges? And the first term, a whole hall of people attacked me because they hate Americans? You want to send me back to that, after what I've done to the academy?"

Jackie cleared her throat. "The headmaster was arrested earlier today. I doubt the police will let a criminal return to a school full of children."

"No, but Edward Mercia just worked out that I'm the leak." I pointed at the door. "Ask your interns if you don't believe me. They've seen the recordings. Don't you think he'll make sure everyone knows about this? With my cover blown, no one will trust me enough to say anything incriminating."

Jackie glanced down and didn't reply. Probably because I'd won the argument.

Rudolph stroked his chin. "It's that or military school."

"Where?" I asked.

"I beg your pardon?"

"Which school?" I snapped. "If it means not going back to Mercia Academy, I'll do it. But when I eventually catch up with Mom, I'll tell her I did everything you asked of me and more, yet you put me in military school because you didn't care what the boys would do to me if I returned."

It was his turn to flare his nostrils. "Very well. If you want to go somewhere else, you'll have to fund it yourself."

Blood drained from my face and settled into my frantic heart. "Y-you would leave me stranded in England?"

"There's a place for you at Mercia Academy." He folded his arms over his chest and stretched out his legs in a display of nonchalance.

I pulled myself out of my seat and walked out on shaky legs. There was no point in continuing this conversation. Until I could accrue enough allowance to buy a plane ticket to New York, I had no choice but to return to Mercia Academy. To the triumvirate's wrath.

My legs felt like wooden pegs as I walked out of the building, and my insides felt raw and hollow, as though someone had scooped them out with a rusty knife. How could Rudolph be so ruthless? Black cabs zoomed past on the red stretches of roads reserved for busses, and I closed my eyes and inhaled cool, spring air laden with exhaust fumes.

"Emilia?" asked a familiar voice.

I turned toward the road. Peeking through the limo window was Marissa, the assistant of the assistant who had escorted me on my first day of the academy.

"What are you doing in London?" She poked her long-nailed hand out of the window and beckoned. "Shouldn't you be at that school?"

"I had to leave."

"Couldn't stand the people?" she asked.

"Something like that." I leaned my hand on the roof of the limo. "Have you seen my mom?"

"She flew across with us but went onto Paris to meet a girlfriend."

My heart sank into my loafers. Why would Rudolph treat me like I was anything but expendable when my own mother didn't give a shit? "Right. Could you tell her I'll be in London for the next few weeks? It's school holidays right now, and I'd love to see her."

Marissa grinned. "Of course, honey."

"Thanks." I didn't hold out any hope that Mom would get in touch. The lifestyle of being the wife of a multimillionaire had clearly gone to her head, and she wouldn't let something as trivial as motherhood spoil her fun. "See you."

As I headed down Fleet Street toward St. Paul's station, I glanced at the buildings of various other British newspapers. None of them would allow an underage girl on an undercover mission, much less force her to return once her cover had been blown. The phone buzzed again. It was probably Edward, telling me I was a bitch.

I pulled it out and gazed at the message on the screen. *Father has been arrested on suspicion of money laundering. FATHER! I hope you're proud that your machinations have brought both the school and the duchy into disrepute. Return to the academy, NOW.*

Guilt gnawed at my insides like a colony of maggots. Even if I replied to explain that I hadn't meant for any of this to affect Edward's poor father, my words would be meaningless. I slipped the phone back into my pocket and waited in line to buy an Oyster card. There was only one person in the world who might be able to give me refuge, and I hoped he was still in London.

CHAPTER 2

Sergei might let me sleep on his sofa until my allowance arrived. It would mean going out with him in the evening as his beard, but by the time the triumvirate found pictures of me in the society pages, they would already hate me for being the leak.

Seconds after I reached the front of the line for the ticket machine, the buzzing of my phone gave me a jolt. My hand twitched toward my pocket. I had to know if there was an update about Edward's dad. The poor man had to be frightened out of his wits to have been arrested. With his dementia, he probably didn't even know why the police had taken him away.

I wrapped my hand around the phone and glanced at the screen. It was a long message from Rita, asking if I had boarded the plane yet. A breath of relief slid from my lungs. She seemed quite excited that I was leaving the country, as opposed to harassed that the triumvirate had stormed our room, demanding answers.

A sharp finger prodded me in the lower back. It belonged to a middle-aged man dressed in a charcoal, pin-striped suit. His sharp features were a younger version of Rudolph's which reminded me of the unfair ultimatum.

His pale, blue eyes flashed. "Are you going to buy a ticket or send text messages?"

"My smartphone is a payment device." I let my gaze flicker down his thin form. "We've moved on from money orders. And from poking girls in the ass."

His cheeks turned red, and he spluttered, "I did no such thing!"

"Why poke a girl at all?"

Breathing hard, he glanced from left to right before storming to another ticket line. I turned around and bought an Oyster card. Since I planned on spending time in London, it made sense to save money buying an electronic, rechargeable ticket.

After paying, I stood at the wall between the ticket machines and sent Sergei a text. *I'm stranded in London. Do you have a spare couch? :)*

Seconds later, the phone buzzed. *This is Andreo. Sergei is playing at the South Bank Center until 23h. Can you get to Sloane Square station?*

Yes. I replied.

One of the guards will meet you outside and take you to our apartment.

The tightness around my neck and torso that I didn't notice before melted away, and I leaned against the wall and exhaled a noisy breath of relief. *Thank you! I'll get there as soon as I can.*

The sun had set by the time I stepped out into Sloane Square, and one of the bodyguards was already waiting. He gave me a nod of greeting and gestured at a street of Victorian mansion apartments overlooking the river. Street lights lit our way, and I breathed hard, trying to imagine which one of these buildings was Sergei's.

Sergei's apartment was a duplex with floor-to-ceiling windows overlooking a suspension bridge lit up by a thousand lightbulbs with views of a park on the other bank of the River Thames. It had an open-plan living area with a kitchen, diner and a bank of leather sofas with views of both a projector TV and of the magnificent vista. The bodyguard showed me to a room the size of my dorm, which he assured me in broken English was unoccupied.

I sat on the bed, pulled out my smartphone, and sent a message to Rita. *My ticket to New York got canceled, and I'm staying with Sergei.*

She replied with, *What about the school in NY your stepfather promised??*

A lump formed in my throat. If I'd allowed Rudolph to send me to military school, I wouldn't be in this mess. *He wants me to return to Mercia and spy.*

They'll kill you.

My heart sank. *I know.* Edward and Blake would restart their campaign of vicious pranks, and Henry would give me disapproving glares if he didn't join them. *But at least I have all of Easter break to work out a way to avoid going back.*

Rita didn't reply. Maybe because I was a lost cause. I stared at Edward's last message. He hadn't messaged again with news about his father, and I doubted that he would give me any updates. I had never meant for my actions to hurt a widower who required round-the-clock care for dementia. Edward had to know that.

I hope you're proud that your machinations have brought both the school and the duchy into disrepute.

My heart spasmed. He had to be feeling as betrayed as I had during my captivity in that basement room. At first, I had been confused that anyone would think me capable of kidnapping Henry, but with Blake's prompting, I had worked out that they had framed me. The pain of that treachery had been unbearable and still stung even today. This morning, I had convinced Edward that I wasn't the leak, gotten a confession of love, then seduced him, only to disappear while he slept.

I had to be the world's biggest bitch.

Rita texted later to say that she'd had to delete my messages because Blake knocked on the door and demanded to see her phone. Hours later, the apartment filled with the sounds of male voices. I stepped into the hallway, padded down the stairs, and hovered by the end of the banister.

Sergei walked through the doors, wearing a black tuxedo with a matching vest and a silver bowtie. His black hair had grown a few inches and hung past his collarbone. He furrowed his brows and stared at me with worried, aquamarine eyes. "Emilia?"

I rushed into his arms. "I'm sorry, but I had nowhere else to go!"

He guided me to the sofas and sat me down. "What happened?"

The entire, sorry tale blurted out. He already knew about the events of the end of my first term, but I told him how I'd gotten revenge on the boys and a few others by revealing their secrets to the Saturday Correspondent. Sergei listened without interruption or judgment, and when I finished by telling him that I'd lost my virginity earlier in the day, he wrapped his arms around me.

"I am so sorry," he murmured into my hair. "These people are continuing to make you suffer."

I drew back and stared into his bright eyes. "Huh?"

"You feel guilty, even after everything they did to you."

"But Edward's father got arrested—"

"Which would have happened eventually when someone else exposed the headmaster."

My mouth dropped open, and a gasp caught in my throat. Sergei was right to some extent. It hadn't been like I was manufacturing stories. Everything I'd shared with the Correspondent had happened of its own accord, but I was still eaten up by guilt. "Friends don't report friends to the papers."

Sergei clasped my shoulders with both hands and gave them a gentle squeeze as though telling me to wake up. Two lines appeared on his brows as he drew them together. "And friends do not frame friends for their own crimes."

"Thanks." I wrapped my arms around his neck. "I really needed that."

Later that evening, my phone buzzed as I was dozing off. I rolled over to the bedside table and glanced at the screen. Edward's text said, *I suppose you've left the country.*

The lack of anger or recrimination in his message made my heart sink. It was as though realization had finally dawned, and he'd resigned himself that I had gone. I closed my eyes and tried to fall back into slumber, but my mind kept dredging up images of Edward's blue eyes, filled with wonder as I surrendered my virginity to him.

My eyes opened, and I bolted upright, pressing a palm over my aching chest. I hadn't counted on hurting him that much, and when the Saturday Correspondent published an article on the papers he had entrusted to me, it would rip out what was left of his heart. I clenched my fists and let out a frustrated breath. If I kept letting thoughts of Edward haunt my mind, sleep would evade me for an eternity.

Mom used to give me a glass of milk when I couldn't sleep. Maybe a drink might clear my mind. I slipped out of bed, padded across the little room, and opened the door.

The mezzanine was dark with only the barest of light at the lower level. As I reached the bannister, a low, male chuckle resounded from below. I peered down to find a shirtless Andreo lying on the sofa with his head thrown back and his eyes squeezed shut. Sergei straddled his thighs, clad in a black robe that exposed his muscular back.

My lips parted, and every ounce of my attention fixated on the two men.

Sergei kissed a path along Andreo's jawline, then sucked on his lover's neck. He held the larger man down by the wrists, making him writhe and strain against his hold. Andreo's low, resonant moan sent tingles between my legs, and I swallowed hard. This was unbelievably hot.

The lower Sergei kissed, the more he exposed of Andreo's tanned, muscular body, and the more those muscles bunched and strained against Sergei's hold. Andreo clenched his teeth and forced out some words in strained Russian. From his tone and the way he bucked against Sergei, he probably wanted an end to the slow teasing.

Sergei chuckled and shuffled further down Andreo's body, revealing the other man's collarbones and muscled pecs. I bit my lip and stifled a moan.

This was so much like the Valentine's party with Henry and Blake. Except they wouldn't have objected to me gaping at them. Sergei pinched Andreo's nipples, making the other man suck in a breath through his teeth and hiss something out in French.

One of Sergei's hands reached down between their bodies, and Andreo let out a sigh of both pleasure and relief. I gripped the bannister and squeezed my thighs together. At any moment, Sergei would go down on his lover, and I'd intrude further on their private moment. I had to leave. Now.

When Sergei's arm started moving, I released my grip on the wood and backed away. I stepped into my room and eased the door shut, careful not to make a sound and let them know I'd been watching.

The drapes of my room were open, revealing the suspension bridge in its illuminated splendor. Its lights reflected on the river, but I couldn't focus on the magical view. Not when I'd seen Sergei and Andreo together. Not when they reminded me so much of Henry and Blake.

I flopped on the bed, a mass of frustration and need. After what I'd just seen, I would never get to sleep. Each breath, every movement, brushed my hardened nipples over the cotton of my nightgown and sent tiny thunderbolts of arousal between my legs. One thigh crossed over the other, and hot pulses of pleasure rippled through my core.

"This isn't working." I parted my thighs and pulled my nightgown up to my hips.

Cool air swirled between my legs, over my clit, reminding me of the wetness in my core. I groaned and reached between my thighs. The tip of my finger skimmed my throbbing nub, and I drew in a breath between my teeth. Even though Sergei and Andreo had triggered this arousal, it seemed rude to think of them while I masturbated, so I cast my mind back to what I'd seen at the Valentine's party.

Cast my mind back to Blake, sprawled beneath a half-naked Henry, kissing him with abandon.

I dipped the pad of my fingertips into my sopping core and gathered enough moisture to let them glide over my throbbing clit in little circles. My nipples tightened, demanding my attention, and I rolled my right one between my fingertips and rubbed harder on my twitching nub.

Blake, with his hands on Henry's tight, muscled ass, invaded my thoughts.

I parted my legs as far as they would go, remembering now the two boys had knelt in front of me, servicing my needs with their fingers and tongues. I increased the pressure on my clit and bit down hard on my bottom lip, imagining the finger belonged to someone else.

In my mind's eye, Blake's full lips wrapped around Henry's length, making the other boy moan and shudder and groan.

The muscles of my core tightened with each stroke of my clit, and pleasure built to the rhythm of my movements. I squeezed my eyes shut and tweaked my nipple, just as Edward had done the day the triumvirate thought they'd seduced me into forgiving them.

Pleasure coiled around my core like a snake, and the world disappeared. There was no more Edward or Henry or Blake. No more double-dealing and treachery. It was just me and my fingers and my quivering core. My fingers continued moving over my clit, and the images in my head jumbled into a mass of muscular bodies quaking with pleasure, just like me.

Then as I pictured my own lips closing over the head of Edward's beautiful, pink penis, my pleasure spiked, and a climax seized my body in a torrent sensations. Every spasm of my core forced out wave upon wave of pleasure, making me moan and shudder until all thoughts of men and the triumvirate retreated to the back of my mind.

CHAPTER 3

The next morning, a knowing smile curved Sergei's lips as he and Andreo sat opposite me at breakfast. One of the bodyguards had brought apricot pastries, and I could barely eat, knowing that Sergei or Andreo had spotted me watching them.

"Ummm…" I bit down on my lip. "Whatever happened with the investigation on your father?"

Sergei's smile faded, and he shook his head. "Alexander deals with these matters."

My gaze flicked to the smallest of the bodyguards, a dark-haired man in his early thirties with hair closely cropped to his scalp. "Sorry for bringing up the subject."

Andreo topped up my coffee from a silver pot, lips quirking into a smile. "Sergei has a concert tonight. Will you accompany us as his beard?"

"Sure," I said with a relieved breath. This would be the last time I'd bring up the subject of his father's poisoning.

I spent the next few weeks attending events on Sergei's arm and appearing in the society pages as his devoted fiancée. Mom didn't text for details, but Dad kept pestering me with questions until I explained that Sergei was just a friend who wanted to drum up a bit of publicity. The pictures, unfortunately, attached the attention of Edward.

Will you return to Mercia Academy next term?

I stared at the phone and gulped. If he had demanded a meeting in London, I would have agreed, but returning to his territory and to all the people affected by the Correspondent articles would be suicide. I tapped the icon for my banking app. My allowance would arrive in a few days, and it would give me enough for a flight back to New York.

A few days before term started, Sergei took me out in the limo to the Claridge's Hotel for breakfast. It was a late Georgian building constructed of red bricks that had probably been built around the same time as the Bourneville's department store. Its grand entrance of white pillars and floor-to-ceiling, art deco windows made me draw in the same awed breath as I had the day the boys had taken me shopping for a ballgown.

As I stepped out of the limo to the crowds of paparazzi, I forced a smile and tried not to think of Henry. I took comfort in Sergei's large hand on the small of my back and walked through the entrance and into the black-and-white tiled foyer.

The dining room was a huge, magnolia-colored space of smartly-dressed tables, decorated with white roses that matched both the table cloths and the pillars. Hanging from the ceiling was an ornate chandelier of flower-bud shapes and glass spirals that looked more like a sculpture than a source of light. Sergei had booked a table by an arched window, behind which photographers gathered to take pictures of us.

Sergei reached across the table and took my hand in his. "A promoter has offered me a three-month tour of Europe. We leave in two days. Will you come with us?"

I chewed my lip and gazed into his earnest, aquamarine eyes. The thought of visiting places like Paris, Vienna, and Rome made my heart flutter, but I couldn't put my life on hold for a fake relationship. "I'm sorry, Sergei. I have my studies."

"I will have to hand back the keys to the owner of the apartment," he said. "Will you return to the United States or stay in London?"

The waiter arrived with our orders, and Sergei let go of my hand. My gaze dropped to my plate of eggs Benedict. My plan had been to stay in his apartment until Mom sent my allowance, but it hadn't materialized, and everyone I messaged had said they couldn't reach her regular phone. Rudolph must have somehow convinced her not to send me any money. I couldn't ask Sergei to buy my ticket. He'd done enough for me, and even if I reached the States, there might not even be a room for me at Rudolph's mansion.

"I'm..." I cleared my throat. "I'm returning to Mercia Academy."

"Are you sure?" He placed a hand on my wrist.

I nodded. "Term starts tomorrow. I'd better go."

Sergei nodded. "Is money your problem? I can—"

"No." A nervous laugh warbled in the back of my throat. Sergei believed the triumvirate thought I was disposable. Admitting that my mother and stepfather also acted like I wasn't worth the expense of pocket money was too much to bear. "I have to face the boys one day. It may as well be now."

He stared at me for a long time, his eyes boring into my soul. Eventually, he sighed. "This would be a good time to stage our break-up."

"Um..." I drew my brows together, trying to work out what he meant. Then my attention dropped to the fake diamond on my finger. I slipped it off to a flurry of camera flashes, and handed it to Sergei, who hung his head. "Don't you think you're exaggerating a little too much?"

"I want to look devastated," he muttered. "Like it will take years to mend my broken heart."

I bit down hard on my lip. If the cameras caught me smiling at his sad display, the press would write me up like some kind of villain.

Later that evening, I sent Edward a text. *I'll be there on Monday.*

His reply was instant. *Take the 9:45 from Victoria. I'll reserve you a seat.*

～

On Monday, Sergei escorted me to Victoria station, this time without the press fanfare. We walked in silence through the busy concourse amidst the cacophony of busy travelers and loudspeaker announcements. The mingled scents from the stores and restaurants made my stomach churn, and I tried not to think of what would await me when I finally arrived at Mercia Academy. We stopped at the platform's ticket barrier, then he wrapped his arms around my shoulders and kissed both cheeks. "If you change your mind, send me a text."

I smiled and stared up into his sad eyes. Apart from Rita, he was the best friend I had made so far in England. "Thanks."

"You are always welcome in my entourage." He whispered the next part into my ear. "And not just as a beard."

I laughed and threw my arms around his neck. "I'll miss you. Thanks again for everything."

The warm glow Sergei left as I boarded dimmed into a flicker the moment the train departed the station. I was doing something I promised Rita I wouldn't do: returning to Mercia Academy. This time, I wouldn't be shunned or ignored by the triumvirate. They would rip me apart and leave what was left of me for the other students to pick through.

My phone buzzed. *Are you on the train?*

Yes.

This had better not be another of your lies.

I stuffed the phone back into my pocket and snarled. Edward was a fine one to call someone a liar.

The train whizzed by countryside, which became greener the closer we got to my destination. My pulse pounded in my eardrums, drowning out the chugging of the wheels on the tracks.

Images of potential scenarios whirled around my mind like a kaleidoscope. Most of them involved ways the students would exact their retribution for leaking stories to the newspapers. Only one of them was a scene where Edward forgave me and repeated his declaration of love. I shook away the false hope and buried my head in my hands until the announcer called out Mercia.

Taking the first step off the train was agony. Palpitations reverberated throughout my body as I made my way out of the station and inhaled warm, fresh country air. Before I could take in the sights of the quaint village of stone-fronted stores, a limo rolled into view, and the back door opened.

My stomach dropped. This could only mean one thing. The triumvirate were in session and ready to exact their vengeance. Nobody stepped out to bundle me inside. I guessed they wanted me to walk to my own gallows.

On feet that felt like lead, I dragged myself to the curb, and stepped inside to meet Edward's wintry glare. The impact was like a kick in the gut, and my breath caught in the back of my throat. I hadn't seen him this livid since the time he upended the table at me.

"I'm…" I cleared my sandpapery throat. "I came as promised."

"Get inside," he said through clenched teeth.

I stepped into the limo and took the seat nearest to the door and furthest away from Edward, who sat upright, breathing loud and deep and fast. The seatbelt around me felt like a leash, but I stared straight ahead, trying not to look at Edward. But in the corner of my vision, he resembled an eagle about to strike.

The driver sped down through the village thoroughfare, but

instead of turning left into the road that led to the academy, he went straight ahead.

My gaze slid to Edward's clenched fists. "Where are we going?"

"I need time with you alone to prepare you for what's to follow," he replied.

A shiver of apprehension ran down my back, and I pictured a gauntlet, but this time, the students carried hockey sticks. My tongue darted out to lick my lips. "What should I expect?"

"The police wouldn't accept any of the documentation we offered them to prove Father's condition, so he remained in a cell for weeks, while their doctors reassessed him. He was released last week on the grounds of diminished responsibility."

A breath of relief slid from my lungs. "I'm gla—"

"Now the entire country knows of his ailment, and vultures are circling us in the guise of well-wishers, hoping to take advantage of his vulnerable state."

Guilt knitted my stomach into knots that stretched up to my gullet. "I'm so—"

"The Board of Governors convened to discuss the future of the academy," he said in a louder voice. "One of the topics of conversation was whether it was worth continuing with a school whose reputation was so tarnished."

I cringed. Even though I hadn't been the one to hand out exam papers to the students of International House, I had passed evidence of the academy's cheating to the Saturday Correspondent. I glanced up at Edward's eyes, but at the weight of his stare, my gaze snapped down to my lap.

"You took matters too far," he said, his voice tight.

My throat flexed. "I realize that now."

"Why?"

A burst of fury seared through all traces of guilt, and my head snapped up. "After you took me back, none of you wanted to clear my name for the kidnapping. I don't care that juvenile records get expunged. You set me up for something that could have gotten me imprisoned for years and didn't have the decency to set things right."

His brows drew together. Before he could speak, I blurted, "Sex doesn't count, otherwise you wouldn't be so hurt about what I did to you."

"You didn't hurt me." He sniffed.

"Do you need more reasons? Nearly blinding me with doctored shampoo, getting me kicked repeatedly by Charlotte Underwood, leaving me in a field in the middle of the night, two counts of false imprisonment... Do I need to continue?"

"No," he said through clenched teeth. "But I told you why I did what I did."

A frustrated breath huffed out of my nostrils. "I get it. Hurting and controlling others made you feel better about your shitty life, but people fight back, and you shouldn't complain when it hurts."

"Why did you return?" he growled.

I'd be damned if I told him I had nowhere else to go. "Because you asked. Repeatedly."

His cold gaze flickered up and down my body then lingered on my breasts. "Blake and Henry are waiting for you in my study. If you think I'm angry, wait until you see them."

CHAPTER 4

We remained silent for the rest of the journey. There wasn't much point in discussing why Henry and Blake were angry. Edward had told them I had either leaked information to the press or had been involved in the coercion of Mr. Frost and Mr. Carbuncle, the two people known to have collaborated with the Saturday Correspondent.

The limo stopped at the front of Elder House, its gardens a deceptively peaceful display of pink and white blossoms. Bile rose to the back of my throat as my mind dredged up what would wait for me inside. Another gauntlet, a baying mob, or a group of everyone who had been hurt by the articles in the Saturday Correspondent.

The driver opened the door, and my heart thudded. I stole a glance at Edward, who wouldn't look at me, and I prayed to whoever was listening that things wouldn't get out of control.

Edward stepped out first and turned to offer his hand. It was as though he knew I would need help walking. I stared into eyes that bored into mine with such intensity, I forgot about impending punishments and became locked in his gaze. They were a storm of clouds reflecting on the surface of the ocean, threatening to drown me in their depths. But he blinked and broke the illusion.

"Come," he said, in a voice so resonant, so commanding, I placed my clammy hand in his.

The touch sent tiny tremors running down every bone in my body. Edward stared down at my hand and creased his brows. The expression was so fleeting, it might have come from my fevered imagination. He helped me out of the limo, and we walked hand-in-hand across the gravel courtyard. Stones crunched underfoot, the sound making my insides writhe with discomfort.

If I endured the ordeal waiting for me beyond the doors, would the boys forgive me, or would they resume the campaign of bullying they had started in my first term?

We stepped through the double doors, through the reception hall beyond, where students bustled through the hallways and up and down the stairs, oblivious to our presence. My breathing shallowed, and I blinked several times.

"What's happening?" I whispered.

Edward glared at me through the corner of his eye. "If you were expecting a welcoming party, then you think less of me than I'd originally feared."

His words stung as hard as a slap. Edward was acting as though the triumvirate hadn't brought any of the public humiliation they'd suffered onto themselves. I stopped walking and placed my hands on my hips. "Perhaps if you three had explained your actions, I might not have taken things too far."

"What?" Edward turned around, fixing me with a dark stare.

I clenched my fists and glowered straight into his eyes. Students in the hallways rushed past, too busy with beginning of term greetings to notice us. Still, I kept my voice to a low hiss. "You were too busy protecting your precious Mr. Frost. I had to learn that he framed me from the Correspondent, and by then, I'd already set everything in motion."

Edward didn't reply, but his eyes softened. Perhaps he was beginning to see the situation from my point of view.

The anger roiling in my gut cooled and faded into the background. Without meaning to, I stepped closer to him and said, "I shouldn't have taken things so far, but can you blame me?"

His face tightened, and he continued down the hallway, leaving me trailing behind, staring at his broad back. I swallowed. Edward seemed conflicted about me. He'd had the entire Easter break with Henry and Blake to work himself into a frenzy about how I'd unjustifiably betrayed the triumvirate, but it had taken a few words for his resolve to waver.

I sucked in a deep breath and wrapped my arms around my middle. Was it too optimistic to expect the other members of the triumvirate to listen to reason?

Edward paused at the door of his study and gave me the tightest of smiles. "Let's wait until the others are present before making excuses, shall we?"

My stomach hardened with dread. So much for my wishful thinking.

He turned the handle and opened the door to his study, revealing an interior darkened by drawn curtains. Leather and coffee and firewood mingled to provide a familiar scent that reminded me of happier times I'd spent in this room. The flames crackling in the fireplace provided illumination, bolstered by two Anglepoise lamps shining on Edward's leather desk. Blake and Henry sat in separate, leather armchairs, each staring up at me with accusing eyes.

Henry was the first to stand. The light of the fire lit the ends of his blond hair, making them appear incandescent. One side of his face was cast in shadow. He stared down at me with the same look he had given me in the early days, like he wanted to dissect me and discover what was inside. Perhaps he did. This was the first time I'd seen him since Mr. Frost's story about the kidnapping had come out.

I lifted my head and tried to meet his eyes, but his gaze was fixed on a spot on my cheek. My heart sank. I had expected shouting. Recriminations, so I could spit out my side of the story and justify my actions, but he remained silent.

Blake pushed himself off his armchair and stood at Henry's left. The ends of his black hair merged with the shadows in the room, making each feature stand out. Dim light exaggerated cheekbones that could slice me in half and a cruel, and showcased a downward slant to his full lips. Once again, my gaze flickered up to meet his eyes, but met expressionless pools of black.

The silence stretched on, each passing moment wringing my guts. From his position by the door, Edward walked around me and stood at Henry's right in the exact formation I'd seen them when we had first met in the first term, on the stairs of the main teaching block. I swallowed hard. "W-what do you want from me?"

"We know why you did it," replied Blake, his voice curling around my senses like smoke. His dark eyes hardened. "But you should understand that no slight against us goes unpunished."

My heart rate doubled, and I gasped out a breath of disbelief. "But we're even. Can't you see that?"

Edward chuckled, a rich, deep sound that promised vengeance. The fine hairs on the back of my neck stood on end. "Why did you come back after what you and your stepfather did?"

I stepped back. "Y-you sent me texts…"

He advanced on me, filling my vision with his cruel, handsome face. "Then I commend you for your obedience."

My gaze flickered to Henry's face. His nostrils had flared, the skin around his green eyes tightened with pain. My throat flexed. He was staring at me as though I had stabbed him in the gut.

I could understand Edward and Blake's animosity. I'd directly encouraged them to incriminate themselves. It was my manipulative words that had goaded Blake into talking treason about the

Prince of Wales in front of the cameras, and my manipulation of Edward's worries that had led him to answer leading questions about International House in front of the cameras. I'd even tricked Edward into handing over vital evidence that had gotten the headmaster and his father arrested.

But I hadn't done anything to Henry. I hadn't coerced Mr. Frost into making a full confession about helping the triumvirate to extort half a million pounds from the Bourneville family by kidnapping Henry.

"You've got a nerve to glare at me like that," I spat.

"Was it your idea to release pictures of Blake and me on the internet?" he asked.

My stomach dropped. "What?"

Henry stalked toward me. "Rudolph Trommel visited my parents with a very interesting video clip from that Valentine's party."

I clapped my hand over my mouth to hide a gasp. Henry and Blake had drunk so much champagne that night. And because of me, they had taken a high thujone absinthe, which had stripped their inhibitions.

What had started with them pinning me to the bed and smothering me with kisses had ended with them kissing and groping each other in front of the hidden camera. All because I'd left them to prompt Blake into talking about International House in front of the balcony camera.

"Why would Rudolph show your parents?" I asked.

"He wanted a refund of the million he paid them to drop the charges against you." Henry clenched his teeth. "With interest. When Mother and Father refused, he released stills on the internet."

"Oh." I glanced away and fixed my gaze on a swirling pattern on the Persian rug. "He blackmailed them."

"Don't pretend you didn't know about it," spat Blake. "Thanks to you, Henry's mother showed them to mine."

My feet shuffled back on their own accord. "I-I'm sorry. But I didn't shoot or release that video."

"What about the interview with an anonymous public school bully?" asked Blake. "It was a repeat of everything I told you on the balcony, twisted to make me look like a bigot."

My mouth dropped open. That was exactly what Jackie had done with the article.

"Don't even deny it." Harsh, guttural bitterness laced Henry's words. "You had that room set up to entrap us. No one else but you could have worked with the Correspondent on that night."

I could deny it, but the evidence proving my guilt was overwhelming. The heat in Henry and Blake's glares made my stomach curdle with a sense of impending doom. Every ounce of moisture in my mouth vanished and reappeared on my hairline. It was bad enough to take the blame for things I had done, but devastating to have them think I'd been involved with the distribution of Henry and Blake's sex tape.

A tiny cough forced its way out of the back of my throat. "You have to believe me. I would never—"

"Stop lying!" Henry bellowed.

I flinched and wrapped my arms around my chest. How could they believe I would allow something so personal on the internet? I glanced at Edward, hoping he would be the voice of reason, but his glower told me he believed me just as guilty as my stepfather. "B-but you framed me—"

"That was Frost, and you know it," Blake growled.

My stomach tightened, and my gaze flickered to his fathomless, dark eyes. The weight of his stare crushed my defiance to dust.

Drawing back my shoulders, I said, "If you hadn't withheld so much information from me, none of this would have happened."

A wall of malevolent silence was my reply. Because I was right. But I was in their territory, outnumbered, with nowhere else to go, and completely at their mercy. I cleared my throat. "What do you want from me?"

"Total and utter obedience," said Henry.

My stomach dropped, and I took another step back to the door. "What?"

"We own you." Blake stepped closer, his dark eyes shining with malice.

"No, you don't." The words came out a bare whisper. "I'll—"

Henry placed a finger on my lips. "If you don't do what we say, we'll release everything we know to the rest of Elder House and leave you to their tender mercies."

Blake walked around me and stood at the door, blocking my only route of escape. "Do you know how furious everyone feels by Carbuncle's supposed betrayal? No one can believe such a well-loved member of staff could leak information about students he served diligently for a decade."

"But they'll believe us if we tell them you sent the journalist who forced Carbuncle to spy for the Correspondence," said Henry.

"You—"

Edward folded his arms across his chest. "You framed an innocent man."

All my trepidation vanished, replaced by righteous anger. "He was corrupt! You saw what he did with that girl."

Henry stepped forward. "Then you should have reported him to the police, not used him as a scapegoat for your own crimes."

I edged back at the vitriol in his words. Blake stood mere inches behind me, his body heat warming my back. "You'd tell everyone I framed Mr. Carbuncle?"

"What do you think they'll do to you when they find out?" Edward asked through clenched teeth.

My body stiffened. They wouldn't be so vindictive... would they? I took another step back. My ass skimmed Blake's hardening crotch. "I don't understand."

Blake's arms wrapped around my waist. "Here's how things will work between us. Unless you do exactly what we say, we'll release evidence into the Mercia-Net that proves you were the leak, and not Carbuncle."

A whimper reverberated in my throat. I still remembered that terrible gauntlet from my first term, and if I didn't want to become the target of every student in the academy, I would have to subject myself to whatever the triumvirate wanted. "Wh-what kind of things will you demand of me?"

"Nothing too onerous." Blake's hand settled over my belly, sending shivers running down my back and between my legs. "Despite everything, we still want you."

"Except you're not taking charge anymore." Henry's finger skimmed my lipline and tried to slip between the seam of my lips.

I clamped my teeth shut. If they thought I would be their sex slave in exchange for their silence, they were out of their minds.

One of Blake's hands rose from my waist and rubbed slow, sensuous circles over my right breast. The sensation made that nipple harden, and the muscles of my core clenched. Heat gathered between my legs, and I stifled a moan.

"What do you want, Emilia?" Edward crooned into my ear. "Will you earn our discretion, or will we tell the school of your treachery?"

Blake's hand made a slow descent down my belly, and his fingertips skimmed the bare skin under the waistband of my skirt. "We're waiting."

Parting my lips, I let Henry slip his finger into my mouth.

"Good girl." Blake ground his erection into my ass. "Now, suck on it."

I closed my eyes, wrapped my lips around his finger and lathed at it with my tongue. This was embarrassing but better than being on my knees in front of them, which was exactly what I would have made them do if I'd been in the position of power.

"Keep your eyes open." Henry pushed the finger further into my mouth.

I glared up into his eyes. The pupils were wide and hungry, bordered by a thin ring of green. Henry's tongue darted out to lick his lips, reminding me of that evening he knelt in front of me behind the oak tree. His breaths were hard and labored and as fast as the pulse pounding between my legs. He stepped closer, filling my senses with his huge body, his citrus and mint scent.

I drew back and turned my head, so Henry's finger slipped out from my mouth. Through ragged breaths, I asked, "Is that all you want? To humiliate me?"

"Private humiliation is only part of the bargain," said Edward. Henry stepped back, giving him the space to stand in front of me and announce, "You're going to repair our reputations."

"How?" My brows drew together.

"Blake's mother has him going to Narcotics Anonymous meetings, in case Rudolph Trommel releases the videos at some point to humiliate the royal family."

"That's wrong," I spat. "How is kissing a boy related to being an addict?"

Edward raised a shoulder. "Mrs. Simpson-West's answer to everything these days is to accuse Blake of being addicted to drugs."

"Thanks to you," said Blake.

"Fine. I'll go with you to your NA meetings." It couldn't be worse than sitting through Mr. Frost's Latin classes.

"And pose for the press."

My brows drew together. "Press—"

"Don't act like you don't love being in front of the camera," Henry snapped. "Your pictures with Bachmann are all over the society pages."

Jerking my head to the side, I pressed my lips together and stared at a small portrait of a knight in armor. One of Edward's ancestors, I supposed. How could I reply to a comment like that, considering I'd gone along with Sergei's plan to become his beard? At the time, I had wanted to create a little intrigue about myself, so that when I returned to Mercia Academy, it would be as the confidante and possibly lover of a famous classical pianist, not just the trollop they'd sent away via a gauntlet.

"Fine," I said with a huffed breath. "I'll pose with you."

Edward cupped the side of my cheek. A tender gesture, until he turned my head back so I could look him in the face. His eyes were as blue and stormy and as cold as clouds over the arctic. "Henry's parents are convinced that he's gay, and they're threatening to disown him if he doesn't produce a suitable girlfriend." Edward prodded me on the shoulder. "You're going to be that girl."

"Why not one of the many sycophants in Elder House like Charlotte?"

"She hasn't returned," said Blake.

"I don't want any of those girls," said Henry. "Only you."

A gust of frustration huffed out of my lungs. "You didn't want me enough to clear my name. Why are you forcing me to be your fake girlfriend?"

His glare hardened. "Who said it would be fake?"

"It would be from my end."

He stepped forward, green eyes blazing. "Will you do it or not? They're in Dubai right now, and I need to contact them to arrange a meeting."

"Alright," I snapped. Their demands were irritating but nothing I couldn't handle. I turned to Edward. "What do you want from me, Mercia?"

"Help with a fundraiser to rebuild the academy's reputation."

My shoulders drooped. "That's it?"

He stepped back. "That's all. You'll come with me to the next meeting of the Board of Governors, and we'll present a few ideas."

I stared after him, head tilting and trying to absorb his every feature. This would be the easiest request of all, but why was his request so unselfish? Keeping the relief out of my features, I made an impatient huff. "Can I go, now?"

"No," said Henry. "You're going to provide us with a little entertainment."

"I'm not sucking anything else."

He snorted. "You won't get our cocks until you beg."

"That's fine with me," I snapped.

Henry's grin turned malevolent. "Next time we have you here, we'll tease you so badly, you'll be crying for us to fuck you."

CHAPTER 5

At lunchtime, I sat at the head table between Edward and Henry, casting my gaze over the rest of the house. We ate the normal fare of a choice of roasted chicken or pork, served with vegetables, roasted potatoes and stuffing. Student slathered on lashings of gravy from jugs at their tables. I cut my chicken breast and sighed. To everyone else, it looked like I was sitting in my usual spot, but the triumvirate had told me I would spend all my hours in the presence of at least one of them unless I wanted my secret exposed.

Just before the waiters served desert, our housemaster, Mr. Jenkins, strolled into the room and stood on the podium on the far right of the table. The man seemed to have lost weight during the Easter break, as his gray suit hung awkwardly off his shoulders. "Welcome back for another term, Elder House!"

Nobody responded. By now, even the mice in the skirting boards had worked out the man had been shirking his housemaster responsibilities.

In the ensuing silence, I glanced at the table usually occupied by Charlotte and her doppelgängers. Wendy, Patricia, and even Alice sat together, but there was no sign of Charlotte. An intern at the Correspondent had mentioned that the family could no longer afford to pay for her tuition fees, and Blake had confirmed earlier that she wouldn't return. I rested my chin on my hand and exhaled my relief. That was one person I wouldn't miss.

Mr. Jenkins' cheeks pinked, and he cleared his throat. "At the end of the lunch bell, please make your way to the assembly block for a meeting with the Board of Governors."

"Where's the headmaster?" Coates, the bulky rugby player with the broken nose and cauliflower ears, stood and ran a hand over his shorn head.

Mr. Jenkins flushed and stepped down from the podium. "I expect the governors will update you on his situation." As he darted out of the room, he said over his shoulder, "Don't forget to go to the assembly block after the lunch bell."

I narrowed my eyes at the retreating man. What was the point of having a housemaster who stayed in his room all day, turned a blind eye to the injustices taking place under his thin nose, and couldn't discipline students? He was more suited to kindergarteners than sixth-formers.

The servers brought a lattice apple pie and custard. I refused a portion. After breakfast with Sergei and his entourage, followed by coffee on the train, my appetite had dwindled. Not running the gauntlet had been a huge relief, but any member of the triumvirate could command me as he wished, and I wasn't sure about the extent of their vindictiveness.

Henry called back the server. "She will have desert." He turned to me and winked. "I don't want you wasting away to nothing."

"Why?" I spat. "Because you think my boobs will shrink?"

His gaze flickered down my to top and lingered over my breasts. "I was more thinking about your arse, but I like the boobs, too."

Edward smirked then turned to Blake and whispered something that made him laugh.

My cheeks burned. How could I have ever become so fond of this pig?

Henry's hand wrapped around my thigh and squeezed. "We should hold weekly inspections. Get out the tape measure to make sure you're staying the same."

"You're really enjoying this," I muttered.

"Not as much as I would enjoy those inspections," he replied. "Eat up."

Irritation fizzled through my veins, making the fine hairs on my skin stand on end. What an asshole.

After lunch, the entire house left the dining hall and walked over the lawn to a Georgian building with the usual tall, symmetrical windows divided into panels. Unlike the other blocks around the law, the assembly hall's oversized porch consisted of a triangular, stone pediment, held up by several columns. It reminded me of the Pantheon.

Edward placed his hand on the small of my back and guided me through the porch into the building's cool exterior, an auditorium with its seats organized around a stage in tiers of concentric half-circles. Students from all houses, ranging from little first years to upper-sixth formers, filled the hall all the way up to the back row, where huge, arched windows streamed in shafts of afternoon light. On the stage sat twelve men and women, each wearing suits. The one in the middle, who I assumed was the new headmaster, was clad in black, academic robes.

We took our seats close to the back, and I ended up sandwiched between Henry and Blake, with Edward sitting on Blake's other side. When everyone was settled, one of the teachers played a tune on the piano, and everybody sang what sounded like the academy anthem. Blake gave me a nudge in the ribs, prompting me to move my lips. At the end of the song, the man in the academic robes stepped forward to a podium on the stage.

"Good Afternoon, staff and students of Mercia Academy."

"Good Afternoon, Mr. Weaver," everyone chorused back.

I studied the man's features. Rita had once spoken about him. He taught Classical Greek and was one of the few members of staff who punished the bullies who had tormented her. My brows rose. At least a good guy would be in charge of the academy for once.

After a few introductions and general greetings, Mr. Weaver spoke. "It's with a heavy heart that I confirm that our former headmaster, Mr. Chaloner, has been charged with money laundering and won't ever return to Mercia Academy."

Chatters broke out across the assembly hall, and I leaned forward to catch Edward's eye, but he stared ahead, a muscle flexing in his jaw. My stomach twisted with trepidation. Was he angry that Mr. Chaloner had left or that the man had even commenced his dangerous venture?

Mr. Weaver raised his hands, indicating he wanted everyone to be silent. When the chatter died down, he continued. "It no longer matters if he is found guilty. If you have followed the articles in the press about International House, you will know that he illegally set up an adjunct to the academy, which made people believe they would receive the premium education available for all legitimate students of our fine establishment."

I rubbed at my temples. The education here was good, but I would hardly call it premium.

"Until we can find a replacement headteacher, we, the Board of Governors, will run the school with the help of an administrator."

Noises of uproar spread across the assembly hall. I glanced around. Everyone except for the triumvirate, who had probably heard about this development from Edward, looked pissed.

I leaned into Blake. "What's the big deal? Chaloner was a hateful crook."

He slipped a hand between my legs. "If you want to know, you can get down on your knees and suck me off."

Heat flooded between my legs, and my cheeks warmed. I

wrapped my hand around his wrist, trying to wrench his hand off on thigh.

He stayed firm as steel, leaned into me and murmured, "We own you, remember. That means we can do anything we like, and you'll just take it. Now, part those pretty thighs, or else."

"You're a bastard," I spat.

He nodded. "Perhaps, but I'm the bastard who holds your leash." He trailed his tongue down the shell of my ear and sucked on my lobe, making my breath hitch. "Do as I say."

While the head of the Board of Governors explained that they had considered options for the school, including closure, I relaxed my legs and let Blake's fingers make a slow descent up the inside of my thighs. He used the most delicious of featherlight touches, pausing to rub small circles that made my core twitch.

Blake's hot breath tickled the side of my neck. "I'm going to stick my fingers in you and make you suck on them. Right in front of the governors."

I bit down on my lip and stifled a moan. The asshole would do anything to make me cry out and humiliate myself, and the worst part was that I didn't want him to stop. An ache formed in my core, which built and built the closer his clever fingers reached their destination.

My legs parted a fraction wider, and the pulse between my legs pounded in time with the throbbing of my nub. Blake's fingers meandered upward at a maddening pace that made slick heat gather between my folds.

"Hurry up," I whispered between clenched teeth.

A deep chuckle reverberated in his throat, and he leaned over to murmur, "As you wish."

When his fingertips brushed over my panties and grazed my slit, pleasure rippled through my core, and my nipples tightened. I let out a shuddering breath, loud enough to catch the attention of Henry at my other side.

Henry huffed a laugh, grabbed my wrist, and placed my hand on his crotch.

I gripped his hot, hardening bulge and squeezed. Hard.

He doubled over and groaned, "Oh, fuck!"

Everyone in the auditorium turned in our direction, but Henry composed himself, while Blake slid his hand back and turned to look at the row behind us. Snapping my legs shut, I placed my hands onto my lap and schooled my features into a semblance of innocence.

Mr. Weaver paused in his speech and glared up at the back of the room, where we sat. "Discipline is something else we will review within the academy. It's my understanding that the previous headmaster allowed the return of expelled students in exchange for donations, but that practice ends now."

I slid down my seat. He was most likely referring to me and how Rudolph had bribed Mr. Chaloner to allow me back to exact my revenge.

Henry leaned into me and whispered, "You'll pay for this when we get you in private."

"I look forward to it," I whispered back.

~

Our first class of the afternoon was English Literature. I sat next to Henry, behind Edward and Blake, and behind us sat Coates, that rugby player from earlier, with Duncan, the boy with the thick glasses who seemed to have subscriptions to every British newspaper.

"I say, Coates," Duncan said in a very loud voice. "Can you believe Bourneville and Simpson-West were having it off with each other?"

I turned around and gave Duncan a sharp look. What the fuck did he think he was saying?

Coates' thick brows drew together. "What?"

"Have you not seen the photos?" asked Duncan.

I turned to Henry, who froze. It could only mean the stills Rudolph had used to blackmail Mr. and Mrs. Bourneville into returning his million dollars were still floating about on the internet.

"What photos?" asked Coates.

Duncan reached into his pocket. "Here, let me show you."

"I'd like to see what's on your phone, too," I said loud enough to attract Miss Oakley's attention.

The old woman strode across the room, lips pursed. Her black robes billowed around her like she was an avenging academic. "Who is playing with mobile telephones in my class?"

I gave Duncan a pointed look. "No one, Miss."

The teacher stretched out her hand. "Give it here."

Duncan cocked his head to the side and gave me a narrow-eyed stare that asked what the fuck I thought I was doing. In the previous term, we had become friends of sorts, but I couldn't let him show anyone the stills from the Valentine's party. He pulled out his smartphone and handed it to Miss Oakley, who walked across the room and placed it in her drawer.

I turned back to Henry and mouthed, "What are you going to do?"

He mouthed back, "I don't know."

"What was this photo you wanted to show me?" asked Coates.

Miss Oakley's shrill voice rang out. "Two demerits each. Silence in class!"

My efforts to quash the photos were futile. By the end of the day, most sixth-formers had seen them, saying they couldn't believe Henry and Blake were lovers. Alice and the doppelgängers were the biggest distributors of the photos, and they didn't care who saw them. It was probably their revenge for the triumvirate treating them like they were their own personal conveniences.

Later, Edward and I strolled along the magnolia tree path under a riot of white and pink blossoms. The sweet scent of citrus wafted down from the breeze, reminding me somewhat of Henry. Up ahead stood Elder House in its ancient glory, and I sighed. So far, the triumvirate's wrath hadn't been nearly as terrible as I had imagined. It probably helped that they still wanted me back.

A gaggle of girls giggled from behind. I glanced over my shoulder to find Alice and the doppelgängers leading a group of younger, female students. "Did you hear he was also in on the act? That's why the trio treated girls so badly."

Patricia sniggered. "They were too much in love with themselves!"

I broke away from Edward, fists clenched. "A few drunken fumbles doesn't make for a relationship. You should know that by now."

Patricia's gaze flickered up and down my form. "What are you? Their beard? With a straight-up-and-down boyish figure like yours, it explains a lot."

I tilted my head to the side and mirrored her eye movement. "Now that Charlotte's gone, you look far less voluptuous. Did you stop stuffing your bra with socks?"

"Did I say you had a boyish figure? I meant that you were a boy." She turned to Wendy, Alice, and the younger students. "Come along, girls. Let's not chat with boys who bat for the other team."

The procession of gossipers walked past with their noses in the air and headed toward the tuck shop. Alice glanced over her shoulder and gave me an apologetic smile.

I shrugged. If she wanted to return to a group of girls who had cast her out once before, who was I to judge? I was firmly entrenched with a gang of bastards.

Edward placed a hand around my waist. "I appreciate your defending our honor, but it's unnecessary. Squabbling over such trivialities will only fuel the rumors."

"Sorry." I huffed out a frustrated breath and met his ocean-blue eyes. "But something about those girls makes me see red."

"I didn't treat them well, and they're lashing out." He placed a hand on my shoulder, eyes shining with compassion. "Just as you did, last term."

Hope swelled in my heart, and a breath caught in my throat. Had Edward already started to forgive me? "I'm sorry things went that far."

He patted me on the backside. "Not as sorry as we're going to make you. Come on, let's go to my study."

Over the next hour, Edward and I sat side-by-side at his desk on leather office chairs working on our prep in companionable silence. I stole a glance at his face. Tendrils of mahogany-brown hair hung over his brow, softening his stern features.

Last term, we had grown so close, and I had seen a glimpse of the kind, sensitive soul beneath the haughty exterior. Now, I couldn't work him out. He delivered his threats so mildly, it seemed like he was just paying lip service to exacting his revenge. And when we were alone, he was his usual, gallant self, albeit a little more reserved. I ached to know how he really felt, but the thought of breaking the peace by bringing up what I had done made my stomach clench.

Later, Blake and Henry knocked on the door. "Dinner?"

Edward shut his book. "Why not?"

I stuffed my books into my satchel, hoping they might allow me to go upstairs later and study on my own. Then we walked in formation through the hallway to the dining room with Henry and Edward in front and Blake taking up the rear with me.

Both Henry and Edward halted at the doors, making us bump into their backs.

"What's happening?" I stood on my tiptoes and looked over their shoulders. At the head table sat Coates and a trio of rugby players with Wendy, Patricia, and Alice.

"What is the meaning of this?" Edward stepped inside.

A hush spread over the entire room, punctuated only by the movements of the servers.

"You heard Mr. Weaver," said Coates. "The school governors want to stamp out all signs of corruption, and that starts with you." The bulky boy folded his arms across his broad chest. "We thought you were arseholes all along, but we went along with you because everyone else did. But last term proved that you're no better than any of us."

"I see." Edward's voice shook with banked rage. "Is that why you saw fit to sit in our seats?"

"That, and we don't like homos lording it over us."

I sucked in a sharp breath. Wendy, Alice, and Patricia gave the boys triumphant smirks. They had probably goaded the rugby players into taking over the head table. I shook my head. Each of the girls up there should have been able to vouch for one or most of the boys, but they remained silent. My gaze flickered to Blake, whose handsome features clenched into a scowl, and Henry, whose body seemed to expand in anticipation for a fight.

"Get out of our seats," said Edward, his voice soft.

With the loud scrape of his chair, Coates stood. "Are you going to make me?"

"If I have to."

Coates walked around the table and swaggered over to meet us at the doorway. From the way the rugby player pulled back his shoulders and thrust out his square shin, he meant business. I darted into the dining room and stood to the side in case the boys came to blows.

Coates squared up to Henry, his captain. The two boys were of equal height, both broad, but Coates had an unattractive bulkiness where Henry was defined. Up close, the rugby player's nose wasn't just flat, it twisted to the side and back again.

"Let's face it, boys." Coates rubbed his cauliflower ear. "Mercia is the heir to a bankrupt duchy that's only worth something because of the academy's ground rent payments. Bourneville will soon become the heir to nothing when his parents discover he'll be producing no little heirs of his own, and Simpson-West is only relevant because his mother is the trollop who landed herself the second in line to the throne."

Blake pushed through Edward and Henry, and swung at Coates, only for the larger boy to grip his fist in one hand and twist him into a wrist lock. I clapped my hands over my mouth and gasped. Henry stepped forward, pulled his arm back, and jabbed Coates in the middle of his flat face, who let go of Blake.

"Of course you'd come to your boyfriend's rescue," Coates said between bloody teeth.

Henry punched him in the gut. "Fuck you."

The other boy doubled over. "You wish!"

Blake punched Coates hard across the face.

Soon, other boys stood from their seats at the head table and rushed over. It would be three against four if Edward decided to fight. Those odds weren't great, considering the boys approaching us were hulking rugby players. I picked up my phone, and with shaky fingers, called campus security.

CHAPTER 6

The fight finished as quickly as it had started because some of the rugby players were loyal to their captain and broke up the fight before campus security arrived. Coates and his friends returned to the head table and wouldn't budge. Technically, it was the table for the housemaster and his staff, so no student had the right to it.

Edward tapped something on his smartphone and stormed out with Henry and Blake on his heels. A pang of sympathy struck my heart, but I remained at the doorway and didn't rush out to give them my support. The only reason those photos were even circulated was that the Bournevilles had lied about the amount of ransom they had paid the supposed kidnappers and made Rudolph pay double to drop the charges against me. When Rudolph approached them with blackmail material, Henry's parents had refused to repay Rudolph, even with the knowledge that Henry was behind the whole scam.

Ignoring the watchful eyes of the other diners, I walked around the room along the ten-foot-tall mahogany wall panels to the table where Rita sat with the scholarship students. One of them had joined Rita and me in the dance lessons the triumvirate had held in the first term, and she gazed up at me with a sunny smile.

I gestured at the seat opposite Rita. "Mind if I sit here?"

"Sit next to me," said a girl from the next table I recognized from the gauntlet. Her hazel eyes sparkled with curiosity.

Rita gestured for me to sit, her brows drawn together with worry. A server rushed over and took my order for a quiche Lorraine and salad.

The hazel-eyed girl leaned toward us on the back legs of her seat, salivating. "Is it true what they're saying about the boys?"

"No," I said.

"But the photos are—"

"You just asked if it was true," I snapped.

She pouted. "I got off with Blake last year, as did most of the girls on this table. I just want to know if he's a homo. I mean, do I have anything to worry about?"

"What do you mean?" I narrowed my eyes.

The girl lowered her gaze and mumbled something incomprehensible. I curled my lip. She was an idiot. A stupid sheep who followed whoever barked the loudest. And right now, it was Coates and the doppelgängers.

"Use your brain," I spat. "In one breath you tell me that you've all fooled around with Blake, and in another, you're asking if he's gay? It's this kind of attitude that makes people afraid to come out."

"Sorry," she muttered. "I thought you might know the facts, seeing as you're their girlfriend or something."

I was about to rant at her when Rita spoke. "Let's not gossip about people behind their backs."

Everyone around the table murmured their agreement and continued eating. I lowered myself into the seat and caught sight of a limo whizzing past the side windows. The boys were either going to Edward's house or to Jean-Paul and Françoise's restaurant to plan their next course of action. A chill ran down my back. I really hoped I didn't factor in any of their schemes.

∼

The next day, the head table was removed from the dining room, leaving everyone to eat in the general area. No matter how much Coates tried to assert his dominance and get it reinstated, it didn't work. Each mealtime, the staff laid special table linen and silverware over whichever table the triumvirate chose, thwarting Coates and the doppelgängers' attempts to appear special.

Over the next few weeks, the triumvirate quashed any attempts by other boys to victimize them by escalating even the smallest of provocations to violence. Soon, everyone, including Coates, knew not to make sly comments within the earshot of Blake, Henry, or Edward unless they were prepared for a fight and the subsequent detentions and demerits.

One morning at breakfast, Coates sauntered up to our table, holding a folded up copy of a tabloid. "Looks like you made the papers, boys."

"What are you rambling about now?" asked Henry.

Coates smoothed out a double-page spread of a pair of the photos that had been circulating on the internet. It had been taken moments after I had left the boys alone on the four-poster. Above them was the headline, *SIMPSON-WEST GAY ROMP*.

I held my breath. Would this result in another fight, or would the boys shrug it off?

Blake stared down at the paper and pursed his lips. "If I had known I would end up in the news again, I would have worn something a little more dignified than the gladiator outfit."

Henry folded his arms across his chest. "I told you to come as a matador."

"Next time, I'll dress as a tango dancer," he replied. "Something to pay homage to my Argentinian roots."

I exhaled my relief. It looked like violence wouldn't break out, after all.

Coates' thick brows drew together. "Don't you care that they've published a picture of you kissing another boy?"

"Why would I?" Blake's brows rose. "You and I both know I've had more girls than you."

The rugby player's face reddened. He turned to me and spat, "How could you hang around with them after what they did?"

I picked up a slice of toast from the silver rack and dipped my knife into the butter dish. "What I don't get is why you're so interested. Are you curious or something?"

Coates' face twisted and he glared from Edward, to Henry, to Blake, and then to me. "Trollop."

I mimed a yawn. "At least I'm getting some, unlike you."

"She's got you there, Coates." Edward raised his glass of orange juice to his lips. "Don't save the image for those long, lonely nights. I doubt that my friends would appreciate the unwanted attention."

The rugby player's nostrils flared, and his lips drew back, revealing clenched teeth. My stomach tightened, and I waited for him to strike, but he crumpled up the paper, threw it on the ground, and stormed back to the table he shared with the doppelgängers.

Because the boys weren't denying the kiss or reacting to the pictures, the gossip quickly died down within the school. But the tabloids continued to post rehashed articles about the Bourneville department store, using the images and news of Henry's faked kidnapping as a segue to attack his parents' business practices.

Things came to a head one Sunday morning, two weeks after the article about Henry and Blake, when Duncan strolled over to our table, holding a one-page announcement in The Times with the Bourneville crest. It declared that Jonas Bourneville, the current Director of Operations in the Middle East, would be groomed to take over the leadership of the Bourneville Group and not the owner's son, Henry Bourneville.

Silence broke out across the dining room. I bit down on my bottom lip and glanced at Henry.

He skimmed the paper and said, "So?"

"Did you know this would happen?" asked Duncan.

"We agreed to it weeks ago. Jonas is my second cousin."

Duncan stared at Henry for several moments before his face fell. "Right. Of course, you did."

When Duncan left, Henry continued eating his scrambled eggs and smoked salmon, his face devoid of expression. If his family had discussed this beforehand, why hadn't one of the triumvirate mentioned it in my presence?

"Henry," I whispered.

"Later."

No one else around the table spoke, but they continued eating their breakfasts. From their blank faces, I guessed that Henry's family hadn't informed him he had been disinherited, and the triumvirate wanted to act as though the announcement wasn't a shock.

Moments later, Coates strolled over, flanked by four members of the rugby team. "The boys have voted me the new captain. Even if you claim to have lots of women, no one feels comfortable having you on the team."

"Right," said Henry between clenched teeth. "Good luck winning without me."

My heart sank, and my gaze dropped to my blueberries and French toast. I had thought that guys like Henry always emerged from scandals unscathed. I'd set in motion an out-of-control train that was still wrecking lives long after the publication of the original articles. Guilt made my shoulders droop. I had thought his parents would only give him a temporary punishment, not a complete disinheritance. My eyes could barely meet Henry's for the rest of our breakfast.

Despite every gaze being locked onto us, the boys took their time eating, still keeping neutral expressions after hearing two sets of bad news. When we had all finished, we stood as a unit and walked to Blake's study.

As soon as the door shut, I turned to Henry and grabbed him by the biceps. "Are you alright?"

He peered down at me, green eyes dull. "This was what you wanted, wasn't it? To see me lose everything."

I bowed my head. "No," I whispered. "I never meant for things to go this far."

"That's the downside to extreme revenge, isn't it?" Edward sat on the Chesterfield sofa. "I'm glad you're here to see the repercussions of your actions."

Irritation flared across my skin, and I stormed across the room and rested my fists on the leather surface of his desk. "Whose fault was it that I went to such lengths in the first place? You all know what you did to me with the help of Mr. Frost. Did you expect me to take it lying down?"

I turned around, trying to catch the gazes of the triumvirate. But they couldn't meet my eyes. Instead, they exchanged embarrassed glances with each other. It was all the fuel I needed for a rant. "And you guys feel so entitled to being bullies, you can't even see that what I did last term makes us even."

"You're forgetting one thing." Blake strode toward me from across the room, his lips curved into a knowing smirk.

"What's that?" I placed my hands on my hips.

"We own you." Blake cupped my cheek. "Body, mind and soul. And at any time, we can command you to do whatever we want. Not only will you accompany Henry to visit his parents, but you'll put on a little show to cheer him up."

I scowled. "Is this the new way of winning an argument? Threats?"

"No." Blake's hand trailed down my neck in the softest of touches that sent a shiver of anticipation down my spine. Then he unfastened the top buttons on my shirt.

Ignoring the heat rushing between my legs, I snapped, "And I have no say in the matter?"

Edward smirked and beckoned at Henry to sit next to him on the sofa. "You could always tell us to stop."

"Would you?" I whispered.

"That's for you to find out," Blake murmured into my ear.

I bit down hard on my lip and forced my breaths to calm as he undid two more buttons and exposed my collarbones and the tops of my breasts.

"Well," said Blake, his voice as smooth and rich as dark coffee. Mischief danced across his brown eyes. "Do you want me to stop?"

I pressed my lips together and jerked my head to the side. The answer was no. I wanted him to continue, but there was no way I would admit that to the triumvirate.

Blake trailed his fingertips over my right breast, making wide circles and avoiding my nipples. I swallowed hard. He was doing this on purpose. Trying to get me riled up and frustrated enough to admit that I wanted this. Wanted him. It was probably his revenge for how badly I had treated him the term before by denying his need for attention. One of his fingertips skimmed my nipple, sending a bolt of electricity down to my core.

I huffed out a breath and gave Blake what I hoped was an irritated glower. "You're not making this easy for me."

Henry snickered. "I can assure you, from where we're sitting, you're making it very hard for us."

My gaze flickered to the sofa, where Henry and Edward sat together, each sporting erections. I licked my lips. "Are you two just going to just watch?"

Edward pressed down on his erection with the heel of his hand. "If you want the three of us together, you'll have to beg."

I shook my head. No matter what Blake did with those nimble fingers, he wouldn't break my composure.

Henry grinned. "Thanks, Blake. This is exactly what I need to forget about my woes."

I pulled a face. Since when was I the entertainment for retired bullies?

"This time, I'll help you disrobe," murmured Blake, "But the next time, you're taking it off at our command."

My thighs quivered, and arousal built between my legs like a persistent ache.

Blake moved to my back as though wanting to give his friends a better view of me in my excited state. He slid his arms over the fabric of my shirt, up my ribs and cupped my breasts, making sure to give them a tight squeeze. I grunted and arched my back. My ass cheeks brushed against his erection, and a groan reverberated in his chest that made the muscles of my core ripple. With a long, shuddering breath, I rested my head back on his shoulder and writhed against him.

"Squeeze her nipples," Henry said in a strangled voice.

Blake rolled my nipples between his thumb and forefinger, making heat flush through my body and settle in my throbbing core.

"Undo four buttons of that blouse, and I'll make you feel really good," Blake murmured into my ear.

Of their own volition, my hands scrambled to unbutton my shirt. Arousal made my head spin, and the pulse between my ears pounded so hard, I forgot to stop at four and unfastened all the buttons. Blake pulled back the fabric, revealing my white, lacy bra to his friends. Henry whistled, and Edward smirked.

"Nice work." He swiped both thumbs against my nipples, making me grind against his erection and clench the muscles of my sopping core. "Do you want my mouth?"

I gave the slightest of nods.

"Where do you want it? Say it out loud, so the others can hear."

I gulped. "O-on my nipples."

"May I take off your bra?"

Before I'd finished nodding, he unhooked my bra and peeled the straps down my arms. The garment fell to the ground, exposing my breasts to the triumvirate. A flush heated my cheeks. So far, only Edward had seen me at this level of undress.

Henry leaned forward, green eyes wide. "Come here."

Blake wrapped his arms around my middle and walked me across the study. He took his seat on the Chesterfield, on Henry's other side, leaving me standing alone before three hungry gazes.

A pleasant shiver ran down my spine. The triumvirate had me half-naked, squirming, yearning for their touch. I was completely at their mercy, and there was not a thing I wanted to do about it.

CHAPTER 7

Henry's gaze roved from one breast to another. "Are you ready to beg for our tongues?"

The heat on my cheeks traveled down between my legs, making my core throb with need. I wanted to say no. To tell them they didn't own me, but the words died in my throat. Henry's gaze flicked up to mine, and the look of hunger burning in his verdant, green eyes made my knees want to buckle.

"Yes," I whispered through clenched teeth.

"Yes, what?" asked Blake from Henry's left. The smirk in his voice told me how much he enjoyed watching me squirm.

"I've lost track of this entire conversation," drawled Edward. "Emilia was supposed to beg for something, but so far all I've heard are monosyllabic answers."

I peered down at the bulge in his pants, and my nipples tightened and ached to be touched. As much as it irked me not to be in charge, I yearned for the triumvirate. All three of them. Together.

"P-pleasure me with your tongues." I gulped. "Please."

"That wasn't so difficult to admit." Satisfaction laced Blake's voice, and his chocolate-brown eyes twinkled with mischief.

"I thought you said you'd make me feel good."

He smirked, letting his gaze linger on my exposed breasts. "All in good time."

"Take off your skirt." Henry's voice was hoarse.

"But you're going to—"

"That inspection I promised." His gaze burned through mine. "And the retribution for squeezing my balls at assembly. It's happening, now. Take off your skirt."

The muscles of my core rippled at his command, and my trembling fingers scrabbled at the buttons on my waistband. Curiosity made my breath hitch. How far would they take this game before they gave me what I wanted? After unzipping my skirt, I released the fabric and let it drop to my feet.

Henry reached out a hand and skimmed his fingertips over my thighs, each touch sending pleasant tingles across my skin. He ran a finger along the lace trimming of my white panties. "Very nice." His voice was breathy. "Now, take off your knickers."

I took a step closer and stood between his spread legs. "If you want them off, you'll have to do it yourself."

"With pleasure." Henry's fingers skimmed my lower belly, reminding me of the time he lay behind me on that filthy mattress and stroked me to orgasm. A hot breath huffed from between my parted lips. He was drawing this out deliberately. Perhaps as revenge for—I pushed away the thoughts of Rudolph's machinations and focussed on the sweep of those fingers against my skin, and on the arousal pounding between my legs.

Henry hooked his fingers beneath the lace and, with a smirk, pulled them down over my thighs and past my knees. The panties landed at my ankles, and I kicked them to the side.

All three pairs of eyes roved up and down my naked form, and I had to force my arms not to wrap around myself.

"Why am I the only one here naked?" I muttered.

Blake smirked. "Because we own you."

Edward picked up the scrap of lace, held it to his nose, groaned, and stuffed them into the pocket of his pants.

I swallowed hard. "Why are you sniffing my panties?"

His blue eyes sparkled with want. "Because you smell delectable."

I squeezed my thighs together and squirmed. Was it that obvious I was aroused?

"Turn around," Henry rasped.

"Why?"

"I haven't had the pleasure of seeing you from this angle."

Rolling my eyes, I turned around to give the triumvirate a view of my ass. They'd probably never seen that before, either. I clasped my arms around my front and squeezed my thighs together.

Blake whistled. "Gorgeous legs."

Henry's large hand cupped an ass cheek and squeezed. "Even better arse. Now," he said in a strangulated voice, "Bend over."

A tingle of apprehension spread across my skin. At the same time, arousal shot through my core and made my nipples throb. I whispered, "What?"

Edward stroked a path down the side of my thigh with his fingertips. "Or you can sit at my desk for the rest of the day and finish your prep... naked."

"And unfulfilled." Blake's smoky voice curled around my hardened nipples.

My tongue darted out to lick my lips. If Blake hadn't gotten me so worked up, I might have taken up Edward on his offer to hide behind the wooden desk. Henry's fingers trailed up and down my ass, and each of his ragged breaths made my skin tingle with the need to be touched... by all six of their hands.

I swallowed hard. There'd be no turning back if I bent over for him, but I'd already gone this far, and this striptease had gotten me so hot and excited for the triumvirate. No matter how much they claimed to be in control, eventually, one of them would crack and give me what I needed.

I placed my hands on my thighs and bent over. Henry drew in a sharp breath through his teeth and scooted forward onto the edge of the Chesterfield sofa. My own breath caught in the back of my throat. No one had ever seen me from this angle. What if they thought badly of me because I'd done as they asked?

With a groan, Henry grabbed both sides of my hips with his large, warm hands. "Fuck, you look so good."

"So wet," said Blake, his fingers trailing up my slit.

Shudders traveled from where his flesh met mine, all the way up my spine. I bit down hard on my bottom lip to suppress a moan.

"Positively delectable." Edward's hand cupped my breast.

"Open your legs." Henry's thumbs parted my outer lips. "I owe you an inspection."

My clit throbbed in anticipation of being touched, and I widened my stance, revealing myself to the triumvirate. A draft blew on my newly exposed flesh, but nothing could cool the humiliation burning under my cheeks. Fixing my gaze up ahead at the empty fireplace beyond Edward's mahogany desk, I calmed my breaths.

"I'm going to stick my tongue into your hole," said Henry.

A shocked thrill of anticipation made a whimper reverberate in my throat.

Edward chuckled. "What happened to the inspection?"

"It's taking place right now," Henry growled.

Excitement rippled low in my belly. All those promises, all those threats, had culminated in this. I turned my head to catch a glimpse of the boys. Edward sat at the edge of his seat, rolling my nipples between his thumb and forefinger. He bent his neck, dark hair covering most of his features, but his entire length jutted through his pants, telegraphing his arousal.

On the other side of Henry, Blake slid his hand over my clit and stroked circles around the sensitive flesh. A frown of concentration settled on his brow as his clever, questing fingers played me like an instrument.

The muscles of my core quivered. I needed Henry's tongue. Now.

Henry leaned forward. His hot breath puffed against my sopping folds, and with the lightest of touches, his tongue skimmed my outer lips, making me cry out with frustration. The tease was drawing this out. He wanted me to plead.

My hands clutched at my knees, and I widened my stance, exposing more of myself to Henry's watchful gaze. Growling with approval, he clamped his lips on one of my folds and sucked.

The muscles of my back stiffened and pleasure surged through my lower half. It wasn't quite where I wanted his mouth, and he knew it. The person who I had become last term would have straightened, taken Edward's get-out clause, and hidden behind my desk to complete my prep, but I'd missed the boys so much. I would never admit that to them, though.

Trying and failing to keep the breathiness out of my voice, I ground out, "Henry... please."

"I suppose I could oblige, since you've asked so nicely," he said with a smirk in his voice.

Henry ran his flattened tongue down the length of my slit, making ripples of pleasure rush up my core.

A gasp caught in my throat. "Now."

Edward scooted forward and gave my nipples a gentle tug, while Blake's fingertips continued rubbing those maddeningly pleasurable circles over my clit. Sparks of delight travelled up and down my thighs, picking up speed with each revolution.

Still clutching at my buttocks, Henry spread me open with my thumbs, further exposing me to his scrutiny. I throbbed with need, and more heat rushed to my core. I was about to yell, when his tongue flickered over my entrance.

A shudder seized me with such intensity, it made my thighs shake. "Oh!"

"See how much she wants this?" said Blake, his voice smug. "We could draw this out forever. How would you like that, Emilia? Being all hot and wet and wanton for us?"

"F-fuck you." I replied through clenched teeth.

Blake chuckled, low and deep.

"Tut-tut." Edward gave my nipple a hard squeeze that sent shards of pleasure down to my already throbbing clit. "What terrible manners. Any more talk like that, and I'll have to wash out your mouth with a bar of soap."

His commanding tone brought up a spark of challenge. My tongue darted out to lick my lips. "I can think of something better you can put in my mouth."

Both Edward and Blake scrambled to their feet, but Edward stood in front of me first. Before I could crow over their own states of arousal, Henry's hot and slippery and oh-so-pliable tongue slipped into my entrance, bringing with it the most intense rush of pleasure. I threw my head back and moaned.

The sound of a zipper brought my attention back to the front. My gaze dropped to the tip of Edward's beautiful, thick penis. A bead of pre-cum glistened at its slit. My mouth watered, and I swallowed back a moan. As Henry tongue-fucked me, I parted my lips and let Edward slip his hard length into my mouth. He tasted of skin and salt and sexiness.

"Emilia," Edward said through panting breaths. "You'll soon learn the consequences of using foul language."

Any reply I might have given him was stifled by his erection reaching the back of my throat, stopping short of my gag reflex. I hummed my appreciation and ran my tongue along the underside of his length.

Blake cleared his throat, and his bulbous tip filled one side of my vision. He was also wet with pre-cum. I wrapped my hand around his length, gathered up the liquid with my thumb, and rubbed it over his perfect prick.

"Yes," Blake hissed through clenched teeth.

As much as I wanted to twist around and grab Henry's dick, I couldn't reach, and I didn't want his inspection to end. Both his large hands spread me wider, and his entire face was buried between my ass cheeks. I might have flushed if I wasn't already feverish from Edward's slow and sensuous slide of his shaft up and down my tongue.

Blake pumped his hips in time with Edward's thrusts, and I squeezed my hand around his thick, pulsing erection, enjoying the way he moaned and shuddered under my touch. For several moments, grunts and groans and slurping moans filled the air, and I breathed hard through my nostrils.

"Ummm…" My lips closed around Edward.

This was so insane. Me, pleasuring the entire triumvirate after everything that had happened between us the previous two terms. I'd moved from hating them to desiring them in my first term, then my lust had turned to loathing. Now, I wasn't sure. Each of them had gotten under my skin, but did they mean to make me earn my forgiveness, or were they setting me up for another fall?

Henry's tongue slid down to my exposed clit and sucked it between his lips, shoving aside my every thought. Spasms rocked my core as my climax hit with the force of a tidal wave. For a moment, my vision blacked out, and my knees buckled, but Henry's strong hands on my hips kept me upright. Blood rushed through my ears, and my nerve endings roared with the intensity of my orgasm.

Both boys quickened their thrusts, and soon, Edward let out a low moan and filled my mouth with warm, bitter fluid. After swallowing, I turned my head to Blake and engulfed his length into my mouth.

"F-fuck!" he moaned with a climax as his semen hit the back of my throat.

Before I could swallow, Henry pulled me down astride his lap and plunged his tongue into my mouth, kissing and slurping up Blake's cum. Our tongues tangled, and I reached down between our pressed-together bodies and pumped his hot, thick erection. My nerve endings still tingled from the aftershocks of my climax, and I squeezed my eyes shut, enjoying the sensations of Henry's tongue in my mouth.

His length thickened and pulsed. Then he broke away, and with a shout, pumped ropes and ropes of cum up his hard, quivering six pack, and over his bulging pecs.

After catching my breath, I asked, "Did I pass your inspection?"

Henry blinked himself back to awareness and smirked. "Unfortunately, you failed. Now, you'll have to suffer through weeks of remedial classes."

I grinned back. "Let's see if I do better next time."

"It might take the entire term to see improvements." Blake ran his fingers down my back.

"And of course, multiple interim inspections." Edward kissed my sweaty cheek.

"Of course." I rested my head on Henry's shoulder and let out a happy sigh. If this was the triumvirate's idea of revenge, I was totally game.

∽

Henry's mood lifted from that session, and he'd only need to give me a side-long look in public to make me flush. For the next few nights, the triumvirate held remedial lessons in Edward's study, each ending with shuddering climaxes. Although none of the boys had brought up their requests to have me fix their reputations, their little games kept them distracted from previous grievances.

One evening, the head table was back on the podium and dressed with different settings. Coates, three of his friends from the rugby team, and all the doppelgängers were in attendance, but the seat in the middle of the table was empty. Edward stiffened for a fraction of a second but continued walking, muttering something under his breath about speaking to the staff. We followed him to a table in the middle of the room.

The servers, led by a middle-aged woman with hair tied into a bun, came to set our table with the special tablecloth, and Edward whispered to the supervisor. "I thought I told you there was to be no more head table."

"You did, Mister Edward." She smoothed down the tablecloth and stepped back to let her colleagues lay the table. "But those students set the table up on their own."

"To what end?" he asked.

"I'm not sure, sir." She took a crystal water jug from an approaching server, laid it in the middle of the table, and scampered away.

The meal continued as normal. We started with a tuna Niçoise salad, followed by beef bourguignon. Coates, Wendy, and Patricia cast us knowing glances throughout the main course. I turned to Edward and asked, "Has anything happened?"

"What do you mean?"

"Those three are acting unusually triumphant," I replied.

He gave me a minute shrug. "They've taken control of the head table. I suppose some people delight in petty victories."

The twist in my gut told me they were planning something else that would turn the tide of their one-sided struggle for dominance over Elder House.

Just before the servers brought out dessert, a blonde figure sauntered through the doors. She wasn't tall, but what she lacked in height, she made up with a voluptuous body. A hush fell across the dining room as she climbed up to the podium and took the seat next to Coates.

Henry squinted. "Is that—"

"Unfortunately," replied Blake.

Edward sighed. "Another intolerable situation."

I chewed the inside of my cheek. "What's going on?"

"Take a closer look at that new girl," muttered Blake.

There was something artificial about her face. Her nose was too straight, lips obviously filled, and the rest of her body seemed too thin to support the weight of those massive boobs. The only familiar things about her were the malevolent, hazel eyes that stared straight at me.

My stomach dropped, and I blurted out loud, "Charlotte?"

She grinned, revealing over-whitened teeth. "One and the same. And from this moment on, I'm the new Queen of Mercia Academy."

The dining room erupted into cheers.

CHAPTER 8

So far, Charlotte's self-styled reign consisted of greeting well-wishers from Edward's usual seat at the head table, and it continued the next day at breakfast. She stood behind the table with her newly bleached hair styled in a bizarre side ponytail that accentuated the strangeness of her new features.

I sat at one of the tables in the middle of the dining room, between Edward and Henry, staring at her from the corner of my eye. "Has she had something done to her eyes? They look different."

"She's wearing mascara," replied Blake. "Remember that time in our second year when she used Wendy's?"

Henry huffed a laugh. "And her eyes swelled?"

Edward cut his kippers with the precision of a surgeon. "What I don't understand is how she was able to return to the academy with her family in so much financial trouble."

I narrowed my eyes at Charlotte. Hadn't she boasted about having met an older man at the Valentine's party? I hadn't taken much notice of it until a fancy package had arrived for her last term. Maybe her bragging wasn't just empty boasts, and she had found herself a sugar daddy.

Charlotte raised a crystal glass and ran her finger over its rim until it sang. When all eyes in the room focussed on her, she cleared her throat. "As the new Queen of Mercia Academy, I say that all students will be equal. There will be no bullying based on physical appearance and no exclusive social events."

The dining room erupted into cheers. Coates, the rugby player, slammed his palm on the table, rattling the china cups in their saucers. He beamed up at her as though she was some kind of sun goddess. Maybe to someone who had recently made inroads with the doppelgängers, she was. A few of the rugby players in the back of the room stood and clapped.

"What the hell is she doing?" I whispered.

Edward's lips tightened. "According to the staff, she arrived early with a few boys to move the chairs and tables into place and then laid the table herself."

I eyed the delicate bone china teapot and matching cups on her table. "She must have gotten those from home."

"I don't get why everyone's following her," muttered Blake.

"Look at Coates," I said. "I'll bet he's wanted Charlotte for ages."

"Ah..." Blake rubbed his chin. "But Charlotte's had her eye on one person for the past few years."

Henry hunched in his seat and squirmed. "I never led her on."

I shot Blake a filthy look. Perhaps he had forgotten that I'd overheard him making promises to Charlotte about a potential relationship with Henry. It still baffled me that he would do such a thing to a friend. "But someone else did."

Blake turned to watch the rest of Charlotte's speech.

She spread her arms wide. "For far too long, everyone in this school has taken direction from a small group of individuals who have held themselves up as exemplary students worthy of leadership." A few grumbles broke out across the room, and she paused for effect. When the students fell silent, she continued. "These false idols have fallen to the pyres of scandal, proving themselves just as fallible as anyone else!"

A group of people sitting a few tables away gave her a round of enthusiastic applause. When no one else joined in, they stopped.

"I say the time has come when we look to ourselves for leadership, and I will show you the way." She raised one fist in the air.

A snort escaped my nostrils. She was happy enough to follow the triumvirate when she thought there was a chance with Henry.

Charlotte placed her hands on her hips. "Did you have something to say, Hobson?"

I rose to my feet. "Actually, I do. You were affected by the scandals, too. What happened to the salary of twelve-thousand pounds your father claimed from the government for secretarial duties performed in Westminster while you were here at school?"

Red blotches appeared on her cheeks. "What would a failed gold digger know about politics?"

"Why don't you tell me how a girl whose father is facing prison for stealing government money got the cash for cosmetic surgery?"

"Get out, you trollop!" Charlotte pointed at the door.

Spreading my arms wide, I said, "When someone has to resort to insults, they've already lost the argument. Be careful who you call a trollop. People might start remembering your cinematic debut from the last school trip."

A few snickers broke out across the dining room, but not enough to make Charlotte run out in shame. I lowered myself to my seat and turned back to my eggs Florentine, ignoring the barrage of insults Charlotte rained down on our table. At least this marked the end of her coronation speech.

∽

The following Saturday after classes, Henry and I took a limo down to London to visit his parents. I buried my nose in a copy of Don

Quixote for the journey, and Henry played games on his smartphone. Without Edward or Blake to act as a buffer, neither of us had much to say to each other. I still bore a grudge from his failure to clear my name for the kidnapping, and he blamed me for his current state of disgrace and disinheritance.

We reached Piccadilly Circus, which was bustling with people enjoying the Spring bank holiday. But instead of stopping outside the main entrance of the store, the car turned down another street.

"Where are we going?" I asked.

"The underground entrance."

I sucked my bottom lip. "Did your parents tell you to use it?"

He turned his face toward the window. "Sales have only just started picking up since they announced Jonas as the heir. The whole country knows my face from those pictures of Blake and me together."

My spine curled into the limo's plush, leather seat. "I didn't put them on the internet."

"Rudolph Trommel did. I know," he replied without casting me a glance. His tone of voice conveyed the unspoken accusation. If I hadn't worked with the Saturday Correspondent, he wouldn't be in this awful position.

Guilt weighed in my stomach and wallowed around like a sick pig. I leaned back in my seat and placed the open book on my lap. My methods had been extreme, but because of Mr. Frost's confession, Jackie managed to get the police to expunge my record, something Henry could have arranged privately with his parents but hadn't.

At the corner of a busy road lined with stores stood a multi-story parking lot emblazoned with the Bourneville crest. The limo drove through its low entrance and turned right, following signs to the basement. It drove down and around the internal ramps until it reached the bottom level, where a roller shutter stood at a wall.

"What's this?" I asked.

"A passageway that leads to the store," muttered Henry.

I pursed my lips. By coming with him and pretending to be his girlfriend, I was doing a damned sight more for him than he had for me when his own actions had thrown me into disgrace. I would have said as much, but I didn't want an argument so close to meeting his parents.

The car drove down a darkened passageway that stretched about two blocks, ending in an underground parking lot that looked more like the garage section of Bruce Wayne's bat cave. Luxury cars stretched out several feet, some of them vintage. I glanced down at my silk blouse and wool skirt. Given their wealth, his parents were probably as grand as royalty.

I cast my gaze at Henry's slacks and polo shirt. "Do I look alright?"

"Relax. They'll love you." He opened the door and stepped out. Unlike Edward, he didn't turn around to offer his hand.

I rolled my eyes and stepped out of the limo. He could be a spoiled, selfish brat at times. Henry stood at the door and stared into what looked like a retina scanner. At the same time, he pressed one of this thumbs onto a fingerprint scanner and spoke a long code of numbers, letters, and words. Eventually, the door clicked open, and we both stepped into a brightly lit corridor with another door at its end.

"This is a lot of security." I glanced at a camera hanging from the corner of the wall like a bat.

"It's the family entrance for when the store is closed," he replied.

We passed through a maze of hallways sectioned by security doors that either required a fingerprint, a retina scan, or a short intercom conversation with the security staff. I wondered if the White House had this level of security. Then we reached an elevator that took us straight to the fifth floor.

It opened up into what I could only describe as a drawing room, but it was the size of our common room in Elder House. Gold leaf paper covered a wall decorated with pillars of black marble. In each section between the pillars hung oil paintings of women in formal wear. One of them had the same nose and golden hair as Henry.

Within the room, about a dozen maroon sofas, edged with gold thread were arranged around walnut low tables, and the whole ensemble was lit by a combination of crystal table lamps and matching chandeliers.

My fingers flew over my mouth to cover a gasp. Because of Mom's marriages, I was no stranger to opulence, but this had a stately flair I'd never seen outside of magazines.

Henry finally took my hand and led me around the edge of the room to another door, which opened into a hallway. "It's over here."

"Is this your family's apartment?" I asked.

"That room is mostly for entertaining. Mother and Father stay here whenever they're in London."

At the end of the hallway, he rang a bell. The hand holding mine let go, and his hand snaked around my waist and brought me close.

I glanced up at Henry, wondering why he felt the need to put on the show behind closed doors, but he leaned down and gave me a peck on the lips. "Did I mention earlier that you look exceptionally pretty today?"

My throat thickened. "You didn't."

A moment later, the door opened, and a middle-aged woman clad in a charcoal-colored pantsuit appeared. She wore her pale, blonde hair off her face, making her features a little severe. After casting me a curious glance, she glared up at Henry.

Butterflies twitched in my stomach. Wasn't anyone going to make introductions?

"Aunt Idette." Henry stepped forward.

She raised her palm. "Don't you Auntie me," she snapped in a slight German accent. "What a mess you have created for your parents. It is bad enough that you stage your own kidnapping but you are frisking with boys, now?"

"This is Emilia Hobson," said Henry in a voice accustomed to being scolded. "My *girlfriend*."

"More likely someone you paid to fool your poor family."

"Actually, she's not." The woman in the portrait with golden hair the exact shade of Henry's walked into the room. She wore a pastel pink Chanel suit with black piping and gold buttons. Unlike Henry's verdant green eyes, hers were an icy blue. "Emilia Hobson is the girl he framed, aren't you, dear?"

A large man stepped into the room after her with a similar frame as Henry's but a little softer around the middle. "Emilia, welcome to our home." Only the tiniest hint of a German accent laced his voice. "I am Oscar, the father of young Henry, and this is my wife, Clara, and my cousin Idette, the International Director of Operations."

"I'm pleased to meet you." My gaze darted to Henry, whose nostrils flared at the sight of his father.

Mr. Bourneville held out his elbow. "Come, dinner is getting cold."

I took the father's arm and glanced at Henry over his shoulder. His mother grabbed his arm, and murmured something at him in a language that sounded like German, but could have been a dialect. Henry shook his head and kept a stony expression.

The next room we entered was a dining room with a table that seated eight but was set for five. Compared to the drawing room, it was very casual. The only things that stood out were the huge gold mirrors that hung above semicircular console tables and the matching candelabras in front of them. Two paintings, each of Mr. and Mrs. Bourneville, hung beside the mirror opposite the head of the table.

Henry's father seated me to his left, with Mrs. Bourneville opposite me, and Henry at my side. Henry reached under the table and held my hand. Within seconds, staff entered the room with plates of food.

"How long have you and Henry been together," asked Mrs. Bourneville.

"Ever since the kidnapping, I suppose." I sipped from the crystal water glass. "Nine days in that room was enough time for us to get to know each other."

"And you had sex with him in that room?" asked Aunt Idette.

Henry's mother pursed her lips, but his father leaned forward.

I gave my head a vigorous shake. "It was filthy!"

Mr. Bourneville narrowed his eyes. "A more relevant question to ask is why the girl who had faced charges for child abduction, that carries a sentence of ten or more, would give Henry another chance."

My mouth opened, but the lie Henry and I had practiced disappeared from the forefront of my mind.

"Unless you're plotting something." Mrs. Bourneville drummed her French-manicured fingers on the table.

I froze. Last term, her words would have been the truth, but I'd already taken my revenge on Henry and the others. Now, I just wanted the boys to stop bearing a grudge.

My tongue darted out to lick my lips. "I returned to Mercia Academy expecting to hate Henry, but I couldn't. That time we spend together as prisoners opened my heart to him, and I saw a side of his personality that only his friends see. It's kind and loving and gentle."

"What do you think of his business between him and Blake?" asked Mr. Bourneville.

"Just boys drinking too much absinthe and having fun," I replied. "I was also in the room with them, and it wasn't a big deal."

The staff took away the first course and brought grilled salmon served with garlic-roasted broccoli, sautéed green beans, and roasted fingerling potatoes. We ate in silence, and I shared a glance with Henry, who gave me a grateful smile.

As soon as the staff took away that course, Aunt Idette's head snapped up. "Why did you forgive him?"

"I didn't at first. But it's hard to explain what happened when I thought we'd been kidnapped. For those nine days and the time after that, I'd never in my life felt closer to anyone." Saying these words made my heart hurt, because they were true. And the worst part was having to admit them in front of Henry. "I couldn't stop thinking about him the entire time we were separated."

"Yet you got engaged to that classical pianist," said Mrs. Bourneville.

"I thought Sergei could mend my broken heart." I lowered my gaze to my plate, wondering whether Henry's mother was addicted to the society columns. "But it turned out that no one could compare to Henry."

Henry leaned toward me and gave me a kiss on the temple. I raised my head and gazed into his verdant, green eyes. For a moment, everything stilled, and I was no longer aware of the dining room or his family. It was just Henry and me, just like it had been our last two days of supposed captivity.

"What a sweet girl." Aunt Idette's sarcasm snapped me out of my Henry-induced stupor.

He smiled. "Not as sweet as you'd think. She made me grovel for a long time."

I tilted my head to the side and smirked. "I intend to make you suffer until I'm satisfied you're truly repentant."

Mr. Bourneville roared with laughter. "Good girl!"

I glanced up and met Mrs. Bourneville's gaze. She gave me her first genuine smile for the day.

My shoulders relaxed. I hadn't completely convinced them, but at least they no longer thought I was an outright liar.

After lunch, we walked back through the maze of hallways holding hands. His family seemed the type who would watch us through the security cameras, so I took the opportunity to bask in his presence. Being with Henry today had been so perfect, and the warmth of his affection couldn't melt the shard of ice still lodged in my heart from his betrayal. The last door clicked shut, and the limo rolled forward from the shadows. Henry opened the door and let me in.

As soon as we settled into the plush, leather seat Henry scooted close, wrapped his arms around me, and kissed the side of my mouth. "You were wonderful! I didn't know you felt so deeply for me."

"Maybe once." I elbowed him hard in the stomach. "But now, you can go to hell."

CHAPTER 9

*H*enry recoiled from the elbow in the gut, and his face slackened into an expression of wide-eyed shock. His broad shoulders drooped, and he seemed to crumple into the leather seat of the limousine. I met his hurt, green eyes with a defiant glare, but he still had the nerve to choke out the words, "What was that for?"

I pushed back the tiny twist of guilt in my belly and snapped, "Didn't you hear a word of what I said to your parents?"

The limousine pulled away and made its slow ascent through the darkened, underground parking lot. The external lights occasionally illuminated the side of his face, exaggerating his wounded expression.

"I…" Henry drew his brows together as though trying to work out the trick in my question. "You said you'd fallen for me in the squat. Was that a lie?"

"No."

"Then why—"

"From the moment I opened my eyes, you knew it wasn't a real kidnapping, but you played along. You watched them inject me with goodness-knows-what, let us sleep on a filthy mattress, and let me wallow in fear and paranoia for nine days."

His shoulders drew up to his ears, and he dipped his head. "We needed the money to help Edward's father."

"I know that now, but why did I have to suffer so much? Why did you let them inject me a second time?"

The limo reached the ground floor and drove out of the low exit into the store-lined street. I kept my gaze on Henry and away from the people outside, bustling from store to store.

He ran his fingers through his hair and sighed. "Paul... Mr. Frost said I had to keep everything as authentic as possible, so you wouldn't guess it had all been a setup."

"And you went along with his plan?"

Henry straightened and raised his blond brows in a look so incredulous, I wondered if I had said something wrong. Eventually, he said, "If I'd told you the truth, you might have gone to the police anyway as revenge for all those pranks the others played."

I snatched my gaze away and stared out of the window. He had a point, but I wasn't going to admit it. The limo rounded Piccadilly Circus. First, we passed the kind of giant, neon signs found in places like Times Square, then moments later, we had a magnificent view of a winged statue with beautiful Georgian buildings in the background. "Is that Eros?"

"It's his brother, Anteros. Some say he's the avenger of unrequited love," Henry replied with a bite to his voice.

The implication hit me in the gut. He thought my shitty attitude was getting in the way of what he wanted. My nostrils flared, and I glared at him through the corner of my eye. "What would he say about love formed under false pretenses?" Before he could speak, I added, "Where were you that time you went missing for a whole day and returned smelling of marijuana?"

He turned away, and adrenaline surged through my veins. If I had to guess, Henry had been relaxing with the kidnappers over takeout and a joint. Probably taking the time to call Edward and Blake to form part two of their plan to buy my silence with affection. I wouldn't have been surprised if Mr. Frost had come down to work out the finer details of how to frame me if everything went wrong.

"I don't know how to make a convincing enough apology to you," he said in a broken voice. "Isn't it enough that I've been disinherited and pictures of Blake and me are floating about the internet?"

All the anger drained out of me, replaced by emptiness. Perhaps it was time to let go of past hurts.

We returned to Elder House in time for the end of dinner. Charlotte toured the dining room like a circling vulture, swooping down on tables to have whispered conversations with each member of the rugby team.

"Why are they all so fond of her?" I asked Henry.

"We called her Butter Face behind her back," he said. "Nice tits, but her face was lacking. I can't think of a reason they'd follow her unless she's offering blow jobs."

I shot him a glare, but he shrugged. "When we returned from our… absence, they were still talking about Blake's video."

I shook my head, got out of my seat and walked toward Duncan's table. The scrawny boy would have an idea of what was really happening. Not even Charlotte would offer to blow the entire rugby team. Double standards meant that actions like that invariably backfired on the girl, and some of the players, like Coates and his cauliflower ears, were gross. Duncan sat alone, picking at his rhubarb crumble and custard while leafing through his pile of newspapers.

"Is this seat taken?" I asked.

Duncan's gaze flicked up over his thick glasses, and his lips quirked with distaste. Probably because I'd gotten Miss Oakley to confiscate his smartphone containing stills from Henry and Blake's sex tape. "Oh, it's you."

That hadn't been a no, so I slipped into the seat next to him. "Why did Alice go back to that group?"

"Changes are taking place within Elder House." Duncan flipped open his copy of The Mail on Sunday and leafed through the tabloid's pages. "Think of it as a paradigm shift. Old gods have fallen and new ones are taking their place. Just as you sat with those tossers last term for protection, Alice has joined Charlotte's team to avoid becoming the victim of the upcoming bloodbath."

I glanced up at Charlotte, who wrapped her arms around one of Coates' battered-looking rugby friends. "What do you mean?"

"I can't say, but it's revolutionary."

My eyes narrowed. "Can't or won't?"

"Won't. The destabilization has been good for me. I finally have cool friends instead of being an outcast."

I glanced around his empty table. If this was his definition of having friends, there wasn't much point in continuing the conversation. "Thanks. I won't trouble you any longer."

As I walked back to the triumvirate through the maze of dining tables, tremors of dread shook the lining of my stomach. No matter what I thought of Charlotte, she was resourceful. That painful and humiliating walk through the gauntlet had been of her design, and she'd even whored herself to Mr. Carbuncle to make it happen. If she was planning a move against me, I had to be extra vigilant.

I reached the table and retook my seat, reporting back that Duncan hadn't said anything useful except for vague hints of Charlotte's plans. A server slid a bowl of rhubarb crumble with cream at my place setting, and I stared into my pudding. If anyone would know what Charlotte had been saying to her supporters, it would be the people at the Saturday Correspondent. Perhaps it was time to power up the burner phone I used to communicate with Jackie.

The next day, our new Latin Master noticed I wasn't doing any of the work. When I explained that I didn't know anything about the language, he sent me out of the class. Taking advantage of the time away from the triumvirate, I rushed to my room, sat on the edge of the bathtub, and called Jackie on the burner phone.

"Emilia!" she rasped. "Have you decided to work with us?"

"It's just a tip off. Charlotte Underwood is up to something nefarious. Did your interns notice her making any plans?"

After a muffled sound of coughing and hacking, Jackie replied. "We've been watching her. So far, she's been promising people tickets to a party to rival the Valentine's Day Massacre."

My shoulders drooped. "Is that all?"

"I need you to find out the name of her benefactor," said Jackie. "Someone's paid over thirty-five thousand pounds to get her back into the academy and financed all the work she's had done on her face."

"Sorry," I said.

"What?" replied Jackie.

"I told Rudolph I wouldn't give him any stories and I meant it. But this thing with Charlotte is personal. If something falls on my lap, I'll pass it on, but I won't go to any efforts after Rudolph reneged on our deal."

Jackie let out a long sigh. "He won't be happy."

I hung up and shook my head. Did Jackie and Rudolph really think I would go sneaking about on their behalf after his colossal betrayal? If they did, they were as crazy as they were corrupt. The lunch bell rang, and I turned off the burner phone, straightened myself up in the mirror, and headed downstairs.

As soon as I reached the dining room, I found Blake in one of the middle tables, glaring into a letter penned in calligraphy script. It was the kind of quality writing paper used in high-class correspondence, but from his expression, it wasn't good news. A shiver of apprehension skittered down my spine. The last time one of the triumvirate received a nasty letter, it had been from the supposed kidnappers. My attempts to help Henry hadn't ended well for any of us.

A hand landed on the small of my back, and Edward's cedar and cypress scent filled my nostrils. "Is everything alright?"

I nodded at Blake. "Something's bothering him."

Edward guided me to what had become the triumvirate's new table. "Let's find out."

"Anything wrong?" Edward pulled out my chair and gave me a warm smile.

Henry strolled in and took the seat opposite mine.

Up at the new head table, Charlotte glowered down at us. Coates sat at her left and murmured something into her ear, but she didn't react. Most likely because she was still preoccupied with ensnaring Henry. I raised my chin and gave her a triumphant smile. All the machinations in the world couldn't get her what she wanted.

Blake sighed and slipped the letter into his pocket. "Mother has told the press I'll be at Narcotics Anonymous in Kensington Town Hall."

Henry shook his head and reached for the crystal water jug. "Why wouldn't you go to one nearer to the academy?"

"You're missing the point," Blake snapped. "Why should I go to one at all?"

He gave Blake's shoulder a squeeze. "At least you'll have company."

Blake's gaze flicked to me, and his lips pursed. "Right."

Bristling, I snatched a bread roll from the middle of the table. "If you think it's a huge imposition for me to come along, I'll stay in the academy. It's not like I wanted to be part of your path to redemption."

"Emilia will be at your side," said Edward.

I curled my lip. "Since when were you my social secretary?"

"Since we own you," said Henry. "Be quiet and finish your lunch."

I flashed my eyes at Henry and stabbed my bread roll. He hadn't been this ballsy yesterday in the back of the limo. Perhaps this was his form of petty revenge for my rejection of his affections. Imagining the roll was his testicle, I tore off a piece with my teeth. Sometimes, he could be such an asshole.

∽

On Sunday morning, I met Blake at the entrance hall. Only the smallest of flames burned in the fireplace because of the warmer weather. Blake stood at the pigeon holes and examined its contents. He wore a navy blazer with stone-colored pants in a fabric that looked like a blend of linen and silk. Only one of the gold buttons of his blazer was fastened, giving him an air of smart-casual chic. I pursed my lips. With his glossy, black hair curving around his high cheekbones, he looked utterly irresistible.

"Are you ready?" I tried to keep the belligerence out of my voice. It was my fault he had to go to Narcotics Anonymous.

"One moment." Blake stuffed a letter in his pocket and placed the other items back into the pigeonhole.

I glanced at the bank of cabinets on the left of the room. Each person's mailboxes were arranged in alphabetical order, so what was Blake, whose last name began with S, doing so close to the end? I was about to ask when he raised his hand. "If you're curious, we can talk later."

Outside, the sun shone out of a cloudy sky, casting the campus in soft light. Pink blossoms covered the magnolia trees leading to the main teaching block, and a slight breeze carried their sweet scent. A limousine pulled up in the driveway by the steps of the house. Blake swept past me and opened the door.

He sat in the car and stuck his nose in the air, looking like he was striking a pose for the camera. "If you think we are friends after what you did, you can think again."

The words landed like a slap, and I reared back. Blake had never expressed this level of vitriol in front of Henry and Edward. Tightening the muscles of my stomach, I raised my chin and sat straighter in the leather seat. "I was done with you months ago, when I realized we never had a friendship."

The limo pulled out from the courtyard, its wheels rumbling over the gravel driveway. I fastened my seatbelt and folded my arms across my chest.

Blake's haughty expression fell. "If I meant nothing to you, why did you bother to come back?"

I huffed an exasperated breath. He was always the first to flirt and to instigate sexual contact. And now, after declaring he wasn't interested in me, he became upset when I didn't fall to his knees and beg to be his friend. The boy was giving me whiplash.

"You're making me regret my choice," I muttered.

After clearing the campus, the limo sped down the long driveway that led to the front gates and then through the fields that led to the village. We sat in silence, each staring out of our respective windows, when Blake twisted in his seat and whirled on me. "Why did you do it?"

"Did I poke you in the ribs and ask you to stand in front of the common room and boast about becoming a prince?" My stomach churned at the lie, as I had all but goaded him into proving his worth.

"Who recorded it?" he snapped.

"You would have noticed me if I had a camera. Maybe one of the many people watching you that evening. How about the types always ready to shoot videos of people making fools of themselves to upload the footage to the Mercia-Net?"

"I find that hard to believe." He turned to stare at the stone-fronted buildings of the village.

"Blake," I snapped. "You're the last person who should complain about being filmed doing something incriminating."

"What?" Annoyance etched his handsome features, and one knee bounced up and down.

I rolled my eyes. Even though I wasn't being completely truthful, his stupidity grated on my last nerve. "Look at what you did to Charlotte. She trusted you, and not only did you trick her into sucking you off, but you recorded it and then played it to everyone and made it look like I'd done it. And you wonder why someone wanted to give you a taste of what it's like to have one's vulnerable moments broadcasted?"

He opened his mouth to say something, then promptly clamped it shut. Likely because any arguments in his defense would make him a hypocrite. I might not have put up the camera above the mantle and I didn't put those words in his mouth, but he had done all the things I had mentioned and worse. He folded his arms and fumed for the rest of the journey, leaving me a jumble of confusion.

Blake was something out of a Henry Wadsworth Longfellow poem about the girl with a curl in the middle of her forehead. When he wanted to be, he was the best of the triumvirate. He was friendly, fun, flirtatious, and so physically dazzling, it was hard to believe he was real. But then there was his horrid side, which craved chaos and loved to set things in motion so he could revel in the resulting car-wreck.

Despite this, there were glimpses of someone who craved love and attention, which gave him a vulnerability some might find endearing. Right now, all I could see was a gorgeous, empty-headed pain in the ass.

With a sigh, I sat back in my seat and pulled out my smartphone. Whatever.

As expected, no messages arrived from Mom, but Dad filled my inbox with emails stuffed with goofy photos of him and the twins. I flipped through them, smiling at the cute pictures. Little Tamara had drawn a picture of her family and included a blonde-haired stick figure that was supposed to be me. Warmth spread across my insides. Even though Dad was half a world away and in no position to help, at least he kept me in his thoughts.

As the limo sped through London, Blake turned to me and spat, "You're two-faced."

"You're hurt because I bested you," I snapped.

"And duplicitous."

A frustrated breath huffed out of my nostrils, and I turned to meet his accusing, chocolate-colored eyes. "If I am, I learned it from you. How many of those pranks did you help with, only to flirt with me afterward? All of them, most Ill bet."

The limo pulled into the front of Kensington Town Hall, a blocky, red brick building consisting of octagonal shapes, where dozens of paparazzi jumped to attention and crowded the car door.

"Oh no." Blake placed his head in his hands. "How may fucking reporters did they contact?"

"Your Mom?" I asked.

"And the palace, most probably. Shit."

All traces of annoyance vanished. It was easy to bicker with Blake when I couldn't see the repercussions of my actions, but the sheer number of reporters jostling each other for the glimpse of the royal rebel made my stomach drop. I had done this. And so had Rudolph. If those stills of Blake hadn't hit the internet, the first scandal would have faded into the background by now.

I unbuckled my seatbelt, scooted across the limo's leather seat and rubbed his back to a panoply of camera flashes. "Come on," I said without moving my lips, just in case one of the nosey fucks outside was recording a video of us for later examination. "We'll get through this together."

Blake raised his head and turned to me, dark eyes shining with gratitude. "I'm glad you're here."

A lump formed in my throat. He should be spitting in my face, not smiling into it. I rubbed my aching chest. If I said too much, I would probably burst into tears. "Sure."

The driver walked around his side of the vehicle and fought his way through the paparazzi to reach the passenger door.

Tiny prickles of nervousness spread across my skin, and my stomach hollowed. This was a different crowd of photographers to the ones I had following me around when I was with Sergei. They probably either belonged to the tabloids or sold their images to such establishments. Some of them jammed themselves and their camera lenses to the window, filling the limo with light. I stole another glance at Blake, whose skin took on the pallor of dead fish.

Once we had waded our way through the riot of photographers and walked through a reception hall consisting of various shades of brown, we entered a sad-looking room, half filled with well-fed, bright-eyed people I suspected were reporters.

The meeting itself was depressing. After the disguised reporters, Blake and I introduced ourselves and got our welcome hugs, we all read from a piece of paper, and the leader facilitated a group discussion. Neither Blake nor I participated but we listened to anecdotes ranging from the sad to the scary to the downright shocking. We exchanged glances. We didn't belong here, and our attendance felt like voyeurism.

When we didn't stay for the coffee and chat after the meeting, half the room followed us out.

"Emilia!" shouted a reporter as we stepped out of the town hall into the bright afternoon.

I raised my head and gave the man a bright smile. "Hello. Are you enjoying the weather?"

"Very nice. Did Blake break up your engagement with Sergei Bachmann?"

Plastering on a wistful smile, I said, "Absolutely not. The distance broke us apart in the end. I was always at school and Sergei was about to start a grand tour of Europe."

"Are you going out with Mr. Simpson-West?" yelled another reporter.

"Blake and I are just good friends."

Blake placed an arm around my waist. "I'd like there to be more. Emilia is an exceptional young woman and one I would love to get to know better."

I gave him what I hoped was a bittersweet smile. "I've already given my heart to Henry Bourneville."

"Emilia!" shouted another reporter. "What can you say about the scantily-clad tryst with Bourneville?"

My smile dropped. "It was between two underaged boys that should never have been published by respectable newspapers."

The driver held the door open, but the reporters and photographers wouldn't let us through to the limo until we told them we wanted to sit down to answer all their questions.

Despite my efforts to make Blake look good while maintaining the facade of being Henry's girlfriend, Blake sat in the seat opposite me and sulked throughout the entire journey.

Fatigue spread through my bones, and I sank into the leather seat, stretched out my legs and watched the freeway whizz past. If Blake wanted a fake girlfriend for the press, he needed to work with someone else. I pulled out my smartphone, replied to a few emails, and glanced at Blake every few minutes. Today had been a rollercoaster of emotions, and I didn't know if things were better between us or worse.

As soon as we reached Elder House, I bolted out of the limo and bounded up the stairs. If the triumvirate objected to my evening off, they could kick down my door.

CHAPTER 10

The next morning, Blake had returned to his usual exuberant self, and we sat around a regular table the staff had dressed with crystalware and fine china. Coates and his group of rugby pals sat at the head table, looking like a group of oversized, clueless dicks without Charlotte and the doppelgängers. Just after the servers had removed my completed plate of scrambled eggs and smoked salmon, Mr. Jenkins approached our table.

"Miss Hobson, may I see you in my office before first bell?"

My gaze flickered to the girls' empty seats at the head table. "Is this some sort of ambush?"

He had the nerve to rear back as though I'd slapped him. Pink blotches rose to his thin cheeks. "O-of course not!"

I twisted my lips, showing him how much I believed him. "Last term, you escorted me to the headmaster's office, where two policemen were ready to arrest me for the most heinous of crimes. I'd count that as an ambush."

His blotches darkened. "I-it's an academic matter."

"Come on." Edward stood and held out his hand. "We'll go together."

I wrapped my fingers around his, enjoying the warmth of our touch, and rose from my seat. Mr. Jenkins trudged out of the dining room, and we followed after him hand-in-hand, stealing glances at each other. For a moment, the betrayals and bitterness faded into the ether, leaving behind the young man who cared deeply for his friends, family, and employees, and the young woman who adored him for it.

A musty aroma filled my nostrils the moment we stepped through the threshold of Mr. Jenkins' office. His curtains were drawn, and even larger piles of paper than before littered his desk. He lowered himself into his seat and gestured for us to sit.

I narrowed my eyes at him. "What's this about, sir?"

He cleared his throat. "Your new Latin master, Mr. Pickering, informs me that he ejected you from his class."

"He did…" I folded my arms across my chest and drummed my fingers on my biceps.

"You now have too many free periods, and that's unacceptable. Either choose another subject or an extracurricular activity to make up the required hours."

"What's available?" I asked.

Mr. Jenkins rattled off a list of subjects, all of which were academic, tedious, and would do nothing for my writing career. When I remained silent, he added, "The following clubs and teams are seeking new members: debating, Gilbert and Sullivan, chess, hockey—"

"Hockey," I said. It was the only topic that vaguely interested me and only because I had played in Park Prep.

"I'll write a note to the Physical Education mistress, and she will get in touch with you with instructions."

On our way back to the dining room, Edward wrapped an arm around my waist. In a low, commanding voice, he said, "Your presence is required at lunchtime."

Memories of the first time we were in his study resurfaced,

where Blake had unfastened the buttons of my blouse and teased my breasts until I unbuttoned the garment open. He had exposed me to Henry and Edward, who had devoured me with their gazes. My nipples twinged in anticipation of Blake's fingers, and my core throbbed at the promise of what would happen when I stripped for the triumvirate.

Keeping the breathiness out of my voice, I asked, "Should I meet you in your study?"

"Outside the former headmaster's office. We're meeting the Board of Governors to discuss my fundraising idea."

"Oh." My libido shriveled at the disappointing pronouncement. We stepped into the dining room, where Charlotte glowered down at us from the head table. "What do you want me to do?"

"You'll sit next to me and smile and nod at everything I say."

I wrinkled my nose. "And the point of that is?"

"Social proof." He pulled out my chair. "You represent the female students, demonstrating that my idea is inclusive to both genders."

"Whatever." I grabbed a triangle of toast from the rack. At least this would be a change from the other tasks of penance I had performed for the triumvirate. This time, I wouldn't be stuck in a limo for hours, listening to him bellyache about how much I'd betrayed him.

∾

After morning classes, I met Edward by the bank of desks outside Mr. Chaloner's old office. A new secretary sat outside the door, who crunched numbers on a calculator. I tried to take a look at her documents, but it was impossible without leaning over the desk and making my spying obvious.

"Emilia," said Edward from behind. "It's this way." He guided me through the hallway on the left of the office and through a wooden door at its end.

Eight of the twelve members of the Board of Governors sat around a wide, rectangular table. At its head stood Mr. Weaver, the man in the academic robes who had spoken in the assembly.

His brows rose. "Viscount Highdown and…"

I glanced over my shoulder for signs of the mysterious viscount, but found no one at our backs.

"Miss Emilia Hobson." Edward placed his hand on the small of my back and guided me to one of the two seats at the end of the boardroom table, opposite Mr. Weaver.

I stole a glance at Edward. No one had told me he was a viscount. I didn't even know what exactly the title meant or why it had been awarded to someone under the age of eighteen.

"Thank you, members of the board, for accommodating me at such short notice," said Edward, his voice clear and commanding. "I would like to propose a fundraiser to generate some good press for the academy to help repair its reputation."

The woman sitting to Mr. Weaver's right steepled her fingers. "I hardly think a charity event will erase the effects of all the negative press the school has received over the past months."

Guilt churned in my stomach, and I slid a few inches down in my seat. If I'd thought my plan of vengeance through, I might not have involved the academy so much. It was hard to anticipate that the cameras would pick up so much corruption when I had only wanted to target Charlotte, the triumvirate, and Mr. Chaloner.

"Perhaps not erase it, Lady Seagrove," said Edward. "But we need something to show the academy in a better light."

"Viscount Highdown is correct," said a rotund man. "Let's give the papers something positive to report on us for a change. What do you suggest?"

"A sponsored run from Mercia Academy to Worthing Pier," replied Edward. "Staff and students can participate for any distance."

"And the charity?"

"More scholarship places."

Mr. Weaver shook his head. "The press might consider that self-serving."

The other board members mumbled their agreement. I gulped. Did they really need to shoot down his idea? I thought it had been great.

"I'm sure the nearest children's hospital will accept a donation," Edward added.

I gave him a nod and an encouraging smile.

Lady Seagrove stroked her chin. "A wonderful idea, but it dilutes the effect of our annual charity sports day."

The room fell silent, and Edward's posture sagged. I let out a long breath. As friendly as this board of directors appeared, I couldn't help thinking that they might have a slight grudge against Edward. Something about the overly cordial tones combined with their polite refusals of his attempts to help told me they blamed him for the scandals that had befallen the academy.

"World Blood Donor Day," I blurted.

Mr. Weaver made a slow blink of incomprehension. "I beg your pardon?"

"It's an international event run by members of the World Health Organization," I said. "My prep school in New York organized a blood donation event to support it."

Edward straightened. "Staff and students old enough to participate can donate, and if it coincides with parents' evening or another summer event, we can get a few parents and alumni to join in."

Lady Seagrove turned to a rotund man sitting on her left. "Your thoughts, Dr. Asgard?"

He gave her a vigorous nod. "Wonderful. We're always looking for more blood. My hospital will be happy to set up a temporary blood donation center on the academy grounds."

Mr. Weaver nodded. "Excellent idea. Thank you very much, Viscount. Let us know your progress in a fortnight."

I held my polite smile. Even though the idea was mine, I was happy for the credit to go to Edward. After the board gave us a polite dismissal, we both stood and walked out of the room. The door clicked shut, and we strolled through the hallway, past the portraits of former headmasters and Mercia ancestors, and toward the main staircase.

Edward wrapped his arm around my waist and beamed. "That went rather well, I think. Thank you for an idea everyone loved."

"Do you think you can forgive me, now?" I asked.

His hand slid down to my hip, and he said in a low voice, "It will take a damned sight more for you to earn absolution for what you brought upon the academy."

Irritation flared across my skin like fire ants. I stepped out of his grip and hurried ahead down the stairs, taking them two at a time.

"You're deluded." I spat.

"What did you say?" his voice echoed in the stairwell.

I whirled around and met his stormy glare. My heart pounded to the beat of a war drum and I clenched my fists. "Do you think all the crap you dished out in the first term counts for nothing?"

Edward's brows drew together. "Of course not, but—"

"I know I took things too far," I hissed. "But you guys hurt me, and if it wasn't for Mr. Frost's confession, you could have damaged my future. We're even." I continued down the stairs, pushed open the wooden door, and stormed down the hallway. Fortunately, classes were still in session, so no one witnessed our whispered spat.

Edward's long strides kept up with mine. "Did you not hear the Board of Governors? Our school's reputation is in tatters. Parents whose children were due to start in the next academic year have relinquished their places."

"Isn't there a waiting list?" I stepped out of the exit into the gravel path and inhaled lungfuls of cool, spring air.

"That isn't the point!" Edward grabbed my arm.

"What is?" I drew closer to him, meeting his cold, blue glower with a heated one of my own. "The three of you are keeping me close to you and exacting a strange kind of retribution. How exactly does that benefit the academy?"

His eyes flashed, and his breathing grew heavy. "We're punishing you."

"You're getting off on it." I jerked my arm out of his grip.

Edward advanced on me, his gaze lingering on my lips. "What if we are? You hurt us the most."

I stepped back, but the wall of the main building blocked me from moving further away. "And you all hurt m—"

Edward grabbed both forearms, pinning me against the wall. A gasp caught in the back of my throat, and before I could protest at the manhandling, his lips descended onto mine in a kiss so soft and aggressive and full of hunger, I couldn't tell if this was a reconciliation or the progression of our fight.

Every nerve ending in my body sang with desire, and my heart pounded with an intensity I felt in my ribs, my breasts, and my nipples. Edward Mercia was kissing me. His beautiful, lips were caressing mine, as though he wanted me, the girl who had left. After everything I had done. After I'd lied to his face and tricked him into handing over files that had gotten his father arrested. The hands holding my arms in place slid down into my blazer and wrapped around my waist, and with a soft moan, I let my eyes flutter closed and shut out the rest of the world.

Melding myself into his hot, hard body, I surrendered further into the kiss, and let his tongue slide between my lips and meet mine. The sensation sent my knees buckling, and I was suddenly glad the wall was at my back to stop me from collapsing like a broken marionette.

He drew back and brushed strands of hair off my face. The pupils of his blue eyes were blown, and he said between panting breaths, "Stay with me tonight. Just the two of us. You won't have to do anything you don't want."

My throat dried, along with all my resentment about not having been forgiven. "A-alright."

A high-pitched cough sounded from behind. Edward glanced over his shoulder, stiffened, and stepped away, keeping his back to the interloper. It was a little first year, dressed in burgundy P.E. clothes, whose flush clashed with her strawberry blonde pigtails.

"Umm..." Heat rushed to my cheeks. I slowed my breathing and fastened the button on my school blazer. "Can I help you?"

"Are you Emilia Hobson?" she squeaked.

"Yes?"

"Miss Shinty says you're to report to the hockey field after lunch."

~

The hockey uniform consisted of items I already had in my cases: a white polo shirt, burgundy gym knickers, a burgundy hockey skirt, long socks, and black sports shoes. I walked over to the hockey field, past the now empty International House building, and around the back of the tuck shop. A group of girls were already running from one end of the pitch and around the goals, guided by a tall hockey coach clad in a 70's style burgundy tracksuit with two white stripes down the sides.

I jogged up to the woman. "Miss Shinty?"

She turned around, revealing buck teeth sent within a gaunt face. "Miss Hobson, I presume?"

"Yes, Miss."

"Your housemaster has already explained your enthusiasm for the game. If you haven't played before, I expect your teammates will get you up to speed." Miss Shinty jerked her head toward the jogging girls. "Run a few laps. When I blow the whistle, put on a blue vest, and you'll join us for a practice match."

I jogged over to join the girls and spotted Patricia, who shot me a nasty glare and ran ahead as though it was a race. It wasn't as if I cared what she thought, so I jogged at a steady pace behind her.

A voice from behind hissed. "What did you do to Henry?" Charlotte appeared from behind and jogged at my side. "He and the others wouldn't spend so much time with a trollop unless you performed some kind of trick."

I shrugged. "If I told you how to ensnare him, what would you give me in return?"

"You're disgusting!" she hissed.

"Says the girl who only knows one type of currency." At her blank look, I added, "According to video evidence, it's not pounds sterling."

Her cheeks turned the color of a baboon's ass. "You pig!"

"You're the one whose mind keeps going to the gutter, not me." I continued around the goal post and quickened my pace. My longer strides should have created some distance between us, but Charlotte sprinted at my side and glared up at me as though I'd taken something that was rightfully hers.

After a few laps of ignoring the self-proclaimed Queen of Mercia Academy, Miss Shinty blew her whistle, and we all separated into our teams. Fortunately, Charlotte's vest was red, meaning I didn't have to play with her.

The game started off with a member of the blue team, a girl from Hawthorn House, whacking the ball toward me. While another member of my team accelerated toward the goal, I dribbled the ball, waiting for the right moment to pass. Someone stuck a stick between my legs and yanked. Hard. I tripped and fell onto my hands and knees.

"Whoops," said Charlotte. "You always seem to land in that position. A trollop should be more careful about sticking out her arse."

Miss Shinty blew her whistle, and growled, "Underwood!"

"Sorry, Miss!" Charlotte ran ahead.

I picked myself up and clenched the stick. The petty little bitch would get a fist in the face if she tried that again. Our team scored, and we continued the game. The girls at Mercia Academy played a little more competitively than we used to at Park Prep, and it had been nearly a year since my last game. Around halfway through the match, another team member passed me the ball again. As I was close enough to the goal, I aimed to score, only to receive a sharp whack across my back.

Pain lightning-bolted across my shoulder blades and I cried out. Memories of being thumped across the back during the gauntlet resurfaced, and I pivoted around and smashed the butt of the hockey stick into my attacker's face.

Charlotte clutched her nose and howled. Blood poured from the spaces between her fingers.

Miss Shinty blew her whistle. "Five demerits, Hobson. Get out!"

I threw down my stick and stormed out of the hockey field. What a bunch of bitches. Always looking after their own.

By dinner time, the entire dining room was filled with rumors that I had maimed Queen Charlotte, she would need reconstructive surgery on her face, and she'd already instructed a lawyer in Manhattan to sue Rudolph Trommel for millions in damages. Even though it was clearly the mutterings of overexcited doppelgängers, I hoped the last part was true. Rudolph had made a profit by associating with me, and I would welcome any excuse to see him bilked.

Later, the servers produced several baked Alaskas, and everyone sang happy birthday to Edward. My jaw dropped, and I leaned into him and whispered, "That's the second important thing about you I've learned today."

He grinned. "What's the first?"

"You're a Viscount."

"A courtesy title because it's one of the titles I'll day inherit." He blew on the flaming pavlova placed in front of him, which turned a delicious shade of caramel.

"You could have at least told me it was your birthday."

"I don't usually celebrate it." He reached under the table and squeezed my thigh. "Stay with me tonight. Maybe we can start a new tradition."

Wendy shot out of her seat at the head table and shrieked, "Charlotte!"

Charlotte hobbled in on crutches and groaned over the students' chatter. A thick bandage wrapped around her head, and an even thicker brace covered her neck. Giant strips of adhesive tape covered the bridge of her nose from one cheekbone to the other. I pursed my lips. How much of that was fake?

"Why does someone who didn't even fall need crutches?" I said out loud.

Charlotte raised a crutch in the air for attention. "I have an announcement."

Henry snorted, and Blake rolled his eyes. "Here we go…"

"I was going to announce this later, but I think now is a better time." Her voice was oddly clear for someone requiring reconstructive surgery on her face. "I'm holding a party to top all previous attempts. Perhaps that's why I was so viciously attacked today."

Grumbles filled the dining room, and I shook my head with disbelief. The girl was utterly shameless.

"Anyway, only the beautiful and the best will be invited, and all elements who have previously subverted the natural order of things will be excluded!"

Male cheers broke out across the room. I was pretty sure she had been referring to the triumvirate, but what on earth did she mean?

CHAPTER 11

The four of us left the dining room shortly after Charlotte's announcement to drink cognac from wide-bottomed snifter glasses in Edward's study. I sat next to Edward on the Chesterfield sofa and sipped from a cup of Irish coffee, made with a sweet, cream liqueur. Blake sat at the armchair on my left, and Henry lounged on Edward's left. A small fire crackled in the fireplace, creating a lovely warm light to the dimly lit room.

"Another year." Henry raised his crystal glass.

Blake glanced at me through the corner of his eye. "An interesting one, though."

I narrowed my eyes. If anyone wanted to throw shade tonight, I would go straight to Edward's room and wait for him outside. "If you don't celebrate your birthday, what do you do instead?"

"Most years, we sat in Edward's room, drinking cognac he either swiped from home or got from Paul." Blake grimaced. "Sorry."

I raised a shoulder. "Hearing about him doesn't affect me at all."

The conversation continued about previous years' birthdays, but they didn't mention Edward's first year, which was around the time his mother had died. I sat back and listened to the boys chat among themselves and discovered that Edward had lost his virginity to Charlotte in their third year, but the experience had been so disastrous, neither of them had touched each other since. Blake's first female lover was a girl who had later been expelled in the third year when they backpacked around France together in the summer term.

Blake turned to me, his eyes dancing with mischief. "And you'll be seventeen when you lose yours."

Edward smirked into his glass, and I flashed Blake a grin.

Blake narrowed his eyes. "What aren't you—" Then his eyes widened. "No! Why didn't you tell us?"

Edward sniffed. "A gentleman never divulges. Besides, we weren't really in the mood at the time to wax lyrical about our wayward fourth."

I sipped my creamy Irish coffee. "You've been quiet, Henry."

He leaned forward and gave me a wistful smile. "I always liked the much older girls. No one in my year or the year above ever appealed, until now."

Edward set down his drink and placed his hand on my thigh. "I'm taking my present up to bed." He yanked me to my feet. "Hurry up and make amends before I decide I don't want to share."

∼

We spent the rest of the evening in Edward's double bed, exchanging slow kisses in our underwear. Edward laid me on my back with my hands on either side of my head and our fingers interlaced. We lay chest to chest, my nipples pebbling against his hard pectoral muscles, as he slowly devoured me with deep strokes of his tongue as though claiming my mouth as his territory.

When he drew back and stared into my eyes with such love, it reminded me of the last time we had been together alone, when he had told me he loved me, and I'd left him to discover that I was his betrayer.

At the time, I'd held back my feelings, but now I was free to say, "I love you, too."

He closed his eyes, and the corners of his mouth curved into a little smile. "Thank you. That's the best gift I could ever have received."

The next morning, I awoke to strong arms wrapping around my middle, muscular legs curled behind mine, and an erection pressed into my ass. A lazy smile spread across my face. Edward. I pushed back against his hardness, making him groan. One of his hands snaked up my front and cupped my bare breast, its thumb and forefingers rolling my nipple. Arousal sparked across my body and through my core in a wave of heat, making me press my legs together and groan. We'd only had sex once, but I missed his touch.

Reaching back, I wrapped my fingers around his erection. "I want it from behind."

He chuckled low and deep and reached for something on the bedside table. "I thought you'd never ask."

The hand not teasing my nipple slid under my waist, and his fingers slipped between my folds, gathering up the moisture. Then he rubbed gentle circles around my clit that made my eyes roll to the back of my head.

"I love how you're so ready for me," he growled.

"Less talk. More dick."

"As my lady commands." He drew back his hips. "One second, while I slip on a condom."

I huffed out a laugh, just as he lined himself up against my entrance and stretched me open. My muscles clenched around his thickness.

He shuddered and stopped moving. "O-oh, fuck."

"What?"

"You're still so tight. I thought Bachmann would have—"

"He was a perfect gentleman and only ever kissed me on the cheek." I backed into Edward's erection, causing him to groan.

"Now, are you going to give it to me good and hard, or will I take it for myself?"

Edward's chuckle rumbled across my back, and he thrust into my core, giving me that wonderful stretch I craved. He pumped in and out, building a rhythm that made me want to howl.

"Is this what you want?" he rumbled.

Humming my approval, I pushed back and forth against him, increasing the friction. His fingers, which made maddeningly light circles over my clit, quickened and the pressure increased until my muscles rippled around him.

"Carry on like that," he said, voice strangulated, "and I won't last long."

With each sweep of his finger, pleasurable tingles built up around my core. I pulsed and spasmed around the length thrusting into me and gasped out, "I'm getting close, too!"

Edward changed the angle of his thrusts, grazing a spot that deepened my pleasure and made it wind and coil like the lever of his gramophone. Panting hard, I dropped my head back onto his shoulder, and clutched at his thrusting hips. He continued teasing my aching, pulsing clit with heavier caresses until the coil snapped and released an eruption of pleasure that kept going and going.

Edward rocked back and forth, his movements prolonging my climax. "Emilia... Fuck."

"Yeah," I said through pants, the spasm of my core muscles showing no signs of ebbing.

His arm clamped around me like a vice, and he thrust hard and fast, making me cry out. Then he stilled and a tremble wracked his entire body. "F-f-fuuuuck!"

I huffed out a laugh. "I never thought I'd hear a viscount use such naughty language."

Edward snickered into my shoulder. "Neither did I."

When Edward softened inside me and withdrew, I sat up and propped my back against the headrest. The first rays of sunlight streamed in through the chink in the curtains, but they were so weak, they provided the barest of illumination. "What time is it?"

"Five, the last time I checked. I wasn't sure if you wanted to be seen leaving my room, so I wanted to give you the opportunity to go before everyone woke."

I ran the back of my fingers down his stubbled cheek and gave him a gentle peck. "Thanks." I leaned over the side of the bed and glanced down at the rug. "Ummm… Where are my clothes?"

"I placed them on the chair hours ago."

"Did you sleep?" I eased myself out of the rug and padded across the room to his desk and chair.

He glanced away. "I… I wasn't sure if you would leave in the middle of the night."

Just as I had the last time we slept together. The thought of him waking to find that I had left Mercia Academy and betrayed his confidence made my heart twist.

Edward closed his eyes and sighed. "I'm sorry."

"What for?"

"Your interventions brought everything with International House to a head before anyone got hurt. After the end of term, vanloads of police and immigration officers stormed the campus and cleared out those too old to belong to a high school. Since the police arrested Mr. Chaloner and exonerated Father, I've slept easier."

Nadia would probably be back home with her fiancé, just as she had wanted. I wrung my hands. "Are you just saying that to make me feel better?"

Edward pulled back the sheets and slid out of bed. The morning light accentuated his high cheekbones, sexy cupid's bow, and strong jawline. My gaze meandered down his smooth, alabaster skin and over the contours of his prominent pecs, tight abdomen, and a dark treasure trail that led to a thick, flushed penis.

"Emilia?" He crossed the room and grabbed my hands. "Some of the so-called international students were very dangerous people who should never have been allowed in polite society, let alone near children. At the end of the raid, the police brought out evidence bags of drugs and weapons... It was a disaster waiting to happen."

My gaze flickered up to meet his earnest, blue eyes, and I blew out a long breath. "Wow."

"Indeed." He clasped my head in his hands and pressed a kiss on my temple.

"Then why were you so angry with me?"

He ran his fingers through his hair and glanced away. "I'm more angry about the mess I'd created and irritated that it took an American girl I had bullied to fix things."

It took me a few moments for his words to sink in. There was one thing I didn't understand. "Why are you blackmailing me, then?"

"Henry and Blake are your blackmailers." He tweaked a nipple. "I'm just along for the ride and to give them a bit of moral support."

I pressed my lips together to hide a smile. "That's not very nice."

His face split into a grin. "Don't tell me you've hated the things they've made you do. I've watched you carefully, and you seem to be having fun."

"That's beside the point." I turned to the chair, took my skirt and slipped it on over my head.

Edward pulled up the zipper. "Play along with them. I'll make them back off if you cause a fuss. It's just taking them a little more time to forgive you."

Irritation flared across my skin. "Even though they—"

He placed his finger on my lips. "I know... None of this would have happened if we hadn't allowed you to take the blame for Henry's kidnapping. And we did a lot of awful things to you before then."

"I'm glad I've gotten through one of your thick heads." I shrugged on my shirt and fastened the buttons.

Edward lay back on his bed with his hands resting behind his head and smirked. "A really good fuck can clear the mind. Blake and Henry would probably tell you the same."

I snorted and stuffed my bra, hose, and panties into the pockets of my blazer, then slung the garment over my shoulder. "They need to adjust their attitudes."

He sat up on the bed and blew me a kiss. "See you at breakfast."

After slipping on my loafers, I backed out of the room and let the door click shut. The hallway was dark, and the floorboards creaked under my feet, but I continued toward the staircase.

"Miss Hobson?" whispered a voice from behind.

I whirled around to find Mr. Jenkins striding toward me in his tartan dressing gown. A pained moan reverberated in my throat. Didn't he have a lodge like Mr. Carbuncle or somewhere else to sleep? I was in no mood to speak to him, so I shook my head and padded down the stairs. The man followed me all the way to the first floor and halfway down the hallway leading to the room I shared with Rita.

"Miss Hobson!" His voice was a whip-crack.

I turned around. "Yes, sir?"

"What were you doing in Mr. Mercia's room?"

"The usual, I suppose." I rubbed the back of my neck and glanced in the direction of my room.

His nostrils flared. "Must I warn you of the dangers of premarital relations?"

"I would have thought all the bullying you allow here is a bigger issue than people over the British age of consent having consensual sex."

His face turned red. "Now, look here—"

"No, you look," I snapped. "You can't just grow a backbone when it suits you. Mr. Carbuncle had a girl in his lodge, and you said nothing to him about premarital relations, or is it all right when an adult male preys on little girls?"

The man's mouth opened and closed. "I will be writing to your mother about your conduct."

"Good luck. Tell her to respond to my texts before I give her a litter of grandkids." I turned around and headed for my room. Mom hadn't bothered to contact me once since I left New York. I doubted that she would chew me out for spending the night with a boy. I unlocked the door and stepped in.

Rita's head snapped up from her bed. "Emilia?"

I shushed her. "It's me."

"Oh." She relaxed back onto her pillow. "Goodnight."

With a smile, I pulled off my clothes and slid under my cool sheets. Her alarm would probably wake her in an hour and a half.

Hours later, the sun blazed through my window, and I grabbed my smartphone. It was eight-fucking-thirty. I groaned and pulled myself out of bed. How could I have slept through all the bells? I jumped into the shower, dried myself off, slipped on a clean uniform, and grabbed my satchel. If I hurried straight to the main teaching block, I might only get two demerits for being late to my first period.

I stepped out of the room, and my gaze caught a white piece of paper at the window end of the hallway. After casting a glance toward the stairs, I walked toward it. If someone had dropped a letter, I needed to place it in their mailbox in case one of the cleaners cleared it away by accident. It was a flyer on thick card stock, printed in gold leaf:

~ Spring Party ~
Saturday 3 June
Penthouse 16, Chelsea Heights
London, SW10 0XG
Doors close at 9:30pm
Dress for sex
RSVP: C.Underhill@MerciaAcademy.com

A palpitation reverberated in my chest. The party was in less than a week! Now, I knew why Charlotte had suddenly become popular with all the boys. The likes of Coates would follow any girl hosting a sex party.

My tongue darted out to lick my lips. This kind of scandal would bury her so deep, she would never resurface. With hands that trembled, I picked the invitation up and stuffed it in my pocket. First period could go hang. I rushed back into my room, turned on the burner phone, and sent Jackie a copy of the invitation.

She texted back immediately, saying she could fit me up with hidden cameras and could put together a team in a van to monitor the party. My mouth dried. Even though I'd told Rudolph my spying days were over, I had to make an exception for Charlotte.

CHAPTER 12

For the next few days, excitement brimmed in my belly, especially when the temperature rose, and Charlotte appeared in the dining hall without the neck brace, head-bandage, and crutches. Only the thinnest of strips adorned her unblemished nose, making me wonder if that had been for show, too. My glee at exposing Charlotte must have shown on my features because one evening after dinner, the boys cornered me in Edward's study.

"You're up to something," said Blake. "I've been watching you."

I lowered myself onto the Chesterfield sofa and folded my hands on my lap. "Whatever do you mean?"

Henry stood in front of me with his arms folded over his broad chest. "Did Bachmann return to the UK?"

I shook my head and stared into his green eyes. "He was in Vienna the last time I checked. Why?"

Blake sat at my side and placed his hand on my bare leg. "Someone's gotten you excited, and it isn't any of us."

"Is this an intervention?" I asked.

"If you like." Edward lowered himself into the leather seat next to mine and grabbed my hand. "You're planning something, and I'm concerned."

I glanced from Edward, up to Henry, and to Blake. Worry etched each of the boys' brows. If their first thought went to Sergei, then they were probably concerned that I no longer wanted to be with them. Or that I might be planning to run away again. Even though I occasionally bickered with Henry and Blake, I wouldn't up and leave them, and I certainly wouldn't do that to Edward. Telling them that would be of no use, because I'd already proven myself a liar. With a sigh, I pulled out the invitation to the sex party.

Edward read over my shoulder. "Why on earth would you need to go?"

"What is it?" asked Henry.

"A bloody sex party." Edward leaned back in his seat.

Blake's hand slid around to my inner thigh. "If it's sex you want. We can provide that. You only have to ask, Emilia, and you'll get more than you can handle."

"No." I squeezed my thighs together. If I let Blake distract me, I'd never get to explain. "There's no way Charlotte's going to find enough girls to attend a party where they'll have sex with her male supporters. I want to find out if she's doing something newsworthy."

With a huffed breath of frustration, Henry threw his hands up in the air. "Didn't you learn anything from last time?"

"Yes." I folded my arms. "Not to call the police if you're trying to frame me for your own crimes." My insides cringed. We were more than even. Why did I keep bringing it up?

Edward's lips thinned. "The academy has already suffered enough scandals for a century."

"And what about the collateral damage?" said Blake. "Everyone misbehaving in that party might be exposed."

"Like Paul," muttered Henry.

I scowled and pushed myself off the sofa. "Mr. Frost was a criminal who got what he deserved."

"Anyway…" Blake stood and placed his hands on my shoulders. "You are hereby summoned to Edward's office on Saturday after classes."

"What for?"

"It's been ages since we've put you in your place," he said in a low, smoky voice. His gaze flickered to my lips. "You're stepping out of line and clearly in need of…"

Heat tingled between my legs. "What?"

"A long, slow, and humiliating inspection." His arms encircled my waist, and his hardness pressed against my ass. A bolt of arousal shot through my core. "With our tongues."

I bit down hard on my lip and glanced at Edward, who gave me a wink and a smirk. It looked like my stint as Edward's birthday present had given them an indication of what they had been missing.

Henry ran a finger down one of my nipples, sending jolts of pleasure sparking down between my legs. At my indrawn breath, his verdant eyes danced with excitement. "We'll have you on the desk."

"On your hands and knees," said Blake.

Edward scooted forward and cupped my ass. "I'll perform the internal inspections, of course."

Heat flooded my body, and the muscles of my core pulsed with need. A horny triumvirate was tempting, but I only had a single chance to deal with Charlotte. I still owed her for the gauntlet and for the countless other pranks she participated in during my first term.

Later, as I walked through the hallway to Creative Writing, I caught sight of one of Coates' friends, a rugby player who stood five feet seven inches tall but had the bulk of someone much larger. The bridge of his nose twisted to the left like a parenthesis symbol and ended in a bulbous tip, and a few of his front teeth had been knocked out. I pursed my lips. Obviously, the team members weren't doing so well without Henry.

The boy grabbed the arm of a younger girl, a fifth year who wore her hair in a blonde bob that framed her delicate features. She and her friends stopped to glare at the rugby player.

"What do you want?" she snapped.

He let go and stepped backward. "You haven't replied to my texts."

I stood close by and pretended to study the plaque beneath the painting of a serious-looking man clad in a gray wig. It curled past the collar of his burgundy velvet jacket down to his shoulders. Apparently, he was one of the headmasters during the seventeenth century.

"What do you expect?" she hissed. "I told you to stop damaging yourself with rugby. You're no good at it, but you didn't listen."

The boy glared at the girl for several moments before saying, "You'll change your tune at Underwood's party."

"What does that mean?" she replied.

I held my breath. What could he think to achieve in less than a week to impress her?

Instead of answering, he walked away with his hands in his pockets. I glared after him. Was he just trying to create a bit of intrigue for himself, or did Charlotte plan something nefarious?

The girl followed after him. "Patterson-Bourke?"

They disappeared into the crowds, and I sent my boys a silent apology. As much as I wanted to play their games, I needed to know what Charlotte had planned.

∼

On Saturday after classes, I rushed back to my room and shimmied on a tank top, skinny jeans, and a leather jacket, then snuck out of the academy grounds in an Uber and took the train to London. It was still light by the time I arrived in Victoria, and I took the number eleven bus to Fleet Street. Not having any allowance since I'd told Rudolph I wouldn't spy for him had taught me the virtues of being frugal.

Jackie waited for me at the Saturday Correspondent's office with Tom, the tech guy, and a group of interns. She made me sit on a desk chair by to bank of computer screens while Tola, the black intern with chin-length braids from the Valentine's Day Massacre, arranged my hair with cameras disguised as hairpins.

Tom watched the screens and instructed Tola to make adjustments to improve the sound quality. Once they were both satisfied with the cameras in my hair, Tom handed me a soda bottle, a watch, and a necklace then explained how each hidden camera worked.

Jackie sauntered back from a cigarette break, reeking of tobacco. I asked her, "Won't anyone else be at the venue with me?"

"We'll send a couple of girls five or ten minutes after we see that it's not a group of brats playing spin the bottle." Jackie smirked. "My interns won't have any trouble gatecrashing if Charlotte Underwood is really holding a sex party."

I blew out a long breath. "This is the last time."

"Yes." Jackie coughed into her fist. "Rudolph is grateful for any assistance you can provide."

Yeah, sure. "Even if it turns out they're only playing spin the bottle, this will still be the last time."

Jackie ran a hand through her bleached hair and pursed her lined lips. "He knows."

"I'm just checking. Last time, he didn't honor our agreement."

"The school is ticking along nicely with Carbuncle's cameras in secret locations." She raised her shoulders. "We only need you to infiltrate Charlotte underwood's party and get the name of her older man."

I narrowed my eyes. That wasn't an answer, but then, no one could really speak for Rudolph.

A delivery guy brought some Chinese takeout, then at eight-thirty, I rode with Tola in the front of Tom's screen-filled van, which she explained would receive footage from my cameras via the internet. A quartet of female interns, clad in party dresses, sat in the back. Tom took the scenic route around London and drove on the roads closest to the River Thames. The traffic wasn't bad at this time of the evening, and I relaxed in the front seat and enjoyed the view. When we sped past Chelsea Bridge, near the mansion apartment Sergei rented, I said, "I thought the party was in Chelsea."

Tola nodded. "It's in Chelsea Harbour, on the other side."

We stopped at an ultra-modern, marina development, complete with its own hotel and train station. As expected, Chelsea Heights was a high-rise block that boasted panoramic balconies that stretched around the entire exterior of the building. My breath caught. Did Charlotte's benefactor live in the penthouse? I pictured Mr. Frost, who had probably made a fortune selling illicit items to wealthy school kids at horrific markups and shook my head. If it was him, he probably only rented the apartment for the sex party.

"Good luck." Tom gave me a thumbs-up as I stepped out of his van. "If things don't heat up after two hours, leave as many cameras lying about as you can and come down."

"Right." I walked toward the building and was about to buzz when a young man walked out from the foyer and opened the door. A breath of relief whooshed out of my lungs. It might have been difficult to explain to whoever was on the other end of the intercom that I was Emilia Hobson, Charlotte's arch enemy, and soon-to-be destroyer. He probably should have asked if I was a resident or guest, but I wasn't going to inform him of his security breach. "Thanks."

The man gave me a nod and strolled out in the direction of Chelsea Harbour station, and I headed for the lift. It arrived as soon as I had called it, and I stepped inside and pressed the highest floor, which was twenty-five. That had to be the penthouse, right? When the elevator reached the top, I walked around the doors, but the numbers only went up to fifteen. I pulled out the invitation to check the address. It said number sixteen, as I had remembered, and the apartment name was correct.

"It was all a fucking hoax," I snarled and headed back to the elevator.

Behind me, a door opened, and heavy footsteps approached.

Before I could turn around, a fist smashed against my temple, and I lost consciousness before I reached the ground.

CHAPTER 13

A throbbing on the left of my face forced me awake, only to find myself lying on my side. I stifled a groan. Déjà fucking vu, except tight ropes bound my ankles and wrists, and I wasn't stuffed in a moving trunk with Henry.

Heavy footsteps, presumably belonging to the bastard who had punched me unconscious, dragged around a room. I would have cracked my eyes open if my head didn't hurt so much. The one on the left was probably swollen shut from the way the flesh seemed to pound in time with my rapid pulse.

Everything ached. The back of my head, my shoulder blades, pelvis, hamstrings, even the backs of my calves. It was as though someone had turned me onto my front and beaten me with a club while I had lain unconscious.

The footsteps approached and stopped close to my head. I swallowed hard, trying not to let the man notice I'd regained consciousness. He crouched down, radiating a sickening warmth over my body and filling my nostrils with the scent of stale tobacco, strong coffee, and mint chewing gum. My nostrils twitched involuntarily.

"Awake are you?" asked a familiar voice.

My right eye opened, and the mustached face of Mr. Carbuncle stared down at me with pitiless, gray eyes. I flinched away, a scream catching in my throat. "What's... Why are you here?"

A hand the size of a bunch of bananas jerked forward and grabbed me by the chin. He bared stained teeth and snarled, "You got me fired."

My heart jumped into my throat and galloped at the speed of a runaway horse. "Th-that wasn't me," I said with my jaw pinned down by the man's thick fingers. "Mr. Chaloner kicked the door down and brought the police. I only came to see what was happening."

"Who else could have grassed but you?"

I exhaled a frustrated breath. Why was he out of prison already? "I..." Wriggling out of his grip was futile. The man was too strong. "I don't know, but if you have a list of suspects, I might be able to help."

Mr. Carbuncle's features smoothed out into a blank expression I'd never seen on his miserable face. He released my chin, wrapped his arms around my neck and hoisted me up into a sitting position. A sharp pain, probably from a bruised hip, spread down my legs, making me wince. Dread rumbled through my insides, and I gulped. There was no one I could blame for his arrest but the former headmaster, but Mr. Carbuncle hadn't found me convincing the first time I had mentioned Mr. Chaloner.

With a rage-filled snarl and an ugly twist of his mouth, he drew back his arm and backhanded me across the face. My head snapped to the side with the force of his blow, then my entire body swayed in the same direction. Pain radiated out from my nose and cheek. I stuck out my elbow, in an attempt to cushion my fall, but when it smacked against the parquet floor, a mix of pain and funny bone tingles shot up my arm.

I squeezed my eyes shut, and tears gathered behind my lids. Where were the interns? Surely they were on their way. Maybe they couldn't find me and were waiting for me to gather some clues.

"Where am I?" I asked for the benefit of the cameras I hoped were still in my hair.

"Tucked away where no one will think to find you," he said with a sneer.

"Mr. Carbuncle..." If the cameras were still running, I was sure they had recognized him by now, but I had to make sure his name was recorded in case I ever got out of this mess alive. "Why are you doing this? I've done nothing wrong."

"That's not what I heard." He laced his fingers through my hair and yanked me back up by the roots. My scalp burned with the pull, and a whimper reverberated in my throat. He shook me so hard, my teeth rattled, and something thin and metallic bounced off my hair and onto the ground. "Now, tell me what you told the bloody cops, or I'll lay into you!"

My heart froze, and ice ran through my veins. If anything happened to those cameras, they might never track me to this featureless room.

"I didn—" He released my hair and slammed his fist into my belly. Pain battered through my insides, and I doubled over with a groan.

He lowered his face to mine, his heavy, excited breaths tickling my ear. "I could go on all day, but something tells me you can take a beating."

My heart slammed against my ribcage. If he threatened to cut my face or something equally as hideous, I might not be able to hold out until Tom and the interns found me. I gasped out a sob. Where were they?

"They tell me you've been fucking those three boys." His large, calloused hand stroked my stinging cheek. "That true?"

"No," I said through clenched teeth.

The janitor's rough, thick-fingered hand skimmed my neck in

a parody of a lover's caress. Disgust rippled up and down my gullet, and I wanted to hurl the contents of my stomach into his face.

I jerked away, but he shuffled onto his backside, and wrapped an obscenely strong arm around my back, holding me in place.

My bound hands automatically rose, to cover my breasts with my forearms, but he slipped his fingers underneath them and wrenched at my nipples. I shuddered and tried shrinking away, but that arm tightened around me, bringing us closer.

"I've always wanted one of these model types," he crooned.

"I'm Edward's girlfriend." Hysteria laced my voice, making my words so high pitched, they sounded like a scream. "Don't you think he'd be upset with what you're doing?"

"Mr. Edward didn't lift a finger to help me when I was on the run from the cops, so he can go fuck himself."

My eyes shuttered closed. Mr. Carbuncle must have outrun them the day we'd caught him with that red-haired girl in the year above. Tears stung the back of my eyes. How could the police have been so incompetent? If I didn't think fast and talk my way out of this… I wouldn't let my mind venture into such dark territory.

He ran his nose up and down my cheek in a sickening rhythm that dragged those rough, stinking bristles over my skin.

"S-sir, so far, you've just hit me," I said. "That's not a big deal. B-but if you go any further than this, you could get into a lot of trouble."

His fingertips moved up to my collarbone.

"How about you tell me what evidence you handed over to the police, and I won't smash your face in," he growled.

My muscles tensed in anticipation of the inevitable blow. At any moment, he would hit me again, but he would do worse if I told him that I had given the Saturday Correspondent the recording of Alice's accounts of what he did to girls. It was my fault he was blackmailed into setting up cameras, my fault there was so much evidence in his lodge against him, and my fault that Mr. Chaloner kicked down his door and let in the police.

"Th-that day, I'd just left Elder House, and I saw the police, Mr. Chaloner and Mr. Jenkins. I was curious, so I followed them. You saw the rest."

"But you knew about my filing cabinet."

"It was the only other piece of furniture in the room apart from your desk. I got curious, after seeing you with that girl. There's nothing more to it."

The hand stroking my collar bone wrapped itself around my neck. "That's all?"

"Y-yes."

He slammed me down onto the parquet, sending bolts of pain shooting from the back of my head. "Fucking lies!"

"N-no!" I cried out.

He slid his hand under my tank top, wafting cool air over my bare stomach and lifting my top to my armpits and exposing my bra. "I suppose I'll have to fuck the truth out of you. I'll bet those wet-behind-the-ears boys haven't taken you up the arse yet."

Panicked, I thrashed out with my bound arms. He jerked his head back. I kicked out with my bound legs and hit him in the shins.

"Little bitch!" he snarled.

"The only way you'll get to touch me is after I'm dead." Every word was a struggle, and I fought against the ache in my jaw and in my rapidly swelling lip to speak. "My dad will have you extradited to California, where they have the death penalty. Would you like that, Mr. Carbuncle?"

"Stop," said a man with a cultured voice. He stood in the doorway with his back to us.

The janitor backed away. "Why do you care what happens to the trollop? She's responsible for ruining both our lives."

"We're here for truth and money, not sex with little girls." I strained to recognize his voice. He was older, but I couldn't tell his age, and he spoke with the same kind of accent as most of the people in the school, except he wasn't as overly posh as Duncan or Coates. "Back away from Miss Hobson."

Mr. Carbuncle gave my left breast a hard squeeze before drawing back. "Fine."

I wriggled, and with my bound arms, wrestled my tank top over my bra and most of my stomach. "Thank you."

"Miss Hobson... Emilia," he said without turning around. "Do you deny passing information to the press about the staff and students of Mercia Academy?"

"I—"

"Before you answer, listen to my theory. The leaks only started after you returned from a tumultuous first term during which you were framed for a crime you did not commit."

I kept my face blank. Mr. Carbuncle crouched at my side on his haunches, his oversized forearms resting on his knees. He leaned forward with an ape-like intensity and examined my expression.

"Your stepfather owns a media company and might have in-roads with the Saturday Correspondent." He chuckled. "The Trommel Group is a mass of subsidiaries and shell companies. Mr. Trommel might well own the newspaper. Who knows?"

My heart flipped. Whoever this man was, he had researched Rudolph but wasn't an insider. I stared at his back, ignoring the ever-approaching Mr. Carbuncle.

"My final piece of evidence is the... Valentines Day Massacre, a cute way to phrase a mass character assassination. You distributed tickets within Mercia Academy, possibly inviting everyone who had wronged you to become drunk and make fools of themselves in front of the cameras."

Realization hit me like Carbuncle's fist to the gut. This had to be Mr. Frost, the sycophantic, drug-dealing Latin Master. How else would he have known the tickets had come from me? I'd even suspected he could be Charlotte's older lover. I lowered my head.

Mr. Frost had masterminded Henry's kidnapping and arranged for all the blame to fall on me if anything went wrong. According to Rita, he was extremely intelligent. The man had probably talked his way out of being charged for his crimes and had somehow recruited Mr. Carbuncle to beat me into submission.

There was no way to win against an opponent like him. Especially with my arms and legs tied.

I cleared my throat. "What do you want?"

"The truth," he replied.

"A-alright." I swallowed hard. "I'll tell you everything I know."

CHAPTER 14

Mr. Carbuncle drew back several inches but remained firmly in my line of sight. Even when crouched, the man's hulking form took up my entire vision. His shoulders quivered with impatience, and he ran a glistening, pink tongue along the underside of that bushy, walrus mustache. His excited breaths echoed in my ears, sending tremors of disgust across my gut. Tendrils of panic twined around my lungs and coiled up my windpipe, tightening with each passing second.

Dots appeared before my eyes, and the edges of the empty room spun. With my wrists still bound by tight ropes, I clutched at my neck and tried to suck in deep breaths, but they stuck in the back of my throat.

"Carbuncle," said the man at the door. "Get the girl a glass of water."

"But she's faking—"

"Do it!"

He swooped forward, and muttered a tobacco-scented, "You'd better not be planning anything."

A cold wave of fear and panic and revulsion seized my muscles, and a pained whimper reverberated in the back of my throat. Would he make one last, defiant snatch of my neck to make his point?

He drew back, taking away his stench, and stood. I kept my gaze on the herringbone pattern of the parquet floor until his footsteps receded through the room. It was only when I spied him shuffling through the doorway that the tightness around my lungs loosened, and I could finally exhale.

"He won't be gone long," said the man at the doorway. His brown hair and broad back offered no clues as to his identity, and neither did the navy blazer he wore with black slacks.

"Where am I?" I asked again for the benefit of the hidden cameras.

"An apartment whose owners will be overseas for the next three months. If you ever want to leave here alive, you'll cooperate with us and answer our questions."

I swallowed hard. Everything throbbed. Even speaking with one side of my lips was a painful effort. "When I tell you the truth, Mr. Carbuncle hits me."

He huffed a laugh. "That hardly seems fair, does it?"

I would have clenched my jaw with frustration if it wasn't already swollen and aching, but blood pounded in my ears. This man treated my situation as a big joke, and the worst part was that I couldn't confirm his identity. I turned my head, hoping that the one remaining camera in my hair might pick up a little footage that could give the reporters a clue about my location. I still didn't understand why they hadn't already gotten the police to kick down the door.

The room was empty, save the paint-stained dust sheet underneath me. It reminded me of a show about a forensics expert and serial killer who was meticulously careful about not leaving his victims' DNA in crime scenes. I shook those thoughts away and focused on what I knew. The mystery man had to be affected badly enough by the leaks to have gotten involved with an abduction, so he was either Mr. Chaloner, our headmaster or Mr. Frost, our Latin master.

"Who are you?" I asked.

"The only person standing between you and Carbuncle's wrath."

I squinted my good eye and whizzed through my options. The police had arrested the headmaster. Last term, I'd seen him in cuffs, being bundled into the back of a police car. And Mr. Weaver from the Board of Governors had said he was facing charges of fraud and money laundering. Would they let someone with links to organized crime out on bail? I would have thought they would try to keep him in custody, so he wouldn't use his Swiss Bank Account money to leave the country.

Maybe it wasn't Mr. Frost. He was more than capable of an abduction like this, but his hair was red and thinning, not thick and dark. But if I were going to commit a crime and didn't want to be identified, I would wear a wig.

I knew two things for sure. One, he didn't want me to see his face in case I recognized him, which meant I might go free at some point. And two, he had collaborated with Charlotte, who had told me about the party and had probably left that fake invitation lying about in the hallway for me to find.

My tongue darted out to lick my lips. "What are you going to do to me?"

"You'll remain here until your stepfather pays a ransom of a million pounds."

All hope of leaving the empty apartment alive drained away with my plummeting stomach. Rudolph only cared about maintaining his reputation. He wouldn't care about something as trivial as a dead stepdaughter. "W-what if he doesn't?"

"According to the article in the Saturday Correspondent, he paid that amount to clear your name after the Bourneville kidnapping that never was."

I gulped. "That was to prevent a scandal for himself."

With a chuckle, the man turned his head to the side a fraction. "What kind of stepfather wouldn't pay the ransom of a seventeen-year-old girl? The longer we keep you here, the more injured and debauched you'll become. I'll issue daily pictures to the press, showing your degradation over time. Rudolph Trommel will not allow the world to know him as a heartless bastard."

My blood turned cold. He'd just given me an important clue. He probably wasn't as affected by the leaks as Mr. Carbuncle but had used it as an excuse to let the janitor attack me. This opened up the possibility of culprits to anyone associated with Charlotte or Elder House. A million-pound ransom had universal appeal, and anyone with a bit of ingenuity could have lured me to the fake party.

But one word stuck in my memory like a skewer.

"Debauched?" I rasped.

"You saw Carbuncle. He can't wait to get his hands on your pretty flesh."

Chills spread across the surface of my skin, and I curled my knees into my chest. "H-have you sent the first ransom note?"

"We'll upload it and a few photos as soon as your bruises turn purple."

I stared down at the ropes encasing my wrists and grimaced at the sheer number of undecipherable knots. They weren't taking any chances. Someone must have told Mr. Carbuncle and the mystery man that I had once freed myself from duct tape.

Mr. Carbuncle returned with an opened can of Diet Coke and placed it by my feet. "Your water's in there. Drink."

Holding up my bound wrists, I said, "I can't pick it up."

"I thought I told you not to bind her arms too tightly," said the man from the doorway.

"She's faking." Mr. Carbuncle stepped closer and cupped his crotch. "Pick it up or I'll give you something else to drink."

Before I could scramble down to reach the can, Mr. Carbuncle nudged it with the tip of his boot along the floor to my hip. I stretched out my fingers, picked up the half-empty can, and pretended to drink. Neither of them had asked me any questions yet, and they didn't seem to like each other much. But if I could get them to argue, maybe I could find an opening and escape.

"Go on then," said the janitor. "Talk."

I coughed a few times and gathered my thoughts. "That day the police raided your lodge, we found bank statements with monthly payments from the Saturday Correspondent."

"Those were planted," spat Mr. Carbuncle. "By you, most likely."

"No." I shook my head. Clearly, the janitor was in denial about having succumbed to blackmail, as he had put the incriminating evidence in the filing cabinet himself. "They were real enough to convince the people in the room. But there were a few checks written out to you that you didn't cash, which proves you might have been involved with the paper against your will."

Mr. Carbuncle didn't answer for several moments, but he continued t heavy, excited breaths that make me cringe. Eventually, he said, "A reporter cornered me at the start of the spring term."

"This is the first I'm hearing of your involvement with the press," said the man at the door.

"You know what reporters are like." I let my voice carry. "They probably found out Mr. Carbuncle had a criminal record and blackmailed him."

"I've never been inside," snapped the janitor.

"Oh." I paused. "Then someone must have told them about what you do with school girls."

Mr. Carbuncle swooped down and snatched my neck with such ferocity, he cut off my supply of oxygen. "Shut your fucking mouth!"

A scream caught in the base of my throat, and my eyes bulged. I batted at his hand with my bound hands and kicked at his legs with my bound feet. Tepid water, presumably from the spilled can, seeped into the fabric of my jeans. I'd hit a nerve, but if I couldn't get him to release his strangling grip, I'd die of asphyxiation.

"Get off her," said the man. "Now!"

"You keep quiet," Mr. Carbuncle snarled through clenched teeth, splattering droplets of spittle onto my face. "Keep quiet, or I'll snap your neck." He lowered his face to mine and gripped harder. His harsh tone implied he would snap my neck later, whether I kept his secret or not.

My eyes bulged, and I tried to move my lips, but no sound came out. With my gaze locked onto his crazed, bloodshot eyes, I nodded.

The janitor released his grip and shoved me so hard, my head bounced on the parquet floor.

"I mean it, Carbuncle," said the man. "If you touch her again today, we'll cut you out of the deal, and you'll get no share in the ransom."

My breaths came in labored pants, and my sore throat convulsed with relief. The man at the door had a business partner. Charlotte, most likely, who had lured me to the apartment building in the first place. But what if he wasn't the headmaster or Mr. Frost? What if he was the man who had paid for Charlotte's academy fees and cosmetic surgeries?

Mr. Carbuncle stepped back, but his scuffed boots remained in my line of sight.

I rolled up to a sitting position and shuffled out from the dust sheet and propped myself up against the wall. If they were going to kill me, they could leave DNA evidence and get themselves caught.

"You were saying, Miss Hobson?" asked the man. "What exactly does Mr. Carbuncle do with girls?"

My gaze flickered to the janitor, who stiffened.

Trepidation skittered down my spine and settled into my roiling stomach. Would the threat of not getting his share of the money be enough to stave off his violent impulses? Did it matter, if the man would allow Mr. Carbuncle to do worse with each passing day Rudolph didn't pay the ransom?

I gulped in several deep breaths to steady myself and spoke. "Wwhen Mr. Chaloner kicked down the door to his lodge, we found him face-down between the legs of an upper-sixth former. That's the bribe he takes from the girls. M-mostly with Ch-Charlotte Underwood and her friends."

The room went silent, and I flinched. When the blows didn't arrive, I peeked up through my lashes. Perhaps the unknown man wanted me intact for the first round of photos, so he could show a daily progression of additional beatings and force Rudolph's hand.

"Charlotte," said the man, his voice laden with menace.

Mr. Carbuncle shot me a venomous look. His hands curled into fists and he jerked forward. "She's lying."

I clamped my mouth shut and raised my bound hands over my face.

"He rapes them?" asked the man.

The janitor's quickened breaths filled my eardrums.

I blurted, "They all come to him willingly and exchange sexual favors for help."

"What kind of... help?" asked the man through clenched teeth.

My gaze flicked up to Mr. Carbuncle. The mustache that took up most of the middle of his face quivered with malevolence. My stomach churned, and I reminded myself that the only way I might get through this ordeal was to create discord among my abductors.

"When a girl forgets her keys and is locked out of her room, she needs to go to Mr. Carbuncle."

The man's back stiffened. "What?"

"No," cried Mr. Carbuncle. "You've got to believe me. I only went with the girls who visited my lodge and wanted something over and above. It was never for things like unlocking doors or replacing lost keys"

"Then what did you do for them?"

The chill in the man's voice made me think he might be more dangerous than Mr. Carbuncle. When his elbow rose as though to pull something out of his inside pocket, I drew in a sharp breath through my nostrils. What if he had a gun? I fixed my gaze on the can of diet coke lying on its side on the dust sheet. While there was still hope of using me for a ransom, he wouldn't shoot me... yet.

"M-Mr. Carbuncle let Charlotte into my room to search it," I blurted. "I caught them on camera. And there was the time she put something in my shampoo, the time she put dye on my clothes, and the time they both arranged for a crowd of students to attack me."

The janitor backhanded me across the face. My head jerked back and hit the wall, and pain ricocheted through my skull. With a nervous, high-pitched giggle, he said, "She'll say anything to make trouble."

"I'm. Not. Lying."

"Shut up!" He booted me in the stomach. Pain lanced through my belly, but it was still less excruciating than the time Charlotte kicked me in the diaphragm. "Or your stepfather will need to pay another million when I make a tape of you choking down my cock."

"Stop," snapped the man. "She'll be unrecognizable with these bruises. Get out and take a cigarette break."

My eyes squeezed shut, and a boulder of regret dropped into my stomach. I'd overplayed my hand, and now the man was more concerned about the ransom money than about Charlotte's virtue.

Mr. Carbuncle stalked out of the room, opened a door and then slammed it shut. It sounded like an external door, but I couldn't be sure.

The man turned around, holding a huge SLR camera in front of his face. One hand held the curved grip underneath the shutter, while the other cupped an oversized lens, obscuring the entirety of his features.

A pained breath whistled out of my lungs. He wanted these photos as high-resolution as possible to capture every detail of my bruises. With photos of my injuries getting worse each day, and the inclusion of a few with Mr. Carbuncle, the man looked to shame Rudolph into paying my ransom.

After the last photo, he turned around and stepped through the open doorway. "I'll be leaving for an hour. Maybe longer. For your own safety, don't say anything while I'm gone to rile Carbuncle."

Terror warbled in the back of my throat. He had his day one photo. Now Mr. Carbuncle would be free to hurt me however he pleased!

"Don't leave," I whispered. "He'll kill me for telling you what he did with Charlotte."

"He won't let you die." The man walked into the darkened hallway. A door creaked open, then a moment later, it clicked shut.

A wave of determination tightened my muscles, and I sucked in a deep breath. If I didn't find a way to leave before Mr. Carbuncle returned from his cigarette break, I probably wouldn't want to live after he'd finished with me.

Sitting with both feet firmly on the ground, I pushed my back into the wall, and used my thighs to propel myself up. The pressure exacerbated the pain around my shoulders, my lumbar, and the back of my head, but I clenched my teeth and forced myself to keep going. Sweat beaded on my brow, and my pulse echoed in my ears, but I ignored everything to push myself to standing.

I hobbled across the room, through the doorway, and into the darkened hall, hoping that the man had left the front door unlocked. It was one of those stainless steel smart door locks with a digital display. I gripped its handle with my bound hands and pulled down.

It was stuck and probably needed an app to unlock it.

A cry of frustration flew from between my lips, and I rushed back to the room. If the apartment wasn't too high off the ground, I would have to jump.

As soon as I crossed the threshold of the room, my gaze locked onto a tall, dark figure standing outside the window. He held his smartphone like a torch, its flash illuminating the empty space.

CHAPTER 15

I froze at the doorway, my heart in my throat, and stared at the dark figure at the window. He was too tall to be Tom, the Saturday Correspondent's tech guy, and wasn't wearing the uniform of a police officer. Whoever he was, he had to be better than an enraged and oversexed Mr. Carbuncle. The man made a shooing motion with his hand, which I interpreted to mean he didn't want me to come any closer.

With a nod, I remained at the doorway. My gaze darted to the front door, which remained closed... for now. How long did it take to smoke a cigarette? Two minutes? Five?

The dark figure tucked his smartphone away, plunging himself in semi-darkness. Then he drew his arm all the way back and punched the glass with his gloved fist. Shards flew into the room and clinked over the parquet floor and onto the electric heater beneath the sill. I clapped my hand over my mouth and gasped. Had he hurt himself? And what the hell was he standing on, a ladder? We had to be several stories high, as there were no views of street lights from beyond the window.

The dark figure hooked his arm through the gap he had created in the broken glass and fiddled with the window lock. After a moment, his arm sagged.

"Emilia," said a familiar, smoky voice. "See if you can open it from your end."

My hands dropped from my face. "B-Blake?"

"Hurry!"

I rushed over to the window, the soles of my boots crunching over broken glass, and twisted a metal lever on the window lock. Like the one on the door, it was stuck fast. I peered at its mechanism and found a tiny keyhole. "It's locked."

"Climb out, then." He raised his head, as though looking over my shoulder. "Hurry, before he comes back."

Jagged shards clung to the window frame, looking like they would slice me open if I dared to climb out. "We have to clear the glass." I glanced over my shoulder at the dust sheet. "Hold on."

Blake picked at the pieces of glass with his gloved hands and threw them down into the room. I picked up the cloth in my arms, rushed back to the window, and with a combination of fingers and teeth, I wrapped it several times around my hands, so it resembled a mitt. While I removed the pieces of glass in the lower part of the window, Blake took care of the ones above. All throughout, my hands shook, and my heart hammered against my chest, urging me to hurry the fuck up before the return of Mr. Carbuncle.

As soon as I cleared all the bottom shards, I wiped the glass from the top of the electric heater, hoping I'd caught the worst of them. "Th-that will have to be enough. We can't risk him coming back."

Blake offered me his gloved hand. "Take it slow," he said in a voice too panicked to be soothing. "I'll catch you."

I stepped forward, but my mind conjured up an image of a long, rubber ladder that would sway like an upside-down pendulum the moment I added my weight to Blake's. One foot stumbled over the other, and a band of panic wound around my chest and squeezed my lungs, making me grip the windowsill.

"W-what are you standing on?" I asked.

"A balcony. Hurry. We still have a way to run."

The tightness around my chest loosened, giving me the courage I needed to crawl out. I grasped Blake's hand and placed a knee onto the electric heater. The movement sent pain lancing across my ribs, making me hiss and flinch.

He drew in a gasp. "Emilia, are you—"

"I-I'm fine," I lied.

With Blake's help, I hoisted my other knee up onto the top of the electric heater. Blake reached through the window and wrapped his arms around my back. His touch aggravated every single bruise on my ribs. A whimper caught in my throat, and I stiffened with the pain.

He stilled. "I've hurt you."

"Keep going," I said between clenched teeth. "Please."

He continued pulling me through, each touch exacerbating my already battered body. Mr. Carbuncle had either bashed me about while I was unconscious, or I'd been too scared to feel the extent of his blows during his interrogation.

My feet cleared the window sill and they landed onto the concrete floor of the balcony with a thud, giving my insides an agonizing jolt that made me double over and clutch my stomach.

"Emilia!" Blake grabbed my arm, his voice breathy with concern.

"I'm fine," I gritted out. "We have to keep moving."

A four-foot-wide, concrete balcony stretched across the side of the building, ending in a metal partition, where it continued over the territory of the next apartment. My stomach clenched painfully at the thought of all that climbing. I could barely walk in my battered condition.

Blake crouched onto one knee. "Get on my back."

I drew back, wrapping my arms around my middle. "But I'll slow you—"

"Now. You're clearly injured and can't move fast."

I edged toward his back and placed my arms over his shoulders. He was right. But I hoped I wouldn't weigh down his movements or cause him to overbalance as he traveled through the balconies. Blake hooked his arms under my knees and stood. My insides groaned with the pain of being jostled, but I pressed my lips together and breathed hard.

Blake turned to the left and hurried toward the barrier separating the apartment from that of its neighbor's. Each footfall made my insides hurt, but I tightened my aching stomach muscles to lessen the impact.

Behind us, a door from deep within the apartment yawned open. My heart jumped into my throat. "He's back!"

Blake scrambled over the partition of the first balcony and sprinted across the second. From further away, another door slammed open.

"Fuuuck!" shouted Mr. Carbuncle.

My insides turned cold, and a whimper reverberated in the back of my throat. "H-hurry," I whispered. "He'll be at the window, now."

Blake didn't reply. He vaulted over the second balcony partition and sprinted across the next. I clung to his back, tightened my grip on his shoulders, and clamped my legs harder around his middle. Each of his movements sent lances of pain through my insides. None of that mattered. Blake might be younger, but he was built like a runway model, not a mountain gorilla like Carbuncle. And I was weighing him down.

Mr. Carbuncle's furious roar made the hairs on the back of my neck stand on end, and he made the pained cry of someone who had just slashed himself on a shard of broken glass.

My breaths quickened, and my pulse thrashed harder between my ears. If he ever caught up with us... Terror blanked my mind, and I focussed on the sounds behind us. The dull thud of heavy feet landing on concrete, a muttered curse, and the stampede of running footsteps.

Blake's thrashing heartbeat reverberated through his back and into my chest, making my own accelerate to match his.

The sound of a body hitting metal, most probably Mr. Carbuncle crashing against the barrier between balconies, made the lining of my stomach tremble. I couldn't look over my shoulder, in case I slowed Blake's movements, but the crash of feet mere yards behind us was indication enough that Mr. Carbuncle had built up his own rhythm of hurdling over the barriers.

Sprint, leap, thud. Sprint, leap, thud. Blake ran like a man chased by a demon. I clung tighter to his torso and closed my eyes, clenching my teeth against the red-hot pain of my organs thrashing within an already agonized body. Tendrils of fear clawed at my spine, as though sent by Mr. Carbuncle himself.

It was probably my fevered imagination, but someone's hot breath warmed the back of my neck, and panting breaths filled my ears.

But when the tips of huge fingers swiped at my back, I screamed.

Up ahead, something creaked. "Did you find—"

Blake swerved left, barreled into someone, and shouted, "Close the door!"

A door slammed shut. Blake tripped, stumbled, and righted himself. Behind me, a key turned in the lock, just as heavy fists pounded against metal and glass.

"What the devil is going on?" asked a cultured male voice.

My limbs, which up until now had been rigid, flopped with relief, and I slid down Blake's back and onto the parquet floor. Adrenaline receded away, and every ounce of pain it had kept at bay surged forward. I curled into a ball on the ground and groaned.

"Emilia!" Blake knelt at my side.

"I-is she alright?" asked the other voice.

"No." Blake's voice broke. "That man out on the balcony hurt her."

"We must call nine-nine-nine!" cried the man.

"I have the sergeant's mobile. They're somewhere in the building."

Overwhelming, red-hot pain settled through my insides, up one side of my face and pounded to the beat of my heart. I squeezed my eyes shut and refused all offers of a drink or a pill or a sofa. Right now, I wouldn't be able to take another jostling.

Everything hurt so much, I thought I would die. Blake knelt beside me, rubbing my hands, one of the few parts of my body that didn't hurt. He murmured to someone on the phone and asked the man in the apartment for his floor and apartment number.

Moments later, a heavy fist pounded on the door. It opened and a group of even heavier footsteps entered the room.

Just as a male voice called my name, I passed out.

~

I awoke, not in a busy emergency room, but in a well-appointed office with a middle-aged man clad in a tweed, three-piece suit, standing over me. Square, horn-rimmed glasses magnified his cerulean-blue eyes, and his thin lips turned down at the corners. The only thing that indicated he might be a doctor was the stethoscope around his neck and two nurses in navy blue uniforms flanking him on both sides.

"Ah, Miss Hobbs," he said in the same kind of difficult-to-understand upper-class accent as Duncan and Coates. "I'm glad to see you're back with us."

My gaze darted around the room. It reminded me somewhat of Edward's study back in Elder House, with its mahogany bookshelves, matching leather desk, and chesterfield sofas, but I lay on an examination table in the corner, and at the wall in front of me was a sink hanging beneath three different types of dispensers. On the other side of the room, certificates adorned the walls along with framed pictures of the skeletal and muscular systems. This had to be some kind of upscale doctor's office.

"My name is George Chumley-Stokes," said the doctor. "Mr. Simpson-West insisted you be brought here for treatment instead of the local A and E. I gave you a mild sedative when you arrived, as you were rather agitated, and you've had X-rays, CT scans, and an ultrasound. Fortunately, there are no cracked ribs or significant internal injuries, but you'll be sore for a very long time."

"But I feel fine." My face was tight.

His eyes softened. "That will be the morphine, my dear. It should last until bedtime, and after that, you'll need to take a course of analgesics and anti-anxiety medications to help you rest."

"Where's Blake?" I asked.

"He's in the waiting room," said the Asian nurse. "Would you like us to let him in?"

I nodded.

Dr. Chumley-Stokes furrowed his brow. "Two police officers are also outside. Are you ready to speak with them?"

"Yes."

A moment later, Blake stepped into the room, his face pale, and eyes bloodshot. As soon as we locked eyes, he flinched. The movement was so slight I might have missed it, if it hadn't sent a bolt of fear through my gut.

"Wh-what's wrong?"

"Enough time has passed for the swelling and bruises to emerge." The doctor clapped his hand on Blake's shoulder and gave him the kind of squeeze that indicated they knew each other extremely well. He said to Blake, "Your young lady is fine and just needs a little rest and care."

Blake's shoulders sagged with relief, and the corners of his mouth flickered into a smile. He crossed the room, sat at a chair beside the examination table, and took my hand. "How are you feeling?"

"Not too bad, considering," I replied.

Before he could say much else, a pair of uniformed officers stepped through the doors. The shorter of them, who wore the flat cap of a sergeant, asked, "Miss Hobson, what can you tell us about Peter Underwood?"

CHAPTER 16

I knew the name, of course. Peter Underwood was Charlotte's older brother. The one she said worked for the Saudi Royal family but had amassed enough gambling debts to ruin the Underwood family fortunes. What I didn't understand was his connection with Mr. Carbuncle.

The police revealed that the Saturday Correspondent had shared recordings of Peter Underwood dragging me across the hallway and down a few flights of stairs into an empty apartment. Because he had positioned me face-down, they were unable to work out exactly how many flights of stairs I'd been moved, and which apartment they had used as their hideout.

All throughout the explanation, Blake stared at me with the kind of tight expression people used to hold themselves back from saying something they would regret. I had no doubt that once the police had left, he would explain how he had managed to find me before them.

The sedative must have still lingered in my system because I remained calm as I told the officers as much as I could, considering

I had been unconscious for most of the ordeal, and they probably had the footage from the camera in my hair. The taller constable wrote down my statement, read it out to me, and got me to sign.

As they stood, I said, "Please tell me you've arrested them both."

The officers exchanged guilty looks. My heart plummeted. They had the camera footage, known I was in an apartment within the Chelsea Heights building, yet they still managed to lose my abductors? What did this mean for my safety?

"We caught Mr. Underwood as he left the building, but we believe Mr. Carbuncle may be hiding in one of the balconies."

"Right," I said. This was the second time bungling cops had let him get away.

One of the nurses escorted them out of the room. Blake scooted forward, his expression pained. "Carbuncle didn't leave the buildings out of any of the exits." Blake wrapped his hand around mine and brought my knuckles to his lips. "I think he scaled down the balconies and escaped while the police were in that man's apartment."

"He could be anywhere."

"We won't let him get close to you again," replied Blake.

My gaze dropped to our joined hands. The sedative muted my feelings, but a little voice in the back of my head admonished me for ignoring the boys' warnings. They had even offered me a distraction to stop me from going to London, but I'd been so determined to expose Charlotte's secrets that I'd run head-first into a trap.

Dr. Chumley-Stokes strolled in, rubbing his hands together. The Asian nurse from before held a small paper bag.

"Right-ho." His gaze dropped to our joined hands and then back to my face. "I have your prescription. One co-codamol every four hours with a maximum of eight a day. Temazepam half an hour before bedtime. No alcohol."

"Thank you, Doctor." I let my eyes close.

"Thank you, Stephen," said Blake.

"Not at all, my boy. I'm just glad the rumors about you weren't true. Hold tight, and we'll arrange transportation to the palace."

My eyes snapped open. "P-palace?"

Dr. Chumley-Stokes furrowed his thick brows. "Kensington, of course. You can't sleep in an uncomfortable dorm with injuries like that, and you're not well enough for a journey of any kind back to Mercia. That won't do at all."

"I'll put you in my room," said Blake.

My insides squirmed. Wasn't that where the former Princess of Wales and her son and daughters had lived before they all died in the London bombing? Even if Blake hadn't told his mother and stepfather that I'd leaked the video of him talking crap about becoming a prince upon the Prince of Wales' death, I was still a foreigner entering a royal palace.

I shot him a worried look. Didn't there need to be a protocol of some sort? Weeks of introductions, vetting, and letter writing? He couldn't just sneak me in like it was just a regular home.

"I-I don't know about this," I whispered.

Blake kissed a spot just above my right eyebrow. "It'll be fine. Mother's up in Balmoral with my stepfather."

"Where?"

"Scotland."

A sigh slid from my swollen lips. Maybe it wouldn't be too bad. Besides, it wasn't like I had any options. The abductors had taken my jacket, which had contained both phones, so I couldn't contact Mom for help. I doubted she would respond, anyway.

Jackie had probably told Rudolph, who would be more interested in the story generated from my abduction than in my wellbeing. Sergei was somewhere in Europe on his tour, and I really didn't want to bother Dad.

"Alright," I said.

The doctor gave me a mild sedative for the journey, and the Asian nurse, who I learned was called Priya, accompanied us in an ambulance all the way to the palace. The morphine dulled my senses, but at some point, armed police detectives boarded the vehicle and inspected it for bombs and whatever else before letting us through the gates. There were a few more inspections, then the nurse moved me to a chair, and Blake wheeled me through hallways wider than those of any grand hotel or museum.

My mouth dried as I took in the crystal chandeliers, damask wallpaper, gilded paintings, and marble sculptures.

"Th-this is where you live?" I whispered.

"Not if I can help it," Blake whispered back.

My gaze rose to a ceiling decorated with gold-leaf cornices and with frescos of patterns I couldn't make out with my slightly blurred vision. The palace was breathtaking, and if I had paid for a tour, I would have been impressed, but this certainly wasn't a home.

After traveling up an old-fashioned elevator with an intricate design etched onto its gold-colored doors and through another maze of corridors, we reached a thick, wooden door and entered a smaller hallway. Its interior reminded me of a regular apartment with cream-colored carpets, alabaster walls, and landscape paintings amidst family portraits. I

f I wasn't so exhausted, I might have taken in more detail, but a combination of the sedative, painkillers, and adrenaline crash made my eyes droop.

Priya walked ahead of us and seemed to know her way to Blake's room, a space larger than the hidden room at the Valentine's party, also with a four-poster bed, but not nearly as cozy. I slumped in the chair, feeling the stirrings of several oncoming aches. Blake rummaged into a chest of drawers, pulled out a set of pajamas, which he left on the bed, and walked out of the room.

"May I change you out of your gown, Miss Hobson?" asked the nurse.

I hummed my agreement and let her move my heavy limbs about until she had removed the robe and gown and changed me into Blake's silk pajamas. Then, with practiced efficiency, she helped me out of the wheelchair and tucked me into a bed that felt like I was floating on clouds. After giving me two pills, she placed my prescription bottles on the bedside table and walked to the doorway.

"I'll return tomorrow to change your dressings." She inclined her head and left the room.

Blake opened the door a couple of inches and knocked. "May I come in?"

A yawn slipped from my lips. "It's your room."

He padded inside, clasping his hands at his stomach. Gone were the usual smiles and confident posture, replaced by the vulnerable expression I'd only glimpsed last term during the times I had deliberately ignored him.

"Is there anything you need?" he asked. "Water, juice, something hot?"

I rubbed the front of my throat. "Water, please."

He gave me a sharp nod and bolted out of the room. My shoulders sagged. After everything he had done for me, why did I make him so uncomfortable?

I wasn't sure how much time passed, but when he returned with the glass of water, my eyelids felt so heavy, I just wanted to close my eyes and sleep for however long it would take my body to heal from Mr. Carbuncle's attacks. Blake placed the glass to my lips, and I let the cool liquid spill onto my tongue and wash away the dry, bitter taste.

"I'm sorry for the part I played in…" He waved his hand at me. "This."

"You weren't the one who told them my location. That was Charlotte."

His face twisted. "If we hadn't pushed you so far in the first term, you wouldn't have gone after us, and Charlotte wouldn't have set her brother onto you."

"Mr. Carbuncle did this."

"And who bribed him to open the door of your room so we could tamper with your things? It was us. Carbuncle would never have paid you much notice if we hadn't been so hell-bent on toying with you."

I stared down at my hands folded over my lap. It was true. They had hurt me. I had hurt them back, and now I was hurt again. But this time, it was even worse than before.

Blake slid his fingers over mine. "Everything that happened last term... the public disgrace, that stint in rehab, and the fallout from this term... I realize now that I brought it all onto myself."

"Are you saying I deserved the beating Mr. Carbuncle gave me?"

"No! Never," his voice was rough. "I'm saying that none of this would have happened if we'd just left you alone. Sorry just isn't enough."

Tears gathered in my eyes and clouded my vision. I continued staring at our entwined hands, not knowing how to respond. Despite the painkiller and sedative, a deep ache formed in my heart and spread up to my throat, which felt raw from screaming. The memories of Mr. Carbuncle's fists and feet and groping hands were too fresh for me to say I forgave anyone, but this was the heartfelt apology I had been seeking all of last term.

Blake drew back, taking away the warmth of his touch. "I'll leave you to rest."

I blinked and raised my head, making the tears drop onto the champagne-colored quilt. "Please, don't go... I want you to stay with me."

He closed his eyes and sucked in a breath so deep, his entire chest expanded. "Emilia, do you know what you're saying?" he asked in a single exhale. "Because—"

"I wouldn't be able to sleep without you at my side."

His gaze darted to the sleeping pills on the bedside, but he didn't comment. "Alright." He licked his lips. "B-but I don't wear pajama tops."

"That's fine."

He walked around the bed and peeled off his clothes. If I wasn't feeling so groggy, I might have enjoyed the show, but a wave of fatigue had just washed over me, causing my eyes to droop. I sank further into the pillows and mattress. A yawn built up in the back of my throat, but my jaws were too stiff to open.

The other side of the bed shifted. Blake climbed in and lay beside me on his back, his arms at his side, and his expression unnaturally neutral.

"Do I look that hideous?" I asked.

"No," he said without looking at me.

"What's wrong?"

"I..." A breath huffed out of his nostrils. "I don't know what to do." His pupils rotated to the corner of his eyes. "Don't laugh."

I don't know why. It was me who was drugged and who'd had the shit kicked out of me by Carbuncle, but a lump of pity formed in the back of my throat. Blake, the incorrigible flirt and consummate man-whore didn't know what to do with a girl he wasn't about to fuck. Blake, who lived in a palace, was the one acting intimidated in the presence of a girl who probably looked like the elephant man.

"Let me lie on your shoulder?" I asked.

He nodded and stretched out his left arm.

I eased myself off Nurse Priya's nest of pillows and laid my head on Blake's shoulder. He was warm and firm and smelled of camphor and spice.

"Do you need more water?" he asked.

My eyes fluttered closed. "I'll have something to drink later."

He gave me another kiss on the forehead. "You know… it's alright to cry."

Warmth filled my heart, radiated throughout my chest, and released the knot of resentment I had held whenever I thought of the part Blake played during Edward and Charlotte's campaign against me in the first term. I clasped his shoulder and squeezed.

"Thank you, Blake."

CHAPTER 17

*B*lake was already out of bed and halfway to the door by the time I awoke within Nurse Priya's nest of pillows. Up ahead, and through the curtains of the four-poster bed, someone outside the room turned the door handle. Before the door swung more than two feet open, Blake jammed one side of his body against it, causing whoever stood behind the door to huff with indignation.

"Master Blake." A man's clipped tones cut through the fog in my mind. He spoke with the haughtiness I'd only ever heard from people who worked in high-class establishments but acted like they could condescend to people who didn't meet their standards. A tray protruded through the gap in the door. "I was informed you were back in residence, and—"

"Breakfast? I'll take that, thank you." Blocking the door with his foot, Blake wrapped his hands around the tray and pulled it out of the man's hands.

"Will the young lady require something to eat?" asked the man, who I assumed was a palace servant.

"There's plenty here for two. *Thank you.*" Blake said the last two words with the tone most used to tell others to fuck off.

I rubbed my fingers over my brow, and the entire left side of my face throbbed. Everything returned in a painful rush. Waking up in agony. Mr. Carbuncle's attacks. That harrowing chase through the darkened balconies. A fog lifted from my mind, taking with it the effects of last night's morphine and codeine, bringing forth a collision of aches and pains. A groan slipped from my lips.

Blake flung his weight against the door and turned a lock. "Emilia!"

I reached for the pill bottles on the side table, but the movement felt like a giant fist slamming into my ribs. I flinched. Through the side of my mouth that wasn't swollen, I asked, "Painkillers, please?"

Blake set down the tray on a side table with a clink of china and silverware, rushed to my side, and handed me a glass of orange juice. He disappeared behind the curtain of the four-poster again and returned with one of the prescription bottles. With hands that shook, Blake unscrewed the bottle, placed a pill between my lips, and brought the glass to the good side of my mouth.

Cold, sweet liquid trickled on my tongue, drenching my dry mouth. It gathered in the back of my throat, dislodging the tablet from where it had stuck, allowing me to gulp the mixture down.

A breath of relief escaped my lungs. Hopefully, it wouldn't take long to work. "Thanks."

"Are you hungry?" he murmured.

"Not really," I slouched back into my nest of pillows. "But I suppose I'd better eat something so the painkiller doesn't hurt my stomach."

Blake turned in the direction of the side table, where he had left the breakfast tray. "There's porridge... And scrambled eggs. Those are soft, aren't they?"

I reached out, ignored the pain radiating through my ribs, and placed my fingertips on his forearm. "Thank you."

"What for?" He turned around, chocolate-brown eyes wide. His messy, black hair flopped over his face, framing his beautiful, high cheek-boned features to perfection.

"For taking care of me."

I thought Blake would smile and say something flirty, but he just stared back with dark, haunted eyes and nodded. He walked back to the tray with his broad shoulders slumped and his head hung low.

Sadness, tinged with a little guilt, washed over me. I dipped my chin to my tightening chest and let out a weary breath. Blake should be feeling proud, not disturbed. He had warned me not to go, then followed me all the way to London and rescued me from a terrible fate, yet he acted like he'd put the bruises on my face and body.

Moments later, he returned with the whole tray and placed it over my lap. Its tall, splayed legs meant that the base of the tray hovered several inches over my body, giving me enough space to turn if I needed it. Whoever had prepared his breakfast had laden it with more than a single person could eat. A bowl of fruit salad, porridge, a full English breakfast, and a rack of toast sat on that tray, along with a small pot of tea, a cup and saucer, a milk jug, butter, marmalade, silverware and condiments.

"Help yourself to anything," he stepped away and wrapped his arms around his bare chest.

"Sit with me," I said.

Blake pulled up a velvet cocktail chair and brought it to my bedside. While I picked at the porridge, he worked his way through every other dish on that tray. As he ate, he stole nervous glances, looking like he wanted to say something. Each time I met his gaze, he would turn back to his food without speaking. There was only so much I could keep down with a stomach that felt like it had been caved in with a battering ram, and when I declared myself finished, Blake left the tray outside and shut the door.

Enough time had passed that the painkiller melted away the bulk of the pain, taking with it a layer of tension. I let my gaze wander around. It reminded me of one of those hotel rooms made up to look like a palace, except this was the real thing. Heavy, champagne-colored silk curtains hung from the four-poster, giving me a glimpse of alabaster walls and the cream carpet I had seen the previous night. Most of the furniture were carved ornamental pieces with gilded bronze handles and ornaments.

The only thing that looked vaguely out of place was a black-and-white photo on the wall, depicting a dark-haired, high cheek-boned woman who could easily have been a model. She stood next to a pale, nondescript man with a curled mustache.

"Are those your parents?" I asked.

Blake returned to the bedside chair and gave me a wan smile. His gaze lingered over the swollen side of my face, which made my fingers twitch to explore the damage. I didn't in case it brought the pain back.

"Yes," he replied. "That's my mother and father on their wedding day."

I eyed her ivory dress with its 1980's shoulder pads and a plunging neckline that dipped down to her sternum. "She's not wearing a wedding dress."

"They married in Chelsea Town Hall. Bridal wear was optional."

"Oh. Were they married for long?"

He glanced down into his clasped hands. "Until the beginning of my second year."

I would have said I was sorry, but some divorces were actually beneficial. For example, Dad didn't realize he had a drug problem until the moment he discovered Mom left and had taken me with her.

"My father's mental state deteriorated when my mother befriended the prince."

I swallowed. During our supposed captivity, Henry had mentioned something about Blake's promiscuous mother driving his father to drink. I kept silent, not wanting to probe. Since the man had died in an alcohol-related car accident, I let it up to Blake to decide if he wanted to continue on the subject.

He rested his forearms on his knees and blew hair out of his eyes through the side of his mouth. "My father described her as the kind of woman who drives men wild but not away. She's a free spirit, I suppose, but he couldn't see that until it was too late."

"I'm... sorry."

His Adam's apple bobbed up and down. "I'm not," he said in a tight voice. "He pinned all his hopes on the one woman who would never stay faithful. And even when she divorced him and married the prince, he couldn't move on. A man should be dignified about these things, but he fell apart in front of the nation."

I chewed my lip. It seemed a little uncharitable to judge someone harshly for being heartbroken, but I held my silence. I'd never seen Dad drunk or high on drugs, or if I had, I couldn't remember, since Mom took me away when I was five. If Blake's family had stayed together until he was twelve or thirteen, he must have witnessed some ugly, scarring scenes.

"I was at school when the worst of it happened. Every time he got into a drunken brawl, it would be emblazoned on the front pages of the tabloids. He lost everything. His wealth, his health, his reputation, and when the palace couldn't do anything else to stop him from self-destruction, he lost his life."

"Oh, I'm so sorry." I reached out for his hand. "Do you remember what he was like before things went wrong?"

"It's hard to tell," he said with a rueful smile. "He was always controlling, and if she didn't listen to him, he'd resort to violence. I don't blame Mother for leaving, although I wished she had done it sooner."

I winced and gave his hand a squeeze. One evening with the likes of Mr. Carbuncle was enough for a lifetime. It was hard to imagine being in that situation for years.

Blake shook his head. "Before I went away to the academy, he would tell me never to get married. That it was the death of all men. I'd probably been too young and wrapped up in myself to notice the cracks in their relationship until I saw evidence of it in the paper."

"Were you friends with Edward and Henry in your first year?"

He smiled. "I got close to Edward when he lost his mother. Our housemaster asked me to drop by his room after prep to keep him company. That was around the time the papers published pictures of Mother and the prince. Maybe he saw the writing on the wall and thought we might need to support each other during the years."

"What about Henry?"

"He was more Edward's friend than mine at first. They both had sports in common. But Henry came through for me a year later, when the papers printed pictures of my mother… in a compromising position with the prince while she was still married to my father. The three of us would fight anyone who dared call her a trollop."

My head snapped up. "That's why you never joined in on the name-calling."

He squeezed his eyes shut. "I should have stopped them. I'm so sorry."

I shook my head. "How can I hold a grudge against you after what you did for me?"

"If I'd gotten there sooner—"

"They might have knocked you out and held you for ransom, too. Then who would have saved us?"

Someone knocked on the door, and Blake rushed to answer it before they turned the doorknob. It was a woman who spoke in hushed tones, asking if she could come in to vacuum. The man from breakfast was with her, demanding to be let in to check the room.

I closed my eyes and sighed. What were they looking for? Drugs? I didn't understand how Blake could tolerate so many interfering busybodies. When Blake tried slamming the door on them, they didn't budge. I rolled my eyes. If whatever they were looking for was a big deal, they would have brought one of the armed detectives.

While Blake bickered with the servants, I studied the picture of his mother and father. His mother stared ahead at the camera, striking a fierce pose, while his father cast her an adoring look that said he was lucky to have married someone so stunning. My heart sank at the thought of how tragically the relationship had worked out. Eventually, Blake told the servants to fuck off, which worked, and they backed away and let him lock the door.

He strolled back with a sheepish grin. My gaze lingered over his strong biceps, prominent pecs with dusky nipples, and tight eight-pack. He didn't have the same bulk of Henry or even Edward, but his muscles rippled tantalizingly with every breath. Instead of sitting back on the chair, he joined me in the bed. I lay on his chest, breathing in his spicy, sandalwood scent and ran my fingertips over the tight ridges of his abdominal muscles.

"I would think that after your mother's infidelity, you wouldn't be interested in sharing me with anyone."

The corner of his lip curled into a smile. "The others each have their reasons for wanting to share a girl, so I can't speak for them. But if I was going to pin everything on one woman, I'd rather have one I shared with my best friends. Henry and Edward are the two people I love most in the world."

"Are they both bisexual?"

"Edward's mostly straight, although he likes to watch. Henry... He's never expressed an interest in anyone else until you."

"Are you and Henry a couple?"

He paused. "Best friends with benefits."

My hand, which had been rubbing up and down Blake's abs bumped his silk-covered erection.

Blake chuckled. "Sorry about that. It has a mind of its own."

A tiny laugh bubbled up in my chest. "I'm not complaining."

Someone rattled the door. Blake raised his head. "Bugger off!"

A mechanism turned, and an elegant woman stepped into the room, her dark eyes blazing. Flanking her were two burly men who were either bodyguards or plain-clothed detectives. From the black hair swept in a messy chignon, dark skin, high cheekbones, and full lips, she could only be one person. Blake's mother.

"Boy," she snapped. "I've just had to take a helicopter from Balmoral because eight different members of staff have called my husband with news that my son is hiding a battered girl in his room. What the hell is going on?"

CHAPTER 18

Mrs. Simpson-West strode to the end of the bed, clad in a teal, one-piece suit I suspected was backless. She wore it with a pearl necklace and a matching tuxedo-style jacket. In real life and up close, the woman was stunning. She combined the slender figure of a young Bianca Jagger with the curves of Mata Hari. Dark, olive skin stretched over sharp, prominent cheekbones that set off huge, ebony eyes framed by long, dark lashes. The only visible scrap of makeup on her face was blood-red lipstick on her full, sensual lips. Long, loose curls hung down from the front of her chignon, framing her face to dramatic effect.

Rolling back to my nest of pillows, I turned my gaze to Blake, not wanting to continue gaping at his mother.

Blake sat up and scowled. "You could have called."

"And missed another one of your antics? Does Henry know of your new proclivity for battering women, or will he read about it in another article of the Sunday Correspondent?"

I bit down on my lip. Did she really think Blake was in a relationship with Henry just because she saw the pictures of them together?

Blake's nostrils flared. "Saturday."

She narrowed her eyes. "What did you say?"

"It's the Saturday Correspondent, *Mother*," he spat the last word like an insult.

I pushed myself up. "Ummmm…"

Mrs. Simpson-West's eyes softened. "Yes, dear?"

"I don't know how to address you."

"Lucia." She gave me a tight smile.

"The Duchess of Surrey," said a middle-aged man in a black uniform who I suspected was the servant who had tried twice to enter the room. "Or Ma'am."

My insides cringed. The English said the word a little differently to Americans, and I didn't want to offend her by pronouncing it wrong. And I didn't want to ask if I needed to call her Lady Lucia in front of the servants and detectives. Blake's silk pajamas covered my body, but everyone could see what had become of my face.

I gave myself a mental slap. None of this mattered. If I didn't speak up for Blake, he'd probably get sent to rehab or have to suffer some other unnecessary penance. "I got abducted by two men last night, and Blake risked his life to save me."

Confusion twisted her elegant features, and she turned to Blake and crossed her arms. I caught sight of her white knuckles, pursed lips, and narrowed eyes and guessed that she was about to ask why he had risked his life for someone he didn't know.

Actually, Mrs. Simpson-West looked the type to object to Blake bringing a stray to the palace, so I blurted out, "I'm not a stranger. My name's Emilia Hobson. I'm—"

"Rudolph Trommel's new stepdaughter," she said.

"Yes." My brows drew together. Did she know Rudolph, or had Blake spoken to his mother about me? "And I'm Blake's classmate."

"And the girl who accompanies me to Narcotics Anonymous meetings," added Blake.

All traces of irritation melted away from Mrs. Simpson-West's face. "Who did this to you?"

"Peter Underwood, the son of the recently resigned Secretary of State for the Supreme Court, and Ernest Carbuncle, the school janitor."

"Are they in custody yet?"

"Only Mr. Underwood the younger," replied Blake. "Carbuncle's still at large."

Mrs. Simpson-West twisted around and addressed a female servant who had held a jug of water on a tray as a pretext to enter Blake's room to eavesdrop. The woman nodded and scurried away.

I glanced at Blake, who shrugged. It looked like he didn't know what his mother was planning, either. She strode up to a young detective, who was built a little like Henry, and spoke to him in soft, flirtatious tones. This time, when I turned to Blake, he scowled. Hadn't Henry told me that the prince had found Mrs. Simpson-West in bed with the chauffeur?

A moment later, the female servant entered and gave Blake's mother a jar. She sashayed around to the bed, dropped it on the bedside table, and examined the labels of my painkillers and sleeping pills. "This is a fast-acting bruise salve, mixed by one of the foremost herbal scientists in the country. I can vouch for its efficacy."

My stomach churned with a mixture of apprehension and revulsion. Why would she still need bruise salve if Blake's father had died four years ago? Blake's body stiffened at my side, and I couldn't meet his gaze. In the back of my mind, I wondered if he had made the same speculations about his mother's relationship with the prince.

I gazed into Mrs. Simpson-West's face but couldn't find a single bruise. "Th-thank you."

She swept out of the room in a cloud of Coco Chanel, taking away her entourage of detectives and nosy servants. As she stepped out of the door, she cast Blake a withering look. "And for God's sake, don't let Henry know about your little indiscretion unless you want to end up with a face like Emilia's!"

My mouth dropped open, and I exchanged a shocked glance with Blake, who rolled his eyes. Did she really think Henry would strike a friend?

The door clicked shut, and my tongue darted out to moisten the undamaged side of my lips. "Blake, do you—"

"Are you thirsty?" He shot out of bed and raced around to the side table, where the female servant had left a jug of water and two glasses. His gaze flickered to the clock. "It's noon. Time for your painkiller."

My shoulders drooped, and I settled into the nest of pillows. If he didn't want to talk about his mother's need for bruise salve, I wouldn't bring up the subject.

The door slammed open, and Henry and Edward burst into the room. As soon as their gazes caught mine, their bodies, and expressions, froze.

My heart sank, and I pulled the silk sheet up around my neck. "Is it that bad?"

"Surprising." Edward enunciated each syllable as though careful not to say the wrong thing. "Blake told us this morning. We came as soon as we could but got delayed at security." He stretched his lips into a bland smile, but it did nothing to hide the pain etched on his features.

I glanced at Henry, who gaped as though he couldn't believe his eyes. After stepping further into the room, he shut the door but didn't move any closer than the foot from the bed. His skin had turned white, and his chest rose and fell like bellows. It was much like the time in the dining room when Coates had twisted Blake in a wrist lock, except this time, there was no one to punch in the face.

Edward walked over to my side of the bed, gave me a peck on the unbruised side of my mouth, and stroked my temple as though I might crumble. His stormy, blue eyes glistened with unshed tears, and he leaned down and kissed me again.

"Thank heavens Blake found you in time." His voice was breathy, like he was trying to hold his emotions down. "I don't know what I would do if—" He shook his head and lowered himself into the bedside chair.

"The doctor prescribed an effective painkiller." I reached out a hand and curled it around Edward's. "As long as I take it every four hours, I'll be comfortable."

He pressed his lips together and nodded. "How are you cop—"

"You should have seen Blake last night." I couldn't face rehashing last night or facing my feelings. Talking about what Mr. Carbuncle had done and how helpless I had felt would only make me feel worse. It was far easier to recount Blake's heroic rescue. "He climbed over all the balconies, searching through all the windows for me with his flashlight."

Blake slipped into bed next to me and rubbed the back of his neck. "My smartphone flash."

I curled my fingers around Blake's. "Then he punched a hole through the window and pulled me out."

He shook his head. "Emilia climbed out by herself. I only helped her land on her feet."

"Then he carried me on piggyback and sprinted through the balconies with Mr. Carbuncle at our heels."

Blake stared back at me with his brows furrowed. "You missed the part where I jumped over those barriers."

I huffed a laugh. Lightning bolts of pain wrapped around my ribs, making me groan and clutch at my sides.

Henry punched his fist into his palm. "Those bastards. If I ever get my hands on Carbuncle, he'll be eating his meals through a straw and shitting through a colostomy bag."

"Language," said Edward. He brought my hand to his mouth and pressed his lips to my knuckles. "How did you know where to find Emilia?"

I blinked several times and stared at Blake, who gazed at Henry with furrowed brows. That was something I had also wondered about before the painkillers had dulled my thoughts.

Blake explained how he had arrived at Chelsea Heights to find a group of girls in party clothes wandering around the top floor and searching through the fire exits. I supposed those were the interns who had ridden in the back of Tom's van. As soon as he discovered there was no number sixteen, he approached the girls, working out that the invitation had been a trap. While the reporters were liaising with the police, Blake knocked on doors until he found someone who recognized him from the papers and was willing to let him in to search the balconies.

All throughout the explanation, Henry stood at the foot of the bed, staring at me with anguish in his green eyes. I couldn't tell if he would burst into tears, fall onto his knees, or smash the room up. He was clearly the most disturbed of the triumvirate and doing the worst job of holding back his feelings.

A soft knock reverberated on the door, and Henry broke away to see who wanted to come in. He opened it to reveal Nurse Priya, dressed in her navy blue uniform.

"Miss Hobson?" she said. "I'm here to check your dressings."

"Right." Blake rolled out of bed and stood in his silk pajama bottoms.

Nurse Priya turned her head and sucked in her cheeks while Blake padded to a mahogany closet and found a robe. He moved onto the dresser, where he pulled out another set of silk pajamas and placed them on the end of the bed before leaving with Henry and Edward.

I pushed my hands onto the mattress and swung out of bed, but a band of agony wrapped around my entire torso and made my muscles seize. Nurse Priya rushed forward and supported my body.

When my feet hit the soft carpet, every single bruise screamed with protest, making me hiss through my teeth.

In Blake's luxurious, marble bathroom, things became worse. An unfeasibly large, purple-black eye stretched across my entire left socket, the start of the bridge of my nose, and ended at my cheekbone. I was lucky he hadn't broken my nose with the force of his punch. Most of the swelling concentrated in the area under the eye, but the rest of the left side of my face puffed and pulled the swollen part of my upper lip down into a permanent expression of melancholy. I looked as though I had developed an oversized jowl.

Dark fingermarks marred my neck from where Mr. Carbuncle had strangled me, and red streaks covered the rest of the skin. The bastard's fingernails had also dug into my flesh, leaving crescent-shaped scabs. If he had held onto my neck for much longer, I would have—I turned from the mirror and let out several gasping breaths.

"Miss Hobson?" asked the nurse.

"I'm fine." The words came out in a gasp. "Just shocked."

"I can perform a bed bath if you're not yet comfortable with seeing the rest of your body," she said.

I gulped. Was she saying that because of what she had seen last night as she put me into the gown, or because of how I had reacted to the sight of my face? "I-I can manage."

When Nurse Priya took off the bandages and revealed my purple skin, I hissed through my teeth and jerked away from the mirror. These bruises must have happened when Charlotte's brother had dragged me down the stairs. I don't remember Mr. Carbuncle hitting me so many times and in so many places that the bruises would have covered me everywhere.

She showed me the kind of tepid water best suited for the early days of bruising and advised me not to turn the shower onto the hottest settings for another two days unless I wanted even more burst blood vessels. I thanked her and climbed into the shower, letting the cool water run over my skin. Everything felt too sore and too raw to apply shower gel, so I didn't stay long and winced as I dried myself off.

The nurse redressed my wounds, helped me into Blake's silk pajamas, and back into the nest of pillows. Just before she left, I asked, "Mrs. Simpson-West said I should use her bruise ointment. What do you think?"

"Wait a few days before applying it, as some of its ingredients might aggravate your open wounds. But it should be fine to rub a small amount on your face four times a day."

"Thanks."

She paused at the door, and her gaze flickered from my face to the carpeted floor.

My brows drew together. "Was there anything else?"

"The abduction made the front page of the papers." Before I could react, she added, "Your name wasn't mentioned, but the article said that Mr. Carbuncle was caught sexually assaulting a girl in Mercia Academy, whose parents are pressing charges. And other girls are coming forward with complaints."

"Oh." I stared into her dark eyes.

"I brought the morning-after pill and an STD test kit. It won't take—"

"H-he didn't go that far," I said. "I mean, he groped me over my clothes and threatened to rape me, but the other man stopped it."

Her gaze dropped to a spot on the end of the bed. "But you were unconscious for some time in your abductors' presence…"

Revulsion shuddered through my belly. Surely, I would have noticed something. Both times I had slept with Edward, I'd felt a pleasant ache afterward. If Mr. Carbuncle had done something to me while I'd been knocked out, I would definitely have felt something. Or he would have gloated about it, at least.

"I didn't feel strange down there when I woke up."

Nurse Priya drew back. "Very well. Everything is healing as it should. I will return tomorrow."

"Thank you."

As the door clicked shut, a mantle of unease settled over my shoulder and seeped into my skin, casting the explanation I'd given the nurse into doubt. Charlotte's brother had been the one to drag me to the apartment. He didn't seem the type to violate a woman while she was unconscious or to allow a man to do it in his presence, but what the hell did I know about him?

I would have to call Jackie to see if she or her interns had noticed anything untoward in the footage.

CHAPTER 19

Later that evening, I insisted that the boys return to the academy. Three pairs of eyes on my hideous face, combined with Henry oscillating between shock and fury, Edward scheming about how to get even with Charlotte and Carbuncle, and Blake's over-attentiveness was too much for me in my current state. The painkillers dulled my senses, and after the shower, the bruises had hardened, making it difficult to speak. Henry and Edward left, promising to call every day, while Blake remained. It was his bedroom, after all.

We spent Monday in silk pajamas, sitting on his chaise lounge with my back leaned against his chest and my head resting on his shoulder. Blake wrapped his arms around me and read stanzas from the poem Don Juan, by Lord Byron. With his perfect, British pronunciation, he brought the work to life, making me giggle at the naughty parts.

I twisted around and gazed into his chocolate-brown eyes, noticing for the first time their flecks of golden brown. "You're a bit like Lord Byron."

His dark brows rose, and a smile curved his full lips. "How so?"

"Mad, bad, and dangerous to know."

Blake's low, deep chuckle vibrated against my back, and he ran a hand down the silk fabric covering my hip. "Don't you think Edward's more byronic than me?"

"Byronic, yes. When I first met him, he was mysterious and moody." I smirked. "You both have Lord Byron qualities."

He placed a kiss on the tip of my nose. "I'll consider that the ultimate compliment. Especially since he had a proclivity for getting ladies into trouble."

I dipped my head and laughed so hard, my ribs ached. Then Blake put down his copy of Don Juan and changed the subject. It turned out that we had more in common than I'd originally thought. Both our fathers had been addicts who had disgraced themselves in the papers, and both our mothers had been models who had married rich. We'd both had our childhoods blighted by divorce, and neither of us had a place we considered home.

During a lull in the conversation, I told Blake what Nurse Priya had said.

His face clouded. "You have to call Tom or Tola and ask to see the footage."

"I don't think I can relive that just yet." I glanced down at my hands. The rope marks on my wrists had already faded into dull streaks of pink.

Blake wrapped his arms around me and pressed a kiss on my temple. "Sorry, I didn't think. If the story has already hit the news, maybe one of those interns has already seen all the footage. Who do you normally speak to at the newspaper?"

I got hold of Jackie, who confirmed that neither man had taken off my clothes or sexually assaulted me while I had been unconscious. She sounded a little distant, and I wasn't sure if it was because she felt bad about what had happened to me or disappointed because Blake had rescued me before the abduction could progress into a more sensational story. She didn't mention Rudolph, and I didn't ask. As far as I was concerned, I was done with the Saturday Correspondent.

On Wednesday, Nurse Priya uncovered my bandages to find that the bruises had healed a lot quicker than she had anticipated, and later that evening, Dr. Chumley-Stokes visited to give me a final check up.

He drew back from my ribcage and smiled. "Ah, the benefits of youth!"

My cheeks warmed as the nurse replaced my bandages. "I also started using Mrs. Simpson-West's bruise salve yesterday."

He grunted his approval. "Marvelous stuff. Well, I'm delighted with your progress. Continue taking the pain-killers every four hours, but refrain from sports or any strenuous activity until you obtain the approval of the academy doctor."

"Yes, sir."

The doctor stood and opened the door.

Blake stepped into the room. "What's the verdict?"

"Miss Hobson is well enough to return to the academy." He clapped Blake on the shoulder and left with the nurse.

∼

On Thursday morning, I lay in the back of his mother's Rolls Royce, stretched out on the seat with my head on Blake's lap. I smiled into Blake's adoring gaze, my heart warm and giddy that he was now looking me full in the face. Most of the swelling on the left side of my mouth had faded, and my gaze flickered down to Blake's lips.

He curled his fingers into my hair and let out a happy sigh. "You're almost like your old self."

I smiled back. "Thanks to you. Who knows what might have happened if you hadn't found me in time?"

"It doesn't bear thinking about." His hand stilled. "Carbuncle is out there somewhere. If he has any sense, he would leave the country, but I think he might return to Mercia."

The lining of my stomach rumbled with dread. "Would he be that stupid?"

"He's that greedy," replied Blake. "If Peter Underwood placed an idea in his head that you're worth a million in ransom, he might seek you out and try again." He reached down and intertwined his fingers with mine. "Each of us has classes with you. We'll make sure you're never alone."

I nodded, caught in his hard gaze. The leather seat beneath me creaked, the sound adding to my trepidation.

"No more sneaking off to be on your own."

My throat dried, and I gulped. "I-I'll be careful."

"At night, you'll sleep in Edward's room. He's the only one of us with a double bed."

"Y-yes." My chest tightened at the thought of Mr. Carbuncle lurking in the grounds, waiting for the right time to catch me unawares. Blake must have been thinking the same as his eyes turned bright, and he swept a shaking hand across his forehead. My chest tightened, and my stomach twisted into several noisy knots.

His brows drew together. "You're hungry."

I placed my hand on my stomach. "But I ate breakfast."

"Not enough, clearly." Blake told the driver to take the next exit out of the freeway and head toward Lake Wessex. "The servants always pack a little hamper when I return to school. We can find a quiet spot and eat there."

Lake Wessex turned out to be a huge body of water surrounding a small island with castle ruins. Brown, marbled ducks swam in the water among black swans with red bills. A group of men swam in the distance, their wet heads glistening in the sunlight. Blake explained this was also a natural swimming pool.

We sat beneath a weeping willow on a woolen picnic blanket with a red tartan pattern interlaced with green and blue, which

Blake explained came from his father's ancestors, the Simpson clan in Scotland.

"This used to be one of my favorite spots when I was younger." A wistful smile touched his lips, and his eyes unfocused. "It would be just Father and me. He would row me to that island and tell me stories of the adventures he had with his chums while at Mercia Academy."

I leaned into his shoulder and raised our laced hands, enjoying how the sun streamed dappled light onto our skin. "Was he there at the same time as Edward's dad?"

"Father was five years older than the duke." He beckoned over a thin boy about our age, dressed in green fishing waders that stretched up to his chest and rubber boots that reached his thighs. "By then, he was already in Elder House so didn't mix with many of the lower year pupils."

The boy rushed over and stood by the edge of the blanket, bouncing on the balls of his feet and making his rubber boots squeak. Blake reached into the inside pocket of his navy jacket, pulled out his wallet, and extracted a twenty-pound note. The boy gave him a jaunty salute and scurried away.

Pushing aside thoughts of how it must feel to see his step-grand-mother each time he used money, I asked, "What are you doing?"

Blake drew back and grinned. "Taking you to Penda Castle, of course."

I glanced across the lake at the ruins and sucked on the right side of my lip. "Isn't that a special place for you and your dad?"

Blake stood and held out his hand. With eyes that shone with sincerity and seemed to stare into my soul, he said, "This is the first time I've been here since before Mercia Academy, actually." I took it, and he pulled me up. Nurse Priya's dressings were so tight, the movement hardly hurt. "Lake Wessex reminds me of empty promises and lost hope. Father should have been able to move on from Mother's betrayal, but he spiraled into despair, and despite numerous interventions, he succumbed to his demons. Whenever I think of this place, it makes me sad. But now I'd like to make some happy memories."

A flock of butterflies fluttered their wings. Something in the tone of his voice told me that he intended for us to be together for a very long time, if not forever. The intensity of his chocolate-brown gaze made my heart quicken, and I turned to the water and watched it ripple over the reflection of the ruins.

Forever was a long time, but after spending days alone with Blake and finally getting to see the real person beneath the mask of humor and flirtation, I found someone I could trust with my heart.

The boy pushed a rowboat around the lake's perimeter and waved us over.

Blake took my hand and led me out from under the willow tree, across a short lawn and to the bank of the lake.

My throat dried. I'd never been in a rowboat before, but Blake was a member of the academy's boat club and had occasionally mentioned wanting to follow his father's footsteps and row for Balliol College in Oxford.

As we reached the boat, I asked, "Have you ever had to worry about kidnapping threats?"

"I have." He stopped a few feet away from the boat and cupped the right side of my face in his hand. "But when the reporters told me you'd been taken, it was the most frightening time of my life."

"I'm sorry for not listening to you," I whispered.

He smoothed the hair off my left temple and tucked it behind my ear. "How were you to know that going to a party in London would result in an abduction?"

My throat thickened, and I swallowed hard. "I should have been more suspicious. This new version of Charlotte is even worse than ever."

"She was always nasty," he replied. "When the tabloids published photos of Mother and the prince while she was still married, she was the first to rally the others to call her a trollop."

The sun disappeared behind a thick cloud, and a cool breeze blew through the cashmere sweaters Blake had lent me for the journey back to the academy. Based on what I had seen of Charlotte in my first term, I would never have guessed that there had been an acrimonious history between her and Blake. "What made her change her attitude?"

"Edward and Henry being on my side, and Mother becoming the Duchess of Surrey by marriage." He continued stroking my hair. "But I never forgot the trouble she started for me."

My lips curved into a half smile, and I placed my hand over his heart. Its slow, steady rhythm quickened. "Is that why you had her suck you off in exchange for getting closer to Henry?"

"Henry would never have been interested in someone so simple-minded. And yes, I wanted her to feel a little of how she and her friends had made me feel during one of the worst times of my life."

I squeezed his hand. "It can't be easy seeing your Mother displayed in the paper like that."

"She was the least of my worries. It was father who kept me up at night."

Something in the background disturbed a flock of ducks, which took flight with noisy quacks. I spotted them flying away in the corner of my eye and turned my gaze back to Blake. Pained lines etched the skin around his eyes, making my heart twist in empathy. "You couldn't sleep because of his drinking?"

He dipped his head. "Not knowing where he was or what he was doing. Strange phone calls late at night, saying goodbye and thanking me for being a good son." A tiny shudder shook his shoulders. "It was terrifying. Mother had washed her hands of him after the divorce because of his violent rages, so he only had me."

I gulped. "That's why she knew so much about bruises?"

"That's part of it. Yes."

I bit down on my lip, waiting for him to elaborate. When he didn't, I asked, "Is she still being—"

"It's not something I can handle right now." Blake blurted the words so quickly, they took a moment for my brain to parse. "I can't persuade her to leave. She loves the attention of being married into the royal family, and nothing will make her let go of that."

"My mom's like that with Rudolph, I think."

"What do you mean?" he asked.

"She hasn't replied to any of my messages since I left the country."

He stilled, and his gaze dropped to the side, as though he didn't know where to look. I couldn't blame him. At least his mother hadn't shoved him out of the palace to cozy up with the prince. And she'd sort of stood by him during the scandals, even if her methods of support had been twisted and sick. Mom had just ghosted me, and if I hadn't had so much shit to deal with at the academy, I might have succumbed to the loss.

"I'm... sorry." He wrapped his arms around my shoulders and gave me a gentle hug. "Did she do the same the last time she married?"

My eyes fluttered closed, and I lost my self in his cedar scent. "No, but that guy was a corporate real estate investor and didn't have the fame or vast fortune of Rudolph Trommel." I shook my head. If Mom wanted to upgrade her life and leave her daughter behind, there was little I could do to change that. "It hurts less each day. Knowing that you and Edward are here for me is enough to negate the effect she's had on my life."

"And Henry," he added in an admonishing tone.

We continued across the lawn and to the lake, where the boy waited for us with an impatient frown. Blake helped me onto the plank at the pointed end of the rowboat, which acted as a seat. Then he took off his jacket, got onto the boat, and the boy pushed it into the water until it was waist deep.

As Blake rowed, he said, "Henry was devastated when Edward told us you were the leak. Last term, he thought you'd settled your differences. It was a huge blow to him to discover you hadn't forgiven him."

I pursed my lips and gazed at his shoulder muscles rippling under his fitted sweatshirt. Right now, Henry was the biggest mystery of the trio. Sometimes the most loving and the one I felt the deepest connection with, and other times, a dismissive lout only interested in sex. "We couldn't agree over getting him to clear my name."

"He had his reasons. If you give him a chance, he'll explain himself."

I shrugged.

Without missing a stroke, Blake fixed me with a hard stare. "Just promise me that you'll stay with one of us at all times, even if it's Henry."

I nodded. "Even if it's Henry."

He continued rowing across the lake until we reached the little island. Up close, the ruins were more intricate than from the other end of the bank. Instead of an empty, stone shell, there were room partitions, indoor arches, and even a staircase that protruded out from the internal walls.

Blake helped me out of the boat, stepped off, and placed a hesitant hand on my waist. His gaze wavered from my eyes to my lips, and his Adam's apple bobbed up and down. It was as though he wanted to kiss me but was afraid I would reject him.

His hand dropped from my waist and wrapped around his chest. "You were right." He gulped. "I did it on purpose."

"What?" I stared into his lowered eyelids.

"Didn't convince you hard enough not to call the police." He rubbed the back of his neck. "It was selfish. Edward had told us both to back off and give you space, and I was sick of all the dance lessons with Yelverton and her friend acting as chaperones. I wanted you to come back the next day and the day after that to talk about the kidnappers."

I blinked a few times. Blake hadn't told me anything new, but I hadn't expected he had wanted us to become closer. "You didn't guess I would call the police, then?"

"I didn't think you would be so decisive, no." He held his body stiff like a person waiting for the blow to strike.

My heart melted. After that extraordinary rescue and the loving care he'd administered over the past days, how could he doubt that I would forgive him? When his eyes flickered to mine, realization slotted into place. Our past, the pranks he had committed against me, were holding him back. Or rather, the guilt he carried for having hurt me so much.

I placed a hand at the juncture of his shoulder and neck. "What you did for me these past few days makes up for everything."

He glanced away. "It wasn't anything special."

I held his head between both hands and turned it toward me, so we stared into each others' eyes. "Listen. No one has ever risked their neck for me the way you did. They could have had knives or guns or another accomplice in a different room, but you rescued me anyway. You weren't satisfied with the police's progress and went looking for me on your own. None of the reporters did that. It was you. So if I say I forgive you for those pranks, I forgive you."

He stepped into my space and pressed his lips onto mine with the gentlest of kisses.

"Swear to me you won't put yourself in danger again," he whispered against my lips.

"I swear it."

CHAPTER 20

Blake and I spent the rest of the afternoon at Lake Wessex. By the time we returned to Elder House, the pain medication, combined with the exhaustion of the day, weighed my limbs and caused my eyes to fall closed. He walked me straight to the room I shared with Rita, opened the door, settled me onto the edge of my mattress, and unfastened one of the Louis Vuitton cases piled at the foot of the bed.

"I'll pack your things," he said.

Rita turned around from her desk, took one look at my bruises, and her face dropped. Her fountain pen fell from her loose fingers and rolled across the floor.

With trembling lips, she asked, "W-where have you been? And who did this to you?" Her gaze darted from me to Blake, and then back to me. "W-was it one of them?"

I shook my head. "I went down to London, and got caught in an ambush." My insides cringed with shame. I hadn't told Rita because she would have begged me not to go and told me that revenge on Charlotte wouldn't be worth the risk of her retribution. "Mr.

Carbuncle did this with the help of Charlotte's brother. Blake came to my rescue."

She clapped her hand over her mouth, her eyes wide. "That's… Did you call the police?"

"They know about it." I didn't want to mention that the Saturday Correspondent had made the call so as not to alert Blake that Rita knew about my involvement with them. I trusted him with my life but didn't trust him with Rita. "Mr. Carbuncle escaped. He's out there, somewhere, and I'm moving in with Edward."

She pulled on her long braid but didn't reply. I wanted to ask her how she hadn't heard anything of the articles in the paper written about Peter Underwood's arrest, but it likely had something to do with the amount of time she spent with her friend in Hawthorn House, who I was beginning to suspect was now her boyfriend.

Blake helped me up to the top floor, where Edward had left his room unlocked. I expect he had already texted ahead about our sleeping arrangements or the three of them had discussed it in the palace on Sunday when Nurse Priya had come to change my dressings. I changed into my nightclothes, settled myself into Edward's bed, and held Blake's hand.

"Thanks for a great day."

He kissed my knuckles. "I'm glad you enjoyed it."

I tucked my arm under Edward's crisp, cotton sheets. Blake stood and pulled off his jacket. "What are you doing?"

"You don't think I'm going to leave you here on your own, do you? This bed is big enough for four. He paused. As long as everyone snuggles close, and the fourth is as small as you."

My lips quirked into a smile, and I scooted back to make space for Blake.

~

I awoke the next morning in Edward's bed, curled around Blake with my head on his bare chest. My leg brushed over the thick erection encased in his silk pajama bottoms, and a low, sensual moan rumbled in his chest. Edward molded his front to my back and slung an arm around my waist. His fingers skimmed the patch of skin between the bandages encasing my torso and the hem of my panties, spreading warmth between my legs. Every muscle of my abdomen relaxed under his touch, and I let out a sigh of contentment. This was the first night I had slept without the sleeping pills, and it was thanks to their presence.

I lifted my head and peered out at the space beyond Blake, half expecting to find a larger body wrapped around him, but there was no sign of Henry. Instead, orange streams of sunlight shone through the chink in the curtain and highlighted his empty spot.

A pang of regret struck my heart and filled my chest with a dull ache. This entire arrangement had started with Henry. Without that time alone in that dingy room, I would never have gotten to know Henry without Edward's hostility getting in the way or without my mixed feelings about Blake's involvement in Charlotte's pranks.

Last night, I had fallen asleep minutes after settling onto Blake's chest, and I hadn't noticed Edward's arrival. Had Henry also entered the room? After I had told him to go to hell the day we visited his parents, he probably didn't think he would be welcome.

After giving me a gentle, morning kiss, Blake went downstairs to get dressed, while Edward offered me the first use of his bathroom. I stood in front of his mirror and scowled at my swollen face. Green now edged the bruises instead of the usual purple-black. Underneath the bandages, the bruises were still a livid purple. Even the passage of time and Mrs. Simpson-West's bruise salves couldn't work miracles.

Edward stepped into the bathroom, froze, and hissed like an angry cat. He fisted his hand over the towel around his waist and breathed hard.

I grimaced at the fading, hand-shaped bruises on my breasts. "You should have seen them a few days ago."

"I'll kill him," he said in a voice as cold as the eyes roving my tapestry of scabs and bruises.

"Not if I get to him first." He opened his mouth to protest, but I spoke first. "But I'll be with one of you and not on my own."

"Yes, you will," he said with a bite in his voice. He raised his gaze, revealing a face etched with worry. "How on earth are you coping with the pain?"

I slipped off my panties, but Edward's gaze didn't waver from my eyes. Damn. I was glad he hadn't seen my body while the bruises had been worse. "The painkillers are great, even though they make me drowsy."

He stepped forward. "Are you sure you should be showering alone?"

My heart skipped a beat. "I could always use a helping hand."

His brows drew together. "This is serious, Emilia."

I gave him a quick peck on the lips and pulled him into the shower. Unfortunately, the shock of my bruises reawakened his gentlemanly instincts, and he washed my body with the professionalism and precision of a surgeon.

After we dressed, we walked hand-in-hand to the dining room, where Henry sat at a table in the middle of the room with Blake.

Sunlight filtered in through the high windows, making the ends of Henry's hair shine like candle flames. As soon as our gazes caught, he rose to his feet and stared at me with widened eyes that traveled around my face, down my neck, and lingered on the fading rope marks on my wrists.

His nostrils flared so quickly, I thought I'd imagined the expression, then he asked, "How are you feeling?"

I sat at his side and placed a hand on his clenched fist. Throughout my assurances, his face tightened into a false mask of calm, and his breathing quickened. I gave his hand a squeeze. "You don't have to do that stiff upper lip thing. You can tell me if you're mad."

"The only person I'm angry with are those two bastards," he said through clenched teeth.

"And that bloody bitch," added Blake. "Who else would have left that fake invitation in your hallway?"

Edward poured me a glass of orange juice for my pain tablet, and I tried to drown out their plans to deal with Charlotte. Somehow, she had worked out that I had been behind the leaks, and she probably now blamed me for exposing her brother's gambling addiction, her father's fall from grace and impending jail sentence, and the resulting sharp decline in her family fortunes. I'd taken my revenge against her too far, and she had retaliated in kind. It didn't mean I wouldn't smash her in the face as soon as I could swing a punch.

Coates and three other boys from the rugby team carried a pair of empty tables and chairs to the podium, getting the space ready for Charlotte's grand entrance. The matron rushed up to admonish them for moving the furniture, but they walked around her like she didn't exist. I rolled my eyes and stirred my porridge.

"They're slipping," muttered Edward. "Last week, they would have had that table ready before anyone arrived."

Blake shook his head. "She probably can't satisfy four rugby boys."

I leaned forward, eyes wide. "You think she's in a relationship with Coates and his friends?"

Henry barked a laugh. "That's what she thinks. You should hear what they say about her in the changing rooms."

"Coates wouldn't cow-tow to someone he didn't respect." Edward cast a disapproving glare on the large boys who had laid the table cloth and were now setting the table with fine china and silverware they'd produced from a box. "What does Charlotte have on him?"

"She's bribing them," I said.

Blake shook his head. "I doubt it. They wouldn't need the money —" His face split into a grin. "Oh, you mean with sex? Coates is a virgin, so…"

Henry snickered. I glanced at Coates, wondering why the triumvirate disliked him. According to Edward, Blake had once put hair remover cream in his sunblock, which seemed like a nasty prank to pull on someone who regularly changed in front of other boys. Maybe Coates was helping Charlotte because he was happy to see the triumvirate dethroned and someone who had hurt him less on the throne.

More students entered the dining room. Whenever their gazes turned to our table, they would catch sight of my face and do a double-take. I didn't care what they thought, since most of them would attack me if prompted to do so by someone they deemed more popular.

At last, Charlotte sashayed into the dining room with the gait of a runway model. Over the weekend, she had darkened her hair to a shade of pale auburn that matched mine. When she took her place at the head table, she curled her lip then pulled out her smartphone and took a picture of my swollen face.

I stilled.

Every ounce of awareness focussed on Charlotte's smug expression. The students' chatter, the clink of forks on plates, Henry's angry, huffing breaths… everything faded into the background, replaced with the roar of blood between my ears. This was the bitch who had arranged that gauntlet, and now she had arranged for her brother and Mr. Carbuncle to abduct me. If Blake hadn't arrived when he did, Mr. Carbuncle would have done much worse. And she had the nerve to smirk.

Someone placed a hand on my arm, and I shrugged it off. In the space of three seconds, I sprung to my feet, crossed the dining room, grabbed the edge of her table, and shoved it hard into her gut.

With a shriek, Charlotte tumbled backward in her chair, but it wasn't enough. As though I'd absorbed Blake's athletic prowess, I vaulted over the upturned table, straddled her chest and grabbed her by the hair.

The noise of the dining room returned in full force. Charlotte screeched and clawed at my hands, but it remained around her fake, auburn hair like a vice.

"You fucking bitch!" I smashed her head against the stone platform. "You sent your brother and Carbuncle to abduct me. Admit it!"

"She's mad," Charlotte screeched. "Coates, Bierson, help!"

The two rugby players moved toward me.

"Touch her, and I'll break what's left of your nose," growled Henry from the other side of the table.

"Whoever records this and uploads a video to the Mercia-Net will suffer," snapped Blake.

I punched Charlotte on the side of her face, but with my limited range of movement from the bruises, I couldn't make enough of an impact.

"Emilia!" said Edward from behind.

"What?" I smashed her head against the platform one more time.

"Attacking Charlotte isn't the answer." He jumped onto the podium and rounded the table. "Even if the evidence points to her being responsible for your abduction, the police won't take an assault lightly."

I clenched my teeth and tightened my grip on her hair.

"I'll press charges," Charlotte yelled. "Then they'll lock you up forever, you crazy bitch!"

"You will do nothing of the sort, unless you want even more information about you leaked to the press," snapped Edward. He held out his hand and in a softer voice, said, "Emilia, let go of Charlotte's hair. We can settle things with her later."

I glanced around into the silence of the dining room. Someone had cleared the upturned tables, and now everyone, staff and students included, stared at me as if I'd turned savage. My fingers uncurled from her brittle hair, and I took Edward's hand. He raised me off a winded-looking Charlotte, tucked me under his shoulder, and wrapped a comforting arm across my back.

Coates stepped toward Charlotte, who stretched out her hand for him to pick her up. Instead, he frowned at me. "You were the girl Underwood's brother got into trouble for kidnapping?"

Her hand dropped to her side, and she didn't answer.

"She left a party invitation near my room with an address in London. When I got there, the number didn't exist. Underwood's brother punched me unconscious and dragged me into an empty apartment. Mr. Carbuncle did the rest."

Coates gaped at Charlotte.

She picked herself off the floor. The buttons of her shirt had burst open, revealing a shocking pink bra. "I-it's a lie."

"How did your brother know where to find Emilia?" asked Blake.

"I already told the police I didn't know!" Charlotte spread her arms wide. "The papers didn't mention Hobson's name. M-maybe my brother got arrested for taking another girl, and Hobson slammed her face in the door to frame me for being involved."

"Those bruises are days old," said someone from within the dining room.

"She could have made them the day the news broke out and hidden all this time."

"No." Rita stood from where she sat with the scholarship students. "Emilia has been missing from our room since Saturday morning."

Charlotte threw her hands in the air. "I didn't say she hid in her room!" She stormed across the podium and hurried down its steps. "H-Hobson's hated me since the day we met. She hates us all. That's why she leaked all that information to the Saturday Correspondent!"

Gasps broke out across the room. I pressed my lips together and sucked in a breath through my flared nostrils. They hadn't reacted to hearing that Charlotte had arranged my abduction, which was typical for the residents of Elder House. They would believe anything about me... Even if it was true this time.

"I saw bank statements with payments from the Correspondent with my very eyes." Edward tightened his arm around me. "There were also checks payable to Carbuncle from the newspaper in his filing cabinet. Everyone, including Mr. Chaloner, was convinced of his guilt before he escaped to avoid charges."

I stilled, and warmth trickled into my heart, making it swell. Edward had defended me, even in the face of irrefutable evidence that I had been the leak. My fingers curled around Edward's side, and I gave him a squeeze I hoped would convey my gratitude.

Charlotte paused at the door and clenched her fists. "Carbuncle was loyal to the school!"

Blake folded his arms. "No... You're loyal to Carbuncle." He shook his head. "Scratch that. You're loyal to his cunnilingus 'stache.

I fought back a wave of revulsion and the memory of the janitor's overgrown, spittle-covered mustache. The rest of the dining room filled with laughter, and Charlotte's face turned the color of her blazer. She picked up a broken plate, threw it at my head, and missed. Someone in the back of the room jeered, and she raced out through the tables and out of the doors. I gave Blake a grateful smile. Between him and Edward, they had averted what could have ended up in a violent mob.

After straightening and smoothing down my uniform, I walked around and off the podium.

Alice rushed over to me, her eyes wide. "Is it true?"

"Yes," I said through clenched teeth. Hadn't she heard me explain everything out loud?

She clapped her hands over her mouth and made a theatrical

gasp. At times like this, it was hard to forget that she was a doppelgänger double-agent. "Why did they do that to your face?"

"They wanted to prove to my stepfather that they meant business. Every day he didn't pay, they would do something worse and release the photos to the press." Edward pressed his palm against the small of my back and steered me away from his former... co-girlfriend, frenemy-with-benefits?

Alice chased after us. "To shame him into paying?"

"Something like that." I sat at the table.

"Do you think she's luring me somewhere?" She rubbed her chin.

"What do you mean?"

"Charlotte's holding a party in London in two weeks. It's the event she's promised will revolutionize Mercia Academy and cement her role as its ruler."

CHAPTER 21

"Alice," said Edward with a long sigh. "I owe you the deepest apologies for the way things happened between us."

She stepped back, eyes wide. "What do you—"

"But if this is another plan to lure Emilia into an ambush, I will destroy you, utterly."

Her bottom lip trembled. "I-it isn't." She turned to me, eyes brimming with tears. "Ask Coates if you think I'm lying. Most boys in Elder and Hawthorn houses have bought their tickets."

Blake's brows rose. "They paid?"

Edward raised his hands. "I don't want to hear it. Alice, leave." She turned around and stormed out of the dining room, and then Edward turned to me. "I want you to stay away from Charlotte. She's likely still in contact with Carbuncle, who will be on the run and desperate for money."

I lowered my gaze to a plate of scrambled eggs and smoked salmon a server had slipped in my place setting. Edward was right, but Charlotte was still up to something, and I didn't just mean my abduction. She had gained a level of overnight popularity that eclipsed the triumvirate and had managed to convince the boys to pay to attend her party. Would it be full of swingers?

"All the reason to go after her." Henry slammed his crystal glass on the table.

My head snapped up. "You want to capture Carbuncle?"

"Beat him bloody, but yes, I suppose I'd have to capture him first."

Blake clapped his hand on Henry's shoulder. "I'll be your second."

"This isn't a duel," snapped Edward. "We're not—"

"Overruled," said Blake.

Henry folded his arms across his chest and gave Edward a sharp nod.

Edward turned to me. "Emilia," he said in weary tones. "Please talk sense into these idiots."

"The party is in two weeks," I said. "By then, I'll have mostly recovered. If we crash it, we can find out what she's up to."

"We can do that, too," said Blake.

Edward's lips flattened with disapproval. It looked like we would be gatecrashing Charlotte's party, after all. He pulled himself out of his seat and stood. "Excuse me, Emilia, while I finalize arrangements for the academy's temporary blood donation center."

As he walked out of the room with his back ramrod straight, Blake stared after him with a frown. "What was that all about?"

"He's pissed off." Henry poured himself a cup of tea and raised the pot as though to ask me if I wanted some. When I shook my head, he poured out a cup for Blake.

"It's World Blood Donor Day next month."

"I don't follow," said Blake.

I reminded Blake and Henry about the penances each of them demanded from me at the start of term. While Blake wanted me to accompany him to Narcotics Anonymous, and Henry asked me to present myself to his parents as his girlfriend, Edward had wanted me to sit next to him in a meeting with the board of governors to present an idea to raise the profile of the academy in the press.

"I remember that now." Henry took a slice of toast from the silver rack.

"That was real?" asked Blake. "I thought he was just trying to get into your knickers."

I shook my head and smiled. Hopefully, Edward would join us in London. If there was a chance to hurt Mr. Carbuncle and have him finally thrown into prison, I would take it, even if it meant missing out on uncovering Charlotte's machinations.

～

The party coincided with Elder House's rugby match against Hawthorn House. We all lounged on the sofas at the front of the common room in protest of Coates ousting Henry as the team's captain. It had been on the grounds of feeling uncomfortable in the changing rooms with someone so obviously gay. Yeah, as if Henry's eye would wander to Coates when he roomed with someone as stunning as Blake.

When the clock struck four, I asked, "What time do they usually come back from a match?"

"Around now, I suppose," said Edward.

"Unless a fight breaks out at the end," added Henry.

Blake snickered. "Which happens about half the time." The common room doors opened, and people streamed in, chatting from the match. "Here they are."

I glanced at everyone who entered, noting some scholarship students and several people I'd seen around the house but who largely kept to themselves. None of the rugby players had arrived, and neither had any of their reserves. I leaned into Edward. "Doesn't everyone usually arrive as a group?"

"They do."

"Then where are Coates, Charlotte, and the other hangers-on?" I asked.

Henry narrowed his eyes. "You don't think—"

"Nobody said the party would take place in the evening." I pushed down on the armrest as leverage to hoist myself up. The bruises still ached a little and had turned green, but I no longer wore dressings or took painkillers.

The others stood, and we walked out of the common room, through the hallway, across the entrance hall, and out of the double doors. A warm gust of citrus-scented air hit us from the direction of the magnolias as we walked down the stone steps.

A squat rugby player limped toward us leaning on a crutch. His left eye was swollen shut, and blood spilled from a head wound that had been wrapped in multiple layers of bandages and stained the front of his shirt. My stomach churned in sympathy for his injuries.

"Patterson-Bourke," said Blake.

The boy's eyes widened, and he clasped his free hand to his chest with the kind of shocked modesty of a girl finding a weirdo in the locker room.

"Don't flatter yourself, you twat," snapped Henry.

Patterson-Bourke's gaze fixed on the one person he probably thought was unlikely to jump his squat, little bones: me. "Wh-what do you want?"

"Where are Underwood and the others?" asked Edward.

He flinched, as though the question was the crack of a whip. Still keeping his eyes on me, he said, "They all boarded the coach."

"Where's it going?" I asked.

"I-I don't know. Underwood didn't tell any of us the address. May I go, please?"

My heart sank. Charlotte had outsmarted me. Again.

"Come on," said Edward. "There's a driveway on the other side of the pitch. Maybe we can find some clues there."

We left Patterson-Bourke quaking on the steps of Elder House under his bout of homophobia and headed down the gravel pathway past International House and toward the playing fields.

"I'm not holding out much hope for finding them," I muttered. "It looks like she's thought of everything."

Blake stuffed his hands into the front pocket of his jeans and kicked a foot-full of gravel. "Me, neither."

"We've got to try something," said Henry.

I pressed my lips together and continued down the path, flanked by Edward and Blake. Even if Charlotte left behind another invitation to a sex party, it would probably lead us into another ambush, or into the deepest dungeon of the Tower of London or somewhere equally as ridiculous.

The afternoon sun shone from the direction of the tuck shop, obscuring my view of the path leading to the fields. A lone figure with flame-red hair emerged from the building, holding a stack of papers. From his petite stature, he looked like a fourth year. I couldn't tell because the sun lit him from the back, obscuring my view of his face.

As we continued along the path, he froze.

Edward placed his hand over his brow and squinted. "That's Blackwell, isn't it?"

"Who?" I asked.

"The four-eyed wanker who hoards all the newspapers," said Blake.

"Duncan?"

"That's him," replied Henry.

I narrowed my eyes. "He told me Charlotte would start a new regime and said lots of other cryptic things about her plans to take over the school."

Henry lengthened his strides. In an uncharacteristically cold voice, he said, "Did he really?"

The red-haired boy turned, dropped his bundle of papers, darted toward the tuck shop, and grabbed a bike. Then he cycled down a path leading toward the playing fields.

I ran a hand through my hair. "What on earth is he doing?"

"He knows something!" Henry picked up his pace and raced after him with Edward on his heels.

I chased after them. Each time my foot landed on the hard gravel, my bruises throbbed as though tiny fists were punching them back to life. I winced and slowed my steps, hoping to lessen the impact. Blake jogged at my side, keeping his gaze on me as though checking that I hadn't collapsed from the effort. We rounded the tuck shop and entered the playing fields, where the ground was softer underfoot and didn't hurt so much. Duncan cycled with the speed and proficiency of someone training for Tour de France.

I turned to Blake and offered him a smile. "Run ahead with the others if you like. I'm fine."

"Not likely," he replied. "It's during situations like these that people get snatched. Henry will—"

Before Blake finished his sentence, Henry leaped through the air and tackled Duncan, bike and all, to the ground. Duncan let out a high pitched shriek.

I winced and slowed my steps. That looked like it hurt.

"See?" Blake walked at my side. "What did I tell you?"

Up ahead, Duncan wriggled out from the wreckage in a strange sort of crab walk, his glasses askew. "S-stay away!"

Edward stalked toward the retreating boy. "You know something about Charlotte Underwood's party, don't you?"

"I won't tell!" he shrieked.

Blake and I caught up with them. As we passed Henry, who was righting the bicycle and checking it for damage, Blake gave him a congratulatory pat on the back. Henry beamed at his friend, but when we locked eyes, his smile faded.

A wave of regret washed over me. If I hadn't treated him so harshly, he wouldn't feel so uncomfortable in my presence. Whereas Blake and I had spent a few days alone in his room, sorting out our differences, I hadn't taken the time to make the effort with Henry. At some point, after we had dealt with Charlotte and her party, Henry and I would have to kiss and make up.

I turned to Duncan. "You once said that things would be better under Charlotte's leadership, but everyone's gone to her party, and you've been left behind with your newspapers. Things haven't worked out to your benefit at all."

Annoyance flickered over Duncan's face, and he opened his mouth as though to argue but schooled his expression then clicked it shut. He had to know I was right. Last term, he sat with Alice, and this term, he sat alone. Just as things had been at the very beginning when the triumvirate led the academy.

"She's organizing an orgy, isn't she?" I asked. Charlotte wasn't the most original of people, and her hoax invitation had said it had been a sex party. Why else would the boys pay to attend?

"H-how did you know?" Duncan squeaked from the ground.

I folded my arms across my chest. "Do the girls know they're being set up?"

He shook his head. "It's not anything as sinister." He gestured at the triumvirate. "Charlotte said she would give boys the opportunities they missed because of wankers like these."

Edward's brows rose. "Wankers?"

"You know what I mean," spat Duncan. "You're just as bad as Simpson-West, stringing along Alice and Patricia and not caring what it did to their friendship."

Edward ran his fingers through his hair. "If I had known they hated sharing, I would have ended things sooner."

"Liar!"

Strangely, I believed Edward. He was more than happy to share me with Blake and Henry. Until the ultimatum, it had probably never occurred to him that Alice and Patricia had accepted crumbs of his affection because they hoped he would one day fall in love with them.

"You knew about this twisted event and kept quiet?" spat Henry.

Duncan's brows drew together. "It's a wonderful opportunity for the rest of us."

"Them, you mean," drawled Blake. "She left you behind."

Duncan's cheeks turned redder than his hair. His bottom lip trembled with the kind of impotent rage I knew well, and his hands curled into fists. I rubbed a hand over my brow. At the start of last term, Duncan was my ally, and I had firmly believed the triumvirate were wankers.

I shot Blake an admonishing look. He didn't have to mock Duncan when we needed his help. "Ignore Simpson-West for a minute. If you paid to attend this party to meet a specific girl you liked, what would you expect from her?"

"Quite a lot, actually." Duncan sat cross-legged on the ground and dusted off his long-sleeved T-shirt.

"Is Charlotte paying the girls to go to this party?" I asked.

His eyes widened. "N-no... but I expect most will be gentlemen about getting the brush-off."

"Patterson-Bourke," I spat.

Henry's brows drew together. "What about him?"

I ground my teeth and snarled. So much had happened since being abducted by Mr. Carbuncle and Charlotte's brother that I had forgotten the strange conversation I had overheard in the hallway. The squat rugby player had grabbed a fifth year girl, demanded to know why she had rejected him, and then said something ominous that had triggered me to walk into that trap.

"Emilia?" Edward tilted his head to the side, staring at me as though I'd had a seizure.

"He told a younger girl she would change her tune at Underwood's party," I spat.

"I don't follow," he replied.

"Charlotte's going to do something to the girls to make sure they satisfy the boys who paid to attend her orgy."

CHAPTER 22

For a moment, everyone went silent as the words soaked in. Even Duncan stared up at me with his jaws slackened. The sun reflected off the lenses of his thick glasses, obscuring most of his expression, but I hoped he realized the need to spill everything he knew about the girls' whereabouts.

Henry grabbed Duncan by the collar and pulled him to his feet. "What happens to the girls targeted by those who aren't gentlemen?"

"This wasn't my party," Duncan squeaked. "Don't blame me!"

"Tell us where it is," I said.

Duncan's body went limp, and he stared into the lawn, pressing his lips together as though they might spill the truth. I turned to Edward, then Blake, then Henry, searching their faces for ideas as to why Duncan wouldn't give us the location of the party. He clearly knew Charlotte's plans.

I scratched at my temple. "Why would you be so loyal to someone who left you behind?"

"Oh, I get it!" Blake wagged his finger at Duncan. "Charlotte was your choice. You've already gotten your 'quite a lot, actually,' haven't you?

His cheeks turned even redder. "A gentleman never tells."

"No, but an idiot does," said Blake.

Henry punched Duncan in the stomach. I winced and wrapped my hands over my belly. "Sorry, old chap," said Henry. "This is taking too long. Tell us the location of Charlotte's party, or I'll turn you into a smudge on the grass."

"Ugh! Alright... alright." Duncan spat on the grass. "It's at the London apartment Charlotte's father owns. The one involved in the expenses scandal."

"Do you have the address?"

He shook his head. "But it will be in one of the Saturday Correspondent articles."

"Let's go," I said.

Edward pulled out his phone and made his way back to Elder House. "I'll arrange a car."

Following him, I pulled my new smartphone out of my pocket. "I'll visit the Correspondent's website."

As I clicked through the articles, Blake walked by my side, keeping a hand on the small of my back. Moments later, someone shrieked. I turned around to find Henry carrying a struggling Duncan over his shoulder. "What are you doing?"

"Bringing him along for insurance."

∼

The five of us sat in the back seat of the limo. Duncan slouched in the seat opposite, nursing a consolation glass of champagne Edward poured for him.

I scrolled down the article and found a picture of a four-story townhouse with a bright red door behind a small monkey puzzle tree. "The address is Erasmus Road, London. But it's a house."

"Divided into flats?" asked Henry.

"Hold on." I scanned the article, scrolled past a picture of the tenant, a furious-looking Asian man, and found a relevant paragraph. "It says here that it's a ground-floor, river-front flat within the division bell, whatever that is."

Edward pressed the limo's intercom and repeated the location to the driver, while Henry explained that the division bell was a boundary set by the British parliament to make sure that its members could reach the building within eight minutes if the emergency bell was rung.

Then he leaned back in his seat. "We've got an hour and a bit to spare before we break up this party. How are we going to spend it?"

"Spin the bottle," said Blake.

"No!" Duncan hugged his champagne glass to his chest.

Nobody took any notice of him. I glanced at Henry. Maybe a game might break the ice between us, and make things easier when we had our conversation later in the evening. "I've got an idea. It's more of a contest, really?"

"I'll win," said Blake.

"Unlikely," replied Edward.

"What is it?" asked Henry.

"Best kisser," I replied. "I'll be the judge."

"That's an easy enough victory." Blake twisted in his seat and pressed his lips onto mine. For a microsecond, my mind went blank. I hadn't expected the competition to start so soon. Then a thrill coursed through my inside, from core to nipples to the tips of my lips. His tongue swept between my parted lips, tasting of champagne.

I kissed back, my heart singing with joy. In these past weeks, I'd seen beyond Blake's beauty and fallen for the protective, loving soul beneath the mask of flirtation and mischief. I slid my hand to his silk-covered, muscled thigh and squeezed.

Blake hummed his pleasure and deepened the kiss. The arm

around my shoulder slid down to my waist and he squeezed, a taste of the delights that awaited me when we returned to Edward's room.

When we broke apart for air, we stared into each other's eyes, both breathing hard. My heart pounded in time with the throbbing between my legs. "That was…"

"Mediocre." Edward pulled me onto his lap. "Here's how to kiss Emilia."

I wrapped an arm around his shoulder to steady myself, and pressed my hand on his chest. Edward wrapped an arm around my back, leaned into my neck and gave me a gentle nip that made me squeal.

"That's cheating," muttered Blake.

Edward ignored him and peppered kisses on my neck. My eyes fluttered closed, and I lost myself to the sensations of how he kissed and sucked and licked my sensitive flesh. When his fingertips skimmed my hardened nipples, I cried out. Blake was right. Edward was cheating, and as the referee of this little contest, I wasn't complaining.

The kisses traveled up to my jaw, and I tilted my head to the side and squeezed his shoulders. I wanted him to hurry and reach my lips. I wanted him to remain kissing me like this forever. Scratch that. I wanted the three of them—together.

His lips made a slow, sensuous ascent up my jaw, and he reached the corner of my mouth. "You're divine, Emilia."

"S-so are you," I said between panting breaths.

Someone to our left huffed his frustration. Blake, most probably. But he'd get his chance to top this kiss in round two.

When our lips finally met in a kiss, it was like a tiny explosion. Sparks of pleasure jolted out from where our flesh met, raced past my nipples, and down to my twitching core. Edward swiped his tongue across the seam of my mouth, and I parted my lips, allowing him entrance. I thought he would take this kiss slowly, the way he had with my neck, but his tongue delved into my mouth deep and devouring and utterly demanding. I surrendered myself to his dizzying kisses, whimpered with each sweep of his tongue.

For a moment, we weren't in a limo. It was just Edward and me and the hardness pressing against my hip. Slickness gathered between my legs, and I shifted about, wishing I had straddled him, so his erection rubbed against my core instead.

Edward held my hips steady and broke the kiss. A flush had crept up his pale skin, and his blue eyes were blown with need. "Any more of that, and I would have come to an explosive finish."

Blake snickered. "Your verdict, Emilia?"

"Oh!" I held onto Edward's shoulders to steady myself. "Very nice… but I might need another go with Blake, as I've forgotten—eep!"

Henry's strong hands lifted me off Edward's lap, and he cradled me in his huge, muscular arms. I placed my palms on his chest, which reverberated with his quickened heartbeat. For several seconds we stared into each other's souls, luxuriating in a closeness we hadn't experienced since our final days in that room.

Henry drew in a sharp breath, and his brows rose in a questioning gaze. He probably wondered if I would include him in this contest after I'd so harshly rejected him the day we had gone to visit his parents. My tongue darted out to moisten my lips, and his eyes tracked the movement. Then I curved my lips into a smile I hoped told him exactly how much I looked forward to this kiss.

"If this is a contest for staring into Emilia's eyes, I'd say Henry's already won," drawled Blake.

Edward snorted a laugh.

"Ignore those dickheads," muttered Henry.

I ran my hands up those glorious, hard pecs, over his collarbones, and up those bulging muscles that extended from his neck to his shoulder. Henry's eyes blazed, and one of his hands slid up from around my waist, over my spine, and cradled the back of my neck.

My lips met his in the softest of kisses. I longed to tell him this wasn't just part of a dumb, best-kisser competition. That I wanted him just as much as I wanted Edward and Blake. Henry's arms tightened around me, bringing us so close, his heart beat for us both. His lips moved against mine in a movement so heartbreakingly familiar, I wanted to sob my relief. I'd missed this. Missed him.

This kiss was infinitely more loving than our encounter behind the oak tree. Infinitely more intimate. Henry's tongue met mine in a series of sweet caresses that made my toes curl, and the throbbing between my legs developed into a pounding need. The hand at my waist slid down to cup my ass, and my core muscles clenched. Hard. And I pressed myself against his growing hardness.

"Your verdict?" asked Blake from beside us.

I broke the kiss and shook my head. "It's escaped my mind. We'll have to start again."

Blake chuckled and leaned close, when someone cleared their throat. I twisted around to find Duncan sitting on the edge of his seat. He had placed his half-full champagne glass in its special holder, and leaned forward, hands clasped.

"H-Hobson." Duncan's voice was breathy, and fog coated the lens of his thick glasses. "Charlotte said I was an exemplary kisser, perhaps I can tender—"

"Stop the car," Edward barked into the intercom.

The limo pulled over onto the side of the freeway.

Duncan's eyes widened. "You don't mean to dump me on the hard shoulder?"

"Take your champagne and sit in the front with the driver," said Edward.

Duncan's lips thinned. "This is exactly why Charlotte's the Queen of Elder House." He grabbed his glass and the entire bottle of champagne, shuffled to the other side of the seat, opened the door, and stepped out into the left-hand shoulder of the freeway. "She's giving all the victims of greedy wankers like you a chance."

Blake pulled the door closed and turned back to me. "What the hell will we find at that party?"

The thought of girls trapped in an apartment with guys who had bought tickets to get close to them sent a shudder down my spine. I climbed off Henry and settled into the seat next to him.

Henry wrapped his arm around me. "Coates might be an idiot, but he and the other members of the rugby team wouldn't fall for a stupid scam like this, much less expect something from any of the girls. They're more likely to intervene if anything gets out of hand."

My mind went back to the comment that injured rugby boy had made to a girl about the party, and I glanced up at Henry, brows drawn together. "Really? They acted like her enforcers."

"They didn't do it for free," said Blake. "Charlotte isn't squeamish about paying lip service, if you catch my drift."

"Is that what she did for you?" I snapped.

He sniffed. "I put a condom on it first."

"I didn't notice."

"That's because you were so dazzled by my cock." He squeezed my thigh.

I nodded. "Yeah," I said in a flat voice. "That was probably it."

The boys continued mocking Blake and his blowjob escapade with Charlotte all the way through London. Eventually, the car stopped at a residential street in Westminster, close to the river, and the driver announced that we had reached our destination. Blake opened the limo door, and we all piled outside. I glanced down a road about four-hundred feet long with over two-dozen monkey puzzle trees on each side.

We hurried down the road, knocking on every house with a red door and a kooky-looking, evergreen tree in front. Very few people answered their doors, and all said they weren't holding a party of any kind. Considering the absence of loud music, I was inclined to agree with them.

Halfway down the road, we found a house fitting the description. Outside stood a sign that read:

BOURNEVILLES
Property Auctions
For Sale By
AUCTION

I opened my mouth to ask if this was one of his family's companies, but clamped my lips shut. It would be indelicate to ask, considering why he had been disinherited. A moment later, Blake gave Henry a consolatory pat on the back, which answered my unasked question.

Edward knocked on the red door, and an Asian man answered. "Hello?"

I scrolled up the Saturday Correspondent article and glanced at the picture of the tenant. It was the same guy.

"Good evening," said Edward. "Is this where Charlotte's party is being held?"

His lips tightened. "Charlotte who?"

"Underwood," said Blake.

Angry, red blotches appeared on his face. "For the last time, I don't know anything about the Underwoods. Now, fuck off, and don't come back again!"

CHAPTER 23

The tenant slammed the door, and Edward stepped away from the house, rubbing the back of his neck. He turned to us, brows raised. "What on earth was that?"

I glared in the direction of the limousine. "Duncan. The slimy little snake sent us on a wild goose chase."

"He didn't count on Henry taking him hostage when he lied," said Blake.

I clapped a hand over my mouth. "What if he escaped while our backs were turned?"

Henry sprinted to the limo, flung the door open, reached inside, and dragged Duncan out by the arm. The smaller boy stumbled across the sidewalk, sloshing the contents of his champagne glass over his front. Rolling my eyes, I followed after them with Blake at my side. Duncan also hadn't counted on getting drunk after being banished with a bottle of champagne.

"What's wrong?" Duncan slurred. "Did Coates and the others not let you in?" Henry gave him a rough shove, and Duncan staggered back, his ass knocking into the side of the limousine. "What was that for?"

Edward advanced on him, his eyes as cold and as sharp as icicles. "You gave us the wrong location."

Duncan clutched the half-full champagne glass to his chest. "Charlotte said it would be at her father's London apartment, I swear."

"Stand aside." Henry pulled him up by the lapels. "I'm going to shake this skinny bastard until he spews out the answer."

"N-no, don't," cried Duncan. "I'll wet myself."

Henry let go of him as though the champagne down the front of Duncan's shirt was urine. "Oh, for goodness' sake!"

Duncan staggered toward a lamp post and fumbled with the flies of his pants.

Everyone, including me, turned their heads.

Ignoring the sounds of urination, I turned to Blake. "Send texts to all the girls at the academy you think Charlotte might have invited. One of them should be able to tell you where they are, especially if they've worked out the boys have paid for their company and have stormed out in disgust."

He frowned but pulled out his smartphone. "Alright."

We all piled into the back of the limo. Duncan sat with us in case he remembered anything he might have overheard. I sent Rita a text in case she had heard from anyone about the party, but she replied straight away to say she hadn't. The only person I could think of was Alice, who had defected to join Charlotte. I sent her a quick text to ask if she was at Charlotte's party.

"Have you heard from anyone yet?" I asked Blake.

"Give them time," he replied. "Parties are noisy, and most girls keep their phones in handbags, so they might not feel anything vibrate."

"I say we interrogate Blackwell," snarled Henry.

"Beat me up all you like." Duncan swigged from the bottle he had brought from the front. "But I don't know any more than you."

Edward rubbed his chin. "All the bus companies local to the

academy might be closed at this time of the evening, but it doesn't hurt to try them."

I nodded and fired up the Google app. While Blake texted every girl in his smartphone, Henry explained that the party could be in any city within driving distance of Mercia county. The only ones I recognized were Brighton, Chichester, Canterbury, and Oxford, but the more places he listed, the more my spirits plummeted.

"Charlotte would hold the party in London," said Blake. "I'm sure of it."

Duncan swigged from his champagne bottle. "She did say her party would rival the Valentine's Day Massacre." He shot me a hurt look. "Thanks for inviting me, by the way."

I let the sarcastic comment wash over me. If he had been at the gauntlet, I would have made sure he'd had a place. But I wasn't about to admit that to an ally of Charlotte.

My phone buzzed, and a message from Alice flashed on the screen. *I'm there, and I've been throwing up all evening. Never mix a cocktail and penicillin.*

My heart flipped. "I've heard from Alice!"

"Where are they?" asked Edward.

"Hold on." *Are you in London?*

On a Thames booze cruise.

"Booze cruise," I said. "She's really sick."

Henry pressed the intercom button. "Head for the Westminster Millennium Pier."

"But you don't know where the cruise is," I said.

"It will be on the Thames, which bisects the entire city. Ask her for the name of the boat or its location."

Which cruise? Where are you?

Forgot the name. We boarded at Butler's Wharf and turned around at Greenwich.

I shook my head. "None of this makes any sense to me." I handed my phone to Henry, who seemed to have the best knowledge of London. "It'll be faster if you ask her the right questions."

Duncan wrung his hands. "Hobson? May I ask what Alice ate?"

"She didn't mention any food. Just that she had a cocktail while she was on penicillin."

He shook his head. "That isn't right. I've mixed alcohol and penicillin, and it didn't have that effect on me."

"Let's focus on finding her." I rubbed my brow and stared as the Houses of Parliament whizzed by.

Shortly afterward, the limo stopped at a pier, and Blake stepped out. Big Ben loomed from the other side of the bridge.

Henry handed me back my smartphone. "I know where they are, but the cruise will likely stop at Butler's Wharf, since it's already turned around at Greenwich. If we head there, we'll catch up with them as they arrive."

"Are you sure we'll make it on time?" asked Edward.

"I've told Blake to find a speedboat." The ominous tone in Henry's voice said he wasn't sure. Not even one bit. He rushed ahead through a line of people waiting to board a river bus.

Edward placed a hand on the small of my back and guided me along the pier. I glanced over my shoulder, partly looking for signs of Mr. Carbuncle. Charlotte might have told him we would use the pier nearest to her father's home. I shook off the paranoid thought. It was too far-fetched, even for Charlotte.

Henry returned seconds later, beckoning us to hurry. Blake had found a boat willing to take us directly to our destination without stopping. We rushed past the people and onto a red speedboat that accommodated twelve passengers. One of the two men in charge handed us yellow lifejackets, and we took our seats. Henry stood in the front with the two men, presumably to make any last-minute arrangements.

The boat's engine roared to life, and Blake took the seat next to me. "They won't stop at any of the eight other piers on their route."

My phone buzzed. I glanced at Alice's message. *All the girls are throwing up!*

I updated the others on the newest development.

"It's strange that she didn't mention the boys being sick," Edward said over the noise of the engine.

Duncan, who sat in the seat in front, turned around. "Charlotte wouldn't poison a cocktail and give it just to girls."

I held the smartphone up. "See for yourself."

The rest of the journey through the Thames was tense. Famous buildings I'd only seen from afar zoomed by, but I couldn't enjoy the sights. Not when anything could be happening to a boatful of girls. Edward tried calling 999 and having ambulances sent to help the girls, but the operator needed the name of the boat and its location. I stared at the screen of my smartphone for several minutes. Alice had gone silent for an agonizingly long time. I tried calling her, but I got transferred to voicemail.

After passing Tower Bridge, the majestic drawbridge consisting of two huge towers connected by a walkway at the top, we reached Butler's Wharf Pier, just as a group of boys rushed en masse off a double-decker river boat and up a ramp. They huddled together at the covered walkway at the top, staring down at the boat. I shook my head and gaped. There were about fifty boys.

Blake leaned across and pointed at a trio of large males at the back of the procession. "That's Coates, that's Bierson, and that's Ellis."

The speedboat stopped behind the party boat, and we piled out and along the pier. My mouth dried to the consistency of sandpaper, and my heart skipped several beats. What the hell would we find on that boat?

Two male crew members blocked the entrance. "No entry, guys. It's a private party."

"Our classmates are in there," I said. "We know the girls are being sick, and need to see what's happened to them."

The larger of the males, who wore a pair of thick-framed glasses, folded his arms across his chest. "Sorry, but the captain says no one's allowed to board."

"Did you at least call an ambulance?" asked Edward.

The crew members exchanged guilty looks and didn't reply.

"For fuck's sake!" Henry barreled through the two men, knocking them aside. Edward rushed after him with me at his heels and with Blake taking up the rear with Duncan.

The moment I stepped into the boat's interior, the acrid stench of vomit filled my nostrils, making me gag. Clapping my hand over my mouth, I stepped aside for Blake and Duncan to pass. We stood at a mezzanine level that looked down on a wooden dance floor with a bar at one end. Tables and chairs ran along the sides, underneath where we stood. Masses of girls either sat at the chairs or knelt on their hands and knees. Each one of them was vomiting or had recently thrown up.

Henry pulled out his phone and spoke to the 999 operator.

After scanning the dance floor for signs of a bleached blonde, I remembered Charlotte had copied my hair color. I looked again but found no sign of her. Or of Alice. I muttered, "Does anyone know first aid?"

"A little." Duncan walked toward a metal stairwell. "We'd better check on the girls and see if any of them need to be put in the recovery position."

We all followed after him, but when we reached the bottom of the stairs, a group of female crew members assured us they had called the ambulances and that the girls were safe. Sirens blared from the distance, and we trudged up the stairs and waited on the mezzanine.

A team of four paramedics stepped into the boat and froze. One of them stepped out, presumably to call for more help, and the others tended to the girls. Moments later, a pair of policemen arrived, who made us wait outside.

I sucked in relatively fresh air and stood with the others by the pier, watching a procession of girls being wheeled or walked up the ramp. Each of them trembled uncontrollably and looked as pale as specters. I swallowed hard. "How could she do this?"

"Do you really think she's capable of something so heinous?" asked Duncan. "Any one of those boys could have spiked the girls' cocktails."

My gaze turned to the group of boys huddled up on the walkway. Eight or so policemen walked among them, taking down details in their notebooks.

Edward wrapped an arm around my waist. "Are you alright?"

"Just horrified," I replied.

A photographer I recognized from the Saturday Correspondent strolled down the ramp, taking photos of the aftermath. The sight of him hovering around like a vulture sent spikes of irritation across my skin. Ignoring the little voice in the back of my mind calling me a hypocrite, I broke away from Edward and approached him. "How did you get here so quickly?"

He flicked his head at the two crew members Henry had pushed aside. "That lot told me."

That's when I noticed they both wore thick glasses. I would bet any amount that Tom's van was parked in a back street, having driven on the roads parallel to the river during its cruise. My hands balled into fists. If the Correspondent had known Charlotte would drug schoolgirls, why didn't they do something to stop it?

I was about to walk over and speak to them when a paramedic wheeled a girl with hair the exact shade as mine. Her head was bowed, and her hair covered most of her upper body, but there wasn't a trace of vomit in that long hair or on her skirt or on her bare legs.

"Charlotte."

She turned her head up at me. Then her eyes widened, and she leaped out of the wheelchair and bolted up the ramp.

CHAPTER 24

Charlotte's four-inch heels clanked up the ramp, and the muscles in her thighs and calves rippled with each rapid movement. For someone in such ridiculous footwear, she made surprising progress. Holding my aching ribs, I chased after her amidst the cheers and the catcalls of the boys being interviewed by the police.

"Emilia!" Blake held my wrist.

"Come on!" I continued running with him by my side. "Overtake me. She's getting away."

"I'm not leaving you," he replied. "Henry's right behind us, and I doubt he'll want you alone either."

Somehow, between the ramp and the waterfront, a wide restaurant-lined sidewalk, Charlotte had taken off her shoes and sprinted ahead. I growled my frustration. Why were the boys being so overprotective at a time like this? We ran past a row of parked ambulances and police vans, at the end of which stood a black cab.

Charlotte waved her arm. "Taxi! Taxi!"

A burst of fury powered my limbs and dulled the pain around

my ribs, and I closed the distance between us. She wasn't going to get away.

Channeling Henry, I leaped through the air and tackled her. "Stupid bitch!"

We both tumbled to the ground. My knees hit the paving stones, sending pain radiating up my thighs. I winced and held onto my quarry.

"Get off me, you trollop!" Charlotte elbowed me in the gut, aggravating my bruises.

I clenched my teeth. "Not until you tell the police and the medics what you put in the girls' cocktails."

She wriggled in my grip like a floundering fish. "Rape," she screeched. "Police!"

Large hands lifted me off Charlotte. "Calm down, Emilia," said Henry. "She's trying to make herself look like the victim."

A male police officer ran over with his female colleague a few feet behind. "What's going on here?"

Charlotte pointed at me. "Didn't you see her assault me? Arrest her!"

"That is Charlotte Underwood, the daughter of Neil Underwood, the disgraced Cabinet Minister, and the organizer of this party," I said between clenched teeth. "She sold tickets to boys from our school, promising them sex with girls they liked. Then to make sure the girls were compliant, she put something in their drinks."

"No," spat Charlotte. "You put the drugs in the punch!"

The policewoman turned to me with her lips pursed, as though I were the liar. "Alright. I need you both to come with me."

"But Emilia wasn't even on the boat," said Edward.

The policewoman raised her brows. "And you are?"

"Edward Mercia, Viscount Highdown." He pulled out his wallet and showed them some ID.

I held my breath and examined the policewoman's face. Surely, that fancy title would sway her.

She inclined her head a fraction. "And you can vouch for this young lady?"

"We all can," said Blake. "She drove down with us in the limousine."

The policewoman blinked as though she recognized Blake from somewhere, then her gaze darted to Henry, and her eyes widened with recognition. She smoothed her features into a neutral expression and asked, "And the other young lady?"

"It's as Emilia said," Edward replied. "Charlotte Underwood organized this party."

Even more police officers arrived and took us all to one side, making sure to separate us from Charlotte. While more ambulances arrived to take the girls away, a huge coach pulled up at the side road. Either it was something that Charlotte had organized, or one of the boys had called their parents to send transportation back to the academy.

Long after the Saturday Correspondent reporters had climbed into Tom's black van and left, and the ambulances had pulled away, we all stayed at the waterfront giving our details to the police. No matter what we said, they wouldn't arrest Charlotte. I supposed they suspected we were bullying her. That, or she had a guardian angel.

The police escorted the boys onto the coach and stopped the traffic on the main road for it to reverse out.

"Good riddance," muttered Henry.

"What a disgusting bunch of bastards," added Blake.

Edward rubbed his temples and sighed. "I'm just grateful for Charlotte's incompetence."

"Just think of what would have happened if she had made the girls compliant instead of violently sick." I shuddered.

A limo pulled into the side road, and the policewoman asked, "Is that your transportation, My Lord?"

"It is," replied Edward.

"Alright, you lot." She hooked her thumb in the direction of the road. "You're free to go."

Duncan sagged. "At last."

Henry placed a protective arm around my waist, reminding me of the reason he had wanted to come down to London. Mr. Carbuncle. Even if the janitor was hiding in an alley, I doubted he would cause trouble with the boys surrounding me and with so many police officers milling about, but I kept close to his side, just in case.

Resting my head on Henry's shoulder, I muttered, "I can't believe she got away with yet another heinous crime."

Henry pressed his lips on my temple and guided me into the limo. My torso ached so much, I slumped into the nearest seat and didn't scoot up.

"We still have a few more weeks until the end of term." Blake stepped in after me and sat at my side. "Plenty of time to even the score."

Edward climbed in and sat next to Blake, and Henry entered and sat on Edward's other side. Duncan was the last to enter, and I exhaled a sigh of relief. I'd probably sleep for the rest of the journey and roll into breakfast late tomorrow on Sunday.

Charlotte stepped into the limo.

"Where do you think you're going?" I snapped.

Her eyes flashed. "You heard the police. They want us out of here."

"Let's leave this area," said Edward. "We can deal with her in a moment."

She gave him a grateful smile and settled into the seat next to Duncan. "Thank you, Edward."

He folded his arms across his chest and didn't reply.

The limo backed out of the side road and drove away from Tower Bridge into a street occupied by offices and very little else. After ten turns, we reached a heavily trafficked road that led to the bridge. Edward clicked on the intercom. "Could you stop the car, please? One of us wishes to leave."

I turned to Charlotte and snarled, "Get out."

Her mouth opened and closed, and she gaped as though we were leaving her in the middle of the Sahara Desert.

"Get out," said Blake, "unless you want Emilia to drag you out by the hair."

"What?" Charlotte glanced through the window. "But it's deserted out there."

"So was that empty apartment with your brother and Mr. Carbuncle," I spat.

"But that wasn't me!"

The driver opened the door, letting in the roar of fast-moving traffic, but Charlotte didn't budge. "Please… Don't leave me out here. What if something happens to me?"

"She has a point, chaps," said Duncan. "It looks rather dangerous out here."

"Then get out and keep her company," I spat.

Duncan lowered his gaze and folded his arms across his chest.

"Alright." She stepped out of the limo. "But if I get hurt, my boyfriend will make your life a living hell, Emilia Hobson!"

"Maybe he can pick you up," I snapped. "Carbuncle might need someone to accompany him on the run."

The driver shut the door, rushed back into his seat, and pulled away, leaving Charlotte on the side of the road, holding her high-heeled pumps. I stared after her, insides still roiling with fury. After everything she had done, I couldn't feel an ounce of pity for the wretched bitch.

Blake slipped his hand into mine. "Are you alright?"

"Much better, now that she's gone."

The limo drove through London and into a familiar street.

"There's the Royal Academy," said Edward.

Blake snickered. "Do you remember getting thrown out for just talking to Emilia?"

"You must not touch the woman of Mr. Bachmann," Henry mimicked in a thick, Russian accent.

I glanced up at the throng of people leaving the royal academy. A few photographers stood on the edges of the red carpet, politely taking photos of the leaving guests. It was nothing like the feeding frenzy I'd endured with Blake in Kensington Town Hall.

One of the guests, a blonde woman sashaying down the red carpet, caught my eye. She stood six-feet tall, wearing the kind of magenta tuxedo dress Mrs. Simpson-West would die for… if only she had the height. Its silk collar and lapels shimmered in the light of the camera flashes.

Just before she entered her car, I glanced at her face, and a boulder of shock hit me through the gut.

"M-mom?"

"Stop the car," said Edward into the intercom.

The limo slowed, but before it stopped, I opened the door and stumbled out.

"Emilia!" someone snarled from the limo.

I ran alongside the row of parked cars, heart racing, my eyes fixed on Mom's car. Her Bentley pulled out from the space, and I ran in the middle of the road, not giving him the chance to overtake me.

"Fuck, Emilia!" shouted Blake from behind.

The car stopped, and I placed my hands on its warm bumper, scrambled around its perimeter, and pounded on the back door.

"What are you doing?" said the stern voice of the driver.

"It's alright." Mom stepped out and beamed. "That's my daughter."

Blake grabbed my shoulder. "You could have gotten yourself killed!"

Mom rushed forward and wrapped me into a Chanel Number

Five-scented hug. My arms hung lifelessly at my sides. How could she act so warm after ignoring me for three terms?

"It's so wonderful to see you," she murmured into my ear. "I know you're busy, but it means so much to me that you changed your mind about coming to London." She drew back and beamed, her gray eyes twinkling with mischief. "Is this Charles? I don't know why you refused to send me a photo. He's gorgeous!"

"Ummm..." Where did she get that name? I exchanged a confused glance with Blake and made introductions. My mind whirred with possibilities. Mom's eyes were as sharp as ever, so I could rule out drugs. Henry and Edward strolled over, and I introduced them to Mom.

Her brows drew together. "You never mentioned any of these handsome devils in your texts!"

My thoughts jumped to Edward's father, and my throat closed up. A car beeped as it overtook the Bentley and beeped again as it overtook Edward's limo.

"L-let's continue this conversation on the sidewalk," I said.

We all moved out of the road, and the boys surrounded me like bodyguards. An idea formed in my head that would explain Mom's strange behavior, but it was too heinous to voice... Yet. I kept her talking, trying to eke out what had happened on her end.

She told me we had texted each other daily, and I updated her with my heavy workload at Mercia Academy but had refused to send her any pictures of myself and my friends. I hadn't received a single text from her, and hadn't told her anything about my life at the academy, so who the fuck impersonated me and gave her all these bogus facts?

"I know what's happened." The words tumbled out of my mouth before I could stop them.

Mom's head tilted to the side. "What are you talking about, darling?"

My mouth opened and closed, and I stared into her smoky eyes.

Mom overreacted all the time. If I told her tonight, she would probably confront Rudolph, and one of two things would happen. Either Rudolph would arrange for Mom or me to get hurt, or he would twist facts around to make me look like a psycho jealous of her own mother's happiness.

Cold fury filled my veins, and I paused, needing time to work out how much Rudolph had done to Mom and me over the last nine months, and how I could pay him back for everything I'd suffered.

Mom's smile faltered. "Darling?"

"It's been a strenuous few hours." I gestured at the boys who still stood behind me like a human shield. "Hey, Mom?"

"Yes, dear?"

"I lost my phone recently and had to get a new one. Can you call my number?"

Confusion crossed her features, but she pulled her phone out from her purse and clicked the icon marked EMILIA.

My phone, which had the same number as before, didn't even vibrate. Someone must have hacked into her smartphone and changed the number she held for me to the impostor's. That same person must also have changed Mom's number, so I wouldn't reach her. With her Manhattan apartment sold, I would have no way of contacting her except via Rudolph.

I schooled my expression and handed her my smartphone, "Why don't you tap your number in here, and I'll call you back?"

"Sure."

Palpitations reverberated in my heart, sending shockwaves of fury through my bones. Fucking Rudolph. Not only had he sent me away to Mercia Academy, but he had changed Mom's number and gotten someone else to impersonate me and exchange messages with her. Was he so insecure about his relationship with Mom that he needed to keep us apart?

She handed back my smartphone, and I held onto her hand.

"Are you happy, Mom?" I asked.

A smile broke out across her face. "I think so. Rudy's so busy with his companies, and I have my functions. It works."

My face remained impassive, but on the inside, my blood boiled with the need for payback. Theories slotted into place in my mind, but I needed time to think. "How long will you be in London?"

"Until Monday morning, then I'll fly to Paris. Why?"

"Because I want to meet you tomorrow. Where are you staying?"

She reached into her purse and pulled out a card for The Dorchester Hotel.

I wrapped my arms around her and whispered, "See you tomorrow. Can we meet for breakfast?"

She kissed my temple and drew back, cupping my face in her hands. Happy tears filled her eyes, and I wondered if she had spent months fretting over why I had been so distant.

"I'd love to," she murmured.

The four of us walked back to the limo in silence, and a bunch of questions rolled to the forefront of my mind. Who told Charlotte I was the Saturday Correspondent leak? Who was rich enough to fund Charlotte's education and pay for her cosmetic surgery? How was Mr. Carbuncle able to disappear, despite being wanted for kidnapping and assault? Who kept making Charlotte's criminal problems go away?

They all had the same answer: Rudolph.

At the time, it had seemed odd that Blake had found me before the reporters and the police. They should have been able to work out which floor I'd been taken by the footage or the number of times I'd been bumped on the stairs. Jackie hadn't once mentioned never hearing Charlotte discuss a party she had been planning in London. Had she known I would walk into an ambush? Why had I been sent up there alone, when there were interns in the back of the van?

Hot, furious breaths steamed out from my nostrils. Everything was consistent with Rudolph's desire to build up the Saturday Correspondent and to separate me from Mom.

If I eventually succumbed to Mr. Carbuncle's rages and died, who would be there to pick up the pieces for Mom? That sick, twisted old fuck. That's who.

I stepped into the limo and leaned back into its leather seat. As soon as the boys had settled in, I clicked the intercom button.

"Turn the car around," I said. "We're going back for the young lady we left behind."

END OF BOOK THREE
READ BOOK FOUR

PAYBACK

KINGS OF MERCIA ACADEMY BOOK 4

CHAPTER 1

The limo drove down Pall Mall, an elegant street of historical, stone-fronted buildings, whose lights resembled something from the nineteenth century. Everyone sitting in the back, Duncan included, turned their gazes in my direction.

I supposed it was rash of me to instruct the driver to turn the car around without informing the others, but the more I thought about it, the more I was convinced Rudolph was behind my recent abduction. I just needed Charlotte to confirm it.

"Emilia?" Edward tilted his head to the side. The artificial lights streaming in through the vehicle's windows made the ends of his mahogany hair shine like rubies. "Anything the matter?"

The limo made a U-turn at the roundabout behind Trafalgar Square, passing the statues of Lord Nelson, the lions, and the fountains. I leaned forward, meeting each of the boys' eyes.

Henry sat on the far left of the limo, the blue spotlights tinting his blonde curls. He furrowed his brow and leaned forward as though needing to examine my features.

Between him and me sat Blake, who narrowed his chocolate-brown eyes. Perhaps pieces of the puzzle were also coming together for him. Out of everyone in this limo, he knew Charlotte the best, even if it was because he believed in keeping his enemies close.

Edward sat on my left, his hand on mine, lending me his strength. Seeing Mom and discovering that someone had impersonated me all this time had been a shock, but it was nothing compared to the realization that Rudolph had been behind everything that had gone horribly wrong this term.

Duncan pushed his thick glasses up his nose, further magnifying his eyes. "What's wrong, Hobson?"

"We're going back for Charlotte," I said.

Relief crossed his features. "I knew you wouldn't leave a lady stranded in the middle of nowhere."

Edward pursed his lips. "A young woman prepared to drug countless others to make them susceptible to a boat-full of boys who have paid for their... attentions is no lady."

Duncan jerked his head to the side and grimaced. My shoulders sagged. He was probably conflicted. He had recently lost his virginity to Charlotte, securing his loyalty, and even in the face of dozens of sick girls being piled into ambulances, he still cared about her.

"I know what she did was wrong," he said, "but surely the authorities—"

"Emilia explained it all to the police officers, and they let Charlotte go," Henry snarled. "Do you call that justice?"

Duncan bowed his head.

"She's guilty of far more than doctoring cocktails." I turned my gaze away from the boy and stared out of the window at the Thames.

The limo sped along the embankment. The green and yellow lights of the Royal Festival Hall reflected on its surface. We passed the Oxo Tower, the Tate Modern, Shakespeare's Globe, and all manner of major landmarks, but none of that mattered. The realization that Rudolph was far more nefarious than I had thought rang in my ears.

Later, as we passed the Tower of London's outer walls and approached Tower Bridge, a lone, female figure shambled down the road, sticking out her thumb at oncoming traffic. My nostrils flared, and my lips curled with disgust. If that girl didn't answer my questions, I would strangle her with my bare hands.

"I'm surprised no one has picked her up by now," muttered Blake.

"She's about to wish someone had," I said through clenched teeth.

The limousine slowed and stopped a few feet ahead of where Charlotte had attempted to hitchhike. She pulled off one of her shoes, hobbled toward us, and opened the door. The roar of a passing motorcycle filled the limo's interior.

"Oh, haha, everyone." She climbed in and settled into the leather seat opposite. "Very funny. I knew you'd come back for me."

From the streaks of faded mascara running down her face, I got the impression she believed she had been stranded. If Mom hadn't revealed that Rudolph was more calculating and malevolent than I'd originally thought, I would have ordered Charlotte out again.

Instead, I turned to Duncan. "Could you sit in the front, please? I want to speak to Charlotte in private."

Duncan crossed his arms, lifted his chin, and gave me his most defiant stare. "Why am I the only one who keeps getting banished? You lot abducted me…"

His words trailed off at the sight of Edward brandishing a champagne bottle. "Blackwell," said Edward. "I suggest you take this and leave."

Duncan reached across, plucked it out of Edward's hands, and opened the door, letting in the sound of traffic. "This is the last time I go anywhere with you wankers."

"What's going on?" Charlotte's mascara-streaked face seemed to pale in the light of the limousine's interior. Her gaze darted from Duncan's retreating back to Henry.

I folded my arms across my chest and glowered at the girl responsible for my abduction. Partially responsible. A pained grimace crossed her features, and she shifted in her seat. She dipped her head, using her pale auburn hair, dyed to match mine, as some kind of shield.

The limousine pulled out and headed over Tower Bridge.

"Everyone blames you for what happened to those girls." I kept my voice even, tamping down the rage simmering in my belly.

Her mouth flapped open. "I didn't drug them."

"But you told the police Emilia did," said Henry.

"Because she tackled me to the ground like a beast."

"You're protecting someone," I said. "Someone who is going to leave you to get the blame and watch the students tear you apart."

She broke eye contact with Henry and picked at her nails. One of her knees bounced up and down.

I leaned forward. "If this person cared about you, he would have sent a car the moment he knew you were stranded in London."

"Who are you protecting?" asked Edward, his voice deceptively mild.

Her chin trembled, and she pressed her lips together in a thin line. I narrowed my eyes. Any display of vulnerability was probably for the boys' benefit. To make them ease off her, but they had seen the state of the girls on that boat. Some of them had been fourth and fifth years too young to drink, let alone to consent to any kind of activities in a sex party.

The limo sped through a restaurant-lined street, where crowds of people drank alcohol outside the pubs. I turned my gaze from the strange sight back to Charlotte, who now hunched forward in her seat.

"Talk," Blake snapped. "Or we'll dump you on the side of the road. Again."

"Philippe de Connasse," she whispered.

I turned to Blake, who shrugged. Charlotte stared at her lap, mascara-tinted tears falling onto her bare legs.

"Would you care to elaborate?" asked Edward.

"Philippe organized the party. He works for the Saturday Correspondent. I met him at your Valentine's Party." She raised her head and fixed me with a venomous stare. "He told me you were the leak who got my father arrested."

I placed my hand over my mouth and frowned. None of this added up. I hadn't met anyone with that name at the Saturday Correspondent and thought Charlotte's mystery lover had been Rudolph.

"Clearly, he lied," said Edward. "How could Emilia uncover details of your father's expenses fraud all the way from Mercia Academy, when the crimes were conducted in Westminster?"

Her nostrils flared.

"A whistle-blower provided all that evidence against your Dad," I said. "She was a former secretary."

Henry leaned forward and showed her the screen of his smartphone. I assumed he had found the article and the name of the woman who had resigned and handed over the evidence to the paper.

"Who is Philippe?" I asked.

"You already met him," said Charlotte. "He was standing outside the boat, making sure the boys didn't get back inside."

I ground my teeth. Henry had shoved two crew members aside to get on the boat. They had worn glasses with frames thick enough to conceal a camera. Philippe really was a member of the Correspondent's staff. But why had Jackie, the editor, been insistent that I uncover the identity of Charlotte's lover if he had been working for her all along? It didn't make any sense.

Charlotte wiped away her tears with the back of her hand. "Everything you blamed me for was his doing. It was Philippe's idea to raise money for Fathers' legal defense by abducting you, not mine."

"Did he also leave that fake invitation near my door?" I snapped.

Her brows lowered into a scowl, and she flared her nostrils. There were no doppelgängers or rugby boys to help her here, and she remained silent.

I folded my arms across my chest. This Philippe story sounded like bullshit. Where did a reporter get the kind of money to lavish on someone as annoying as Charlotte? Very few people had the type of wealth that could pay for cosmetic surgery and Mercia Academy tuition fees. And Charlotte's helpless victim act was a sham, too. Even if Philippe was the driving force behind my abduction and the disastrous sex party, he couldn't have achieved any of this without Charlotte's full cooperation.

"Where does this Philippe live?" snarled Henry.

She shrugged. "We only met in hotels."

"How convenient," muttered Blake.

"Give me his number, and we'll arrange a meeting tonight," said Henry.

Charlotte tapped a few buttons on her smartphone and handed it to Henry, who called his number. Hot, angry breaths streamed through his nostrils as he waited for Philippe to answer.

I swallowed hard. Charlotte didn't seem the type to throw a wealthy benefactor under the bus. Maybe he really had abandoned her as she had claimed. What if this Philippe was the person behind recent events? A million-pound ransom was a big enough motivation to do anything, and if he planned on keeping the money for himself, it made sense that he would set things up for Charlotte, her brother, and Mr. Carbuncle to get the blame.

"He's not answering," said Blake. "Who are you protecting?"

"No one," whispered Charlotte.

I lowered my head and stared into my hands. Charlotte had met someone at the Valentine's Day Massacre, which had been staffed by employees of the Correspondent dressed as waiters. Maybe she was telling the truth, and I was too blinded by hatred to see it.

"Hello?" asked a male voice on the speakerphone.

My heart jumped.

Henry held the phone out to Charlotte.

"Philippe," she said in a wheedling tone. "You left me to get the blame, and Emilia hurt me again."

"I am sorry, ma chérie," he crooned in a French accent. "That girl has always hated you. She is the cause of everything that has gone terrible in your life."

Charlotte shot me a hateful look. I glowered back.

She made a whining noise at the back of her throat. "But why did you have to leave me to the police?"

"Did they arrest you?" he asked a little more urgently.

"No, but—"

"What did you tell them?" he asked.

"I said Emilia put something in the girls' cocktails."

Philippe's throaty laugh filled the limousine, and blood pounded in my ears. Who the fuck was this guy, and why did he take such delight in hurting me? Edward curled his fingers around mine and pressed a kiss on my temple, but it did nothing to distract me from the odious Frenchman.

Henry made an urgent hand signal at her, and she nodded.

"When can I see you?" she asked in a baby voice.

"Soon, ma petite puce. Soon."

"What should I tell everyone when we get to school? They're all going to think I did it."

"Keep to your wonderful fiction," said Philippe. "Emilia poisoned the drink because she was jealous not to have been invited. And she needed a follow-up article for the Saturday Correspondent to discredit you and to drum up ill will toward your father before his trial."

My teeth ground together, and blood rushed through my ears.

The worst part about Philippe's plan was that the students of Elder House would believe Charlotte's version of events and not mine. Ignoring Blake's comforting hand on my back, I leaned forward, met her hazel eyes, and mouthed, 'tonight.'

Charlotte tried to wheedle an invitation to his hotel, hovel, wherever this troll was staying, but he said it wasn't possible. I stopped listening to Philippe's excuses. He was obviously a conman, using Charlotte as his cat's paw, but I still couldn't work out why someone I had never met hated me so much.

Philippe hung up, and Charlotte turned to me. "You see? It was him all along."

"Where does Rudolph Trommel fit into this?" I asked.

Charlotte tilted her head to the side. "He's your stepfather. I've never met him."

I didn't reply. All evidence might point to this mysterious Frenchman, but something about him still didn't ring true.

We finished the rest of the journey in silence. Charlotte's posture straightened with triumph, the boys sat back with pensive expressions, and my mind whirred like the mechanism of a malfunctioning pocket watch. Was there a link between Philippe and Rudolph or between Rudolph and Charlotte? I couldn't see it, but I could feel it deep in my gut. The only trouble was working out the details.

We reached Elder House just before midnight. The limousine's tires crunched on the gravel courtyard outside the ancient building. Duncan left the limo first and staggered up the stone steps, still holding the champagne bottle.

Charlotte reached out her hand. "Phone, please."

"You'll get it back tomorrow." Edward opened the limo door. "Get out."

With a huff, Charlotte climbed out and stormed into Elder House.

"I'm going to search through her messages." Edward squeezed my hand. "Why don't you go up to my room with Blake?"

"Do you need any help?" I asked.

"Get some rest," said Henry. "I'll work with him."

While Edward and Henry retreated to Edward's study to rifle through Charlotte's phone, I walked up the wooden staircase to Edward's room with Blake. Ever since Mr. Carbuncle had evaded the police in Chelsea Heights, the boys hadn't let me out of their sights. My heart weighed heavily in my empty chest, and my stomach felt like a lead weight. After a night like this, I really needed company.

Blake squeezed my hand as we reached the darkened top floor. His life had been as chaotic as mine. His father had been an alcoholic, and mine had been addicted to drugs. Both our mothers had married powerful, unscrupulous men and both of us felt slightly estranged from our mothers as a result.

"You must have worsened your injuries from wrestling with Charlotte." Blake's whisper echoed through the hallway.

"Probably," I muttered. "Though I didn't feel it at the time."

He chuckled. "Adrenaline blocks pain. You should see some of the bruises Henry gets after a rugby match." He turned the key in the lock and opened the door to Edward's room, letting out a cloud of sandalwood-scented air.

In a smoky voice that curled around my libido, he said, "Let me help you out of those clothes and tend to your wounds."

CHAPTER 2

Blake and I made slow love, only pausing to change the condom after he had climaxed. Pushing away the unsolved pieces of the puzzle that was Philippe, I fell asleep in the comfort of his embrace. It was the same way I'd lain in his arms when I had been too traumatized to sleep on my own. It had been exactly what I'd needed. A break from all the unpleasantness of the evening.

I drifted to sleep in his arms feeling content and secure until soft kisses on my neck pulled me from my slumber, and a gentle hand stroked circles over my belly. Warmth spread across my insides and pooled between my legs. I sighed against Blake's broad chest. At any moment, an erection would rub against my ass, and Edward would wait for me to arch before sliding into my core for our usual morning screw.

When I didn't feel him against me, my eye peeped open. Pale sunlight streamed in through the window, indicating that only a few minutes had passed since dawn.

"Edward, don't you ever sleep?" I murmured.

"We need to leave soon if you want to make it in time to meet your mother for breakfast," he replied.

A bolt of panic shot through my veins. My eyelids snapped open, and I bolted upright, jostling Blake. "Mom!"

"What?" Blake slurred.

All three of us piled into the bathroom for the longest quick shower of my life. The cubicle was barely wide enough to accommodate three, but the temperature of the water and the heat of our bodies more than made up for it. Taking up the middle spot, I soaped the boys with shower gel and gripped their erections with both fists.

Edward shuddered, and Blake let out a gasping breath.

"Ready?" I turned from Edward's blue eyes to Blake's chocolate brown.

They both gave me eager nods.

I tightened my grip on their thick, pulsing lengths and made slow, twisting actions with my wrists. Blake shivered under my touch, and Edward let out a low moan that went straight to my core.

With the slowest and most deliberate of movements, I moved my hands back and forth along their erections, reveling in the way they pulsed and lengthened under my touch. They were both of an equal length, except Edward was thicker along the shaft, and Blake thicker at the head.

The shower gel lathered over their lengths, easing the glide of my hands over their flesh. I tightened my fingers around their erections, and both Blake and Edward let out appreciative moans that made my insides ripple with delight. My tongue darted out to lick my lips. If we'd had the time, I'd be on my knees in front of them, taking their dicks in my mouth. Heat pulsed between my legs, and I bit down hard on my lip as my hands faltered at the thought of tasting them both.

"Can't handle us?" said Blake with a chuckle.

"Just thinking about swirling my tongue over your cock-heads." I ran my thumbs over both their slits. Edward's skin there was silkier than Blake's, who had a slightly rougher texture I ached to explore. "It's a shame we have a prior appointment."

"Not fair," Blake moaned.

Edward snickered. "I'm sure Emilia can give us a blow by blow demonstration in the limo."

A laugh bubbled up to the back of my throat, and I quickened my movements.

Their breaths came in shallow pants, and I varied my ministrations. A squeeze at the base, a twist at the head, each time, I reveled in the boys' gasps and moans and shudders.

"Which of you will last the longest?" I asked.

"At this rate," said Blake between clenched teeth. "Neither of us."

I flicked a strand of wet hair from out of my face. "That's high praise, coming from you."

Edward slid his fingers between my legs and circled my clit, sending pleasure sparking from my core. "I think you'll climax first."

"Ha!" Blake bent at my chest, closed his lips around my nipple, and sucked. The muscles of my core tightened with each gentle flick of his tongue. With his other hand, he rolled my nipples between his fingers.

A moan reverberated in the back of my throat. If it wasn't for the shower's constant stream of hot water, sweat would have broken out on my skin. Sensations swirled through my insides and gathered in my core, which ached with need. This was so unfair. Two of them working on me while my hand movements faltered.

"I thought Emilia said she could handle us both," Blake murmured with my nipple still in his mouth.

Edward rubbed the pad of his thumb over my clit while his index finger delved into my folds. "She never actually said she could."

"Fuck," I gasped out.

Edward's relentless fingers continued playing me like I was some kind of toy that dispensed moans and shudders at his command. His fingers pumped in and out of me, making the muscles of my core spasm and clench and twitch.

I tried to focus on the lengths pulsing in my grip, on making the boys climax first, but Blake's tongue and Edward's fingers kept bringing me back to reality. There was no winning with them working together to turn me into a moaning, twitching mess.

Warm water beat against my face like a summer storm.

Blake's dark chuckle caressed my core. "Let go, Emilia. Let us take you to a well-earned climax. There's no shame in losing to us."

Edward huffed a silent laugh.

"Alright," I said between panting breaths. "But winning when it's two against one doesn't count."

"Of course, it doesn't." Blake's answer was too smooth and silky to be heartfelt, but who cared with that hand kneading my breast? "Relax… I want to see you come."

A spasm released all the built-up pleasure in a wave of sensation that arched out from my core, swept down every limb, and crashed against each nerve ending. My shoulders seized, both hands curled tighter around the boys' erections, and I rocked back on my heels. Blake's arm around my back kept me steady, but the next spasm tore a moan from my lips.

My muscles pulsed around Edward's fingers, and his thumb stilled but maintained the pressure on my clit. As I convulsed through this seemingly endless climax, the boys continued thrusting, their slick lengths sliding back and forth against my tight grip.

Wave after wave of pleasure rocked my body. I couldn't explain why this climax was so intense. A release of all the pent-up pressure from the night before, perhaps? Edward groaned first—closely followed by Blake, and they both came to shuddering, spasming climaxes.

My core continued twitching. "I may have started first, but I was the last to finish."

～

Henry had already left to take an early train with Duncan to visit the girls in the Accident and Emergency department of Guy's Hospital and would join us later with an update on their progress. After an enjoyable drive, where I got a chance to taste the boys as I had fantasized in the shower, the limo stopped at the Dorchester Hotel, opposite Hyde Park.

The Dorchester was more modern than I had imagined, with none of the architectural features I'd become accustomed to at Mercia Academy. With terrazzo slabs covering the walls instead of bricks or stone-cladding, it reminded me of one of the hotels on Park Avenue. But when we stepped out of the limo and entered the vast, black-and-white tiled lobby, its art deco features made me catch my breath.

"She'll probably be at the Promenade." Blake gestured at a long, open space on the right. It was wider than any hallway I'd ever seen and consisted of three rows of mahogany tables with elegant, green chairs. "Mother often comes here for afternoon tea."

"Let's see if she's here." Edward placed an arm around my waist, and the three of us made our way to the Promenade.

For a Sunday, the dress-code at the Dorchester seemed to be smart-casual. Edward and Blake fitted in wearing the same kind of dark blazers and smart pants as the other men. Feeling slightly disheveled from the boys' double-teaming in the limo, I stared down at the creases on my ivory, linen sundress, and tamped down the butterflies in my stomach.

Edward's hand rubbed up and down my back. "Are you alright?"

I gulped a mouthful of air and nodded. It wasn't like this was a college interview. I was only going to see Mom. And she hadn't really ignored me for the entire three terms I'd been in Mercia Academy.

Mom sat at the bar, clad in a sleeveless dress, which was cut in the same style as the black Givenchy number Audrey Hepburn wore in Breakfast at Tiffany's. Except Mom's was champagne-colored and knee-length. She swept her blonde hair into a chignon, showing off a swan-like neck encased in a triple-strand, pearl choker.

"She looks even more breathtaking in daylight," murmured Blake. "I see where you get your outstanding beauty."

A warm glow filled my insides. Mom was the supermodel, but it was nice of him to compliment my looks. "I would have said the same for you if your Mom hadn't burst in on us with an entourage."

Edward chuckled. "This sounds like a fun story."

"It wasn't," Blake and I replied at the same time.

"We'll take a separate table and join you afterward." As we neared the bar, the warmth of Edward's hand left the small of my back.

My steps faltered. "Why?"

"You both have a lot to discuss," said Blake. "We won't intrude on your reunion."

Mom stood and swept me into a Chanel Number Five-scented hug. "I worried all night that you would cancel at the last minute like you did that time I returned from Fashion Week and two months ago when I went to Paris."

I ground my teeth and held my silence. She didn't know the person at the other end of her texts wasn't me, and I wanted to ease her into the whole revelation that she'd married a psychopath.

After she exchanged polite greetings with Blake and Edward, one of the waiters guided us to a table set with a pristine white cloth and elegant silverware.

Mom placed her hands on the cloth and glanced across the room. "What happened to Charles? Are you dating one of those two boys instead?"

I rubbed the side of my neck, and a sheepish smile crossed my face. "Both of them, actually."

Her gray eyes widened. "And they know?"

I nodded.

Her gaze lingered over Blake and Edward, who were currently shooting furtive glances in our direction. The corner of Mom's lip curled into a smile. She probably thought I'd been going out for ice cream with the boys and exchanging chaste kisses under the magnolia trees or something equally as innocent.

Grandma had been a child of the sixties and had experienced her fair share of men. However, Mom had met too many predators in the modeling scene and only dated with a view to marriage. She'd brought me up with similar values, but they'd crumbled into dust the moment I had met the triumvirate.

When she had finished scrutinizing the boys with her eyes, she leaned back in her seat and raised her brows. "That explains why you never had time to see me."

"Mom," I leaned across the table and placed my hand in hers. The pleasant notes of the piano filled the air, contrasting with what I was about to tell her. "Those texts you've been receiving weren't from me."

"What?" She reached under the table where she had left her purse and placed it on her lap. After unzipping it, she placed her hands into its depths and pulled out her phone. "That's impossible. You and I have texted nearly every day."

"Did you ever call?" I asked.

"Yes, but you either didn't pick up, or the line was so bad, I couldn't hear a word you said." She slid the phone across the white tablecloth. "See for yourself."

I scrolled through the fake texts. Whoever had impersonated me had taken phrases I had used in previous texts to Mom and changed things up a word here and there to suit the situation. The imposter had presented him or herself as someone who had immediately made friends within Mercia Academy and was too busy catching up with subjects such as Latin and Classical Greek to return to New York for the holidays or to meet Mom in London.

The piano paused to a smattering of applause, leaving me alone with my thoughts.

Whoever had impersonated me had even taken photos of a bedroom, shopping sprees, stacks of books, parks, and British meals with quippy messages about toad in the hole, cock-a-leekie soup, and spotted dick. The skin around my eyes heated, and my insides felt as though they'd been scraped out by Rudolph's grasping, wrinkled, liver-spotted hands. This was probably the work of an enthusiastic, young intern.

"I sent you phone calls and texts." My voice broke. "All this time, I thought you were too caught up with in being Mrs. Trommel to bother with me."

Her jeweled hand reached across the table and covered mine. "I'm not sure what's going on, but no matter who I marry, you'll always come first."

A lump formed in my throat. When we were young, it was just her and me, living in that cramped Brooklyn apartment. Mom would leave me with a neighbor whenever she was lucky enough to get modeling work. But it had been fun. Mrs. Williams had daughters my age, and I had loved the sleepovers. I'd never felt neglected until she had married and decided to send me to an exclusive prep school.

The piano restarted, ending the silence, but the melodic sounds did nothing to soothe my nerves.

"Are you sure you sent them to me?" Mom asked in a voice as soft as a hug. "My number hasn't changed."

Rudolph must have gotten one of his minions to change the number I had for Mom on my phone to make it look like she wasn't communicating with me. His home was full of servants. One of them could have snuck into my room while I was asleep or in the shower and done the deed.

"It's an impostor," I whispered.

Mom's lips turned down. "I traveled down to Mercia in October and spoke to the headmaster, but he told me you were on a school trip."

A pang of sadness struck my heart. I reached for the napkin and twisted its ends, anything to distract me from the oncoming tears. Maybe she thought I was lying to cover up having snubbed her all year. It was as though she couldn't believe anyone would go so far to impersonate me, and she was scrabbling for other explanations. After the events of this term and the last, I was willing to believe anything of Rudolph. Mom had probably only seen his charming side.

The waiter strode out from beside the bar and took our orders. As soon as he left, I turned my attention back to Mom. "I didn't send any of these texts."

Her brows drew together. "They sounded like the kind of things you would say." In a smaller voice, she added, "I wondered if you resented me for not insisting that you stayed in New York."

My shoulders drooped, and I slumped into my seat. I had resented her for a lot of things, but it had been my decision to go to England, even though I had secretly wished she had seen through Rudolph's attempt to keep us apart by sending me abroad.

With a long sigh, I said, "Someone's put a wedge between us, and I think I know who."

"Rudolph," she snapped.

"Huh?" I hadn't expected her to come to that conclusion so quickly.

"Every time we traveled to Europe, I would ask to stop at Southampton." Mom balled her fists, looking as though she wanted to slam them on the table.

"Why?"

"It's the nearest airport to Mercia Academy. Rudolph would make an excuse and offer to drop me off at one of the London airports. I suppose he needed time for his impostor to fabricate a convincing excuse for why we couldn't see each other."

The waiter placed an egg-white omelet in her place setting, and she murmured her thanks. It was a far cry from the usual graceful appreciation she would show serving staff, but I guessed she was in shock.

I thanked the waiter for my avocado toast with poached egg, something I hadn't eaten since coming to England. How much should I tell her about recent events? There was the gauntlet and my being framed for Henry's kidnapping, but the events of the second term had made what I had suffered back then insignificant.

"Emilia," said Mom. "What else aren't you telling me?"

I poked my poached egg and stared at the yolk bleeding out into the avocado. Was there any point in rehashing my experience with Mr. Carbuncle and breaking her heart? Even though suspicions about Rudolph lingered in the forefront of my mind, I kind of believed that Philippe was behind the kidnapping.

Since he worked for the Saturday Correspondent, he knew that Rudolph had paid the Bournevilles a million pounds not to press charges against me for Henry's abduction. It would make sense in his twisted mind that Rudolph would pay the same amount to stop pictures of the battered face of his stepdaughter from appearing in the press.

Before I could muster up an answer, Mom's phone rang. A scowl crossed her delicate features. "If that's him checking up on me…"

"Mom!" I dropped my fork. "Don't confront him, yet."

"Why not?" she hissed. "All this time, he's been keeping us apart. I want to know why!"

"Isn't it obvious?"

"What?"

"He wants you to himself." Her bullish expression remained in place, and I added, "Plus, you don't know what he'll do to either of us if you accuse him without all the facts."

Mom sniffed. "Alright. I'll hold my silence until I hear the full story. But if that old degenerate has done anything else, I'll wring his scrawny neck."

I blew out a sigh of relief. When Mom was agitated enough, there was no stopping her temper.

"Hello," she said with an impatient snap in her tone.

The male voice at the other end of the phone spoke.

Mom's features melted into a pleasant smile. "Oh. How are you, Philippe?"

CHAPTER 3

A palpitation seized my heart. It reverberated through my chest and shook me to the marrow. Suspicion joined in and kicked me in the gut. Philippe. I turned to where the boys sat at another row of the Promenade and waved them over. Blake and Edward exchanged confused looks and rose from their seats.

The pianist tinkled a relaxing tune, but the sounds only made my muscles tense. I needed to hear what this Philippe was saying. Mom continued a pleasant conversation with Philippe, and I leaned across the table, straining to listen to his voice. Her delicate brows scrunched into a quizzical frown, and she tilted the phone, so I could hear.

"Monsieur cannot spare the private jet and would like to know if a first-class ticket on British Airways will suffice," said the same, creepy Frenchman from the night before.

My lips tightened. Philippe had to be more than an employee of the Saturday Correspondent. Blake and Edward stood by our table, both seeming to recognize Philippe's voice.

Mom's expression turned from quizzical to worried, and she

said, "Can we continue this conversation later in the afternoon? I'm having problems with my order."

"Of course," said the smooth voice from the other side of the line. "A bien tôt, Madame."

She clicked the End button and gestured for the boys to sit. "What's wrong?"

"Who's Philippe?" I asked.

"Rudolph's European Personal Assistant," she replied. "Why?"

A mixture of triumph and disgust rippled through my insides. It wasn't a pleasant sensation, but vindicating, all the same. Turning to Mom, I said, "There's a girl at my school who lured me to London with a fake party invitation."

Mom clutched at her chest, her breathing ragged. "What happened?"

My mouth opened and closed as I formed the best way to skim over being beaten and groped by Mr. Carbuncle. The more I hesitated, the more her face slackened until she looked like she'd been punched.

"Blake rescued me and took me to Kensington Palace," I blurted.

"Kensington—" Her gaze darted to Blake. "What on earth is going on?"

Blake, who sat in the seat next to Mom, placed a hand on her wrist. In a soothing voice, he said, "Two men employed by Philippe abducted Emilia and wanted to hold her for ransom." The tone sounded so well-practiced, I wondered if he had used it often on his mother. "I found her less than an hour after she was taken and carried her away to safety."

Mom's brows drew together. "Anyone who works closely with Rudolph would know never to cross him."

The waiter who had been tending to Blake and Edward paused at our table. He leaned into Edward, and after a whispered conversation, he walked back through the Promenade and disappeared behind the piano.

Blake turned back to Mom. "We believe Mr. Trommel instructed Philippe to organize the kidnapping, perhaps in revenge for a disagreement he had with Emilia."

Mom's eyes bulged, and she turned to me, her expression a mask of slack incredulity. Her arms wrapped around her middle, and she asked, "Disagreement?"

I told her all about how I had volunteered to get revenge on some classmates by gathering information on them to be published in his failing newspaper. The waiters brought the boys' plates, and we continued breakfast, albeit at a much slower pace. Mom's face turned from furious to pale to disgusted. As I told her about him forcing me to return to Mercia Academy after my cover would have been blown, she bowed her head with the weight of my news.

"I didn't know." Her chest rose and fell with rapid breaths. "He's known for being ruthless in business, but I didn't think it would carry over to his personal life."

My stomach twisted into a knot, and a tight fist of guilt clutched at my heart. "Sorry for piling this all on you. But I'm fine. I survived."

She shook her head. "None of this would have happened if I hadn't remarried."

"Mrs. Trommel," said Blake. "I'm sure you wouldn't have married him if you had known the extent of his malevolence."

"I would never have even spoken to him if I knew he was capable of all these things." With hands that shook so hard the glass clanked against her rings, Mom brought her water glass to her lips and sipped.

"Then your guilt is misplaced," added Edward.

"Rudolph will pay for what he did to you," Mom snarled.

I exchanged nervous glances with Edward and Blake, wondering if they were thinking along the same lines as me. We'd all contributed to this sorry situation. The triumvirate had framed me for Henry's abduction, which had attracted Rudolph's wrath. Then I had negotiated to work with the Saturday Correspondent to exact my revenge, inciting Rudolph's greed. The articles had been lucrative and had ruined the lives of many, and when I had wanted to stop, I supposed Rudolph had used Philippe's connection with Charlotte to hurt me.

Blake leaned forward. "What if this Philippe was acting without Rudolph's authority?"

Edward frowned. "Then why did Philippe engineer the booze cruise? It looks like he wanted to produce material for the paper."

"I'm certain he was working under Rudolph's instruction," said Mom. "Some of his assistants carry out unpleasant tasks. He once arranged a vehicle accident for a manager who had embezzled funds from one of his companies." She pressed her lips together as though she'd already said too much.

We sat in silence, picking at our breakfasts. Mom ordered a bloody Mary with extra vodka and breathed hard through her nostrils. "The police need to know."

I slumped in my seat and stared at the remnants of tomato juice in her empty glass. "He'll only bribe them."

"So far, everyone under his protection has evaded prosecution," said Edward.

I raised a shoulder. "Deep pockets go a long way in escaping justice."

Henry arrived at the table, also dressed in a blazer and slacks. He took one look at our downcast expressions and frowned. "Am I interrupting?"

I shook my head. "Sorry, Mom. Let me introduce you to everyone again."

This time, I gave a little background on each of the boys. Mom had met Blake's mother at a few social events, and she seemed impressed that Edward's father was the Duke of Mercia. She also recognized Henry's last name from the department store. "Henry's just returned from visiting the girls who drank the doctored cocktails at the booze cruise."

"How are they?" Mom asked in a voice that sounded hoarse with unshed tears.

"Some have already been discharged. Mr. Jenkins was there." Henry turned to Mom. "He's our housemaster. He and the house matron took most of the girls back to the academy, but a few others are still being kept for observation."

We all blew out collective breaths of relief. Mom called over and ordered another bloody Mary and whatever else we wanted. Henry ordered a full English breakfast.

I sipped from my glass of orange juice. The sweet liquid coated my bitter tongue and moistened my dry throat. "What about the others who had to stay?"

"From what I heard, those are the ones who drank the most. They're being kept back for observation, as the drugs haven't left their systems."

"They overdosed," I snarled.

Mom shook her head. "I can't stay married to that monster."

"Can you wait a little longer?" I asked.

"Why?"

"He'll ask why you're divorcing him." My hands clenched into fists. "If you tell Rudolph it's because he was behind my abduction, he'll become cautious. I want to make him suffer for everyone he hurt."

Her gaze darted around the table. "He's dangerous. I don't want you to provoke—"

"Mom, please. Just give us some time. If we can't work out a way to make him pay without attracting his attention, I'll drop it."

"He's already gone after Emilia once," said Blake. "Delaying divorce proceedings a little longer will give us the chance to stop him."

Mom twisted her napkin. She seemed to be mulling over our

proposal, but the way she blinked too quickly and the confused twist of her lips told me she couldn't decide whether to give me the chance to exact some revenge against Rudolph.

Edward cleared his throat. "Mrs. Trommel—"

"Call me Melinda," she said.

Edward inclined his head. "If it seems like Emilia's actions will attract negative attention from Rudolph or his agents, I will personally put an end to proceedings for her own protection."

Mom swallowed. "How long do you need?"

I glanced from Henry to Edward, to Blake, asking them a silent question. The conversation stopped while the waiter brought a large plate laden with poached eggs, sausages, bacon, black pudding, tomatoes, and grilled mushrooms.

After the waiter deposited a jug of orange juice on our table, Edward spoke. "Term ends in two weeks. After that, Charlotte will leave Mercia, and we won't see her until the start of the next academic year."

I turned to Mom. "Can you hold off until then?"

She pursed her lips. "He's expecting me back in New York next week, but I suppose I can tell him I want to go to Casablanca for a fashion expo."

"Don't tell anyone you saw me," I said.

A tiny smile broke across her lips. "I wouldn't want to ruin the surprise when he finally gets what he deserves."

Mom changed the subject from Rudolph and asked a bunch of questions about what life was really like at Mercia Academy. The impostor had given her the impression that the faculty provided weekly excursions to London for shopping and trips to the theater. Skipping over the bullying and the prejudice and the scandals, I told her about the beautiful buildings and the quaint village outside the academy.

Later, we walked back to the black-and-white tiled lobby. Mom needed time to check in for her flight which was in two hours, and we needed to work out a way to make Rudolph hurt.

After the boys hugged Mom goodbye, she held me back and whispered, "Is Henry…?"

"I'm dating him, too."

"Be careful." Mom glanced at where the triumvirate stood by the Dorchester's revolving door. "They all seem to love you. Make your choice soon before you break the other boys' hearts."

I stared up into Mom's gray eyes. How could I say this without her freaking out in the middle of the hotel lobby? "We're all together."

She gave me the oddest look. It was one-part wonder, two-parts concerned, and three-parts scandalized. "You're sleeping with them all?"

"Not yet."

Her nostrils flared. "Emilia Faye Hobson," she whisper-shouted. "What did I tell you about safe sex?"

"Shhh!" I glanced around the lobby. No one was listening, but the conversation was embarrassing enough. "We're being careful."

Her expression pinched, and she brushed off a piece of imaginary lint on my shoulder, storm clouds forming in her eyes in an expression that I recognized as her building into a rant. "I should hope so—"

"Mom," I snapped. "If it wasn't for them, I would never have survived the past few weeks. They've done so much for me."

She jerked her head to one side as though slapped. Then she sighed. "More than I have."

"Don't blame yourself." I squeezed her hand. "I thought you were ignoring me, too."

Her chest deflated with a sigh. "But I'm your Mother…"

"Is there anything you can tell me about Rudolph that might help us get our revenge? Something personal?"

"Hardly." She made a soft snort. "We haven't even consummated our marriage. After we announced our engagement, his pre-marriage blood test was positive for syphilis. I wanted to break things off, but he persuaded me not to make him lose face."

I narrowed my eyes. "Persuaded or threatened?"

She shook her head. "Don't worry about me. I'll be fine as long as I keep the confidentiality clause in our prenup."

"But you've just told me."

"And you won't tell anyone else."

I shook my head. The wounds Mr. Carbuncle had inflicted were reminder enough of the brutality of Rudolph and his agents. "What does the prenup say?"

Mom raised a shoulder. "I get nothing if I file for divorce in the first year and a sizable chunk of his fortune if he's unfaithful. But to hell with Rudolph and his dirty money. I'll file for divorce the moment you get your revenge."

A plan hatched in the back of my mind. "Is there any way you can hang on until the end of August?"

"Emilia!" She stepped back.

My hand closed around hers. "Don't leave yourself empty-handed. If we work things out, you might get that sizable chunk."

After bidding Mom a tearful goodbye, Henry insisted that we cross the road and walk through Hyde Park to clear our heads. We stepped out of the Dorchester, crossed the busy street, and entered an expanse of green that reminded me of Central Park. Long paths meandered around a lawn dotted with huge oak trees, and the scent of roses filled my nostrils. People sat on blankets, jackets, directly on the grass, either having picnics or enjoying the sunshine.

The boys took off their blazers, and I strolled between Henry and Edward toward a body of water in the distance.

"At least this is one place we know isn't bugged," muttered Henry. "Rudolph seems to have tentacles everywhere."

I shook my head. "He must have planned to turn against me from the start if he'd gotten his assistant to seduce Charlotte."

"He's always steps ahead of us. How do we get back at him?"

"We can start by sweeping the academy for surveillance devices," said Blake.

"I have Carbuncle's map of cameras," added Edward.

"How?" asked Henry.

"It was in his filing cabinet." Edward slipped his hands in his pockets and offered me his elbow. "I placed magnets on as many of the cameras as I could find to block the signals."

"You didn't tell us that," said Blake.

"I wasn't really thinking straight during the Easter break," he said.

The sadness in Edward's voice squeezed at my heart. That had been at the height of my betrayal, and I still cringed every time I thought of my actions. "Edward, I'm—"

"Don't. We've had this conversation countless times. You've forgiven us, and we've forgiven you. Let's not rehash it."

Without meaning to, my gaze traveled to Henry, and I met his verdant, green eyes. Unease settled in my stomach like a flock of butterflies flailing in a flood of guilt. I'd had the chance to speak with Edward and Blake about our first two terms, but every time Henry and I were alone, either lust or resentment took the forefront, and we never got the chance to open our hearts. He gave me the saddest of smiles, and my heart sank into the abyss of drowning butterflies.

At some point, I would need to get him alone to resolve our differences.

Up ahead, a group of boys around our age played five-a-side football. I smiled at the laughter and boisterous cheers of the scoring team. So close to the end of term, we should be having fun in the sun, not scheming ways to protect and avenge ourselves from my psychotic stepfather.

"Who thinks Charlotte knows Philippe works for Rudolph?" Blake raised his hand.

"She told me her boyfriend had the power to make my life miserable." I stared into a group of swans swimming close to the edge of the water. "The way she said it implied that this man had some kind of power over me."

"Like access to a stepfather," said Edward.

"I think she's sleeping with them both," said Blake.

Henry chuckled. "You'd go to any length to disparage that girl."

He shrugged. "It doesn't mean I'm wrong."

A shudder of disgust rippled through my gut. It was bad enough thinking of Mom kissing that old reptile. But I couldn't see someone my age, not even Charlotte, going anywhere near Rudolph turtle-face Trommel.

"I'd rather not think about that girl's nocturnal activities," said Edward, his voice clipped.

I dipped my head to hide my smile. Whatever fumble he had shared with Charlotte when he was thirteen must have been disastrous. A group of cyclists sped past on the nearest path, blowing whistles. One of the riders had the same mousy ponytail Charlotte used to sport before she changed her hair color.

"We already know how to get back at Charlotte," said Henry. "The girls will destroy her when they return from the hospital."

"But Rudolph and Philippe will be a challenge."

"A sex scandal," I said. "If we can tie Charlotte and Rudolph together—"

"What's the age of consent in New York?" asked Blake.

"Seventeen," I said. "Why?"

His shoulders sagged. "It's sixteen over here. I was hoping we could prove that one or both of them seduced an underage girl to get her to entrap another underage girl into a violent abduction."

"What if they took her somewhere with a higher age of consent?" I asked.

Henry barked out a laugh. "There's no way we can convince

Charlotte to fuck an old man in England, let alone a place where it's illegal for her to have sex."

"She's already sleeping with Philippe," I said. "She's upset enough that he's allowing her to take the fall for spiking the girls' cocktails. We just have to get her to lure him overseas."

"It's fifteen in France," muttered Blake.

"Fourteen in Italy," added Henry.

"Eighteen in California," I said.

All three of the triumvirate turned to stare at me.

"What?" I asked.

Edward sighed. "If we had a year to cajole Charlotte and the stomach to encourage such a liaison, it might be a workable idea. But we don't. Let's not waste any more time on this line of thinking."

As we continued toward the lake, the people lying on the grass wore fewer clothes, and at the banks, they sat on towels and wore swimsuits. Henry explained that this part of the lake was a natural swimming pool, and the entire body of water was built during the reign of King George II.

I pulled my gaze away from the bathers and tried to think up ways to get even with Rudolph. We threw out ideas, ranging from recording Rudolph's gloating confession to outright poisoning him, each as ridiculous as the other.

Edward ran his fingers through his mahogany hair. "Regardless of what we decide, Carbuncle is still at large and still being hidden by Philippe or Rudolph. At any time, our enemies can use him as a weapon against you."

His warning sent a chill through my bones that not even the midday sun could warm.

CHAPTER 4

The only way I could describe Monday morning was desolate. Thick clouds covered the sky, so no natural sunlight streamed into the dining room's tall windows. That, combined with the ten-foot-tall mahogany panels and lack of burning fireplaces made the room appear dull. It didn't help that a quarter of the girls were missing, reminding me of the darkness that had permeated the academy.

Many of the boys I had seen leaving the booze cruise sat together as though giving each other moral support. Coates, Bierson, and a few of the rugby boys gathered around a table at the back, leaving the dais bare.

"Have you noticed all the sex party wankers sitting together?" Blake glowered at Henry's former rugby teammates.

Henry grunted. "They're probably ashamed of themselves."

Edward poured himself a cup of earl grey from a china teapot, releasing the fragrant scent of bergamot. "Hopefully, they realize the danger of paying for access to unwitting girls."

"Let's hope so." I shot Patterson-Bourke a filthy look. He was the stout rugby boy with no talent for the sport who had implied to a fifth-year girl that she would warm to him at Charlotte's party. His words and tone of voice had indicated that he knew exactly what would happen.

The chatter dulled to a tense silence, and I glanced around to see what had caused everyone to stop talking.

Charlotte stood at the doorway with a crutch under one arm and the other in a loose sling. I sucked in a breath through my teeth. The wretched cow fought me with the strength of a bull last night when I had tackled her to the ground. This had to be one of her sympathy-getting tactics. I straightened, ready to call her out on her deception, but Edward placed a hand on my forearm.

"Don't distract the rest of the house from their grievance," he whispered. "If you speak up against her, some might take her side over yours and forget her transgressions."

I gave him a sharp nod and turned back to my spinach and cheese omelet. "Will you reclaim the head table?"

Edward shook his head, the faintest of smiles curving his full lips. "There's no need for such an ostentatious display. Thanks to the three of you, I have everything I need."

"Hear, hear." Blake nodded. "The most damning of our secrets are out, and we've survived unscathed. His Grace has the best care money can buy, Chaloner has disappeared to hell and taken his mobsters with him, and we have a beautiful bedwarmer who suits all our tastes."

My head snapped up. "Did you just compare me to a hot water bottle?"

"She's more like a koala," said Edward.

"Or a limpet," added Blake.

Suppressing a smile, I said, "If that's how you feel about my snuggling, I won't bother."

My eyes caught Henry's, who dropped his gaze to his scrambled eggs and kippers. A twinge struck my heart, making me snatch my gaze away and grab a piece of toast from the rack.

Anyone could tell he felt left out. It wasn't like I had told him he wasn't welcome in Edward's room, but seeing me battered and bruised at the palace had shaken him.

Blake had apologized for his role in my framing and subsequent detention, saying that he now realized that it had driven me to seek revenge and led me into even more trouble. Henry, however, hadn't yet spoken with me about that incident.

I turned my attention back to Charlotte, who still stood at the doorway, making her best impression of Charles Dickens' Tiny Tim. My lips turned downward. It was an effort to not say something scathing. What was she waiting for, an invitation?

She wrapped her arm— sling and all— around her middle, accentuating her huge breasts, and hobbled on her single crutch over to our table. "Blake," she said in a small voice. "May I talk to you?"

"About what?" he grabbed a slice of toast from the rack and slathered it with butter.

Her gaze darted around the tables, where people had stopped to glare at her. "It's... personal."

I clamped my lips together and clenched my teeth. It made no sense that Charlotte would try to confide in the person who had filmed her sucking him off and then broadcast it to the whole of Elder House. In case this was an attempt to rile me up and start a fight to garner sympathy for herself, I focused on my eggs.

"I'm all ears." Blake crunched into his toast.

Charlotte let out a frustrated huff. "Blake, I—"

"Whatever it is," he said, "I'm not interested unless you're here to tell us the truth about who you're working with."

"Blake—"

"You have a short memory." Blake snapped. "How many girls have you lured into perilous situations?"

She didn't answer.

"Don't approach us until you're ready to tell us everything you've done behind the scenes to hurt Emilia and the other girls."

~

In English Lit, Miss Oakley handed out copies of Nathaniel Hawthorne's The Scarlet Letter. A flush stained her sallow cheeks, and she pulled off her robe and lay it on her desk. "Now, I know it's not British, but since we have an American in our ranks who can relate to this tale, I thought we might indulge in this wonderful piece of literature for the next fortnight."

I rolled my eyes. Would this old lady ever stop comparing me to prostitutes and fallen women? At least this was better than her Pretty Woman analogy.

She clapped her hands together. "Can one bright spark tell me about the theme of this story?"

Charlotte's hand shot up. "It's about a woman who ended up ostracized for trying to do the right thing."

The teacher's pale eyes gleamed, and she smacked her thin lips. "Do explain."

"Hester fell in love and got pregnant out of wedlock. In enlightened societies, this isn't of any consequence. However, in puritan times, they forced her to wear the mark of an adulteress."

"Yes, yes." Miss Oakley edged closer to Charlotte.

"Hester was mistreated by her peers." Charlotte stood and addressed the class like she was the lecturer and not the salivating old woman behind her. "Sometimes, a person is just ahead of their time. Look at Galileo? He was arrested for heresy for being a misunderstood genius, and it took nearly a century for people to realize that he had been right all along."

A few of our classmates whispered among themselves, and I caught a few people offering murmured words of support. I turned around and stared at the girls who had been drugged, but none of them spoke up or even cast Charlotte a glare.

My pulse pounded like a war drum. Blood roared through my ears, and the part of me who believed that scoundrels like Charlotte always landed on their feet bristled. I clenched my fists and ground my teeth. Nothing about her being shunned at breakfast had been undeserved. She'd set up dozens of girls to be date-raped, and some of them still suffered in hospital beds.

"Miss Oakley, I have a question."

The old woman's eyes sparkled. Probably because she considered me the subject-matter expert on all things scandalous. And it was all thanks to Charlotte, who had placed red ink on my skirt and informed her that I'd bled from rough sex.

"Yes, Miss Hobson?"

"Does the heroine of The Scarlet Letter trick other women into following in her example?"

The old woman shook her head. "Hester Prynne was more virtuous than the puritans who ostracized her."

Edward tugged at my arm, probably to repeat his warning from breakfast about publicly calling Charlotte out, but I ignored him. Her stupid Galileo speech seemed to be swaying the weak-minded sheeple who had called me names just to follow the example of the triumvirate. The drugged girls hadn't said a word against Charlotte, out of fear or embarrassment, I didn't know, but I couldn't stand to listen to that girl's bullshit any longer.

I nodded. "I think that drugging other girls in the village and trying to sell them to the men would justify the heroine becoming a pariah."

"Oh, Miss Hobson." The teacher pulled at the lapel of her tweed jacket. "You really ought to read the book. Hester Prynne didn't—"

"But that's what Underwood did." I turned around and glared into Charlotte's sneering face. "And she sold tickets to the boys, promising them success with girls who had shunned them."

Miss Oakley backed toward her desk. "Miss Hobson, that's rather harsh and potentially slanderous—"

"I was there." Alice shot out of her seat. "There were bottles of lager for the boys and a fruit punch on the bar for the girls. I only had a few mouthfuls of it and got sick."

Grumbles filled the room, and Charlotte collapsed into her seat. "H-Hobson is a liar."

Irritation flared across my skin. I was about to call Charlotte a liar and a conspirator to commit date-rape when someone knocked on the door, silencing the class.

A prefect from the year below poked his head inside. "Sorry to interrupt. Underwood is wanted in Mr. Weaver's office."

Charlotte's body sagged with relief. She hopped out of her seat, walked part-way to the door, then hobbled back to fetch her crutch.

I ground my teeth. She was such a shameless fraud. And nothing was being done to take her to task for drugging all those girls. I didn't, for one minute, believe that Philippe had placed the drugs in the punch without her knowledge. She would never have sold tickets to a party where boys thought they would have sex with girls unless she knew there would be a way to make the girls compliant.

∽

At lunchtime, Charlotte walked into the dining hall, holding some papers. Mr. Carbuncle's replacement, a much older man with a Santa Claus beard, Mr. Jenkins, and two policemen followed her inside. The new caretaker held a toolbox and a stepladder.

"I hope this is about the doctored drinks," I muttered into my glass of sparkling water. "Maybe they've found her stash of illicit drugs."

"Not quite," replied Edward.

Charlotte glanced at the piece of paper and pointed at a spot on the mantelpiece. The caretaker placed his ladder against the wall and climbed up. He turned to the police and nodded before climbing back down to rifle through his toolbox.

"Does anyone know what's going on?" I asked.

"I made a deal with Charlotte," said Edward.

"When?" asked Blake.

"Just before the first period, he replied. "I wouldn't mention her involvement in the drugging to the board of directors in exchange for her volunteering to show Mr. Rigley the location of all the hidden cameras."

Blake chuckled. "Did she know the police would accompany her?"

Edward raised a shoulder. "Even I didn't know they'd make an appearance. Perhaps Mr. Weaver called them."

My gaze darted back to the fireplace. "But it kind of looks like she might have planted the cameras."

"That's a small price to pay for not being expelled." Edward sliced into his salmon steak.

I glanced around the tables, my stomach lining trembling with apprehension. What if Charlotte publicly accused me of being the leak again? Everyone stopped eating to stare at the group by the fireplace. When the caretaker pushed aside a picture frame and removed the first camera, noises of uproar filled the dining room.

Mr. Jenkins strode into the room with his palms raised. "Ladies and gentlemen, please keep your voices down. Miss Underwood has kindly brought to our attention a security breach we believe is responsible for the recent spate of bad publicity surrounding Mercia Academy."

I slid further under the table. Based on the sneers being sent her way, she might not want to return to school in September.

"Miss Hobson." Mr. Jenkins hovered by my table. "There's a pressing matter I wish to discuss with you."

Dread lined my belly with a layer of cold lead. Charlotte might have convinced him that I had been the one who had set up those cameras. I glanced at Edward in a silent request to accompany me to the housemaster's office. My few interactions with Mr. Jenkins revealed him to be the kind of man who sided with bullies simply to get an easier life.

Edward and I stood, and the three of us walked out of the dining room to Mr. Jenkins' room. The musty scent of old paper filled my nostrils and made me cough. Even more documents than before piled his desk, and I wondered how he got any work done. He sat at desk chair and groaned.

"Sir?" I said.

"The school received a letter from Rudolph Trommel's office, explaining that this would be your last term here at Mercia Academy. Will you return to Park Preparatory? We need somewhere to send your records."

A jolt of panic shot through my heart. What the fuck was the old bastard planning this time? I exchanged a confused look with Edward and turned back to Mr. Jenkins. "I'm returning here next year."

Our housemaster leaned back in his creaky desk chair. "That's not what the letter says."

"Was it written by my mom?"

He rubbed the back of his silver hair. "No, but—"

"Rudolph didn't adopt me. He has no say in where I study." Now that Mom knew about his behind-the-scenes machinations, and I had her number, there was no way I would get nervous over this matter.

His cheeks pinked. "I do beg your pardon, but if you wish to maintain your place at Mercia Academy, your parents or guardian must inform us in writing no later than two weeks after the end of term."

"Thank you for the information," said Edward in his most cordial tone.

We both stood and marched out of the room.

"Is this a preemptive strike?" Edward asked.

"I think so."

Edward shook his head. "Let's discuss this tonight, outside the academy."

My hands balled into fists. If we didn't come up with a way to stop Rudolph soon, I was screwed.

CHAPTER 5

Rudolph's latest stunt soured my mood for the rest of the day. I couldn't even focus in class, earning me two demerits from Mr. Weatherford in Creative Writing for daydreaming. I couldn't tell whether Rudolph's attempt to withdraw me from Mercia Academy was revenge for refusing to supply him with new stories or a warning. Maybe he knew I was plotting against him with the triumvirate.

By the last lesson, Spanish class, my thoughts had become so paranoid, I pictured Rudolph and Philippe holding Mom at gunpoint for some imagined slight.

Henry and I sat in the back of the classroom, translating a passage of El Buscón by Francisco de Quevedo. I pulled out my phone and sent Mom a text to ask how she was doing, hoping to get a response in a few hours.

Just as I slipped the phone in the pocket of my blazer, it buzzed with her reply. She was shopping in Paris and would soon leave for Casablanca to stay with friends. My shoulders sagged with relief, and I focused on our translation.

As soon as the bell sounded, indicating the end of the school day, I stuffed my books in my bag and shot out of my seat.

Henry grabbed my wrist. "Where are you going in such a hurry?"

"I can't stop thinking about that letter he sent the school. What if there's a deeper meaning?"

With a sigh, he placed his books in his satchel. "He doesn't strike me as the kind who sends cryptic messages."

"He isn't."

Henry stood. "Perhaps the letter means exactly what it says: he's no longer willing to fund your education."

I blew out a long breath, and we walked out of the classroom together into the hallway. A gaggle of first years crowded around a bank of lockers, seeming less tiny than they had been in September. Many of them, who had started the academic year with blazers a size too large, now fit into their clothes. I smiled and turned back to Henry, who looked down at me with concern in his green eyes.

"Come on." I slid my hand down his arm and interlaced our fingers. "Let's meet the others."

We walked under the magnolia trees holding hands. Only a few pink flowers remained on their branches, now replaced by dense, green foliage. The faint scent of citrus wafted down to us through their canopy, but it did nothing to soothe my frayed nerves.

I glanced up at Henry, who turned his gaze down to me and smiled. It was a bitter-sweet curve of the lips, perhaps a more cheerful variation of the British stiff upper lip, but it struck at my heart.

A flock of butterflies took flight in my belly, urging me to use this opportunity to patch up our relationship. "Henry, I—"

"Let go of my person!" screeched a voice from behind.

A gang of fifth-year girls crowded around Charlotte. I recognized a blonde girl whose hair was cut in a bob from a conversation I had overheard earlier in the term. Patterson-Bourke, the shortest rugby player in the school, had accosted her in the hallway for having dumped him.

"Finally decided to show your face?" said the blonde. "What do you have to say for yourself after nearly killing us with a cocktail of drugs?"

Charlotte flung her arm out in my direction. "That American trollop put the drugs in your drinks. If you want retribution, go to her."

I rolled my eyes. That girl's desperation knew no bounds.

The blonde placed her hands on her hips. "The trollop wasn't even on the boat."

Her friend snuck up behind Charlotte and yanked at her hair. "You promised us the Yank wouldn't be there, so we know you're lying!"

My heart sank at the irony. I had endured so much to stop Charlotte from exploiting these girls, yet they still despised me. Maybe this was why Edward hadn't wanted me to speak up against Charlotte. Little had changed since the first term. The other students had only stopped calling me names because I was now under the protection of the triumvirate.

"Ignore them." Henry placed an arm around my shoulder and walked me further along the path of magnolia trees.

Blake and Edward stood outside the steps of Elder House, still clad in their school uniforms. The limo waited at the side of the building.

Edward raised his brows in silent question about how I was faring following Rudolph's letter. I tilted my head to the side and grimaced to indicate that I was still freaked out.

"We're going to Maison Saint-Nazaire."

I pictured the friendly old French couple who ran the quaint, little restaurant in the village. "We're seeing Jean-Paul and Françoise?"

Blake beamed. "He made us something special but told me it was a surprise."

The tightness in my shoulders unwound. An evening away from Charlotte sounded like heaven.

∽

After a round of effusive hugs and kisses, Françoise led us to the table by the kitchen, which she explained the boys had used since the Duke of Mercia had brought them over as first years. I sat next to Henry and opposite Blake, while Edward sat opposite Henry. Françoise served a round of Kir Royal, the most delicious aperitif of crème de cassis, which I learned was a blackcurrant liqueur, and champagne. A few diners sat at the front, but there was enough space between us so they wouldn't overhear our conversation.

The first dish was bouillabaisse, a rich, garlicky stew made from a dizzying array of seafood ingredients, served with bread Françoise had baked in her special baguette oven.

As Françoise poured us glasses of sauvignon blanc, she turned to Edward. "Your father was here today with his friend. It was good to see him."

Edward straightened. "How was he?"

"Happy, and that is all that matters, no?" The old woman retreated into the kitchens.

Edward leaned across the table and clasped Henry's hand. "I can't thank you enough." Emotion choked his voice. "What you have done for Father has been beyond my wildest expectations."

Henry shook his head. "There's no need—"

"I know what it cost, and there has never been a truer friend than you."

"Hear, hear." Blake raised his glass of sauvignon blanc.

I peered at Henry under my lashes, pondering the nature of the sacrifice he had made. Edward might have been referring to getting disinherited, but I couldn't be sure. It wasn't a subject I wanted to raise because I had endangered their plans by calling the police.

Later, Jean-Paul brought a pot of cassoulet, a rich casserole containing a variety of meats, beans, and sausages, which he had made using the recipe of a chef who worked for the Bourneville Group. Françoise brought a vintage Chateauneuf du Pape that had arrived earlier in the day from France. As she chatted with Edward and Henry in rapid French, I leaned over to Blake and asked, "What's this sacrifice Edward was talking about?"

"Sacrifice?" he whispered back.

"Edward said the kidnapping incident cost Henry something."

His brows drew together. "That time you followed him into the bushes on our school trip. One of Bingham's assistants knocked you out, and they argued about what to do with you."

My gaze flickered to Henry, who was still deep in conversation with Françoise. "Go on."

"Mr. Frost and the others gave Henry a choice," Blake continued. "If he left you behind in that clearing to wake up naturally, the deal was off, and Edward wouldn't get the help he needed for his father."

I nodded. It made sense since I would raise the alarm and get them all caught.

"But if Henry brought you along, it would ruin the friendship you'd built up. Even though I made the first move, Henry was the first to start liking you."

"Oh." I dipped my head.

Blake leaned across the table and whispered, "If you've already forgiven Henry, give him a sign. While I love guarding your naked body at nights, it's not the same without him in the room, don't you think?"

I nodded. "I've been meaning to speak with him."

"Do it sooner, rather than later." He leaned back and winked.

We ate the cassoulet in silence, occasionally making appreciative comments about the rich, meaty, and intensely flavorful dish. Afterward, we were all too full for tart tatin, Françoise's pudding of the day, so she brought a bottle of Sauternes, a dessert wine from Bordeaux.

Blake raised his glass in a toast. "To love and to wine and to laughter. To forgiveness, to cassoulet, to a happy ever after."

Françoise threw her head back and laughed while we clinked our glasses. My eyes were locked with Henry's for several rapid heartbeats longer than I'd held the others' gazes, and my throat dried. The naked hunger on his face and the unspoken want in his eyes made the pulse between my legs pound.

"Back to serious matters." Edward's commanding tone cut through the tension. "We have ten days to deal a blow to Rudolph, and so far, he seems to be ahead."

"Will your mother be able to afford next year's tuition fees without help?" asked Blake.

"Possibly," I replied. "Although I don't know whose money she uses to buy all those fashions."

"She seems like an intelligent woman," said Blake. "I'm not mentioning any names, but I know of a former model whose husband doesn't give her access to cash but allows her to spend unlimited amounts on fripperies. She has a little side-business where she uses his cards to make expensive purchases and sells the items to other women for fifty percent of their worth in cash."

My brows rose. Mom would yell at me if I suggested she run a scam like that, and I wouldn't dare bring up such a subject. In case Blake had been referring to his mother's arrangements with the prince, I said, "Rudolph probably has an assistant account for every item she's purchased."

Blake raised a shoulder. "Quite possibly."

"I say we corner him somewhere and beat him senseless," said Henry.

A laugh bubbled up in my throat. "That can be our plan B."

Blake leaned forward, brown eyes gleaming with mischief. "The sex scandal is probably the best way to get to him. Let him see what it's like to be drugged and groped at a party."

Edward held his napkin to his mouth. "Who will volunteer to be the groper?"

"You can do it," said Blake.

Edward raised his brows. "Why not Henry?"

"My tastes are extremely limited." Henry turned to Blake. "You do it."

I clapped my hand over my mouth and laughed. Heaven would be the four of us sitting around the table enjoying Jean-Paul's cooking and Françoise's wine, with the boys bantering over silly subjects like penis sizes and who would grope Rudolph Trommel.

We walked back to the academy through the village of quaint shops. The sun hung low in the sky, casting long shadows on the sidewalk. Edward and Blake walked ahead at double speed, chatting amiably about some musician I'd never heard about, leaving Henry to walk by my side on the pretext of protecting me from Mr. Carbuncle, who could be lurking anywhere.

Henry's hand brushed mine, each touch sending tiny shivers down my spine. We had gone to Maison Saint-Nazaire together once before. Slept in the same bed. Been intimate on several occasions, but there was a newness about strolling alongside him. The kind of butterfly-wings-tickling-the-stomach-lining feeling that I couldn't explain. My pulse pounded in my ears, drowning out the sounds of our footsteps, and I glanced up into his beautiful face. A mop of blond curls obscured his brow, but I imagined he was as nervous as I.

At this time of the evening, when most of the village stores were closed, only a few older students and villagers walked the streets. The occasional car drove past, but the thoroughfare was mostly silent. I glanced up at Henry, trying to think of something to say, but my mind went blank.

My tongue darted out to lick my lips. Since I had rejected him when he tried to kiss me after we visited his parents, I had to make the first move. I stretched out my index finger and brushed his hand.

The touch of his finger on mine sent a surge of heat between my legs. I sucked in a sharp breath through my teeth. What was it about Henry that made my libido race from zero to horny bitch? It had to be that large, athletic body, because right now, I was picturing him naked and pinning me to a mattress. Our fingers intertwined, and he held my hand.

We headed toward the long, straight road that led to the academy. If I didn't speak now, I might lose my chance. "Henry."

"Emilia," he said at the exact same time.

We both exchanged identical smiles. This was such a rom-com cliché, it was ridiculous. Avoiding endless rounds of 'you first. No, you.' As we turned the corner, I cleared my throat and said, "Do you think we can—"

"Blake!" screeched a voice in the distance. "Edward!" Charlotte sprinted toward us like a Tasmanian she-devil in her hockey skirt and a low-cut top that offered her ample breasts no support.

My heart sank. If she had abandoned the crutch and sling, then it meant she'd already thought up something more dastardly than faking an injury. I glanced at Henry, the object of her desire, and sighed. Why couldn't Charlotte take her ostracism like a woman and eat cheese sandwiches in her room?

Charlotte crossed her arms over her chest as she ran. Presumably to pin down her boobs to stop them from thrashing about. I rubbed the back of my neck and wondered if she regretted not wearing a sports bra.

Up ahead, Blake turned back to us and shrugged.

Henry groaned. "What does she want?"

"Nothing good," I muttered.

Charlotte stopped in front of Blake and Edward, her light auburn hair darkened with sweat. My brows drew together. Had she been run out of Mercia Academy for her transgressions? She doubled over, resting her forearms on her knees.

"Is there a reason why you're crouching in such an unseemly manner?" Blake tilted his head to the side. "You look like you're about to give birth."

Fat tears ran down her cheeks, and she clasped her hands to her chest. "I-it's Rudolph."

A jolt of adrenaline shot through my heart. "Rudolph?"

Ignoring me, she turned to Edward. "I lied. He's my sugar daddy. Philippe and I just slept together a few times before he made the introduction."

I sucked in a breath through my teeth but kept quiet. Any word from me, and Charlotte would turn belligerent and not want to reveal anything useful.

"Why are you admitting this now?" asked Blake.

She turned to Edward. "Those cameras you had me point out to Mr. Rigley and the police." She puffed out a breath. "Rudolph called, and he was furious. He says he won't pay for Father and Peter's criminal defense."

I held my breath, waiting for her to reveal more.

"Did you explain that you did it because Philippe left you with the blame for poisoning those girls?" asked Edward.

Her lips formed a thin line, and she didn't reply. Rudolph was far too wily to instruct his own official PA to put date-rape drugs in the cocktails of underage girls. I'd bet Charlotte did it herself and botched the doses.

Edward and Blake exchanged knowing glances.

"I want revenge." Charlotte folded her arms across her chest and glanced at Henry. "And you're going to be the ones to help me."

CHAPTER 6

Wiping the sweat off her brow, Charlotte sashayed past Blake and Edward and toward Henry. Her gaze flickered down to our joined hands. Hatred flared across her features for a microsecond, too quick for the eye to process, but it made my stomach drop with trepidation. Acting as though she wasn't bothered by our closeness, she directed her widest smile at Henry.

I pressed my lips together and tried not to pull a face. Charlotte was telling the truth about Rudolph being her sugar daddy, and I had no reason to doubt her claim. Everything made sense: the tuition fees, the nose job, the liposuction, and lavish gifts. He needed her to hurt me, so he could hurt Mom who he either secretly resented, secretly wanted to control, or both.

Inhaling deep, calming breaths through my nostrils, I stepped closer to Henry. She might be the key to getting our revenge on Mercia, but I wouldn't let her take advantage.

"Henry." She stopped in front of him and pouted. "You're the only one I can speak to on this subject."

He stiffened. "You're better friends with Edward and Blake than with me."

"They've been horrid." She continued in a babyish tone that seemed more whiny than sexy. "Edward kicked me off the head table, and Blake broadcasted a video of me to a whole campsite."

My eyes rolled toward the sky. Now she acknowledged that Blake was behind the blowjob video? I was the one who got a mug of hot cocoa in the face and a kick to the diaphragm for his prank.

"What do you have to say?" he asked.

Charlotte shook her head. "I won't confide in anyone else but you."

A pained look crossed Henry's features. It was clear that he wanted to walk past her, but we had struggled to find a way to hurt Rudolph before term ended. I imagined he felt conflicted.

"Why don't the two of you sit in the back of the car and discuss Charlotte's plan?" Edward gestured at the approaching limousine.

"Great idea." Charlotte held out her hand and turned toward the limo. "Come on, Henry."

Henry gazed down at me. "What do you think?"

"If she tries to touch you, stop the car and walk out. Then she'll have to deal with me."

His handsome features morphed into one of those crooked smiles that looked like he was trying not to laugh. The thought of me protecting his virtue probably amused him, but I was serious. Charlotte had gone to desperate lengths in the past to get her claws into Henry. There was more to her attraction than the Bourneville fortune. She still wanted him after he had been publicly disinherited. I expected she'd spent so long watching Henry on the rugby field and fantasizing about his powerful, sexy body, that she'd worked herself into a full-blown obsession.

The limo stopped on the side of the road. Charlotte opened the back door and sat inside, stretching her legs out on the leather interior, giving Henry no choice but to brush past them or walk around to the other side.

A tractor trundled toward us, pulling a pallet full of hay piled about eight bales high. Dust and bits of dried grass flew out from the bundles. I glowered at Charlotte's smirking face. What convenient timing.

Henry stepped over Charlotte's outstretched legs, and I headed toward the front passenger door.

"What are you doing?" Edward wrapped his hand around my wrist.

"This is the girl who uses date rape drugs and gives people blowjobs in exchange for information about Henry. I'm not leaving him alone with her."

Edward let go of me and sighed. "Henry can look after himself."

"That's dashed my plans of licking Armagnac off your naked body." Blake's dark eyes twinkled with mirth. "You know, he's escaped worse tackles than Charlotte's."

"Rugby's different. Henry would never elbow a girl in the gut, no matter how annoying or gropey. I have to keep an eye on her." I opened the limo's front door. The driver, who wore a flat cap with his black suit, gave a nod of greeting.

Blake climbed in after me. "Move up. Someone has to be there to make sure the catfight doesn't get out of control." He turned to Edward. "Are you coming?"

"I have a report to prepare for the Board of Governors," he replied. "But I'll see you tonight."

The limo sped down the road, leaving Edward on the narrow sidewalk. I leaned to the side and watched him in the rearview mirror, strolling toward the academy with his hands in his pockets. "Why didn't he come with us?"

"Watching Charlotte making a fool of herself for the thousandth time with Henry isn't anyone's idea of fun," replied Blake.

"Except yours."

"I can never get enough of seeing that girl fail." He twisted in his seat and slid open a panel.

"You want an English Rose, not American pigweed." Charlotte's nasal voice grated on my nerves.

I turned and peered through the gap. Henry wasn't in sight, and I assumed he sat on the driver's side to get as far from Charlotte as possible.

She leaned toward him with her skirt hiked up around her hips, exposing her stout, muscular thighs. Her shirt was unbuttoned to the sternum, showcasing a cleavage that would make a Hooters model weep with envy. "I just want what's best for you."

After an annoyed huff, Henry said, "If you don't get to the point about Rudolph Trommel, I'm leaving and walking to the academy."

Blake gave me a gentle nudge and raised his brows in an expression that said, 'See? I was right about Henry.'

A tiny smile curved my lips. I hadn't been worried about Henry succumbing to Charlotte's dubious charms. Even someone as oblivious as Mr. Jenkins could tell that Henry had no interest in her. But Charlotte was capable of the most heinous acts, and I didn't want her alone with anyone I cared about. I reached into my pocket.

Blake snickered. "Getting a gun?"

I pulled out my smartphone and pressed the voice recorder app. "I want to make sure we don't miss anything useful in between her clumsy attempts at seduction."

"Hobson's fucking Edward and Blake" Charlotte pulled off her tie. "Did you know that?"

I ground my teeth. What business was it of hers, and how did she find out?

"Stop that," said Henry. "What is this plan you have to get even with Rudolph Trommel?"

"Don't you care that she spends her nights in Edward's room with Blake, while you're left all on your own?" She spread her legs.

"I'll bet she's not wearing any knickers," Blake muttered into my ear.

"Right," Henry snarled through clenched teeth. "Driver, stop the car, please."

I folded my arms and nodded my approval. Charlotte was deluded if she thought Henry would show the slightest bit of interest in her. He hadn't in all the years she had been pursuing him, and nothing had changed except that her actions had repulsed him even more. The car slowed to a stop outside the academy gates, and the sound of a car door opening filled the back of the limo.

"Wait!" she screeched. "I'll tell you everything you need to know."

"Button up, pull your skirt down, and move right back to the other end."

"Henry…" she crooned.

"Do it!" he hissed.

I jolted. The only time I had seen Henry lose his temper was the time Coates had put Blake in a wrist lock. Even then, he had just stepped forward and punched the other boy in the face. Even that time when boys threw slurs at the triumvirate, Henry hadn't become as worked up as Blake or Edward.

"What do you want to know?" she asked with a pout in her voice.

"When did your relationship with Rudolph Trommel start?"

As the limo continued through the academy grounds and beyond, Charlotte told a long, rambling tale starting with how juicy Henry had looked in his fireman stripper costume at the Valentines Day party. She revealed that she had seen the four of us disappear into the hidden room and had tried to follow.

Blake leaned into me and muttered, "Thank fuck she didn't work out how to use the secret lever."

I shuddered. That would have made for a disastrous evening.

Charlotte explained that Philippe had approached her at the secret entrance and took her to another room for sex. After that, he had sent gifts to her at the academy in exchange for used panties.

"Do you think he gave them to Rudolph?" whispered Blake.

My lips curled. "I don't want to think about it."

On the weekend after she had discovered her father wouldn't be able to pay her tuition fees, Philippe had invited her down to London, where she met Rudolph. I narrowed my eyes. When I visited the Sunday Correspondent office at the end of last term, one of the interns had mentioned that she'd seen a video of Charlotte confiding in someone that she wouldn't return to the academy. The meeting must have happened then.

Loud sobbing filled the back of the limo. "I-I was so desperate. Father was scrambling around, selling assets to pay his criminal defense lawyers, and he didn't care what happened to me. Rudolph offered me everything I thought I wanted."

"What do you mean?" asked Henry.

She hiccuped. "R-Rudolph said he would pay off Peter's casino debts and fund Father's legal defense."

"What did he want in return?"

"Girls."

"What?" Henry choked out.

I twisted around in my seat and gaped through the gap in the panel. This had to be an exaggeration. Rudolph wouldn't be stupid enough to ask Charlotte to bring him underage girls.

"He said his wife didn't understand him, and they slept in separate bedrooms. He was lonely and needed a little company."

I drew in a sharp breath through my teeth. Mom had told me she hadn't slept with the syphilitic lizard, but I hadn't thought he would go so far as to approach some as young as Charlotte. "Why didn't he just marry someone else?"

"Because he's twisted," muttered Blake.

"And you gave him this company for money?" asked Henry.

Charlotte dipped her head. "You make it sound sordid. I didn't sleep with him out of enjoyment. I needed to continue my education, and he was desperate to hurt his wife."

Henry remained silent. How could anyone reply to a comment like that?

"Rudy wasn't a good sugar daddy. All he could talk about was getting payback. Payback for the gold digger who married him and didn't love him enough. Payback for his insane bitch stepdaughter who was going to get herself killed."

A boulder of shock hit me in the gut, and the blood drained from my face.

"What?" said Blake.

"What did you say?" said Henry.

She paused as though she hadn't revealed something heinous. "You mean Hobson? Rudolph told me she was a slut who would sleep with anyone. It would get her into trouble one of these days."

I grimaced. Something told me he had been laying the foundations for his kidnapping plot, rather than bitching that I would get an STD.

Charlotte sniffled. "He was picky, too. He listed all my flaws and said I would only reach his standards with liposuction, rhinoplasty, and collagen implants."

"Ouch," said Blake.

A dull ache filled my chest, and I wrapped my arms around my middle. All this time, I had thought Charlotte had demanded the cosmetic surgery when Rudolph had been the one who had demanded she alter her features. "He's sick."

Blake shook his head. "I almost feel bad for the girl."

"Did you have sex with him during the Easter break?" asked Henry.

Charlotte shook her head. "I was still recovering from my surgeries, but we watched each other over video chat."

"How many times did you meet him in real life?"

"A few times." She paused, either because what she would say next was terrible, or because she wanted to draw out the suspense.

"Philippe would meet me in London and take me to Rudolph's suite."

"What did you do for him?"

"Everything," she said in a broken voice. "Oral. Anal. Whatever he wanted. I kept thinking about helping my family, not about myself. Rudolph is ugly, and—"

"Whose idea was it to lure Emilia into that trap?" asked Henry.

My gaze flickered down to my app, which still recorded her confession.

"Not mine," she replied. "Rudolph told me Emilia had been his little spy for the Saturday Correspondent, but she was doing a poor job and needed to be taught a lesson. He asked me to meet Carbuncle and to present a scheme for him to get enough money to survive while hiding from the police."

"But you left that invitation in her hallway," said Henry.

Charlotte sniffled. "If Emilia didn't show up in Chelsea Heights, Rudolph wouldn't help my family."

"How did your brother get involved?"

"He went to mother, demanding that she sell her jewelry because someone he owed threatened to cut out his liver. I asked Rudolph for money, and he suggested that Peter make himself useful. The plan was to have an anonymous kidnapper send Hobson's pictures to the Correspondent every day until Mr. Carbuncle was finally caught."

Nausea seized my insides in its slimy grip, and I doubled over. Reading between the lines, it looked like Rudolph had planned to have Mr. Carbuncle murder me or leave me in a state close to death. I blew out a long, shuddering breath. "Why does he hate me so much?"

Blake rubbed my back. "He hates your mother for not sleeping with him."

I bit down on my lip. What if Mom refused to go to bed with Rudolph long after he'd gotten a clean bill of health for syphilis?

That should be grounds for divorce, not vengeance. It looked like Rudolph was trying to hurt her by isolating us both and having me killed in the most grisly manner.

"I-It was terrible," said Charlotte. "He's like an emaciated chicken with loose skin. If you saw how much Viagra he had to take—"

"I don't need the details," snapped Henry. "Where is he hiding Carbuncle?"

"He didn't say," Charlotte replied in a small voice.

Henry changed the subject, and they discussed options for getting her revenge on Rudolph. I could barely absorb the words as I kept thinking about Mom. Did she know how much Rudolph resented her for her refusal to sleep with him? From Mom's carefree demeanor, I didn't think she did.

Eventually, Henry and Charlotte concocted the idea of a honey trap, where Charlotte would go on Skype and entice Rudolph to say something incriminating, such as how he had instructed Philippe to recruit Mr. Carbuncle and Peter Underwood to abduct me.

I sank lower into my seat and watched the fields stretching through vast expanses of the Mercia estate. A dull ache settled at the bottom of my roiling stomach, adding to my nausea. "What kind of long, twisted game is he playing?"

Blake patted my thigh. "He wants to deliver his revenge at the right time."

I bowed my head. "That's how it looks to me, too."

He squeezed my hand. "But we'll stop him. He won't hurt you or your mother."

I stared at my phone. As soon as Charlotte finished talking, I would send the recording to Mom and tell her to watch her back.

CHAPTER 7

The limo driver drove around the block and pulled into the courtyard outside Elder House. The second the vehicle stopped, Henry opened the door and stepped outside. Charlotte remained in the back seat, presumably to adjust her skirt and button her shirt. Without waiting for Blake or me to exit, Henry bolted up the steps to Elder House and disappeared through the wooden double doors.

I thanked the driver then stepped out after Blake. He turned to me, his dark brows creased with concern. "Try not to worry about your mother. She'll be out of Rudolph's reach until she decides to return from Morocco."

We walked up the stone steps, through the double doors, and into the reception hall. The stone construction of Elder House meant that its interior was cooler than the outside, which was great for summer. Blake walked to his mailbox on the far left, while I checked mine in the middle. A manilla envelope lay in my mailbox.

I pulled it out. "What's this?"

"Does it say who it's from?" Blake pulled out a thick envelope made of quality paper stock out of his own mailbox. He turned it around to reveal the calligraphy script. "No prizes for guessing who has written to complain about my conduct."

My brows drew together. "But you haven't done anything wrong."

He flashed me a grin so wide, it made my heart flip-flop. Blake was such a handsome rascal. "Not yet."

I shook my head, and we walked arm-in-arm through the hallway to Edward's study. Henry paced back and forth in front of the fireplace, his face a mask of disgust. Edward sat at his desk and tapped on his laptop, doing his best to ignore Henry's wordless ranting.

Blake smirked. "Take one for the team."

"Easy for you to say," Henry snarled. "She isn't salivating all over you."

"No, but she often salivated over my cock."

"Blake," all three of us snapped at the same time.

He waved us away and sat on the Chesterfield. "You all love it when I talk dirty." Pulling me down onto his lap, he wrapped his arms around my waist and murmured, "Especially you."

"Not when it's about Charlotte Underwood." I slapped his muscled chest.

"I concur," muttered Edward, still staring at the screen of his laptop.

"Anyway," I squirmed on Blake's lap. "Henry won't have to take one for the team because I'll be there to chaperone."

"Good." Henry strode to the door. "We're meeting her in her room."

"Now?"

"She told me to meet her in five minutes. That was ten minutes ago."

I slid off Blake's lap and slapped at the hand reaching for my ass.

"One second," said Edward. "I've just downloaded the Stealth app. Fire it up before using Skype and video-call Charlotte. It will record everything that takes place on Skype. As soon as you activate stealth mode, you will become invisible, and she can call Rudolph without him noticing you're also on the line." He handed me his laptop. "It will also give you an excuse to be present."

"Thanks." I hugged the computer to my chest. Whatever Charlotte had planned would be designed both to entrap Rudolph and seduce Henry.

Henry and I left Edward's study and ascended the stairs to the girls' floor. He walked with the gait of a condemned man, a grim expression on his face. "I don't know what she's going to want me to do."

I placed a comforting hand on his arm. "I'll be there to supervise. Feel free to walk out once she has Rudolph in front of the camera."

Charlotte's room was larger than the one I shared with Rita and had a great view of the lawn, main teaching block, and the path of magnolia trees. Rugby posters covered the walls of the left side of the room, depicting blond and ginger-haired players with muscular physiques like Henry's.

She wore a parody of the Mercia Academy uniform. Under her burgundy blazer, a fitted shirt strained against her curves, and her skirt barely skimmed her crotch. Long, white socks finished off the outfit, making me wonder how many times she had dressed up like that for the camera. With her hair in two bunches, abnormally straight nose and bee-stung lips, she looked like a porno version of a schoolgirl.

Her laptop was balanced on her desk chair and pointed toward the bed. As soon as we stepped into the room, her malevolent glare raked over my form. "What's she doing here?"

"Someone has to make sure you're well lit," I said. "And to record the blackmail material."

"Fine. Just don't ogle me."

I snorted. "As if."

After opening Edward's laptop, I fired up the Stealth app and connected to Charlotte on Skype, making sure to silence the speakers to avoid feedback. The screen divided into two segments. Charlotte on the right and me on the left. She positioned herself on the bed for the camera and preened. The glare of the sun coming in from the window affected the quality of the picture, so Henry drew the curtains, and I turned on the desk lamp, creating softer lighting.

She crossed her legs. "How do I look, Henry?"

"Ready," he muttered.

I clicked the stealth-mode button, and my image disappeared from the screen. "Call Rudolph whenever you like."

Screen Charlotte leaned forward, fiddled with the mousepad on her laptop, then clicked a button. The Skype app made a dialing sound, and a few seconds later, a close-up of Rudolph's jowly face appeared on the screen. He blinked a few times before his expressionless face morphed into a wide grin of unnaturally bright teeth.

"Darling," he purred.

Anger burned in my veins, and acid roiled in my stomach. This bastard was the root of everything that had gone wrong in my life. If he hadn't coerced Mom into marrying him so he could save face, I would have still been in Park Prep, enjoying a carefree life with Noelle. My heart sank. In all the turmoil, I'd lost touch with my former best friend.

"You've been a very naughty girl." His voice became a low purr that made all the hairs on the back of my neck stand on end.

Charlotte leaned into the camera, arms squishing her ample breasts together. She swung her shoulders from side to side, making her cleavage waltz. "Rupee, I had no choice. Those horrible boys gave me Mr. Carbuncle's map and told me to tell the acting headmaster about the hidden cameras."

"How do I know you're telling the truth?" he used a mock-stern tone he probably only reserved for playtime.

"Can't I prove myself to you?" she said, full pout in her baby voice. "I'm just a young girl who makes mistakes."

Rudolph's chuckle sent a shudder down my back. "A young girl who requires a stern punishment."

I glanced up at Henry, whose gaze was fixed on me. His lips turned down, and one side of his nose wrinkled in a rictus of disgust.

"I wish you were here," she crooned.

"So do I." Rudolph's voice became breathy. "Turn around and show me your panties."

My brow furrowed. She was supposed to trick him into admitting that he had sent Mr. Carbuncle after me. How the hell did the conversation turn to her underwear?

Charlotte twisted around on the bed and positioned herself on her hands and knees, the back of her pleated gray skirt facing the camera. She flipped up the garment, revealing a skimpy thong, its white crotch already wet with arousal. I shook my head. For all that talk of Rudolph being disgusting, she was certainly enjoying herself now.

"Very good," he said, voice breathy. "Now give yourself a hard spanking."

I stepped away from the screen and stared at Henry. The corner of his mouth curled into a smile, and I smiled back. This was ridiculous. Watching two of my worst enemies have Skype-sex. In all the fuss about Charlotte, we hadn't had a chance to have our heart-to-heart.

Ignoring the sounds of slapping, Charlotte's fake whoops of pain, and Rudolph's excited words of encouragement, I laced my fingers with Henry's. The arousal I had felt earlier after the restaurant receded to the back of my mind, dampened by the activities in the room.

"Good girl," said Rudolph. "Now, sit down."

Rudolph's voice broke me out of my Henry-induced stupor, and my gaze snapped to the screen. I blinked several times to focus my eyes, not quite believing what I was seeing. Rudolph had somehow zoomed out his webcam, so it showed him sitting on the leather armchair of a hotel room, naked and with his legs akimbo. His withered right hand pumped an angry red penis that stretched like elastic with each movement. It was probably still flaccid while he waited for the help of Viagra.

"Will you help me with my woes?" Charlotte crooned.

"That depends entirely on you, my dear." Rudolph frowned down at his unresponsive member.

Charlotte leaned into the camera and fluttered her lashes. "What do you mean?"

"If you please me on camera, I will consider your request."

She made an exaggerated pout. "What shall I do?"

"Those big jugs straining through your blouse, the ones with the thick, juicy nipples… I want to see them."

Charlotte unbuttoned her shirt, and I twisted my fingers, indicating for Henry to turn his head. He turned his back to Charlotte, who now sat on the bed with her shirt undone. Her enormous boobs bulged out of a skimpy, red bra that barely covered her nipples. I winced, wondering if she suffered from back strain.

"Pull out those udders," said Rudolph, his voice hoarse. "I want to see you suck on them."

I squeezed my eyes shut and tried to ignore Charlotte's slurping sounds and the urgent pounding of Rudolph's fist hitting his groin.

For the next few minutes, we stood with our backs to Charlotte, staring into the opposite wall. Wet sounds of her dildo sliding in and out of her core filled my eardrums, as did Rudolph's grunts and groans. The slimy tendrils of disgust warred with the warm fires of triumph. With this video, we could humiliate Rudolph and ruin his reputation. Mom would get a chance to divorce him on the grounds of infidelity, and we'd be free of the psychopath.

Charlotte made loud porn-star cries as she reached what I suspected was a fake climax, and Henry wrapped his hand around mine and squeezed. I glanced up into his scrunched features. He probably thought this was as ghastly as I did.

Rudolph made a strange gurgle in the back of his throat then let out a noisy gasp. "Good girl. I will be in touch with your next assignment."

"Wait," said Charlotte. "I thought you would finance Father's legal defense if I did this."

"It's a start. Standby for further instructions, my dear." Skype made a hanging up sound, indicating the end of the video call.

"Did you get the recording?" Charlotte asked through clenched teeth.

"One second." Skipping my eyes over the figure on the screen, I minimized Skype and double-clicked Stealth. The video I had recorded popped up. "Yes. I've got it."

"Send me a copy," she snapped. "And turn around while I get changed."

I hadn't been looking at her, anyway. Tiny sniffles filled the air. It was hard to tell if Charlotte was genuinely upset or making the noises to garner Henry's sympathy.

Part of me felt responsible for her predicament. If I hadn't sent the Correspondent a recording of Alice telling me about her brother's gambling problems, they wouldn't have published a damning exposé on her family. And Charlotte's father's secretary might not have decided to blow the whistle on his embezzlement.

I blew out a long breath. It was too late for self-blame. Charlotte had hurt me with the doctored shampoo, the gauntlet, and other pranks, and I'd acted in revenge. Then she and Rudolph had conspired to get me abducted by Mr. Carbuncle. I would say she had gotten retribution.

It took a while for Charlotte to put on her clothes. Henry stood as still as death, still staring at the opposite wall, while I walked to the window and inhaled lungfuls of fresh air. Rudolph was stringing Charlotte along. He had given her just enough to carry out the tasks he wanted while dangling the carrot of paying her family's legal fees.

"Are you decent, yet?" I asked.

"Henry," she said. "Did you see me?"

"No," he replied.

I turned around in time to catch her features falling, and she clutched the sides of her dressing gown and stormed into the bathroom.

As soon as the door slammed shut, Henry strode to the door. "I have to get out of here."

I closed Edward's laptop, tucked it under my arm, and rushed after him. "What's wrong?"

"Nothing." He opened the door and rushed down the hallway.

"Henry." I hurried after him. At the top of the stairs, I grabbed his arm.

He rolled his eyes up at the ceiling, features pinched with annoyance. "What?"

My gaze dropped to the slight bulge in his crotch. A blank wall of shock closed in around my brain, and my mouth gaped open. "Charlotte and Rudolph turned you on?"

"Of course not." He continued down the stairs.

"Then why—"

"It's been a long time, and my dick has a mind of its own, alright?"

My brows drew together. Ever since Blake had brought me back from the palace, he had spent every night with Edward and me. I barely remembered the last time I'd been intimate with the triumvirate. I think it was a week before the ambush, which was an eternity ago.

Guilt clutched at my heart. Even though there was space for Henry in Edward's bed, I hadn't made an effort to ask him to join us. And after everything I had been through, he wouldn't have imposed.

As we reached the ground floor, I murmured, "Henry, if you want—"

"Leave it." He hurried down the hallway. From the dim lights illuminating the space, it was probably close to curfew. The common room door opened, letting out a few stragglers.

My mouth opened and closed. "I'm trying to invite you—"

"Emilia." He opened the door to Edward's study. "Now is not the time."

Blake stuck his head through the door. "Have you finished?"

I nodded.

"You're wanted upstairs." He stepped out and offered me his arm.

"Are you coming?" I turned to Henry.

He shook his head. I tried to meet his eyes, but he muttered goodnight and stepped inside.

I turned to Blake, heart heavy. Despite my intentions to clear the air with him, things kept getting in the way. A long sigh escaped my lungs, and I took Blake's arm.

"Problems?" he asked.

"I need to make up with Henry."

We walked back along the hallway and up the stairs. "He feels responsible for everything that's happened to you."

"But it wasn't—"

"I know." He kissed me on the cheek. "Henry wants to make amends, and he feels that words won't be enough."

CHAPTER 8

The next morning, Edward's movement as he rolled out of bed jostled me awake. I blinked my eyes open and lifted myself off Blake's chest. He stood with his back to the window, and pale streams of sunlight made the ends of his mahogany hair shine like burnished copper. As he stretched and yawned, my eyes tracked gorgeous, tight biceps that led to beautifully shaped pecs. His movements deepened the grooves of his six-pack, making his abdominal muscles even more prominent. The pulse between my legs twitched awake.

"Good morning." The corner of Edward's mouth lifted into a half-smile. The kind that said he knew exactly what I was doing, and if I wanted some, I only had to ask nicely.

I dropped my gaze past the dark treasure trail that led from his bellybutton to the thicket of pubic hair, to the organ between his legs. His long, thick penis jutted out in a state of arousal, its head flushed and ready to be sucked.

My tongue darted out to lick my lips. Sometimes, it was hard to believe that I had three outrageously sexy boyfriends.

Edward turned around and walked into the bathroom,

displaying a sculpted back that tapered down to tight glutes and long, muscular legs. The pulse between my legs quickened, and my breath came in shallow pants. When the sound of a shower reached my ears, my lips curled into a smile, and I swung out of bed to make my way to the bathroom.

Wet Edward was infinitely more delicious than dry Edward. The spray of the shower slicked his hair back, accentuating his strong jaw and defined cheekbones. Water streamed over his alabaster skin, down to that beautiful, jutting length.

Edward turned and smirked. "May I remind you of what you said the last time we showered with Blake?"

An excited breath caught in the back of my throat, then my mouth watered. I had wanted to get on my knees and swirl my tongue over that angry cock-head. Now was my chance. I strode across the bathroom, into the shower cubicle and sank to my knees. It was cramped, and warm water cascaded down on my head and shoulders, but I paid none of it any mind. Edward stepped back to give me more room, and I shuffled forward, gaze glued to that lengthening, thickening organ.

He laughed. "Emilia, I—"

Whatever he was about to say was cut off by my mouth engulfing the head of his prick.

Edward drew in a sharp breath, and warm triumph spread through my chest. It was always fun to have him fall apart at my command. As promised, I swirled my tongue around his cock-head, making sure to lick the sensitive underside. Edward hissed through his teeth, and the muscles of my core made a pleasurable ripple in response.

He tasted delicious, a heady combination of freshwater and salty precum that made me moan around my mouthful.

Edward's hand cupped my jaw, and his hips made tiny thrusts. "Take it." His voice strained. "Take it all."

Relaxing my jaw, I let his gorgeous length slide down to the back of my throat. Edward drew back and forth in a steady, gentle rhythm. Each time he withdrew, I lathed my tongue against the ridge on his underside and made him gasp.

The warm arousal pooling between my legs developed into a pleasant ache that throbbed in time with Edward's appreciative moans. I reached down between my legs, between my sodden, slick folds and ran my fingertip over my needy clit.

"Emilia," he groaned.

His deep voice brought pleasure rippling through my core muscles, which tightened with every caress of my throbbing nub. I bobbed my head up and down on his shaft against the thrust of his hips, increasing the friction and increasing the intensity of his moans. My fingers moved over my clit in the same rhythm, and it felt like I was experiencing the same intense pleasure as Edward. We continued this steady pace until Edward broke my concentration with a loud, strangulated moan.

He was close.

And judging by the pleasure building around my clit, so was I.

I rubbed myself harder, pleasure thrashing against my core like an out-of-control river held back by a dam. Edward's thrusts quickened, and I relaxed my throat, letting him deepen our connection. My tongue lashed at the underside of his dick, teasing out his climax.

"Emilia!"

Warm, thick pulses of fluid hit my tongue and slid to the back of my throat. The familiar taste, combined with his fevered groans, broke the dam of pressure around my core and released a flood of sensation. Breathing hard, I swallowed his essence with a satisfied moan.

After he caught his breath, Edward helped me to my feet and held me to his chest. His strong arms wrapped around my middle and kept me in place. "I should jostle you awake more often."

"Don't you dare." I tilted my head and gave him a playful peck.

Edward's chuckle reverberated against his chest, and his hands slid down to my ass. "I suppose it's only good manners to return the favor."

"Actually, there's no need."

He drew back and fixed me with his smiling, sapphire eyes. "Why not?"

"I took care of myself while I was on my knees."

Desire flared in his eyes, and his hardness pressed against my belly. "In that case, why don't you bend over, and I'll slip you something I think you'll like."

"Not without a condom!"

He chuckled. "Maybe later, then." Bending to pick up one of the bottles, he said, "I'll shampoo you if you return the favor."

"Alright." I held out my hand.

Edward placed a large blob of shampoo into my palm. "There's a board of director's meeting today."

"Do you want me to come?"

Brushing his erection against my belly, he pressed a kiss on the tip of my nose. "Of course. You're still under our command."

"Very funny." I rubbed the shampoo between my palms and ran my hands over his slick hair. "What will you say when they ask you about Charlotte?"

"The truth."

My hands stilled. "But you promised you'd keep quiet about her role in the booze cruise in exchange for her owning up about the hidden cameras."

His erection softened. "How many of those girls' futures would be ruined if her cocktail hadn't made them violently sick?"

"Ugh. You're right. Sorry to bring up such a distasteful subject."

"It's fine. I'd been forming a nefarious plan involving Blake that would have made us late for first period. The mention of Charlotte is exactly the splash of cold water on the dick I needed to focus on the upcoming meeting."

Later that day, Edward and I sat in front of the Board of Governors. It took a few minutes for them to reach the agenda item of Edward's academy fundraiser. Dr. Asgard reported that his hospital could get a temporary blood donation center set up for the academy's sports day, which would maximize the number of donations.

As the board was pleased with the progress, Mr. Weaver decided to move up Edward's report on the events of the weekend. I cringed as he explained to all twelve board members and a secretary, how Charlotte had extracted money from several boys for the promise of a chance with the girls of their dreams. He detailed the events of the evening, starting with a clue he had gathered from another rugby player, and ending with the police and ambulance service taking the girls away.

Mr. Weaver frowned. "While I commend the ingenuity of you and your friends, Viscount, I do wish you had filed a report with campus security."

"Yes, Chairman," replied Edward, his voice stiff. "However, if we had acted as you have suggested, there would be no representative to inform the police of what really happened. Moreover, the events took place after academy hours, where my friends and I were free to leave the campus as we saw fit."

Mr. Weaver glanced at Lady Seagrove, who pursed her lips but remained silent. This time, they couldn't fault him on his actions.

Edward inhaled a deep breath through his nostrils. "Unfortunately, there might be another report in the papers about Saturday's events. We saw a newspaper photographer with a Saturday Correspondent lanyard around his neck."

I chewed down on the inside of my lip, hoping they wouldn't blame Edward for this fiasco.

Lady Seagrove sniffed. "This Charlotte Underwood is the same young lady responsible for the removal of the cameras around the academy?"

"She is."

"How did she know of their location?" Dr. Asgard rubbed his chin.

"Charlotte is a close associate of the former caretaker, Mr. Carbuncle."

Each member of the Board of Governors stiffened at the mention of the former caretaker's name.

Lady Seagrove blurted, "Perhaps this young lady has been unduly affected by her association with that reprobate. Reprimanding her at this stage might lead to another exposé."

Her words hit like a slap to the face. Did they think Charlotte was one of Mr. Carbuncle's victims? She was his fucking accomplice! I sucked in a breath, ready to say something, but Edward placed a calming hand on my wrist.

The Board of Governors dismissed us, and we walked through the marble hallways of the main teaching block. My fists clenched and unclenched. Why did Charlotte always land on her feet? Rudolph was the only person who could handle her, and I wouldn't wish that slimy reptile on anyone, including Charlotte.

We stepped out of the building into the sunny morning. I was about to launch into a full-blown rant about Charlotte when Edward's phone rang.

He pulled it out of his pocket and frowned. "It's Father's nurse."

Clamping my mouth shut, I gave him a sharp nod and held my breath. I knew very little about dementia, except that it was a condition that caused memory loss and confusion in old people. I had no idea how dangerous it was when it affected younger victims.

With a concerned frown, Edward answered the phone. The nurse did most of the talking, and with each word, Edward's face twisted with confusion. At the end of the conversation, he stared at the phone as though not quite believing what he had heard.

A few people leaving the main teaching block paused to stare. Charlotte might have been one of them. The hair dyed like mine was unmistakable, but there was no time to bother with her when palpitations squeezed at my heart. "What's wrong? Did something happen?"

"Father's having a lucid day," he said, voice dreamlike.

I wrapped my hand around his. "Go to him!"

"Come with me."

"Of course."

As we raced through the campus, Edward called for the limo. At a time like this, neither of us wanted to make the long trek through the estate to Edward's house.

～

The Duke of Mercia sat in the garden under a gazebo, clad in a burgundy, silk dressing gown complete with tailored shoulders, lapels, and cuffs. He wore a white shirt under the garment, opened halfway down to the sternum, and a matching cravat.

We walked across the lawn and, as I got a closer look at the duke, my stomach dropped. I had expected him to be a man in his fifties, but he looked about thirty-five. "He's so young."

"Thirty-eight," said Edward. "Thirty-three when diagnosed. The doctor said it was a particularly early case of young-onset dementia."

I squeezed Edward's hand, and we continued toward the gazebo. The duke was deep in conversation with a man the size of Henry, who wore a white polo shirt and slacks. This had to be the nurse paid for by the ransom money.

When the duke turned to us, my breathing hitched. His handsome, regal features were nearly identical to Edward's except for slightly paler eyes and a dimple on his chin.

"Edward," he said with wonder in his voice. "You look well."

"Father." Edward's face broke into a smile. "It's wonderful to have you back."

The duke shook his head. "Apparently, it's all thanks to my new nurse. He insisted we try an experimental medication Dr. Asgard didn't think would work."

Edward turned to the nurse and inclined his head in thanks.

I stood back, throat thickening, watching their interaction. Although warmth shone in their eyes, and it was clear that the duke hadn't properly seen his son in years, neither reached out to touch the other. I suppose this was a manifestation of the aristocratic, British stiff upper lip.

The duke raised his head and fixed me with curious, aquamarine eyes. "I see you've brought a young lady."

Butterflies writhed through my insides as I remembered how much everyone had hated me for being American. Would Edward's father also reject me for the same reason? Swallowing hard, I shot Edward a helpless glance.

"Father, please meet Emilia Hobson, who joined us this year from Park Preparatory, New York. Emilia, this is my father, the Duke of Mercia."

"Indeed?" The duke's brows rose. "How d'you do?"

"How d'you do, Your Grace," I repeated.

His face broke into a smile. "Call me Alfred! And do join us for lunch."

As if summoned by an invisible force, the butler walked across the lawn with a brass hostess trolley laden with an entire baked salmon, a quiche, and a variety of mouth-watering salads.

While he served out generous portions, Edward updated his father on recent events, carefully steering away from the estate's financial difficulties and from the recent scandals that had rocked the school. The duke listened and made suggestions for areas where the staff could improve, and I sucked in an excited breath. If the medication worked, would Edward's father be able to take back some of the burden?

The duke turned to me. "To which family do you belong, Emilia?"

I scrambled for an answer. Mom and Dad came from humble beginnings, and I didn't want to seem like an interloper. "The Jensens. My father's family came to the States last century from Denmark, and my mom's originally from Connecticut. She's married to Rudolph Trommel now."

"Indeed?" The duke's brows rose. "Trommel is a fascinatingly ruthless businessman. My father had dealings with an associate of his, who worked in the publishing industry. A former Mrs. Trommel obtained a million-pound deal to write her memoirs of being married to the mogul, and Trommel quashed it before she even got pen to paper. I understand that he now makes everyone he encounters sign confidentiality agreements."

My eyes widened. "Really?"

He tilted his head to the side. "You haven't?"

"Emilia is still seventeen," said Edward. "I doubt that such a contract would be enforceable on a minor."

The duke chuckled. "I expect not, and he'll have a jolly hard time trying to make you sign one when you turn eighteen unless you work for him in some capacity!"

Realization dropped into my stomach like a lead weight. Was this why he had offered me an internship? To get me to sign one of his non-disclosure agreements when I turned eighteen? The more I learned about Rudolph, the more disgusting I found the old creep. Perhaps he was waiting until neither Mom nor I could expose him before making us both suffer.

The duke remained lively throughout lunch. He gave me a tour of his house and gardens, pointing out items of historical interest. The pride and enthusiasm for his family history shone in his bright, blue eyes and in his voice. He displayed a level of exuberance I'd never seen in Edward.

I squeezed Edward's hand and gave him a warm smile. It was no surprise he was so serious when he lived under a cloud of bereavement, family illness, and the thieving, conniving Mr. Chaloner. Maybe a few more days like this in the summer would lift his spirits.

At the end of the tour, we stood in a marble reception hall nearly identical to the one in the main teaching block. The duke turned to his nurse and chuckled. "I'm a terrible influence. Shouldn't you both be in lessons?"

"We have free periods this afternoon," I lied.

"Then it's lucky for me." He turned to the butler. "Afternoon tea for four, Reginald."

We retired into a drawing room with views of a garden of pink roses climbing over arched frames among a riot of rose bushes of every color imaginable. Later, Reginald the butler brought in a three-tiered cake stand containing finger sandwiches, scones, macarons, and delicate cakes. As he poured us cups of tea from a china pot, the duke asked, "Are you still chums with little Henry?"

Edward smiled. "Henry's six-four now, and the captain of the rugby team."

"That little cherub?" His face broke out into a wide grin. "I'd like to see that!"

Edward pulled out his smartphone and swiped through his pictures until he found a group he had taken during one of the rugby matches. "Bring him along the next time. And Blake."

Later, as the sun dipped behind a group of fluffy clouds, the duke's eyelids grew heavy, and the nurse announced it was a side effect of his medication and time for his nap. We left and made our way back to the academy on foot.

I looped my arm through Edward's as we walked along a gravel path bordering the woods. "Will the new drug cure him?"

Edward shook his head. "There's no cure for his condition. Unfortunately, drugs only reduce the symptoms."

We passed a small meadow of blue, purple, and pink wildflowers. Edward let go of my hand. Beyond it, men wearing khaki jackets stared up into the skies. One of them pointed a long-barreled shotgun at a flock of passing birds, while the other carried what might have been a dead pheasant. I couldn't tell from the distance.

I intertwined my fingers with his. "I'm so glad you got the chance to speak with him."

"As am I. It's been years since he last recognized me." He stopped by the edge of the path and pulled out his penknife.

"What are you doing?"

"Picking you a bunch of flowers." Edward walked farther into the meadow.

A large hand clamped around my mouth, and a thick arm looped around my waist. Panic spiked through my heart, and adrenaline surged through my veins. The stench of alcohol and stale tobacco filled my nostrils. I jerked in my assailant's grip, but he was too strong, too determined.

This could only be one person: Mr. Carbuncle, who had come to abduct me for his million-pound ransom.

I let out a scream through my nose. Edward shot out from among the wildflowers and raced toward me with murder in his eyes.

"Carbuncle," Edward roared. "Let go of Emilia, or I'll have you shot."

Still with his arms crushing me to his apish chest, Mr. Carbuncle turned and ran into the woods. I wriggled and jerked and thrashed in his grip.

"Stay still," he hissed into my ear. "Don't move, or I'll make things worse for you."

A gunshot pierced through the air, and everybody froze.

CHAPTER 9

The former caretaker's heart pounded against my back as though trying to break through my ribcage. My own heart skittered, needing an escape, and rapid breaths concertinaed in and out my lungs. His filthy hands clamped harder around my mouth, and the acrid scent of strong urine and stale tobacco burned through my sinuses. My eyes watered, both from fear and from the stench.

No other gunshots followed the first, and Mr. Carbuncle turned around, still clutching me to his chest. Now, I was both his captive and his shield.

The two men in khaki hunting clothes sprinted forward. The one carrying the gun pointed his rifle at us.

"Come any closer, and I'll wring the whore's neck," snarled Carbuncle.

A shudder ran down my spine, and sweat poured down my brow.

"Fredrickson is an excellent marksman," said Edward, his voice cold. "If you continue to hold Miss Hobson, I will order him to shoot."

"Then he'll shoot her," shouted the former caretaker.

My eyes darted to Fredrickson, and I sent him a silent plea to shoot. I would rather take my chances on his skills than on the mercy of Mr. Carbuncle.

Mr. Carbuncle's rasping breaths filled my ears. He hoisted me up, so I covered most of his head, and the thick bristles of his mustache rubbed against my ear. Disgust rippled through my insides, and my stomach heaved.

"What are you doing?" barked one of the huntsmen. "Stop that!"

"Put. Her. Down," snarled Edward.

No matter how much I tried to wriggle out of his grip, Mr. Carbuncle held on tighter.

Edward turned to Fredrickson. "Aim for the elbow of the arm with the hand clamped around her mouth. If he flinches and turns around, aim for his back."

Mr. Carbuncle threw me down onto the ground. I fell onto my hands and knees and stayed low. As he sprinted into the woods, gunshots filled the air. None of them were accompanied by the sound of a heavy body hitting the ground. My heart sank, but a pained bellow from behind the trees filled me with vicarious triumph.

When I turned around, it was Edward holding the gun. I hadn't seen him this furious since the time he flipped over the head table. He handed it back to Fredrickson and strode toward me, his eyes softening. The two other men sprinted past into the woods, presumably to capture an injured Mr. Carbuncle.

"Are you hurt?" Edward knelt at my side, hands reaching for my arms but not quite touching. It was as though he was afraid of exacerbating any injuries.

"Fine, I think." The bruises around my torso from my time in London twinged from the rough handling, and Mr. Carbuncle's foul, tobacco scent lingered in my hair, on the back of my blazer, and under my nose. "Though I think I'll need another shower."

He pulled me up to my feet and wrapped his strong arms around my shoulders. "I thought we would have to shoot him with you in his arms."

At his touch, all the tension in my muscles drained into the ground, and I let out a long, relieved sigh. Edward's cedar and cypress scent filled my nostrils, and I melted against his hard body. If he hadn't been there... My mind didn't want to explore the possibilities. Tears welled behind my eyelids. I was with Edward and safe.

"I'm glad you managed to get him," I murmured. "Where did your shot hit?"

"I'm not as accurate as Fredrickson. The gun was filled with birdshot, so he'll be left with small, lead pellets embedded in his back."

"Which means he'll have to go to a doctor to get them out."

"Or a vet." Edward pulled out his phone and called a number. Moments later, he reported the incident to someone who sounded like campus security, and then he called the police.

The two men emerged from the woods. "He had a vehicle at the east driveway leading out to Highdown Hill," said Fredrickson. "We heard him leave and saw the tracks. He was too far away to get a registration, but it was a white pickup truck."

Edward thanked the men and turned to me, his eyes stormy. "Sorry."

I drew back and frowned. "What for?"

"I left you to pick those flowers."

Shaking my head, I placed a hand on the side of his face. It was typical of him to carry too much responsibility on his shoulders, but this was ridiculous. We had been less than ten feet apart. "Did you know Mr. Carbuncle was lurking behind the trees?"

A breath huffed out of his nostrils. "Of course not."

"Then there's no need to apologize. We were unlucky, and he caught us off-guard. If it wasn't for you alerting the others, he would have taken me away."

A few minutes later, campus security arrived in two vehicles. After we had given them an account of what happened, one of the officers drove us through the estate, back to the campus. Edward turned to me in the back seat. "I want you to carry something with you, in case he strikes again."

The muscles of my throat flexed. "He will."

"Did he say?"

"He works for Rudolph, doesn't he?" I said. "Rudolph and Philippe could have set this up as another way to lash out, like the letter Rudolph wrote to Mr. Jenkins about withdrawing me from the academy."

When the car stopped outside Elder House, Edward walked me to his study and poured us both a tumbler of brandy for the shock. Even though I knew I was safe in Elder House, my hands couldn't stop shaking. Mr. Carbuncle had nearly taken me. If he had succeeded, there would be no Peter Underwood to stop him from doing precisely what he had threatened.

I sagged onto the leather Chesterfield, tears clouding my vision. I had ruined Mr. Carbuncle's life by exposing what he had done with the sixth-form girls, and now, he wanted to ruin me. Edward sat at my side, rubbing comforting circles on my back and whispering words of reassurance, but the tremors wouldn't stop. I'd developed a phobia of Mr. Carbuncle, and I wasn't sure of the cure.

Two police officers arrived and interviewed us both in Mr. Jenkins' dusty room. Our housemaster remained silent throughout the interview, his face paling at the mention of the gun. It might have been because he worried about Mr. Carbuncle's wellbeing, but I no longer cared. Mr. Jenkins was firmly on the list of people I didn't trust.

After the junior officer had taken my statement, he said, "We've already sent out warnings to local vets, General Practitioners, and hospitals with Carbuncle's description. If he seeks medical attention for his shotgun wounds, they'll inform us."

Nodding, I swallowed hard. As much as I wanted to believe in the efforts of the police, Rudolph had helped people, myself included, escape justice with his money and influence.

I returned to Edward's study and slumped on the leather sofa. All the adrenaline drained out from my system, leaving me hollowed out and raw. Even when the academy medic visited to give me a checkup, I couldn't muster enough graciousness to offer him more than a muttered thanks.

Edward sat on my left, and Blake arrived later to sit on my right. I rested my head on Blake's shoulder and stared straight ahead at the trees outside the window. Even his warm, comforting familiarity failed to snap me out of my overwhelmed state.

Henry stepped into the room, his face grave. "I heard what happened." He held out his hand. "Come with me."

Edward shot out of his seat. "I hardly think this is an appropriate time for a date."

"A change of scenery." He pulled me out off the sofa. "We're going to London and staying at the apartment, behind guards more effective than campus security."

∾

Henry stroked my hair for the entire journey while I dozed on his chest. Somehow, his presence and the moving vehicle provided a level of security I hadn't gotten from sitting in Edward's study.

As the limo passed Marble Arch, Henry's phone buzzed.

"What's that?" I murmured.

"Hold on." He shifted a bit and pulled his phone out of his blazer pocket. "It's from Blake."

I scanned the smartphone's screen. Blake's message read:

Mr. Underwood was arrested for trying to leave the country while on bail. Charlotte wants to sell her story to the tabloids. She has already secured an agent and two offers. Her copy of the video will be used as evidence.

Annoyance rippled through my insides. "Fuck."

Henry's lips thinned. "You can't use Charlotte's video to blackmail him anymore, but this will still lead to Rudolph's ruin, and the adultery will give your mother grounds for divorce. Right now, you need to focus on yourself."

We traveled through the public parking lot, through the underground passageway under the stores, and into the Bourneville private parking lot. The maze of hallways and security doors that led to the upstairs apartment didn't seem as daunting as the first time I had visited.

When we stepped into the giant drawing room of black marble pillars, crystal chandeliers, and gold-embroidered furniture, Mrs. Bourneville stepped out from the far doors. She wore a maroon, snakeskin leather jacket with a camel-colored, bodycon dress. Golden hair, the exact shade of Henry's, cascaded down to her shoulders, framing her delicate features to perfection.

"Henry? I didn't expect to see you."

He leaned into me and muttered, "Sorry. Mother told me she was in Milan."

I wrapped my arm around his bicep. "It will be nice to catch up with your mom."

Mrs. Bourneville crossed the room and yanked Henry down for a kiss. "We arrived a few hours ago." She drew me into a tight hug. "It's a wonderful surprise to see you both. Have you come for dinner?"

Henry turned to me and shrugged. "We can always eat at one of the restaurants downstairs if you're not up for company."

"Up here's fine," I replied.

Mrs. Bourneville beamed. "Well, food will be ready in an hour. Change out of your uniform and put something on." She stared down at my empty hands. "Did you bring any clothes?"

I shook my head. In my desperation to leave Mercia Academy, I hadn't really thought we would need to dress for dinner.

"We'll go downstairs and find you something to wear. Who's your favorite designer?" Before I could reply, she waved her manicured hand. "It doesn't matter. We can try a selection and see which you like best."

Mrs. Bourneville looped her arm through mine and walked us through the drawing-room to another elevator. I glanced over at Henry, who walked behind us, his lips quirked into a smile. I smiled back. At least he would be coming with us.

She placed her entire right hand on a scanner at the side of the elevator. It beeped, and she looked into a tiny reader that scanned her retina. After that, she tapped in a code and spoke into the intercom. "Yes… Clara Bourneville here with Emilia Hobson, a guest."

"Henry?" said a voice from behind. "Did you come to discuss your inheritance?"

Mr. Bourneville stepped out of another door with Henry's Aunt Idette in tow. They both wore identical navy blue trouser suits, but Aunt Idette wore a red pussy bow around her collar instead of a necktie.

Henry's brows drew together. "I'm giving Emilia a change of scenery after an intruder nearly snatched her in Mercia Academy."

Aunt Idette placed her hands on her hips. "Another kidnapping?" Contempt edged her voice. "What do you children need money for this time?"

I bristled. "It wasn't faked."

"Henry, we need to have words."

"I'm escorting Mother and Emilia through the—"

"Do you think you can do a better job than our security staff?"

Henry scowled but didn't reply.

His father turned to me. "Emilia, please be assured that a pair of armed bodyguards will escort you through the door when you step out of the lift."

Mrs. Bourneville placed a hand on my arm. "There's no need to be afraid. Henry brought you here because the security is world-class."

I glanced around the opulent room. Henry hunched his shoulders, and a muscle in his clenched jaw flexed with annoyance. His mom gave him an encouraging smile, which he didn't notice.

Mr. Bourneville kept his gaze steady, with only the drumming of his fingers an indication of his impatience. Aunt Idette's narrowed eyes darted around the room, and her mouth puckered as though she'd tasted something sour.

A lead weight of guilt sank my heart into my stomach. If it wasn't for me, Mr. Bourneville wouldn't have disinherited Henry. If there was a chance for him to make amends with his father and regain his birthright, I couldn't be selfish and insist he stayed at my side.

Giving Henry what I hoped would be a reassuring smile, I said, "I'll be fine in the store."

Mrs. Bourneville pressed the elevator button, and the doors opened. We both stepped in, and she selected the middle button, which wasn't even labeled.

As the elevator descended, she said, "It's wonderful to see you here with Henry, considering your rocky start."

"We went through an awkward patch, but things are getting better."

She shook her head. "I wish he had come to me for help with his friend's father instead of getting you implicated in such a convoluted plot."

Before I could answer, the doors opened into a short hallway. Two guards with body armor under their suits stepped forward. Guarding the entrance further on was a pair of regular security guards who wore black uniforms and matching caps with the Bourneville crests.

My throat dried. While their presence evaporated any fears I had about Mr. Carbuncle following me to London to finish the job he had started, I couldn't help but wonder why Mrs. Bourneville needed a pair of bodyguards.

Pushing those thoughts aside, I walked alongside Henry's mom though the doors and into the store. She took me to the designer concessions department, where I had shopped with the triumvirate for my gown.

Mrs. Bourneville stopped at Amanda Wakely and picked out a floor-length wrap dress in a luxurious, green silk that matched Henry's eyes. "This would look divine on you."

I gulped. It seemed more like the sort of gown Mom would wear. "Will it be a formal dinner?"

"Smart-casual for the men. Anything goes for the women." She winked. "If you wear that, I'll put on my Diane Von Furstenburg maxi."

My stomach twisted. I loved dressing up, but after today, I was in the mood for something understated. At the end of the row of concessions stood on a mannequin wearing a knee-length, asymmetric dress in caramel satin.

I nodded in its direction. "What about that one?"

She tilted her head to the side. "A bit young but—" A delicate huff escaped her nostrils. "What am I talking about? You're only sixteen."

"Seventeen," I said.

"Of course. I forget that Henry is younger than his friends." She looped her arm through mine. "Let's go and try it on, then we can accessorize."

Shopping with Mrs. Bourneville reminded me of the days I would spend with Mom before she remarried. Back then, she couldn't afford to shop in a London department store, but there was a togetherness that I thought I'd lost forever. With Mrs. Bourneville, it was like I was her best friend, daughter, dress-up doll, and the source of gossip for her favorite subject: Henry.

The ladies' shoe department had a special, where they served a glass of champagne for every customer who made a purchase. As soon as the server, a middle-aged lady, caught sight of Mrs. Bourneville, she rushed over with two glasses.

"Thank you, Felicity. May I introduce my son's girlfriend, Miss Emilia Hobson of New York?"

The older woman's brows rose for a microsecond, as though the pictures of Henry and Blake's romp had been etched in her mind, but the expression disappeared so quickly, I almost imagined it.

She inclined her head. "I'm very pleased to make your acquaintance, Miss Hobson."

By the end of the shopping spree, I had a pair of nude shoes, a chunky cuff bracelet in rose gold, and a matching pair of teardrop earrings. She would have bought me more, but I really wanted to see Henry.

∼

Mr. Bourneville's angry rant filled the air as we stepped out of the elevator and walked through the parlor. I turned to Mrs. Bourneville, who sighed. "I had hoped they would reconcile their differences by now, but it seems Oscar's temper has flared again."

I chewed my bottom lip and gripped the handles of my shopping bags. "Is he always like this?"

Her gaze fell. "With Henry, yes."

"And now you want to antagonize Trommel?" yelled Mr. Bourneville from beyond the door.

"Why?" screeched Aunt Idette.

Henry muttered something I couldn't hear. Largely because he wasn't screaming at the top of his voice.

My heart rate doubled. Why were they talking about Rudolph? Mrs. Bourneville and I hurried through the door and down the hallway. We reached a white door and stopped.

"What did you say, boy?" snarled Mr. Bourneville.

"I can't believe it," said Aunt Idette.

"You brought this on yourself," Henry replied. "First, you swindled him by saying the ransom was twice the amount you paid out, then you refused to refund him. That's why he released those pictures onto the internet."

"What nerve," growled Mr. Bourneville. "You, who stole from your family and then slapped us in the face by taking it up the arse from a boy."

"The nerve of that boy!" said Aunt Idette.

I raised my hand to push open the door. To storm into that room and halt that awful conversation.

Mrs. Bourneville held me back. "Henry has to learn to stand up to his father," she whispered. "Or he will be a follower his entire life."

My shoulders sagged. I'd never seen Henry in this light before. In the academy, he had been the captain of the rugby team and one of the triumvirate. Edward appeared to be the leader of the trio, but I couldn't tell whether it was because of his natural leadership or because he had been friends with Blake and Henry before they had become friends with each other. I shook off those thoughts. Henry wasn't a follower, he was just... quiet.

Mr. Bourneville continued his rant, with Aunt Idette acting as hype-man with loud agreements and the occasional jibe.

"Get out of my sight," Mr. Bourneville snarled.

Mrs. Bourneville grabbed my arm and pulled me into a powder room. Her shoulders drooped, and her face flushed with sadness. "Do you see what I mean?"

I ran a hand through my hair and sighed. What could I do to help Henry stand up to his father?

CHAPTER 10

Doors opened and slammed. Mrs. Bourneville leaned over the counter and dabbed at her eyes. I stared down at the powder room's marble floor tiles and shuffled my feet. Poor Henry. His shitty father seemed to blame him for everything that had happened with Rudolph, even when it was Mr. Bourneville who had angered Rudolph twice.

Henry's mom placed a comforting hand on my back. "I'll show you to his room."

"Thanks."

She walked me down the hallway, past the room where Mr. Bourneville and his spiteful cousin sniped about Henry's imagined shortcomings. We stopped at a door close to the end, and Mrs. Bourneville gave it a soft knock.

"What?" he said.

She opened the door a fraction. "Go to him. Maybe you can say something to inspiring. Everything I've tried has failed."

I stepped through into the mingled scents of leather and citrus. The bedroom was a mix of charcoal, brown leather, and ivory sheepskin that reminded me somewhat of Edward's study at Elder

House. Henry sat with his back to the door on a leather ottoman at the end of the bed.

"Henry?"

His shoulders sagged, and his hands clutched the edge of the ottoman. "I can't believe you heard."

"Why did you let your father talk to you like that? You'd never put up with that crap at the academy."

He blew out a long breath through his nostrils. "I don't know."

I crossed the room and placed a hand on his bicep. "You just don't want to admit the reason why."

"Maybe not."

A convulsion seized the back of my throat, and I placed a knee on the leather ottoman and wrapped my arms around Henry's broad shoulders. What on earth had happened between Henry and his father to cause this level of animosity?

"Do you remember when I told you I'd been kidnapped on my way to Mercia Academy?" asked Henry.

A dull thud reverberated through my heart, and cold dread filled my insides. Pushing away speculations of what terrible thing might have happened when he had been abducted as a child, I forced out a long breath. "D-did they hurt you?"

"The kidnappers weren't too bad. It's what happened afterward that really stung." He dipped his head and stared into the sheepskin rug. "They dropped me off on a country road late at night. I wandered around for hours, thinking they had left me in the middle of nowhere to die. By the time the security staff found me, I was inconsolable. Father slapped me and said I was a disgrace to the Bourneville name."

Bile rose to the back of my throat. "But you were only eleven."

"Ten."

"How's someone that young supposed to protect himself from grown attackers when your driver couldn't?" I drew back and stared into his mournful, green eyes.

"I'd had self-defense lessons since I was tiny, and he made me study martial arts. I was no good at it. Hated every moment. Father kept telling me he had enemies who would come at him through his weakest link."

"Why didn't he assign you bodyguards if he was so worried?"

A huge sigh gusted out of his lungs. He pulled himself off the ottoman, crossed the room, and turned his back to me. "That's a question he'll never answer. He just recites the same old crap he did since I was five: I'm weak, useless, a burden."

I followed after Henry and grabbed his wrist. "But you're nothing like that."

"Those voices never go away," he said, still not looking me in the face.

I wrapped both arms around his broad body and inhaled his mint and citrus scent.

Henry slipped his arm around my waist and kissed the top of my head. "That night in the Peak District when you followed after me, we should have called off the kidnapping."

I drew back to stare into his eyes and listened. Maybe now, I'd understand more about what had gone through his mind at that time.

He lowered his gaze to my collarbone. "But my mind kept going back to Edward's father. He was great when we were young, and now he can't even recognize his own son. I wanted to help, but Father wouldn't let me access my inheritance early. So, when Paul... When Mr. Frost knocked you out, he wanted to move you to another field even farther away than the night before, but I didn't want you to get hurt, so I suggested we bring you along."

I stepped closer and rested my head against his shoulder. This was the longest I had ever heard him speak. "Whose idea was it to inject me?"

"Paul's, of course. He wanted to make sure you didn't wake and raise the alarm." His Adam's apple bobbed up and down. "I'm so sorry for that and sorry for letting him convince the others in the squat into blaming you if anything went wrong."

Any residual anger I'd held about the kidnapping drained out of me. I'd finally gotten what I had sought from Henry, a heartfelt apology.

"I really did feel something for you during those days." He guided me to the edge of his bed, sank down on the mattress, and positioned me between his legs. "A lot, actually."

"What happened the day you disappeared?" I stepped into his personal space and slid both hands over the muscles on the sides of his neck.

Henry stared up at me through green eyes that glistened with remorse. "Paul arrived to discuss what to do if you ever called the police. He told the people in the squat to blame you. I went along with it because I didn't think you'd seen anything useful enough to lead to an arrest."

"I was awake when we left the car, cataloging landmarks, like Mulberry Terrace, the three-story house, and the photographer with the dreadlocks," I said.

He groaned. "If I'd known that, I would have explained our plans."

Warmth spread across my chest. Finally, I understood Henry. I leaned down and pressed a kiss against his temple. "I also get why you didn't confide in me. You didn't want to jeopardize helping Edward's father. He was lucid today, and I couldn't believe someone could be struck down so young." All the air left me in one outward breath. "Now I wish I hadn't taken matters into my own hands and contacted the police."

He wrapped his arms around my waist and squeezed me around the middle. "You were worried. And I must have sounded flippant."

"I thought you and Blake had gone crazy." A laugh bubbled up in my throat. "The excuses you made for not being scared of the kidnappers were so frivolous."

He drew back and fixed me with his earnest, green eyes. "From now on, there'll be no lies or half-truths. If I can't tell you something, I'll just say."

"And I won't sneak about behind your back."

He pulled me onto his lap and wrapped both arms around my waist. A comfortable silence stretched out between us, and all the tension from the day melted away.

In this bedroom, in this secure apartment, and in his warm, firm embrace, I finally felt safe. If only we could stay here forever and never leave until the police caught Mr. Carbuncle and arrested Rudolph. But a nagging voice in the back of my head told me that it was time for me to unburden myself.

"I'm sorry, too."

He stilled. "What for?"

"This whole mess you're in is because of me. If I hadn't worked with the Saturday Correspondent, Rudolph would never have gotten that footage of you and Blake, and he wouldn't have released it on the internet."

"I blame Rudolph and Father for that part, not you."

I dipped my head. "Can we call a truce?"

His lips spread into a smile. "I thought you'd never ask."

Henry gave me a gentle kiss on the lips. It was probably meant as a peck, but I snaked my arm around his neck and held him in place before he could withdraw. Now that we had really spoken about out grievances, I wasn't about to let him go.

His strong lips moved against mine in a series of toe-curling caresses. I moaned, and his tongue slipped between my lips. His tongue caressed mine, each stroke causing tingles of pleasure between my legs.

He adjusted me onto his lap, so my legs straddled his, and my knees sank into the mattress. We sat chest-to-chest, drinking each other in. This was the closest I had felt to him since our time in that dingy room. The first time in months, we had expressed affection in the form of a kiss instead of out of lust.

My heart fluttered with the wing-power of a hundred butterflies. This was new. Exciting, even better than it had been the first time around.

I pulled back and stared into his forest-green eyes. My face reflected in pupils widened into vast pools of black. "I've missed you."

"Not as much as I've missed you," he replied.

His hardness pressed against my core, and I writhed on top of him, enjoying the way tiny bolts of sensation sparked from my nub.

Henry placed both hands on my hips and groaned. "I can't get enough of you."

I felt the same way. His tongue twisted and curled around mine, eliciting the most delicious sensations. My core, aching and needy, writhed against his clothed length. It was nice, but not enough. I wanted more.

Desire made my hands shake, and need made the muscles of my core twitch. I unbuttoned his shirt and ran my hands over his hard, muscular chest. This was the first time in an eternity that I'd gotten the chance to explore him without the others.

Henry shouldered off my blazer, pulled my shirt from the waistband of my school skirt, and reached under the fabric. His fingertips skimmed the fevered skin of my back.

"I can't believe we're doing this under your parents' roof," I murmured. "What will your father say?"

"I'm past caring." Securing my legs around his waist, he stood and walked around to the other side of the bed, where he laid me on my back.

My gaze trailed down prominent pectoral muscles, a six-pack I wanted to explore with my tongue, and down a treasure trail of golden hair that led to the waistband of the gray pants of his academy uniform. His erection strained against the fabric, and I stretched out my arms to unleash it.

Henry stepped back. "Ladies first."

With as much speed as I could muster, I divested myself of my shirt, skirt, and loafers, leaving myself in an ivory silk lace bra and matching panties. "Your turn."

Henry pulled off his shirt, pants, and boxers. His beautiful, thick length jutted out from pubes as blonde as the hair on his head. I licked my lips and stretched out my arm, eager for him to unwrap the rest of me.

He stepped forward and straddled my hips. "Have I ever told you how beautiful you are?"

My lips curved into a smile. "I never get tired of hearing it."

His kisses trailed down my neck to my collarbone. I reached down and wrapped my fingers around his thick erection and slid my hand over its length. Henry groaned into my ear. "If you continue like that I'm going to come all over you."

A giggle bubbled up in my throat. "I don't mind."

After removing my bra, he slid off my panties and parted my legs, exposing my throbbing clit and sopping, wet folds. "You look good enough to eat."

Before I could respond, he lowered his head between my thighs and ran his tongue along the length of my slit. A bolt of pleasure sent shockwaves of sensation through my core, making my body jolt with surprise.

Henry raised his head and fixed me with a gaze so heated, shivers of pleasure skittered down my spine. "Like that, do you?"

I bit down on my lip and nodded.

His hands spread me open even wider, exposing me fully to his gaze. This wasn't the sweet Henry who stroked my belly and massaged me to a shuddering climax. This was the Henry from the start of the term. Henry from the inspections he had conducted in Blake's study. The one who had made me take off my panties and display myself to him and his friends. My breath caught, and the muscles of my core trembled with delicious anticipation.

When his tongue swirled around my nub, the sensation was so intense, I flinched away. Henry continued circling and flicking and lapping at my clit, holding me in place with those strong hands, and not letting me wriggle out of the way of his relentless tongue.

"H-Henry…" Whatever I wanted to say died in my throat. It was a mixture of the most exquisite pleasure, bordering on pain. Pain from the pressure expanding behind my clit, around my core. Pressure that seemed to have no end, yet I didn't want it to stop.

He continued his sweet torture until my vision went white, and the pressure burst, releasing a torrent of ecstasy that made me open my mouth in a silent scream. Through the pounding in my ears, I heard the tear of a foil wrapper. Seconds later, while I was still riding my climax, Henry entered me in a smooth, hard thrust. The movement made the muscles of my core clamp hard against his length.

I let out a shuddering moan. "B-but I thought you were a virgin."

"You're forgetting, I have a very experienced roommate." His hips moved in a slow circle that sent pleasant ripples through my core.

The intensity made me groan and arch into his chest. Blake. I imagine he was quite a handful. "Have you two—"

"All the way." He pulled out of me and slid back in, building up a steady rhythm

My thighs tightened around his hips, and my pelvis rocked against his thrusts, creating a delicious friction that made my eyes roll to the back of my head. Each downward thrust rubbed his pelvis against my clit, and each time he ground against me, the muscles of my core spasmed against his length.

Henry continued this rhythm of grinding and stroking and delicious, hard thrusts. I held onto his hard glutes with both hands, enjoying how they flexed as he fucked.

"You're terrific," he murmured into my ear.

I squeezed his ass cheeks. "I wanted to do this with you from the moment I saw you in that stairwell."

His movements faltered, and he pressed his lips on mine in a dizzying kiss that lasted until I was breathless. While his tongue caressed mine, that gorgeous, thick erection massaged the muscles of my core to submission. It was wonderful. It was ecstatic. I could have made love with him like this all night.

Henry's pelvis resumed its delicious grind against my nub. I squeezed my eyes shut and writhed against him, pleasure exploding around my core and sending a flurry of stars shooting behind my eyelids.

"W-what was that?" I gasped out.

"You liked it?" He ground against me, and this time, my nipples tightened against his chest.

"Don't stop."

Each movement sent shockwaves of pleasure that traveled up my torso and into my nipples, then down the insides of my thighs until they reached my toes. I tightened around him and bucked. This had to be my g-spot. Somehow, Henry had found it, and now he was giving me the most excruciating pleasure of my life.

My nails dug into his ass cheeks—I couldn't help it—and Henry shuddered. He pulled out, then thrust forward in tight, circular motions. I bit down hard on my bottom lip. Was that how he and Blake had sex? They had looked so hot together at the Valentines' Party.

"Keep going," I said through clenched teeth.

"Fuck," he gasped out.

Henry continued this maddening back and forth circular movement that hit my clit with one stroke and caressed that sensitive spot in my core with another. Sweat poured down my brow, and I panted at having been suspended in pleasure for so long without release.

I squeezed my eyes shut and quickened my movements. Henry did the same, and flashes of pleasure lit up my nerve endings. They kept sparking and flaring until the deepest spasm rocked my core and squeezed Henry so hard, I worried it might hurt.

"Ugh!" Henry's upper body convulsed, and a low, deep moan filled my ears and reverberated in his chest. His erection thickened and trembled with tiny shudders.

A second orgasm blazed through my body, making me clench and pulse around him in a series of never-ending tremors.

As Henry softened, he drew back, green eyes bright. "Give me a minute," he said between panting breaths. "I'm going to fuck you until my prick falls off."

CHAPTER 11

I lay beneath Henry and breathed hard. That second round had been even more intense than the first, but we had spent too long in the bedroom. Mrs. Bourneville would be livid if she knew we hadn't made an effort to get changed. My gaze wandered around his bedroom at the charcoal-colored walls, lit by gilded sconces and floor lamps. There was no sign of a clock, but I found a bookshelf of leather tomes and gold-framed paintings of rugby players wearing nineteenth-century uniforms.

Henry cupped my breast and kneaded it with his large hand. "One more."

I pressed both hands on his broad shoulders and gave his immovable body a shove. "What about dinner?"

He placed a kiss on the tip of my nose. "I'll eat you."

A laugh huffed out of my chest. "Behave yourself. Your mom's probably holding up dinner. What if she gets impatient and sends someone to fetch us?"

"You are right," said a female voice through the door, the slight German accent giving it a creepy edge. "But his father sent me."

My heart jumped into my throat, and I stiffened. Who the fuck was that?

"Aunt Idette," Henry growled. "How long have you been standing out there?"

"Long enough to hear you engaging in fornications with a young girl!" she snapped. "You had better get dressed and face your father."

"Sorry," I whispered.

He drew back, brows furrowed, blond curls in disarray. "What for?"

"I should have stopped us before things got too far."

He snorted. "Nothing would have stopped me from fucking you. Not even father standing in the middle of the room." Henry rolled off me and sat up. "I've wanted you for months."

The dim lighting from the wall sconces accentuated the bulge of his muscles while deepening where they formed grooves, such as the dips that separated his six-pack. My throat dried. He looked like something out of a photoshoot, including for the knowing smirk. "Want a shower?"

I squeezed my eyes shut, trying not to think about all the things I had done while showering with Blake and Edward, and all the things I would like to do with a hot, wet, and naked Henry. "A quick one."

Henry's dark chuckle made my nipples tighten with anticipation. My eyes snapped open, and I gave him what I hoped was a severe glare. "I mean it. Your aunt's outside, waiting for us. No messing about."

"Of course," he said in a voice too smooth to be believable.

I stepped off the bed and padded across to one of the many doors around the large room. The first one I opened led to an impressive, walk-in closet of open rails laden with garments, mahogany shelves, and a leather lounge chair.

"That's the wardrobe." Henry wrapped his arms around my waist and guided me out of his closet. "Here's the bathroom." He walked me to the next door down.

It opened up into what I could only describe a stone room. Charcoal-gray slate lined the walls and the floors, with black marble forming the worktops. In one corner hung a stainless-steel shower head the size of a platter, and opposite stood a huge bathtub large enough to fit two.

"We're already in enough trouble today," he murmured into my ear. "Why don't we go for a long soak?"

It was tempting, but Aunt Idette's cruel voice still rang in my ears. The thought of her bursting into the bathroom while Henry and I soaped each other down dried up all my enthusiasm for getting in that tub. I turned back to Henry and said, "Another time. Let's hurry and see if we can still make it for dinner."

After the quickest and most platonic shower I'd ever taken with any member of the triumvirate, we dried off. Henry entered his walk-in closet while I rifled through the shopping bags with a fluffy towel over my head.

I slipped on the caramel satin dress and nude shoes Mrs. Bourneville had chosen and added the rose-gold earrings and matching bracelet. Then I rushed back to the bathroom and blew-dry my hair, so it didn't look so much like a stringy mess.

I stepped out into the bedroom. Henry stood by the door, clad in a navy jacket that was clearly tailored to fit his muscular physique. He wore it with a blue-and-white striped shirt, unbuttoned to the collarbones, and a pair of fitted, ivory slacks. My gaze flicked up to his face. Caramel-colored curls, still damp from the shower framed his tan skin and highlighted his sharp cheekbones. I swallowed hard. He was so fucking handsome. How could I have resisted him for so long?

Henry's green eyes gleamed with delight. "You look like a girl who's just been fucked."

I smirked. "You look like a boy who's just been robbed of his virginity."

"Yes, yes," growled Aunt Idette from behind the door. "Save the lovey-talk for the dinner table, so we can all enjoy it."

Henry rolled his eyes. "Go away."

"What's wrong with her?" I mouthed.

"She's Father's minion and agrees with everything he does," he whispered back.

I checked myself in the mirror and frowned. My hair wasn't quite dry but was passable, but my swollen lips and flushed cheeks were incriminating. Henry hadn't been joking when he said I looked like I'd been fucked.

"I can't go out like this!"

He strolled over and combed through my hair with his fingers, making it even more of a mess. "There. It's very Brigitte Bardot, now."

I shoved his fingers away and tried to smooth out of the auburn rats' nest on my head. "Do you have a brush or something?"

His arm wrapped around my waist, and he guided me to the door. "Let's go."

"To dinner?"

"Another hotel."

"Don't you think your mother—"

"She'll understand." He turned the door and pulled it open.

Mr. Bourneville stood in the hallway next to Aunt Idette, his face the color of her burgundy pants suit. Aunt Idette's features were twisted into a smirk of triumph.

I furrowed my brows. Why on earth would she be pleased Henry was in trouble again?

Mr. Bourneville bared his teeth. "Of all the stunts you've pulled, this has to be the most desperate."

"What are you talking about now?" Henry snapped.

My heart resounded in my chest. The sounds of Mr. Bourneville's angry breaths filled the hallway. His hazel eyes burned with a fury so fierce, I glanced away. My eyes dropped to Aunt Idette, who mirrored his body language, only with that manic look of glee in her eyes.

Schadenfreude.

It was a German word that meant the delight in someone else's misfortune. Aunt Idette had it in droves. I blocked out the father-son stand-off to focus on what I knew about the peculiar woman. Wasn't she the mother of Jonas Bourneville, the person they announced in The Times would become new heir to the business? If her son had already been given Henry's birthright, why was she hell-bent on destroying what little goodwill he had left with his parents?

"What is this," his father snarled. "A desperate ploy to prove you're not queer?"

My mouth dropped open. Most fathers would object to their sons having sex with girls under their roof, not the motivations behind the act.

Aunt Idette placed her hands on her hips. "He thinks he can earn back his inheritance by fornicating with his beard."

Anger surged up from my gut and rushed to my cheeks. "Excuse me?"

Her malevolent gaze snapped to me. "What did he offer you for this stunt? Another new coat?"

"You're deluded," I snapped.

"Aaaah!" Aunt Idette clapped her hands together. "I understand."

"Tell me," said Mr. Bourneville, "because I don't know what is happening to my son."

"Stockholm Syndrome," she said.

My eyes bulged. "What?"

Aunt Idette paced the hallway like she was the female Sherlock

Holmes about to announce a great feat of deductive reasoning. She rubbed her chin and said, "This little fool fell for Henry during the fake kidnapping. Why else would she still be by his side after he blamed the whole spectacle on her? Now, she is under the delusion that she can replace Blake, Henry's true love."

"This is ridiculous." I turned to Henry, urging him to put the bitter woman in her place, but he remained silent, his eyes locked on those of his father.

Aunt Idette raised her chin. "Tell me I'm wrong!"

"You've twisted everything to ridiculous conclusions." I tried to make eye contact with Henry's dad, but he continued glaring at his son. "Henry had a drunken fumble with another boy, and now you think he'll never give you an heir and needs to be disinherited. When he finally sleeps with a girl, you think he's doing it to get his inheritance back."

Mr. Bourneville turned to me, his brows furrowed. "What is she talking about?"

I shot Henry a look and flashed my eyes. Now was the time to say something in his own defense.

He folded his arms across his broad chest and thrust his chin up. His lips were clamped so tight, they appeared thin and pale.

"Typical," Aunt Idette waved her hands in the air. "The boy gets his friends to do his talking. This one is just another Blake!"

I bared my teeth and whirled on Mr. Bourneville. "You're all too deluded to see that this old witch has a vested interest in keeping you apart. Who stands to benefit if Henry falls from grace? She does… along with her son, Jonas!"

Mrs. Bourneville stood at the end of the hallway, breathing hard. From the way she nodded, it seemed like she agreed with everything I had said.

I yanked on Henry's arm, silently urging him to speak, but he stared at a spot on the wall.

"Henry, take Miss Hobson and leave," snarled Mr. Bourneville.

Shoulders sagging, I exhaled a disappointed sigh but hitched them up again and straightened my posture. What had happened to Henry? At one point during my argument with Aunt Idette, Mr. Bourneville had seemed interested in hearing his side.

My gaze flickered to the end of the hallway to Mrs. Bourneville, who gave me a watery smile and mouthed, 'thank you.'

The smile I gave Mrs. Bourneville was apologetic. Perhaps by squaring up to Aunt Idette and raising my voice, I had taken away Henry's chance to fight back. That time when Coates and the other rugby boys had occupied the head table, he had been ready to defend his friends and had even lashed out at Coates for holding Blake in a wrist lock. Maybe I needed to stand back and let Henry build up whatever emotional reserves he required to make a stand against Mr. Bourneville.

After hugging Henry's mom goodbye, we walked through the maze of hallways in silence. Cameras were everywhere, and I had no doubt Aunt Idette would be at the control room, scraping up things to use against Henry.

Guilt weighed my heart, and regret weighed my steps. This wasn't the first time I had contributed to Henry's estrangement from his family, but I hoped it would be the last.

As soon as we reached the underground parking lot and climbed into the limo, I settled next to Henry and held his hand. "Why didn't you stand up to your father?"

He leaned forward and stared into his lap. "You don't know what he's like."

"A bully?"

"It's always the same with him. I'm not good enough. Not strong enough. Not as impressive as Jonas."

The limo drove through the dark passageway under the stores that led to the multistory parking garage. As it ascended the ramps to street level, I wrapped an arm around Henry's broad shoulder.

"How old is your cousin?"

"Twenty-nine."

"And how long has your dad compared you to him?"

With a weary breath, Henry shook his head and gazed out of the window. The limo exited into the still-bright evening, where shoppers and tourists still occupied the streets.

"For as long as I can remember. It doesn't matter what I do, Jonas will always be better."

"Of course he'll be better," I said.

Straightening, he turned to me with pained eyes. "What do you mean?"

"He's thirteen years older than you. When you got kidnapped at ten, I'll bet your father said Jonas would never have gotten snatched. He would have been twenty-three, then. That's hardly a fair comparison."

His shoulders drooped. "You sound like Mother."

"Because she's right." I twisted in my seat and grabbed Henry's forearms with both hands. "If you want your father to stop talking shit about you, stand up to him."

"I will."

"Should we turn the limo around?" I asked.

Henry shook his head. "Give me some time."

I rested my head on his shoulder. If I thought a single conversation could undo years of his father's brainwashing, maybe I was as deluded as Aunt Idette had said. If Henry's mother couldn't do it after years of trying, I didn't have a chance.

"Let's go back to the academy. I think we'd both sleep better with Blake and Edward."

※

By the time we reached Elder House and climbed up the stairs to Edward's room, it was empty. We walked down to his study, opened the door, and stepped into a cloud of cigar smoke mingled with the fruity, caramelized scent of Armagnac.

Edward lay on the Chesterfield sofa with a newspaper over his head. Blake sat on the floor with his back propped on the sofa, legs sprawled over the Persian rug. At his sides lay two open laptops.

"Guys?" I said.

Blake blinked his eyes open. "Emilia, you're looking well, but what are you doing back so soon?"

"It's a long story." Henry pulled Blake to his feet.

"Did you have any trouble in London?" Blake stretched and yawned. His shirt rode up, revealing a tantalizing glimpse of his dark treasure trail.

"You could say that." Wrapping my arms around Blake's middle, I pressed my lips on the juncture of his neck and shoulders. I inhaled Blake's cedar and spice scent and sighed. "What have you been researching?"

"Something Father mentioned." Edward pushed his newspaper to one side and sat up. "Rudolph Trommel went to great lengths to stop his former wife from publishing a memoir featuring him, but back then, he had no ties to England."

I bit down on my lip. "He owns at least one paper here, even if it's through a shell company."

Edward swung his legs off the sofa and onto the Persian rug. "I don't think we can rely on Charlotte's exposé even reaching the press."

"You think he'll block it?" I asked.

"More like bribe the paper not to release that article," said Blake.

Edward drew a hand through his mahogany hair. "He might even have blackmail material against the owners of all the major papers in the UK."

I turned to Henry, who scowled. "Do you still think we can use it for blackmail material?"

Henry rubbed his chin. "I think we should hand it to your mother's lawyers and be rid of the twat."

"Edward and I worked out another angle," said Blake.

Edward reached down to the mahogany coffee table by the Chesterfield and picked up an old copy of the Times. "Rudolph has left Peter Underwood in prison without bail and likely without a legal defense. It says here that he was the mastermind behind your abduction, but we know that's not true. Why not see if he's willing to reveal who hired him?"

Suppressing a shudder, I wrapped my arms around my middle. "How can we contact him?"

"He's at Brixton Prison."

Blake wrapped an arm around my shoulder. "Charlotte has agreed to let us tag along when she visits him tomorrow."

My brows drew together. "Can we trust her?"

"No." Blake kissed my temple. "But we can trust her to want to do right by her family."

Edward put down the paper and stood. His brows creased, and storm clouds filled his eyes. He wrapped his hand around mine. "You don't need to come with us," he said in his gentlest voice. "After that business with Carbuncle earlier today, I can't imagine you wanting to visit his accomplice."

My gaze traveled from Henry to Blake to Edward. All three of the boys wore the same grave expressions I'd seen when they had visited me the day after Blake had rescued me from that abandoned apartment.

"I can handle seeing Peter Underwood," I said.

"Are you sure, Emilia?" asked Edward. "You don't need to—"

"I'll be fine." My voice was firmer this time. It wasn't like I was meeting him in a dingy basement or anything. We'd be in a prison, surrounded by guards. There might even be a glass screen separating us. "Besides, I think he's had enough time to realize he's been abandoned by Philippe. He'll be pissed enough to reveal his other accomplice."

"Very well," said Edward. "We will set off tomorrow."

Tamping down the apprehension writhing in my gut, I gave him a sharp nod. It looked like Henry wasn't the only person who needed to face his demons.

CHAPTER 12

The next morning, I awoke wrapped around Henry and with Edward spooned at my back. Blake lay on his side with his head on Henry's chest, just as I had lain on Blake since we had slept together at the palace.

Sunlight streaming from the window played across their muscled bodies, making them look like they were in some kind of artistic movie shot by Andy Warhol or some other connoisseur of male beauty. Warmth spread across my chest. We were complete… almost.

Threats still hung over our heads. Mr. Carbuncle was still at large, probably madder than before and blaming me for getting shot. Then there was Rudolph, the most diabolical of all. That malevolent old bastard had coerced Mom into not breaking their engagement and then resented her for failing to jump into bed with his syphilitic self.

A sigh slid from my lips. If only I had known this before and not played into his hands by working for the Correspondent. I'd only opened the door to more creative ways for him to exact his revenge on Mom.

I was so glad she would be away in Casablanca when the shit hit the fan.

Edward's erection brushed against my ass. He murmured into my ear, "You're awake."

"And you're hard." I reached behind me and wrapped my fingers around his hot, thick length.

I slid my hand back and forth along Edward's hot erection, enjoying the way it twitched and lengthened at my command. His quiet gasp sent a frisson of excitement down to my core, and I squeezed my legs together.

My grip tightened, which made him hiss, and I swirled the pad of my thumb on his cock-head. A bead of precum glistened on his slit, and my tongue darted out to lick my lips.

Edward's breaths shallowed, his full lips parted, and his chest rose and fell like bellows. A smile curved my lips. A year ago, if anyone had told me I'd be in bed with a viscount, the son of a British prince, and a sexy rugby player, I would have laughed in their faces. Yet here I was, teasing Edward Mercia to distraction.

Edward rocked his hips with each movement of my fist, his precum lubricating my fingers. As Edward build up a steady rhythm, my eyes fell on Henry. He lay on his back, fast asleep and oblivious. With my free hand, I reached under the covers and grabbed his thick erection.

Blake's hand closed around mine, and he propped himself up on his elbow. "Let me. He loves to be worked up this way."

Still pumping one fist around Edward's length. I withdrew my hand and pulled back the sheets, exposing Henry's beautiful, hard body. His prominent pecs rose and fell with each breath in sync with the bunching and relaxing of his six-pack.

Groaning, Edward flung a hand over his head. "I can't watch this."

Blake chuckled. "Afraid you'll shoot your load over Emilia in ten seconds?"

"Ha."

Blake lowered his head to Henry's erection. "Edward's the ultimate voyeur."

"And you're an exhibitionist," he replied through clenched teeth.

Mischief shone in Blake's eyes as he wrapped a hand around Henry's waist and pressed a kiss on the other boy's massive pec. Henry didn't respond. Not even when Blake's tongue swirled around his nipple and teased the other until it darkened. Not even when Blake's hand slid down Henry's tight abs, and he threaded his fingers through the other boy's blonde pubes.

The pulse between my legs pounded, and my breath quickened. I'd seen them both at the Valentine's party, and I had seen Sergei and Andreo that time from the mezzanine of their apartment. But this was the first time I would witness two boys together in daylight.

"Emilia." Edward's voice was strained. "Loosen your grip."

I relaxed the fist pumping up and down Edward's erection and slowed my movements.

"Changed your mind, then?" Blake trailed kisses down Henry's six-pack, over his prominent hip bones, stopping at the level of his crotch.

"I can't miss this." Still thrusting into my loose fist, Edward raised his upper body off the bed and peered over my shoulder.

Henry's erection lay flat against his tight stomach, thick and slumbering, his foreskin fully retracted and exposing a bulbous cock-head. I licked my lips, partially wishing it was me who got to worship that gorgeous erection and partly in anticipation of what Blake would do next.

His dark eyes met mine, the look in them saying 'you're next.' Arousal heated my core, and wetness slicked my folds. Then he swiped his tongue along Henry's length from base to tip.

Edward's groan went straight between my legs, and he thrust into my closed fist. "Looser, Emilia… Looser."

I untightened my fingers. Watching Blake and Henry together and getting jerked off would bring anyone over the edge.

Blake's hand cupped Henry's heavy balls, and he massaged them between his fingers. At the same time, he swiped that tongue up and down Henry's shaft, pausing to flick the underside of the other boy's darkening head.

Henry still didn't respond.

"He loves being woken up this way," murmured Blake.

When Blake wrapped his full lips around Henry's erection and sucked at the tip, Henry didn't even twitch. All the moisture in my throat traveled south to my slick core. This was so unbelievably hot.

I brought my free hand between my legs and circled my clit with my index finger. Blake's tongue lashed at the underside of Henry's cock-head with vigorous strokes, and I stimulated my nub with the same rhythm.

"Take him all the way in," Edward said with a groan.

I would have said the same thing, but Edward's hand snaked around my front, and his fingers slipped underneath my hands and between my wet folds. An inaudible gasp left my lips.

"Let me..." he growled into my ear.

I moved my hand away, and his fingers glided over my clit, sending sparks of pleasure flying down my thighs, up to my belly, and into my core.

Blake's head bobbed up and down Henry's length, his full lips stretching around his mouthful. At the same time, he rubbed his prick against Henry's muscular thighs.

It was hard to concentrate with Edward fingering my sensitive bundle of nerves, and his erection sliding back and forth in my fist. His hot breaths filled my ear and sent tiny shivers of pleasure down my back, and at the same time, Blake continued to pleasure an oblivious Henry.

A low, resonant moan reverberated in Henry's chest and made the muscles of my core ripple. My gaze flicked up to his face, but he remained fast asleep. Edward's fingers circled my clit with cruel precision, never stopping, never easing up.

"He's such a heavy sleeper and probably thinks it's a dream," said Edward, his voice strained.

Up and down, up and down, Blake went on that beautiful, thick shaft. Henry's breaths deepened. I licked my lips. Maybe Henry was getting close. Edward's thrusts quickened, and he increased the pressure of the fingers circling my nub.

My eyes rounded, my nipples tightened, and the muscles of my core clenched.

Pleasure coiled around me like a constrictor, squeezing and squeezing until I couldn't breathe. Then when I could take no more, the most intense orgasm squeezed out of me in a series of undulating contractions that radiated pleasure down to every nerve ending from scalp to toes.

Edward continued teasing more and more sensations, stretching out my climax until it reduced to the tiniest of trembles. A whimper of satisfaction escaped my lips.

Then Henry bolted upright, eyes flying open. "Oh, fuck!"

As Blake laughed around Henry's length, I clamped my fingers around Edward's dick, and he thrust against my grip, letting the tip of his erection rub against my ass. Edward's erection pulsed in my hand, and with a low, shuddering moan, ropes and ropes of thick, pearlescent fluid shot out of his slit and landed on my hip.

Still thrusting against Henry's lower body, Blake's muscles bunched, and he gasped out his climax.

I slumped on the mattress and licked my lips. "Synchronized orgasms? I'm impressed."

～

We left for Brixton Prison at lunchtime, aiming to arrive in London in time for the last available slot for the day. Five of us sat in the back of the limo. Henry at the far end, with Edward, Blake, and me forming natural barriers between him and Charlotte. After all the stunts she had pulled, I didn't want her getting a whiff of him.

Sergio's latest concerto played in the speakers, an energetic piece that reminded me of a storm. According to Musical Opinion magazine, he was touring Russia. I wondered if his security guy had gotten any closer to discovering the identity of the person who had poisoned his father.

"Prison's no place for a trollop, you know," said Charlotte.

I shot her a glare. "After your video sex with a man older than a giant tortoise and with a body to match, I'm surprised you have the nerve to throw accusations about."

She sagged in her seat. "Sorry… Force of habit."

"Take no notice," whispered Blake. "She's faking."

I nodded. The only thing I could trust Charlotte to do was watch out for her family and stick a knife in the backs of everyone else.

Brixton Prison was a dreary, early-nineteenth-century building behind tall, brick walls that were bolstered by miles of barbed wire and what might have been an electrified fence. As the limo pulled up outside the gates, the lining of my stomach trembled. It would be me, Charlotte, and Henry visiting Peter Underwood.

"Will you be alright?" Edward asked.

I nodded, and Blake gave me a peck on the lips. "Be careful."

Henry wrapped an arm around my waist. "Let's go."

He opened the door of the limo and helped me out. We turned toward the entrance when Charlotte stumbled across the sidewalk. I shared a glance with Henry. This was the same girl who had sprinted away from me in six-inch heels. I doubted that she was incapable of stepping out of a limousine.

"You could have at least helped me." Charlotte ran her hands down her blazer and shot me a venomous glare. "Why do they all like you?"

"Shouldn't we focus on the matter at hand?" I muttered. "Helping your brother?"

Henry placed a hand on the small of my back and guided me through the first of the security checks. My mind kept flashing back to that terrible night when Mr. Carbuncle had threatened to rape me, and how Peter Underwood had only cared that the former caretaker didn't do it in his presence.

He had even left me to email some photos, knowing that Mr. Carbuncle would soon return from his cigarette break. Even though he'd been duped and double-crossed by Philippe, as Rudolph would never have paid a ransom for something he had set up, I couldn't feel much sympathy for the man.

"Edward spent years stringing along my best friends, yet you arrive and swoop him up and his friends. How did you do it?"

My gaze darted to the female security officers who checked our ID before directing us to a bank of lockers. "Focus, Charlotte." I hissed back.

Her lips puckered as though I had insulted her. Ignoring her expression, I asked, "You brought your brother into the scheme to abduct me, right?"

"Philippe told me—"

"Now he's in prison because Rudolph's abandoned him. Let's focus on seeing how much of the blame we can push where it belongs."

She cast her eyes at Henry, who had just returned from the lockers, and whispered, "Alright."

There were more people in the waiting room than I had expected. At times like this, I would have people-watched, but my stomach churned with a combination of dread and guilt. I should have kept my revenge to dumb pranks, like hair remover in Charlotte's conditioner or something that would only affect the people I had wanted to hurt. By striking too deeply and aiming at their families, I had brought the wrath onto myself.

I sat on a plastic chair and stared at my loafers. When I had passed information about Peter Underwood's gambling addiction to the Saturday Correspondent, it had set off a chain of events that had uncovered his father's expenses fraud and created a national scandal.

"Are you alright?" Henry wrapped an arm around my back.

I nodded. "Just getting mentally prepared."

The prison guards led us to a visitors hall, consisting of rows of plastic tables and chairs. Half the tables were occupied by male prisoners clad in gray sweatshirts and jogging bottoms. I looked around for the man who had abducted me, but I didn't recognize anyone.

Charlotte's shoulders tensed, and she walked to the far side of the room. Henry and I followed, my heart in my throat and pulsing so hard I thought it would burst.

I recognized the man who hugged Charlotte. Right now, he looked haggard with a fat lip and a fading bruise on his cheek, but I'd seen him before. He had opened the door for me in Chelsea Heights before I had gotten a chance to ring the apartment bell. He had probably been lying in wait for me the entire evening.

Peter Underwood's brow lowered into a frown. "What's she doing here?"

"Helping us," Charlotte replied.

"Can she be trusted?"

"Philippe withdrew his financial assistance. We're on our own."

Surely she meant to say Rudolph? I opened my mouth to ask but clicked it shut. Watching and listening at this stage might give me the answers I needed.

Peter closed his eyes and let out a long breath. "Bastard." He turned to me. "Will you pay for our lawyers? It's the least you could do after leaking our family business to the press."

I bristled, and Henry placed a comforting hand on my knee. That entitled prick was even worse than his sister. "Isn't that a question for the secretary who went to the Correspondent with all that evidence against your father?"

His lip curled into an ugly sneer. "What are you here for, then?"

"I want to make a complaint against Rudolph Trommel for my abduction, but I won't be able to prove anything unless I have witnesses. Are you willing to testify that you were working for him?"

He raised both shoulders and spread his arms wide. "I'll say anything if it results in a lighter sentence."

Frustration welled up in my insides. "Did you meet Rudolph?"

"No." He gave his sister quizzical look. "I worked with Carbuncle and a man called Philippe, but I can say we worked with Rudolph if it will help me."

My shoulders slumped. "No one will take you seriously if you fabricate claims that can be refuted with alibis," said Henry. "Can you testify that Philippe was behind the abduction?"

"Yes, but I thought you were trying to pin this on Rudolph," he replied.

"Philippe works for Rudolph," said Charlotte.

Peter reared back and glowered at his sister. "Why didn't you tell me this?"

She dipped her head.

"Answer me!" he roared.

A fist clenched at my heart, and I winced. By instinct, I raised my arms to my chest. Peter Underwood hadn't hurt me while I had been conscious, but being in his presence made my skin crawl.

One of the prison guards stepped forward, and Henry raised his palm. "It's just a discussion that's gotten out of hand."

The guard stood over Peter. "Watch yourself."

Peter's nostrils flared. "If you had told me, I would have asked why a mogul would have his own stepdaughter kidnapped," he said through clenched teeth. "I would also have asked why he would want photos of the girl plastered all over the papers to extort ransom money from himself."

"Sorry."

"You were so blinded by your hatred for the girl that you brought me into this harebrained plot. I thought it was a chance to pay off my debts with a bit extra to help Father, not a crusade to hurt another schoolgirl."

It was my turn to bow my head. Charlotte wasn't the only person whose desire for revenge had turned into an out-of-control monster.

"Now, look at me." He leaned forward and whispered. "Behind bars with murderers, pedophiles, and men who dominate others with rape."

My throat thickened, and I gulped.

Peter Underwood turned to me. "I already planned on telling the authorities everything I knew about this Philippe fellow. Now that I know he was working for Rudolph all along, and this was a sick game they'd concocted to push the blame onto me for hurting you, I'll do everything I can to help."

"Thank you," I murmured.

He turned to Charlotte. "Did you even think about the impact that dragging me into your vendetta would have on me? How could you?"

"How could you?" she spat. "Look at what your gambling has done to the family. Mother and Father sold all their assets to pay off your casino bills, and now Father's in trouble for fraud. All because of you!"

My insides cringed. All this time, I hadn't anticipated that Charlotte was capable of such malice toward her own brother. I turned to Henry and grimaced.

He gave me an equally awkward glance in return and mouthed, 'Are you alright?'

Nodding, I tried to tune out the family dispute. It was hard to feel sympathy for Peter Underwood, even if Charlotte had kind of set him up. If Blake hadn't come to my rescue, I might not have left that apartment alive.

With a long sigh, I let my gaze wander to a man chatting with his wife and toddler daughter. At least Peter had agreed to do the right thing, even if he was motivated by self-interest.

CHAPTER 13

While Henry updated Blake and Edward on the conversation we had with Peter Underwood, Charlotte wept the entire journey back to Mercia Academy. I peered at her through the corner of my eye.

"I'll bet you consider this a victory," she spat, "But it's not!"

"I'm just trying to make sure those out to hurt me get punished. Mr. Carbuncle tried to abduct me yesterday."

"He should have taken you." Charlotte wiped her face with the back of her hands. "Maybe you'll learn a bit of humility after spending a few days in his basement."

"What did you say?" asked Blake.

Face paling, she broke eye contact. "Nothing."

"Did you tell him where to find Emilia?" asked Edward.

Something niggled at the back of my mind. I closed my eyes and took a deep breath. So much had happened yesterday—the blow job with Edward in the shower, the Board of Governors, meeting Edward's father, Mr. Carbuncle, sex with Henry, confronting Aunt Idette—it was hard to keep track of everything. But where had I seen Charlotte, and would she have known where I would be in the afternoon?

The memory rolled to the forefront of my mind, and my eyes snapped open. "She walked past us when we stood outside the main block," I said to Edward. "Charlotte heard me tell you to go home and visit your father."

She cringed. "I didn't tell him to snatch you."

Blake shot out of his seat and grabbed Charlotte by the chin. Through clenched teeth, he growled, "Where is he?"

My hands clapped over my mouth. I'd never seen Blake so angry.

She jerked out of his grip. "I don't know!"

"You're still in contact with him!" he snarled.

Edward grabbed his arm. "Blake—"

Blake shook him off. "No! This fucking bitch set Emilia up for a horrific beating that left her broken and unconscious. Then she called Carbuncle so he could do it again!"

Henry wrapped both arms around Blake's middle and hauled him into his seat. "Don't do it."

Blake twisted himself around in Henry's grip and met his eyes. "But you should have seen—"

"I know," he said in a soft, soothing tone. "But hitting Charlotte isn't the answer."

Her eyes roved over the pair. "You're a couple." Wonder filled her voice. "Those pictures weren't a drunken one-off. You love each other!"

"Don't change the subject." I kicked her in the shin, making her shriek. "Where's Mr. Carbuncle hiding?"

She clamped her lips together.

"Right." I slammed my fist into my palm. "When I've finished with you, someone else will have to pay for a new nose job, because you'll look like Coates."

Edward placed a hand on my arm. "Emil—"

"Don't stop me." I shook him off. "If Fredrickson hadn't been there with the gun, Mr. Carbuncle would have raped and murdered me by now."

His hand dropped away. Because he knew I was right.

The limo sped along the freeway, and the roar of the air conditioning matched the roar of blood between my ears. Charlotte was the queen of setting people up. If she had done it to her brother, I had no doubt that she was the driver behind Mr. Carbuncle's latest attack. If she didn't give us something, I would take out all my anger on her face and see how Rudolph liked her the next time he wanted an online booty call.

Ducking her head, Charlotte clapped both hands over her nose. "I don't know where he is," she wailed. "I swear on my brother's life."

"Considering you got him embroiled in an abduction plot where he would take the fall, I doubt that you value his anything," muttered Blake.

She raised her head to reveal tear-streaked, hazel eyes. "He lives with his mother in Estermere village. A-a-and I have his number."

"Where's his basement?" I pictured an abandoned bunker, deep underground. The type psychopaths and serial killers converted into their lairs.

"At his mother's house," she snapped. "Where else?"

Leaning forward, Edward held out his hand. "I suggest you give me Mr. Carbuncle's phone number and his mother's address."

Charlotte reached into the pocket of her blazer and then hesitated.

"It looks like you want the National Health Service to perform your facial reconstructive surgery," Blake muttered.

With a pout, Charlotte pulled out her smartphone. "I suppose you want his mother's phone number, too?"

"I'll take it myself," said Edward.

She handed it to Edward.

"Security code?"

"Six-six-sixty-nine."

"Typical," muttered Blake.

Edward tapped the security code and texted the numbers onto his own phone. After pressing the home button, he swiped through the screens and looked through her apps. "Is that all the information you have on Carbuncle?"

"Yes."

Blake sneered. "Where do you meet him to get your pussy licked?"

"Blake!" she screeched.

"You have to be getting it somewhere."

Her face twisted with faux-disgust. "Like you're getting it from Henry?"

He smirked. "And Emilia."

"Answer his question," said Edward. "Where are you meeting him for trysts?"

Charlotte's lips pressed together in a tight line. If she hadn't been in the limo that was doing seventy miles per hour on the freeway, she would probably have stormed out with her nose in the air. I'd seen her do it every time she had felt cornered in the dining hall. But she was trapped without her doppelgängers and without her rugby boys for moral support. And I was furious enough to break her nose. And this time, I wouldn't need a hockey stick.

After several tense moments, her shoulders fell. "He still has his key to the caretaker's lodge."

"Thank you." Edward slipped the phone into his pocket.

"That's mine," she screeched. "What are you doing?"

"Making sure you don't arrange any more attacks."

A huge breath of relief whooshed out of my lungs. With Charlotte unable to contact Mr. Carbuncle, a layer of stress fell off my shoulders. I wasn't completely safe by any measure, but at least the former caretaker wouldn't have the advantage of advance knowledge of my whereabouts.

The best part of having Charlotte's phone was that we could

now impersonate her and lure Mr. Carbuncle out of his hiding-place. I thanked Rudolph for teaching me that sneaky trick.

∼

It was late evening by the time we reached Mercia Academy, and a warm, forest-scented breeze meandered around the campus, carrying with it the faint scent of wildflowers. Charlotte stormed into Elder House, presumably to sulk about her confiscated phone, and we walked across the lawn for a change in scenery. As it was dinnertime, only a few people strolled around the campus.

As we approached the music block, the scent of lavender filled the warm, evening air and instantly calmed my frayed nerves. Henry placed an arm around my shoulder, while Blake and Edward strolled at my side. I almost wished Mr. Carbuncle would ambush me here with the triumvirate around me. The three boys would give him a pummeling he would never forget.

The garden behind the music block was a riot of fragrances and colors. Pink roses, orange echinacea flowers, and ornamental onion grew among the lavender shrubs. We walked along the meandering gravel path crunching stones underfoot.

Blake rubbed his chin. "We should pay Carbuncle's mother a visit and see if he's hiding in the basement."

"The police will have visited his family home to check on his whereabouts," said Edward. "Carbuncle is probably sleeping in his pickup truck."

"Are there lots of places he could hide it?" I asked.

"Countless," replied Edward. "The entire South Downs is larger than the entire landmass of Greater London, and there are numerous farms, estates, garages, and warehouses where he could hide. The only way to catch him is by luring him out."

"Or taking something he considers precious," said Blake.

My brows drew together. "The only thing he seemed to value was his job."

Edward sighed and ran his fingers through his hair. "All those bribes we paid him over the years to facilitate our pranks. He probably has the funds to do anything."

There wasn't much I could say to a statement like that, considering I had suffered the brunt of some of those pranks in my first term. Blowing out a long breath, I stared ahead at a drinking fountain styled to look like a cast-iron podium and tried to think of something else.

Live-in staff at Mercia Academy, such as caretakers and housemasters, were given food and accommodation. Anyone with a frugal mindset could save most of their salary. If they took bribes or sold illicit items to students, they could amass a tidy sum. In addition to whatever nest-egg Mr. Carbuncle might have accumulated, he was probably taking bribes from Philippe. I couldn't think of any other reason why he came after me a second time.

Turning to Blake, I said, "Do you have any ideas for what Mr. Carbuncle might value?"

He raised a shoulder. "Let's visit his mother's home and work out if he kept anything of worth there."

"Tomorrow," said Edward. "We've already missed all our afternoon classes. Even with the end of term so close, we can't afford to fall too behind."

∼

The next morning at breakfast, Charlotte approached us, her eyes red-rimmed. She turned her body to Henry, who pretended he couldn't see her. I stiffened. At any minute, she would get frustrated at his lack of attention and lash out at me.

"What now?" asked Blake, his voice weary.

"Did I get any messages on my phone?"

"I turned it off," replied Edward. "Why?"

"Mother sent me an email." Her voice shook. "Peter has been attacked in prison. I-it's really bad."

I sucked in a breath through my teeth. "Is he alright?"

People from other tables turned to stare, and a hush spread across the dining hall. It seemed like everyone wanted to listen to Charlotte's latest news.

When she didn't answer, my intestines twisted into tight knots. I resented him for getting involved in that kidnapping plot, but I wouldn't wish a brutal beating on anyone. "Do you have any news on his condition?"

"Do you think Rudolph arranged it?" whispered Henry.

"It's an uncanny coincidence," added Blake.

I leaned forward, trying to catch her eye. "Is he in a regular hospital?"

"What do you care?" she spat.

My shoulders dropped. "Sorry for asking."

"What happened?" asked Edward.

She shook her head. "Nobody knows. The guards found him last night half-battered to death." Then her gaze landed on me. "If you had stayed in your own country, none of this would have happened."

The words struck like a punch to the gut. There was a grain of truth in what she said, but she was wrong. If it was anyone else, I would have let the comment slide, but Charlotte was no stranger to arranging violent ambushes.

Straightening, I met her square in the eye. "You chose to drag your brother into this. What did you think would happen to him when I got released?"

A tiny voice in the back of my head, combined with the defiance in her eyes, said that she hadn't expected me to leave that apartment alive. I pushed away those thoughts. As long as I stayed with the boys, no one else could hurt me.

Charlotte sniffed. "And my agent emailed to say the newspapers withdrew their offers."

"There's the answer to your mystery," said Blake.

She tilted her head to the side. "What are you talking about?"

"You went behind our backs and decided to use the videos for yourself. What if Rudolph bribed your agent to bury the footage? Your agent was only ever going to receive a percentage of what the papers would give you. Rudolph could have made him a better offer and decided to teach you a lesson through your brother."

Her bottom lip trembled. "Are you saying I was the cause of what happened to Peter?"

I turned and slashed my hand over my throat in the universal sight to say cut it out, but Blake continued speaking. "Rudolph knows someone is out to get him. Because you took that footage to an agent, all evidence points toward you."

She turned to Edward. "This is all your fault."

"Do elaborate," he drawled.

"You told me to pull down the cameras."

"And you knew those cameras were linked to the Saturday Correspondent." He glanced up. "Did you think you were the exception to Rudolph's wrath?"

From the way she winced, I wondered if she had believed she was special to Rudolph.

"You four are making me look stupid."

Henry's head shot up, and he gave her a 'who, me?' look. He hadn't said a single thing, but Charlotte blamed him all the same.

Slumping in my seat, I placed my fork on my plate of summer fruits and Belgian waffles. Watching Charlotte rant just made me tired. Everything was backfiring on her, and she was spiraling out of control. Although she had made me feel like that at the gauntlet and when she had arranged for my abduction, I couldn't feel much pity for her.

"What did I ever do to you?" she hissed at me.

"If you have to ask, I can't explain," I replied.

"You're a bitch." She balled her fists and raised her voice, so even the kitchen staff could hear. "If I ever get the chance, I'll repay you five-fold for what you've done!"

"Look in the mirror, Charlotte," said Blake. "You might see the real culprit within your blinkers."

"Ten-fold!" she stormed out of the dining room with her ponytail flying.

I rested my chin in my hand and sighed. Would Charlotte's brother change his mind about implicating Philippe or would the prison beating serve as ample warning not to involve Rudolph or his assistant?

CHAPTER 14

The next morning, as we walked through the dining room's double doors, Rita sat straighter in her seat and raised her hand in a wave. Warmth spread through my chest. Ever since I had moved out of our shared room, we hadn't had a chance to chat. She spent most of her time in Hawthorne House with her boyfriend, and I had my hands full with all the drama unfolding in my life. With a smile, I waved back and turned to Henry. "I think Rita wants to tell me something."

"I'll come with you," he replied.

"No need," I said, "Unless there's another entrance to the dining hall I haven't noticed."

"The kitchens," said Blake and Henry at the same time.

"Ah." I looped my arm around Henry's bicep. "Then we'll go together."

As Blake took his seat at the middle table set up with special china and silverware, Henry and I continued across the room. A few people, mostly those who had been at the gauntlet, raised their heads to stare but didn't comment. I kept my gaze off them and continued toward the table Rita shared with the other scholarship students.

"Emilia?" Alice beckoned me over as I passed. She sat opposite Duncan, who had his usual pile of papers next to his plate. Excitement filled her face, and she bounced on her seat. Whatever she was about to share would be good.

As soon as I paused, Alice blurted out, "Did you hear? The Port of London Authority has shut down the boat company because of Charlotte's booze cruise."

I frowned. "Don't tell me they're getting the blame for the doctored cocktails?"

"A few of the parents have decided to go after the company since it had a duty of care to their passengers to provide potable drinks."

"Oh, no." I turned to Henry.

"Do the parents know what really happened?" he asked.

"It's hearsay." Duncan shrugged. "Charlotte's denying everything, of course. No one actually saw her do it. Now, she's telling everyone that someone else named Philippe organized the cruise and absconded with the money."

Irritation flared through my insides. An entire company with boats and employees and other obligations would have to close down because Charlotte couldn't admit the truth. She could even have blamed the poisoning on Philippe to protect the innocent company, but she chose to let an innocent party get the blame. Someone in a nearby table snorted with laughter, adding to my foul mood. It just reminded me of Charlotte not taking what she had done to the girls, and now the boat company, seriously.

Pursing my lips, I tamped down the anger simmering in my belly. It looked like Charlotte would get away with drugging all those girls the same way she got away with leading me into that trap.

"Thanks for letting me know." My words came out strained. "I hope the doctored cocktail didn't interfere with your course of antibiotics."

Alice let out a weary sigh. "I'm fine. It's just so unfair that the most she's suffering is a mild snubbing. By next year, everyone but the affected girls would have forgotten about the booze cruise, and she'll think of another way to regain her popularity."

"That's what I'm afraid of," I said before heading over to Rita's table. There wasn't much else to say with people at the surrounding tables eavesdropping. "See you later."

Rita sat with the usual group of scholarship students. She stood and met me halfway. Her gaze darted to Henry, but the sight of him at my side didn't change her pleasant expression. I suppose his easy-going personality made him the least threatening of the triumvirate.

I walked around and wrapped my arms around her narrow shoulders. "Hey, Rita. It's been so long."

Her hug was a tight squeeze of the arms and not the usual relaxed embrace. I drew back and stared into huge, deep brown eyes ringed with dark circles. Two lines appeared between her brows, and tension tightened her features.

"What's wrong?" I whispered.

Rita gulped. "I heard some noises outside last night and looked out of the window. At first, I thought it might have been someone from Hawthorne House, but I saw a large man prowling around the building, trying to force his way in."

My stomach dropped. "Do you think it might have been—"

"I don't know," she blurted as if the word Carbuncle was too horrific to hear. "But I called campus security, and four officers came right away. They stayed for ages with dogs and torches. Then the dogs led two of the handlers away toward the back of the building."

"In the direction of his lodge," said Henry.

I glanced up into his concerned features, framed by a halo of golden hair. "What else?"

"Campus security called me back." Rita rubbed at her heart, making me wonder if she had gotten any sleep after seeing that prowler. "They assured me that whoever had been there had left and said I probably shouldn't look out of the windows at night."

"Seriously?" asked Henry, his voice flat.

"That doesn't sound promising at all," I muttered.

The muscles in Henry's jaw tightened. "They should have called the fucking police!"

Rita flinched, and I stepped in front of Henry and placed an arm on her shoulder. "Thanks so much for telling me. You might want to sleep in Hawthorn House from now on. If he was outside your window, he was probably looking for me."

"T-that's what I thought," she whispered. "I won't sleep another night in that room. But you need to be careful, too."

A sigh slid from my nostrils. "Thanks, Rita. And I'm sorry that this business with him is affecting you."

She wrapped her arms around my neck and gave me a tight squeeze. "Take care of yourself, and don't wander around on your own."

I trudged back to our table, my aching heart sinking to my stomach. It was obvious that Mr. Carbuncle would strike again, but I never thought he would resort to breaking into Elder House at night. Henry wrapped a comforting arm around my middle, lending me his warmth and protection. My muscles relaxed at his touch, but the thought of Mr. Carbuncle returning to finish what he had started rolled around my head like a millstone and ground the last of my peace of mind to dust.

Blake and Edward sat opposite each other, observing me with concerned faces. Blake tilted his head to the side, while Edward's posture remained rigid.

"What did she say?" Blake's gaze flickered from my eyes to Rita's table.

I took my seat and stared at my empty plate. "It's Mr. Carbuncle."

Henry sat opposite. "You don't know that for sure."

While Henry poured us both a cup of tea, I repeated Rita's account of last night's events. Blake and Edward's faces hardened as I spoke. Neither of them shared Henry's optimism. A regular burglar would break into the empty International House or one of the other houses at the edge of the campus. It had to be Mr. Carbuncle.

When I finished, Blake shook his head. "He's becoming more of an immediate danger than Rudolph."

My shoulders sagged. "We need to do something about him."

"He hasn't yet replied to my text from the confiscated phone," said Blake. "When he does, I'll arrange a trap."

Nodding, I brought my cup of tea to my lips. Hopefully, Charlotte hadn't found a way to tell him we were now in control of her phone.

Edward picked up a slice of toast from the rack. "I've just introduced myself to Mrs. Carbuncle, saying that I am a concerned student who would like to meet her to see what I can do to help her son. She told me she'd be delighted to join us for afternoon tea at the village teashop."

⁓

We arrived at Muriel's Tea Rooms at four o'clock, which was apparently the time everyone decided to visit. A young server led us to tables Edward had reserved. The plan was to have Blake and me at a nearby table observing, while Edward and Henry poured on the charm. I ordered a slice of chocolate fudge cake, Blake ordered the strawberry shortcake, and we waited for Mrs. Carbuncle to show her face.

At quarter-past four, an elderly woman arrived at Muriel's Tea Rooms, wearing a worn, tweed suit with a brown blouse, and an oversized chiffon scarf with a houndstooth pattern. Her thinning, silvery hair was pulled back from her face into a severe bun, but it only highlighted her soft features.

"That can't be Mrs. Carbuncle." I leaned into Blake and whispered, "She doesn't look like him at all."

"It has to be her," he whispered back. "All the other old ladies arrive in pairs or gangs."

I glanced around the tea room at the groups of elderly women sitting around the tables enjoying afternoon tea served in tiered cake stands. He was right. My gaze traveled back to the old lady, who glanced around the room until she spotted Edward and Henry, sitting at the table for four next to ours.

She strode across the room at a brisk pace, considering her walking stick. Edward and Henry stood at the same time. While Henry pulled out the old woman's chair, Edward gave her a dazzling smile. "Mrs. Carbuncle, I presume?"

The old woman offered her hand. "How wonderful to meet you, Viscount Highdown."

Edward pressed his lips on her knuckles. "Please, call me Edward."

With cheeks flaring brighter than the strawberries on the shortcake, Mrs. Carbuncle took her seat and gave Henry an admiring gaze. "And who is this handsome fellow?"

"Henry Bourneville, at your service." He gave her a gallant bow and kissed her hand.

"Not the Bourneville Bourneville's from London?"

"The very same," he said in a deep voice that made my nipples pebble.

Mrs. Carbuncle clapped her hands over her flushed cheeks. "And you say you're acquaintances with my Ernest?"

Rolling his eyes, Blake placed a huge chunk of strawberry shortcake in his mouth.

"We've known him since we were eleven." Henry nodded his thanks to the server, who placed a butterfly-patterned tea set on the table. "Edward has known your son for longer, as he's lived on the academy grounds his entire life."

The old woman's eyes shone with pride. "He never said, but that's my Ernest for you. Rubs shoulders with the high class and is never one to boast."

"Rubbing more than shoulders with the girls, I would say," drawled Blake.

I gave him a kick under the table. Snickering, Blake poured me a cup of Lady Grey tea from a pot patterned with pink roses and took another bite of his cake.

Mrs. Carbuncle fluttered her eyelashes. "What can a humble lady like myself do for you, young sirs?"

"We're trying to find him," said Edward. "Someone fired birdshot at the poor fellow, and we believe he requires urgent medical attention."

"It's nice of you boys to worry about Ernest, but he came to me late one night for help. I used my tweezers and fillet knife and a whole bottle of Dettol."

I set down my teacup and gaped at Blake, who narrowed his eyes and smirked.

"Did you get it all?" asked Henry.

She rubbed the side of her face. "As much as I could. I wanted to do more, but he refused, the stubborn ass."

The server brought scones, finger sandwiches, and a slice of every cake available in the tea shop.

The old lady's eyes gleamed. "Which one is mine?"

"We didn't know what you liked." Henry raised the milk jug in silent question. When the old woman shook her head, he poured the tea. "Why don't you take a bite of each?"

Edward raised the bowl of lemon slices, and the old woman gave a vigorous nod.

"I wish those two would stop fucking about and interrogate the old battle-ax," muttered Blake. "Can't they tell she's putting on airs and graces for show?"

"Quiet." I pushed my chocolate fudge cake to his side of the table.

Blake picked up his fork and cut himself a huge chunk. The corners of my mouth curled into a smile. I didn't know he could be subdued so easily.

Mrs. Carbuncle raised the cup to her lips with her pinky finger up, while Edward and Henry drank their tea without the pretensions. I chewed on my lip, hoping they would get to the point, but this was a delicate matter. If I was on the run from the police, Mom wouldn't reveal my location to strangers, even if they were as handsome and as cultured and as well-connected as Edward and Henry.

The old woman raved about the cakes and brought up her recipe for a lemon drizzle pudding. Blake, who had finished my chocolate fudge cake, melted into a stupor of boredom. My own eyes glazed, and I slumped in my seat, marveling through my daze at how the boys remained attentive through Mrs. Carbuncle's monologue. It was hard to tell if she knew about her son's crimes or if she believed him to be innocent of all accusations.

"It's lovely to be out and about," she said. "The local police have kept me a virtual prisoner."

Blake and I jolted awake.

"What do you mean?" asked Edward.

"Poor Ernest had a bit of trouble with a nasty American trollop at the school. Apparently, she wanted access to another girl's room and threw herself at my boy."

Edward tutted. "How distasteful."

Henry's face blanked.

After declaring the orange marmalade cake delectable, Mrs. Carbuncle leaned forward. "Do you know what she did next?"

"I dread to think," replied Edward.

"She got all the other little girls to report him to the police for hanky-panky."

My brows lowered. Mom used to play a catchy old Madonna song called Hanky Panky. I leaned into Blake and whispered, "Does that mean spanking?"

"In this context it means fucking," he murmured. "Or close to it."

I ground my teeth. That lying bastard. And how could Mrs. Carbuncle believe any woman with good eyesight and a sense of smell would throw themselves at her grimy gorilla of a son and then take such drastic revenge because he turned her down?

"Why are policemen harassing you?" asked Edward.

She sniffed. "They think I know his whereabouts, but I don't. He's a great outdoorsman, my Ernest. He took his sleeping bag and might be anywhere."

Blowing out a breath, Edward shook his head. "I'm certainly glad this trollop didn't get the better of dear Mr. Carbuncle."

"But I'm the one who suffers." She took a bite out of the red velvet cake. "Do you know reporters came to my house, wanting to take photos? And a seedy Frenchman called Philip."

"Philippe?" asked Henry.

"How did you know?"

He shrugged. "Je parle Français."

Mrs. Carbuncle pressed a napkin to her lips. "They teach you all sorts in that Mercia Academy, don't they? It was where the aristocrats used to go to school when I was a girl. I wanted to work in the kitchens, but they said I wasn't qualified."

"And the academy is poorer for not being graced by your lemon drizzle pudding," said Edward.

"He could charm the knickers off a goat," muttered Blake.

"So can you," I whispered. "Let's pay attention."

"Does Mr. Carbuncle have connections in France?" asked Henry.

"No." She reached for one of the finger sandwiches. "But each time this Phillip leaves an envelope for Ernest, the police come to visit days after."

I swallowed a chunk of citrus peel in my lady gray. Mr.

Carbuncle probably used Mercia as a base with his mother's address as a pick-up point for his instructions. Since he had his mobile, he likely visited his mother whenever Philippe left a package. But what the fuck did Philippe send him?

"I think he's the trollop's fancy man, set out to get his revenge. He's always getting my boy into trouble."

I rolled my eyes.

Edward placed his hand on his heart. "It's a travesty that so many should harass an innocent woman. Why don't you stay in my guesthouse for a few days? It overlooks the mansion's rose gardens, and we have a butler available to tend to your needs. You can see it as a sort of holiday until the trollop is caught and reprimanded."

Her scone dropped to the china plate. "Y-you would do that for me?"

My jaw dropped to my chest. I leaned forward and whispered, "Edward's kidnapping an old woman?"

"I believe he's treating her to a luxury holiday she'll never forget," said Blake.

"Edward," said Henry. "Why don't you escort Mrs. Carbuncle this evening in your limousine?"

"I'll be ready at seven o'clock," said the old woman. "Do you think they'd let me take home the cakes I didn't eat?"

A boulder of dread rolled through my belly. What would Mr. Carbuncle say if he knew we had taken his mother?

CHAPTER 15

Henry, Blake, and I decided to conduct a little mission of our own. If we could find one of the envelopes Philippe left for Mr. Carbuncle, we might be able to better implicate Rudolph in their crimes. At six-thirty, we set off in separate vehicles.

Estermere village wasn't as quaint as the village by Mercia Academy. According to Edward, our village shops received a lot of patronage from the academy, the duchy, and all the buildings were listed by the government as warranting preservation for special interest. Potholes marred the main thoroughfare of Estermere village. Tall, plastic trash cans stood on the sidewalks outside flat-fronted cottages with brick facades marred by water damage and satellite receivers.

Blake, who had been taught to drive by one of the royal bodyguards, drove a jeep behind Edward's limo. Henry and I sat in the front seats, tracking our progress with Google maps on my smartphone.

"They're going to park in a moment." I squinted at the screen.

"Turn right onto… Scratchy Bottom Street, and we'll walk the rest of the way."

The boys snickered. Henry said, "It's still a better place name than Shitterton, Happy Bottom, and Shaggs."

"You're making that up." I placed my phone into my pocket. We had all dressed similarly for the occasion: black, long-sleeved tops and black pants.

"They're in Dorset." Blake pulled up by the street sign. "Edward brought us there in our second year to take a look."

I undid my seatbelt. "What did you find?"

Henry opened the front passenger door and stepped out. "Nothing worth the journey, but the fish and chips weren't bad."

"He liked the cockles and mussels," said Blake. "And the spotted dick."

Pushing aside the mental image to concentrate on our mission, I grabbed them both by the hands, and we stood at the corner to watch Edward step out of the limo and knock on a door covered in peeling, red paint.

Mrs. Carbuncle answered the door, carrying a leather suitcase almost half her size. Edward gave her a gallant bow and took her case. Then he led her to the limousine and handed the suitcase to the driver, who carried it to the trunk.

"Let's hope she doesn't return for the kitchen sink," muttered Henry.

"That's why I brought these." Blake reached into the pocket of his black jeans and pulled out a handful of unused stockings.

"Why do you have those?" I whispered.

"Don't ask," they both replied at the same time.

If we weren't about to commit the crime of breaking and entering, I would have pressed for more information. But since Mr. Carbuncle could be anywhere, including close by and watching his mother's house, I kept my mouth shut and slipped on a pair of leather gloves.

When the limo disappeared down the road and out of the village, we walked through the street, acting as though we were on our way to visit a friend. Henry knocked on the red door, waited, and stepped back. Blake slid in front of him and forced open the lock with a credit card.

A breath caught in my throat. "Where did you learn that?"

"One time at the palace, everyone was bored of waiting for Mother and the prince to emerge from their chamber. To pass the time, a pair of detectives taught me the basics of lock picking."

The door swung open, and the scent of strong air freshener filled my nostrils. Wincing, I stepped into a darkened hallway. Floorboards creaked with every step. I turned the knob of the first door and entered.

Threadbare, floral sofas took up most of the room, and a fluffy, brown rug made up of four sheepskin covered splintery, wood floors. A thick envelope lay on the side-table. Henry picked it up and placed it in a bag.

"We should search his bedroom," I said. "He's bound to keep something incriminating up there."

Upstairs was a bathroom with a dark purple toilet, sink, and bath, complete with a bidet. Mauve, damask carpets covered the ground, along with fluffy, aubergine bathmats.

"There's only one toothbrush," I spotted a plastic brush with splayed bristles standing in a grimy, enamel mug.

"Indicating that she lives alone," added Henry.

"Indicating that Carbuncle lives here part-time," said Blake. "His mother would have packed hers for her little trip."

A chill shuddered down my spine. "I think you're right." That was an excellent observation, although I'd seen Mr. Carbuncle's teeth up close, and it wouldn't surprise me if this was the only toothbrush he owned. I turned around and glanced through the bathroom door into the upstairs landing. "We'd better hurry in case he decides to visit."

The next room was a pink bedroom with a quilt-covered bed that obviously belonged to Mrs. Carbuncle. I opened the next door, which contained a water tank and mauve towels on a shelf.

"Where does he sleep?" I muttered.

"In that bed with his mother?" asked Blake.

"Charlotte mentioned a basement," said Henry.

A tight fist of apprehension clenched my stomach. "What if he's already down there, lying in wait?" I could imagine him happily telling his mother to stay at Edward's and using her time away to snatch me. My mind conjured up images of being suffocated to death, then melted in a bathtub of acid. "It rained last night. What if he got fed up with sleeping in his truck and snuck home?"

"One of us will stay on the downstairs landing while you and the others go down and investigate," said Blake.

"I'll go down with you." Henry balled his hands into fists. "If he's there, he won't last long."

Worry rippled through my insides. Henry and Mr. Carbuncle were both of an even height, but while Henry had the build and musculature of a heavyweight boxer, the former caretaker was built like a mountain gorilla and likely had the strength of the criminally insane.

"Are you sure you can take him on?" I whispered as we descended the creaky staircase.

His blond brows rose. "You doubt me?"

"Mr. Carbuncle is a man on the run. He's got nothing to lose."

Blake placed a comforting hand on the small of my back. "I've seen Henry fight four rugby players and still come out looking pretty. He can handle Carbuncle."

"Don't call me pretty." Henry strode to the end of the darkened, downstairs hallway.

We reached a set of stairs that led underground. Blake huffed and folded his arms. "Between Emilia's fretting and Henry's semantics, we'll be here until Carbuncle comes to pay mummy dearest a midnight booty call."

I wrapped my hand around Henry's, and we walked down a set of rickety wooden stairs. The surface of the wood crunched under my feet, making me wonder if it meant woodworm. What we stepped down into was more like an underground pantry than the dungeon of a psychopath. Wooden shelves lined one side, mostly laden with cleaning supplies and empty preserve jars.

"That's where he must sleep." Henry pointed the flashlight of his smartphone at a folded z-bed propped against the wall, which was mostly covered in blankets.

Next to it stood a chest of drawers. I crossed the room and opened the first one. Photos filled the entire drawer. One of them was from the Valentine's party. I lay on the four-poster bed, kissing Henry on the mouth while Blake sucked on my collarbone. Every ounce of blood drained from my face. "How did he get this?"

Another photo had been taken through the window of Edward's study. I was naked and bent over, Henry's head was between my ass-cheeks, my free hand gripped Blake's erection, and my lips were wrapped around Edward's prick. A cold mix of fear and disgust skittered over the lining of my stomach and climbed up my gullet. I gulped several mouthfuls of air and clutched the drawer.

"Two sets of people are supplying him with photos," I gasped out. "The Correspondent, and someone with access to the academy."

"What the fuck?" Henry grabbed handfuls of photos and stuffed them in the bag.

Shaking off my speculations, I filled Henry's bag with photo after incriminating photo of myself and the triumvirate. Even if it was evidence vital to a case against Mr. Carbuncle, I didn't want pictures like that of me circulated anywhere.

The other drawers contained old clothes, worn shoes, and faded porn magazines of women with 1980's bouffants.

BANG, BANG, BANG, BANG!

My heart jumped into my throat. It was Mr. Carbuncle!

"This way!" Henry yanked me up the stairs. At the top, he grabbed Blake and ushered us to the kitchen at the back of the house.

Blake pulled out his credit card and tried the back door. He couldn't wedge it open. "F-fuck!"

"Mum?" Mr. Carbuncle shouted through the letterbox. "You in the toilet?"

Henry kicked aside the doormat and found a key. Blake swooped down and picked it up.

BANG, BANG, BANG, BANG!

Each knock on the front door reverberated through my bones and chilled me to the marrow. "Hurry!"

Mr. Carbuncle groaned. "Don't make me have to go back to the car to get my keys!"

Blake unlocked the door. I shoved it open and let in the fresh air. The overgrown lawn stretched a hundred feet to a row of spruce trees that formed a green barrier. Heart ticking like a bomb about to detonate, I sprinted between Henry and Blake through knee-length grass to the end, where we fought our way through the trees' dense, pine-scented foliage. Behind them stood an ivy-covered brick wall even taller than Henry.

Blake scrambled up its front and sat on top. He leaned down and stretched out his arm. "Come on."

I grabbed his hand, and Henry hoisted me up. Within seconds, I was up and over the brick wall and landing on the other side in a crouch. Henry's bag fell at my feet, followed by Henry, and we raced down the street.

"Where did we park the car?" asked Blake.

"This way!" I pointed toward the main road.

As Blake drove back through the country roads, and my heart stopped feeling like it was about to explode, a realization slapped me in the back of my head. There were three of us this time. "We might have been able to overpower Mr. Carbuncle and force a confession out of him."

"No way," they both said at the same time.

"Why?" I picked a spruce needle out of my hair.

"If I caught a pair of scoundrels in my mother's house with her missing, I would kill them," said Henry. "He would have had rage on his side or used you as leverage."

"I suppose so." My gaze drifted into the distance. The setting sun cast an orange haze over the horizon, reflecting its golden light off the fields and trees. That had been so close.

"After seeing those photos, I don't want him within ten miles of you."

"What photos?" asked Blake.

"They're in the bag," I muttered. "Let's not touch anything until we have a fire going at Edward's."

"That bad?"

"Worse."

∽

Blake took the long way back to Mercia Academy in case Mr. Carbuncle decided to get into his pickup truck and drive around the village and surrounding roads to find his mother. By the time we arrived, the campus was deserted, as it was dinner time. We reached Edward's study, but he wasn't there.

"He's probably still charming old Mrs. Carbuncle." Blake strode to the mantlepiece and placed dried logs in the fireplace. "What do you want to do with those pictures? Burn them or take a look?"

I stared at the bag. "After seeing the first few pictures, I'm not sure I want to see the rest."

Henry sat on the Chesterfield sofa. "We need to know if they're camera stills provided by someone at the Correspondent—"

"From Philippe." Blake added tinder to the logs and lit a match.

Lowering myself on the leather seat next to Henry, I turned to the window and stared out into the courtyard. "Or if someone's been sneaking around taking photos with their camera or smartphone."

"How are we going to tell the difference?" asked Henry.

"The angles," I said. "And those pictures printed in the Correspondent were a little grainy."

"So were the pictures of us from the Valentine's party."

My shoulders sagged. I wish I hadn't helped with that stupid, fucking party. If I hadn't been so blinded by destroying the triumvirate in my second term, none of this would have happened. Not only had I ruined Henry and Blake's standings with their families, but my acts of revenge also would never stop backfiring. And now I was the star of Mr. Carbuncle's newest stash of porn.

"Don't look so guilty," said Henry. "I'm not dwelling on it, and neither should you."

Blake pressed a kiss on my temple. "Mr. Bourneville would have found a reason to disinherit Henry regardless of whether those pictures had come out or not."

The door opened, and Edward stepped in, still clad in his navy blazer and dark slacks. I would have admired his handsome, brooding looks and the way his mahogany hair framed his aristocratic features if those terrible pictures weren't still fresh in my mind.

His gaze turned to the lit fireplace. "Isn't it a bit warm for a fire?"

Henry held out the bag. "Carbuncle arrived to visit his mother, but we managed to snatch some damning evidence before we escaped."

Edward took the proffered bag and pulled out a photo. His eyes widened. "Good Lord."

My spine curled toward my knees, and I stared at my lap. Was it worse than the pictures of me I'd seen? "Are they camera stills?"

"This one looks like it was definitely taken from over there." Edward pointed at the window.

A lead boulder of dread rolled in my stomach. I'd hoped my initial assessment of the photos had been wrong. Because the implications were unthinkable.

I whispered, "He must have been peeping at us."

"Or it could have been Charlotte," said Blake.

"Never underestimate the depth of that girl's malice." Edward placed the picture in the bag and picked out another. "Or her depravity."

Curiosity built in my chest, and I couldn't hold back any longer. "Let me see."

Edward sat beside me on the Chesterfield, sandwiching me between himself and Henry. Blake stood over us, his dark brows furrowed into a frown. Most of the photos Edward pulled out had come from someone standing behind the window and taking advantage of the gap in the curtain. But there were a few of me crouching on the ground surrounded by students. Someone pulled up my skirt, exposing my panties, while others punched and kicked and pulled my hair. I swallowed hard. The gauntlet.

"The IT people were supposed to delete those from the servers," said Edward.

"Someone must have downloaded them before that," added Henry.

"Or Charlotte took them herself."

I shook my head. "She was on the other side of the crowd, waiting for me outside with her little gang."

Henry wrapped a strong arm around my shoulders and pulled me into his warmth. "Nothing like that will happen to you again as long as we're around."

Blake plucked the photos out of my fingers. "You shouldn't look at these. And we're not handing them to the police."

"Those incompetent buffoons?" Edward patted my thigh. "Absolutely not." Then he stood. "The fire is ready. I'll burn these and keep anything that might prove useful."

"What will we do next?" I croaked.

"Step one of our plan is complete. We have Mrs. Carbuncle in our grasp, and she has no means of contacting her son."

Blake huffed a laugh. "By now, he'll be frantic with worry about his mother. Let's give him a day to stew, then we'll tell him to surrender to the nearest police station and make him confess to being employed by Philippe and Rudolph to abduct and assault you."

A lump formed in my throat. "Is Mrs. Carbuncle alright?"

Edward threw another photo onto the fire. "I walked her to the kitchens, where Reginald served her a meal of pan-fried trout with a glass of Pinot Gris. She was most charmed by his gentlemanly ways."

A long breath slid from my lungs. The old woman was probably having the time of her life and didn't even know her son would think she was abducted.

"I hope this works because it could backfire very painfully."

CHAPTER 16

The next day in English Literature, I could barely concentrate on Miss Oakley's lecture on The Scarlet Letter. Last night's adventure preyed on my mind, and those compromising photos made the pancakes and maple syrup I'd had for breakfast churn in my stomach.

I glanced over my shoulder at Blake and Henry, who sat together at the pair of desks behind us. How had they felt when the photos of them together had reached their parents? Powerless, angry, violated? I had hurt them. Exposed their secret to the entire country. Yet they had still forgiven me.

My shoulders slumped, and I doodled on a sheet of paper. I wasn't sure I could forgive whoever had sent those pictures to Mr. Carbuncle.

Edward's phone beeped and broke me out of my reverie.

Miss Oakley stopped talking and glowered around the room. "How many times must I inform you that telephones are not permitted in the classrooms?"

At the other side of the room, Coates shot up his hand. "Miss, the sound came from Bourneville's direction."

I rolled my eyes and leaned into Edward. "Isn't it enough that he took Henry's place as the rugby captain? Now, he wants to get him into trouble?"

"He really is the most pathetic creature."

Holding onto the lapels of her black professor's cloak, Miss Oakley strode to our side of the room, her face a mask of determination. She stopped at Henry's desk and held out her palm. "Hand it over."

Henry tilted his head to the side. "I beg your pardon?"

"Your phone," she snapped.

He tapped his blazer pockets. "I left it in my room today."

Blake leaned forward and flashed her a dazzling grin. "Should I remind him to bring it to the next class?"

Miss Oakley's cheeks pinked. "Of course not." She glanced around. "The next person whose forbidden phone interrupts my lecture will have it confiscated."

As she ambled back to her desk, Edward pulled out his phone, held it under the table, and glanced at the screen. His eyes widened, and the tiniest of smiles curved his lips.

I couldn't see his screen from that angle, so whispered, "What's happened?"

"I set off a google alert for Philippe's name." He tapped the screen. "Philippe de Connasse was arrested last night on suspicion of abduction."

A thrill of triumph surged through my insides and exploded like a Roman skyrocket. "Where was it reported?"

"The Saturday Correspondent's website."

My jaw dropped. "Why would Jackie put something like that in the paper?"

"It's actually a report on police brutality. They used excessive physical force when apprehending Philippe in their offices."

"Good." I leaned back in my seat and raised my head to feign attention to Miss Oakley's lecture.

Jackie, the Saturday Correspondent's editor-in-chief, had asked me last term to uncover the identity of Charlotte's benefactor. But I had been too angry with her and Rudolph to do the paper any favors. What if she had been trying to warn me all this time that Rudolph was planning something too nefarious for her to stomach? I shook off those thoughts. If Jackie had been serious about warning me, she would have sent me more apparent clues.

The bell sounded, and Edward walked me to my next class, Creative Writing, which was located on the top floor in one of the classrooms by the atrium, a beautiful glass dome that opened up a shaft of sunlight that spread across the mezzanine and down to the ground floor.

As we strolled down the hallway toward the marble staircase, Edward placed a hand on the small of my back. "Have you and Henry resolved your differences yet?"

I paused. So much had happened since Henry and I had discussed the events of the first term—the argument with Aunt Idette and Mr. Bourneville, visiting Peter Underwood in Brixton Prison, and the theft of Mrs. Carbuncle and subsequent raid on her house—it was hard to remember that we had spent time together mere days ago.

"Yes," I said. "We kissed and made up."

His brows drew together. "You don't sound convinced."

"I am..."

It took a while to put the words together. The kidnapping incident was in the past. I'd resented him the most because he was the only member of the triumvirate I'd fallen for before the betrayal. He hadn't redeemed himself in my second term due to the pact he had made with his friends and accomplices. Something else still niggled.

"Have you met Mr. Bourneville?" I asked.

"I have." Edward's tone was biting.

"He's a bully."

"I concur."

"Why can't Henry stand up to him? Last term, you three defended yourselves against homophobic attacks and slurs, but he didn't argue back against his father and aunt's accusations."

As we ascended the first flight of marble stairs, I told him my theory about his Aunt Idette, and how she had probably poisoned Mr. Bourneville's mind.

Sunlight streamed in through narrow windows and gave the ends of Edward's mahogany hair a fiery, paprika glow. He shook his head. "I'll have to show you pictures of Henry before his growth spurt. He was one of the smallest boys in the year even up until the third year. I think his father's disapproval stems from that."

"Are you serious?"

"Unfortunately, I am."

"But Henry's bigger than him, now."

Edward shrugged as we reached the second-floor landing. "Mr. Bourneville is set in his ways. But I think the disinheritance might be good for Henry. It's one less threat the old man can hang over his head."

The thought of that toxic pair berating Henry sent a flash of irritation across my skin. "I don't understand why he didn't just tell him to fuck off."

"Henry tends to be more protective over his friends than over himself." Edward's voice was grave. It made me wonder if he'd had this conversation with Blake. "Perhaps if Mr. Bourneville threatened his friendship with one of us, Henry would speak up."

I nodded. Henry wasn't the type to abandon a friend in peril.

Edward hummed, and we continued up the stairs. By now, most of the younger students had disappeared into their classrooms. A few stragglers who had likely come from other blocks dashed up the stairs, but since Edward's Economics class was also located on the top floor, we took our time.

"When will we contact Mr. Carbuncle?" I whispered.

"Let him stew for the rest of the morning." Edward held the door open that led to the atrium. "We can send a message from Charlotte's phone this evening, telling him we have urgent news about his mother and to meet us at the usual place."

"Does Mrs. Carbuncle have a cellphone?" I stepped through the door and squinted against the glare of the sun.

"Just the landline." We continued around the curved hallway of the atrium level until we reached the door to my classroom. He gave me a peck on the cheek. "I need to speak to Mr. Williams after Economics. Wait for me here until I come to collect you."

∽

Perhaps the incident with campus security and their dogs had spooked Mr. Carbuncle. He didn't reply to the text Edward sent from Charlotte's phone. Henry and Blake stayed up to stake out the caretaker's lodge, while Edward and I went to bed at ten because we had to wake up early for the academy's sports day.

Edward's kisses on my neck woke me from a pleasant dream of wrapping my lips around Henry's length and teasing him awake while Blake pounded into me from behind. As I untangled myself from under Henry's muscular arm, Edward shuffled off the bed and headed for the bathroom. He wrapped a towel around his hips, obscuring my view of his muscular ass.

"What time is it?"

"Seven, I'm afraid." He glanced over his shoulder. "Dr. Asgard's people will arrive at the lawn in a moment."

I swung my legs off the bed and cast Henry and Blake a wistful look. Blake curled himself around Henry's left side and let out a contented sigh. At the sound of water running in the shower, I turned around and headed to the bathroom to get ready for sports day. Hopefully, we would have time to relax when Edward had fulfilled his duty at the blood donation booth.

After a quick shower, we dressed and left Elder House. Henry and Blake were still sleeping, although I suspected Blake was pretending so as not to be roped into volunteering for sports day.

The sun shone across the campus as we walked hand-in-hand across the great lawn, and a lemon-scented breeze blew in from the magnolia trees on our left. Dozens of people gathered on the lawn, setting up stalls and their canopies, and even a huge marquee.

Some members of the Board of Governors stood around a large, red-and-white trailer emblazoned with the logo of the National Health Service. I was about to comment on the size of the vehicle when I spotted a short figure chatting with Mr. Weaver and Lady Seagrove.

My lip curled. "What's Charlotte doing here?"

Squeezing my hand, Edward blew out a breath. "Despite everything, she's still a prefect. Unfortunately, that means she's also aware of opportunities to make herself appear less heinous."

"I don't understand why she hasn't been expelled."

"Her name is on the list of girls who made complaints about Carbuncle. She's also struggling with two incarcerated family members and is currently being ostracized for organizing a school booze cruise that went horrifically wrong. Imagine how it would look if they threw her out in the middle of her A-Levels."

I shook my head. "What happened to Mr. Weaver's speech about tightening up discipline? She can't be allowed to act out because her dad and brother are in jail."

Edward rubbed the back of his neck. "It wouldn't surprise me if she wasn't connected to one or more of the Board of Governors."

"It wouldn't surprise me if she wasn't sleeping with one or more of them, either."

He snorted a laugh. "Don't let them hear you say that."

"As if."

Dr. Asgard stepped away from the group and bounded toward us with his hand outstretched. He pumped Edward's hand and greeted him like an old friend. It was then I remembered that the doctor was also the duke's physician. The doctor guided us through the trailer's cool interior, which contained four beds. A nurse and six paramedics bustled about inside, getting ready for the arrival of the donors.

Charlotte stepped in behind us with Lady Seagrove. "I'm so glad Edward decided to implement my suggestion of a blood donation day. We need to contribute more to public health."

Annoyance flared through my insides, and I clenched my fists. Edward wrapped an arm around my waist and squeezed. His signal for me to keep my cool. I gave him a subtle nod. There was no way I would make a scene in front of the Board of Governors, but there was also no way I would let Charlotte make herself look good by stealing our idea.

"Why don't you be the first to donate?" I said.

Dr. Asgard swept his arm toward one of the beds. "It's wonderful to see such enthusiasm in the young!"

Charlotte's face paled. "You first."

"Why don't we all donate at the same time?" said Edward.

Charlotte glared at me as though I'd insulted her in front of the Board of Directors. "Will you excuse me for a moment?"

Before anyone could reply, she turned on her heel and hurried out of the trailer. I clenched my teeth, trying to keep my face neutral. Why didn't that girl just do everyone a favor and fall down a ditch?

The doctor guided us through the blood donation process. Mr. Weaver volunteered to donate, and Lady Seagrove pursed her lips. After a few tense moments, she agreed to participate.

I lay back on the bed and smiled. If Charlotte hadn't rushed out, the arrogant old aristocrat might not have felt under pressure to give her precious, blue blood.

Afterward, one of the paramedics set up an awning at the side of the trailer, along with tables and chairs. Edward and I stood in the shade, handing out leaflets on blood donation, welcoming donors into the trailer, and handing out drinks and snacks to everyone who had donated blood. At some point in the morning, Henry and Blake arrived to donate, but they disappeared soon after to get snacks.

Sports day turned out to be more of a village fete with the occasional game than a day dedicated to sports. Parents, staff, villagers, and the press wandered around the great lawn, sampling produce. Most gathered in the giant refreshments marquee set up at the far end, between the tuck shop and Elder House.

"Doctor!" shouted a shrill voice. Charlotte led a procession of two-dozen boys from the sixth and upper-sixth years across the lawn. "I've found some donors."

Dr. Asgard rocked back on his heels. "Jolly good, Miss Underwood. With your proactivity, we may run out of blood bags!"

Raising her chin, she shot me a triumphant glare. "Yes. I've been working hard while some have been sitting in the sun handing out drinks."

"Does that mean you're ready to donate?" I folded my arms across my chest.

"She was waiting for us." Coates slung an arm over her shoulder and guided her into the trailer.

Edward and I shared puzzled looks. Since when had Charlotte made up with all the boys she had scammed into that disastrous booze cruise?

As Charlotte's entourage waited in line to donate, I turned my attention to the charity auction. Outside the main teaching block, Mr. Jenkins sounded more confident than usual on the stage, announcing items on the microphone which his wife held up for display.

"Ladies and Gentlemen," he said, voice breathy with excitement. "My next item is a six-person hamper containing bone-china crockery, stainless-steel cutlery, and a cashmere picnic rug. And of course, it comes with two bottles of vintage champagne, a vast selection of liqueurs, meats, patés, cheeses, and preserves. It comes with a weekend stay at the Mountbatten golf-course and spa, and is generously donated by Mr. Oscar Bourneville!"

As applause broke out across the lawn, both our heads turned to the outdoor auction.

I clapped my hand over my mouth. "Don't tell me he's here?"

"Over at the front," Blake said from behind. "Turning around so everyone can see him."

"Bloody hell," Edward said under his breath.

"Why's he here?" I turned to find Blake standing in front of our table of blood donation leaflets.

"Likely to show the world that he isn't a heartless bastard." Blake wrinkled his nose. "Because going to your son's sports day makes up for informing him of his disinheritance via a one-page announcement in The Times."

I shook my head. "Do you think he wants Henry to grovel for a piece of the Bourneville fortune?"

"Probably."

The hamper ended up selling for five-thousand, four-hundred-and-fifty pounds. Mr. Bourneville walked onto the stage, clad in a cream boating blazer that showed off his broad frame and thick biceps. He handed the hamper to the winner and made a pompous-sounding announcement about an upcoming summer sale at his department store.

Afterward, he strolled around the lawn with Mrs. Bourneville on his arm. She wore a wide-legged pastel blue jumpsuit with a wrap-around top that showed off her golden hair and slim figure and she held a contrasting sienna-yellow clutch. Her face lit up as they approached.

"Of course," muttered Mr. Bourneville. "My degenerate son's lovers would have to be friends."

"Mr. Bourneville, are you here to donate?" Edward gestured at the entrance of the blood donation trailer.

The older man narrowed his green eyes.

Blake stepped forward. "I was going to make a witty remark about getting blood out of a stone, but I was distracted by Mrs. Bourneville's beauty."

"How are you, dear?" Mrs. Bourneville exchanged air kisses with Blake.

"Better for seeing you."

With a disgusted snort, Mr. Bourneville rolled his eyes. I pushed a leaflet into his hand, and I walked around the table to greet Henry's mom.

"And Henry?" asked Mrs. Bourneville.

"Unburdened, I'd say." Blake shot the older man a filthy look.

Henry's mom exchanged hugs and kisses with Edward and me, while Mr. Bourneville cast impatient glances around the stalls. He probably didn't want to admit he was looking for Henry.

I stepped back and gave him my sweetest smile. "Are you going to donate, sir? There's a reporter inside, interviewing donors."

With a grunt, he walked up the trailer stairs. I glared at his broad back. He obviously wanted something from Henry if he was flaunting his wealth at Mercia Academy. As far as I knew, Henry hadn't asked for his inheritance back. Did Mr. Bourneville want his son to beg?

"Where's Henry?" I asked.

"Getting the Pimms and lemonade." Blake nodded in the direction of the refreshment tent, where Henry emerged with a large jug of fruit cup.

Mr. Bourneville stormed down the stairs and beckoned for Henry to meet him behind the trailer. Henry rolled his eyes, gave his mother a quick peck on the lips, and walked around to the back. Blake rushed after Henry to unburden him of his tray.

The older man cleared his throat. "The summer holiday starts next week. I've arranged a job for you on the shop floor of our Hong Kong branch. If you perform to my satisfaction, I may—"

"I've decided to pursue a career in professional rugby," said Henry.

Mr. Bourneville snorted. "Nonsense. They kicked you off the team."

"And they've lost every match since. I'll challenge Coates for my position at the start of next year."

The egg-and-spoon race started, and cheers filled the lawn. I snuck around the trailer to get a view of proceedings. Mr. Bourneville's face darkened as though he was building himself up to a rant. Henry turned around, seeming to have ended the conversation.

"Don't walk away from me." Mr. Bourneville grabbed Henry by the arm.

Henry spun and head-butted his father straight in the face, making the older man grunt and staggered back. My hand rose to my chest. I was pretty sure his mom wanted Henry to use words, rather than violence, to stand up to his father, but Mr. Bourneville seemed to have gotten the message.

Henry's dad strode out from behind the trailer, clutching his hand over his bleeding nose. "Clara, we're leaving."

Mrs. Bourneville turned around and winked. "We'll be between Tokyo and Hong Kong this summer. The London flat and European villas are at your disposal."

"I hope you're not upset—"

She rushed up at him and threw her arms around his neck. "I've been waiting years for you to knock that pompous ass on his behind. Things will be different the next time you meet."

"Clara!" Mr. Bourneville hissed.

"Bye, boys. Bye, Emilia." She spun on her heel and hurried down the magnolia path.

I stood on my tiptoes and gave Henry a kiss on the cheek. "Well done."

Blake clapped him on the back. "You showed him."

"Oh, fuck," said Henry.

"What?" I glanced up into his paling face, and his wide, green eyes staring at a point beyond his retreating parents.

An even taller blonde clad in a white summer dress walked along the magnolia path. Her face was obscured by huge, black sunglasses, but her willowy figure could only belong to one person.

"Mom?"

Behind her walked four well-built men in suits, who were obviously bodyguards. But it wasn't them who made the blood drain from my face. It was the decrepit old man who walked beside her.

Rudolph. Fucking. Trommel.

CHAPTER 17

The cheering from the egg-and-spoon race faded to a dull roar as every ounce of my concentration focussed on Rudolph. My pulse pounded in my ears to the beat of a war drum. What was he doing here… with Mom? Something terrible must have happened if she had left Casablanca. My mind jumped to Dad and the twins, but they were fine. I'd just seen a goofy photo he had taken the day before of the twins riding on his back.

Rudolph strode toward us with his head held high, jowls merging into a turkey neck that disappeared into a crisp, white shirt. Unlike all the other visitors who wore lightweight clothing, Rudolph wore a navy, pinstriped suit, indicating that he meant business. Even Mr. Bourneville pulled his wife behind him and stepped aside to let him pass.

My gaze darted to Mom, whose expression was as blank as a barbie doll's, and her posture equally as stiff. A lump formed in my throat. Did he threaten her life… or mine? After everything I had learned about that reptile, I wouldn't be surprised if one of the bodyguards towering over her held a gun to her back.

"What the bloody fuck?" muttered Blake.

"Everybody, stay calm," said Edward. "I doubt that Rudolph will make any moves in front of so many witnesses."

"But his bodyguards might," I muttered.

"They're probably armed," added Blake.

Henry stepped in front of me, blocking my view of the approaching procession of doom. "Don't go with them, no matter what they say. Even if they threaten your mother's life."

My gaze flickered up his back. "Henry—"

"She wouldn't want you to endanger yourself on her account."

"Let's not speculate until Rudolph has declared his intentions." Despite his calm words, Edward's voice strained with tension.

We didn't speak while Rudolph took an eternity to close the distance. Neither of us handed out blood-donation brochures to passers-by.

Clearing my throat, I examined Mom's expressionless features. This stoic act wasn't like her at all, as she had the worst poker face ever. Scenarios whirred through my mind. Maybe Rudolph had drugged her into submission, or he'd gotten his guards to hit her where the bruises wouldn't show.

Ignoring my rising panic, I croaked, "H-hi, Mom. What brings you to Mercia Academy?"

"Good afternoon to you," said Rudolph.

I ignored him and continued staring at Mom, who pressed her lips together as though not wanting to give anything away. My throat dried. "M-mom?"

"Your mother has received a terrible shock, isn't that right?" said Rudolph.

My hands balled into fists. If I had to look into his face, I would probably punch it. "What are you talking about?"

Rudolph turned his head toward the nearest bodyguard. "Axel—"

"Don't do this." Mom made a strangled noise in the back of her throat.

"I've tried to protect you from the worst of your daughter's transgressions." Rudolph gave Mom a pat on the arm. "This time, she has gone too far. She doesn't care for my authority or yours. This picture is an incentive for her to come quietly… and without her three paramours. Now, Axel, please display the images."

A stone ball of dread formed in my stomach, and I held my breath, bracing myself for digital versions of Mr. Carbuncle's pictures.

Blake wrapped his hand around my bicep. "You can't go with him."

One of the bodyguards pulled out a large smartphone, tapped a few buttons, and showed pictures of a spacious, green park complete with its own pond. My brows drew together, and I squinted at the screen. The palm trees in the background indicated that it wasn't Hyde Park or anywhere in London, and my gaze flickered up to Rudolph's twinkling eyes.

Axel swiped at the screen, and another picture came up. My little brother and sister, Tony and Tamara.

I swallowed hard. "Why are you showing me this?"

"As I said to my devoted wife, it's an incentive for you to listen to my proposal."

"If anything happens to me, everyone in the academy will know you took me away."

He inclined his head. "My men won't stop your boyfriends from following at a distance."

I walked the long way around the table and wrapped my arms around Edward and whispered, "I've got pepper spray in case things get ugly, and my phone is set to share my location."

"Stay safe and stay quiet." Edward drew back and cupped my face in his hands. "Listen to what he has to say, and don't provoke him."

With a nod, I broke away and walked at Mom's side down the path to the main teaching block. The magnolia trees overhead provided shelter from the sun, but sweat beaded on my brow.

Another guard stood at the doors to the main teaching block. He opened the doors, and we walked through the marble hallway. I tried turning around to see if the other guards allowed the boys to follow. Through the nearly solid barrier they formed, I caught a glimpse of Henry's shoulder.

Another guard opened the door to the main entrance and guided us to a black limo that looked more like a hearse. He opened the door to reveal an L-shaped seat and a huge screen at one end of the vehicle's interior. Playing on its screen were videos and pictures of the boys and me, mostly taken by someone outside the window of Edward's study but some were the drunken kiss I shared with Blake and Henry at the Valentine's ball.

Bile rose to the back of my throat. "Where did you get these?"

"A young lady at your academy was overjoyed to help me monitor your activities," said Rudolph.

"Charlotte," I said between clenched teeth.

Rudolph's wrinkled face broke into a smile. "She speaks highly of you."

Mom turned her head away from the images. "Rudolph, please, stop."

"You have to see what kind of girl she's become." The old man tried to turn her head back toward the screen but wasn't strong enough to get Mom to move.

"Get off her." I lurched forward, but one of the bodyguards blocked me with a meaty arm.

Rudolph beckoned at another guard, who forced Mom's head up, making her cry out. I tried shoving my way to reach Mom, but the guard holding me back was as immovable as an oak.

The old reptile sat back and steepled his fingers. "As you see, my darling, your daughter has fallen into a disorder of compulsive and indiscriminate promiscuity."

Whoever had set up this portfolio had made closeups of the boys, so it looked like I was with more than three partners. The editor had even mixed pictures of me hugging Sergei and Andreo or getting close to other people. There were also images of Tola, from the Saturday Correspondent, helping me into my corset dress.

"I'm not sleeping with all these people," I snarled.

Rudolph widened his rheumy eyes. "Do you mean to suggest that's a body double or clever CGI?"

My gaze flicked to a video of Edward taking me from behind while I tried to fit both Blake and Henry in my mouth. It was from a different angle to the others, likely taken from behind the door. Charlotte must have wedged the lens of her smartphone through the keyhole.

I glanced at Mom, who held her head in her hands. Her torso shook as though she was wracked in shame and misery. The sight of her crying was like a kick in the gut. I might have implied that I was having sex with the boys, but I had neglected to share that it was at the same time.

"You need help." Rudolph leaned over and patted my knee. "There's a specialist in Drochia, Moldova, who deals with precocious promiscuity, and he is willing to take you on in his clinic."

Mom's eyes bulged. "A mental hospital?"

"Indeed." His thin lips broke into a wide grin that revealed teeth too white and too even to be anything but dentures.

"Having three boyfriends doesn't make me crazy," I said.

"I beg to differ," said Rudolph. "You have routinely spied on and recorded your classmates in a bid to avenge yourself against schoolyard pranks, and on numerous occasions, you've attacked a young woman you deemed to be a rival."

One of the bodyguards tapped his smartphone, and a slideshow of Charlotte's body appeared on the screen. Hand and finger-shaped bruises marred her arms, her thighs, and her breasts.

My mouth dropped open. It was clear that whoever she had slept with had treated her too roughly. "I didn't do that."

"Moreover, you're a danger to yourself." He clicked his fingers, and the same bodyguard changed the screen to images of my swollen and bruised face.

I hissed through my teeth. This was the photo Charlotte had taken of me the first day I returned from the palace.

Mom clapped her hands over her mouth to smother a cry. Her eyes shone with tears.

"I'm sorry to shock you, my darling," Rudolph crooned. "In the middle of her promiscuous episodes, Emilia got herself mixed up with older men whose sexual tastes ran toward the sadistic."

The guard brought picture after picture of me in my battered state. Some were those Peter Underwood had taken after Mr. Carbuncle had beaten me up. A few were of me still unconscious, propped up against the wall with what I could only guess was the former caretaker's erection pointing at my mouth.

Mom closed her eyes and sobbed, "No more."

"Do you see why I staged this intervention?" Rudolph sounded genuinely concerned. "If we don't do something about our wayward daughter, she's likely to get herself killed in pursuit of sexual thrills."

Mom bowed her head.

"M-Mom?"

She raised her palm. "I-I just can't talk to you, right now."

"But those men were working for—"

"Emilia," she snapped. "Please."

My stomach plummeted. Mom acted as though we hadn't bumped into each other in London two weeks ago, and I hadn't explained to her Rudolph's every machination. I had glossed over what Mr. Carbuncle had done, as I hadn't wanted her to worry. However, was it too much of a stretch to accept that I was sleeping with the boys at the same time? Or had Rudolph convinced her I had gone crazy?

With a triumphant grin, the old reptile wrapped his arm around Mom's shoulders. "There, there, my darling. Rudy will take care of your little problem, and you'll be happy again."

I ground my teeth. By happy, Rudolph likely meant willing to sleep with him. His addled mind seemed to think that I was the cause of Mom's refusal to consummate their marriage. Not his syphilis diagnosis and not his coercing her to continue the engagement and be married long enough for him to save face.

My hands shook, and a dull ache spread from my gut, up to my chest, and to the back of my throat. I clasped together my sweaty palms and laced my fingers. Mom was either drugged, brainwashed, or playing along. None of those roles meshed with her quick temper and passionate nature.

A spasm squeezed my throat. What if she agreed to send me away to Moldova? I didn't know anything about the country except that it once used to be part of the Soviet Union. I doubted that this institution would provide me with any kind of treatments that would leave my mind intact.

"M-mom?"

"I need time." She dabbed her tears with a handkerchief. "And a second opinion."

Rudolph's smile dropped. "Isn't this evidence enough to prove Emilia's mental instability?"

"She's not going anywhere until I have her personally assessed by my own doctor and not through an expert who has seen a few pictures."

Hope sprung in my chest. Even if she wasn't playing along, this would buy me time to work out my next move.

"Darling." Rudolph leaned forward and held her hand. "I think you're making a mistake."

"And I'm getting her a second opinion with a doctor in Britain or the States," she said. "We'll use the time between now and the end of term to contact experts in juvenile mental health and get a diagnosis based on an assessment."

Rage flashed in his eyes. It lasted quicker than a heartbeat, but it made my stomach drop. His expression smoothed out into his usual wrinkled, expressionless mask. "Very well, my darling, but I will keep some guards stationed in Mercia for Emilia's protection."

"Is that really necessary?"

"I insist," he said through clenched teeth.

"May I return to the academy, please?" I held my breath.

Rudolph glowered at me with a cold glower that chilled me to the marrow. "Of course, Emilia. We'll be staying at Elfwynn House until the end of term. In the meantime, please try to stay away from bad influences and don't break your mother's heart."

He nodded at the guard outside, who opened the limousine door, letting in warm, fresh air. Henry stepped forward, but the guard held out his palm, indicating for him to proceed no further.

Mom raised her head and mouthed, "Go."

"Ummm... Bye." I stepped out onto the curb and passed Rudolph's guard. My legs shook so much, I practically collapsed on Henry's chest.

"What happened?" He held me up with his strong arms.

"Let's go back to Elder House," I whispered.

"What about your Mother?"

"She told me to leave." I glanced over my shoulder. The guard stepped into the limo, and the vehicle pulled out. "So far, Rudolph only wants to hurt those closest to her." I pulled on his arm, and we hurried toward the main teaching block. "Where are Blake and Edward?"

"They took a jeep to the gatehouse in case they needed to follow you through the streets."

I blew out a breath of relief and pulled my phone from the pocket of my blazer. My hands shook so much, I couldn't tap in my passcode.

"Do you want to call them?" he asked.

I nodded.

Henry pulled out his phone and called Blake, who said to meet them in front of Elder House. I clamped my lips together and didn't speak. It would take ages to make sense of what had just happened and to explain the reason behind Rudolph's machinations. We walked through the main teaching block in silence. Henry stared down at me, as though waiting for me to say something.

We stepped out of the building, into the busy sports day fete. The sounds of younger children whooping mingled into the cheers of the crowds watching a race on the lawn that I couldn't see. I met his green eyes and forced a smile, even though nausea churned in my belly.

In the shock of seeing that compilation of stills and video, I'd forgotten to mention that I had a copy of Rudolph's Skype-sex session. We continued down the path of magnolia trees toward Elder House.

Charlotte jogged after us. "Henry, did you see—"

"Not now," he snapped.

She overtook us and blocked our path, eyes blazing. "What's wrong with you?"

Henry pulled me to his side and continued past her along the magnolia path.

"If you walk away from me, you'll regret it," her voice shook. "I've spent years trying to get your attention. You were aloof and unattainable, and the few flirty glances you sent my way kept me going."

"Charlotte," he said in a weary voice. "Give up. You were never my type."

"Because you like pretty boys. Like Blake Simpson-West and Emilia Hobson," she snapped.

Charlotte's petty digs slid over me like a breeze, and I stared straight ahead, gaze fixed on Elder House. She was nothing compared to Rudolph, a madman who would keep coming at me until I was no longer in a state—mental or otherwise—to fight back. Then there was no telling what he would do to Mom.

As we continued past, she spat, "You wouldn't know what to do with a real woman if she sat on your face!"

Pausing, Henry glanced over his shoulder. "I hope you find what you're looking for because it isn't me."

Charlotte staggered back and sat on a bench with the brass plaque dedicated to Nicodemus Underwood. Up ahead in the distance, the jeep pulled up outside Elder House. We didn't stick around to see what she would do or say next.

I wrapped my fingers around the hand propping me up by the waist and exhaled. "Right now, I need you, Blake and Edward to take my mind off this mess."

CHAPTER 18

*B*lake reversed the jeep round to the side of Elder House. He and Edward hurried out and met us at the end of the path of magnolia trees. Edward's posture relaxed a few inches, presumably from relief, and Blake pressed his hand on his chest and sagged.

Tension settled over my shoulders and wound my muscles so tight, I could barely look from left to right. I rubbed the back of my neck and grimaced. My problems had only just begun, and I couldn't see a way out. I doubted that any of the triumvirate would approve of my short term plan, but right now, I just wanted to lose myself for a few minutes before facing the insurmountable.

As soon as Henry and I got close enough, Edward's brows creased, and his lips thinned.

Blake folded his arms across his chest. "What happened?"

I swallowed hard. My predicament was a form of karma. Everything I had done in my second term kept backfiring, and I was in the biggest trouble of my life.

Henry gave me a gentle squeeze around the waist. "Should we go to Edward's study?"

"Upstairs. The bedroom's more secure." At least no one would be prowling around outside the window of the top floor.

Blake exchanged a puzzled look with Edward, who gestured for me to go inside. More people than I had expected milled the hallways and staircase. Perhaps sports day wasn't a fun prospect for sixth formers. If it hadn't been for Edward's blood drive, I probably wouldn't have attended, either.

We reached Edward's room, and I blurted out the basics. Rudolph had mixed a bunch of random images and footage with videos of me either having sex with two or more of the boys or closeups that made it look like I was promiscuous with other boys.

I dipped my head. "He said I was a danger to myself and showed Mom the pictures taken after Mr. Carbuncle attacked me."

Blake winced. "Emilia…" He shook his head. "I have no words. Is this another attempt to drive a wedge between you and your mother?"

"He wants me committed."

Henry placed his hands on my shoulders. "What?"

"Mom's trying to buy time. I think she's trying to change Rudolph's mind."

Edward's nostrils flared. "It's important now more than ever that we collect as much evidence against that tyrant as we can." He turned to Blake. "Let's see if we can get in contact with Carbuncle and persuade him to report his association—"

"Wait." I placed both hands over my ears. "Can we discuss this afterward?"

Henry rubbed my back. "After what?"

I turned toward him and placed a hand on his broad chest. "Make me forget. Even if it's just for a few minutes."

"Emilia." Even without looking at Edward, I could hear the frown in his voice. "Don't you think we should discuss this?"

I slipped off my blazer and hung it on the doorknob, making sure it obscured the keyhole. Anyone wanting to spy on us could film the lining of my jacket. When I turned around, Edward, Blake, and Henry stood in a row, each giving me puzzled stares. I unbuttoned my shirt. Henry frowned, Edward pursed his lips, and Blake's gaze flickered to my lacy, cream bra.

When I unzipped my skirt and let it fall to the ground, Henry's eyes blazed, Edward's nostrils flared, and Blaze pressed the heel of his hand against his crotch.

I hooked a thumb under my bra strap and eased it down my shoulder. "Will one or more of you get me off, or will I have to do it myself?"

"Sometimes, a hard fuck is what a girl needs to clear her head." Blake circled his arms around my waist and nuzzled my neck. He ground his hardening length into my belly, making me melt. "Let's give her what she wants, and we can deal with Rudolph later."

I ran my tongue across my bottom lip, and Henry's green eyes tracked the movement. His breathing quickened, and his Adam's apple bobbed up and down. He was conflicted. The business with Rudolph was dire, but I needed release. Now.

Henry cast Edward a furtive look.

"Just kiss me," I whispered. "We can plan later."

Blake cupped my breasts. "Forget about those two." He rolled my nipples between his fingers and murmured, "They're limp under pressure. I can give you what you need."

Edward snorted. "Don't denigrate level-headedness and knowing one's priorities."

"Edward's right," said Henry. "We need a way to fight back."

Blake brought strong, demanding lips to mine. He wrapped his arms around my waist and the back of my head as though he could kiss my worries into oblivion. It was working. Sensations sparked from my lips and ignited a fire that seared through my immediate concerns. I moved my lips against Blake's as he pressed our bodies together so tight, I melted into the hardness crushed against my belly.

A moan slipped from my lips. This kiss was exactly what I needed. It was warmth and passion and delicious decadence, more so under the gazes of Edward and Henry.

"For goodness' sake," muttered Edward. "There's a time and a place for everything."

Blake's hand slid under the lace of my panties, and his fingers skimmed my clit. I moaned into his kiss.

"We may as well help him out," said Henry, his voice breathy. "The sooner she gets what she wants, the sooner we can focus on what's important."

Blake's rich, smoky chuckle reverberated against my chest. "How gallant." Still kissing me, he unbuckled his belt, while I worked on the buttons of his shirt. "Once I've slipped on a condom, I'll pound you so hard, you won't even remember your own name. How about that?"

Out of the corner of my eye, I spied Henry stripping off his clothes. I couldn't get enough of his hard, tanned, sculpted body, but right now, I wanted attention from all three of the triumvirate.

Edward stood against the far wall, glaring at us with unrestrained hunger. He held his posture rigid, as though giving into me would be a terrible defeat. Blake broke away from the kiss, only for Henry to step in front of me with a huge erection straining up to his belly button.

I licked my lips. "Is that for me?"

Henry snickered. "Don't finish it all at once. You've got to leave room for dessert."

I wrapped my fingers around Henry's thick length and sucked on his bulbous tip.

Henry groaned and bucked his hips. "Take it all in."

He didn't need to ask me twice. I slid my lips over his expanding length and groaned around my mouthful. My tongue ran across the ridge of flesh under his head, and he let out a long, shuddering moan.

At the same time, Blake positioned me by the bed and ran the tip of his erection along my hot, wet slit.

I gasped out a breath, and Henry's prick fell out of my mouth. Edward cleared his throat. My gaze dropped to the bulge in his pants. "Come over here."

He frowned. "Emilia, this is—"

I made a show of licking my lips. "You know how much I like your taste, right?" A hard thrust from Blake made my eyes roll to the back of my head. "I want to feel you sliding down my tongue."

Edward rolled his eyes but took a step closer. His erection strained the fabric of his pants.

"Never mind him." Henry gripped his erection and gave it a couple of hard tugs.

I took the hint and parted my lips. He slid back into my mouth, over my tongue, and down to the back of my throat. Still keeping my eyes on Edward, I gave Henry's dick an appreciative hum.

Desire flared in Edward's blue eyes. I bobbed my head, encasing Henry's erection until it reached the back of my throat. Henry let out a low, shuddering groan that went straight to my clit. Sucking in my cheeks, I drew my head back along his length and moaned.

Blake continued his steady pace, stretching and filling me with thrusts that made my breasts jiggle. "You're so fucking tight. How are you ever going to take two of us at the same time?"

"Huh?" I said around Henry's dick.

Henry chuckled. "We've had this fantasy for ages. One of us would lie on the bed while the girl straddles him. Then the other would enter her from behind, giving her two cocks.

Blake's fingers dug into my hips, and he pumped into me with hard, steady strokes. "How would you like that, Emilia? Two of us stretching you wide..." He pulled out a few inches, making my muscles clench around him. "Filling you like nothing has ever filled you before?"

My eyes fluttered closed. Two penises at once? The thought of being stretched even further made me groan with the desire for more.

Blake bent over my back and cupped my breasts with both hands. He swiped a thumb over my nipple, making it pebble. "And the third will fill your mouth, just like Henry's doing now."

I tried to imagine boys sliding in and out of me at different rates. My core muscles fluttered around Blake's length, adding to the waves of pleasure he continued to incite with every movement. I thrust back with my hips, increasing the friction.

"I think she likes the idea," said Edward from much closer than before.

My eyes snapped open. A naked Edward stood in front of me, stroking his flushed-looking erection. A bead of precum glistened at its tip, and a thrill of excitement surged to my clit. I knew he would change his mind and join the fun.

Drawing back from my mouthful of Henry, I wrapped my fingers around Edward's prick, making him hiss. As I lapped at Edward's slit, Henry positioned himself a little to the left, so the heads of their erections faced each other.

I held onto both their pricks and rubbed their tips together, enjoying how the glistening organs slid over each other. Edward's skin was paler than Henry's—usually alabaster but the blood coursing through his beautiful, thick erection darkened it to a flushed pink. Henry's golden skin was the same, except his cockhead had darkened to an angry red.

I flattened my tongue and ran it along the undersides of their joined erections, making them both shudder.

Blake snickered. "Crossing swords is alright if there's a girl involved. Isn't that what you once said, Woody?"

"I'm helping things along," Edward said, his voice breathy. "As you quite rightly stated, the sooner she gets what she wants, the sooner we can plan what to do next."

Blake's right hand left my breast, slipped over my ribs and belly, then settled between my legs. He rubbed gentle circles over my clit, which sent bolts of sensation traveling up to my navel and down my thighs. My muscles clamped around his thick erection, and he timed the movement of his fingers with his thrusting in and out of my core.

Sweat gathered on my brow, and Blake continued his delicious combination of deep thrusts and caressing fingers over my throbbing nub. The hand on my breast now rolled my nipple in a series of tight movements which my body interpreted as intensely pleasurable.

"Lucky girl gets to play with two cocks," mused Blake.

"Mmmm." I lapped at both organs and ran my fingers along their lengths.

Both Edward and Henry's hips rocked against my hands, adding to the friction.

Blake's thick erection pleasured me from the inside, while his fingers played with my sensations as though he was manipulating an instrument. My body tensed and shuddered at his attention, and at the same time, the two gorgeous, heavy pricks demanded my concentration. A happy sigh escaped my lips. This was exactly the distraction I needed. With Edward in the mix, I could focus on the triumvirate and not my troubles.

A giggle bubbled up in the back of my throat. If anyone told me at the beginning of my first term that I would be naked in front of the triumvirate, I would have laughed in their faces. But here I was twitching and shuddering under Blake's ministrations and lapping at Edward and Henry's cock-heads while sliding my fingers up and down their pulsing lengths.

"I'm not going to last." Blake's hands dropped away from my nipple and clit and clenched my hips. After a few hard pumps, he shuddered and moaned. Through harsh breaths, he said, "The sight of you taking two cocks tipped me over the edge."

"Allow me." Edward broke away and walked around to my back.

After a bit of shuffling around and the tearing of a foil wrapper, Blake slid out, and Edward slid in.

Blake's tongue slid against my clit. A cry escaped my throat, muffled by Henry's dick in my mouth, and my core muscles clamped around Edward's thick length.

Both Henry and Edward moaned.

I clenched at the comforter and panted. With Blake's tongue curling and swirling about my sensitive bundle of nerves, I wasn't sure how much longer I would last.

Edward continued thrusting in and out, while Henry took control of the blowjob and slid himself back and forth out of my mouth. I drew back and curled my tongue over his engorged head, enjoying the little moans and shudders I elicited from every stroke.

Blake's tongue lapped at my throbbing clit, making me clamp even tighter around Edward. Sensations more intense than I had ever felt radiated from the joining of our flesh, and I moaned around Henry.

I lost focus, and spots danced before my eyes. With Edward pumping into me, Blake licking me senseless, and Henry making those slow, sensual slides in and out of my mouth, I could barely remember my name, let alone how I ended up being the center of attention for three hot guys.

Pleasure built up around my clenching and shuddering core, expanding and intensifying to a point that teetered on agony. It was too much. I tried to tell Blake to ease off with that tongue, but Henry's erection deep in my mouth smothered my words to incoherent moans.

My legs, which were splayed open to accommodate both Blake and Edward, trembled with the onslaught of sensations. My arms shuddered, yet the boys continued plundering my body. Two sets of fingers—I don't know whose—tugged at my nipples, and something within me snapped.

Light flashed before my closed eyes, and spasm after spasm of sensations pumped out from my clenching and twitching core. My hips trembled with each mighty convulsion, squeezing Edward's gorgeous, thick erection.

"Argh!" Edward's fingers dug into the flesh of my hips, and he thrust once, twice, three times, and shuddered. His hand rested between my shoulder blades, splayed fingers curling into my flesh.

Blake's tongue slowed to the gentlest of movements, intensifying the pleasure radiating from my clit and core. I gulped and groaned around my mouthful.

Henry moaned and thrust to the back of my throat with long, deep strokes. His erection thickened, trembled, and spurted bitter, creamy fluid into the back of my throat. I swallowed my mouthful and moaned around his twitching length.

He slid out from my lips, and my head flopped to the mattress. "T-thanks," I said between panting breaths. "M-maybe we can build up to that double-penetration thing over the summer? It sounds fun."

The gong sounded for dinner, and Edward cupped my ass cheek. "Time to eat."

"I want a chateaubriand. Let's go to the Saint-Nazaire," said Blake.

Henry hummed his agreement. "Steak au poivre, gratin dauphinois, crème brûlée."

"That sounds lovely!" I climbed over Edward, who deliberately tangled our limbs and held me for a few seconds. After I gave him a peck on the lips, he let me go. I padded across the wood floor to the corner of the room, where I kept my Louis Vuitton cases, and put on a pair of panties, skinny jeans, and a fitted tank top.

Edward's gaze lingered on my breasts, and a smile curled his lips. "And there's always Armagnac à l'Emilia."

I narrowed my eyes and placed my hands on my hips. "That sounds like drinking Armagnac off my body."

"Out of her belly button?" Henry threw on a rugby shirt and jeans.

"I can think of better places." Blake pulled on a pair of jeans and a T-shirt. He threaded his fingers through his hair and somehow managed to style it.

Chuckling, Edward slipped on a pair of boxers and walked across the room. He wrapped his arms around my middle and pressed a kiss on the juncture of my neck and shoulder. "Did that help?"

I closed my eyes and sighed. "Until I climaxed, but the nerves are creeping back." Twisting in his arms, I rested my head on his shoulder and inhaled his cypress and cedar scent.

"It's understandable." He hugged tighter. "But Rudolph can't legally take you away without the consent of your mother."

"But illegally..." said Blake.

"We won't let you out of our sight." Henry embraced me from behind and kissed the crown of my head. "We can spend summer in one of the villas. There's one near Valencia in case you want to practice your Spanish."

"Or we can spend the summer in Largs Castle." Blake reached between them and ruffled my hair. "It's my stepfather's private residence."

"That might be an option," said Edward. "We can take a car and drive up to Scotland. Pay for petrol with cash, in case Rudolph decides to trace our cards, and stay there until term starts."

Unease settled in my stomach. Hiding from Rudolph wasn't the answer. "He knows where my brother and sister live. I'm sure he'll do something to them if I disappear."

Everyone's shoulders sagged. Edward groaned. "Apart from murdering him ourselves, what can we do?"

Henry's nostrils flared. "He's a fragile, old man. One punch, and—"

"It's manslaughter," said Blake. "There's an article on one-punch killings on the BBC website."

"Even if you don't kill him, he has the power to ruin you." I wrapped my arms around my middle. "Maybe we can visit Philippe in prison and see if he's willing to testify against Rudolph."

Edward sighed. "It's worth a try, but I fear that Rudolph already has a contingency plan to deal with those who know his deepest secrets. Something more binding than a non-disclosure agreement."

Blake shouldered on a blazer. "What about Charlotte's honey—"

My eardrums reverberated with the boom of a gunshot.

Chunks of wood splintered from the door. Before I knew it, Henry yanked me down and threw himself over my body. Ice flooded my veins. This had to be one of Rudolph's guards, come to drag me to that asylum in Moldova.

I raised my head and found Mr. Carbuncle storming toward us with a sawed-off shotgun, his bloodshot eyes boring into mine. Terror seized my heart in its crushing grip. I couldn't breathe, couldn't scream, couldn't tell Henry to run. By the time I forced in a breath, the caretaker slammed the butt of his gun on Henry's head. His entire body went limp, and he crushed me under his weight.

A scream ripped from my throat, and I placed my hands on Henry's shoulders, trying to get out from under him. My blazer lay a few feet away. If I could reach it and the pepper spray, it might buy some time for campus security to arrive—or the police.

With an almighty kick, Mr. Carbuncle shoved Henry aside, grabbed my wrist, and yanked me to my feet. Blake rushed at him, but the man pushed him hard into the wall.

"Stop," I cried.

"Carbuncle." Edward pointed something at the man. I couldn't see what, but he said, "Let go of—"

Mr. Carbuncle aimed his gun at Edward and fired.

Cold shock hit me in the gut. My legs gave way, and I fell to my knees. He had shot Edward in retaliation for Edward shooting him.

Mr. Carbuncle picked me up and threw me over his shoulder. He ran down the stairs like a rampaging bull, shoving screaming students aside. Each movement aggravated the remnants of the wounds he had given me a month ago, and nauseating contractions seized my stomach. I emptied its contents over the man's broad back, but he didn't flinch, didn't falter.

He reached the downstairs hallway and raced through the entrance hall.

"I will not condone this behavior in Elder House," cried the voice of Mr. Jenkins. "Stop, before I call campus security!"

Bitter loathing rippled through my insides, and dregs of puke spilled from my lips. Mr. Carbuncle was long past reasoning. He had shot Edward. Mr. Jenkins needed to call for a police swat team, not threaten him with a group of underworked security staff.

The caretaker whirled around and fired his shotgun. "Fuck off, you sanctimonious ponce!"

Even with my pulse pounding in my skull, and with my ears ringing from the gunshots, I heard the unmistakable thud of a body hitting the ground.

Screams filled the hallway, and adrenaline filled my veins. I writhed in his grip and nearly fell off, but his arm secured me in place.

Mr. Carbuncle sprinted through the entrance hall and out of the double doors, where a jeep awaited with its engine still running. Panic crushed my windpipe and cut off my air. If I got into that vehicle, he could take me anywhere. Images flashed before my mind of forests, out-of-the-way fields, and the bottom of a ditch. I thrashed my arms and legs, but he flung the passenger door open and threw me inside.

My head hit the dashboard, and everything went black.

CHAPTER 19

The pounding in my head overwhelmed my senses. It was like I had a boom-box instead of a brain. Reverberations of intense pain struck with each beat of my pulse. My ears rang as though I'd fallen asleep next to a siren, and something scratchy irritated my back. It could have been a blanket, or it could have been an ant's nest. Right now, it was a struggle not to drown in the fog of pain and confusion and nausea threatening to engulf me back into unconsciousness.

A rough hand massaged my breast, a tongue lapped at my nipple, and bristles brushed against the surrounding skin. Shivers of revulsion scattered across my skin like an army of centipedes, and memories of the shooting slammed back to the forefront of my mind. I wanted to open my eyes, but the thought of seeing that man's face up close was too much to bear.

"M-Mr. Carbuncle..." I whispered. "S-stop."

He raised his head from my chest and let in a gust of fresh air.

"You smell like you've just been fucked." His breath ghosted over my skin, bringing with it the mingled stench of strong alcohol and stale tobacco.

Nausea swirled in my stomach. It spasmed, but nothing came out. I turned my head and tried to escape his scent, but it was a futile effort.

Mr. Carbuncle shifted, so his mustache tickled my ear. In a breathy, excited voice, he whispered, "I wanted to fuck you while you were sleeping, but then I'd miss those little expressions."

Pain mingled with relief, and shallow breaths moved in and out of my lungs. He hadn't removed my jeans—yet. I cracked an eye open to examine my surroundings, but the man straddled my thighs and lay on top of me, resting his weight on his limbs. His bulk blocked my view of everything except an ancient tree whose branches curled and twisted on a ground consisting of bare soil. The sun hung low in a cloudy sky, indicating that hours had passed.

I clenched my teeth, still not daring to look at him. "Why are you doing this?"

"Do you know how many times I've wanked over your pics? Can't get enough of them. Wanted to see you up close." He ran the tip of his tongue along the shell of my ear.

All the muscles of my upper body seized. I cried, "Stop!"

"This time, there won't be no Peter to interrupt us."

"D-did my stepfather pay you to do this?" I gasped out. "I-I have money in my account. You can take it all if you leave me alone."

"Trommel?" He cupped my breast. "Once I've sent the ransom letters, old Rudolph will pay a fortune to have you back."

My stomach dropped. He didn't know. Didn't know that Philippe had set up the original abduction as a way to make me suffer. Didn't know that Rudolph would use me as a tool to control Mom. The old bastard would probably leave me in Mr. Carbuncle's clutches until I was dead.

"D-didn't you hear?"

"Hear what, cock-slut?" He ran his huge hand down my belly and slipped his thick fingers into the waistband of my jeans.

I wriggled and jerked, trying to throw off his filthy hand. "Peter and Philippe are in jail—"

"I heard about Pete." His fingers skimmed the lace of my panties.

"But Rudolph paid Philippe to arrange the kidnapping."

Mr. Carbuncle's hand stilled, and he said nothing for a tense moment. "Why the fuck would he have his own stepdaughter abducted and beaten up?"

"H-he was planning to draw the story out for weeks to sell more newspapers." My mind whirred for ideas. I got the impression that he would empathize with Rudolph if I told him the syphilis story. "And hurting me was a favor to Charlotte. She was sleeping with Philippe and Rudolph."

"The dirty fucker," he snarled. "He won't pay out, then?"

"But I will." My throat convulsed. "If you let me go, I'll give you everything in my bank account."

Mr. Carbuncle drew back, taking away his awful hand. I filled my lungs with warm, fresh air and glanced from left to right at my surroundings. Bare-branched, twisty trees stretched out for several yards and beyond them was what looked like a forest.

"You can do online banking, right?" He ran his tongue along the underside of his bushy mustache.

"Yes, but the account with all the money needs a signature for withdrawals."

"Then I'll keep you until we can get to a branch on Monday." His gaze flickered down to my bare breasts. He reached back at a spot by his feet and retrieved a tub of vaseline. "Bought this for you in case we had trouble getting you loose enough for anal. There's a lot we can get done until then."

Panic exploded across my chest, and adrenaline filled my veins. I thrashed my arms, but the ropes encasing my wrist kept them above my head. Whatever happened, I couldn't let Mr. Carbuncle touch me. "S-sir! You have to let me go."

He pinched my nipple so hard, pain radiated across my chest and made me wince. "Why's that, then?"

"He took my mom hostage."

I snatched my gaze away from the overgrown mustache obscuring the middle third of his face. Ideas, images, memories scrambled through my mind, looking for anything I could use to stop the caretaker from proceeding with his plan. My desperate mind latched onto the visual of Mrs. Carbuncle stepping into Edward's limousine.

"That's what Rudolph's good at," I said. "Taking. Mothers. Hostage."

The tub of vaseline fell to the forest floor.

"What did you say?" he whispered.

"He took my mom hostage."

My throat dried, and my pulse beat so hard against my eardrums, it drowned out the sounds of the birds. I had to make this explanation as convincing as possible so he would think about his own mother.

"M-mom went to another country to hide from that brute, but he brought armed bodyguards to find her. Rudolph came to the academy today and tried to make Mom sign some papers to have me institutionalized."

Still keeping those wild eyes on my face, Mr. Carbuncle rose to his feet. My stomach lurched. Would he kick me in the belly for lying as he had done in that abandoned apartment?

A gut-wrenching silence stretched out for an eternity while the caretaker remained rooted to the earth. Tiny tremors twitched across his face, and his lips twisted under his unkempt mustache.

I squeezed my eyes shut and let out a trembly breath. There was no telling what was going on in the mind of that lunatic. Right now, I had to be careful with what I said next. Pushing the kidnapped mother angle might make him wonder how I knew Mrs. Carbuncle was missing. If I told him outright that Rudolph had taken his mother, then he might punish me for not telling him earlier.

"Fuck," he snarled.

Without meaning to, my eyes snapped open, and my gaze traveled up from the dungarees pooled around his ankles, over bowed legs covered in a thick coating of matted hair, and to a deflating, mushroom-shaped penis that curved out of a nest of pubes as bristly as his walrus mustache.

My gaze skipped past a bristle-covered beer belly, and outsized pecs with the largest nipples I'd seen on a man, to his stricken face. "S-sir? What's wrong?"

"My mum."

I held my breath, praying to whoever was listening that he would come to the right conclusion. When he didn't speak, I said, "D-do you think Rudolph might track her down?"

A strangled noise rumbled in Mr. Carbuncle's throat. "He's got Mum."

"Bring her along if you're worried about her," I said, playing ignorant. "Or take her to a bed and breakfast if you're concerned about Rudolph's violent bodyguards. The money in my account should cover the costs."

"You don't understand." He balled his hands into giant fists. "My mum's been missing for days."

I turned my head. "Oh, no. Were you close?"

"Why are you talking about her as if she's already dead?" he roared.

My heart jumped into my throat. I'd overdone it. "S-sorry! It's just that he had Charlotte's brother badly beaten in prison for saying Philippe organized my abduction. He'll probably have Philippe killed for knowing his secrets. If Rudolph is holding your mom, he probably doesn't want you to testify against him and Philippe."

Mr. Carbuncle pulled his dungarees up to his chest, clipped on their fastenings, then paced within the shelter of the twisted tree.

He paused and stared at me. "I don't suppose he'll take you in exchange for mum?"

"M-maybe."

"Where does he live?"

"New York, but they're staying at Elfwynn House."

He grabbed a handful of my hair. "You'd better not be fibbing, or I'll keep you here and fuck that virgin hole till your insides fall out of your arse."

My anus clenched with terror. "I wouldn't lie about something so important."

"Good." He pulled out a hunting knife and slashed the ropes around my wrists. "You're coming with me."

My numb arms fell onto my belly with a thud. Unpleasant tingles ran up and down them as my empty veins filled with blood. With fingers I could no longer feel, I pulled my tank top down over my exposed breasts. I tried scrambling away, but he had lashed one of my ankles to a tree in a series of complicated knots.

"Run, and I'll shoot you in the back." Mr. Carbuncle fastened a bandolier belt around his hips, picked up his shotgun and reloaded it with ammunition. Memories of him bursting into Edward's room resurfaced, and a tight fist of sorrow clenched at my heart.

Choking back a sob, I asked, "Sir?"

"What?" He adjusted his bandolier.

"Did you shoot Edward?"

"Shot at him, yeah."

Tears filled my eyes, and pressure squeezed at my chest from where I forgot to breathe. Dwelling on Edward's predicament would do me no good. I would only fall into grief, but I had to know. I wouldn't be able to concentrate on escaping if I kept speculating on his fate. "Did the bullet hit him?"

"I'll be fucked if I know," he muttered.

Disappointment mingled with relief as I blew out a breath through my nostrils. Edward might be unhurt, after all.

* * *

Mr. Carbuncle sped his pickup truck through winding country roads lit by the setting sun that led to a highway. Rolling hills stretched out on all sides, giving me the impression we were driving through the South Downs, a national park Edward had described as the size of London.

I looked out for signs of police and helicopters. A man had barged into a school, shot at the Viscount of Highdown, attacked two other boys, abducted a girl, and possibly killed a housemaster. Where were the search parties?

Cold despair seeped through my skin, penetrating me to the marrow. What was wrong with the British police? If this was New York, the whole place would be flooded with officers. But Mr. Carbuncle kept evading justice, only to keep striking back.

He threw my phone into my lap. "You're going to call that cunt of a stepfather and tell him to meet me outside the hotel."

"Yes, sir," I whispered.

I pulled out my phone and stared at the screen. "There's no signal."

"Wait, then," he growled.

Muttering under his breath, Mr. Carbuncle took a swig from a stainless steel flask. I rubbed my sore wrists. Had he always been this insane or had recent events pushed him into this madness?

My mind raced through scenarios. The best case was that we hit a roadblock, and the police gunned him down in a rain of bullets. But he would probably use me as a shield. The most likely situation would be that Rudolph convinced him that he didn't have old Mrs. Carbuncle, and he talked the former caretaker into taking me away with his blessing.

The text message alert indicated we were back within signal range. It was from Henry.

"There," he growled. "You can call him now."

"I have to look up the number for the Elfwynn House."

"Call his fucking mobile!"

"He only gives out the numbers of his personal assistants. Please... you remember how long it took to contact him when Mr. Chaloner expelled me? I need to look up the number of Elfwynn House on the internet. It's going to take much longer to go through a PA."

"Try anything funny, and I'll throttle you."

"Y-yes, sir."

Henry's text said he was on the road with Blake, tracking me through my phone. There was no mention of Mr. Jenkins, Henry's head wound, or whether Edward was alive or dead.

I replied with, C thinks Mrs C abducted. Will confront R in Elfwynn Hse.

"Did you find it?"

"There are two bed and breakfasts with that name. I'm just going to Google Maps to make sure I call the one closest to the academy."

He snarled. "It's the one in Mercia, you daft bint."

"Ah... Sorry." I entered the name into Google. "Found the number."

It took a lot of half-truths and wrangling for the receptionist to put me through to Rudolph's room. By the time she agreed, the muscles of my neck and shoulders cramped with tension. The phone rang again, and I exhaled a long breath.

"R-Rudolph?"

"Who is this?" asked another male voice.

"Emilia Hobson, his stepdaughter."

After a long moment of silence, Rudolph's voice purred, "Emilia, to what do I owe this pleasure?"

"I thought about what you said, and I want to meet."

"Tomorrow at eight for breakfast—"

"No!" I blurted. "It's urgent. You were right about my nymphomania. I just had sex with three boys and I almost had anal with a fourth. P-please… I need help."

Rudolph's low chuckle filled my belly with revulsion. "You naughty girl," he said in the same tone he had used in Charlotte's honey trap. "I'll send a car."

"A-actually, I'm on my way. Will you meet me in the lobby? Please don't tell Mom. I can't let her see me in this state."

He paused. "I'll book a room, so we can discuss the matter in private. Ask for Rudy Prong." He laughed at his own joke. "It's more subtle than Rudy Ramrod, don't you think?"

Nausea battled with self-disgust, and I forced out the words, "Y-yes, sir."

Rudolph hung up, and I slipped my phone into the pocket of my jeans.

"Did he agree to meet you?"

"He's booking a private room."

Mr. Carbuncle dumped his pickup truck in an overgrown field, where a red jeep waited. Swigging from a huge bottle of booze, he dragged me out, shoved me into the passenger seat and drove off. Every ounce of hope drained from my body. The police would be looking out for a white truck, not a red jeep. Tears filled my eyes and dread filled my belly as I pictured Mr. Carbuncle's face when Rudolph convinced him that he hadn't stolen his mother.

We reached the gates of Elfwynn House after sunset. Iron lamps lit a long driveway that led to a massive, timber-framed mansion with white-washed walls and paneled windows. I scanned the vehicles parked next to the courtyard and found no police cars. Why wasn't that a surprise?

He pulled up outside the double doors, downed the rest of his bottle, and slurred, "I'll keep the shotgun trained on your back. Walk inside, find Rudolph Trommel's room, and don't try anything dumb."

The decorative wooden interior of the venue faded into a blur.

Over the next few minutes, I struggled to stay upright, struggled to retain my composure, and struggled to find the room in the name of Rudy Prong. Even walking up the stairs was a struggle with a lunatic's hot, alcoholic breath on my back. I eventually located the room and knocked on the door.

The voice behind it purred, "Come in."

"You first," whispered Mr. Carbuncle.

Sucking in a deep, fortifying breath, I prayed to whoever was listening that Rudolph had brought his bodyguards and that they would shoot at the first sight of the shotgun. I pushed the door open to find Rudolph lounging on the bed clad in a crimson satin robe with gold lapels. My eyes skipped to the corner of the room, where a camera stood on a tripod, and a bottle of champagne sat in a bucket.

"Good evening, darling." He sat up and fumbled at the belt of his robe.

Mr. Carbuncle shoved past me and punched Rudolph square in the face. "What the fuck did you do to my mum?"

The old man fell back on the bed, his body bouncing on the mattress.

Wincing, I backed out of the room.

The caretaker turned around and grab me by the arm. "You're going nowhere." He threw me onto the bed, and I landed next to Rudolph. "Where is she?"

Rudolph clutched his bleeding nose. "Who are you?"

Mr. Carbuncle lurched forward and grabbed Rudolph by the lapels. "The man whose mother you took. Where is she?"

I rolled off the bed and landed on the floor.

"I don't know what you're talking about," said Rudolph.

"Philip works for you, yes?"

"If Philippe offended you, visit him in prison," cried Rudolph.

"You said his name right. That means you know him!" Mr.

Carbuncle shook the old man so hard, his dentures fell out of his mouth and bounced on the wood floor.

My heart jumped into my throat. At any moment, Rudolph would tell the crazy caretaker I was lying, and I'd be the one getting beaten.

As Mr. Carbuncle pummeled into Rudolph, not giving him a chance to catch his breath, I crawled to the foot of the bed, where he had left his shotgun. With the greatest of care, I picked up the weapon and edged to the corner of the room. Mr. Carbuncle rained blow upon blow on Rudolph, reminding me of something Henry and Blake had once discussed: one-punch killings.

It was cold. It was heartless, but if Rudolph survived this beating, he would do more than have me sent to a mental institution in Moldova. If I escaped this hotel room and Mr. Carbuncle gave chase... I shook my head. It would be brutal.

With my free hand, I reached into my jeans pocket, called 999, and left the phone on the floor, hoping that the operator would eventually work out what was happening and trace the call.

CHAPTER 20

Mr. Carbuncle pummeled into Rudolph, and I sank into the corner at the side of a wingback chair, hugging his shotgun to my chest. It was as though the caretaker had fallen into a rage so blind, he'd forgotten that he needed Rudolph lucid enough to answer his questions. The caretaker's grunts filled the air. Each smack of his fists into Rudolph's flesh made my stomach leap into my throat, and each blow landed with such force that Rudolph's legs jumped.

The door rattled with the weight of a pounding fist. "Mr. Trommel?" said a male voice. "Are you alright?"

"Sir?" shouted another male voice.

My heart pounded so hard, reverberations traveled down every nerve ending in a series of tremors that made every limb shake. A fleeting thought crossed my mind that I wouldn't be able to handle the gun if Mr. Carbuncle turned his anger on me and that I might hurt myself, but if I moved and attracted his attention, he might turn his fury onto me.

"Sir, we're coming in."

A long breath shuddered out of my nostrils. I wished they would burst through the door instead of just talking about it.

Mr. Carbuncle stepped back and stared at Rudolph's still body. His broad shoulders and barrel-shaped torso expanded and contracted with loud, harsh breaths. From my position on the floor wedged at the side of the chair, I couldn't tell if Rudolph was still breathing.

The caretaker turned around, his eyes wide and showing their whites, and bared his crooked teeth. "What happened to my mum?"

I opened my mouth and screamed.

With an almighty crash, the door flew off its hinges. Three huge bodyguards rushed into the room and tackled Mr. Carbuncle to the bed. The force of them hitting the mattress knocked Rudolph off onto the floor.

Another bodyguard reached down and snatched the shotgun from my arms. With a few deft movements, he removed the shells, placed the weapon on a nearby table, and yanked me up by the arm. "Tell me what happened, girl."

Mr. Carbuncle's outraged roar filled the room and made the hairs on the back of my neck stand on end. The bundle of men rolled off the bed in the direction Rudolph had fallen. A second later, the former caretaker scrambled out from behind the bed and leaped to his feet.

I clapped my free hand over my mouth. "D-don't let him get away again!"

"M-Mr. Trommel?" said one of the bodyguards from behind the bed.

"Mr. Trommel!" the other shouted.

The bodyguard holding my arm tightened his fingers. "Talk!"

Hysteria filled my lungs and made my eyes bulge. Mr. Carbuncle dashed out of the door, and none of the wretched bodyguards tried to stop him. "No!"

A heartbeat later, the sound of a fist smacking into flesh had the caretaker staggering back into the room, clutching his nose. Henry stormed after Mr. Carbuncle, and with lightning-fast speed, he slammed his fist into the side of the caretaker's head.

I sucked in a breath and whispered, "H-Henry."

"Fuck!" The caretaker fell onto his ass, his back hitting the foot of the bed.

Behind him, the bodyguards lifted Rudolph's still body onto the mattress. The old man's robe gaped open, revealing a wrinkled chest, and his head lolled to the side. I wasn't sure if he was unconscious or dying or dead.

A heartbeat later, a fist flew past my face and into the jaw of the bodyguard holding my bicep. The man let go and staggered into the dresser. Blake pulled me into his arms and hurried to the other side of the room. "Emilia, are you hurt?"

"N-no," I gasped out.

"Y-you fucking ponce." Mr. Carbuncle pulled himself up.

"Eat this." With another fist in the face, Henry knocked him down to the floor.

Mr. Carbuncle's eyes rolled to the back of his head, just as one of the bodyguards pushed Henry aside and pummeled the unconscious caretaker with the butt of his handgun.

My nostrils flared. Those guards were only good for maltreating women and attacking men who couldn't fight back.

Henry strode across the room and wrapped his arms around me. "Emilia, did he do anything to hurt—"

"Not really." I gazed into his verdant green eyes, and a fist clenched at my heart. Something terrible must have happened in the bedroom because only two of the triumvirate had come to my rescue. "But where's Edward?"

"A and E," said Blake.

I whirled around. "What?"

"Campus security stormed Elder House as we were leaving to

track your phone. They saw Edward's arm and held him back for the ambulance. We didn't stick around."

"But is he alright?"

"It's just a flesh wound," said Henry. "The bullet only skimmed his body, but he hit his head while dodging it."

My muscles sagged with relief, and all the tension left my body in a dizzying rush. Blake held me upright and turned us to where the bodyguards still took their anger out on Mr. Carbuncle. One of them stamped on his knee, making the man wake up with a pained bellow.

Behind him, Rudolph lay on the bed, his face a bloody mess, his chest unmoving. My throat dried. Why weren't his bodyguards performing CPR or calling for an ambulance?

"Drop your weapons!" A police officer clad in bullet-proof armor stepped into the room holding a semi-automatic rifle. Flanking him were two other officers carrying guns.

After rounding up the bodyguards, the paramedics arrived, took one look at Rudolph and told us all to leave.

What happened next was a blur of paramedics rushing in and out Rudolph's room, bringing in oxygen tanks and a defibrillator. After a paramedic measured my blood pressure and other vital signs, the police took our statements. What I told them was mostly the truth, that a drunk and paranoid Mr. Carbuncle had abducted me for ransom but changed his mind when he thought Rudolph had taken his mother in revenge for kidnapping me last term.

A policeman tracked down Mom, who rushed down the crowded hallway and enveloped me in a Coco Chanel-scented hug. "They just told me that man abducted you again." She stepped back and scanned my face and body. "D-did he hurt you?"

I shook my head. "Apart from a bump on the head and a few bruises on my wrists."

She called over a paramedic, who sat me in their suite and checked me for signs of a concussion. Henry and Blake came along and murmured to each other while Mom fretted, and the paramedic retook my blood pressure.

Just as the paramedic left, Edward rushed through the door. The bodyguard grabbed at his arm, but Mom told him he was a friend.

Edward shot the man a cold look and crossed the room. "I came as quickly as I could."

I jumped out of my seat and wrapped my arms around his neck. Edward's familiar cedar and cypress scent engulfed my senses and wiped away the last of my tension. It was one thing to hear that the gunshot wound hadn't been fatal, but it was another to see him in the flesh.

"How did you find us?" I murmured.

"Henry's been keeping me updated throughout the evening." He pressed a kiss on my lips. "I'm so glad you're unhurt."

A knock reverberated on the door. The bodyguard opened it and stepped aside.

"Mrs. Trommel?" A different paramedic stepped into the room. "I'm afraid I have bad news. Despite our best efforts, Mr. Trommel died at ten-fifty-five."

Mom clapped both hands over her face. "No... No!"

"I'm very sorry," said the paramedic.

"Can I see him?" she asked.

"Yes... Of course."

When we left Mom's suite, police, paramedics, and hotel staff still occupied the hallways. Mom intertwined her fingers with mine, and we walked together with Edward, Henry, and Blake at our backs. My heart beat a steady thrum, and I kept my breaths even. My mind couldn't decipher whether the situation was fortunate or fucked-up.

Rudolph Trommel was dead.

Beaten to death by Mr. Carbuncle.

I'd have thought that with Rudolph gone and Mr. Carbuncle finally arrested, my heart would soar and steps would lighten. But guilt roiled through my stomach, filled my chest and made the back of my throat ache as though I had spent the entire night screaming. Rudolph had suffered a brutal death, and it was entirely my fault.

My gaze darted to Mom, and I gulped. How would she react if she knew I had been the reason why Mr. Carbuncle had come to Elfwynn House? Would she understand, or would she believe I was as twisted as Rudolph had suggested in the limo?

The policeman outside the door to Rudolph's second room opened the door. Rudolph lay on top of the bed with his satin rob splayed open. Someone had kindly placed a towel over his genitals, but a plastic breathing tube remained in his mouth.

Mom clapped her hand over her chest and gasped. "I didn't think he would look so bad."

"Mr. Carbuncle wouldn't stop hitting him," I whispered. "Then, three of the bodyguards jumped Mr. Carbuncle, and a fight broke out on top of Rudolph."

She pressed her lips together. Eventually, she spoke to the corpse on the bed. "That must have really hurt... Just like when Mr. Carbuncle abducted Emilia."

I glanced over my shoulder at the boys, who exchanged puzzled looks.

"We'll never go on that honeymoon you wanted to Bora Bora." Mom shook her head, voice choked. "Emilia won't get the chance to see your doctor associate in Moldova, but I'll make sure she gets that Ivy League education you promised, the internship, and the job."

I bit down on my lip. It almost sounded like she was gloating.

Her lips curled into a smile. "Goodbye, Rudolph. My daughter and I will take good care of your empire." She turned to us, eyes bright. "Have you eaten? The room service menu here is excellent."

On Monday morning, we staggered into the dining hall, red-eyed and delicate from spending Saturday night and the whole of Sunday at a suite in Elfwynn House. According to the boys, Edward's room was a mess of plaster from the shooting, and a team of maintenance staff would need a day to patch it up. After having alcohol with every meal, including breakfast, and finishing off the evening with champagne and cigars that Rudolph had bought for a thousand dollars apiece, I was ready for an English breakfast with lots of tea.

As we took our seats, Mr. Weaver crossed the room and stood at the dais. Next to him was Dr. Asgard and a nurse from yesterday's blood drive. "Good morning, Elder House. It's with a heavy heart that I announce that your housemaster was shot on Saturday and is in critical condition at West Mercia Hospital."

My shoulders drooped, and a pang of sadness filled my chest. The one time Mr. Jenkins had tried to stand up to someone in the wrong, he had received a gunshot wound. If he ever returned to teaching, he would become more reclusive than ever.

The Chairman of the Board of Governors cleared his throat. "I am impressed with the number of people who donated blood, but I have delicate news related to the endeavor. Dr. Asgard, if you please."

The doctor stepped forward, clasping his hands over his stomach. "As many of you are aware, we took samples from each person who donated blood, and these samples underwent screening for infections, antibodies, and viral markers."

Silence spread through the dining hall. I leaned forward, trying to anticipate the nature of this delicate news.

Doctor Asgard cleared his throat. "A significant number of donors tested positive for strains of syphilis."

I cringed. Chatters broke out across the tables. Someone at the back of the room dropped a plate.

The doctor raised his palms. "There's no cause for alarm. It's perfectly treatable with penicillin injections, but I must reiterate the importance of practicing safe sex."

"Abstinence," said Mr. Weaver. "Sexual activity is against the regulations of Mercia Academy for this very reason."

The academy medic rubbed the back of his neck. "From our analysis, it appears that the condition was spread by one individual."

A few girls shot Blake dirty looks, but he stared ahead, unaffected.

"To safeguard the privacy of those who tested positive, we have placed envelopes in everyone's mailboxes. Those who tested negative or didn't donate blood will find blank sheets of paper instead of test results."

Everyone rushed to the entrance hall. A tiny voice in the back of my head wondered if I had caught anything from Mr. Carbuncle. I'd been unconscious in his presence twice, and although both times I had awoken wearing my jeans, it didn't guarantee that he hadn't done anything nefarious.

I reached into my mailbox and pulled out a white envelope. All around me, people were doing the same, so I retreated to the fireplace and pulled up the flap.

Rita walked up to me, her face pale. "A-are you alright? I can't face looking at mine."

"Let's swap, then." I gave her a smile. It looked like the boy she had been visiting in Hawthorn House was her boyfriend, after all. "I'll open yours if you open mine."

With a nod, we exchanged envelopes. I tore Rita's open and pulled out the sheet of paper. Hers was blank. She handed me mine, which was also blank.

Her posture slumped. "That's a relief."

My gaze traveled to Henry, who held up a blank piece of paper, and then to Edward, who did the same. At the far right of the room, Blake brandished his blank sheet. "See?" Blake told no one in particular. "It wasn't me who spread the syphilis. Look somewhere else."

A group of boys huddled in the corner. Coates, Bierson, and Patterson-Bourke from the rugby team. Among them were other rugby players, a few boys I'd never really spoken to, and Duncan, the scrawny boy with thick glasses who subscribed to every newspaper.

In the middle of the huddle of boys stood a pale-faced Charlotte.

Blake strolled up to us at the fireplace, mischief shining in his chocolate-brown eyes. "This will be interesting."

"What?"

He turned me to the door, where boys from Hawthorn house walked into the entrance hall, many of them holding letters instead of blank pieces of paper. They all glowered in the direction of Charlotte.

I shook my head. "She couldn't have—"

"It looks like she did," said Blake.

"What's going on?" asked Rita.

I grimaced. "Do you remember how Charlotte returned with sudden popularity and a nose job? That's how she gained so many allies so quickly."

Blake rubbed the back of his neck. "I feel bad about broadcasting that blowjob video. It contributed to both her popularity and the degradation of the academy's genito-urinary health."

"I doubt it would have made a difference to that rabble." Edward leaned against the fireplace's marble surround.

Henry shook his head. "They'll tear her apart."

"Where is she?" Alice led a group of girls, including Patricia, Wendy, and a bunch of others who I recognized from the disastrous booze cruise.

"Actually," drawled Blake. "It looks like the girls will get there first."

EPILOGUE

The limo pulled out in front of the main building of Mercia Academy, and Mom and I stepped out to a riot of paparazzi. Mr. Carbuncle's murder trial started the next morning, and the press had followed our every move since we had arrived in Mom's new private jet.

I wore my usual blazer but with one difference. A tiny prefect pin to match Edward's. The board of governors had been so impressed with the positive press generated by the blood drive, that they decided I would be a perfect replacement when they expelled Charlotte for spreading a particularly resistant form of syphilis.

Mom towered over me in her Louboutins, their red soles the only flash of color in her outfit. She wore a black, one-button tuxedo jacket with matching cigarette pants that lengthened her already long legs.

"Work hard this year." She wrapped her arms around me. "And try not to get distracted from your studies."

"You too." I gave her a peck on the cheek and whispered, "Say hi to Bruno, Dimitri, and Maurice."

Her lips pressed together in a thin line, but the roundness of her cheeks told me she was trying not to laugh. Ever since the boys and I had vacationed with her in Bora Bora, she had been determined to gather her own 'harem of hunks' to act as personal assistants and bodyguards.

She drew back. "If you need anything, send me a text."

"I will."

Once Mom stepped back into the limo, the reporters rushed toward their vehicles, presumably to follow Mom to London, where the trial was due to start at the Old Bailey.

The academy's stone-fronted building was no longer as imposing as I had found it on my first day. With a smile, I ascended the stone steps, pushed open the mahogany door, and stepped into the marble hallway. The vast space stretched out in front of me, and I headed toward the middle of the building.

A mixture of former headmasters and Mercia ancestors stared down at me through gold-framed portraits, giving me a warm feeling of belonging. I had survived my first year in a British boarding school, which was more than I could say about Rudolph.

I took the rounding, twisting staircase to the first floor, just as I had on my first day. When I rounded a corner, Blake, Edward, and Henry stood at the top of the flight. My mouth went dry, and butterflies caressed the lining of my stomach. Even though I'd dated them for nearly a year, seeing them together still made my heart skitter in time with the pulse between my legs.

Blake stood on the left, his full lips curling into a smile that made me lick my lips. Mischief sparkled in his chocolate-brown eyes, and I couldn't help the tiny shiver of anticipation that skittered down my spine.

Edward gazed down at me with warm, sapphire eyes that reflected the depth of his affection and caused my heart to swell with love. The bullet wound on his bicep had healed entirely, leaving a scar that would fade in time.

Henry stood on the right, his blond hair curling around his face like a gilded frame. My gaze roved down from his startling green eyes to his kissable lips, and down to his powerful, muscular body that was encased in tight, rugby whites.

My tongue darted out to lick my lips, and I had to clench my hands by my sides to keep from groping him in the stairwell. "Why aren't you in your uniform?"

"It's customary for the sports teams to wear their kit on the first assembly. By the way, Mr. Ellis saw our abysmal final tern results, and he's made me the captain."

Pride swelled in my chest. Everything was back to normal.

Blake gave Henry a playful nudge in the ribs. "Getting the St. Mary's sports scholarship also didn't hurt."

I gasped. "You got in?"

Henry flushed and raked a hand through his blond curls. "Father's furious that I've ditched retail for a life of professional rugby."

"Congratulations!" I hurried up the stairs and wrapped my arms around his neck. Henry's mint and citrus scent engulfed my senses, turning my bones to jelly. He was his own man now, and Mr. Bourneville was the one begging him to return to the fold.

Edward clapped Henry on the back. "This calls for a celebration."

"Your place?" asked Blake.

"Father's got guests tonight," replied Edward. "I'd suggest the cottage, but Mrs. Carbuncle is still in residence."

I drew back from Henry's embrace. "How about Elfwynn House?"

"Sounds like a plan!" said Blake.

Someone cleared their throat. Mr. Weaver stood behind the boys with his arms folded across his chest. He wore black, academic robes over his usual suit, with a sash emblazoning the Mercia crest, indicating that his position of acting headmaster was now permanent.

Blake stepped aside, and the older man passed us down the stairs, but at the bottom, he turned around.

"Hurry along, Mr. Mercia and Miss Hobbs," said Mr. Weaver. "I need you both in place at the assembly hall for the announcement of head boy and girl."

My eyes widened, and a shocked breath whooshed out of my lungs. I glanced at Edward, whose lips curled into a satisfied smile.

"Of course, sir." Edward descended a few steps and offered me his arm.

I followed after him and looped my arm around Edward's.

We walked out of the stairwell and into the hallway, and I replayed the new headmaster's words. I completely understood the Board of Governor's choice of head boy. Edward had always been concerned about the reputation of the academy, and he was a direct descendant of its founder. But me? I'd only been studying here for a year.

Mr. Weaver pushed open the double doors, and we all stepped out into the September day. A lemon-scented breeze meandered in from the magnolia trees on the far right of the lawn, whose leaves had turned a dazzling mix of ambers and golds over the fall.

We strode across the lawn to the assembly hall, which stood proudly on the left of the campus, a stone building whose entrance consisted of columns holding up a triangular pediment, much like the Pantheon in Rome. Blake walked on my left, Edward on my right, and Henry on the far right of our procession.

I leaned into Edward and whispered, "Did you know I'd become the head girl?"

"Didn't you ever wonder why I brought you to all those board of governors' meetings?" he murmured back.

"For moral support?"

"And with a view of having you at my side when I performed my head boy duties."

"Otherwise it would have been Charlotte or someone equally as ghastly," muttered Blake from my other side. "The academy is better with you at the reigns."

A mixture of joy and pride swelled in my heart. This time last year, I had joined Mercia Academy as the outcast—a foreigner who couldn't fit in and was hated for being a trollop. Now things were different. My ivy league education was guaranteed, and now I'd been awarded the highest accolade in Mercia Academy.

Not only was I surviving my time at a British boarding school, but I was also thriving.

And best of all, I had three beautiful boyfriends who loved me as much as I loved them.

END OF KINGS OF MERCIA ACADEMY
READ BULLY BOYS OF BRITTAS ACADEMY

FROM SOFIA DANIEL

Thank you for completing Emilia's story! If you enjoyed Kings of Mercia Academy, please take a moment to leave a review. A sentence or two can make the difference to a book!

Want teasers for upcoming books? Join my reader group, Sofia's Study Group.

Wicked Elites (Bully Boys of Brittas Academy)
Captured (Royals of Sanguine Vampire Academy)
Cruel Games (Knights of Templar Academy)
Fae Trials (Royal Fae Academy)

www.SofiaDaniel.com